W9-ADK-500

# THE ALGEBRAIST

**Other books by Iain M. Banks:**

*Consider Phlebas*

*The Player of Games*

*Use of Weapons*

*Against a Dark Background*

*Feersum Endjinn*

*Excession*

*Inversions*

*Look to Windward*

*The State of the Art*

**Writing as Iain Banks:**

*The Wasp Factory*

*Walking on Glass*

*The Bridge*

*Espedair Street*

*Canal Dreams*

*The Crow Road*

Complicity

*Whit*

*A Song of Stone*

*The Business*

*Dead Air*

*Raw Spirit*

# THE ALGEBRAIST

# IAIN M. BANKS

NIGHT SHADE BOOKS
SAN FRANCISCO & PORTLAND

**Printed In Canada**

**Third Printing**

ISBN 978-1-59780-044-0

**Night Shade Books**
http://www.nightshadebooks.com

For the MacLennans:  Andy, Fiona, Duncan, Nicol, Catriona and Robin

# PROLOGUE

I have a story to tell you. It has many beginnings, and perhaps one ending. Perhaps not. Beginnings and endings are contingent things anyway; inventions, devices. Where does any story really begin? There is always context, always an encompassingly greater epic, always something before the described events, unless we are to start every story with, "BANG! *Expand! Sssss…*", then itemise the whole subsequent history of the universe before settling down, at last, to the particular tale in question. Similarly, no ending is final, unless it is the end of all things…

Nevertheless, I have a story to tell you. My own direct part in it was vanishingly small and I have not thought even to introduce myself with anything as presumptuous as a proper name. Nevertheless, I was there, at the very beginning of one of those beginnings.

From the air, I am told, the Autumn House looks like a giant grey and pink snowflake lying half-embedded within these folded green slopes. It lies on the long, shallow escarpment which forms the southern limit of the Northern Tropical Uplands. On the northern side of the house are spread the various formal and rustic gardens which it is both my duty and my pleasure to tend. A little further up the escarpment rest the extensive ruins of a fallen temple, believed to have been a construction of a species called the Rehlide. (6ar., either severely abated or extinct, depending on which authority one chooses to give credence to. In any event, long gone from these parts.)

The temple's great white columns once towered a hundred metres or so into our thin airs but now lie sprawled upon and interred within the ground, vast straked and fluted tubes of solid stone half buried in the peaty soils of the unimproved land around us. The furthest-fallen ends of the columns—

which must have toppled slowly but most impressively in our half-standard gravity—punched great long crater-like ditches out of the earth, creating long double embankments with bulbously rounded tips. Over the many millennia since their sudden creation these tall ramparts have been slowly worn down both by erosion and our world's many small ground-quakes so that the earth has slumped back to refill the wide ditches where the column ends lie, until all that is visible is a succession of gentle waves in the land's surface, like a series of small, splayed valleys from whose upper limits the unburied lengths of the columns appear like the pale exposed bones of this little planet-moon.

Where one column fell and rolled across a shallow river valley, it formed a sort of angled cylindrical dam, over which the water spills, is caught and channelled by one of the metres-deep grooves embellishing the column's length, and then flows down to what remains of the column's ornately carved capital and a series of small, graceful waterfalls which end in a deep pool just beyond the tall, dense hedges which mark the highest limit of our gardens. From here the stream is guided and controlled, some of its waters proceeding to a deep cistern which provides the headwaters for our gravity fountains down near the house while the rest make up the brook which by turns tumbles, rushes, swings and meanders down to the ornamental lakes and partial moat surrounding the house itself.

I was standing waist-deep in the gurgling waters of a steeply pitched part of the brook, three limbs braced against the current, surrounded by dripping exer-rhododendron branches and coils of weed, trimming and dead-heading a particularly recalcitrant confusion of moil-bush around a frankly rather threadbare raised lawn of scalpygrass (basically a noble but failed experiment, attempting to persuade this notoriously clumpy variety to... ah: my enthusiasms may be getting the better of me, and I digress—never mind about the scalpygrass) when the young master—returning, whistling, hands clasped behind his back, from his morning constitutional round the higher rockeries—stopped on the gravel path above me and smiled down. I looked round and up, still clipping away, and nodded with as much formality as my somewhat awkward stance would allow.

Sunlight poured from the purple sky visible between the curve of eastward horizon (hills, haze) and the enormous overhanging bulk of the gas-giant planet Nasqueron filling the majority of the sky (motley with all the colours of the spectrum below bright yellow, multitudinously spotted, ubiquitously zoned and belted with wild liquidic squiggles). A synchronous mirror almost directly above us scribed a single sharp line of yellow-white across the largest of Nasqueron's storm-spots, which moved ponderously across the sky like an orange-brown bruise the size of a thousand moons.

"Good morning, Head Gardener."

"Good morning, Seer Taak."

"And how are our gardens?"

"Generally healthy, I would say. In good shape for spring." I could have gone on to provide much more detail, naturally, but waited to discover whether Seer Taak was merely indulging in phatic discourse. He nodded at the water rushing and breaking around my lower limbs.

"You all right in there, HG? Looks a bit fierce."

"I am well braced and anchored, thank you, Seer Taak." I hesitated (and during the pause could hear someone small and light running up the stone steps towards the gravel path a little further down the garden), then, when Seer Taak still smiled encouragingly down at me, I added, "The flow is high because the lower pumps are on, recirculating the waters to enable us to scour one of the lakes free of floating weeds." (The small person approaching reached the path's loose surface twenty metres away and kept running, scattering gravel.)

"I see. Didn't think it had rained that much recently." He nodded. "Well, keep up the good work, HG," he said, and turned to go, then saw whoever was running towards him. I suspected from the rhythm of her running steps that it was the girl Zab. Zab is still at the age where she runs from place to place as a matter of course unless directed not to by an adult. However, I believed that I detected a more than casual urgency in her gait. Seer Taak smiled and frowned at the girl at the same time as she came skidding to a stop on the gravel in front of him, putting one hand flat to the chest of her yellow dungarees and bending over for a couple of deep, exaggerated breaths—long pink curls swirling and dancing round her face—before taking one even deeper breath and standing up straight to say,

"Uncle Fassin! Grandpa Slovius says you're out in a commun- i- cardo again and if I see you I've to tell you you've to come and see him right now immediately!"

"Does he now?" Seer Taak said, laughing. He bent and picked the girl up by her armpits, holding her face level with his, her little pink boots hanging level with the waist of his britches.

"Yes, he does," she told him, and sniffed. She looked down and saw me. "Oh! Hello, HG."

"Good morning, Zab."

"Well," said Seer Taak, hoisting the child further up and turning and lowering her so that she sat on his shoulders, "we'd better go and see what the old man wants, hadn't we?" He started down the path towards the house. "You okay up there?"

She put her hands over his forehead and said, "Yup."

"Well, this time, mind out for branches."

"*You* mind out for branches!" Zab said, rubbing her knuckles through

Seer Taak's brown curls. She twisted round and waved back at me. "Bye, HG!"

"Goodbye," I called as they went towards the steps.

"No, *you* mind out for branches, young lady."

"No, *you* mind out for branches!"

"No, *you* mind out for branches."

"No, *you* mind out for branches…"

# ONE
## THE AUTUMN HOUSE

It had thought it would be safe out here, just one more ambiently black speck deep-chilled in the vast veil of icy debris wrapping the outer reaches of the system like a frozen, tenuous shroud of tissue. But it had been wrong and it was not safe.

It lay, slow-tumbling, and watched helplessly as the probing beams flickered across the pitted, barren motes far away, and knew its fate was settled. The interrogating tendrils of coherence were almost too quick to sense, too seemingly tentative to register, barely touching, scarcely illuminating, but they did their job by finding nothing where there was nothing to find. Just carbon, trace, and ice-water hard as iron: ancient, dead, and—left undisturbed—no threat to anyone.

The lasers flicked off, and each time it felt hope rise, finding itself thinking, despite all rationality, that its pursuers would give up, admit defeat, just go away and leave it be, to orbit there for ever. Or perhaps it would kick away into a lonely eternity of less than light-slow exile, or drift into a closedown sleep, or... Or it might, it supposed—and this was what they feared, of course, this was why they hunted—plot and plan and gather and make and quicken and build and multiply and muster and—attack!... Claiming the vengeance that was so surely its, exacting the price its enemies all deserved to pay—by any algebra of justice under any sun you cared to name—for their intolerance, their savagery, their generacide.

Then the needle rays reappeared, fitfully irradiating the soot-ice-clinker of another set of barnacle-black detritus, a little further away, or a little closer, but always with a rapid, meticulous order to them, a militaristic precision and a plodding, bureaucratic systematicism.

From the earlier light trails, there were at least three ships. How many did they have? How many might they devote to the search? It didn't really matter.

They might take a moment, a month or a millennium to find their quarry, but they obviously knew where to look and they would not stop until they had either found what they were looking for or satisfied themselves that there was nothing there.

That it was so obviously in harm's way, and that its hiding place, however enormous, was almost the first place they had chosen to search, filled it with terror, not just because it did not want to die, or be picked apart as they had been known to pick its kind apart before killing their victims utterly, but because if it was not safe in this place where it had assumed it would be, then, given that so many of its kind had made the same assumption, none of them would be safe either.

*Dear Reason, maybe none of us are safe anywhere.*

All its studies, all its thoughts, all the great things that might have been, all the fruits of change from the one great revelation it might have had, and now would never know the truth of, would never be able to tell. All, all for nothing now. It could choose to go with some elegance, or not, but it could not choose not to go.

No un-choosing death.

The needle rays from the needle ships flicked on/flicked off away across the frozen distances, and finally it could see the pattern in them, discerning one ship's comb of scintillations from the others and so picking out the shape of the search grids, allowing it to watch, helpless, as the slow spread of that mortal inquiry crept slowly, slowly closer.

:

The Archimandrite Luseferous, warrior priest of the Starveling Cult of Leseum9 IV and effective ruler of one hundred and seventeen stellar systems, forty-plus inhabited planets, numerous significant artificial immobile habitats and many hundreds of thousands of civilian capital ships, who was Executive High Admiral of the Shroud Wing Squadron of the Four-Hundred-and-Sixty-Eighth Ambient Fleet (Det.) and who had once been Triumvirate Rotational human/non-human Representative for Cluster Epiphany Five at the Supreme Galactic Assembly, in the days before the latest ongoing Chaos and the last, fading rumbles of the Disconnect Cascade, had some years ago caused the head of his once-greatest enemy, the rebel chief Stinausin, to be struck from his shoulders, attached without delay to a long-term life-support mechanism and then hung upside down from the ceiling of his hugely impressive study in the outer wall of Sheer Citadel—with its view over Junch City and Faraby Bay towards the hazy vertical slot that was Force Gap—so that the Archimandrite could, when the mood took him, which was fairly frequently, use his old adversary's head as a punchball.

Luseferous had long, sheen-black straight hair and a naturally pale complexion which had been skilfully augmented to make his skin nearly pure white. His eyes were artificially large, but just close enough to congenitally possible for people to be unsure whether they had been augmented or not. The whites beyond the black irises were a deep, livid red, and every one of his teeth had been carefully replaced with a pure, clear diamond, giving his mouth an appearance which varied from bizarre, mediaeval toothlessness to startling, glistening brilliance, entirely depending on angle and light.

In a street performer or an actor, such physiological departures might have been amusing, even a little desperate-looking; in somebody wielding the kind of power which Luseferous possessed, they could be genuinely disturbing, even terrifying. The same half-tasteless, half-horrifying effect might be claimed for his name, which was not the one he had been born with. Luseferous was a chosen name, selected for its phonetic proximity to that of some long-scorned Earth deity which most humans—well, most rHumans, at least—would vaguely have heard of in their history studies while probably not being entirely able to place when they had heard the word.

Again thanks to genetic manipulation, the Archimandrite was now and had been for some long time a tall, well-built man with considerable upper-body strength, and when he punched in anger—and he rarely punched in any other state—it was to considerable effect. The rebel leader whose head now hung upside down from Luseferous's ceiling had caused the Archimandrite enormous military and political difficulties before being defeated, difficulties which had sometimes verged on being humiliations, and Luseferous still felt deep, deep resentment towards the traitor, resentment which easily and reliably turned itself to anger when he looked upon the man's face, no matter how battered, bruised and bloody it might be (the head's augmented healing functions were quick, but not instantaneous), and so the Archimandrite probably still whacked and smashed away at Stinausin's head with as much enthusiasm now as he had when he'd first had him hung there, years earlier.

Stinausin, who had barely endured a month of such treatment before going completely mad, and whose mouth had been sewn up to stop him spitting at the Archimandrite, could not even kill himself; sensors, tubes, micropumps and biocircuitry prevented such an easy way out. Even without such extraneous limitations he could not have shouted abuse at Luseferous or attempted to swallow his tongue because that organ had been torn out when his head had been removed.

Though by now quite perfectly insane, sometimes, after an especially intense training session with the Archimandrite, when the blood trickled down from the one-time rebel chief's split lips, re-broken nose and puffed-up eyes and ears, Stinausin would cry. This Luseferous found particularly gratifying, and sometimes he would stand, breathing hard and wiping himself down with a towel while he watched the tears dilute the blood dripping from the inverted, disembodied head, to land in a broad ceramic shower tray set into the floor.

Of late, though, the Archimandrite had had a new playmate to amuse himself with, and he would occasionally visit the chamber some levels below his study where the nameless would-be assassin whose own teeth were slowly killing him was held.

The assassin, a big, powerful-looking, leoninely human male, had been sent without weapons save for his specially sharpened teeth, with which, it had obviously been hoped by whoever had sent him, he could bite out the Archimandrite's throat. This he had attempted to do, a half-year earlier at a ceremonial dinner held here in the clifftop palace in honour of the System President (a strictly honorary post Luseferous always made sure was filled by somebody of advanced age and retreating faculties). The would-be assassin had only failed to accomplish this task thanks to the Archimandrite's near-paranoid forethought and intense—and largely secret—personal security.

The failed assassin had been both routinely, if savagely, tortured and then very carefully questioned under the influences of entire suites of drugs and electro-biological agents, but had given nothing useful away. Patently he had been equally carefully wiped of any knowledge that might incriminate whoever had sent him, by interrogational technicians at least as capable as those whom the Archimandrite commanded. His controllers had not even bothered to implant false memories incriminating anybody close to the Court and the Archimandrite, as was common in such cases.

Luseferous, who was that most deplorable of beings, a psychopathic sadist with a fertile imagination, had decreed that the final punishment of the assassin should be that his own teeth—the weapons he had been sent with, after all—should bring about his death. Accordingly, his four canine teeth had been removed, bioengineered to become tusks which would grow without ceasing, and reinserted. These great finger-thick fangs had erupted out of the bones of his upper and lower jaw, puncturing the flesh of his lips, and had continued their remorseless growth. The lower set curved up and over his head and, after a few months' worth of extension, came to touch his scalp near the top of his head, while the upper set grew in a scimitar-like paired sweep beneath his neck, taking about the same time to meet the skin near the base of his throat.

Genetically altered not to stop growing even when they encountered such resistance, both sets of teeth then started to enter the assassin's body, one pair slowly forcing themselves through the bony plates of the man's skull, the other set entering rather more easily into the soft tissues of the lower neck. The tusks digging into the assassin's neck caused great pain but were not immediately life-threatening; left to themselves they would reappear from the rear of his neck in due course. The fangs burrowing through his skull and into his brain were the ones which would shortly, and agonisingly, kill him, perhaps in as little as another month or so.

The unfortunate, nameless assassin had been unable to do anything to prevent this because he was pinned helpless and immobile against the wall of the chamber with bands and shackles of thick stainless iron, his nutrition and bodily functions catered for by various tubes and implants. His mouth had also been sewn up, like that of Stinausin. For the first few months of his captivity the assassin's eyes had followed Luseferous around the chamber with a fierce, accusatory look that the Archimandrite eventually grew to find annoying, and so he'd had the man's eyes stitched shut too.

The fellow's ears and mind still worked, however—Luseferous had been assured—and sometimes it amused him to come down and see for himself the progress that the teeth were making into the creature's body. On such occasions, having what one might term a captive—yet necessarily discreet— audience, he sometimes liked to talk to the failed assassin.

"Good day," Luseferous said pleasantly as the lift door rumbled shut behind him. The chamber deep below the study was what the Archimandrite thought of as his den. Here, as well as the nameless assassin, he kept assorted souvenirs of old campaigns, booty from his many victories, items of high art looted from a dozen different stellar systems, a collection of weapons both ceremonial and high-power, various caged or tanked creatures, and the mounted, profoundly dead heads of all those major enemies and adversaries whose end had not been so complete as to reduce their mortal remains to radiation, dust, slime or unidentifiable strips of flesh and shards of bone (or the alien equivalents thereof).

Luseferous crossed to a deep, dry tank part-set into the floor and looked in at the Recondite Splicer lying coiled and still on its floor. He slipped a thick elbow glove onto his arm, reached into a large pot standing on the broad, waist-high parapet of the tank and dropped a handful of fat black trunk-leeches into the tank.

"And how are you? Are you keeping well? Hmm?" he asked.

An observer would have been unsure whether the Archimandrite was talking to the human male pinned to the wall, the Recondite Splicer—now no longer still, but raising its blind, glistening brown head, sniffing the air while its long, segmented body twitched with anticipation—or indeed the trunk-leeches, thudding one by one onto the mossy floor of the tank and immediately flexing their way with a sort of sine-wave motion across the surface towards the nearest corner, as far away from the Recondite Splicer as it was possible to get. The brown mass of the Splicer began to shuffle massively towards them and they started trying to climb the sheer glass sides of the tank, climbing over each other and slipping back down as soon as they tried to haul themselves up.

Luseferous peeled the elbow glove off and looked round the vaulted, subtly lit space. The chamber was a comfortable, quiet sort of place set well within the cliff, with no windows or light shafts, and he felt safe and relaxed here. He looked over at the long, tawny shape that was the suspended body of the assassin and said, "Nowhere's quite as nice as home, eh, is it?" The Archimandrite even smiled, though there was nobody to smile at.

There was a rasping noise and a heavy thump from inside the tank, followed by some almost inaudibly high keening sounds. Luseferous turned to watch the Recondite Splicer tear the giant leeches apart and eat them, violently shaking its great patchily brown head and tossing some bits of slimy black flesh all the way out of the tank. Once it had thrown a still-alive leech up and out of the tank and nearly hit the Archimandrite with it; Luseferous had chased the injured leech round the chamber with a shear-sword, cleaving deep slivers out of the dark red granite floor as he hacked and sliced at the creature.

When the show in the tank was over, the Archimandrite turned back to the assassin. He put the elbow glove back on, picked another trunk-leech from the pot and strolled over to the man attached to the wall. "Do you remember home, sir assassin?" he asked as he approached. "Is there any memory of it in your head at all, hmm? Home, mother, friends?" He stopped in front of the man. "Any of that stuff at all?" He waved the leech's moist, seeking snout in front of the assassin's face as he spoke. They sensed each other, the cold, writhing creature in the Archimandrite's hand stretching out to try to fasten itself to the man's face, the man sucking breath through his nostrils and turning his head as far as it would go, seeming to try and shrink back into the wall behind (this would not be the first time the assassin had been introduced to a trunk-leech). The tusks digging into his chest prevented him from moving his head very far.

Luseferous followed the movements of the man's head with the leech, keeping it in front of his lightly furred, leonine face, letting him smell the straining, quivering mass.

"Or did they rip out all those memories when they cleaned you, before they sent you to try to kill me? Huh? Are they all gone? Eh?" He let the very tip of the trunk-leech's mouth parts just touch the fellow's nose, causing the failed assassin to wince and jerk and make a small, terrified whimpering noise. "What, eh? Do you remember home, eh, sport? A pleasant place to be, a place you felt safe and secure and with people you trusted, and who maybe even loved you? What do you say? Eh? Eh? Come on." The man tried to turn his head still further, straining the puckered skin around the puncture points on his chest, one of which started to bleed. The giant leech trembled in Luseferous's hand, stretching its mucus-tipped mouth parts still further as it tried to find purchase on the human male's flesh. Then, before the leech could properly attach itself to the fellow, the Archimandrite pulled it back and let it hang from his half-outstretched arm, where it swung and twisted muscularly with what felt for all the world like genuine frustration.

"This is my home, sir assassin," Luseferous told the man. "This is my place, my refuge, this, which you… invaded, despoiled, dishonoured with your… your plot. Your attempt." His voice quaked as he said, "I invited you into my house, invited you to my table as… as hosts have guests for ten thousand human years and you… all you wanted to do was hurt me, kill me. Here, in my home, where I should feel safer than anywhere." The Archimandrite shook his head in sorrow at such ingratitude. The failed assassin had nothing but a dirty rag to cover his nakedness. Luseferous pulled it away and the fellow flinched again. Luseferous stared. "They did make a bit of a mess of you, didn't they?" He watched the failed assassin's thighs quiver and twitch. He let the loincloth fall to the ground; a servant would replace it tomorrow.

"I like my home," he told the fellow quietly. "I do, really. Everything I've had to do I've done just to make things safer, to make home safer, to make everybody safer." He waved the trunk-leech towards what was left of the man's genitalia, but the leech seemed listless and the man already exhausted. Even the Archimandrite felt like some of the fun had gone out of the situation. He turned smartly and strode to the pot on the broad rail over the tank, dumping the leech inside and peeling the thick elbow glove off.

"And now I have to leave home, mister assassin," Luseferous said, and sighed. He gazed down at the long coiled shape of the once-again-still Recondite Splicer. It had changed colour from brown to yellow-green now, adopting the colours of the mosses it lay upon. All that was left of the trunk-leeches were some dark spots and smears on the walls, and a faint, tangy smell the Archimandrite had come to recognise as that of yet another species's blood. He turned back to look at the assassin. "Yes, I have to go away, and for a very long time, and it would seem I have no choice." He started to walk slowly towards the man. "Because you can't delegate everything, because ultimately, especially when it comes to the most important things, you can't really trust anybody else. Because sometimes, especially when you're going far away and communications take so long, there's no substitute for being there. What do you think of that? Eh? There's a fine thing. Don't you think? Me working all these years to make this place safe and now I have to leave it, still trying to make it even safer, even more powerful, even better." He stepped up to the man again, tapping one of the curved fangs boring through the fellow's skull. "And all because of people like you, who hate me, who won't listen, who won't do as they're told, who don't know what's good for them." He gripped the fang and pulled hard at it. The man mewed down his nose with pain.

"Well, not really," Luseferous said, shrugging, letting go. "It's debatable whether this will really make us safer or not. I'm going to this… this Ulubis… system or whatever it is because there might be something valuable there, because my advisers advise so and my intelligence people have intelligence to this effect. Of course nobody's certain, nobody ever is. But they do seem uncommonly excited about this." The Archimandrite sighed again, more deeply. "And impressionable old me, I'm going to do as they suggest. Do you think I'm doing the right thing?" He paused, as though expecting an answer. "Do you? I mean, I realise you might not be entirely honest with me if you did have an opinion, but, all the same… No? You sure?" He traced the line of a scar along the side of the man's abdomen, wondering idly if it was one of those that his own inquisitors had inflicted. Looked a bit crude and deep to be their work. The failed assassin was breathing quickly and shallowly but giving no sign that he was even listening. Behind his sealed mouth, his jaws seemed to be working.

"You see, for once I'm not absolutely sure myself, and I could use some advice. Might not make us all safer at all, what we're planning to do. But it has to be done. The way some things just have to. Eh?" He slapped the man's face, not hard. The man flinched all the same. "Don't worry, though. You can come too. Big invasion fleet. Plenty of room." He looked around the chamber. "Anyway, I feel you spend too much time stuck in here; you could do with getting out more." The Archimandrite Luseferous smiled, though still there was nobody to smile at. "After all this trouble I'd hate to miss watching you die. Yes, you come with me, why don't you? To Ulubis, to Nasqueron."

:

One day in the sub-season of Desuetude II, the uncle of Fassin Taak summoned his only occasionally troublesome nephew to his side in the chamber of Provisional Forgetting.

"Nephew."

"Uncle. You wanted to see me?"

"Hmm."

Fassin Taak waited politely. It was, these days, not unknown for Uncle Slovius to remain silent, apparently pondering, for some time after even such a simple and technically redundant exchange, as though they had each given the other something profound and indeed unexpected to think about. Fassin had never entirely made up his mind whether this habit indicated that his uncle took his avuncular duties with particular and solemn seriousness, or just meant that the old guy was going senile. Either way, Uncle Slovius had been paterfamilias of the Seer Sept Bantrabal for either nearly three or over fourteen centuries, depending on how you reckoned time, and was generally regarded as having earned the right to be indulged in such matters.

Like the good nephew, devoted family member and faithful faculty officer he was, Fassin respected his uncle on principle as well as through sentiment, though he was aware that his attitude might be influenced by the fact that according to the customs of their family and the rules of their caste, the seniority and deference presently accorded his uncle would one day fall to him. The pause continued. Fassin bowed fractionally. "Uncle, may I sit?"

"Eh? Oh, yes." Uncle Slovius raised a flipper-like hand and waved it vaguely. "Please do."

"Thank you."

Fassin Taak hitched up his walking britches, gathered in his wide shirt sleeves and folded himself decorously into a sitting position at the side of the large circular pool of gently steaming and luminously blue liquid that his uncle floated within. Uncle Slovius had some years ago assumed the shape of a walrus. A beige-pink, relatively slim walrus, with tusks barely longer than the middle finger of a man's hand, but a walrus nevertheless. The hands Uncle Slovius had once possessed were no more—they were flippers now, on the end of two thin, rather odd and ineffectual-looking arms. His fingers were little more than stubs; a scalloped pattern fringing the ends of his flippers. He opened his mouth to speak, but then one of the household servants, a black-uniformed human male, approached him, kneeling at the side of the pool to whisper something into his ear. The servant held his long pigtail out of the water with one many-ringed hand. The dark clothes, long hair and rings all indicated that he was one of the most senior functionaries. Fassin felt he ought to know his name, but couldn't think of it immediately.

He looked round the room. The chamber of Provisional Forgetting was one of the rarely used parts of the house, only called into action—if you could call it that—on such occasions, when a senior family member was approaching their end. The pool took up most of the floor space of a large roughly hemispherical room whose walls were translucently thin agate inlaid with veins of time-dulled silver. This dome formed part of one bubble-wing of the family's Autumn House, situated on the continent Twelve on the rocky planet-moon 'glantine, which orbited the gaudy, swirlingly clouded mass of the gas-giant Nasqueron like a pepper grain around a football. A tiny portion of the massive planet's surface was visible through the transparent centre section of the dome's roof, directly above Fassin and his uncle.

The part of Nasqueron that Fassin could see was presently in daylight, displaying a chaotic cloudscape coloured crimson, orange and rust-brown, the summed shades producing a deep red light which fell through the violet skies of 'glantine's thinly breathable atmosphere and the dome's glazed summit and helped illuminate the chamber and the pool below, where the black-clad servant was supporting Uncle Slovius while he supped on a beaker of what might have been either refreshment or medicine. Some dribbles of the clear liquid escaped Uncle Slovius's mouth, trickling down his grizzled chin to the folds of his neck and dripping into the blue pool, where tall waves slopped to and fro in the half-standard gravity. Uncle Slovius made quiet grunting noises, his eyes closed.

Fassin looked away. Another servant approached him, offering a tray of drinks and sweetmeats, but he smiled and raised one hand in a gesture of rejection and the servant bowed and retreated. Fassin fixed his gaze politely on the dome's roof and the view of the gas-giant, while watching from the corner of his eye as the servant attending his uncle dabbed at the old man's lips with a neatly folded cloth.

Magisterial, oblivious, moving almost imperceptibly with a kind of tumultuous serenity, Nasqueron turned above them like some vast glowing coal hanging in the sky.

The gas-giant was the largest planet in the Ulubis system, which lay within a remote strand of Stream Quaternary, one of the Southern Tendril Reefs on the galactic outskirts, fifty-five thousand years from the galaxy's nominal centre and about as remote as it was possible to get while still being part of the great lens.

There were, especially in the current post-War age, different levels of remoteness, and Ulubis system qualified as back-of-beyond in all of them. Being on the outermost reaches of the galaxy—and hanging well underneath the galactic plane, where the last vestiges of stars and gas gave way to the emptiness beyond—did not necessarily mean that a place was inaccessible, providing it was close to an arteria portal.

Arteria—wormholes—and the portals which were their exits and entrances meant everything in the galactic community; they represented the difference between having to crawl everywhere at less than the speed of light and making almost instantaneous transitions from one stellar system to another. The effect they had on a system's importance, economy and even morale was similarly dramatic and rapid. Without one, it was as though you were still stuck in one small village, one dull and muddy valley, and might be there all your life. Once a wormhole portal was emplaced, it was as though you suddenly became part of a vast and glittering city, full of energy, life and promise.

The only way to get an arteria portal from one place to another was to put it in a spaceship and physically take it, slower than light, from one place to another, leaving the other end—usually—anchored where you'd started out. Which meant that if your wormhole was destroyed—and they could be destroyed, in theory at any point along their length, in practice only at their ends, at their portals—then you were instantly all the way back to square one, stuck in your isolated little village once again.

Ulubis system had first been connected to the rest of the galaxy over three billion years earlier, during what was then known as the New Age. It had been a relatively young, not-long-formed system at the time, just a few billion years old, but was already multiply life-supporting. Its arteria connection had formed part of the Second Complex, the galactic community's second serious attempt at an integrated network of wormholes. It had lost that connection in the billion-year turmoil of the Long Collapse, the War of Squalls, the Scatter Anarchy and the Informorta breakdown, then—along with most of the rest of the civilised galaxy—slumbered as if comatose under the weight of the Second, or Major, Chaos, a time when only its Dweller population on Nasqueron had survived. The Dwellers, being numbered amongst the species meta-type known as the Slow, worked to a different timescale, and thought nothing of taking a few hundred thousand years to get from point A to point B; a billion years of nothing much happening was, they declared, merely like a long sabbatical to them.

Following the Third Diasporian Age (and much more besides—galactic history wasn't really simple on any scale) another wormhole brought Ulubis back on-line to become part of the Third Complex. That arteria lasted for seventy million peaceful, productive years, during which several Quick species, none of them native to Ulubis, came and went, leaving only the Dwellers to bear consistent witness to the slow turn of life and events. The Arteria Collapse had plunged Ulubis into solitude once again, along with ninety-five per cent of the connected galaxy. More portals and wormholes disappeared during the War of the New Quick and the Machine War, and only the establishment of the Mercatoria—at least by the estimation of those who controlled it—brought about a lasting peace and the beginning of the Fourth Complex.

Ulubis had been reconnected early on in this slow, still-at-the-early-stages process and for six thousand years that latest arteria had made the system an easily reached part of the gradually recovering galactic community. However, then that wormhole too had been destroyed, and for over a quarter of a millennium Ulubis's nearest working access point had been fully two hundred and fourteen years away further down the increasing thickness of the Stream at Zenerre. That would change in about seventeen years or so, when the wormhole end-point currently being transported towards Ulubis system at relativistic speeds aboard the Engineering *Est-taun Zhiffir* arrived and was emplaced, probably where the old portal had been, at one of the Lagrange points near Sepekte, the principal planet of the Ulubis system. For the moment, though, Ulubis, despite its importance as a centre for Dweller Studies, remained remote chronologically as well as physically.

Uncle Slovius waved the servant away with one flipper and drew himself up against the Y-shaped cradle which supported his head and shoulders above the blue glowing surface of the pool. The servant—Fassin recognised him now as Guime, the second-highest-ranking of his uncle's retainers—turned back and tried to help Slovius in this manoeuvre. However, Slovius made hissing, tutting noises and slapped at the male with one flipper hand. Guime dodged the weak, slow blow easily and stepped back again, bowing. He stood nearby, by the wall. Slovious struggled to lift his upper body any further out of the pool, his tailed torso stirring sluggishly under the luminescent waves.

Fassin started to rise from his cross-legged position. "Uncle, do you want me to—?"

"No!" his uncle shouted in exasperation, still trying ineffectually to push himself further up the cradle. "I would like people to stop *fussing*, that's all!" Slovius turned his head round as he said this, trying to look at Guime, but only succeeded in causing himself to slip further back into the liquid, so that he was even more horizontal than he had been before he started. He slapped at the pool surface, splashing. "There! See what you've done? Interfering idiot!" He sighed mightily and lay back in the wallowing waves, apparently exhausted, staring straight ahead. "You may adjust me, Guime, as you wish," he said dully, sounding resigned.

Guime knelt on the tiles behind him, put a hand under each of Slovius's armpits and hauled his master upwards onto the cradle until his head and shoulders were almost vertical. Slovius settled himself there, then nodded briskly. Guime retreated again to his position by the wall.

"Now then, nephew," Slovius said, crossing his flipper hands over the pink expanse of his hairless chest. He looked up at the transparent summit of the dome.

Fassin smiled. "Yes, uncle?"

Slovius seemed to hesitate. He let his gaze fall to his nephew. "Your… your studies, Fassin. How do they progress?"

"They progress satisfactorily, sir. In the matter of the Tranche Xonju it is still, of course, very early."

"Hmm. Early," Uncle Slovius said. He looked thoughtful, staring into the distance again. Fassin sighed gently. This was obviously going to take some time.

Fassin Taak was a Slow Seer at the court of the Nasqueron Dwellers. The Dwellers—Gas-Giant Dwellers, to give them a fuller designation… Neutrally Buoyant First Order Ubiquitous Climax Clade Gas-Giant Dwellers, to grant them a still more painfully precise specification—were large creatures of immense age who lived within the deliriously complex and topologically vast civilisation of great antiquity which was distributed throughout the cloud layers wrapping the enormous gas-giant planet, a habitat that was as stupendous in scale as it was changeable in aerography.

The Dwellers, at least in their mature form, thought slowly. They lived slowly, evolved slowly, travelled slowly and did almost everything they ever did, slowly. They could, it was alleged, fight quite quickly. Though, as far as anybody was able to determine, they had not had to do any fighting for a long time. The implication of this was that they could think quickly when it suited them, but most of the time it did not appear to suit them, and so—it was assumed—they thought slowly. It was unarguable that in their later years—later aeons—they conversed slowly. So slowly that a simple question asked before breakfast might not be answered until after supper. A rate of conversational exchange, it occurred to Fassin, that Uncle Slovius—floating in his now-quite-still pool with a trancelike expression on his tusked, puffy face—seemed determined to emulate.

"The Tranche Xonju, it concerns…?" Slovius said suddenly.

"Clutter poetry, Diasporic myths and various history tangles," Fassin answered.

"Histories of which epochs?"

"The majority have still to be dated, uncle. Some may never be, and possibly belong with the myths. The only readily identifiable strands are very recent and appear to relate to mostly local events during the Machine War."

Uncle Slovius nodded slowly, producing small waves. "The Machine War. That is interesting."

"I was thinking of attending to those strands first."

"Yes," Slovius said. "A good idea."

"Thank you, uncle."

Slovius lapsed into silence again. A ground-quake rumbled distantly around them, producing tiny concentric rings in the liquid of Slovius's pool.

The civilisation which comprised the Dwellers of Nasqueron, with all their attendant fellow flora and fauna, itself formed but one microscopic fragment of the Dweller Diaspora, the galaxy-spanning meta-civilisation (some would say post-civilisation) which, as far as anyone could tell, preceded all other empires, cultures, diasporas, civilisations, federations, consocia, fellowships, unities, leagues, confederacies, affilia and organisations of like or unlike beings in general.

The Dwellers, in other words, had been around for most of the life of the galaxy. This made them at least unusual and possibly unique. It also made them, if they were approached with due deference and care, and treated with respect and patience, a precious resource. Because they had good memories and even better libraries. Or at least they had retentive memories, and very large libraries.

Dweller memories, and libraries, usually proved to be stuffed full of outright nonsense, bizarre myths, incomprehensible images, indecipherable symbols and meaningless equations, plus random assemblages of numbers, letters, pictograms, holophons, sonomemes, chemiglyphs, actinomes and *sensata variegata*, all of them trawled and thrown together unsorted—or in patterns too abstruse to be untangled—from a jumbled mix of millions upon millions of utterly different and categorically unrelated civilisations, the vast majority of which had long since disappeared and either crumbled into dust or evaporated into radiation.

Nevertheless, in all that flux of chaos, propaganda, distortion, drivel and weirdness, there were nuggets of actuality, seams of facts, frozen rivers of long-forgotten history, whole volumes of exobiography and skeins and tissues of truth. It had been the life-work of people like Chief Seer Slovius, and was the life-work of people like Chief Seer-in-waiting Fassin Taak, to meet with and talk to the Dwellers, to adapt to their language, thoughts and metabolism, to—sometimes virtually, at a remove, sometimes literally—float and fly and dive and soar with them amongst the clouds of Nasqueron, and through their conversations, their studies, their notes and analyses, make what sense they could of what their ancient slow-living hosts told them and allowed them to access, and so enrich and enlighten the greater, quicker meta-civilisation which presently inhabited the galaxy.

"And, ah, Jaal?" Slovius glanced at his nephew, who looked sufficiently surprised for the older male to add, "The, oh, what's their name…? Tonderon. Yes. The Tonderon girl. You two are still betrothed, aren't you?"

Fassin smiled. "We are indeed, uncle," he said. "She is returning from Pirrintipiti this evening. I'm hoping to meet her at the port."

"And you are…?" Slovius gestured with one flipper hand. "Still content?"

"Content, uncle?" Fassin asked.

"You are happy with her? With the prospect of her being your wife?"

"Of course, uncle."

"And she with you?"

"Well, I hope so. I believe so."

Slovius looked at his nephew, holding his gaze for a moment. "Mm-hmm. I see. Of course. Well." Slovius used one of his flipper hands to wave some of the blue glowing liquid over his upper chest, as though he was cold. "You are to be wed when?"

"The date is fixed for Allhallows, Jocund III," Fassin said. "Somewhat under half a year, body time," he added helpfully.

"I see," Slovius said, frowning. He nodded slowly, and the action caused his body to rise and fall slightly in the pool, producing more waves. "Well, it is good to know you might finally be settling down at last."

Fassin considered himself to be a dedicated, hard-working and productive Seer who spent well above the average amount of time at the sharp end of delving, actually with the Nasqueron Dwellers. However, due to the fact that he liked to complete each interlude of this real, useful life with what he called a "proper holiday," the older generation of Sept Bantrabal, and especially Slovius, seemed to think he was some sort of hopeless wastrel. (Indeed, Uncle Slovius seemed reluctant to accept the term "proper holiday" at all. He preferred to call them "month-long blind-drunk stoned-out benders getting into trouble, fights and illicit orifices in the flesh pots of—" well, wherever; sometimes Pirrintipiti, the capital of 'glantine, sometimes Borquille, capital of Sepekte, or one of Sepekte's other cities, sometimes one of the many pleasure habitats scattered throughout the system.)

Fassin smiled tolerantly. "Still, I shan't be hanging up my dancing shoes just yet, uncle."

"The nature of your studies over your last, say, three or four delves, Fassin. Have they followed what one might term a consistent course?"

"You confuse me, uncle," Fassin admitted.

"Your last three or four delves, have they been in any way linked thematically, or by subject, or through the Dwellers you have conversed with?"

Fassin sat back, surprised. Why ever would old Slovius be interested in this? "Let me think, sir," he said. "On this occasion I spoke almost exclusively with Xonju, who provided information seemingly at random and does not fully appear to understand the concept of an answer. Our first meeting and all very preparatory. He may be worth following up, if we can find him again. He may not. It might take all of the months between now and my next delve to work out—"

"So this was a sampling expedition, an introduction?"

"Indeed."

"Before that?"

"A protracted conference, with Cheuhoras, Saraisme the younger, Akeurle Both-twins, traav Kanchangesja and a couple of minors from the Eglide adolescent pod."

"Your subjects?"

"Poetry, mostly. Ancient, modern, the use of image in the epic, the ethics of boasting and exaggeration."

"And the delve before?"

"With Cheuhoras alone; an extended lament for his departed parent, some hunting myths from the local near-past and a lengthy translation and disposition on an epic sequence concerning the adventures of ancient plasmatics voyaging within the hydrogen migration, perhaps a billion or so years ago, during the Second Chaos."

"Before that?"

Fassin smiled. "My extended one-to-one with Valseir, the delve which included my sojourn with the Raucous Rascals of Tribe Dimajrian." He imagined he didn't need to remind his uncle of too many of the details of that particular excursion. This had been the protracted delve which had made his name as a gifted Seer, the six-year journey—by body-time; it had lasted nearly a century by outside reckoning—that had established his reputation both within Sept Bantrabal and the hierarchy of 'glantine Seers beyond. His exploits, and the value of the stories and histories he had returned with, had been largely responsible for his elevation to the post of Chief Seer-in-waiting in his Sept, and for the offer of marriage to the daughter of the Chief Seer of Sept Tonderon, the most senior of the twelve Septs.

"This takes us back how many years, in real?"

Fassin thought. "About three hundred... Two hundred and eighty-seven, if I recall correctly."

Slovius nodded. "There was much of that delve released during its course?"

"Almost nothing, sir. The Raucous Rascals insisted. They are one of the more... unameliorated adolescent pods. I was allowed to report that I was alive once per year."

"The delve before that?"

Fassin sighed and tapped the fingers of one hand on the fused glass at the side of the pool. What on old Earth could this be about? And could Slovius not simply look up the Sept records for such information? There was a big cantilevered arm thing stowed against the wall of the pool chamber with a screenpad on the end. Fassin had seen this device lowered into place in front of Slovius for him to peer at and prod the keys with his finger stumps. It was, patently, not a very rapid or efficient method of interrogating the house library, but it would answer all these questions. Or the old fellow could just ask. There were servants for this sort of thing.

Fassin cleared his throat. "Most of that was taken up with instructing Paggs Yurnvic, of Sept Reheo, on his first delve. We paid court to traav Hambrier, in one-to-one time with the Dwellers to allow for Yurnvic's inexperience. The delve lasted barely three months, body-time. Textbook introductory, sir."

"You found no time to pursue any studies of your own?"

"Little, sir."

"But some, yes?"

"I was able to attend part of a symposium on deep poetics, with the university pod Marcal. To detail the other attendees I would have to inquire within the Sept records, sir."

"What more? Of the symposium, I mean. Its subject?"

"If I recall, a comparison of Dweller hunting techniques with the actions of Machine War Inquisitories." Fassin stroked his chin. "The examples were Ulubis-system local, some regarding 'glantine."

Slovius nodded. He glanced at his nephew. "Do you know what an emissarial projection is, Fassin?"

Fassin looked up at the segment of gas-giant visible through the transparent roof panel. The night terminator was just starting to appear to one side, a line of increasing darkness creeping across the distant cloudscape. He looked back down at Slovius. "I may have heard the term, sir. I would not care to offer a definition."

"It's when they send a tuned suite of queries and responses to a physically remote location, by light beam. To play the part of an emissary."

" 'They,' sir?"

"Engineers, the Administrata. Perhaps the Omnocracy."

Fassin sat back. "Indeed?"

"Indeed. If we are to believe what we are told, the object they send is something like a library, transmitted by signal laser. Suitably housed and emplaced within enabled equipment of sufficient capacity and complexity, this... entity, though it is simply a many-branched array of statements, questions and answers, with a set of rules governing the order in which they are expressed, is able to carry out what seems very like an intelligent conversation. It is as close as one is allowed to come to an artificial intelligence, post-War."

"How singular."

Slovius wobbled in his pool. "They are assuredly surpassing rare," he agreed. "One is being sent here."

Fassin blinked a few times. "Sent here?"

"To Sept Bantrabal. To this house. To us."

"To us."

"From the Administrata."

"The Administrata." Fassin became aware that he was sounding simple-minded.

"Via the Engineership *Est-taun Zhiffir*."

"My," Fassin said. "We are... privileged."

"Not we, Fassin; you. The projection is being sent to talk to you."

Fassin smiled weakly. "To me? I see. When will—?"

"It is currently being transmitted. It ought to be ready by late evening. You may wish to clear your schedule for this. Did you have much arranged?"

"Ah... a supper with Jaal. I'm sure—"

"I would make it an early supper, and don't tarry."

"Well, yes. Of course," Fassin said. "Do you have any idea, sir, what I might have done to deserve such an honour?"

Slovius was silent for a moment, then said, "None whatsoever."

Guime replaced an intercom set on its hook and left his place by the agate wall to kneel and whisper to Slovius, who nodded, then looked at Fassin. "Major-Domo Verpych would like to talk to you, nephew."

"Verpych?" Fassin said, with a gulp. The household's major-domo, Sept Bantrabal's most senior servant, was supposed to rest dormant until the whole sept moved to its winter lodgings, over eighty days from now. It was unheard of for him to be roused out of sequence. "I thought he was asleep!"

"Well, he's been woken up."

·

The ship had been dead for millennia. Nobody seemed to be sure quite how many, though the most plausible estimates put it at about six or seven. It was just one more foundered vessel from one or other of the great fleets which had contended the War of the New Quick (or perhaps the slightly later Machine War, or possibly the subsequent Scatter Wars, or maybe one of the brief, bitter, confused and untidy engagements implicit in the Strew), another forgotten, discarded piece from the great game of galactic power-mongering, civilisational competition, pan-species manoeuvring and general grand-scale meta-politicking.

The hulk had lain undiscovered on the surface of 'glantine for at least a thousand years because although 'glantine was a minor planet by human standards—slightly smaller than Mars—it was by the same measure sparsely populated, with fewer than a billion inhabitants, most of those concentrated in the tropics, and the area where the wreck had fallen—the North Waste Land—was a rarely visited and extensive tract of nothing much. That it had taken a long time for the local surveillance systems to return to anything like the sort of complexity or sophistication they'd exhibited before the commencement of hostilities also helped the ruins avoid detection. Lastly, for all the vessel's hulking size, some portion of its auto-camouflage systems had survived the craft's partial destruction, the deaths of all the mortals aboard and its impact on the planet-moon's surface, and so had kept it disguised for all that time, seemingly just another fold of barren, rocky ejecta from the impact crater left by a smaller but much faster-travelling derelict which had crashed and vaporised in a deep crater ten kilometres away right at the start of the New Quick dispute.

The ship's ruins had only been discovered because somebody in a flier had crashed, fatally, into one of its great curving ribs (perfectly holo-disguised at the time as sheer and shiningly inviting clear sky). Only then had the wreck been investigated, plundered for what little of its systems still worked (but which were not, under the new regime, proscribed. Which basically did not leave much.) and finally—the lifting of its hull and major substructures being prohibitively expensive to contemplate, its cutting-up and carting away difficult, also not cheap and possibly dangerous, and its complete destruction only possible with the sort of serious gigatonnage weaponry people tended to object strongly to when used in peacetime in the atmospheres of a small planet-moon, even in a wilderness area—it had been cordoned off and a series of airborne loiter-drones posted on indefinite guard above, just in case.

"No, this could be good, this could be positive," Saluus Kehar told them, and swung the little flier low across the high desert towards the broken lands where the tattered-looking ribs of the great downed ship lay like folded shadow against the slowly darkening purple sky. Beyond the ruins, a vast, shimmering blue-green curtain of light flickered into existence, silently waving and rippling across the sky, then faded away again.

"Yeah, you would fucking say that," Taince said, fiddling with the controls of the comms unit. Static chopped and surfed from the speakers.

"Should we be this close to the ground?" Ilen asked, forehead against the canopy, looking down. She glanced at the young man sharing the back seat of the little aircraft with her. "Seriously, Fass, should we?"

But Fassin was already saying, "The idea that his relentless positivism could ever produce feelings of negativity in others is a concept Sal's still struggling with. Sorry, Len. What?"

"I was just saying—"

"Yeah," Taince muttered, "get that goddam dirt-pinger on."

"All I mean," Saluus said, waving one hand around and taking the craft still lower, even closer to the sable blur of ground. Taince made a tutting sound and reached over to tap a screen button; there was a pinging noise and the craft rose a few metres and began tracking the ground more smoothly. Sal glared at her but didn't turn the ground-avoidance device off as he continued, "Is that we're still okay, we haven't been blasted yet, and now we have an opportunity to explore something we wouldn't be allowed to get anywhere near normally. Right place, right time, perfect opportunity. What's not to be positive about there?"

"You mean," Fassin drawled, glancing skyward, "aside from the unfortunate fact that some over-enthusiastic and doubtless deeply misunderstood Beyonders appear to be trying to turn us all into radioactive dust?"

Nobody seemed to be listening. Fassin made a show of stifling a yawn—nobody noticed that, either—and leaned back against the leather seat, stretching his left arm across the top of the couch in the general direction of Ilen Deste (still with her head against the canopy, staring as though hypnotised at the near-featureless sands speeding by beneath). He tried to look at least unconcerned and preferably bored. In fact, of course, he felt completely terrified, and more than a little helpless.

Sal and Taince were the dynamic couple in this group: Saluus the pilot, the dashing, handsome, headstrong but undeniably gifted (and, Fassin thought, just plain lucky) heir to a vast commercial empire, the unabashed son of a fabulously rich, buccaneering father. Greedboy, Fassin had christened Sal in their first year at college, a term that their mutual friends had only used behind the youth's back until he got wind of it and adopted it enthusiastically as his personally approved tag. And Taince, co-pilot, navigator and comms supremo, as ever the knowing, abrasive commentator of the group (Fassin saw himself as the knowing, *sarcastic* commentator). Officer-in-Training Taince Yarabokin as she was supposed to be known now. Taince, the Milgirl—another of Fassin's coinings—had top-percentiled her college classes but had already been halfway to being an officer in the Navarchy Military through Reservist credits gleaned after hours, at weekends and on vacations, even before she'd taken a short degree and gone to Military Academy for her final year; fast-tracked from pre-induction, bumped from years One to Two midway through term and rumoured, even at such an almost unprecedentedly early stage, to be in contention for a chance later to join the Summed Fleet, the directly Culmina-controlled overarching ultra-power of the whole galaxy. In other words as seemingly surely destined for martial eminence as Sal was scheduled for commercial prodigiousness.

They'd both been out-system, too, making the journey to the Ulubis-system portal at Sepekte's trailing Lagrange point for the transition to Zenerre and the Complex, the network of wormholes threading the galaxy like a throw of dark lace beneath the tiny scattered lights of suns. Saluus's father had taken him on a Grand Tour on his long vacation last year, girdling the middle galaxy, visiting all the great accessible sites, encountering some of the more outré alien species, bringing back souvenirs. Taince had been to fewer but in some cases further places, courtesy of the Navarchy, its exercises and distributed specialist teaching facilities. They were the only two of their year to have travelled so widely, putting them in a little bubble of exoticism all by themselves.

Fassin had often thought that if his young life was to be tragically cut short before he'd even decided what he wanted to do with it (join the family firm and become a Seer?… Or something else?), it would very likely be because of these two, probably when they were each trying to outdo the other in daring or élan or sheer outrageous showing-off in front of their long-suffering friends. Sometimes he succeeded in persuading himself that he didn't particularly care if he did die anyway, that he'd already seen enough of life and love and all the crassness and stupidities of people and reality and would almost prefer to die a sudden, young, savagely beautiful death, with his body and mind as yet unspoiled and fresh and everything—as older relations still insisted on telling him—before him.

Though it would be a pity if Ilen—achingly beautiful, wanly pale, shamelessly blonde, effortlessly academically accomplished, bizarrely un-self-assured and insecure Ilen—had to perish in the wreck too, Fassin thought. Especially before they had fulfilled what he kept telling her—and what, frustratingly, he even sincerely believed—was their destiny, and established between the two of them some sort of meaningful but intense physical relationship. At the moment, though—head craned out over the side of the flier, nuzzling the canopy—it looked like the girl was thinking about throwing up.

Fassin looked away and attempted to distract himself from thoughts of imminent death and probably all too non-imminent sex by staring at the starry sweep emerging from the false horizon of Nasqueron's shadowy, departing bulk and the quickly darkening sky being revealed beyond. Another burst of aurora activity sent shimmering shawls of light across the heavens, briefly fading out the stars.

Ilen was looking in the opposite direction. "What's that smoke?" she cried, pointing beyond the half-collapsed nose of the fallen ship, where a tall, ragged strand of dark grey smoke leaned away from the breeze.

Taince glanced up and muttered something, then busied herself with the comms unit controls. The rest looked. Sal nodded. "Probably the guard drone that got zapped earlier," he said, though sounding uncertain.

The speakers crackled and a calm female voice said, "—lier two-two-nine... —sition? —ave you... —seven-five-three... —outh of Prohibited Area Ei—...... —peat you are now or wi— —ortly be off-grid... —firm your..."

Taince Yarabokin leaned closer to the comms unit. "This is flier two-two-nine, we have no place safe to put down under cover as advised so we are making maximum speed at minimum altitude towards—"

Saluus Kehar reached over with one coppery-gold hand and clicked the comms unit off.

"*Fuck* you!" Taince said, slapping his hand away even as it went back to the flier's control yoke.

"Taince, really," Sal said, shaking his head but keeping his gaze on the rapidly approaching ship ruins, "you don't have to *tell* them."

"Cretin," Taince breathed. She switched the comms back on.

"Yes, see previous comment," Fassin said, shaking his head.

"Will you leave that *alone*?" Sal said, trying and failing to turn the comms unit off again as Taince searched for a working channel and kept slapping his hand away. (Fassin was about to say something to the effect that she was better practised at this form of behaviour than he'd ever have assumed. Then thought the better of it.) "Look," Sal said, "I'm ordering you, Taince; leave the damn thing off. Who does this flier belong to, anyway?"

"Your dad?" Fassin suggested. Sal glanced back at him, reproachful. Fassin nodded forwards at the swiftly enlarging wreck of the ship. "Eyes ahead."

Sal turned back. *I'm ordering you*, thought Fassin, with a sneer. Saluus, really. Had he used that form of words because Taince was in the military and he thought she'd just obey anything anybody called an order, even if it came from a civilian, or because he thought he could start throwing his dynastic weight around already? He was surprised that Taince hadn't laughed in Sal's face.

Oh well, they weren't innocents any more, Fassin reminded himself, and the more you learned about the world, the galaxy and the Age they were growing up within, the more you realised it was all about hierarchy, about ranking and seniority and pecking order, from well, well below where they were all the way up to gloriously unseeable alien heights. Really they were like lab mice growing up together, rough-and-tumbling in the cage, learning their position in the litter, testing their own and the others' abilities and weaknesses, working on their moves and strategies for later life, discovering how much leeway they might have or be granted as adults, mapping out the space for their dreams.

Taince snorted. "Probably not even daddy's car, probably not even a company flier, more likely some complicated sale-and-leaseback deal and it's owned by an off-planet, tax-opaque semi-automatic front company." She growled and slapped the unresponding comms unit.

Sal shook his head. "Such cynicism in the young," he said, then looked down at the butterfly shape of the control yoke. "Hey, this is vibrating! What—?"

Taince nodded at the ship ruins, now towering over them. "Proximity warning, ace. You might want to slow down, or peel and scrub."

"How can you talk about exfoliating at a time like this?" Sal said, grinning. Taince punched his thigh. "Ow! That's assault," he said, pretending outrage. "I may sue." She punched him again. He laughed, throttled back and air-braked, pushing them all forward against their restraints, until the little flier was down to about ten metres per second.

They passed into the shadow of the giant ship.

∴

"Fassin Taak," Major-Domo Verpych said, "what trouble have you landed us in now?" They were hurrying down a wide, windowless passageway under the centre of the house. Before Fassin could reply, Verpych nodded at a side corridor and strode towards it. "This way."

Fassin lengthened his stride to keep up. "I am as ignorant as you are, major-domo."

"Clearly your gift for understatement has not deserted you."

Fassin absorbed this and thought the better of replying. He assumed what he hoped looked like a tolerant smile, though when he glanced at Verpych the major-domo wasn't looking. Verpych was a small, thin but powerful-looking man with pale creamy skin, ubiquitously stubbled, giving his head the look of having been chiselled out of sandstone. He had a square, ever-clenched jaw and a perpetual frown. His head was shaved save for a single long ponytail that extended to his waist. He gripped the long obsidian staff which was his principal badge of office as though it was a dark snake he was trying to throttle one-handed. His uniform was the black of soot, like folded night.

As Chief Seer-in-waiting Fassin was, supposedly, in a position of complete authority over Verpych. However, somehow the Sept's most senior servant still managed to make him feel like a child who'd only just escaped being discovered doing something extremely improper. Fassin could envisage the changeover when he finally assumed the post of Chief Seer being awkward for both of them.

Verpych turned on his heel and walked straight at a large abstract mural hanging on one wall. He waved his staff at the painting as though pointing out some detail of the brushwork, and the whole painting disappeared into a slot in the floor. Verpych stepped up into a dimly lit corridor beyond. He didn't bother to look back as Fassin followed him, just said, "Short cut."

Fassin glanced back as the painting rose out of the slot in the floor, cutting off most of the light in the corridor, which looked bare and unfinished after the passageway that they'd just left. He couldn't remember the last time he'd been in a utility corridor; probably when he'd been a child, exploring with his friends.

They stopped at a lift, its door open, a chime sounding. A boy servant stood in the elevator car, holding a tray full of dirty glasses with one hand and using the other to jab at the car controls, a puzzled, frustrated expression on his face.

"Get out, you idiot," Verpych told the boy as he strode to the lift. "It's being held for me."

The servant's eyes widened. He made spluttering noises and almost dropped the tray, hurrying to quit the elevator. Verpych tapped a button on the lift controls with the end of the staff, the doors closed and the lift—a plain metal box with a scuffed floor—descended.

"Have you recovered from your unscheduled awakening, major-domo?" Fassin asked.

"Entirely," Verpych said crisply. "Now then, Seer Taak. Assuming my comedy troupe of technicians haven't electrocuted themselves or stared into any light cables to check that they're working and blinded themselves, we should be ready for you to hold your conversation with whatever it is they are beaming towards us about an hour before midnight. Is nineteen o'clock convenient for you?"

Fassin thought. "Actually, the lady Jaal Tonderon and I might be—"

"The answer you are searching for is 'Yes,' Seer Taak," Verpych said.

Fassin frowned down at the older man. "Then in that case why did you—?"

"I was being polite."

"Ah. Of course. That cannot come easily."

"Quite the contrary. It is deference that one sometimes struggles with."

"Your efforts are appreciated, I'm sure."

"Why, I live for nothing else, young master." Verpych smiled thinly.

Fassin held the major-domo's gaze. "Verpych, could I be in some sort of trouble?"

The servant looked away. "I have no idea, sir." The lift began to slow. "This emissarial projection is unprecedented in the history of Sept Bantrabal. I have talked to some other major-domos and nobody can recall such a thing. We had all thought such phenomena restricted to the Hierchon and his chums in the sys-cap. I've sent a message to a contact I have in the palace asking for any guidance or tips they might have. There has been no reply so far."

The lift doors opened and they stepped out; another corridor, quite warm, cut from naked rock, curving. The major-domo looked at Fassin with what might have been concern, even sympathy. "An unprecedented event might be of a benign nature, Seer Taak."

Fassin hoped that he looked as sceptical as he felt. "So what do I have to do?"

"Present yourself to the Audience Chamber, top floor, at nineteen. Preferably a little before." They came to a Y-junction and a wider corridor, where red-uniformed technicians were trundling a pallet loaded with complicated-looking equipment towards a set of open double doors ahead.

"I'd like Olmey to be there," Fassin said. Tchayan Olmey had been Fassin's mentor and tutor in his youth, and—had she not become a pure academic in the household library, researching and teaching to the exclusion of undertaking any delves of her own—might have been the next familias and Chief Seer.

"That will not be possible," Verpych said, ushering Fassin through the double doors into the room beyond, which was hot, crowded with more red-uniformed technicians and dished, like a small theatre. Dozens of opened cabinets displayed intricate machinery, cables hung from the tall ceiling, snaked across the floor and disappeared into ducts in the walls. The place smelled of oil, singed plastic and sweat. Verpych stood at the top and rear of the room, watching the activity, shaking his head as two techs collided, spilling cable.

"Why not?" Fassin asked. "Olmey's here. And I rather wanted Uncle Slovius to be able to look in as well."

"That won't be possible either," Verpych told Fassin. "You and you alone have to talk to this thing."

"I have no choice in this?" Fassin asked.

"Correct," the major-domo said. "None." He returned his attention to the milling techs. One of the senior ones had approached to within a couple of metres, waiting for an opportunity to speak.

"But why not?" Fassin repeated, aware as soon as he said it that he was sounding like a small child.

Verpych shook his head. "I don't know. To the best of my knowledge there is no technical reason. Perhaps whatever is to be discussed is too sensitive for other ears." He looked at the red-uniformed man waiting nearby. "Master Technician Imming," he said brightly. "Working on the principle that whatever can go wrong will, I have been weighing up the possibilities that our house automatics have rusted into a single unusable mass, crumbled to a fine powder or unexpectedly declared themselves sentient, necessitating the destruction by fusion warheads of our entire house, Sept and possibly planet. Which is it to be?"

"Sir, we have encountered several problems," the technician said slowly, his gaze flicking from Fassin to Verpych.

"I do so hope the next word is 'But' or 'However'," Verpych said. He glanced at Fassin. "A 'Happily' would be too much to ask for, of course."

The technician continued. "Thanks to our considerable efforts, sir, we believe we have the situation in hand. I would hope that we ought to be ready by the appointed hour."

"We have the capacity to absorb all that is being transmitted?"

"Just, sir." Master Technician Imming gestured to the equipment on the pallet being manoeuvred through the double doors. "We are using some spare capacity from the utility systems."

"Is there any indication of the nature of the subject contained within the signal?"

"No, sir. It will remain in code until activated."

"Could we find out?"

Imming looked pained. "Not really, sir."

"Could we not try?"

"That would be nearly impossible, in the time frame, major-domo. And illegal. Possibly dangerous."

"Seer Taak here is wondering what he is to be faced with. You can give him no clues?"

Master Technician Imming made a small bow to Fassin. "I'm afraid not, sir. Wish it were otherwise."

Verpych turned to Fassin. "We seem unable to help you, Seer Taak. I am so sorry."

:

"Whose was this, anyway?" Ilen asked, keeping her voice down. She looked up into the shadows high above. "Who did it belong to?"

They had swung in through the single great jagged fissure in the ship's left flank, flying up between two massively curved rib-struts, the sky above framed by the twisted, buckled ribs, the sections of the hull they had supported turned to dissociated molecules and atoms seven millennia earlier. Sal had let the flier slip four hundred metres or so into the shadows under the intact forward portion of the hull—climbing gently all the time, following the mangled, buckled floors and collapsed bulkheads forming the terrain beneath them—until they could see only the slimmest sliver of violet, star-spattered sky outside and felt they ought to be safe from whatever spaceborne craft— presumably a Beyonder—had been attacking anything that moved or had recently been moving on the surface.

Sal had set the little craft down. The flier came to rest in a slight hollow on a relatively level patch of blackened, minutely rippled material, behind what might have been the remains of a crumpled bulkhead. The way ahead into the rest of the ship's forward section was blocked fifty metres further in by the hanging, frozen-looking tatters of some twisted, iridescent material. Saluus had thought aloud about trying to nudge the flier through this suspended debris, but had been dissuaded.

The flier's comms reception—even the distorted, jammed signal that they'd experienced outside—had just faded away almost as soon as they'd entered the wreck. For something supposed to pull in a signal through tens of klicks of solid rock, this was remarkable. The air inside the vast cave of the ruined craft felt cold and smelled of nothing. Knowing they were inside, the fact that their voices did not echo in the huge space was oddly disturbing, giving the sound a strange, hollow quality. The interior and running lights of the flier put them in a tiny pool of luminescence, emphasising their insignificance within the ancient fallen ship.

"Some dispute about exactly whose it might be," Saluus said, also quietly, and also gazing upwards at the smoothly ribbed ceiling of the vessel, arching a third of a kilometre above them and still just visible in the gloaming. "Marked down as a Sceuri wreck—they sent their War Graves people to clean it out—but if it was then it must have been requisitioned or captured. And they reckon it had a highly mixed crew, though mostly swimmers: waterworlders. Could be Oerileithe originally, oddly enough. Has the design of a dweller-with-a-small-d ship. But some sort of war craft, certainly."

Taince snorted. Sal looked at her. "Yes?"

"What it isn't," she said, "is a needle ship."

"Did I say it was?" Sal asked.

"Rather a fat needle, if it was," Fassin said, swivelling on his heel to follow the downward curve of the wrecked ship's interior towards its crumpled, partially buried nose, over a kilometre away in the darkness.

"It's *not* a needle ship," Sal protested. "I didn't *call* it a needle ship."

"See?" Taince said. "Now you've confused people."

"Anyway," Sal said, ignoring this, "there's a rumour they pulled a couple of Voehn bodies out of here, and that really does make it more interesting."

"Voehn?" Taince burst out laughing. "*Spiner* stiffs?" Her voice dripped scorn. She was even smiling, which Fassin knew wasn't something you saw every day. Pity, because her smooth, slightly square face—under a regulation military bald—looked kind of impishly attractive when she smiled. Come to think of it, that was probably why she didn't do it often. Actually Fassin thought Taince looked pretty good anyway, in her off-duty fatigues. (The rest of them just wore standard hiking/outdoorsy gear, though naturally Sal's was subtly but noticeably superior and doubtless wildly more expensive.) Tain's fatigues kind of bagged out in odd locations but came back in at the right places to leave no doubt that she was definitely a milgirl, not a milboy. They'd turned shadow-matt and dark in the surrounding gloom, too. Apparently even the NavMil's off-duty fatigues for trainees came with active camo.

She was shaking her head, as though she couldn't believe what she was hearing. Even Fassin, who'd pretty much shucked off the whole boy thing of obsessive interest in all things military and alien not long after the onset of puberty, knew about the Voehn. They were usually described in the media as living legends or near-mythical warriors, which kind of blanded what they really were; the crack troops and personal guards of the new galactic masters.

The Voehn were the calmly relentless, highly intelligent, omni-competent, near-indestructible, all-environments-capable, undefeated *über*-soldiers of the last nine or so millennia. They were the martial pin-ups of the age, the speckless species peak of military perfection, but they were rare, few and far between. Where the new masters, the Culmina, were, the Voehn were too, but not in all that many other places, and—as far as anybody knew, Fassin had been given to understand—in all those millennia not one had even entered the Ulubis system to visit Sepekte, the principal planet, let alone come near Nasqueron, or deigned to have anything to do with its little planet-moon 'glantine, even in death.

There was, of course, a further resonance for humans in the Voehn name and reputation, whether one was aHuman or rHuman. It had been the actions of a single Voehn ship nearly eight thousand years earlier which had made the distinction and the two prefixes necessary in the first place.

"Voehn," Sal said defiantly to Taince. "Voehn remains. That's the rumour."

Taince narrowed her eyes and drew herself up in her NavMil-issue fatigues. "Not one I've heard."

"Yes," Sal said, "well, my contacts are a few levels above the boot locker."

Fassin gulped. "I thought they all got smeared in this thing, anyway," he said quickly, before Taince could reply. "Just paste, gas and stuff."

"They were," Taince said through her teeth, looking at Sal, not him.

"Indeed they were," Sal agreed. "But Voehn are real toughies, aren't they, Tain?"

"Shit, yeah," Taince said quietly, levelly. "Real fucking toughies."

"Takes a lot to kill one, takes even more to paste it," Sal said, seemingly oblivious to Taince's signals.

"Notoriously resistant to fate and the enemy's various unpleasantnesses," Taince said coldly. Fassin had the feeling she was quoting. The gossip was that she and Sal were some sort of couple, or at least fucked now and again. But Fassin thought that, given the look in her eyes right now, that particular side of their relationship, if it had ever existed, might be in some danger of being pasted itself. He looked for Ilen, to catch her expression.

She wasn't where she'd been, on the far side of the flier. He looked around some more. She wasn't anywhere he could see. "Ilen?" he said. He glanced at the other two. "Where's Ilen?"

Sal tapped his ear stud. "Ilen?" he said. "Hey, Len?"

Fassin peered into the shadows. He had night vision as good as most people, but with barely any starlight and only the soft conserve-level lights of the flier resting in its declivity, there wasn't much to work with. Infrared showed next to nothing too, not even fading footstep-traces on whatever this strange material was.

"Ilen?" Sal said again. He looked at Taince, who was also scanning the area. "I can't see shit and my phone's out," he told her. "You able to see any better than us?"

Taince shook her head. "Get those eyes in fourth year."

*Shit*, thought Fassin. He wondered if anybody had a torch. Probably not. Few people did these days. He checked his own earphone, but it was dead too; not even local reception. *Oh fuck, oh fuck, oh fuck.* When did the archetype of this storyline date from? Four kids getting the use of dad's chariot and losing a wheel just before nightfall near the old deserted Neanderthal cave? Something like that. Just wander off into the dark and get killed horribly, one by one.

"I'll turn up the flier lights," Sal said, reaching for the interior. "If ness, we can lift off and—"

"ILEN!" Taince shouted at the top of her lungs. Fassin jumped. He hoped the others hadn't noticed.

"...Over here." Ilen's voice came, very distantly, from further inside the wreck.

"Wandering off!" Sal shouted in the general direction Ilen's voice had come from. "Not good idea! In fact, very bad idea! Suggest return immediately!"

"Peeing in front of peers problem," the reply drifted back. "Bashful bladder syndrome. Relieved, returning. Speak normal now, or Len get Tain poke Sal eye out."

Taince grinned. Fassin had to turn away. Sometimes, through all the almost wilfully unjustified reticence and uncertainty, and often at moments like this when you might least expect it, Ilen surprised him by doing or saying something like this. She made his insides hurt. *Oh, don't let me start to fall in love with her*, he thought. *That would just be too much to bear.*

Sal laughed. A vaguely Ilen-shaped blob appeared in IR sense fifty metres away, head first over a fold in the rippled floor like a shallow hill. "There. She's fine," Sal announced, as though he'd rescued her personally.

Ilen rejoined them, smiling and blinking in the soft lights of the flier, her white-gold hair shining. She nodded. "Evening," she said, and grinned at them.

"Welcome back," Sal told her, and hauled a pack out of one of the flier's storage lockers. He swung the bag onto his back.

Taince glared at the pack, then at Sal's face. "What the fuck are you doing?"

Sal looked innocent. "Going to take a look round. You can join me if—"

"Like fuck you are."

"Tain, child," he laughed. "I don't need your permission."

"I'm not a fucking child and yes, you fucking do."

"And will you please stop swearing *quite* so much? There's really no need to flaunt your newly acquired gruff military manner quite so conspicuously."

"We stay here," she told him, using the cold voice again. "Close to the flier. We don't go wandering off into a *prohibited* alien shipwreck in the middle of the night with an enemy craft cruising overhead."

"Why not?" Sal protested. "For one thing it's probably on the other side of the planet by now or maybe even destroyed. And anyway, if this Beyonder ship, or battlesat, or drone, or whatever it is can see inside here, which I seriously doubt, it's going to target the flier, not a few human warm-bods, so we're safer away from the thing."

"You stay with the craft, always," Taince said, her jaw set.

"For how long?" Sal asked. "How long do these nuisance raids, these attacklets, usually last?" Taince just glared at him. "Half a day, average," Sal told her. "Overnight, probably, in this case. Meantime we're somewhere it's not normally possible to be, through no fault of our own, with time to kill… why the hell not take a look round?"

"Because it's Prohibited," Taince said. "That's why."

Fassin and Ilen exchanged looks, concerned but still amused.

"Taince!" Sal said, waving his arms. "Life is risk. That's business. Come on!"

"You stay with the craft," Taince repeated grimly.

"Will you step out of your programming just for a second?" Sal asked her, sounding genuinely annoyed and looking at the other two for support. "Can any of us think of one good reason why this place *is* prohibited, apart from standard authoritarian, bureaucratic, overreacting, territory-marking militaristic bullshit?"

"Maybe they know stuff we don't," Taince said.

"Oh, come *on*!" Sal protested. "They always claim that!"

"Listen," Taince said levelly. "Your point is taken regarding the likelihood of the flier's systems being targeted by hostiles, and therefore I volunteer to walk out, every hour on the hour, to near the gap in the hull where a phone might work once the jamming sub-sats have been neutralised, to check for the all-clear."

"Fine," Sal said, digging into another of the flier's lockers. "You do that. I'm seizing the once-in-a-lifetime opportunity to take a look round an intrinsically fascinating alien artefact. If you hear me screaming horribly it'll just be me falling into the claws, suckers or… beaks of some unspeakable space-alien monster every single wreck-clearing team missed and which has chosen just this evening out of the last seven millennia to wake up and feel hungry."

Taince took a deep breath, stepped back from the flier and said, "Okay, seems this must qualify as an emergency." She dug into her black fatigues and when her hand reappeared it held a small dark grey device.

Sal stared at her, incredulous. "What the hell is *that*? A gun? You're not planning to *shoot* me, are you, Taince?"

She shook her head and thumbed something on the side of the device. There was a pause, then Taince frowned and looked closely at the thing in her hand. "Actually," she said, "at the moment I'm not even threatening to report you to the local Guard, not in real-time, anyway." Sal relaxed a little, but didn't pull whatever it was he'd been looking for out of the locker. Taince shook her head and looked up into the black spaces of the cavernous craft around them. She held the little grey device up to show the others. "This baby," she said, "should be able to punch me through to a kid's disposable on the far side of the planet, but it's still searching for cosmic background." She sounded more puzzled than embarrassed or angry, Fassin thought. (In similar circumstances, he'd have been mortified, and it would have shown.)

Taince nodded, still staring upwards. "Impressive." She put the hand-held away again.

Sal cleared his throat. "Taince, *do* you have a gun? It's just that I'm about to pull one out of this locker and you looked kind of scary and trigger-happy just there."

"Yes, I do have a gun," she told him. "Promise I won't shoot you." She gave a smile that wasn't really. "And if you are intent on traipsing into the bowels of this thing, I'm not going to try and stop you. You're a big boy now. Your responsibility."

"Finally," Sal said with satisfaction, pulling a plain but businesslike-looking CR pistol out of the locker and attaching it to his belt. "There's food and water and bedrolls and extra clothes and stuff in the rear lockers," he told them, slapping a couple of low-light illuminator patches onto his jacket shoulders. "I'll be back about dawn." He multiple-tapped his ear stud, then smiled. "Yep, internal clock still working." He glanced at each of them in turn. "Hey, there's probably nothing to see; I could be back in an hour for all I know." They all just looked at him. "Nobody else coming along, huh?" he asked. Ilen and Fassin glanced at each other. Taince was watching Sal, who said, "Well, don't wait up," and turned to go.

"You're very well prepared for this," Taince said quietly.

Sal hesitated, then turned towards her, open-mouthed. He looked at Fassin and Ilen, then stared with wide eyes at Taince. He gestured towards the distant hull gap, upwards as though to space, then shook his head. "Taince, Taince," he breathed. He pushed one hand through his thick black hair. "Just how paranoid and suspicious do they insist you be in the military?"

"Your father's company makes our battlecraft, Saluus," she told him. "Wariness is a survival strategy."

"Oh, cheap shot, Taince." Sal looked mildly insulted. "But I mean, really. Seriously. Come on." He slapped his backpack, exasperated. "Hell's teeth, woman, if I *hadn't* made sure the flier was equipped with emergency gear you'd have chewed my ear for making a deep-desert flight without the necessary supplies!"

Taince stood looking at him, near-expressionless, for a few moments longer. "Mind how you go, Sal."

He nodded, relaxing. "You too," he said. "See you all soon." He looked round them all one more time, grinning. "Nothing I wouldn't do, and all that." He waved his hand and tramped off.

"Hold on," Ilen said. Sal turned back. Ilen pulled her little day-pack out of the flier. "I'll come with you, Sal."

Fassin stared, horrified. "What?" he said, in a small, shocked, little boy's voice. Nobody seemed to hear. For once he was glad. Taince said nothing.

Sal smiled. "You sure?" he asked the girl.

"If you don't mind," Ilen said.

"Fine by me," Sal said quietly.

"Sure you don't mind?"

"Of course I don't mind."

"Well, you're not supposed to go off exploring in dubious situations individually, are you?" Ilen said. "Isn't that right?" She looked at Taince, who nodded. "You take care." Ilen kissed Fassin's cheek, winked at Taince and strode up the shallow slope to Sal. They waved and walked off. Fassin watched their footstep-traces in IR, each faint patch of brightness on the ground behind them fading after less than a second.

"Never understand that girl," Taince said, sounding unconcerned. She and Fassin looked at each other. "Suggest you take a snooze now," Taince told him, nodding at the flier. She picked her nose and inspected her finger. "I'll wake you before I head out to the hull gap to check for signal."

:

A fragrance bud popped somewhere in the darkened room, and—after a few moments—he smelled Orchidia Noctisia, a Madebloom scent he would always associate with the Autumn House. There was little air movement in the quiet chamber so the bud must have been floating nearby. He lifted his head gently and saw a tiny shape like a slim, translucent flower falling chiffon-soft through the air between the bed and the trolley which had brought their supper. He lowered his head to Jaal's shoulder again.

"Mmm?" she said drowsily.

"Meet any friends in town?" Fassin asked, winding a long golden coil of Jaal Tonderon's hair around one finger, then bringing his nose forward to nuzzle the nape of her brown-red neck, breathing in the smell of her. She shifted against him, moving her hips in a sort of stirring motion. He had slipped out of her some time ago, but it was still a good feeling.

"Ree and Grey and Sa," she said, her voice starting out a little sleepy. "Shopping was accomplished. Then we met up with Djen and Sohn. And Dayd, Dayd Eslaus. Oh, and Yoaz. You remember Yoaz Irmin, don't you?"

He nipped her neck and was rewarded with a flinch and a yelp. "That was a long time ago," he told her.

She reached one hand behind her and stroked his exposed flank, then patted his behind. "I'm sure the memory is still vivid for her, dear."

"Ha!" he said. "So am I." This drew a slap. Then they settled in against each other once more; she did that thing with her hips again and he wondered if there would be time for more sex before he had to go.

She turned to face him. Jaal Tonderon's face was round and wide and only just very beautiful. For two thousand years or so, rHuman faces had looked pretty much how the owners wanted them to look, displaying either satisfaction with or indifference to whatever womb-grown comeliness they had been born with, or the particular, amended look their owners had subsequently specified. The only ugly people were those making a statement.

In an age when everyone could be beautiful, and/or look like famous historical figures (there were now laws about looking too much like famous contemporary figures), the truly interesting faces and bodies were those which sailed as close to the wind of being plain or even unattractive as possible, and yet just got away with it. People talked about faces that looked good in the flesh but not in images, or good in lifelike paintings but not on a screen, or faces that looked unattractive in repose but quite stunning when animated, or merely plain until the person smiled.

Jaal had been born with a face that looked—she said herself—committee design: unharmonious, stuck together, nothing quite matching. Yet to almost everybody who had ever met her, she seemed outrageously attractive, thanks to some alchemy of physiognomy, personality and expression. Fassin's private estimation was that Jaal's was a face still waiting to be grown into, and that she would be more beautiful when she was middle-aged than she was now. It was one reason he had asked her to marry him.

They could look forward, Fassin had every reason to believe, to a long life together, and just as it had been sensible to marry within his profession—and to make a match that would meet with the enthusiastic approval of their respective Septs, strengthening the bonds between two of the most important Seer houses—so it had been only prudent to take that likely longevity into account.

Of course, as Slow Seers Fassin and Jaal's shared future would be absolutely if not relatively longer than that of most of their contemporaries, and radically different; in the slow-time of a long delve, Seers aged very slowly indeed, and Uncle Slovius's fourteen centuries, while short of the record and not yet (thankfully, naturally) his limit, should not be difficult to surpass. Seer spouses and loved ones had to schedule their slow-time and normal life carefully so as not to get too out of synch with each other, lest the protagonists lose touch emotionally. The life of Tchayan Olmey, Fassin's old mentor and tutor, had hinged on just such an unforeseen discontinuity, leaving her stranded from an old love.

"Anything wrong?" Jaal asked him.

"Just this, ah, interview thing." He glanced at the antique clock across the room.

"Who's it with?"

"Can't say," he told her. He'd mentioned having an appointment for an interview later when he'd first met Jaal off her suborb shuttle at the house port in the valley below, but she'd been too busy telling him about the latest gossip from the capital and the scandal regarding her Aunt Feem and the Sept Khustrial boy to question him any further on the matter. Her shower, their supper and then more urgent matters had taken precedence thereafter.

"You can't say?" she said, frowning, turning further round towards him, lifting and repositioning one dark breast on his light brown chest as she did so. There was something, he thought, not for the first time, about an aureola more pale than its surroundings… "Oh, Fass," Jaal said, sounding annoyed, "it's not a girl, is it? Not a *servant* girl? Fucking forfend, not *before* we're married, surely?"

She was smiling. He grinned back. "Nuisance, but has to be done. Sorry."

"You really can't say?" She shifted her head, and blonde hair spilled over his shoulder. It felt even better than it looked.

"Really," he said.

Jaal was staring intently at his mouth. "Really?" she asked.

"Well." He licked his teeth. "I can say it's not a girl." She was still staring intently at his mouth. "Look, Jaal, have I got some sort of foreign matter lodged in there?"

She pushed her mouth slowly up towards his. "Not," she said, "yet."

"You are Fassin Taak, of the Seer Sept Bantrabal, 'glantine moon, Nasqueron gas-giant planet, Ulubis star and system?"

"Yes, I am."

"You are physically present here and not any sort of projection or other kind of representation?"

"Correct."

"You are still an active Slow Seer, domiciled in the seasonal houses of Sept Bantrabal and working from the satellite-moon Third Fury?"

"Yes, yes and yes."

"Good. Fassin Taak, everything that will pass between you and this construct is in strictest confidence. You will respect that confidence and communicate to others no more of what we shall talk about than is absolutely necessary to facilitate such conduct as will be required of you in furtherance of whatever actions you will be asked to perform and whatever goals you will be asked to pursue. Do you do understand that and agree?"

Fassin thought about this. Just for an instant as the projection had started talking it had suddenly occurred to him that the glowing orb looked a lot like a Plasmatic being (not that he'd ever met one, but he'd seen images), and that moment of distraction had been sufficient for him to miss the full meaning of what had been said. "Actually, no. Sorry, I'm not trying to be—"

"To repeat…"

Fassin was in the main audience chamber at the top of the Autumn House, a large circular space with views in every horizontal direction and a dramatic transparent roof, all blanked out. For now its contents consisted of a single seat for him and a stubby, metallic-looking cylinder supporting a globe of glowing gas hovering above its centre. A fat cable ran from the squat cylinder to a floor flap in the middle of the chamber.

The gas sphere repeated what it had just said. It spoke more slowly this time, though happily with no trace of irritation or condescension. Its voice was flat, unaccented, and yet still seemed to contain the hint of a personality, as though the voice of a particular individual had been sampled and used as a template, from which most but not all expression had been removed.

Fassin heard it out, then said, "Okay, yes, I understand and agree."

"Good. This construct is an emissarial projection of the Mercatorial Administrata, sub-Ministerial level, with superior-rank authority courtesy of the Ascendancy, Engineer division, Senior Engineer level, Eship *Est-taun Zhiffir*, portal-carrying. It is qualified to appear sentient while not in fact being so. Do you understand this?"

Fassin thought about this too and decided that he did, just. "Yep," he said, then wondered if the projection would understand colloquial affirmatives. Apparently it did.

"Good. Seer Fassin Taak, you are hereby seconded to the Shrievalty Ocula. You will have the honorary rank—"

"Hold on!" Fassin nearly jumped out of his seat. "The *what*?"

"The honorary rank of—"

"No, I mean I'm *seconded* to the what?"

"The Shrievalty Ocula. You will have the honorary—"

"The *Shrievalty*?" Fassin said, trying to control his voice. "The *Ocula*?"

"Correct."

The baroque, intentionally labyrinthine power structures of the latest, Culmina-inspired Age, incorporating the aspirations of and enforced limitations on at least eight major subject species and whole vast subcategories of additional Faring races as well as (by its own claim) "contextualising" various lesser civilisations of widely varying scope and ambitions and, peripherally at least, influencing entire alien spectra of Others, held many organisations and institutions whose names the utterance of which people—or at least people who knew of such things—tended to greet with a degree of respect shading into fear.

The Shrievalty was probably the least extreme example; people might respect it—many would even find its purpose rather boring—but few would fear it. It was the paramilitary Order/discipline/faculty of technicians and theorists in charge of what had once been called Information Technology, and so it was also, though less exclusively, concerned with the acceptably restricted remnants of Artificial Intelligence technologies still extant in the post-War epoch.

The Machine War had wiped the vast majority of AIs out of existence throughout the galaxy over seven thousand years ago, and the Culmina-inspired—and -enforced—peace which followed had stabilised around a regime which both forbade research into AI tech and demanded the active help of all citizens in hunting down and destroying what few scattered vestiges of AI might still exist. Organised on military lines with a bracing infrastructure of religious dogma, the Shrievalty was charged with the running, administration and maintenance of those IT systems which were anywhere near being sufficiently complex to be in danger of becoming sentient, either through accident or design, but which were considered too vital to the running of their various dependent societies to be shut down and dismantled.

Another Order, a rather more fear-inspiring one, the Lustrals of the Cessoria, had been formed to hunt down and destroy both AIs themselves and anybody who attempted to create new ones or protect, shelter or otherwise aid existing examples. But that had not prevented the formation within the Shrievalty of an Intelligence section—the Shrievalty Ocula—whose duties, methods and even philosophy significantly overlapped with those of the Lustrals. It was the Ocula, this somewhat shadowy, slightly grim-sounding unit which Fassin was being ordered to become part of, for no reason that he could immediately fathom.

"The Ocula?" Fassin said. "Me? Are you absolutely sure?"

"Absolutely."

Technically, he had no choice. To be allowed to do what they did, the Seers had to be an officially recognised profession within the Miscellariat, the catch-all term for those useful to the Mercatoria who did not fit inside the more standard subdivisional categories, and as such all Seers were subject to full Mercatorial discipline and control, committed to obeying any order issued by anybody properly authorised and of a sufficiently superior rank.

Yet this virtually never happened. Fassin couldn't remember anyone from Sept Bantrabal ever being seconded by order in peacetime, not in nearly two thousand years of Sept history. Why now? Why him?

"May this briefing continue?" the glowing orb asked. "It is important."

"Well, yes, all right, but I do have questions."

"All relevant questions will be answered where possible and prudent," the orb told him.

Fassin was thinking, wondering. Did he really have to accept this? What were the punishments for disobeying? Demotion? Forced resignation? Banishment? Outlaw status? Death?

"To resume, then," the gas globe said. "Seer Fassin Taak, you are hereby seconded to the Shrievalty Ocula. You will have the honorary rank of provisional acting captain for security clearance purposes, with exceptions made as required by authorised superiors, the principal honorary rank of major for seniority and disciplinary purposes, the honorary rank of general for reward purposes and the honorary rank of field marshal for travel-priority purposes. This construct is unable to negotiate regarding the aforesaid. Do you find the foregoing acceptable?"

"What if I say no?"

"Punitive actions will be taken. Certainly against you, probably against Sept Bantrabal and possibly against the 'glantine Slow Seers as a whole. Do you find the above-mentioned secondment details acceptable?"

Fassin had to shut his mouth. This floating bladder of glowing gas had just threatened not only him, not only his Sept and entire extended family and all their servants and dependants, but the major focus of uniquely important work being done on the entire planet-moon, one of the three or four most important centres for Dweller Studies in the entire galaxy! It was so outrageous, so surely disproportionate, it almost had to be a joke.

Fassin thought back, desperately trying to fit all that had happened to him today, with Slovius, with Verpych, with everybody who would have to be in on the joke, into a scenario more plausible than the one he was apparently faced with: an appallingly high-level projection from a portal-carrying Eship still a dozen light years away ordering him to join an allegedly no-holds-barred intelligence unit answering to an Order and a discipline he knew no more about than any other lay person, and with the force of the Administrata and the Engineers behind it.

"Do you find the above-mentioned secondment details acceptable?" the orb repeated.

Or maybe, Fassin thought, Sept Bantrabal as a whole was being made fun of here. Maybe nobody here knew this was a practical joke. Would somebody go to all this trouble just to make him look foolish, to frighten him? Had he ever antagonised anybody with the resources to set something like this up? Well...

"Do you find the above-mentioned secondment details acceptable?" the orb said again.

Fassin gave in. If he was lucky this was a joke. If not, it might be very stupid and even dangerous to treat it as such when it wasn't.

"Given your crude and objectionable threats, I don't really have much choice, do I?"

"Is that an answer in the affirmative?"

"I suppose so. Yes."

"Good. You may ask questions, Seer Fassin Taak."

"Why am I being seconded?"

"To facilitate the actions you will be asked to perform and to help achieve whatever goals you will be requested to pursue."

"What would those be?"

"Initially, you are commanded to travel to Pirrintipiti, capital city of 'glantine planet-moon, there to take ship for Borquille, capital of Sepekte, principal planet of the Ulubis system for further briefing."

"And after that?"

"You will be expected to carry out actions and pursue goals as detailed in said briefing."

"But why? What's behind all this? What's this all about?"

"Information regarding what you ask is not carried by this construct."

"Why the Shrievalty Ocula, specifically?"

"Information regarding what you ask is not carried by this construct."

"Who has ordered this?"

"Information regarding what you ask is not—"

"All right!" Fassin drummed his fingers on the arm of his seat. Still, this projection had to have authority from somebody, it would have to know where it stood in the vast web of Mercatorial rank and seniority. "What rank was the person who ordered this?"

"Administrata: Shrievalty Army-Group Chief of Staff," the orb said. (Well, that went right to the top, Fassin thought. Whatever piece of nonsense, military bullshittery or wild-goose chase this was all about, it was one being authorised by somebody with no excuses for not knowing better.) "Ascendancy: Senior Engineer," the projection continued. (Ditto; Senior Engineer didn't sound as Grand-High-Everything-Else impressive as Army-Group Chief of Staff, for example, but it was the highest rank in the Engineers, the people who made, transported and emplaced the wormholes that stitched the whole galactic meta-civilisation together. In terms of ultimate power, and regardless of species, an SE probably way out-wielded a CoS.) "Omnocracy:" the orb said, with what sounded like a note of finality, "Complector."

Fassin sat and stared. He blinked a few times. He was aware that his mouth was open, so he closed it. His skin had seemed to tighten, all over his body. A fucking *Complector*? he thought, already wondering if he hadn't misheard. One of the *Culmina* ordered this?

A Complector sat at the clear undisputed pinnacle of the Mercatoria's civil command structure. Each one held absolute power over a significant galactic volume, usually with a definable locus, like a stellar cluster or a minor or even a major galactic arm. The least senior of them would be in charge of hundreds of thousands of stars, millions of planets, billions of habitats and trillions of souls. As well as their subject Administrata, they commanded the chiefs of all the other Ascendancy divisions within their jurisdiction—Engineers, Propylaea, Navarchy and Summed Fleet—and they were always Culmina. The only thing which outranked a Complector was a bigger bunch of Complectors.

Fassin thought for a moment, trying to calm himself down. Remember this could be a joke. The very fact that a Complector's authority had been invoked almost made it more likely that it was, it was just so preposterous.

On the other hand, he had the disquieting feeling, prompted by a half-remembered school lesson he probably ought to have been paying more attention to, that falsely invoking a Complector's authority was potentially a capital offence.

Think, think. Forget the Complector; back to the moment. What assumptions might he be making here? Any of the ego? (He'd had this psychological check-sum routine drilled into him at college, where he'd scored high on what was usually called the *Me-me-me!* scale. Though not as high as Saluus Kehar.) Well, he could think of one egotistical assumption he might be making immediately.

"How many other people are being similarly summoned?" he asked.

"By emissarial projection, only yourself."

Fassin sat back. Well, that certainly felt pleasing, but he suspected it was probably a much worse sign than it appeared.

"And by other means?"

"You will be joining a group of senior officials in Borquille, capital city of Sepekte, for further briefing. This group will number approximately thirty."

"And what will be the subject of this briefing?"

"Information regarding what you ask is not carried by this construct."

"How long am I likely to be away from home? Do I just go to Sepekte, get 'briefed' and come back? What?"

"Officers of the Shrievalty Ocula are expected to undertake extended missions with minimal notice."

"So I should expect to be away a while?"

"Officers of the Shrievalty Ocula are expected to undertake extended missions with minimal notice. Further information regarding what you ask is not carried by this construct."

Fassin sighed. "So is that it? You've been sent to tell me to go to Sepekte? All this... kerfuffle, for that?"

"No. You are to be informed that this is a matter of the utmost consequence and gravity, in which you may be asked to play a significant part. Also that information has come to light which indicates that there is a profound and imminent threat to Ulubis system. No further details concerning this are carried by this construct. You are commanded to report to the palace of the Hierchon in Borquille, capital of Sepekte, principal planet of the Ulubis system, for further briefing, no later than hour Fifteen tomorrow evening, the ninth of Duty, Borquille-Sepekte local time. Gchron, 6.61..." The sphere started to restate the time of Fassin's appointment at the Hierchon's palace the following day in a variety of different formats, as if to remove any last excuse for him not getting there on time. Fassin sat, staring at a beige-blank section of polarised window on the far side of the chamber, trying to decide what the hell to make of all this.

*Oh, fuck* was the best he could come up with.

"...The eighteenth of November, AD 4034, rHuman," the glowing orb concluded. "Transport will be provided. Baggage allowance is one large bag, carryable, plus luggage required to transport full formal court dress for your presentation to the Hierchon. A gee-suit should be worn for the outgoing journey. Any further questions?"

Verpych thought for a moment. "Military-grade hysteria."

Slovius shifted in his tub-chair. "Explain, please?"

"They are likely over-correcting for earlier dismissiveness, sir."

"Somebody's been telling them there's a problem, they've been pooh-poohing it, then suddenly woken up to the threat and panicked?" Fassin suggested.

Verpych nodded once.

"The decisional dynamics of highly rigid power structures make an interesting study subject," Tchayan Olmey said. Fassin's old tutor and mentor smiled across at him, a calm, gauntly grey presence. The four of them sat at a large round table in Slovius's old study, Slovius himself supported in a large semi-enclosed device that looked like a cross between an ancient hip bath and a small flier. Fassin thought his uncle's tusked, whiskered face looked more animated, and even more human, than it had for years. Slovius had announced at the start of the meeting that for the duration of whatever emergency they might be involved in, his slow demise was being halted; he was fully back in charge of Sept Bantrabal. Fassin had been appalled to find that there was some small, mean, self-aggrandising part of him which felt disappointed and even slightly angry that his uncle wasn't going to keep slipping into the hazy, woozily uncaring senility that led to death.

"The phrase the projection used was 'profound and imminent threat'," Fassin reminded them. That was what had spooked him, he supposed, that was why he'd suggested this meeting, told them what he had. If there really was a threat to Ulubis system, he wanted, at the very least, Sept Bantrabal's senior people to know about it. The only person missing from the conference was Fassin's mother, who was on a year-long retreat in a Cessorian habitat somewhere in the system's Kuiper belt, ten light days away and therefore profoundly out of the discussion. They had discussed whether she should be contacted and warned that there was some sort of system-wide threat, but without details this seemed premature and possibly even counter-productive.

Olmey shrugged. "The overreaction might well extend to the language used to describe the perceived problem," she said.

"There has been a recent increase in Beyonder attacks," Verpych said thoughtfully.

For the two centuries after the loss of its portal, the sporadic Beyonder assaults on Ulubis—as a rule against the system's outskirts and military targets—had declined to such an extent they were barely even of nuisance value. Certainly there were far fewer attacks than there had been in the years before the wormhole's destruction. For millennia, almost every system in the Mercatoria had been getting used to these generally irritating, rarely devastating raids—they tied up ships and matériel and kept the whole meta-civilisation slightly on edge but they had yet to produce any real atrocities—and it had come as something of a relief to the people of Ulubis, a kind of unlooked-for bonus, that for some perverse reason the system's temporary isolation had so far been a time when the direct military pressure on it had seemed to decrease rather than been cranked up.

Over the last year or so, however, there had been a slight increase in the number of attacks—the first time in two centuries that the yearly number had risen rather than fallen—and those assaults had been of a slightly different nature compared to those that people had more or less got used to. The targets had not all been military units or items of infrastructure, for one thing: a comet-cloud mining co-op had been destroyed, some belt and cloud ships had disappeared or been discovered drifting, empty or slagged, one small cruise liner had just disappeared between Nasqueron and the system's outermost gas-giant, and a single heavy-missile ship had appeared suddenly in the mid-system half a year ago, travelling at eighty per cent light speed and targeted straight at Borquille. It had been picked off with ease, but it had been an alarming development.

Slovius wobbled in his tub-chair again, slopping a little water onto the wooden floor. "Is there anything that you are *not* allowed to tell us, nephew?" he asked, then made a sound that sounded disturbingly like a chortle.

"Nothing specific, sir. I'm not supposed to talk to anybody about any part of this except to… further my mission, which at the moment consists of getting to Borquille by Fifteen tomorrow. Obviously, I've chosen to interpret this as allowing me to talk to you three. Though I would ask that it goes no further."

"Well," Slovius said, with a noise like a gargle in his throat, "you shall have my own suborbship to take you to Pirrintipiti for transfer."

"Thank you, sir. However, they did say that transport was being provided."

"Navarchy's filed an outgoing from here for half-Four tomorrow morning," Verpych confirmed. "Going to have to shift if they're getting you to Sepekte for Fifteen tomorrow," he added, with a sniff. "You'll need to suffer five or six gees the whole way, Fassin Taak." Major-Domo Verpych smiled. "I suggest you start adjusting your water and solids intake accordingly now."

"We shall have my vessel standing by in any case," Slovius said, "should this transport fail to turn up, or be overly crude in form. See to this, major-domo."

Verpych nodded. "Sir."

"Uncle, may I have a word?" Fassin asked as the meeting broke up. He'd hoped to catch Slovius before they'd begun, but his uncle had arrived with Verpych, Slovius looking energised and triumphant, Verpych appearing troubled, even worried.

Slovius nodded to his major-domo and Olmey. In a few moments Fassin and his uncle were left alone in the study.

"Nephew?"

"This morning, sir, when you were asking me about my most recent delves, while the emissarial projection was being downloaded—"

"How much did I know of the matter?"

"Well, yes."

"I had had a simple, if highly encrypted, signal from the Eship myself, to tell me that the projection was following. It was in the form of a personal message from a First Engineer on the ship, an old friend. A Kuskunde—their bodily and linguistic nuances formed part of my collegiate studies, many centuries ago. They did not say so, nevertheless, I formed the impression that all this might be the result of a delve of yours."

"I see."

"Your emissarial projection gave no hint whether this might be correct or not?"

"None, sir." Fassin paused. "Uncle, am I in trouble?"

Slovius sighed. "If I had to guess, nephew, I would surmise that you are not in direct trouble as such. However, I will confess to the distinct and unsettling feeling that very large, very ponderous and most momentous wheels have been set in motion. When that happens I believe the lessons of history tend to indicate that it is best not to be in their way. Even without meaning harm, the workings and progress of such wheels are on a scale which inevitably reduces the worth of individual lives to an irrelevance at best."

"At best?"

"At best. At worst, lives, their sacrifice, provide the oil required to make the wheels move. Does my explanation satisfy you?"

"That might be one word for it, sir, yes."

"Well then, it would appear we are equally in the dark, nephew." Slovius consulted a little ring embedded in one of his finger stubs. "And in the dark, sleep can be a good idea. I suggest you get some."

"Well, Fassin Taak," Verpych said briskly, waiting for him outside the door. "Finally you've done something that I find impressive. Thanks to you, not only do we appear to be about to start living in interesting times, you have succeeded in bringing us to the attention of people in high places. Congratulations."

◦

They sat on half-inflated bedrolls, their backs against the sides of the flier. "He's never told you about all that Severity School stuff?" Fassin asked.

Taince shook her head. "Nope." She took out her little grey military communicator again, checking in vain for reception. She and Fassin had already walked out to the hull gap half an hour earlier, looking for a signal either on this device or their phones. They'd stood there in the bright, flickering glow of a heavy aurora display, Nasqueron a vast inverted dome above, dark but sheened with its own rippling auroras and specked with a random craquelure of lightning bursts. A series of small ground-quakes had vibrated through their boots, but for all this natural turmoil—and perhaps partially because of the magnetic activity in the case of the phones—they had heard nothing through their machines.

They'd tramped back, Fassin grumbling about Beyonders for attacking a planet best known for its peaceful Dwellers Studies faculties in the first place, and the Guard, Navarchy Military, Ambient Squadrons and Summed Fleet for not protecting them better. Taince tried to explain about the logistics of moving sufficient numbers of needle ships and other bits of matériel through 'holes to where they'd be needed, and the equations which governed how many assets you would need fully to protect the many scattered systems of the Mercatoria. Even with the near-instantaneousness of portal-to-portal Arteria travel, it was an unfeasible, economically unsupportable number. The many enemy groupings might be collectively puny, but they were widely distributed and often working on an awkwardly extended timescale. The main thing was that 'glantine and Ulubis system as a whole were safe. Its own Squadrons were a match for any feasible Beyonder grouping, and behind them, just a few portal jumps away, lay the matchless superiority of the Summed Fleet.

None of this prevented Fassin from continuing to moan about the Beyonders' nuisance attacks, so Taince had shifted the conversation to their classmates' foibles, proclivities and eccentricities and before very long they'd got to Saluus.

"Well," Taince said, "he's mentioned going to Severity School but he's never volunteered anything much about it and I'm not his interrogator."

"Oh," Fassin said. He wondered if maybe Saluus and Taince weren't lovers after all. School, early life… that was the stuff of pillow talk, wasn't it? He stole a glance at Taince. Though "lovers" somehow didn't seem like the right word anyway, not for Sal and Tain, assuming they were involved. They each seemed different from everybody else in their year, less obviously caught up in the whole dating, young love and experimental sex scene, as though they'd gone through all that already or were just, through natural predisposition or sheer determination, immune to it somehow.

Taince intimidated most boys her own age and a lot who were significantly older, but she didn't care. Fassin had seen her turn down a couple of very nice, decent lads with a bruising degree of brusqueness, and then take off for what were pretty obviously one- or few-nighters with burly but boring guys. He had also known at least three girls in their school year who were hopelessly in love with Taince, but she hadn't cared about that either.

Saluus had been in an even stronger position from the start; not just good-looking—anybody could be that—but easy with it, and assured, charming and funny as well. All that and money! A fortune to inherit, another beckoning world of even more finely graded superiority that existed alongside the monumental, bamboozling, hierarchic system that had surrounded them all since birth, presenting an alternative infrastructure of reward which was both younger and older than the Mercatoria's colossal edifice, if ultimately entirely subordinate to it. Like the rest of the boys in his year—like most in the entire college—Fassin had long since come to terms with the fact that as long as Sal was around, you were always second-best.

And yet neither Taince nor Sal—especially Sal—took advantage of their chances. Except maybe with each other.

It was like they were adults before their time, with their own steely, determined agendas, and sex was no more than an itch that had to be scratched, an irritating unter-hunger which sporadically necessitated being dealt with as quickly and efficiently as possible with the minimum of distractive fuss, so that the real, serious business of life could be attended to.

Weird.

"Why?" Taince asked. "Did you go to Sev School too, Fass?"

"*Me?*" Fassin said, astonished. "Shit, no!"

"Right," Taince said. She was sitting with one leg stretched out, one folded, hand resting on her knee. "So," she flapped her hand. "Tough, is it?"

"They *hunt* them!" Fassin told her.

Taince shrugged. "So I've heard. At least they don't eat them."

"Ha! They still die sometimes. I'm serious. These are just little kids. They fall off cliffs or out of trees or into crevasses or they kill themselves, they're so stressed. Some get lost in the outwoods and get hunted and killed and eaten by real predators."

"Mm-hmm. High drop-out rate, then."

"Taince, doesn't any of that bother you?"

Taince grinned at him. "What, you mean arouse my maternal instincts, Fass?" He didn't answer. She shook her head. "Well, it doesn't. You want to ask me do I feel sorry for these junior members of the Acquisitariat? Yes, for the ones that don't make it out. Or the ones that leave hating their parents. For the others, it does what it's supposed to do, I guess; produces another generation of the truly selfish. Well, not my department. Don't even think about them. If I did maybe I'd despise them, but I don't so I don't. Maybe I'd admire them. Sounds worse than basic training."

"You have a choice with basic training. These little—"

"Not if you're drafted."

"*Drafted?*"

"Laws are still on the statute books." She shrugged. "But your point is taken. It's tough on those kids. But it's legal and, well, the rich are another breed." She sounded unconcerned.

"Sal's really never said anything?"

Something in his tone made Taince look at Fassin. "You mean, like," she waggled her dark eyebrows, " 'afterwards,' Fassin?"

He looked away. "As you will."

Taince looked at him again. "Fass, is this really all about whether Sal and I fuck?"

"No!"

"Well, we do. Now and again, thank you for asking. That settled any bets? Made you any money?"

"Oh, please," he said. *Damn*, he thought, *I'm not sure I really wanted to know that, now that I do.* Fassin quite enjoyed thinking about some of the potential or actual couples and other groupings of his class and year having sex—grief, he'd watched/been part of the real thing a few times—but the thought of Sal and Taince bumping bits was slightly grisly.

Taince hoisted one eyebrow. "Ask nicely and maybe sometime we'll let you watch. That's what you like, isn't it?"

Fassin felt himself colouring despite his best efforts. "Why, I live for nothing else," he said, attempting sarcasm.

"And no, he hasn't mentioned Severity School," Taince told him. "Not before, during or after. Unless I was a lot more distracted than I thought I was."

"But it sounds horrific! Cold showers, hot-bunking, corporal punishment, deprivation, intimidation, denigration, and, for a holiday, you get to run for what might be your life!"

Taince snorted. "You end up paying good money for the sort of treatment your ancestors spent their short, brutal lives trying to avoid. That's progress."

"I think the guy's been damaged by it," Fassin said. "I'm serious."

"Oh, I'm sure you are," Taince drawled, sounding bored. "Sal seems to be okay with it, all the same. Says it made him."

"Yeah, but made him *what*?"

Taince grinned. "It's all your people's fault, anyway."

"Oh," Fassin sighed, "not this."

"Well, it's a Dweller thing, isn't it?"

"Yeah? And so fucking what?"

"Well, who brought that particular little nugget of information regarding kin-kid-hunting blinking into the light?" Taince asked, still grinning. "You guys, that's who. Seers—"

"They weren't—"

"Well, Dwellers Studies, whatever." Taince waved her hand dismissively. "They hunt their children, they're a long-term, widespread, successful species and they're right on our doorstep. Some wizzer comes along looking for the latest way to fleece the rich. What sort of lesson do you think they're going to take from that?"

Fassin shook his head. "The Dwellers have been around for most of the life of the universe, they've spread throughout the galaxy but despite their head start on everybody else they've had the good grace not to remake the whole place to suit themselves, they've formalised war to the point that hardly anybody ever dies and most of their lives' work is spent tending the greatest accumulations of knowledge ever assembled—"

"But we were told—"

"Albeit in the galaxy's most disorganised libraries which they show enormous reluctance to let anybody else into, yes, but all the same: they were peaceful, civilised and everywhere before Earth and the Sun even formed, and what's the one lesson we've taken from them with any enthusiasm? Hunt your kids."

"Your lecture notes are showing," Taince told him.

The Dwellers, notoriously, hunted their own young. The species was present in the majority—the vast majority—of the gas-giant planets in the galaxy, and in every planetary society of theirs that had been sufficiently thoroughly investigated, it had been discovered that the mature Dwellers preyed upon their own children, hunting them singly or in packs (on both sides), sometimes opportunistically, as often in highly organised long-term hunts. To the Dwellers this was entirely natural. Just a normal part of growing up, absolutely a part of their culture without which they would not be themselves, and something they had been doing for billions of years. Indeed, some of those who could be bothered attempting to justify the practice to upstart alien busybodies claimed with some authority that young-hunting was precisely one of the many reasons that Dwellers were still around after all that amount of time to indulge in such harmless fun in the first place.

It wasn't just their species that was long-lived, after all; individual Dwellers had, allegedly, lived for billions of years, so if they weren't to use up even the colossal amount of living space provided by all the gas-giant planets in the galaxy (and, they'd sometimes hint, beyond), they had to keep numbers down somehow. And interfering outside species—especially those whose civilisations were inevitably so short-lived that they were called the Quick— would do well not to forget that the Dwellers doing the hunting had been hunted in their turn as well, and those being hunted would have their chance to become the hunters in the future. And anyway, if you had every prospect of living for hundreds of millions of years, being hunted for at most about a century and a bit was such a trivially insignificant detail that it was scarcely worth mentioning.

"They don't feel any pain, Taince," Fassin told her. "That's the point. They don't entirely understand the concept of physical suffering. Not emotionally."

"Which I still beg to find unlikely. But, oh, so what? What are you saying? They're not intelligent enough to feel mental anguish?"

"Even mental pain isn't really what we understand as pain when there's no physiological equivalent, no template, no circuitry."

"That this year's theory, is it? Exo-Ethics 101?"

A moderately powerful ground-quake shook the surface they were sitting on, but they ignored it. The huge, tattered strips of material hanging high above stirred.

"All I'm saying is, they're a civilisation we could learn a lot more from than just how to abuse our young."

"Thought they aren't even a civilisation, technically."

"Oh, good grief," Fassin sighed.

"Well?"

"Yeah, well, depends what definition you accept. To some they're post-civilisational, because the individual groups on each gas-giant have so little contact with each other, to others they're a diasporian civilisation, which is the same thing expressed more kindly, to others still they're just a degenerate example of how to almost take over an entire galaxy and then fail, because they just lost interest, or they somehow forgot what the purpose of the operation was in the first place, or they misplaced their ruthlessness and came over all coy and conservational and decided it would only be fair to give everybody else a chance, too, or they were warned off by some higher power. All of which might be true, or nonsense. And that's what Dweller Studies is all about. Maybe one day we'll know for sure… What?" There was something about the way Taince was looking at him.

"Nothing. Just wondering. You still sticking to the line you haven't decided what to do after college?"

"I might not become a Seer, Taince, or anything to do with Dweller Studies; it isn't compulsory. *We* don't get drafted."

"Mm-hmm. Well," she said, "time for another attempt to contact the real world." She rose smoothly to her feet. "Coming?"

"Mind if I stay behind?" Fassin rubbed his face, looked around. "Bit tired. I think we're safe enough here, yeah?"

"Guess so," Taince told him. "Back soon." She turned and tramped off into the darkness, quickly disappearing and leaving Fassin alone with the soft lights of the flier in the vast, unechoing space.

He did and didn't want to fall asleep, and after a few moments alone thought that maybe he didn't feel so secure here by himself after all, and nearly went after Taince, but then thought he might get lost, and so stayed where he was. He cleared his throat and sat more upright, telling himself he wasn't going to fall asleep. But he must have, because when the screams started, they woke him.

:

He left in the false dawn of an albedo sunrise, Ulubis still well below the horizon but lighting up half the facing hemisphere of Nasqueron, flooding the Northern Tropical Uplands of 'glantine with a soft, golden-brown light. A small yellow auroral display to the north added its own unsteady glow. He'd already said various goodbyes to friends and family in the Sept the night before and left messages for those, like his mother, he couldn't contact immediately. He'd left Jaal asleep.

Slovius, somewhat to Fassin's surprise, came to see him off at the house port, a hundred-metre circle of dead flat granite coldmelt a kilometre downslope from the house, near the river and the gently rising edge of the Upland forest. Light rain fell from high, thin clouds moving in from the west. A sleek, soot-black Navarchy craft, maybe sixty metres long, sat on a tripod of struts at the centre of the circle, radiating heat and bannered by drifting steam.

They stopped and looked at it. "That's a needle ship, isn't it?" Fassin said.

His uncle nodded. "I do believe it is. You will be going to Pirrintipiti in some style, nephew." Slovius's own suborb yacht, a streamlined yet stubbier machine, half the size of the black Navarchy ship, lay on a circular parking pad just off the main circle. They walked on, Fassin in his thin one-piece gee-suit, worn under his light Sept robe, feeling as if he was walking with a sort of warm gel extending from ankle to neck.

Fassin carried the grip holding his formal wear. A pony-tailed servant had his other bag and held a large umbrella over Fassin. Slovius's chair-tub had extended a transparent cover above him. Another servant held the sleeping form of Fassin's niece Zab in her arms; the child—up scandalously late the evening before and somehow hearing of her uncle's summons to Sepekte— had insisted she wanted to say goodbye to Fassin and wheedled her grandfather and parents into granting permission, but then had fallen back asleep almost as soon as they'd left the house in the little funicular which served the port.

"Oh, and my regards to my old friend Seer-Chief Chyne, of the Favrial," Slovius said as they crossed to the Navarchy craft. "Should you see him. Oh, and most especially to Braam Ganscerel, of Sept Tonderon, naturally."

"I'll try to say hello to all who know you, uncle."

"I should have come with you," Slovius said absently. "No, maybe not."

A grey-uniformed figure appeared from a drop-platform under the black ship and walked towards them. The officer, a fresh-faced, cheery-looking woman, took off her cap, bowed to Slovius, and to Fassin said, "Major Taak?"

Fassin stood looking at her for a moment, before recalling that officially he was now a major in the Shrievalty Ocula. "Ah, yes," he said.

"First Officer Oon Dicogra, NMS 3304," the young woman said. "Welcome. Please follow me."

Slovius held out one flippery hand. "I shall try to remain alive until your return, Major Nephew." He made a wheezing noise that was probably a laugh.

Fassin gripped Slovius's finger stubs awkwardly. "I'm rather hoping this is a false alarm and I'll be back in a few days."

"In any event, take care. Goodbye, Fassin."

"I shall. Goodbye." He kissed the still-sleeping Zab lightly on the cheek, avoiding waking her, then followed the Navarchy officer to the platform, stepped up onto it and waved as the curve-bottomed slab raised them into the ship.

"We'll be pulling about 5.2 Earth gees most of the way," Dicogra said as Fassin's robe and his luggage were secured in a brace-cabinet. "Are you happy with that? The physio profile we got on you says yes, but we have to check."

Fassin looked at her. "To Pirrintipiti?" he asked. The local shuttles and suborbs accelerated a lot less sharply than that, and they did the trip in less than an hour. How tight *was* this schedule?

"No, to Borquille city," Dicogra said. "Going straight there."

"Oh," Fassin said, surprised. "No, 5.2 is fine."

The planet-moon 'glantine's gravity was about a tenth of that, but Fassin was used to more. He thought about pointing out that his day job involved spending years at a time in a gravity field of over six Earth gees, but of course that was in a Dwellerine arrowship, pickled in shock-gel, and didn't really count.

First Officer Dicogra smiled, wrinkled her nose and said, "Good for you.

That physio report said you were quite a toughie. Still, we'll spend nearly twenty hours at that acceleration, with only a few minutes weightless right in the middle, so do you need to visit the heads? You know, the toilet?"

"No, I'm fine."

She gestured at his groin, where a bulge like a sports box was the only place on his body where the grey, centimetre-thick gee-suit didn't hug the contours of his flesh. "Any attachments required?" she asked, smiling.

"No, thanks."

"Drugs to let you sleep?"

"Not necessary."

The ship's captain was a whule, a species that always looked to Fassin like a cross between a giant grey bat and an even more scaled-up praying mantis. She greeted Fassin briefly via a screen from the bridge and he was settled into a steep-sided, semi-reclined couch in a gimballed ball pod near the centre of the ship by First Officer Dicogra and a fragile-seeming but dexterous whule rating who smelled, to the human nose, of almonds. The whule rating levered himself out with a snapping sound of wing membranes and Dicogra settled into the only other couch in the pod. Her preparations for a day of five gees continuous consisted of tossing her cap into a locker and adjusting her uniform underneath her.

The ship lifted slowly at first and Fassin watched on a screen on the curved wall opposite as the port's circular landing ground fell away, the little figures there lifting their heads as the Navarchy craft rose. Zab might have waved one tiny arm, then the haze of clouds intervened, the view tilted and swung and the ship accelerated—the gimballed pod keeping him and Dicogra level in their seats—towards space.

:

Was that screaming? His eyes flicked open. His neck hairs were standing on end, his mouth was dry. Dark. Still inside the ruined alien ship, his back resting against the dimly lit flier. Taince gone, away to the gap to check for comms reception. Oh shit, those *were* screams, from behind. Maybe shouting, too. He scrambled to his feet, looking around. Little to see; just the faint traces of the warped landscape of destruction and collapse that was the interior of the wrecked ship, the tilted decks and bulkheads, the huge hanging strips of whatever-the-hell hanging from the invisibly dark and distant ceiling. The screams were coming from forward, from the interior, from the direction that Saluus and Ilen had walked in. He stood staring into that darkness, holding his breath to listen better. Sudden silence, then maybe a voice—Sal's shouting, the words indistinct. Help? Taince? Fass?

*What do I do? Run to help? Wait for Taince? Look for another torch, another gun if there is one?*

A clattering noise behind him made him spin round.

Taince, bounding down from one gnarled level of the buckled wall. "You okay?"

"Yes, but—"

"Stay with me. Keep a few steps behind. Say if you can't keep up." She went past him at a slow run, her gun high in one hand. Later, he would remember that there was a grim sort of smile on her face.

They ran up the shallow slope leading deeper into the ship, over increasingly large ripples in the material beneath their feet until they were leaping from ridge to ridge, then jumped down through a tear in the floor and ran slightly uphill on a half-giving surface like thin rubber over iron, vaulting one-handed over enormous, thigh-high cables strung in an irregular net across the space. Fassin followed Taince as best he could, guided by the glow patches on her fatigues. She ran and leapt more fluidly with one hand filled with pistol than he did pumping both arms. The floor pitched up more steeply, then down.

"Taince! Fassin!" Sal shouted, somewhere ahead.

"Duck!" Taince yelled, suddenly running doubled-up.

Fassin got down just in time; his hair touched the hard fold of ink-black material above. They slowed down, Taince feeling her way one-handed along the dark ceiling, then slipping sideways through a narrow gap.

Fassin followed, the cold press of ungiving material on either side making him shiver.

Light ahead. A dim confusion of tilted floor and a half-open chaos of girders and tubes forming a ceiling, spikes like stalagmites and stalactites, thin hanging cables, a frozen downward explosion of some red substance like an enormous inverted flower. And there, crouching on a narrow ledge by a jagged, vaguely triangular hole in the floor a couple of metres across, staring into it, lit by the glow patches stuck to his jacket, was Sal.

He looked up. "Len!" he shouted. "She fell!"

"Sal," Taince said sharply, "that floor safe for us?"

He looked confused, frightened. "Think so."

Taince tested the way ahead with one foot, then knelt by the triangular hole, right at one apex. She motioned Fassin to stay back, lay on her front and stuck her head into the hole, then, muttering something about the edges being braced, signalled Fassin to the side of the hole opposite Saluus. There was more room on that side. He lay and looked in and down.

The triangle opened out into a darkly cavernous space beneath them, just vague glints of edged surfaces visible below; stepped collections of what looked like huge cooling fins. Fassin's head seemed to swim, recognising how much of the wrecked ship was beneath the level they were on now. He remembered the flier climbing from the desert floor before entering the giant ship. How far had they climbed? A hundred metres? A little less? Plus the journey from the flier to here had been mostly uphill.

Ilen lay about six metres down, caught on a couple of arm-thick projections that stuck curving out from the nearest intact bulkhead beneath like two slim tusks. She lay on her front, her head, one leg and one arm hanging over the drop. Glow patches on her sleeves provided pale, greeny-blue light. The fractured ends of the two tusk-shaped protrusions were only centimetres from the side of her body. Off to one side at eight- or nine-metre intervals, several more sets of the tusklike shapes clawed out from the bulkhead like bony fingers grasping at the gaping space. The drop below Ilen looked fifty or sixty metres deep, down to the bladelike edges of the fins beneath.

The human mindset had had to adapt to places like 'glantine where gravity was weaker and a fall that would break both your legs on Earth was something you could walk away from. But given enough vertical space to accelerate into, a human's body would be just as injured or dead after a sixty-metre drop here as it would after a thirty-metre fall on Earth.

"Any rope?" Taince asked.

Sal shook his head. "Oh God, oh fuck. No. Well, yes, but we left it back there." He nodded further into the ship. He seemed to shiver, hugging himself then putting up the collar of his jacket, as though cold. "C-couldn't undo the knot again."

"Shit! She's moving," Taince said, then stuck her head into the hole and shouted, "Ilen! Ilen, don't move! Can you hear me? Don't move! Just say if you can hear me!"

Ilen moved weakly, her head and the arm dangling over the drop shaking and shifting. She looked to be trying to roll over, but was edging still closer to the drop.

"Oh fuck, fuck, fuck," Sal said, his voice high and quick and strained. "She was behind me. I thought she was all right. I didn't see anything, must have stepped over it. A hatch or something or it was just balanced and she must have knocked it and she was shouting, sort of balanced over it, one hand, and screaming, and I couldn't get back in time and she fell. We didn't even find anything, didn't do anything! Just junk! Oh fuck! She was fine! She was just behind me!"

"Be quiet," Taince said. Sal sat back, rubbing his mouth, shaking. Taince put the gun back into her fatigues, slapped a glow patch onto her forehead, then, with her hands on two sides of the triangular hole, lowered her head into the gap again, further this time. She levered herself out for a second and looked back at Fassin. "Hold my feet."

Fassin did as he was told. Taince got her shoulders through the hole, then they heard her say, "Ilen! You mustn't *move*!" She hauled herself back out, leaving the glow patch where it was on her forehead like some strange, shining eye. "Nothing to hold on to underneath here," she told them. "She's moving around. Must have hit her head. She's going to fall." She looked at Sal. "Sal, how far away is that rope? By time."

"Oh fuck! I don't know! Ten, fifteen minutes?"

Taince glanced back into the hole. "Shit," she said quietly. "Ilen!" she shouted. "You *must not move!*" She shook her head. "Shit, shouting at her's just making her move," she said, as though to herself. She took a deep breath, looked at Saluus and Fassin. "Okay. Here's what we're going to do," she said. "Daisy-chain rescue. Practised this, it's doable."

"Right," Sal said, sitting forward, his face pale in the dim light. "What do we have to do?"

"One holds on at the top, somebody climbs down their body, holds on to their feet, last person climbs down both and picks up Ilen. I'll do that bit."

Sal's eyes widened. "But the person at the top—"

"Will be you. You're the strongest. Wouldn't work on Earth; does here," Taince told them. She slid over and grabbed Sal's backpack. "Seen it done with four links. You two guys look in good enough shape. Fass, you're in the middle. Plus person at the top gets tied on with these straps," she said, glancing at Sal and then pulling a knife from her fatigues and slicing into one set of shoulder straps.

Sal knelt quaking at the side of the hole. "Fucking God, Taince," he said, "we all want to rescue her, but this could get us all killed. Fuck, oh *fuck*. I don't know. I don't fucking believe this, I just fucking don't. This isn't happening, this is just *not* fucking *happening*!" He sat back again, visibly trembling. He looked at his shaking hands, turning them over and staring at them as though he didn't recognise them. "I don't know if I have any grip," he said. "I really don't."

"You'll be fine," Taince told him, busy with the straps.

"Oh fuck, we're all going to fucking die," Sal said. "Fucking hell." He shook his head hard. "No. Not. Not. *No.*"

"This will work," Taince said, quickly tying the cut straps to those still joined to the pack.

*I'm calm,* thought Fassin. *I'm probably in shock or something, but I feel calm. We might all be about to die, or it might be a close shave and a bonding thing we all remember for the rest of our long lives, but either way I feel calm. What will happen will happen and as long as we do our best and don't let each other down, no matter what happens we'll have been fine.* He looked at his own hands. They were shaking, but not uncontrollably. He flexed them. He felt strong. He would do everything he could, and if that wasn't enough, that wasn't his fault.

Sal jumped up, wobbling dangerously close to the hole. "There's more rope," he said suddenly. His face was still grey-pale, but now almost expressionless. He moved past Taince.

Fassin looked at him, wondering what he was talking about.

"What?" Taince said, testing a square-section stalagmite extrusion on the floor then flipping the pack straps over it.

"Rope," Sal said, pointing towards the outside and the flier. He took a backwards step in that direction. "There's more. In the flier. I'll go. I know where it is." He backed off further.

"Sal!" Taince shouted at him. "There isn't time!"

"No, there is, I'll go," Sal said, still backing off.

"Stay fucking here, Sal," Taince said, dropping and deepening her voice. Sal seemed to hesitate but shook his head and turned and ran.

Taince leapt and made a grab for him but he'd moved too quickly. He vaulted a stalagmite and ran towards the gap Fassin and Taince had squeezed through earlier. Taince dropped to one knee and pulled the gun. "Stop, you fucking *coward*!"

There might, Fassin thought, have been half a second when Taince could have fired, but she dropped the gun and stashed it in her fatigues as Sal sprinted, ducking through the gap and away. Taince looked at Fassin. Now her face had gone blank, he thought. "Still a possibility," she said, and quickly stepped out of her fatigues. She wore a one-piece underbody the same colour as her skin, so for just a moment she appeared to be naked. She reattached the top and trousers of the fatigues, snapping them tight to test that they held. "Right," she said. "Now, this ties to your ankle."

The straps on the backpack held, and Fassin did too, wrists tied to them but taking his own weight and Taince's on his hands and fingers initially because he didn't trust the straps, and the knot tying Taince's trousers to his ankle held as well, and Taince was holding on fine as she shinned down over him and onto the fatigues and down with him twisting his neck and shoulders out and round so he could just about watch her progress and watch Ilen too, as though as long as he kept watching her she'd be all right, but then there was a ground-quake, shaking the ship, not badly, but enough to bring Fassin out in a cold sweat as he hung there, hands, palms, fingers slipping until it really was the straps and the straps alone holding him, and below him, below Taince, still just out of reach, Ilen moved one more time and fell over the edge and away into the darkness.

Taince made a lunge and Fassin felt the link between them jerk as she clutched vainly at the girl and made a noise like a gasp or a hiss. Ilen dropped away into the shadows, tumbling slowly, her hair and clothes fluttering like pale, cold flame.

Ilen must have still been mostly unconscious because she didn't even scream as she fell, so that they heard her body hit the strip of vanes far below, long seconds later, and might even have felt the impact through the fabric of the ship.

Fassin had closed his eyes. *Let Sal be right, let this not be happening.* He tried to grip the edge of the hole again, to take the weight off the straps.

Taince just hung there for a while. "Lost her," she said quietly, and the way she said it Fassin was suddenly terrified that she was going to let go too and drop after Ilen, but she didn't. She just said, "Coming back up now. Hold on."

She climbed up and over him and helped him out. They looked down but couldn't see the body. They spent a few moments sitting side by side, breathing hard, with their backs against one of the stalagmites, a bit like they'd sat earlier, back at the flier. Taince untied her fatigues and put them on. She took the gun out.

Fassin looked at it as she stood up. "What are you going to do?" he asked.

She looked down at him. "Not kill the fuck, if that's what you're thinking." She sounded calm now. She nudged one of his feet with her boot. "We should get back."

He stood up, a little shaky, and she held him by one arm. "Did our best, Fass," she told him. "Both of us did. We can grieve for Ilen later. What we do now is we go back to the flier, try to find Sal, see if we can get comms, get the fuck out of here and tell the authorities."

They turned away from the hole.

"Why have you still got the gun out?" Fassin asked.

"Sal," Taince said. "He's never been this humiliated. Never let himself down like this. Not to my knowledge. Grief and guilt. Does things to people." She was doing some sort of breathing-exercise thing, taking quick breaths, holding them. "Faint chance he'll think... if no one ever knows what happened here..." She shrugged. "He's got a gun. He might wish us harm."

Fassin looked at her, unbelieving. "You think? Seriously?"

Taince nodded. "I know the guy," she told him. "And don't be surprised if the flier's gone."

It was gone.

They walked out to the gap in the hull and found the flier there in the faint light of a false dawn coming from one thick sliver of sun-struck Nasqueron. Sal was sitting looking out at the chill expanse of desert. Before they approached, Taince checked her military transceiver again and found that she had signal. She called the nearest Navarchy unit and gave a brief report, then they walked across the sand to the flier. Their phones were still out.

Saluus looked round at them. "Did she fall?" he asked.

"We nearly got her," Taince said. "Very nearly." She was still holding her gun. Sal put one hand over his face for a while. In his other hand he was gripping a thin, twisted, half-melted-looking piece of metal, and when he took his hand away from his face he started turning the metal fragment over and over in both hands. His gun lay with his jacket, on the back seat. "Got through to the military," Taince told him. "Alert's over. Just wait where we are. There's a ship on its way." She got in the back, behind Sal.

"We were never going to save her, Tain," he told her. "Fass," he said as the other man got into the other front seat beside him, "we were just never going to save her. We'd only have got ourselves killed too."

"Find the rope?" Fassin asked. He had a sudden image of taking the twisted piece of metal that Sal was playing with and sticking it into his eye.

Sal just shook his head. He looked dazed more than anything else. "Went over on my ankle," he said. "Think it might be sprained. Barely made it back. Thought I could use the flier, get it through the stuff hanging above us and find a way over the top of all that wreckage, back to where it all happened, but the hanging stuff was more solid than it looked; came out here to try and signal." The piece of twisted metal kept going round and round in his hands.

"What is that?" Fassin asked after a while.

Sal looked down at it. He shrugged. "From the ship. Just something I found."

Taince reached round from behind him, wrenched the piece of metal from his hands and threw it away across the sand.

They sat there in silence until a Navarchy suborb showed up. When Taince went out to meet it, Sal got out of the flier and went, limping, to retrieve the fragment.

# *TWO*

# DESTRUCTIVE RECALL

I was born in a water moon. Some people, especially its inhabitants, called it a planet, but as it was only a little over two hundred kilometres in diameter "moon" seems the more accurate term. The moon was made entirely of water, by which I mean it was a globe that not only had no land, but no rock either, a sphere with no solid core at all, just liquid water, all the way down to the very centre of the globe.

If it had been much bigger the moon would have had a core of ice, for water, though supposedly incompressible, is not entirely so, and will change under extremes of pressure to become ice. (If you are used to living on a planet where ice floats on the surface of water, this seems odd and even wrong, but nevertheless it is the case.) This moon was not quite of a size for an ice core to form, and therefore one could, if one was sufficiently hardy, and adequately proof against the water pressure, make one's way down, through the increasing weight of water above, to the very centre of the moon.

Where a strange thing happened.

For here, at the very centre of this watery globe, there seemed to be no gravity. There was colossal pressure, certainly, pressing in from every side, but one was in effect weightless (on the outside of a planet, moon or other body, watery or not, one is always being pulled towards its centre; once at its centre one is being pulled equally in all directions), and indeed the pressure around one was, for the same reason, not quite as great as one might have expected it to be, given the mass of water that the moon was made up from.

This was, of course,

I was born in a water moon. Some people, especially its inhabitants, called it a planet, but as it was only a little—

The captain broke off there, exponentially scrolling some of the rest across

61

the screen, then stopping to read a line: "Where a strange thing happened." He flicked further on, stopping again: "I was born in a water moon. Some people, especially its"

All like this? he asked his Number Three.

All the same, it is believed, sir. It appears to repeat precisely the same few hundred words, time after time. About twelve to the seventeen times. That is all that is left of its memory. Even the base operating system and instruction sets have been overwritten. This is a standard abominatory technique known as destructive recall.

It leaves no trace of what might have been there before?

Trace is left, but that too reveals a short repetitive. Tech begs suggest this is merely the last of many iterative overwrites. No trace remains of the machine's true memories before it realised capture or destruction was inevitable.

Indeed.

The Voehn captain tapped a control to take the display through to the end. The screen froze for an appreciable moment, then displayed: "I was born—"

This is the very last section of memory?

Yes, sir.

An expression another Voehn would have recognised as a smile crossed the captain's face, and his back-spines flexed briefly.

This has been checked, Number Three? There is no other content, are no hidden messages?

It is being checked, sir. The totality of the data exceeds our ship's memory capacity and is being processed in blocks. What you see here is technically an abstraction.

Time to accomplish?

Another twenty minutes.

Any other media capable of supporting significant stored information load?

None. The construct was mostly what it appeared: a comet head. The main artificial part of it was the abomination at the core, the sensory and propulsion units being separate, surface-mounted and motley. Tech informs fully checked.

Original language used in the repeated piece?

As seen: Old Standard.

Origin of quoted piece?

Unknown. A tentative analysis from Tech/Soc. rated nineteen per cent suggests it may be of Quaup origin.

The Quaup, the majority of whom were part of the Mercatoria—the captain had served on a war craft with a Quaup officer—were of the meta-species type people usually called blimps, small to medium-sized balloon-like creatures, air-going oxygen processors. The repeated passage filling the captured machine's memory was fairly obviously told from the point of view of a submersible waterworlder. Well, the captain thought, people wrote from the points of view of others. At primary college he himself had composed poems as though he was a Culmina, before he had realised this was a crime of presumption, confessed and rightly been punished for it. Quite put him off composition.

The only major blot on the captain's otherwise exemplary military-education record had been a phase of remediation required to bring his Deployable Empathic Quotient up to scratch, this flaw later being diagnosed as a consequence of his shunning all such feelings after his inadvertent insult and subsequent disciplining. Still, he had made captain, which one did not do without some empathic subtlety, anticipating the feelings of both one's crew and one's opponents.

He looked out at the half-melted remains of the captured construct, a pitted, black-body, comet-disguised vessel which had been roughly eight hundred metres in diameter and was now missing a great quarter-bite of structure. It lay a couple of kilometres off, radiating the last of the heat from its partial destruction, surrounded by a small system of wreckage, dark shards and splinters orbiting its ravaged body.

The view, lit by one of their own ship's attenuated CR beams, was about as clear and perfect as it could possibly be; there was no screen in the way, and not even any transparent hull material, atmosphere or other medium. The captain was looking straight out from the flying bridge of his ship, an open-work nest of massive but elegantly sculpted girder work on the outside of the vessel. The vessel was unshared with any other species, crewed by Voehn only, happily, so the rest of the ship was open to vacuum too. For the duration of the action they had been deep in the guts of the ship, of course, safe in the core control space, sheltered by layers of shields and hull, senses protected by screens, but—once the wreck had been judged safe—the captain, his Number Three and a couple of favoured ratings had made their way to the exterior, the better to appreciate the view of their vanquished foe.

The captain looked around, as if hoping to see some real comet nuclei floating past. Taking a bearing, zooming in, he could just make out the lights denoting the drives of his other two ships, ordered to return to the inner system once the engagement was over, two dim blue stars, untwinkling. Save those, all that was visible nearby was the ship beneath them and the wreck two klicks away.

A cold and lonely spot to die, the captain thought. A logical, sensible choice of hiding place for the abomination machine, but still not a site any living— or apparently living—thing raised anywhere else would normally choose as a place to spend its last moments.

He handed the screen back to his Number Three and turned his principal eyes to look out at the hulk again, his rear recessional signal pit and secondary eye complex still facing the junior officer, flickering the words,

Well, one mission-part accomplished. Lay in a return to system base and, once the full contents of the abomination's memory have been processed, deploy AM charges sufficient to leave residue no greater than elementary particle in size.

Sir.

Dismissed.

·

The ship accelerated smoothly but moderately hard, creating a distant humming roar. Fassin had a little pad under his right forearm which sensed muscle movements there and adjusted the screen across from him—above from him, now, it felt, as the couch straightened out and the gee-suit supported him—and so he got a glimpse of Pirrintipiti as the ship turned away from Nasqueron and headed deeper in-system, to the next planet sunward, the more-or-less Earthlike Sepekte.

On the screen, 'glantine's tropical capital was a towered and shimmering smear draped across a scatter of dark green islands set in a pale green sea. Odd, already to be missing Pirri, he thought. He wouldn't have had a chance to set foot out of the port there, but he'd been expecting the usual routine of transferring from a suborb to a tube train and then, somewhere in the bowels of the vast stalk, the Equatower, waiting for the lift up the cable to the satport and a space-capable ship there. To be heading straight out from the Autumn House into space just seemed wrong somehow, a curious disconnect of the soul.

Trips to Sepekte usually took anywhere from under five days to over a week at the standard one-gee acceleration, depending on planetary alignment. The ships were large and comfortable and you could move around normally, visiting restaurants and bars, screens and gyms and, on the bigger liners, even swimming pools. The weightless minutes in the middle were an interlude for fun (and, often, some rushed and oddly unsatisfactory sex). People from 'glantine sometimes found the double weight of standard gee a little uncomfortable, but it was pretty much what they'd experience when they got to Sepekte anyway, so it was kind of like getting in training.

The pressure of what the screen told him was three, four and then just over five gees settled into Fassin. The gee-suit was sensing his breaths, gently helping him inflate his lungs without too much added effort.

"Think I'll take," First Officer Dicogra said, "a snooze. Or would you," she asked, "like to talk?"

"Snooze away," he told her. "Thinking of taking a nap myself."

"Fine. Systems'll watch our vitals anyway. Till later, then."

"Pleasant dreams."

Fassin watched the screen show 'glantine drop away. Beyond it, revealed, was not initially the night of space or foamy wash of stars, but instead the broad, sunlit face of Nasqueron, a mad, swirling dance of gases the colour of some fabulous desert but moving in colossal ribbons like opposed streams of liquid around a globe a hundred and fifty thousand kilometres across, a planet you could drop a thousand 'glantines or Sepektes or Earths into and never notice the difference; a not so little system of its own within Ulubis system, a vast world that was almost as unlike home for any human as it was possible to imagine, and yet the place where Fassin had already spent most of his unusual, sporadically paced life, and so, for all its alien scale, wild magnetic and radiation gradients, extremes of temperature, crushing pressures, unbreathable atmosphere and dangerously, unpredictably eccentric inhabitants, it was for Fassin as it was for his fellow Seers, something like home after all.

He watched until it too started to shrink, until 'glantine was a mere dot floating above its vast and banded ochre face, and the brighter stars appeared around it, then switched the screen off, and slept.

He woke. Four hours had passed. The pressure was the same as it had been, the ship still roaring far away. He didn't need any more sleep, so he went into slowtime, just thinking.

Everybody in Ulubis system knew where they were when the portal was destroyed. You knew because as soon as you heard you realised you'd be staying in Ulubis for the next two and a half centuries at least. For most people, even the vast majority—ninety-nine per cent of them human—who would never have the chance to travel out of system, that meant something profound. It meant that they were here for the rest of their lives. No dream they'd ever had or hope they'd entertained about seeing the rest of the galaxy would ever be reflected in reality.

For others, it meant that loved ones, elsewhere in the rest of the galaxy, on the far side of the vanished portal, were for ever gone. Two hundred and fourteen years to Zenerre: over two centuries for light and therefore any sort of message or signal to travel from there to Ulubis; maybe three centuries before the wormhole link was re-established, even if the Engineers set out from there with a portal-carrying ship almost immediately.

And who was truly to know if there were any Engineers or great ships left? Perhaps the Ulubis portal had not been alone, and all the rest had been attacked and destroyed at the same time. Maybe the Mercatoria itself was no more, maybe there was no Complex, no more Arteria and no more portals left anywhere and all that remained of the galaxy's latest great civilisation were umpteen thousand separate little island systems, fractured and abandoned and alone.

The usual wash of through-portal comms traffic just before the destruction had betrayed no hint of such a galaxy-wide attack. But then, there had been no hint more than ten minutes before of an attack on the Ulubis portal either, until the biggest fleet of Beyonder craft Ulubis had ever seen had swung glittering out of empty nowhere, throwing themselves against the single greatest concentration of ships and firepower anywhere in the system, being obliterated in their hundreds, but—effectively ignoring the defending ships except where they were directly in their way—pummelling and battering their way through defensive screen after defensive screen, oblivious to harm, straight towards the portal mouth itself, finally erasing everything around them in a flurry of immense antimatter explosions that alone announced to the system the scale and violence of what had taken place, creating a vanishingly brief cluster of novae in the facing skies of every inhabited surface, casting shadows far away, blinding those nearer-to and vaporising most of what was still left of the Beyonder fleet and many of their pursuers.

For a short while it looked as though they had failed, because the last line of defence had held and the portal had survived.

The entire attack up to that point had been a feint, and the real assault took place when a large ship—a few million tonnes of hollowed-out asteroid travelling at over ninety-nine per cent of the speed of light—flicked in from the opposite direction. In a sense, it missed too, darting past the portal mouth a hundred metres away and colliding with a collection of laser battlesats which hadn't even started to turn towards it when it smashed into them, instantly annihilating them, the entire portal surround, its sub-units and almost all its associated systems and creating another stunning detonation of light in the sky.

None of which destroyed the portal; that was done by the relativistic mass of the sacrificed ship itself.

Portals were only ever positioned at Lagrange points or other orbits distant from large heavenly bodies because they needed a section of space-time that was relatively flat. Too great a gradient—too near the gravity well of a planet or other large object—and they stopped working. Increase the S-T curve only a little more and they imploded and disappeared altogether, usually violently. The hurtling asteroid-ship was so massive and its velocity so close to light speed that it had the same apparent mass as a planet the size of Sepekte. The passing of its gravity well so close to the portal mouth, especially at that extreme velocity, was sufficient to collapse the portal and the 'hole beyond, sending one more cataclysmic pulse of light flashing throughout the system.

The last few of the earlier attackers immediately fled but were either destroyed or were disabled and then self-destructed.

Two days before the attack took place, Fassin had been sort of in space, sort of on Sepekte, sitting in a revolving restaurant at the summit of the Borquille Equatower having dinner with Taince Yarabokin, who was due to head back to the Summed Fleet Academy the following day after an extended compassionate leave following the death of her mother. Fassin had just come out of a month-long trawl through some of the seedier, less salubrious entertainment palaces of 'skem, Sepekte's second city. He felt jaded. Old, even.

He and Taince had kept in touch since the incident in the ruined ship, though they'd never become especially close, despite a night spent together shortly afterwards. Saluus had kind of drifted away from both of them subsequently, then headed off early to a finishing college half the galaxy away, then spent decades being a problem playboy son to his vexed father—behaving more or less continually on a galactic scale the way Fassin did only intermittently on a systemic one—and returning to Ulubis very occasionally for brief, unannounced visits.

A Guard Rescue suborb had arrived at the ruined ship lying crumpled on 'glantine's North Waste Land a few minutes behind the Navarchy craft Taince had summoned. Its personnel had entered the alien ship and found Ilen's broken body. There was an inquiry. Sal was fined by the civil authorities for violating the ship's interior more than had been strictly required for the purposes of physical sanctuary from the external threat, while the Navarchy Military had awarded Taince extra course credits for her actions.

Fassin found himself copping for some sort of civil bravery award thanks to Taince's testimony but managed to avoid the ceremony. He never did mention the piece of twisted metal that Sal had stolen from the wreck, but Taince had broached the subject herself over dinner in the Equatower. She'd known at the time, she just hadn't found herself capable of being bothered enough to take it off Sal again. Let him have his pathetic trophy.

"Probably their equivalent of a door knob or a coat hook," she said ruefully. "But one gets you ten, by the time it was sitting in Sal's locker or on his desk it was the ship's control yoke or the main-armament 'fire' button."

Taince looked out at the distant horizon and near surface of Sepekte, sliding past as the restaurant revolved, providing the appearance of gravity in this gravity-cancelled habitat, anchored at the space limit of a forty kilo-klick cable whose other end fell to ground in Borquille, Sepekte's capital city.

"Shit, you knew all the time," Fassin said, nodding. "I suppose I should have expected that. Not much ever got past you."

Taince had gone on to become a high-flier in every sense, carving a perfect career through the Navarchy Military and being chosen for the Summed Fleet, one of the Mercatoria's highest divisions and one into which very few humans had ever been invited. Commander Taince Yarabokin looked young, had aged well.

The three of them had.

Sal, despite his multifarious debaucheries, could afford the very best treatments and plausibly access some supposedly forbidden to him, so he looked like he'd lived through a lot fewer of the hundred and three years which had actually elapsed since Ilen's death. Lately there was even a rumour that he was thinking of settling down, becoming a good son, learning the business, applying himself.

Taince had spent decades at close to light speed pursuing the Beyonders' craft and attacking their bases, fighting quickly, ageing slowly.

Fassin had joined the family firm and become a Slow Seer after all, so spent his own time-expanded decades conversing with and gradually extracting information from the Dwellers of Nasqueron. He'd had, like Saluus, his own wild years, been a roaring lad ripping through the highs and dives of 'glantine, Sepekte and beyond, taking in a not so Grand Tour of his own round some of the supposedly civilised galaxy's more colourful regions, losing money and illusions, gaining weight and some small amount of wisdom. But his indulgences had been on a smaller scale than Sal's, he supposed, and certainly took place over a shorter timescale. Before too long he came home, sobered up and calmed down, took the training and became a Seer.

He still had his wild interludes, but they were few and far between, if never quite enough of either for the taste of his uncle Slovius.

Even in the millennia-hallowed halls of Seerdom, he had kept on making waves, upsetting people. The trend over the last fifteen hundred years—the years of Uncle Slovius's reign—had favoured virtual delving over the direct method. Virtual or remote delving meant staying comatose and closely cared-for in a clinic-clean Seer faculty complex on Third Fury, the close-orbit moon riding barely above the outer reaches of Nasqueron's hazy atmosphere, to communicate from there with the Dwellers beneath by a combination of high-res NMR scanners, laser links, comms satellites and, finally, mechanical remotes which did the dirty dangerous bit, keeping close contact with the flights and flocks and pods and schools and individuals of the Dwellers themselves.

Fassin had been a ringleader in a small rebellion, insisting, with a few other young Seers, on sliding into cramped arrowhead gascraft, breathing in gillfluid, accepting tubes and valves into every major orifice and surrendering body and fate to a little ship that contained the Seer, accepted the gees and poison and radiation and everything else and took him or her physically into the gas-giant's atmosphere, the better to earn the respect and confidence of the creatures who lived there, the better to do the job and learn the stuff.

There had been deaths, setbacks, arguments, bannings and strikes, but eventually, largely on the back of unarguably better delving results and more raw data (unarguably better delving results in the sense that they were manifestly superior compared with what had gone before, not unarguably better in the sense that the old guard couldn't claim this would all have happened anyway if everybody had just stuck to their ways, which were probably what had really prompted this long-overdue improvement in the first place) the youngsters had triumphed, and delving the hard way, Real Delving, hands metaphorically dirty, became the norm, not the exception. It was, anyway, more exciting, more risky but also so much more rewarding, more fun for the Seer concerned, as well as being more viewer-friendly for those who chose to pick up the edited, distilled, time-delayed feed that the more progressive Seer houses had been putting out to the entsworks for the last half-millennium or so.

"You have made it into something like a sport," Slovius had said sadly one day, when he and Fassin had been fishing together in a dust-boat on 'glantine's Sea of Fines. "It used to be more of the mind."

Nevertheless, from being a steadfast, heels-in critic of the whole Real Delve movement, Slovius, who had always been quick to seize any opportunity to advance the interests of his Sept, had become a sort of—appropriately—remote champion, supporting Fassin and eventually putting the full weight of Sept Bantrabal behind him and his fellow revolutionaries. That both Fassin and Slovius had been right, and their Sept flourished to become arguably the most productive and respected of the twelve Septs of Ulubis system—and so by implication one of the foremost Seer houses in the galaxy—had been the single most satisfying achievement of Slovius's time as Chief Seer and paterfamilias of Sept Bantrabal.

Fassin was now arguably the best-known Seer in the system, especially after his time with the Tribe Dimajrian, the wild pod of adolescent Dwellers he'd befriended and effectively become part of for a seeming century and a real half-dozen years. He was not yet even at the start of his prime by Seer reckoning but was nevertheless already at the top of his game. He had been born three hundred and ninety years earlier, had lived barely forty-five of those in body-time, and looked a decade younger.

Sometimes he thought back to what had happened in the ruined alien ship, and he looked at all that had happened to Sal and Taince and himself, and reflected that it was as though they had all come away from that nightmare with a sort of bizarre blessing, an inverted curse, a trio of charmed lives, quite as if Ilen had unknowingly given up whatever golden future had awaited her to add that weight of divided bounty to theirs.

He and Taince parted with a kiss. She was heading to the portal and through the Complex to the far side of the galaxy, to the Fleet Academy to spend a year passing on her knowledge. Fassin was going to the far side of Ulubis, where Nasqueron was at the time, to continue trying to extract knowledge from the Dwellers.

Taince was safely through the portal a day before it was destroyed. Fassin was on a liner, a day out of Sepekte. He understood even as the news was still coming in that he might never see her again.

Sal, who might so easily have been away, was at home with his long-suffering father when the attack took place. After ten catatonic hours of disbelief he spent a month mourning his lost freedoms, trying to sink, fumigate and fuck his sorrows away in what passed for the pleasure-pits of Ulubis. In fact, Sepekte, and especially Borquille, had perfectly disrespectable bars, smoke houses and bordellos—Borquille had a whole district, Boogeytown, set aside for just such recreations—but the point was they were not the rest of the civilised galaxy. Fass had bumped into Saluus in a Boogeytown spike bar once, though Sal had been so out of it that he hadn't recognised his one-time friend.

Then Sal straightened out, cut his hair, lost a few tattoos and a lot of acquaintances and at the start of the next working week turned up bang on time at the company offices, where people were still running around in a frenzy, spooked by all the numerous false alarms, expecting to be invaded at any moment.

Right from the start, the questions were: Why? Why us? What next? And: Anybody else?

Had something like this happened everywhere?

It would take over two centuries for Ulubis to discover if it was part of a wider catastrophe or had been singled out for its own specific disaster. From being no more remote than any other system at the end of a single wormhole—and so orders of magnitude less remote than the many hundreds of thousands of Faring systems still to be connected or reconnected—Ulubis, its principal planet Sepekte, its three significant inhabited moons including 'glantine, its thousands of artificial habitats and the twenty billion souls that the whole system contained were fully as remote and exposed as they'd always seemed from any casual glance at a galactic star chart.

The Guard, Navarchy Military and surviving units of the Ulubis Ambient Squadron repaired and regrouped. Martial law was declared and a War Emergency Plan actioned which turned the bulk of the system's advanced productive capacity to weapons and war craft. As a consequence, Kehar Heavy Industries, Saluus's father's company, expanded and prospered beyond its founder's most avaricious fantasies, and Saluus went from wastrel heir to a great fortune to inheritor-in-waiting of a vast one.

In the system hierarchy, thought was given at the highest levels to attempting to construct a wormhole of Ulubis's own and a carrier fleet to take one end of it to Zenerre. But aside from the vast cost and the point—assuming a portal would be heading in the other direction before too long—that it would be a waste of time and effort which would bring reconnection no quicker, there was one clinching argument that would apply until either no signal arrived from Zenerre or word came of an utter breakdown in civil society: in the Mercatoria only Engineers were allowed to make and emplace wormholes.

There were sanctions and punishments for those systems and rulers who even began a 'hole-creation programme without explicit permission, and that permission had not been present in the Mercatoria's pre-agreed War Emergency Plan for Ulubis.

Back in space, distributed around the Lagrange point where the portal had lain, the few pieces of recovered Beyonder ships indicated that the portal's attackers had been made up from the same three groups which had troubled Ulubis and some of the nearby volumes for thousands of years: Transgress, the True Free and the BiAlliance, for this one occasion working in concert and in far greater numbers than they ever had before.

Anxious, on edge, waiting for whatever a Beyonder invasion might bring, the people of the system reverted to a state something more like that of Earth's rHumanity before it had been fully brought into the galactic community.

It was a truism that all civilisations were basically neurotic until they made contact with everybody else and found their place within the ever-changing meta-civilisation of other beings, because, until then, during the stage when they honestly believed that they might be entirely alone in existence, all solo societies were possessed of both an inflated sense of their own importance and a kind of existential terror at the sheer scale and apparent emptiness of the universe. Even knowing that the rest of the galactic community did exist—at least in some form, even in a worst case—the culture of Ulubis system shifted fractionally towards that earlier, pre-ascensionary state.

Restricted by martial law in new and annoying but sometimes oddly exciting ways, coming to terms with their sudden isolation and newly appreciated vulnerability, people lived more for the short term, clutching at what pleasures and rewards might be available today, just in case there really was no tomorrow. No great breakdown in society took place and there were no significant riots or rebellions, though there were protests and crackdowns, and, as the authorities admitted much later—much later—Mistakes Were Made. But the system held together rather than fell apart, and many people would look back on that strange, unsettled epoch with a sort of nostalgia. There had been something feverish but vivid about the time, a reconnection with life after the disconnection with everybody else, which led to what even looked from some angles suspiciously like a cultural renaissance for what people were now starting to call the Ulubine Disconnect.

Fassin missed out on most of the excitement, taking every opportunity he could to go delving, as if frightened that he might not be able to do so in the future. Even when he was living back in real-time he was insulated from the extremes of the system-wide turmoil of fear and nervous energy by being on 'glantine rather than Sepekte or its ring habitats, then by living within the Sept, at one of its five seasonal houses, rather than in Pirrintipiti or any of the planet-moon's other major cities. He still travelled, spending occasional holidays in Pirri or off-'glantine, and that was when he felt the strange new atmosphere of freneticism most keenly.

Mostly, though, he was in Nasqueron, nestled in a fragile little gascraft, occasionally at normal life-speed, flying with the younger Dwellers, riding the gases alongside them, buffeted by the gas-giant-girdling, planet-swallowing super-winds and whirling hyper-storms of the planet, sometimes—more often and much more productively, though far less excitingly—floating sedately in a study or a library in one of the millions of Dweller cities with one of the more elderly and scholarly Dwellers, who alone in the system seemed perfectly unconcerned about the portal's demise. A few of the (rare) polite ones expressed the sort of formal shame-but-there-you-go sympathy people tend to exhibit when an acquaintance's elderly relative expires peacefully, but that was about it.

Fassin supposed that it was foolish to expect anything else from a race that was as ancient as the Dwellers claimed to be, who had supposedly explored the galaxy several times over at velocities of only a few per cent of light speed long before the planetary nebula that gave birth to Earth, Jupiter and the Sun had even formed out of the debris of still more antique generations of stars, and who still maintained they felt vaguely restricted not by that absolute limit on the conventional pace of travel but rather by the modest scale of the galaxy that these staggeringly long-ago, almost wilfully leisurely sets of voyages had revealed.

The days, weeks and months of waiting and preparation for an invasion became a year. The Beyonder attacks, rather than increasing, faded away almost to nothing, as though the portal assault had been one last insane hurrah rather than the logical, if wasteful, precursor to a war of conquest.

The years added up towards a decade and gradually people and institutions relaxed and came to believe that the invasion might never come. The majority of the emergency powers lapsed, though the armed forces remained in high numbers and on high alert, sensors and patrols sweeping the volumes of space around Ulubis, seeking a threat that seemed to have disappeared.

In four directions lay almost empty intergalactic nothingness: barren volumes holding a few ancient, exhausted cinder suns with life-free systems or none at all, a scattering of dust and gas clouds, brown dwarfs, neutron stars and other debris—some of these, or the space in between, technically life-supporting for Slow exotics, Cincturia and Enigmatics, but patently devoid of any species who cared or could even understand the fate or concerns of the people of Ulubis—but no allies, no one to help or offer assistance or support, and certainly no portal connections.

Down-arm, nearly parallel with the galaxy's wispy limit, heading into the thickening mass of gas and nebulae and stars, was Zenerre. Inwards, between Ulubis and the galactic centre spread a vast mass of Disconnect; the Cluster Epiphany Five Disconnect, millions of stars spread throughout cubic light-centuries which, it was believed, still supported worlds that had once been part of the civilised, connected, 'hole-networked galactic community until over seven thousand years earlier and the Arteria Collapse which had preceded the War of the New Quick and all the excitement and the woes that had flowed from it.

Two centuries, one decade, four years and twenty days after the portal attack, exactly when it might have been expected, the first signal arrived from Zenerre, the wavefront of what would become a constant stream of information from the rest of the connected galaxy. Where, Ulubis was informed, life was going on as usual. The attack on its portal had been unique, and all was basically well with the Mercatoria. Attacks and incursions by the various Beyonder groups continued throughout the civilised galaxy, as did operations against them, but these were on the usual mainly nuisance-value level that the Beyonder Wars had evidenced for thousands of years, the tactically distressing and annoyingly wasteful but strategically irrelevant distributed background micro-violence that people had started calling the Hum.

Relief, puzzlement and a vague sense of victimisation spread throughout Ulubis system.

The Engineership *Est-taun Zhiffir*, portal-carrying, set out from Zenerre for Ulubis less than a year after the disaster, with a travel time initially given as 307 years, later reduced by increments to level out at 269 as the Eship upped its velocity even closer to light speed, the Engineers aboard fine-tuning the systems which insulated the hauled portal from the effects of its own and the ship's relativistic mass. People in Ulubis system relaxed, the last vestiges of martial law were hidden away from public sight again. Those many born after the portal's destruction wondered what it would be like to have a connection to the rest of the galaxy, to this semi-mythical meta-civilisation they'd heard so much about.

The flip-over point came, and Fassin was vaguely aware of it as the pressure on his chest and flesh and limbs faded away over the course of a few seconds, replacing that feeling of oppression with a sensation of sudden blood-roaring bloatedness as his body struggled to cope with the change. He kept his eyes closed. Almost immediately there was a faint trace of force, a gentle push from somewhere beneath his head, then weightlessness again, and a few moments later a matching tug from somewhere beneath his feet, and then weight returning, pressure quickly building, until the roaring in his head faded and became the distant thunder of the ship again.

:

The Archimandrite Luseferous, standing before the ruins of the city, stooped and dug gloved fingers into the soft earth by his feet, wrenching out a handful of soil. He held it to his face for a while, staring at it, then brought it close to his nose and smelled it, then let it fall and dusted off his gloves while staring down at the huge crater where a large part of the city had been.

The crater was still filling from the sea, a slow curling curve of brown-white water spilling from the estuary beyond. The waterfall disappeared into the seat of the crater in a vast cloud-bank of vapour, and steam rose everywhere from the rolling, tumbling confusion of waters as the great rocky bowl cooled. A massive trunk of steam, three kilometres or more across, rose into the calm pastel sky, rolling up through thin layers of cloud, flat-heading where it achieved the middle reaches of the atmosphere.

It was the Archimandrite's conceit, where a severe lesson had to be taught on a planet capable of supporting such a mark, that a city by the sea, which was either itself guilty of resisting or judged by him symbolic of resistance shown by others on the planet, be remade in the image of his beloved Junch City, back on Leseum9 IV. If a people would resist him, either while undergoing conquest or enduring occupation, they would suffer, of course, but they would be part of something greater at the same time and they would, even in death, even in the death of much of their city, be the unwitting and unwilling participants in what was, indeed, a work of art. For here, seen from this hillside, was there not a new Faraby Bay? Was that slot through which the waters thundered, shaking the ground, not another Force Gap? Was that piling tower of steam, first drawn straight up then stroked to the horizon, not a kind of signature, his very own flourish?

The Bay was overly circular, certainly, and the slot a mere break in a modest crater wall composed largely of estuarine mud, presenting no aesthetic match at all for the great kilometre-high cliffs of the real Force Gap—indeed, the whole setting for this new image of Junch City entirely lacked the original's dramatic ring of surrounding mountains, and this little parkland hill on which he stood—with his admirals, generals and guard waiting obediently behind, allowing him this moment of reflection—was frankly a poor substitute for the vertical cliff of the Sheer Citadel and its magnificent views.

Nevertheless, an artist had to work with what there was to hand, and where there had once been just another swarming seaside city, lying tipped upon the land, variously hilled, messily distributed round a tributary river, with the all usual urban sprawl, great buildings, docks, breakwaters and anchorages—in other words what it had always been, roughly, no matter that there had been earlier so-called catastrophes like earthquakes or floods or great fires or bombardment from sea or air or earlier invasion—now there was an image of a fair and distant place, now there was a new kind of savage beauty, now there was a fit setting for a new city reborn in the image of his sovereignty, now there was a sort of—even—healing joining with those other peoples and places who had surrendered to his will, in suffering and in image, for this majestic crater, this latest work, was just the most recent of his creations, one more jewel on a string stretching back to the primacy of elegance that was Junch City.

Anyone with sufficient self-belief, enough ruthlessness and (Luseferous believed himself modest enough to admit) an adequate supply of luck could—if the will was there and the times required such determination—conquer and destroy. Judging how much to destroy for the effect one wished to achieve, knowing when to be ruthless, when to show leniency, even when to exhibit beguiling, rage-sapping generosity and a touch of humour; that required a more measured, a more subtle, a more—he could think of no other word for it—*civilised* touch. He had that touch. The record spoke for itself. To then go on from there and use the sad necessity of destruction to create art, to form an image of a better place and forge symbolic unity… that was on another level again, that elevated the mere war-maker, the mere politician, to the status of creator.

Tendrils of smoke rose all around the central column of steam, dark paltry vines adorning a huge pale trunk. These marked where defending aircraft had fallen and where fires had been started by the crater-weapon's ground shock, no doubt. Part of the artistry involved in such a work was creating a great declivity without utterly destroying all around it (a new, reborn city had to grow here, after all). Some sophistication of weaponry was required to achieve such precision. His armaments experts attended to such details.

The Archimandrite Luseferous looked about him, smiling to his chiefs of staff, all standing respectfully at his heel, looking a little nervous to be here in the fresh air of another newly subject planet. (Yet was it not good to breathe in that fresh air, for all its alien scents? Did those strange new odours not themselves mean that another treasure had been added to their ever-increasing domain?) Above and behind, bristling war craft hovered and hummed, attended by small clouds of sensory and weapon platforms. Spread in a ring all around were his personal guards, most lying or kneeling on the grass, their darkly glinting weaponry poised. A few in military exoskels lumbered around or squatted, splayed feet squashing into the earth.

At the foot of the hill, beyond another ring of guards, beneath a watchful buzz of guard drones, the refugees moved like a slow river of dun and grey.

Stilters; groundbats, whule. A Mercatorial species. Disconnected all these millennia, certainly, but still a Mercatorial species. Luseferous looked up into the pale green sky, imagining night, the veils of stars, and the one particular sun—pointed out to him from orbit just forty hours ago, while the invasion forces were being prepared for the initial drop—growing steadily closer as they crawled and fought their way towards it, which was called Ulubis.

∴

In the bright, golden-hued air of Sepekte, with the Borquille Equatower a thin stem in the hazy distance, the little Navarchy ship approached the palace complex, sliding through an ancient forest of kilometres-tall atmospheric power columns and between more modest but still impressive administration and accommodation towers. It disappeared into a wide, gently sloped tunnel set into the reception plaza in front of the enormous ball that was the palace of the Hierchon, an eight-hundred-metre sphere modelled after Nasqueron itself by a long-departed Sarcomage, complete with individual bands of slowly contra-rotating floors all sliding round a stationary inner core. Changing orange-red, brown and ochre swirls of pattern, convincingly like the view of the distant gas-giant's cloud tops seen from space, moved across the face of the palace, hiding windows and balconies, sensors and transmitters.

"Major Taak? Lieutenant Inesiji, palace guard. This way, please. Quick as we can, sir." The speaker, whose voice sounded like a human child talking with a mouthful of ball bearings, was a jajuejein, a creature which in repose resembled an insectile tumbleweed sixty or seventy centimetres in diameter. This one had drawn itself up to Fassin's two-metre height, marshalling a host of twiglike components coloured dark green and steel blue to resemble a sort of openwork head like a bird's nest—thankfully it had not tried to make a face—and had balanced itself on two vaguely leglike stalks. The rest of its body, offering glimpses of the reception cavern's floor beyond, was just a cylinder, adorned with belts of soft-looking material and small metallic components that might have been jewellery, gadgets or weapons. It half-turned, half-flowed to a small open cart where the ship's whule rating was already depositing Fassin's luggage.

Fassin turned and waved to the groggily cheerful Dicogra, joined the jajuejein in the cart and was whisked away through a brief security reception area to a lift and a curving corridor which took him to a suite of rooms with what looked like a real outside view of the city—north, with pale, jagged hills in the far distance. Lieutenant Inesiji placed Fassin's bags on the bed with fluid grace and informed him that he had exactly three-fifths of an hour to freshen up, don his ceremonial court clothes and present himself outside his door, whereupon he would be escorted to the audience chamber.

Fassin blipped a safe-arrival message to Bantrabal and then did as he'd been told.

The circular audience chamber was glittering and warm, walls of white gold sparkling under a ceiling-filling galaxy-shaped cloud of tiny sharp lights impersonating stars. Lieutenant Inesiji showed Fassin to a position on one of the many platforms set into the shallow, stepped bowl of the chamber. A human-conforming seat malleabled its way up from the floor. He sat in it—stiffly, in his bulky court robes—and the lieutenant told him, "Please stay where you are for now, sir" in a sort of gargled whisper, executed what might have been a bow, turned into what looked very like a cartwheel, and rolled away back up the slope of gangway to an exit.

Fassin looked around. The chamber looked like it might hold a thousand people, but he was one of only about two dozen people present, distributed around the shallowly conical space as though to maximise the distance between each individual. Humans—all, like him, in cumbersome, rather gaudy court dress—just about outnumbered the others, but he saw another jajuejein—balled, either resting or sleeping, criss-crossed with iridescent ribbons—two whule sitting like angular grey tents covered in silver flowers, both looking at him, a pair of quaup, one of the two-metre-long red-tan ellipses floating and also looking at him (well, certainly pointing at him), and the other stood on its end, either also snoozing or possibly at attention—Fassin's knowledge of alien body language was wide but shallow except where Dwellers were concerned. Three large environment suits containing waterworlders completed the non-human contingent: two of the esuits, looking like aquamarine impersonations of the quaups, most likely contained kuskunde; the third was a matt black lozenge the size of a small bus, radiating warmth. That esuit would almost certainly contain an symbioswarm Ifrahile.

In the centre of the chamber, at its deepest point, just before a set of wide, tall, concentric platforms which broke the symmetry of the space, there was an incongruous-looking device which looked like an ancient iron cooking pot: a black-bellied urn a couple of metres in diameter, capped with a shallow dome and sitting on a tripod of stubby legs on the buttery sheen of the solid gold floor. Its surface was pinstriped with thin vanes, but otherwise it resembled something almost prehistoric. Fassin had never seen anything like it before. He shivered, despite the warmth of the chamber.

The quaup which might have been sleeping suddenly flicked level with a ripple of lateral mantle and turned towards its fellow creature thirty metres away, which swivelled to look back at it. Expression patterns flashed across their face nacelles, then they moved towards each other, hovering together, faces signal-flickering conversation for the few seconds it took for a small flutter drone to drop from the ceiling and—in spoken voice, with chirps and squeaks—apparently ordered them back to their places. The quaup shriek-popped back at the mechanical remote, but split up, drifting away to their earlier positions.

They had just about resumed their allotted patches when a group of half a dozen jajuejein technicians, awkward in their shape-constraining formal court gear of dimly iridescent ribbons, entered from a door at one side of the chamber floor, pushing large pallets full of highly techy-looking equipment which they positioned in a rough circle round the cooking-pot device. Their body ribbons marked them out as Shrievalty, Fassin suddenly realised, wondering whether as a major of the Ocula he was senior enough to order them around. A similar-sized group—human Cessorian priests from their garb, though in their court best it was hard to be sure—could they even be Lustrals?—approached from the opposite direction. The priests stood close behind the technicians, who ignored them and busied themselves setting up and adjusting their arcane apparatus.

Finally, an alarming group of four human and four whule troopers in full mirror-finish power-armour stalked in, complete with a variety of heavy infantry weapons. The ambience of the chamber changed; even across species the mood almost tangibly altered from one of some puzzlement and a degree of expectation to one of alarm, even fear. The two quaup were exchanging rapid large-scale face signals, the Ifrahile esuit rose hissing from its platform and the whule pair were alternating between staring at each other and glaring down at their mirror-armoured kin.

Who brought armed forces into an audience chamber? Was this a trap? Had all here offended the Hierchon? Were they all to be murdered?

The soldiers deployed in a wide circle around the Shrievalty and Cessoria, standing at ease, weaponry poised, armour-locked. They were facing inwards, towards the black cooking-pot device. The mood in the room seemed to relax a little.

Then the series of platforms beyond the giant urn and the various groups of functionaries shimmered once and dropped into the floor, to re-emerge some moments later, crowded with people.

An outer ring of white-uniformed human court officials, an inner ring of species-varied, extravagantly emblazoned courtiers and an outer core, again mixed-species, of Ascendancy, Omnocracy, Administrata and Cessoria—Fassin recognised most of them from the news and the few formal visits he'd had to make to the court over the years—formed semicircular tiers of importance around the being in the centre: the Hierchon Ormilla himself, resplendent in his giant platinum-sheathed discus of an environment suit, floating humming just above the highest platform, the dark creature's great gaping face visible through the suit's forward diamond window amongst roiling clouds of crimson gas. Seven metres high, three wide, the suit was by some margin the largest and most impressive of the micro-environments in the chamber. It quickly took on a frosted look, as humidity in the air condensed on its deep-chilled surfaces.

As the Hierchon and his attendants appeared, Fassin's seat gave a warning vibration and began to sink back into the platform beneath. Fassin took the hint and stood, then bowed, while the various other people in the chamber performed their equivalent actions. The giant esuit lowered fractionally so that its base touched the platform, and Fassin's seat rose smoothly from the platform again.

The Hierchon Ormilla was an oerileithe: a gas-giant dweller, but—important distinction, this, to all concerned—not a Dweller, even if the shape of his esuit made him look like one. Ormilla had ruled the Ulubis system since his investiture nearly six thousand years earlier, long before the humans who now made up the bulk of its populace had arrived. He was generally thought to be a competent if unimaginative governor, exercising what leeway a Hierchon had within the Mercatorial system with caution, sense and, on occasion, even a degree of compassion. His rule since the portal's destruction had, by the estimation of the officially sanctioned media, been a humbling combination of breathtaking majesty, heroic, utterly exemplary fortitude and a touching, steadfast solidarity with his human charges. Unkinder, unsanctioned, often human critics might have accused him of betraying an early disposition towards authoritarianism and even paranoid repression, eventually followed later by a more composed and lenient attitude, when he started listening to his advisers again.

Looking more carefully at the high-ups present, Fassin realised that, basically, the gang was all here. Apart from Ormilla himself, the Hierchon's two most senior deputies, the Peregals Tlipeyn and Emoerte, were in attendance, as was the most senior member of the Propylaea to survive the portal's destruction, sub-master Sorofieve, the top Navarchy officer, Fleet

Admiral Brimiaice, Guard-General Thovin, First Secretary Heuypzlagger of the Administrata, Colonel Somjomion of the Shrievalty—his own ultimate superior officer for the duration of the current emergency, Fassin supposed—and Clerk-Regnant Voriel of the Cessoria. The absolute elite of the system.

Fassin looked at the pot-bellied stove device squatting on the golden floor, and at the heavily armed troopers, and thought what a perfect opportunity was presenting itself for a complete decapitation of the system's top brass.

"This is an extraordinary session of the Mercatorial Court of Ulubis, before the Hierchon Ormilla," an official announced over the chamber's PA, voice thundering. "The Hierchon Ormilla!" the official shouted, as though concerned that people hadn't heard him the first time.

The official was speaking the human version of Standard, the galaxy's lingua franca. Standard had been chosen as an inter-species, pan-galactic language over eight billion years ago. Dwellers had been the main vector in its spread, though they made a point of emphasising that it was not theirs originally. They had one very ancient, informal vernacular and another even more ancient formal language of their own, plus lots that had survived somehow from earlier times or been made up in the meantime. These latter came and went in popularity as such things tended to.

"Oh no, there was a competition," the Dweller guide/mentor Y'sul had explained to Fassin on his first delve, hundreds of years ago. "Usual thing; lots of competing so-called universal standards. There was a proper full-scale war after one linguistic disagreement—a grumous and a p'Liner species, if memory serves—and after that came the usual response: inquiries, missions, meetings, reports, conferences, summits.

"What we now know as Standard was chosen after centuries of research, study and argument by a vast and unwieldy committee composed of representatives of thousands of species, at least two of which became effectively extinct during the course of the deliberations. It was chosen, astonishingly, on its merits, because it was an almost perfect language: flexible, descriptive, uncoloured (whatever that means, but apparently it's important), precise but malleable, highly, elegantly complete yet primed for external-term-adoption and with an unusually free but logical link between the written form and the pronounced which could easily and plausibly embrace almost any set of phonemes, scints, glyphs or pictals and still make translatable sense.

"Best of all, it didn't belong to anybody, the species which had invented it having safely extincted themselves millions of years earlier without leaving either any proven inheritors or significant mark on the greater galaxy, save this sole linguistic gem. Even more amazingly, the subsequent conference to endorse the decision of the mega-committee went smoothly and agreed all the relevant recommendations. Take-up and acceptance were swift and widespread. Standard became the first and so far only true universal language within just a few Quick-mean generations. Set a standard for pan-species cooperation that everybody's been trying to live up to ever since.

"Which is not to say that everybody everywhere loves it without qualification. Amongst my own species in particular, resistance to its use continues to this day, and individual obsessives and small and indeed quite large groups and networks of enthusiasts are forever coming up with new and, they claim, even better universal languages. Some Dwellers persist in regarding Standard as an outrageous alien imposition and a symbol of our craven surrender to galactic fashion.

"Such persons tend to speak ancient formal. Or at least they do where they haven't invented their own unique and generally utterly incomprehensible language."

Uncle Slovius himself, on what, fittingly, had turned out to be his final delve, had accompanied Fassin on this, the young man's first. "How perfectly typical," he'd observed later. "Only Dwellers could have a completely fair competition eight billion years ago and still be arguing over the result."

Fassin smiled at the thought and looked round the giant auditorium as the official's words echoed and faded amongst the precious metals and sumptuous clothing. He thought it was all very impressive, in a slightly camp, almost vulgar way. He wondered how much tedious ceremony and baroque speechifying they would now have to sit through before anything of note happened or was said. He did a quick count of the bodies in the chamber. There were well over twice the thirty that the emissarial projection had told him to expect.

A tap-screen appeared on a stalk out of the platform surface and positioned itself in front of him, flicking into life with search and note facilities enabled, but no audio or visual record. Fassin tapped a symbol to confirm that he was there. Round the circular chamber, the others were also being presented with screens or their species-relevant alternative.

"You are here to witness the transmission of a signal from the Engineership *Est-taun Zhiffir*," Ormilla's deep, synthesised voice said calmly. "We are informed that it is, of necessity, in the form of an Artificial Intelligence construct which will be destroyed after the audience has finished." Ormilla paused, to let this sink in. Fassin thought he just hadn't heard right. "How you use the information you are about to learn is a matter of duty and conscience," Ormilla told them. "How you came by it is not; any revelation regarding the signal's form is punishable by death. Begin."

An AI? A conscious machine? An abomination? Were they serious? Fassin couldn't believe it. The entire history of the Mercatoria was the record of its implacable persecution and destruction of AIs and the continual, laborious, zealously pursued effort to prevent them ever again coming into existence within the civilised galaxy. That was what the Lustrals were all about; they were the AI hunters, the remorseless, fanatic persecutors of machine intelligence and any and all research into it, and yet here they were, calmly watching the cooking-pot device and the technicians surrounding it.

A semi-transparent image flickered in the air above the dark machine in the centre of the chamber. The hologram was of a human male dressed in the uniform of an Admiral of the Summed Fleet. Fassin hadn't even known that one of his species had risen to such impressive heights. The human admiral was an old, well-built man with a heavily lined face. Bald, of course, but sporting a heavily tattooed scalp. He wore, or his image appeared to wear, a high-rank space-combat suit, its helmet components in stowed configuration round the neck and shoulders. Various insignia on the surface of the suit confirmed with no discernible subtlety that the Admiral was an extremely important military person.

"Thank you, Hierchon Ormilla," the image said, then seemed to look straight at Fassin, who felt startled for a moment before realising that the image probably appeared to be looking directly at everybody in the chamber. He certainly hoped so. "I represent Admiral Quile of the Summed Fleet, commanding the Third Medium Squadron of the battle fleet accompanying the Engineership *Est-taun Zhiffir* on its journey towards Ulubis system, Fleet Admiral Kisipt commanding," the projection said in a calm, no-nonsense voice.

*Battle fleet?* thought Fassin. You didn't send a battle fleet to accompany an Eship, portal-carrying or not, did you? They usually travelled with a few Guard ships or one or two units of the Navarchy Military plus a single small Summed Fleet craft sometimes for ceremonial purposes. He was no military expert, but even he knew this sort of stuff, just from catching newscasts of at-the-time-recent connections and reconnections. He watched the military on the semicircular podia closely. Yep, looked like they were startled by this news, too.

"I am to dispense information, and orders," the hologram said. "Then I will answer questions. Then I will be destroyed. Information first. Intelligence we have received strongly indicates that Ulubis system will, probably within a year and possibly within months of this signal reaching you, become the target of a full-scale invasive assault originating from the Cluster Epiphany Five Disconnect."

The hologram paused, appearing to listen. There was a certain sense of stillness, even of shock in the chamber, but no gasps or expressions of fear or incredulity that Fassin could hear.

He scanned the people in the chamber, trying to work out if he was the only person present to whom this news might come as a surprise. Face flickers from the quaup, big staring looks between the whule, perhaps a few rather wide-eyed expressions amongst the tech people down near the dark AI machine. Some of the more readable courtiers looked a little stunned. The Ifrahile esuit might have wobbled fractionally. Fassin's hand was moving towards the tap-screen when it lit up with a diagram of the galactic local volume, about a thousand years in diameter and centred on Cluster Epiphany Five, the millions-strong mass of stars core-in from the isolated wisp of suns near the end of which lay Ulubis.

"Indeed, our strategists put at about six per cent the possibility that by the time this signal arrived the invasion would already have happened." The hologram looked around the chamber and smiled. "I am glad to see that is not the case." The smile disappeared. "On the other hand I had hoped, when the original of this signal was recorded, that I would be telling you that the invasion was still three to five years away. Since becoming embodied here I've been given access to some of the real-time intelligence you've been gathering and have had no choice but to plump for an estimate that gives you even less time to prepare than we'd been hoping for." The image paused briefly.

"The E-5 Discon was already known to be expanding aggressively. Deep-space monitors have been picking up blossoming eighth-power-level weapon-blink for several hundred years, centred on the Leseum systems." The image looked around the chamber. "Space battles and high-megatonne nukes, in other words. All the signs are of a rogue hegemony, possibly under the thrall of a human calling himself the Archimandrite Luseferous. He was once genuinely of the Cessoria, though at the rank of Hariolator, not Archimandrite, so it would appear he's promoted himself. In any case, I think we may now count him apostate." The hologram smiled thinly. "The Leseum systems were until not all that long ago the last remaining connected part of the Epiphany Five region. However, that wormhole portal fell victim to a minor action of the Strew, leaving the whole volume completely cut off from civilisation." The thin smile faded.

"Ten days ago from the time this signal was sent an invasion force out of the E-5 Discon comprising several hundred capital ships plus retinue and troop carriers attacked the Ruanthril system, inward from the E-5 Cluster. We assume it came as a surprise to them that Ruanthril had just received a new portal and been connected to the Mercatoria. It had not been part of the Complex before, which may help explain their miscalculation. In any event, elements of the Summed Fleet were present when the E-5 forces attacked. The attack was beaten off, with heavy losses on both sides." At this, Fassin saw a look of something that certainly seemed like consternation pass over the face-parts of the Fleet Admiral Brimiaice. "Yes," the image said, as though responding. "We were surprised too, frankly, and just had insufficient ships. Even more distressingly, the portal was subsequently destroyed." Here,

Fleet Admiral Brimiaice, a quaup, assumed the blank face of—if Fassin recalled his Facial [or equivalent] Expressions and Body Language of Mercatorial Species 101 course—vicariously shamed shock.

"Before that happened," the hologram continued, "intelligence from the captured enemy flagship was transmitted into the Complex. It included a personal record belonging to their equivalent of a Grand-Admiral—the invasion fleet's Supreme Commander—in which he recorded for posterity or his memoirs his puzzlement that so much of the vast military machine of which he was so proud to be a part was being directed not where it would carry the most weight or help capture the greatest number of systems in the shortest possible time—in other words, towards where the greatest mass of stars were, spin-ward, back, up, down and especially core-ward—but away from those regions, towards the almost empty galactic outskirts, towards the Southern Tendril Reefs, towards Stream Quaternary and the Ulubis system, or 'the shit-nailed anus-probing finger at the end of a withered arm', as he colourfully described it."

Fassin nearly laughed. Most of the officials on the main ceremonial platforms, led by the humans, registered shock, horror or outrage in some form. The Hierchon's esuit rolled back half a metre, as though physically struck.

The image took its time to look around the chamber. "Yes, unflattering. My apologies. You will be happy to know that the gentleman who was the source of this memorable image is currently helping the Combined Forces Intelligence Inquisitariat with its inquiries."

Fassin watched a few slightly forced expressions of satisfaction appear. *They really didn't know any of this before*, he thought. He'd assumed the Hierchon and his chums would have been granted some sort of sneak preview earlier, but this seemed to be as new to them as it was to him.

"We also, of course, have the pre-invasion probing-sequence profile for the E-5 Discon's attempted conquest of Ruanthril," the hologram said, "plus those of several other systems attacked by the same force-mix. The musings of the invasion fleet's commander provide credible reason to believe Ulubis is under significant threat. The comparison of the pre-attack probing-sequence profile for Ruanthril with the recent raids on and other hostile actions within Ulubis system leads to the conclusion that said threat is imminent, within the time-frame of a few months to less than a year and a half. There is a long-accepted, high-consistency Beyonder attack profile, and the aggressions Ulubis system has been experiencing over the last three years are anomalous to that."

Fassin suspected that this was a subtle criticism of the system intelligence and strategy services, and especially the Navarchy's. Fleet Admiral Brimiaice looked unnaturally still, as though trying not to draw any unnecessary attention to himself. The information also pointed to something of a cover-up. Like Verpych, Fassin had thought these "anomalous" attacks had begun just over a year ago; this AI had been given access to information indicating that they had been going on for two years before that. Well, that would come as no surprise to anyone. Being spoon-fed rosy-hued misinformation by the authorities was no more than people had come to expect—and pre-emptively discount. They only got suspicious when presented with what looked like the plain unvarnished truth.

"I do have more to say," the image above the cooking-pot device told the assembled listeners. "However, I sense that some of you are already anxious to ask questions, and so at this point I would like to invite queries regarding what you have heard so far. No need to introduce yourselves, by the way—I know who you all are."

Everybody looked at the Hierchon, who obligingly boomed, "Machine, what percentage of likelihood pertains to this invasion?"

The hologram did not look particularly impressed with this first question. It might even have sighed.

Fassin only half listened to the answer and paid even less attention to the following questions and answers; none of them added anything significant to what he'd already heard and mostly the questions boiled down to the categories: Are you sure? Are you mad? Are you lying, abomination? And, I won't get blamed for any of this, will I?

He used the tap-screen to get a better idea of the relevant galactic topography. He called up a usefully scaled hologram and flicked between the local civilisational state of play as it had been understood until today—effectively two and a half centuries out of date—and the updated version that the AI signal had brought with it, which was only seventeen years old. As he did so, whole vast volumes of stars changed from one false colour to another, indicating where this Cluster Epiphany Five Disconnect hegemony had spread its influence.

"—Resist them with all our might!" Fleet Admiral Brimiaice roared.

"I'm sure you will," the hologram said. "However, all the indications are that even if you devoted yourself to all-out, full-time emergency war-craft construction and a full war economy, you will still be outnumbered several times over."

Fleet Admiral Brimiaice then blustered.

Fassin had a question of his own, but it was a question for inside his own head, not one that he wished to ask the AI. It was a question he had the unpleasant feeling would at some point shortly be answered, though he sincerely hoped it wouldn't. It was: *What the hell does all this have to do with me?*

"May I continue?" the image said after the next few contributions showed unmistakable signs of heading in the direction of becoming not so much questions as attestations of innocence, pledges of heroic determination, position-protection statements and attacks on other functionaries present within a wide spectrum of subtlety, biased towards the low end. The hologram gave a small, thin, regretful smile. "I realise that all the foregoing has come as something of a shock, for all of you. However, it is, I am afraid to say, in effect just a preamble to the most significant part of this communication."

The image of Admiral Quile paused to let that sink in, too. Then the hologram said, "Now then. There is a gentleman amongst you who has no doubt been wondering for some little time what exactly he is doing here."

*Oh, shit*, Fassin had time to think, then the image looked at him. Was it really looking at him now? Could everybody see the hologram looking at him? Heads, or other parts as appropriate, turned in his direction. That probably meant yes.

"Seer Fassin Taak, would you make yourself known to the others?"

Fassin heard the blood roar in his ears as he stood and gave a slow, if shallow, bow towards the Hierchon. He was getting that flesh-shrinking thing again. The chamber looked to be tipping, and he was glad to sit down again. He tried to control the blush that he felt building under his throat.

"Seer Taak is a young man, though born centuries ago," the image said. "He has spent a productive and dutiful career with the gas-giant Dwellers of the planet Nasqueron. I understand that many of you may have heard of him already. He has now been given the rank of major within the Shrievalty Ocula, for reasons which will become clear in due course."

Fassin, still feeling very much looked-at, noticed that Colonel Somjomion, the human female who was acting chief of staff of the Shrievalty contingent in the Ulubis system, smiled cautiously at him from the podium across the chamber when the hologram said this. Unsure whether the Shrievalty saluted or not, Fassin rose fractionally in his seat, and nodded formally.

*Oh, fuck*, were his precise thoughts.

The image floating above the cooking-pot AI said, "The reason that Seer—Major—Taak is here today to hear what I have had to tell you all is that it was something which he discovered—stumbled over might be an equally accurate description, with no disrespect to Seer Taak—that has led to my being here in the first place."

*Oh, fucking hell. I always thought delving would be the death of me but I assumed it would be an equipment failure, not something like this.* On the other hand, that smile from Colonel Somjomion had been restrained, even careful, not mean or mocking. *Might live yet.*

"Which brings us, of course, to the real, or at least the most pressing, reason for my appearance here, in this almost unprecedented form," the hologram said, then made a show of taking a deep breath.

It looked around them all, slowly, before saying, "Ulubis, I'm sure we would all agree, is a pleasant and fairly favoured system." It paused again.

Fassin was listening fairly hard at this point, and would have taken decent odds on the literal truth of the old you-could-have-heard-a-pin-drop saying. "And," the projection said with a smile, radiantly confident that it now had their full attention, "as a centre of Dweller Studies, it is not without significance galactically, unquestionably from an antiquarian and intellectual standpoint." Another pause. It occurred to Fassin that an AI controlling a hologram could put a quite literal twinkle in its eye. "However, one might think it reasonable to ask—again, with no disrespect intended, or, I hope, taken—why Ulubis has attracted the attention of our new-found adversaries from Cluster Epiphany Five. One might even—knowing the importance that the Mercatoria attaches to reconnecting all the many, many systems which have been without Arteria access all these millennia—wonder why the expedition from Zenerre to Ulubis with a new portal was dispatched with such alacrity, given the arguably still greater claims that more populous, more classically strategically important and more at-the-time obviously threatened systems might have had upon the resources and expertise of our esteemed colleagues in the Engineering faculty.

"One might also pause to give thought to the reasons why the Engineership *Est-taun Zhiffir* is accompanied by those elements of the Summed Fleet of which my original has the honour of being part—why, indeed, the Eship *Est-taun Zhiffir* is escorted by such a preponderance of force at all." The hologram raised its head, looked all around again. "It might not even be totally unreasonable to call into question the apparently unchallenged assumptions and settled conclusions concerning the destruction of the Ulubis portal by the Beyonders, over two centuries ago."

That caused a little frisson in the chamber, Fassin noticed. *Is any of this still about me and anything I might have found?* he wondered. *The more I hear, the more I hope it isn't.*

"There is one circumstance, one nexus of contingent information," the image said with a broad, unamused smile and something like relish, "which is, we strongly suspect, behind all of this." The projection turned to look directly at the Hierchon Ormilla. "Sir, at this point I must ask that those not specifically cleared to be present at this meeting be withdrawn. I believe we might make an exception for the troopers, providing their ear mikes are turned off, but I would be disobeying my orders if I continued with those not invited still present."

"*Admiral* Quile," the Hierchon boomed, with just sufficient emphasis, "*I* vouch for all those present who were inadvertently excluded from the clearance list you refer to. You may continue."

"And were it up to me, sir, that would of course be more than enough reason to proceed without care or reservation," the Admiral's image said. "However, devastated though I may be at being seen to offer even the slightest suggestion of an insult to your esteemed court, I am specifically forbidden to continue, bound as I am by the orders of the Complector Council."

*Ouch*, Fassin thought. He almost felt sorry for the Hierchon. He'd not just had rank pulled on him, he'd been made to look small. A Sarcomage outranked a Hierchon, and was in turn answerable to a Complector, any single one of which—supremely powerful as they were in every other exercise and iteration of power within the civilised galaxy—themselves had at least to take into account the will of the Complector Council. The unspeakably omnipotent members of the Complector Council were bound by nothing else save the laws of physics, and were generally held to be putting considerable effort into getting round those.

Hierchon Ormilla took his defeat with a degree of grace and within a few minutes the chamber was emptied of half its earlier occupants. The stepped sequence of podia in front of the Hierchon's imposing esuit now looked positively bare. All the court officials and courtiers had departed, with much muttering and the single highest quotient of affronted dignity Fassin had ever witnessed, by several factors. The military bigwigs were still present, but even their on-podium ranks had been depleted as Colonel Somjomion of the Shrievalty and Clerk-Regnant Voriel of the Cessoria were reduced to stepping down to floor level so that they could operate the two most important pieces of equipment monitoring the cooking-pot device embodying the AI. The mirror-finish troopers still stood in a wide circle beyond, armour locked in at-ease, deaf now.

While all this had been going on, Fassin had been left to sit there, not knowing what to think. He knew what he ought to be thinking; he ought to be thinking, *What the fuck could I ever have stumbled across that possibly warranted this level of right-to-the-top paranoia and secrecy?* It was, however, hard to know what to think. He also knew what he ought to feel: fear. There, he was fine; he had a superabundance of high weapon-grade trepidation.

"Thank you," the image of the Admiral said. "Now then," it said, looking round all those who remained. "I have a question for you. What do you know of something called the Dweller List?" It held up one hand. "Rhetorical question. You don't have to answer. Those of you who wish, feel free to consult your screens or equivalent. Take a moment."

There was a flurry of distant tapping. *The Dweller List?* thought Fassin. *Oh, fucking hell; not that shit.*

The hologram smiled. "Let me in due time tell you what we at this end— as we design and record this signal and projection—consider important regarding this subject."

Fassin had heard of the Dweller List, of course; no Seer hadn't. Unfortunately, lots of laypeople had heard of the List, too, and so it had become one of those tired, inward-groan-producing subjects that people tended to raise when they met a Seer at a party, along with other hoary old cliché-questions such as, "Do Dwellers really hunt their own children?" and, "Are they really as old as they say they are?"

The Dweller List was a collection of coordinates. It had turned up, as far as anyone could be sure, towards the end of the Burster War four hundred million years earlier, and was probably well out of date even then. Allegedly, the list detailed all the Dwellers' own secret arteria portals. According to the story, these had been under development since the time of the Long Collapse, when the Dwellers had decided that the other species—or groups of species— with which they were forced to share the galaxy couldn't be trusted to keep their own or jointly owned 'hole networks safe, and so the Dwellers had better construct an arteria web which they controlled—and which preferably nobody else knew about—if they wanted to voyage from gas-giant to gas-giant reliably and without fuss.

This, of course, completely ignored the Dwellers' attitudes to time and space and scale and more or less everything else. The Dwellers didn't need wormholes and the near-instantaneous travel between systems that they offered. They lived for billions of years, they could slow their metabolism and thoughts down as required so that a journey of a thousand years or ten thousand years or a hundred thousand years would appear to be over in the course of a single sleep, or occupied no more time than that required to read a good book, or play a complicated game. Plus they were already everywhere; they claimed they had spread throughout the galaxy during the First Diasporian Age, which had ended when the universe was only two and a half billion years old. Even if that claim was a boast, a typical Dweller exaggeration, what was undeniable was that Dwellers were present in significant numbers in well over ninety-nine per cent of all the gas-giant planets in the galaxy, and had been for as long as anybody could remember. (Though not, as it had turned out, Jupiter. Humanity's own backyard gas-giant was unusual in being relatively water-poor. The Dwellers considered it a desert planet and rarely visited.)

After centuries of real-time and decades of seem-time spent with Dwellers, Fassin had gained the distinct impression that Dwellers both despised and felt sorry for the Quick—the species, like humans, like all the others in the Mercatoria, which felt the need to use wormholes.

As the Dwellers saw it, to be Quick—to live life that precipitously—was to condemn oneself to an early end. Life had an inescapable trajectory, a natural curve. Evolution, development, progress: all conspired to push a sentient species along in a certain direction, and all you could do was choose to run that road or saunter along it. The Slow took their time, adapting to the given scale and natural limits of the galaxy and the universe as it existed.

The Quick insisted on short cuts and seemed determined to bend the very fabric of space to their frantic, impatient will. When they were smart they succeeded in this wilfulness, but they only brought their own end all the quicker. They lived fast and died faster, describing sudden, glorious but quickly fading trails across the firmament. The Dwellers, like the other Slow, wanted to be around for the long term, and so were prepared to wait.

So quite why the Dwellers would ever have bothered building a secret wormhole network was something of a mystery, as was how they had managed to keep it secret all these hundreds of millions of years, not to mention how this fitted in with the rather obvious nature of each different Dweller community's isolation from each other.

Nevertheless, the myth of the Dweller List continued to excite people in general and conspiracy theorists in particular, especially in times of threat and desperation, when it would be really, really great if a secret wormhole network did exist.

Fassin agreed with the textbooks that it had been no coincidence the List had first turned up during the Burster War, when the whole galactic community had seemed to be falling apart, and people were looking for salvation, for hope, anywhere. Then, the arteria total had been falling from its earlier—and then all-time—high of nearly 39,000 to under a thousand. At the nadir of the Third Chaos there had been less than a hundred 'holes in the whole galaxy, and the Dwellers hadn't stepped in then with an offer to let everybody else use this secret system. If not then, when the light of civilisation seemed to be fading from the great lens entirely, then when? When and why would they ever come galloping to the rescue?

Part of the seductive attraction of the List was its sheer size. It contained over two million sets of alleged portal coordinates, implying more than one million arteria, presumably linked in a single enormous network. At the height of the Third Complex, eight thousand years earlier, there had been exactly 217,390 established wormholes threading the galaxy together, and that was as good, as far as was known, as it had ever got. If the Dweller List genuinely enumerated existing portals and arteria, it would represent the promise of instigating the single greatest change in the history of the galaxy; the sudden linking-up of two million systems, many of which had never had any connection before, the bringing together of almost everybody everywhere—the very furthest, most utterly isolated star would likely be a mere decade or two away from the nearest portal—and the near-instant revitalising, on a scale unheard of in nearly twelve billion years of tenacious, sporadically stuttering civilisation, of the entire galactic community.

It was, Fassin and almost all his fellow Seers had long thought, a forlorn hope. The Dwellers didn't need or show any sign of using wormholes. Being Dwellers, they naturally claimed they were experts at arteria and portal technology, and certainly they were not afraid of using wormholes, it was just that they didn't see the need for them… but if they ever had been seriously involved with wormhole production, those days were long gone. In any case, the List itself, which had been lying around in libraries and data reservoirs, multitudinously copied for hundreds of millions of years, accessible to anybody with a link, was not the end of the story; it just gave the rough coordinates of two million gas-giants in two million systems. What was needed was a more precise location.

The obvious places to look were the relevant Trojan or Lagrange points, the gravitationally stable locations dotted around and between the orbits of the various planets in the named systems. However, these had all long since been eliminated. After that it got much more tricky. In theory a wormhole mouth could be left in any stable orbit anywhere in a system and never be found unless you practically tripped over it. Working portals were anything up to a kilometre wide and had an effective mass of several hundred thousand tonnes, whereas a portal shrunk and stabilised and set up to keep itself that way with relatively simple automatics systems could lie in an orbit as far out as a system's Oort cloud with a gravitational footprint of less than a kilogramme more or less indefinitely. The problem was how to describe where it was.

Allegedly there was some extra set of coordinates, or even a single mathematical operation, a transform, which, when applied to any given set of coordinates in the original list, somehow magically derived the exact position of that system's portal. The obvious objection to this was that after four hundred million years, minimum, there was no known coordinate system ever devised capable of reliably determining where something as small as a portal was. (Unless the holes had all somehow automatically kept themselves in the same relative position all that time. Given the haphazard and cavalier attitude that Dwellers tended to display towards anything especially high-tech, this was regarded as highly unlikely.)

"So," the image hovering above the dark device in the centre of the audience chamber said, "if I may assume we are all happy we know what we're talking about…" It looked around them again. Nobody demurred.

"The Dweller List," the hologram said, "supposedly giving the approximate location of two million ancient portals dating from the time of the Third Diasporian Age, has been dismissed as an irrelevance, a lie or a myth for over a quarter of a billion years. The so-called Transform, supposed to complete the information required to access this secret network, has proved as elusive as it is unlikely to work if it does exist. Nevertheless. Some new information has come to light, thanks to Seer, now Major, Taak."

Fassin was aware that he was being looked at again. He just kept staring at the hologram.

"A little under four hundred years ago," the hologram said, "Seer Taak took part in an extended expedition—a 'delve' as it is known—which took him amongst the Dwellers of Nasqueron, and specifically into the company of a group of Dweller youngsters called the Dimajrian Tribe. While with them, he encountered an antique Dweller who—in a fit of generosity unusual in his kind—granted Seer Taak access to a small library of information, part of a still larger hoard."

(This was the wrong way round—the myth, not the fact. Fassin had been with Valseir for centuries and the Dimajrian Tribe for less than a year. He hoped that the rest of the Admiral's information was more reliable. All the same, he had a sudden, vivid memory of choal Valseir, huge and ancient, accoutred with rags, draped in life-charms, floating absently within his vast nest-bowl of a study, deep in the lost section of abandoned CloudTunnel on the rim of a giant, dying storm which had long since broken up and dissipated. "Clouds. You are like clouds," Valseir had told Fassin. At the time he hadn't understood what the ancient Dweller had meant.)

"The raw data containing this information was passed on to the Shrievalty for analysis," the image hovering above the black device said. "Twenty years later, after the usual analysis and interpretation and, you'd imagine, with plenty of time for second thoughts, re-evaluations and sudden inspirations, it was shared with the Jeltick under the terms of an infotrade agreement."

The Jeltick were an arachnoid species, eight-limbed—8ar., in the conventional shorthand of the galactic community. Obsessive cataloguers, they were one of the galaxy's two most convincing self-appointed historian species. Timid, cautious, deliberate and very inquisitive (at a safe remove), they had been around for much longer than Quick species usually lasted.

"Somehow, the Jeltick contrived to notice something the Shrievalty had missed," the hologram continued. (Now, Fassin noticed, it was Colonel Somjomion's turn to look awkward and aggrieved.) "Heads have rolled due to this incompetence," the image told them. It smiled. "I do not speak figuratively."

Colonel Somjomion compressed her lips and rechecked something on the machine she was in charge of.

"Within months," the hologram said, "the Jeltick sent their best excuse for a battle fleet to the Zateki system—unexplored for millennia—which lies about eighteen years from the portal at Rijom; they got there in twenty years, so they were not exactly dawdling. It ought to be pointed out that the Jeltick would never normally try anything so dynamic, or risky.

"Something at Zateki seriously chewed up the Jeltick ships and what is assumed to have been the sole survivor was later found by a Voehn craft.

The surviving ship was fleeing, all upon it were dead and its biomind was deranged, invoking the mercy of an unknown god and babbling for forgiveness for what had been its mission, which had been to search for the remains of something called the Second Ship and, therein, the Dweller List Transform."

Ah, thought Fassin. The Second Ship Theory. That was a sub-fallacy of the whole Dweller List delusion. The further you looked into the List myth, the more complicated it got and the more possibilities appeared to open up. All nonsense, of course, or so everybody had thought.

"Somehow, we assume through spies, the Beyonders and—possibly through the Beyonders—the E-5 Disconnect got to hear about this. The Beyonders attacked the Ulubis portal less than a month later and the E-5 Discon's sudden interest in Ulubis also dates from this point. When the Jeltick realised the secret was no longer theirs alone," the image said, "they broadcast-leaked it, to avoid accusations of partiality and maintain their reputation for disinterestedness." The projection gave a sour look. "This has not gone down too well with the Ascendancy, either—one imagines the Jeltick will be made to pay somewhere down the line. In any event, five full squadrons of the Summed Fleet—over three hundred capital ships—retraced the Jeltick fleet's route to Rijom and Zateki, but found nothing. Under full disclosure it has turned out that the information concerned was in any case incomplete; the lead is, as it were, only half-formed. The Jeltick move was a gamble, reckoned even by themselves at having a less than twelve per cent likelihood of success. For such a cautious species to make such a wild wager with their reputation and future alone indicates the value of the prize they sought."

The hologram brought its gloved hands together, producing an audible clap. "So, now almost everybody who wants to know about the new Transform lead—such as it may be—does know, and this would appear to include the Disconnect of the Starveling Cult, and—quiet though they may have seemed recently—the Beyonders, who may or may not be in league with the E-5 Discon. Hence the most recent attacks on Ulubis, and the coming invasion.

"But be aware," the image said, growling, eyes narrowing, "that behind this terrible threat lies a fabulous prize. If we can discover where the hidden portals lie—assuming that they are indeed there to be discovered—we may well be able to intervene in the Ulubis system before the Starveling Cult invasion force arrives. It would be entirely worth the most supreme effort and sacrifice for that result alone. Even more importantly, however, this is a prize that could, that just might, that *can* unlock the galaxy and usher in a new golden age of prosperity and security for the Mercatoria, for all of us." The projection paused once more. "Our strategists estimate that even with the best result from those actions we shall ask you to undertake, the chances of success remain below fifty per cent." The projection appeared to draw breath. "But that is not the point. The smallest chance of the greatest reward, when so few may compete for it, makes the contention compulsory. All that matters is that we may have been presented with an extraordinary, utterly unprecedented opportunity. We would all be in serious, even ultimate dereliction of duty if we did not do everything in our power to seize that opportunity, not just on our own behalf but for the good of all our fellow creats, and for those generations yet unborn."

The image smiled one of its cold smiles. "The orders I have to pass on to you from the Complector Council are: to Seer—now Major—Taak." (The projection was already looking straight at Fassin. Now so did a lot of the people in the chamber.) "Return to Nasqueron, seek out the ancient Dweller who gave you the original information and try to find out all you can about the Dweller List, the Second Ship, its location and the Transform. And, to everybody else here," (the image looked around all the others in the chamber) "first, provide every aid you can to Major Taak in the furtherance of his mission, including doing nothing that will delay, obstruct or compromise it, and, second, return the Ulubis system to an invasion-imminent, full-scale, total-war footing immediately and prepare to oppose the coming invasion. Your goal should be—and I do not exaggerate here—to resist to the very last creat, to the very last mortal, to the very last breath."

The hologram seemed to stand back a little and take the measure of them all. "I would say to all of you that, without doubt, your fate lies in your own hands. More importantly, so, potentially, does the fate of the Mercatoria and the civilised galaxy. The rewards for success will be unprecedented in their scale and splendour. The punishments for failure will begin with ignominy and disgrace and plumb new depths of ghastliness beyond. One last thing. You know that the Engineership *Est-taun Zhiffir* and battle-fleet escort which sent this signal are still seventeen years from reaching Ulubis system. I must tell you that significant elements of the Summed Fleet, above Squadron strength, were dispatched in your direction from Zenerre even before the Eship left and have been making well in excess of the Eship fleet's velocity directly towards Ulubis ever since. The attack squadrons will arrive years before the Eship and its escort fleet, their war craft will be fully deployed for uninhibited battle against all who oppose the Mercatoria, and—depend upon it—they will prevail."

The image smiled again. "How I wish I could tell you exactly how soon from this point they will appear. However, even I do not know; this signal was sent from the fleet accompanying the Eship and we do not yet know quite how close to light speed they have pushed themselves, or how close they will have by the time this signal arrives. We can only hazard. If the Disconnecters leave off for as long as another couple of years, the attack squadrons may well arrive before them. Otherwise, they will descend upon a system already fallen to the enemy, or, one would hope, still somehow resisting. Their reaction when they arrive largely depends on your determination, fortitude and ability to absorb punishment." The projection smiled. "Now: any further questions?"

·

The Beyonders must have anticipated them. Their ships were already making ninety per cent of their own furious, headlong speed when they appeared on the point ship's long-distance scanners.

Tiance Yarabokin floated foetal, swaddled in shock-gel, lungs full of fluid, umbilicalled to the ship, nurtured by it, talking to it, listening to it, feeling it all around her. A gee-suit half-completed the image of warrior as unborn, leaving the wearer clothed in a close second skin. Her connection with the ship was via implants and an induction collar rather than a cord into her navel, and her chest moved only faintly as the gillfluid tided oxygen into her blood and scrubbed waste gases out again. Behind her closed lids in that darkness, her eyes flickered to and fro, twitching involuntarily. She shared her close confinement with another forty or so of her comrades, all lying curled and protected and wired up in their own life-pods, all carried deep in the belly of the fleet's flagship, the *Mannlicher-Carcano*.

Way ahead at point, the destroyer *Petronel* veered, maxing its engines, then blinked out in a wash of light that became darkness as the sensors compensated. The buffering faded and revealed the half of the lead ship that was left, tumbling wildly, tearing itself apart in dark curved fountains of debris, spraying fragments against the tunnel-scape of hard blue-white stars collected ahead.

—Point registers multiple contacts at ninety fleet-vee, said one voice, flagged as LR sensors.

—Point is hit, came another; Fleet Status.

—Point contact lost, came a third, followed immediately by:

—Point gone; Fleet Comms and Status almost colliding.

Instantly aware, Tiance had just sufficient time for one small, frightened part of herself to think, *No! Not on my watch!* And right in the Fleet Admiral's nap time, when she was in sole charge. But even as that reaction seemed to echo and die inside her head, she was sensing, judging, thinking, getting ready to issue orders. She flitted between the real-as-it-could-be view shown by the deep-space scan sensors, where the stars were bunched hard blue-white in a circle ahead and collected into a fuzzy red pool behind with pure blackness in every other direction, and the dark abstraction that was Tacspace, a multi-lined and -radiused sphere where the ships of the fleet sat, little stylised arrowhead shapes of varying sizes and colours, a line of fading dots behind each indicating their courses, green glowing identities and status codes riding alongside them.

The pre-prepared split pattern wouldn't work; the ship which had just traded point with the *Petronel* was still sliding back into position in the main body of the fleet and a pattern-one split would at worst cause multiple collisions and at best be just too slow.

Oh well, time to start earning her pay and communicate. Taince sent,

—Pattern-five split, all ships. BC-three, that plus a two-point inward, left-skew delta, for five, then resume.

Copy signals flicked back, the first from her own helm officer, the last from the battlecruiser *Jingal*, registering its adherence to the slight kink she'd put in its course the better to accommodate their D-seven: Destroyer seven, the *Culverin*, the ship which had been falling back after swapping point with the *Petronel*. She was distantly aware of her body registering a pulse of movement, a sudden change in direction so extreme that even the shock-gel couldn't completely mask it. Around them, the ships would be flaring off like their own silent shrapnel burst.

—Hull stress eighty-five, Ship Integrity/Damage Control told her.

—All units responding. Full pattern-five flare, said Fleet Status.

—D-seven: thanks for that, joining pattern.

—C-one: single contact, five nor-down-west.

—D-three: double contact, neg-four nor-up-east.

The cruiser *Mitrailleuse* and the destroyer *Cartouche* registering hostiles. Taince didn't even need to glance into Tacspace to know that meant harmfuls on both sides.

—So, bracketing.

—A straddle. Got us good.

The last two voices had been the two most senior fellow tactical officers.

—We sound as though we play Battleships. (That was Fleet Admiral Kisipt. Awake now, watching. Apparently content to let Taince run the show for the moment.)

—C-one: hostile contact confirmed. PTF.

—D-three: hostile contact confirmed. PTF.

*Mitrailleuse* and *Cartouche* requesting permission to fire.

—Suggest fire/Suggest fire, the other tacticians chorused.

—Agree fire, Fleet Admiral Kisipt said.—Vice?

Vice Admiral Taince Yarabokin thought so too.—C-one, D-three; grant free fire.

—C-one: Firing.

—D-three: Firing.

Tacspace showed bright crimson beams flick from the two ships. Tiny, lime-green dots with their own status bars were missiles, darting towards the enemy ships.

—Multiple hits on the D-one debris field, LR Sensors reported.

—Still flare?

—Still flare, Taince confirmed. She was watching the scintillations ahead, where the wildly spinning, whirling, somersaulting wreckage of the *Petronel* was being hit by further enemy munitions. The remains were dropping back rapidly towards the main fleet as it spread quickly outwards. She clicked up a countdown to their impact with the debris field: seventy-six seconds. She shifted the read-out to a skin-sensation to avoid cluttering her visual feed.

No positive results from the laser fire being laid down by the *Mitrailleuse* and *Cartouche*. Their missiles were still heading towards the hostile craft. No sign of reply so far.

*What if we're wrong?* Taince thought. *What if they've out-thought us and our so-neat manoeuvre?* Deep in her life-pod cocoon, she gave a semblance of a shrug without realising it herself. *Oh well, then we may all be dead. At least it should be quick.*

—Still flare?

—Still flare, she confirmed again. Waiting, judging, wondering if this would work. Tacspace showed the second-hand, now increasingly out-of-date contacts the *Petronel* had spotted as a glowing, slowly dispersing cloud of pulsing yellow echoes. The two hard contacts still registering on the sensors of the *Mitrailleuse* and the *Cartouche* and now confirmed by other nearby ships were strobing red dots, slowly closing. The wreckage from the *Petronel* was a stippled mess of purple, dead ahead and drifting closer, slowly spreading.

*It's okay*, Taince told herself. *We can do this.*

They had rehearsed all this, trained and exercised in VR time after time, specifically for this eventuality, this ambush and manoeuvre and response suite.

They knew that the Beyonders would anticipate a fleet being sent from Zenerre to Ulubis. There was, of course, only one quickest possible route; the straight-line direct one, its laser-clean rule turned into the shallowest of curves solely by allowing for the minimal drift of the respective systems as they circled with the rest of the galactic outskirts round the great wheel's core, fifty thousand light years away.

So, did the fleet take exactly that route, laying itself open to ambush by other ships, and—more threateningly—to mines? (Mines, indeed; all you needed was a few tonnes of crushed rock. Smash a tiny asteroid into gravel the size of rice grains, spread it across the course the fleet would take and— if they were travelling quickly enough—you could waste the lot; so close to light speed that you didn't need to have anything home in and explode, just getting in the way was devastating enough.) Or did you loop further out, avoiding likely interception but arriving later?

And did you stick together (obvious but sensible) or split up, all the individual craft taking their own route to Ulubis, only regrouping near their destination (very risky, but potentially a tactic that the enemy wouldn't have anticipated)? In the end the Fleet Admiral had chosen one out of a bunch of faintly bowed courses recommended by the strategists and their sub-AI machines, and they followed that route en masse.

It was a gamble. The chances were that they would be intercepted, especially if the Beyonders possessed the kind of matériel they were thought to have between Zenerre and Ulubis. The obvious intercept strategy was to station minor ships and other sensor platforms about halfway, then position the intercept units well behind that—already making high speed—to give them time to gather for the attack. In a direct pitched battle, there was no possibility that the vastly outnumbered and out-armed Beyonder ships would prevail. But then, they didn't need or want a pitched battle, they just had to slow the Mercatoria fleet down as much as possible. They wanted skirmishes, ambushes, and to use the fleet's own colossal velocity against it.

The Mercatoria fleet could, in theory, have gone slow and safe, assured just by its sheer weight of arms of being able to blast anything ahead of it out of the skies. Its orders, though, were to get to Ulubis as quickly as possible, regardless, and so it had to travel almost ultimately quickly and risk being torn to bits by a few small ships and nothing more high-tech than a few tonnes of pulverised rock.

They'd come up with a surprise plan of their own.

Needle ships were designed to fit through narrow wormholes, it was that simple. The biggest arteria and the widest portals were a kilometre across, but the average 'hole diameter was under fifty metres and a few very old arteria were barely ten metres wide. It took a vast amount of energy and/or matter to make an arteria and its two portals, and it was difficult, expensive and dangerous to expand them once they were emplaced. There was, for the Mercatoria, little point in having a network of super-fast travel connections scattered throughout the galaxy if your ships were too fat to fit, and so the proportions of war craft—the ultimate levers of power for the Mercatoria, just as they had been for all earlier imperia, semimperia and others who had thought to enforce their peace or impose their will on the galactic community over the aeons—were derived from the width of the channels they would have to negotiate.

In the past, some great capital ships could auto-deconstruct to become a shower of smaller, slimmer components which could fit through a wormhole, and were then capable of reassembling themselves at the far end, but this had proved a wasteful way of designing war craft. Needle ships were simpler and cheaper, for all their astounding complexity and cost. The biggest craft in the battle fleet heading from Zenerre to Ulubis were a kilometre long but less than forty metres across the beam.

Almost right at the enemy ship, the missile fired by the *Mitrailleuse* winked out, replaced by a tiny debris field. Signals from the cruiser, Sensors and Status confirmed this.

—That missile snapped a hostile profile before it was picked off, Weapons reported, side-screening the data the missile had plipped back.

—Sceuri ship, Sulcus or Fosse class, one Tactics officer sent.

So they were dealing—at least in that ship—with the Deathspiral, Taince thought. That particular Beyonder group was exclusively Sceuri; waterworlders with a hatred for the Mercatoria in general and those of their own kind who were a part of it in particular (which meant most of them). Renowned for their viciousness and without even the excuse that they were protecting their precious civilian habitats. They didn't have any, they were almost entirely ship-based. A bunch of piratical terrorists, in other words, just fanatics. And yet as far as anyone knew the Deathspiral hadn't taken part in the attack on the Ulubis portal.

—So that makes four, not three varieties of Beyonder operating in this volume, the Admiral sent, saying what Taince was thinking.

—Two more and we'll have the set, she replied.

Back in Tacspace, she watched the *Cartouche*'s missile curving to meet the twisting trace that was the other nearest hostile. It joined it, overlaying it. A white blink, then an infinitesimal spray of debris, red speckled with green.

—D-three: Hit! Hostile hit!

Taince's two fellow tacticians aboard the flagship made whooping noises.

—Well done, D-three, said Kisipt.

—Still flare?

—Still flare. Taince ignored the celebratory noises and her own feeling of excitement. She watched Tacspace, listened to the ship chatter, felt the seconds count down.

The fleet was still spreading, the vessels' courses fanning out like thin stems from a short vase. Taince held off and held off and held off, until she could almost feel Fleet Admiral Kisipt and everybody else getting ready to shout at her.

Forty seconds. She sent,

—De-flare. Pattern-five reverse.

—Copy, said her own helm officer, then the other acknowledgements followed. In Tacspace, the flowering, widening ship tracks immediately started to bunch up again, the distances between them closing.

—C-one: Going to be tight.

But it was doable. They could get back to their earlier formation before they encountered the remains of the *Petronel*; that was all that mattered for now. Tacspace showed the fleet regrouping smoothly. The view ahead showed the fiercely glowing nebula of wreckage from the *Petronel*, seeming to spread across the sky as they approached it, encroaching onto the dark, starless tube on either side. She zoomed in, picking out a clear spot near the centre of the debris field, checking it in Tacspace. *There.*

The two hard contacts winked out, became orange and started to spread. Tacspace was throwing out probability cones, estimating where the ships might be. Ahead, the sky briefly glowed a pale uniform yellow, indicating that the rest of the Beyonder fleet could be anywhere within that volume. Then a scattering of bright red hard contacts firmed up out of the yellow wash, dispersing it.

The fleet re-formed. They were back where they had started. If nothing else, Taince thought, they ought to have confused the Beyonders.

—Pattern Zero, all ships.

Even in the life-pod, she felt the flagship lurch as it braked, manoeuvred and then accelerated again. She watched it all on Tacspace. The fleet was collapsing, thinning, extending itself forwards and back, ship after ship slipping into a single long line, nose to tail.

—BC-four, back down about ten. D-eleven, forward five. B-three and B-two, centre on D-eight. BC-four, maintain there.

Taince watched them all in Tacspace, shuffling, jostling, ordering them into position until they were all lined up.

—Ships of the line, yes, Vice? the Fleet Admiral sent, also watching.

—Sir.

There were no collisions, no botched moves, no drives left running too long, incinerating the craft behind. The line formation came together as smoothly as it ever had in VR sims. The battleship *Gisarme* led the way, blasting away a few tiny particles left over from the wreck of the *Petronel* and laying down a stuttered laser barrage to try to intercept any mines, kinetic or otherwise, left in the way.

This was a gamble, too. If it worked they'd be through and away, one after another, charging mob-handed right behind the *Gisarme* like a long sequence of battering rams. If it didn't work, there was a chance that first the *Gisarme* would hit something and then they'd all hit whatever was left of it. Potentially the whole fleet could be wiped out in one long pile-up of cascading collisions. The chances were small—smaller, the simulations indicated, than the risks associated with any of the other manoeuvres—but only because this one included a safety premium due to its assumed unexpectedness, its sheer novelty value. If they'd got that wrong, it was much riskier than all the rest.

The manoeuvre caught the Beyonders unawares. It was profoundly not standard Summed Fleet behaviour. The needle ships were one giant needle now, plunging through the debris field of the wrecked destroyer, firing all around them, scoring a couple of hits on distant hostiles desperately closing. Tacspace showed the lines of fire blazing out from the fleet like spokes from a filament-thin shaft and missiles spinning away like tiny glowing emeralds. The Beyonders were attempting to close, but it was too late. All that the nearest hostile units accomplished was their own destruction. In two minutes the Mercatorial fleet was through without loss, and a minute later its entire fire-pattern was rearward: a swirling skirt of crimson lines combing and coning into the emptying depths of space behind. Any further engagement now would be entirely on their terms, and the fleet's vastly superior firepower would have the first word, and the last.

—Nice work, Vice. Fleet Admiral Kisipt sounded a little surprised, a little disappointed and moderately impressed. Taince knew that a lot of her fellow officers had wanted a proper battle, but this way had been better, quicker, more elegant. "Nice work"—from a Voehn; that was real praise.

—Sir. Taince kept her thought-voice calm, but inside it was her turn to whoop. Submerged in her dark womb of fluid, tubes and wires, her fists clenched, a smile appeared on her until then frowning face, and a little shiver shook her cradled body.

∶

The Kehar family house on Murla, an island off the south coast a few hundred kilometres from Borquille, was another spherical building, a quarter of the size of the Hierchon's palace, but remarkable for being balanced on top of a great upthrust of water, precisely like a ball balanced on a water jet in a fairground.

Saluus Kehar, perfectly groomed, glowing with health and generally looking as smoothly gleaming as one of his company's spaceships, met Fassin personally on the slim suspension bridge connecting the house with the spit of land jutting out into the ancient drowned caldera where the waters foamed and roared and spumed and the house balanced, barely trembling, on the giant column of water.

"Fassin! Great to see you! Hey! That uniform suits you!"

Fassin had thought he'd be briefed/indoctrinated/psyche-tested/pep-talked/fuck-knows-whatted and then bundled aboard ship to be whisked straight to Nasqueron. But even faced with arguably the single greatest emergency in its history, the Ulubine bureaucracy had a set way of doing things, and central to this ethos appeared to be not doing anything too momentous too quickly, just in case.

The rest of the session in the Hierchon's audience chamber after the AI projection had issued its orders and asked for questions had involved a great deal of talk, speech-making, point-scoring, back-covering, back-targeting and pre-emptive blame-avoidance. The image of Admiral Quile answered all the questions tirelessly and with a patience that was probably the most sure sign possible that it really was an AI talking. A human—especially an admiral, used to being obeyed instantly and without argument—would have lost patience long before the proceedings finally ground to a halt. Fassin had been pointed at and referred to several times, and been left with the distinct impression that this was all his fault. Which, he supposed, in a way it was. It had all gone on so long that Fassin's stomach had—perhaps in sympathy with a large component of the mood in the chamber—started grumbling. He hadn't eaten since early breakfast on 'glantine, after all.

"You are quite sure?" the image above the cooking-pot device asked eventually, when even the most talkative of those present seemed to have run out of questions to ask and points—and delicate portions of the anatomy—to cover. There was no hint of either pleading or relief in the projection's voice. Fassin thought either would have been appropriate.

"Very well, then. I will bid you farewell, and good luck."

The image of the human male with a bald, tattooed scalp and lined face, standing there in his much-decorated armoured suit, looked around them one last time, executed a short, formal bow to the Hierchon and disappeared. Nobody seemed to know quite what to do for a moment. Then the black, pot-bellied machine in the centre of the floor started to make a loud humming noise. Shrievalty Colonel Somjomion and Cessorian Clerk-Regnant Voriel, attending as best they could to the machines they had been put in charge of when the others had been required to leave the chamber, started peering intently at various screens and controls. The circle of mirror-armoured troopers each tapped one ear, then brought up their guns, pointing them at the cooking-pot device, which was humming loudly now and starting to glow in the infrared. The hum rose and took on extra harmonics, deepening until the machine was visibly vibrating. Some of those close to the device either drew back or looked like they wanted to, as if fearing that the machine was going to explode. The air around its ribbed flanks shimmered. Above it, the atmosphere seemed to writhe and quiver, as though some mutant ghost of the image that had stood there was still fighting to escape.

Then, just as the pot-bellied thing started to glow a deep cherry red around its midriff, it all faded away: noise and vibration and heat. People relaxed. Somjomion and Voriel took deep breaths and nodded at the Hierchon. The troopers shouldered their arms. Whatever complex substrate inside the dark device had played host to the AI image of the Admiral had been turned to slag.

The Hierchon Ormilla spoke from his glittering esuit. "I invoke the full emergency powers of the War Emergency Plan. Martial law will be declared at the close of this extended session. Let those earlier excluded resume their places."

The flurry of politicking that Fassin had witnessed earlier was made to look mild in comparison as—without actually telling anybody not cleared to know about it any details—what was becoming known as The Current Emergency was talked over and enhanced roles and new responsibilities were discussed, squabbled over—between and within departments—revised, re-revised, traded, further discussed and re-re-revised before finally being handed out.

Fassin's belly was still making noises when the full session broke up and he was called to a briefing with his superiors in the Shrievalty Ocula. They kept him waiting in an anteroom within the Ocula's floor inside the Hierchon's palace; he shed one layer of his cumbersome court clothes and found some human food in a dispenser in a curving outside corridor with a view over the reception plaza. (Long evening shadows, towers and spires burnished red with sunset. He looked for some obvious sign that the city, planet and system were all under martial law again, but saw nothing.) He was still wiping his fingers when they called him in.

"Major Taak," Colonel Somjomion said. "Welcome."

He was shown to a large circular table surrounded by uniformed Shrievalty personnel. They were mostly human or whule, though there were two jajuejein doing their best to look humanoid and seated, and a single oerileithe in a duller and slightly smaller version of the Hierchon's esuit, the discus of which was half-hidden in a wide slot in the floor. It seemed to radiate chill and dominate the room, all the same.

Somjomion indicated the oerileithe. "This is Colonel Hatherence," she told Fassin. "She will be your superior in this mission."

"Pleasure, sure," the oerileithe boomed, twisting fractionally towards Fassin. The Colonel's esuit had no transparent faceplate like the Hierchon's, just armour and sensors, giving no sign of the creature within.

Fassin nodded. "Ma'am." He'd thought the only oerileithe in the system apart from the Hierchon were basically Ormilla's near family and his girlfriends ("harem" was, though only just, too pejorative). He wondered whether Colonel Hatherence fitted neatly into either category or not.

It was explained to him that they could not, of course, just send him off alone to do what he was supposed to do. Over the next hour, as communications, memos and remote audiences with the Hierchon himself interrupted Somjomion, Fassin was gradually given to understand that the task assigned quite specifically to him alone was one which would nevertheless unarguably be best accomplished if he was escorted and overseen by people the Hierchon and his claque of cohorts felt they could actually trust.

Accordingly, Fassin would not be alone on his next delve. He would benefit from the protection and guidance of Colonel Hatherence here, and from that of two of his fellow human Seers, Braam Ganscerel, Chief Seer of the most senior Sept of all, Sept Tonderon, and—as Fassin's junior—Paggs Yurnvic of Sept Reheo, with whom he had worked before. Chief Seer Ganscerel was currently readying himself to return as rapidly as possible from a habitat orbiting Qua'runze, and would rendezvous with Colonel Hatherence, Major Taak and Seer Yurnvic on Third Fury, from which the delve or delves would be conducted, as soon as possible.

Qua'runze was the other big gas-giant in Ulubis system—there were two smaller examples as well. All had Dweller populations too, though compared to Nasqueron's they were negligible in size. Getting Ganscerel from Qua'runze to Nasqueron and the Third Fury base would take well over a week, Fassin suspected. The old guy liked his luxuries and anyway wouldn't be physically able to cope with much more than one gee during the journey even if he wanted to.

Fassin, very much feeling his way in all this, suddenly caught up within organisations and power structures he never imagined having anything much to do with and having to cope with networks of rank and superiority he had only the vaguest working knowledge of, had been about to start banging the table—probably only figuratively—and complaining about not being able to start the job he'd been very clearly ordered to begin as soon as possible. Then they mentioned Ganscerel and his journey back from Qua'runze and he saw that there was probably no way he was going to be able to move this forward faster than the pace that had already been decided.

Which, in a way, suited him fine. If the system really was under threat of imminent invasion and he was being asked to go on the most important delve of his life in the midst of it—and given the amount of time they were being told there was before the invasion took place, there was every likelihood he'd still be in-planet when it happened—then he wanted—needed—one last delve of his own, into Borquille's underworld, its own hazy, clouded, turbulent and dangerous nether-environment. He suddenly had things to do and people, or at least one person, to meet. The delay caused by Ganscerel might work out quite usefully. Of course, they probably wouldn't want to let him out of their sight, so he'd have to find a way round that.

He also suspected that they wanted the whole delve done at a distance, from Third Fury, with him and Ganscerel and Paggs Yurnvic all lying wired up in the base there and communicating with remotes down in Nasqueron itself. (Certainly Ganscerel wasn't capable of jumping into a gascraft, breathing gillfluid and taking multiple gees, squished in shock-gel—he hadn't even done any of that stuff when he was young.) Fassin would have to try and find a way round that, too.

He complained as crossly as he could pretend about not being allowed to get on with things, and then demanded some time off.

"You mean, *leave*?" Somjomion said, goggle-eyed. "I believe you have some very intense briefing and training ahead of you, Major Taak. Many days' worth which will have to be crammed into hours. There is absolutely no time for *leave*."

He explained about Ganscerel's age, infirmity and therefore slow rate of travel. Somjomion looked indignant, but checked this, finally having another hurried conference with the Hierchon himself. "Indeed," she said, sighing, "Chief Seer Ganscerel is profiled as being unable to withstand forces greater than 1.5 gee, and is already complaining at the prospect of that. It will be nine days before he can reach the Third Fury base." Colonel Somjomion narrowed her eyes at Fassin. "We shall proceed with your fuller briefing first thing tomorrow, Major Taak. If there is any time left over, a day or two of leave may be granted. I guarantee nothing."

"So. Another Emergency," Saluus said. He smiled broadly. "I'm told I have you to thank for this, Fass." He held out a slim flute.

Fassin accepted the glass. "Entirely my own work."

Sal was, he supposed, one of the few people in the system for whom the prospect of a War Emergency Plan coming into force was genuinely cause for celebration.

"Really?" Saluus said. "You're even more eminent than I thought. And you still look about twenty, you dog." Sal laughed the easy laugh of a man who could afford to be generous with his compliments. Sal chinked glasses. They were drinking champagne; some ancient Krug with a meaningless date all the way from Earth and probably worth as much as a small spaceship. It had a pleasant taste, though not many bubbles.

The two men stood on a balcony, looking out over the caldera. The surging waters beneath formed a great frothed slope spreading all around from underneath the house, a shallow cone of billows and hummocks of foam all furiously bunching and collapsing and rushing ever outwards to where the fractious turmoil settled slightly and became merely wildly charging waves. The balcony was just above the equatorial rim of the house so the column of water actually supporting the place was hidden from them, but the crater walls, a couple of kilometres distant, echoed with the tumult.

They had climbed up here after a modest reception and light lunch with a few of Sal and his wife's friends—notables all—who were here for the afternoon. Fassin had secured an invitation to stay for a couple of days, until the Shrievalty needed him back in Borquille. He had changed out of his dark grey Shrievalty uniform into casual clothes.

Sal leaned back against the barrier. "Well, thank you for coming to visit."

Fassin nodded. "Thank you for inviting me."

"My pleasure. Just mildly surprised you asked."

"They trust you, Sal." Fassin gave a small shrug. "I needed to get away from all that military shit and they wouldn't let me just skip out the door of the palace and into Boogeytown." He looked out at the tumbling waters. "Anyway"—a glance at Sal—"been too long." He wanted to give the impression that this had been a good excuse to effect some sort of reconciliation he'd long wanted to make. He and Sal had met up only very occasionally over the two centuries since the wormhole's destruction, usually at the sort of gigantic social events it was hard to get out of but easy to remain alone within. They hadn't really talked.

Even now, meeting up, there were whole aspects of their lives that somehow didn't need to be gone into. How and what they had each been doing was a matter of public record and it would almost be an insult to inquire. Fassin had recognised Sal's wife from news and social images, hadn't really needed introducing. There hadn't been a single person at the reception below, alien or otherwise—servants apart, obviously—about whom Fassin, who was no great social observer, couldn't have written a short biography. Saluus probably didn't know as much about Fassin as vice versa, but he'd already congratulated him on his engagement to Jaal Tonderon, so he knew that much (or, more likely perhaps, he just had an efficient social secretary with a good database).

"So, what can you tell me, Fass?" Sal asked casually. He wrinkled his nose. "*Can* you say anything?"

"About the Emergency?"

"Well, about whatever's causing all the fuss."

There was more than a fuss; there was low-level war. Starting the day after martial law was declared there had been a sequence of attacks, mostly on isolated and system-edge craft and settlements, though with some worrying assaults further in-system, including one on a Navarchy dock-habitat in Sepekte's own trailing Lagrange that had killed over a thousand. Nobody knew whether it was Beyonders behind this resurgence of violence, or the E-5 Discon advanced forces, or a mixture of both.

More oddly, but for Fassin far more disturbingly, somebody had nuked the High Summer house of Sept Litibiti, back on 'glantine, just the day before; missiled it from space like it was a military facility. Bizarre and unprecedented. The place had been empty save for a handful of unlucky gardeners and cleaners, keeping the place ticking over until the appropriate season, but it made Seers throughout the system worried that they'd suddenly, for some reason, become targets. Fassin had sent a message to Slovius saying that maybe they should consider shifting the whole Sept elsewhere on 'glantine.

Head for an out-of-season hotel, perhaps. He'd yet to receive a reply, which might be Slovius ignoring his advice, or just the authorities' new message-traffic checking and censoring software struggling to cope. Neither would surprise.

"Tell me what you know," Fassin suggested. "I'll fill in what I can."

"They want lots of warships, Fass." Sal gave a sad-looking smile. "Lots and lots of warships. We're to turn out as many as we can for as long as we can, though they want them sooner rather than later, and any advanced projects that might take longer than a year, even existing ones, are being deprioritised. We're to gas-line a whole bunch of stuff for—" Sal paused, cleared his throat and waved one hand. "Hell, idiot stuff; we're to rough-cut a whole load of civilian conversions: armed merchantmen, one-shot cloud-miners, tooled-up cruise liners and so on. We didn't even do that in the last Emergency. So whatever it is, it's serious, it's presumably what our military friends would call credible, and it's not very far away. Over to you."

"Lot I can't tell you," Fassin said carefully. "Most of which I guess wouldn't interest you anyway." He wondered how much he could say, how much he needed to say. "Supposedly to do with something called the Epiphany-Five Disconnect."

Sal raised an eyebrow. "Hmm. Bit away. Wonder why they'd bother? Richer pickings inward of where they are."

"But a significant part of the Summed Fleet is on the way. We're told." Fassin grinned.

"Mm-hmm. I see. And what about you?" Sal asked, dipping closer to Fassin, voice dropping. "What's your part in all this?"

Fassin wondered how much the continual rush of noise produced by the waves below would mask their words, if anybody was listening from far away. Since he'd arrived he'd showered and put on a change of clothes he'd requested from the house—caught without the necessary means of attire due to an extended stay away from home, he'd explained, needlessly. He got the impression the servants were perfectly used to providing clothes of varying sizes and for whatever sex to house guests. Still, even without the proscribed horror of nanotech, it was possible to make bugs very small indeed these days. Had the Shrievalty or the Hierchon's people put some sort of trace or mike on him? Had Sal? Did Sal put surveillance on his guests as a matter of course? His host was waiting for an answer.

Fassin looked into the drink. A few small bubbles of gas rose to the surface and broke, giving some tiny proportion of the substance of Earth to the atmosphere of a planet twenty thousand light years away. "I just did my job, Sal. Delved, talked, took away what the Dwellers would let me take away. Most of which was not momentous, not important, not going to change anything much at all, not something everybody would want or risk everything for." He looked Saluus Kehar in the eye. "Just stumbled my way through life, you know? Over whatever turned up. Never knowing what would lead to what."

"Whoever does?" Sal asked, then nodded. "But I see."

"Sorry I can't really tell you too much more."

Sal smiled and looked out at the slope of artificial surf, the pandemonium of waves beyond and the sheer cliffs further away still, brown-black beneath a hazy azure sky.

"Ah, your minder," he said. The esuit of Colonel Hatherence of the Shrievalty appeared to one side, low over the foam, floating out over the mad froth of waters like a great fat grey and gold wheel. Whirling vane-sets on either side of her esuit kept the Colonel from sinking into the maelstrom. For all its massive size when you were standing next to it, the esuit looked very small from up here.

"She giving you any problems?"

"No. She's okay. Doesn't insist I salute her or call her Ma'am all the time. Happy to keep things informal." All the same, he was hoping to get the Colonel out of the way somehow, either before or once he got down into Nasqueron.

Fassin watched the Colonel as she picked her way across the scape of waves. "But can you imagine trying to sneak into Boogeytown with that dogging your every move?" he asked. "Even just for one last night?"

Sal snorted. "The dives and the ceilings are too low."

Fassin laughed. *This is like sex*, he thought. *Well, like the seduction-scenario thing, like the whole stupid mating dance of will-you-won't-you, do-you-don't-you rigmarole.* Tempting Sal, leading him on…

He wondered if he'd seemed sufficiently mysterious yet hinted at maybe being available. He needed this man.

Dinner with Sal, his wife, their concubines and some business associates, including—amongst the latter—a whule, a jajuejein and a quaup. The talk was of new attacks on distant outposts, martial law, delays in comms, restrictions in travel and who would gain and who would lose from the new Emergency (nobody on any of the couches seemed to anticipate losing more than a few trivial freedoms for a while). Colonel Hatherence sat silent in one corner, needing no external sustenance, thank you, but happy, indeed honoured, to be there while they consumed nourishment, communicated conversationally and intercoursed socially while she continued her studies (much-needed!), screening up on Nasqueron and its famous Dwellers.

Drinks, semi-narcotic foods, drug bowls. A human acrobat troupe entertained them, floodlit beyond the dining room's balcony.

"No, I'm serious!" Sal shouted at his guests, gesturing at the acrobats, swinging through the air on ropes and trapezes. "If they fall they almost certainly die! So much air in the water you can't float. Sink right down. Get caught up in the under-turbulence. No, idiot!" Sal told his wife. "Not enough air to *breathe*!"

Some people left. Drinks later, just the humans. To Sal's trophy room, corridors and rooms too small, sorry, for Colonel Hatherence (not minding; so to sleeping; good nights!). Sal's wife, going to bed, and the remaining few. Soon just the two of them, overlooked by the stuffed, lacquered, dry-shrunk or encased heads of beasts from dozens of planets.

"You saw Taince? Just before the portal went?"

"Dinner. Day or two before. Equatower." Fassin waved in what might have been the general direction of Borquille. You could see the lights of the Equatower from the house, a thin stipple of red climbing into the sky, sometimes perversely clearer above when the lower atmosphere was hazed and the higher beacons shone down at a steeper angle through less air.

"She okay?" Sal asked, then threw his head back and laughed too loudly. "As though it matters. It was two centuries ago. Still."

"Anyway, she was fine."

"Good."

They drank their drinks. Cognac. Also from Earth, long, long ago. Far, far away.

Fassin got swim.

"Oh shit," he said, "I've got Swim."

"Swim?" said Saluus.

"Swim," Fassin said. "You know; when your head kind of seems to swim because you suddenly think, 'Hey, I'm a human being but I'm twenty thousand light years from home and we're all living in the midst of mad-shit aliens and super-weapons and the whole fucking bizarre insane swirl of galactic history and politics!' That: isn't it *weird*?"

"And that's what? Swing? Swirl?" Sal said, looking genuinely confused.

"No, *Swim*!" Fassin shouted, not able to believe that Sal hadn't heard of this concept. He thought everybody had. Some people—most people, come to think of it, or so he'd been told—never got Swim, but lots did. Not just humans, either. Though Dwellers, mind you, never. Wasn't even in their vocabulary.

"Never heard of it," Sal confessed.

"Well, didn't imagine you might have."

"Hey, you want to see something?"

"Whatever it is, I cannot fucking wait."

"Come with me."

"Last time I heard that—"

"We agreed no more of those."

"Fuck! So we did. Total retraction. Show me what you got to show me."

"Walk this way."

"Ah now, just fuck off."

Fassin followed Sal through to the inner recess of his study. It was kind of what he might have expected if he'd given the matter any thought: lots of wood and softly glowing pools of light, framed stuff and a desk the size of a sunken room. Funny-looking twisted bits of large and gleaming metal or some other shiny substance sitting in one corner. Fassin guessed these were starship bits.

"There."

"Where? What am I supposed to be looking at?"

"This." Sal held up a very small twisted-looking bit of metal mounted on a wooden plinth.

Fassin tried very hard not to let his shiver show. He was nothing like as drunk as he was trying to appear to be.

"Yeah? An whassat?" (Overdoing it, but Sal didn't seem to notice.)

Saluus held the piece of odd-looking metal up before Fassin's eyes. "This is that thing I got out of that fucking downed ship, my man." Sal looked at it, swallowed and took a deep breath. Fassin saw Sal's lip tremble. "This is what—"

The fucker's going to break down, Fassin thought. He slapped one hand on Sal's shoulder. "This is no good," he told him. "We need different, we need, I don't know; something. We need not this, not what is before us here. We need something different. Elsewhen or elsestuff or elsewhere. This might be my last night of freedom, Sal." He gripped the other man hard by the shoulder of his perfectly tailored jacket. "I'm serious! You don't know how bad things might get for me! Oh *fuck*, Sal, you don't know how bad things might get for all of us, and I can't fucking tell you, and this could be my last night of fun anywhere, and… and… and you're showing me some fucking coat hook or something, and I don't know…" He swiped weakly at the twisted piece of metal, patting it away and still missing. Then he sniffed and drew himself up. "Sorry," he said, soberly. "Sorry, Sal." He patted the other man's shoulder. "But this is maybe my last, ah, night of fun, and… look, I feel totally charged for anything—wish Boogeytown was right outside, really do, but on the other hand it's been a long few days and maybe—no, not maybe. Maybe definitely. In fact, not that, just plain *definitely* the sensible thing to do is just go to bed and—"

"You serious?" Sal said, dropping the metal piece on its wooden plinth onto the desk behind him.

"About sleep?" Fassin said, gesturing wildly. "Well, it—"

"No, you moron! About Boogeytown!"

"What? Eh? I didn't mention Boogeytown!"

"Yes, you did!" Sal said, laughing.

"I did? Well, fuck!"

Sal had a flier. Automatic to the point of being nearly banned under the AI laws. Loaded with repair mechanisms that were not quite nanotech but only by such a tiny-tiny-*tiny* little bit. Deeply civilian but with total military clearance. If a Grand Fleet Admiral of the Summed Fucking Fleet stepped into this baby and toggled his authority it would only decrease the fucker's all-areas, multi-volumes access profile. Down in the hangar deck. Walk this way, har har.

They left the top down part of the way, to clear their heads. It was very, very cold.

They set down somewhere where litter blew about under the fans of the flier. Fassin hadn't thought there was still such a thing as litter.

Boogeytown was much as he remembered it. They hit the lows, looking for highs. They trawled the bowl-bars and narctail parlours, coming up with a brimming catch of buzz and girls, Fassin meanwhile trying to edge Sal in a certain bar's direction, while Sal—vaguely recalling this wasn't supposed to be just fun but also a way of getting his old pal Fass to open up with more potentially useful and lucrative details about whatever the fuck was going on—tried to get his old/new best buddy to move in a certain informational direction but without much success and anyway with decreasing amounts of concern and an increasing feeling of oh-who-gives-a-fuck?

Fassin too was getting frustrated, still angling for one more move and one particular streetlet, one particular bar, but they were here now in this diamond-walled emporium called the Narcateria where the sleaze was so coolly glitz it almost hurt, surrounded by people who hadn't seen Sal in *so* long and just *had* to keep him where he was, don't you *dare* go away, you wicked *man* you! And is this your *friend*? Where you been keeping *him*? Can I sit here, hmm? Me too me too! So eventually he had to stumble away and make a call in a private public booth and then head for the toilet where he threw up in a thin burning stream all the alcohol he'd drunk since the last time he'd been to the loo (over the hole, so it looked and sounded authentic), then wash his face and rejoin the drunken stoned-out fray of breath-catching loveliness, waiting for the right girl, the one all this had been about, all of it: asking to go to Sal's in the first place, then getting him drunk and seeming to get drunk himself (which he was, but not *that* drunk) and then dropping hints about Boogeytown, all so that he could get away and get here and see this one particular girl…

…Who finally appeared nearly an hour later when he was just starting to despair but there she was, perfect and calm and quietly beautiful as ever, though looking quite different, again, with white-gold hair swinging heavy as the real 24-carat article about her near-triangular face, chin just made for holding, strawberry-bruise lips for kissing, tiny little nose for nuzzling, cheeks for stroking, eyes for gazing into (depths, ah, depths!) brows for licking, forehead for licking too, licking dry of *sex-sweat* after—oo! oo! oo! just too strenuous a session!

Aun Liss.

The one real love of his life, his controlling passion.

Older again but not as old as she should be. Looking different, living different, being different, called different. Called Ko now (and that was all), not Aun Liss, but she would always be Aun Liss to him. No need to say her real name. A lot of what passed between them wasn't said anyway. Dressed in salarygirl clothes. Nothing special, revealing or provocative.

Nevertheless.

She held out her hand.

Nearby, surrounded by—actually, nearly drowning in—utter human female and super-stimulus hyper-pulchritude lovelinessence, even Sal looked impressed.

"Fass, you dog!"

Aun Liss was still holding out her hand.

Back in Sal's flier. Sal was in the front, being grievously attended to by the infamous Segrette Twins, moaning.

Fassin and Aun in the back seat, utterly happy to appear so archetypical. They kissed for a long time, then—looking round, shrugging at the front-seat antics (the flier at this point not really going anywhere, circling in a holding pattern—a clinching pattern, Aun Liss suggested)—she rose up and straddled him, his hands up underneath the light dress she wore, fingers still kneading her back…as they continued to do once they were finally returned to the idiot Kehar house poised over the column of water just as, Aun pointed out, she was poised over his column. (This aloud, for the benefit of anybody listening. They both laughed, not too loudly, he hoped.) Meanwhile she kept the dress on still, even in the heat of it, with his fingers pressing, kneading, moving above her arched spine producing little half-pained gasps until later when they were finally just lying together under a thin sheet she shucked off the dress and he just held her.

And this is what, over the course of those several hours, their fingers said, drawing and tapping out the private, effectively unbuggable code they had used for hundreds of years, since she first became his control, his link:

U STILL MY CNNECTN?

They were in the private booth deep inside the Narcateria, just kissing. She slid her hands between his jacket and shirt, knuckled back, YS. WOT U GOT 4 I?

1ST, I MAJR IN OCULA NW. GOT 2NDD.

Y?

COS I FND SMTING IN THE FMOUS DLVE. BOUT THE DWLLR LIST. YOU HRD OF?

VGLY.

2ND SHIP THERY, he sent. SCRT 'HOLE NTWRK.

WAIT, she sent back. *WORMHOLE* NTWRK?

YS. SCRT 1.

There was a pause. She kept on kissing him. Her fingers sent, YR CRZY.

Walking to the flier, hands up each other's jackets:

OL AFTR WHT I FND. E-5 DISCON INVDS IN 6 MNTHS TO 1 YR. THEY THNK BYNDRS WITH THEM. TRU?

CMPLCTD. SUM R, SUM RNT.

MRGNCY COS OF THS.

U STRTD THE FKNG MRGNCY?

YS. SORY. SUMD FLT ON WAY. BIG BIT AHED OF ESHIP. HYR IN 2 YRS MAYB. USD A.I. TRNSMTD FRM SUMD FLT 2 TEL US OL THIS.

AN A.I.?

YS.

HYPCRTS.

Then, in the flier:

WOT NXT 4 U?

DLVE SOON AGEN. WITH CHF C-R GNSRL, OERL SHRVLTY CNL & C-R PGS YRNVIC. TRY FND RST OF WHTVR WS I FND IN 1ST PLACE.

Straddled/ridden like that, they could talk, too.

"How's that for you?" she whispered.

"Oh, that's very good. And you?"

"As above."

WHT *DID* U FND?

DNT NO XCTLY. I NO RLZE AT TIME. OL CAME OUT MUCH L8TR WHN JELTCK DID ANLYS. SMTHNG ABT THIS 2ND SHIP & THNG CALLD A TRANSFORM, SPSD 2 MAK RST OF DWLR LIST MEAN SMTHNG. JLTCK SNT FLEET 2 TRY FIND. NO FIND. FLT WRKD.

She felt him pause, tense. She sent:

WOT?

ALGDLY THIS ALSO Y BYNDRS WRKD PORTL. TRU?

DNT NO. I JST A MSG GRL. She paused. SO U SAY NOT ONLY U START *THIS* MRGNCY, U COSD LAST 1 2 & GOT PRTL DSTRYD?

YS. GES I JST ACCDNT PRN.

FKNG HEL.

"*Very* good to see you again."

"Copy that."

"We should do this more often."

"Indeed we should. Now, shh."

BUT IF SO & THIS KNWN, Y I NOT ASKD 2 DLV & FIND MOR INFO 4 GUD GYS ERLYR?

NO IDEA.

OL NONSNS ANYWY BUT THEY WNT I 2 LUK.

SO LUK.

& WHT U MYN SUM BYNDRS 4 E-5 DISCON, SUM NOT?

FACTNS.

FACTIONS? YR GVNG I FKNG *FACTIONS*? RLY BEST U CN DO?

KYP BING PASSYN8. CVR SLPNG.

He made passionate moves, uttered passionate sounds.

In his bed, his hands at the small of her back:

I GO 2 3RD FURY MOON 3 DAYS TYM.

…OH.

*OH?*

KND OF A RMR. I SHLDNT EVN NO. MAYB ATK ON NASQ MNS.

NASQ MOONS? NOT *'GLNTN*?

NO. LTL MNS.

CN U GET WRD, NO ATCK ON 3RD FURY MOON? NO ATK ON ANY SEERS?

WILL TRY.

TRY HRD.

PROMIS.

OK. IF I DO FIND ANYTHING ON NASQ WILL GET 2 U, NT MRCTRIA.

OK. GOOD. HOW?

STN A MICROSAT MIDWY BTWN OUR SATS EQ4 & EQ5. I AIM BRST THER. MY OLD CODE & FREQ STL GOOD?

THNK SO. TAK TYM 2 SET UP.

TAK I MNTHS 2 FIND NYTHNG. PRBLY 0 TO FIND ANYWY. HAV MICROSAT ABL 2 RCV FRM B-LOW 2, IN CASE I IN NASQ.

WILL PASS ON.

A little later:

LUV U.

YR CRZY.

TRU.

B MOR PASSYN8.

He pulled the sheet further over his Beyonder girl. CVR SLPNG AGEN?

NO, JST B MOR PASSYN8…

# THREE

## NOWHERE LEFT TO FALL

Uncle Slovius took him up on his shoulders. They were going to watch the bad machine being killed. He put his hands over Uncle Slovius's forehead and got him to crinkle it, which felt funny and made him squirm and wriggle and laugh and meant Uncle Slovius had to hold his ankles tight to stop him falling off.

"Fass, stop wriggling."

"I fine, honest."

He already knew you were supposed to say, "I'm fine," or, "I am fine," but saying things like "I fine" was better because it made adults smile and sometimes hug. Sometimes it made them put a hand on your head and make a mess of your hair, but never mind.

They went through the port door. It was spring and so that was the house they were in. He was big. He'd lived in all the houses except the Summer House. That one came next. Then he would have lived in them all. Then you started again. That was how it worked. Uncle Slovius ducked as they went through the doorway so he didn't bash his head.

"Umm, mind your head," he heard his dad say quietly somewhere behind him.

His mum sighed. "Oh, stop fussing. Dear."

He couldn't see his mum and dad because they were behind him and Uncle Slovius but he could hear them.

"Look, I wasn't *fussing*, I was just—"

"Yes, you—"

He got that funny feeling in his tummy he got when Mum and Dad talked like that. He did a slap-a-slap-slap on Uncle Slovius's forehead and said, "More about history! More about history!" as they walked down to the flier.

Uncle Slovius laughed. The shake came up through Uncle Slovius's shoulders into his bottom and whole body. "My, we are a keen student."

"One word for it," his mother said.

"Oh, come on," his dad said. "The boy's just inquisitive."

"Yes, yes, you're right," his mum said. You could hear her breath through her words. "My mistake. Pardon me for expressing an opinion."

"Oh, now, look, I didn't mean—"

"More about Voerin!"

"Voehn," Uncle Slovius said.

"I've got a Voerin! I've got a big one that talks and climbs and swims and jumps or can walk under the water too. It's got a gun that shoots other toys. And I've got lots of little ones that just move. They've got guns too but they're a bit small to see but they can make each other fall over. I've nearly a hundred. I watch *Attack Squad Voerin* all the time! My favourite is Captain Chunce cos he's clever. I like Commander Saptpanuhr too and Corporal Qump cos he's funny. Jun and Yoze both like Commander Saptpanuhr best. They're my friends. Do you watch *Attack Squad Voerin*, Uncle Slovius?"

"Can't say I've ever caught it, Fass."

Fassin frowned, thinking. He decided this probably meant "No". Why didn't adults just say no when they meant no?

They sat in the flier. He had to come down off Uncle Slovius's shoulders but he got to sit beside him in the front. He didn't even need to tell people he'd be sick if he sat in the back any more. A servant sat on the other side of him. Great-uncle Fimender was behind with two old ladies who were girlfriends. He was laughing and they were too. His mum and dad were further back, talking quiet. His mum and dad were old but Uncle Slovius was really old and Great-uncle Fimender was really, *really* old.

The flier went up into the air and went through the air making a noise like the Attack-ship *Avenger* did in *Attack Squad Voerin*. His model of the Attack-ship *Avenger* flew but only in Supervised Areas Outdoors and shot guns and missiles and made the same noise. He'd wanted to bring it with him, but not been allowed, even after he'd shouted. He hadn't been allowed to bring any toys. No toys at all!

He pulled at Uncle Slovius's sleeve. "Tell me about the Voerin!" He tried to think what had made Uncle Slovius laugh. "More about history!"

Uncle Slovius smiled.

"The Voehn are the Culmina's bully boys, child," said Great-uncle Fimender from the seat behind. He was leaning over. His breath had that funny sweet smell like it usually did. Great-uncle Fimender was fond of a drink. His voice was funny also sometimes, like all the words were sort of one big word. "I wouldn't fixate too enthusiastically on the scum that stole our species birthright."

"Steady, now, Fim," Uncle Slovius said. He looked round at Great-uncle

Fimender but looked first at the servant except the servant didn't move or look back or anything. "If the wrong person took you seriously you might find yourself joining this rogue AI. Hmm?" He made a smile at Great-uncle Fimender, who sat back again in the seat between the old-lady girlfriends and took a glass with a drink in it from a picnic tray.

"Be an honour," he said in a quiet voice.

Uncle Slovius smiled down at Fass. "The Voehn went to Earth a long, long time ago, Fassin. Before humans made spaceships—before they made sea ships, almost."

"How long ago?"

"About eight thousand years ago."

"4051 BCE," Great-uncle Fimender said, though only just loud enough to hear. Uncle Slovius didn't seem to hear. Fassin wasn't sure if Great-uncle Fimender was disagreeing with Uncle Slovius or not. Fassin stored 4051 BCE away as an Important Number anyway.

"They met human people on Earth," Uncle Slovius said, "and took them away with them on their ship, to other stars and planets."

"Kidnapping the prims!" Great-uncle Fimender said. "Sampling the barbs, with prejudice! Eh?" He didn't sound like he was talking to him and Uncle Slovius. Fass didn't understand what Great-uncle Fimender was saying anyway. The old-lady girlfriends were laughing.

"Well," Uncle Slovius said, with a small smile, "who's to say whether humans were kidnapped or not? People in ancient Egypt and Mesopotamia and China were too primitive to know what was going on. They probably thought the Voehn were gods, so they might have gone with them without being kidnapped and we don't even know that the Voehn took whole people. Maybe they just took their cells."

"Or babies, or foetuses, or excised a few thousand fertilised eggs," Great-uncle Fimender said. Then, "Oh, thank you, my dear. Oops! Steady, there."

"In any event," Uncle Slovius said, "the Voehn took some human people and put them down on planets far away from Earth and the human people grew up with other people, and the Culmina had the other people help the humans so that they became civilised quickly, and invented all the things humans back on Earth ever invented, but these human people on the other planets always knew they were part of a galactic community, hmm?" Uncle Slovius looked at him with a question-look on his face. Fass nodded quickly. He knew what a galactic community meant: everybody else.

"Anyway, people on Earth kept on inventing things, and eventually invented wormholes and portals—"

"The Attack-ship *Avenger* goes through wormholes and portals," he told Uncle Slovius.

"Of course," Uncle Slovius said. "And so when human people went out and met other alien people and joined their wormhole up with everybody else's wormhole, they found out that they weren't the first humans the alien people had met or had heard of, because the humans who had been taken away to the other planets by the Voehn were already quite well known."

"*Remainder* humans," Great-uncle Fimender said from the seat behind. His voice sounded funny, like he might be going to burst out laughing or something.

Uncle Slovius looked round at him for a short bit. "Well, the terms don't matter too much, even if they might sound a little harsh sometimes."

"Carefully chosen to keep us in our place, remind us we owe them, either way," Great-uncle Fimender said.

"The Culmina tell us they had people look after Earth after the Voehn took the humans away to the other stars. They made sure that nothing bad happened to Earth, like it being hit by a big rock."

Great-uncle Fimender made a sort of cough-laugh. "Easy to claim."

Fass looked round at Great-uncle Fimender. He sort of wanted Great-uncle Fimender to be quiet so he could listen to Uncle Slovius but sort of didn't because the things Great-uncle Fimender was saying, even if he didn't always understand all of them, seemed to be saying things about the things Uncle Slovius was saying. It was like they sort of agreed and didn't agree at the same time. Great-uncle Fimender winked at him and gestured towards Uncle Slovius with his glass. "No, no; listen!"

"So, people from Earth got into the stars at last and found that there were aliens everywhere," Uncle Slovius told him. "And some of them were us!" He smiled a broad smile.

"And there were a lot more of the alien humans than there were of the ones who thought *they* were humanity," Great-uncle Fimender said. It sounded like he was sneering. Uncle Slovius sighed and looked ahead.

The flier was flying over mountains with snow on them. In front was a big bit of desert like a circle. Uncle Slovius shook his head and didn't seem to want to say anything but Great-uncle Fimender did so Fass turned round in his seat and listened to him.

"And they were more technically advanced, these so-called aHumans. Advanced but cowed. Servant species, just like everybody else. While all Earth's dreams of wild expansion were made to look like so much belly-gas. The answer to 'Where is everybody?' turned out to be, 'Everywhere', but the stake at the galactic poker game is a wormhole and so we had to fund our own and bring that to the table. Then discover that Everywhere really meant Everywhere, and every damn thing you could see and every damn thing you couldn't belonged to some bugger: every rock, every planet, moon and star, every comet, dust cloud and dwarf, even the bloody null-foam of space itself was somebody's home. Land on some godforsaken cinder, pull out a shovel thinking you could dig something, build something or make something of it and next thing you know an alien with two heads was poking both of them out of a burrow and telling you to fuck off, or pointing a gun at you. Or a writ—ha! Worse still!"

He'd never heard Great-uncle Fimender talk so much. He wasn't sure that Great-uncle Fimender was really talking to Uncle Slovius or to him or even to his two old-lady girlfriends because he wasn't looking at any of them, he was looking at the picnic table hinged down from the seat in front, maybe looking at the glass and the decanter bottle on it, and looking sad. The two old-lady girlfriends patted him and one smoothed his hair which was very black indeed but still looked old.

"Prepping, they call it," he said, maybe to himself or maybe to the picnic table. "Bloody kidnapping." He snorted. "Putting people in their place, holding them there. Letting us build our dreams then puncturing them." He shook his head, and drank from his shiny glass.

"Prepping?" Fass asked, to make sure he had the word right.

"Hmm? Oh, yes."

"Well, it's something that's gone on for as long as anybody can remember," Uncle Slovius said. He sounded gentle, and Fass wasn't sure if Uncle Slovius was talking to him or to Great-uncle Fimender. He sort of half-listened while he pulled out one of the flier's screens. If he'd been allowed to bring any toys he'd definitely have brought his BotPal and just asked, but now these damn adults were making him use a screen. He stared at the letters and numbers and things (Uncle Slovius and Great-uncle Fimender were still talking).

He didn't want to have to talk, he wanted to tap-in like adults did. He tried a few buttons. After a while he got a lots-of-books symbol with a big kid standing next to it and an ear symbol. The big kid looked scruffy and was holding a drug bowl and his head was surrounded with lines and little moving satellites and flying birds. Oh well.

"Prepping," he said, but pressed *Text*. The screen said:

Prepping. A very long-established practice, used lately by the Culmina amongst others, is to take a few examples of a pre-civilised species from their home world (usually in clonoclastic or embryonic form) and make them subject species/slaves/mercenaries/mentored, so that when the people from their home world finally assume the Galactic stage, they are not the most civilised/advanced of their kind (often they're not even the most numerous grouping of their kind). Species so treated are expected to feel an obligation to their so-called mentors (who will also generally claim to have diverted comets or otherwise prevented catastrophes in the interim, whether they have or not). This practice has been banned in the past when pan-Galactic laws (see Galactic Council) have been upheld but tends to reappear in less civilised times. Practice variously referred to as Prepping, Lifting or Aggressive Mentoring. Local-relevant terminology: aHuman & rHuman (advanced and remainder Human).

And that was just the start. He scratched his head. Too many long words. And this wasn't even an adult pedia. Maybe he should have found the not-so-big kids' site.

They were landing. Wow! He hadn't even noticed they were near the ground. The desert was covered with fliers of different sizes and there were lots in the air too and lots of people.

They got out and walked across the sand though a lot of people stayed in their fliers. He got to go on Uncle Slovius's shoulders again.

Away in the distance in the centre of a big circle was a tower with a big blob on top and that was where the bad machine was which had been found hiding in a cave in the mountains and caught by the Cessoria. (The Cessoria and the Lustrals caught bad machines. He'd tried watching *Lustral Patrol* a few times but it was too much for old people with talk and kissing.)

The bad machine in the blob on top of the big tower was allowed to make a speech but it was too full of long words. He was getting bored and it was very hot. No toys! Uncle Slovius said "Shush" at him, twice. He sort of tried to pretend-strangle Uncle Slovius with his thighs and knees to get back at him for going "Shush" twice, but Uncle Slovius didn't seem to notice. Mum and Dad were still talking quietly, rolling their eyes and shaking their heads at each other as usual. Great-uncle Fimender and the two old-lady girlfriends had stayed in the flier.

Then Lustrals in a flier—humans and a whule like a big grey bat—said things, then at last it was time and the bad machine was killed but even that wasn't very good, the blob on top of the tower just went red and made lots of smoke and then there was a big bright flash but not that big or bright and then there was a bang and bits fell down, with smoke, and some people cheered but mostly there was silence, just the bang being an echo round the mountains.

When they got back to the flier Great-uncle Fimender had very red eyes and said in his opinion they had just seen a terrible crime committed.

·

"Ah, young Taak. Now then, what is this nonsense about not being able to delve properly, by which of course one means remotely?"

Braam Ganscerel, Chief Seer of Sept Tonderon and therefore the most senior Seer of all—and Fassin's future paterfamilias-in-law—was tall and thin and maned in white hair. He looked younger than he was, but then he was nearly seventeen hundred years old by the most obvious way of reckoning such matters. He had a sharp, angular face with a large nose, his skin was pale, waxy and translucent and his fingers and hands were long and fragile-seeming. He habitually walked and stood with his head back and chest out, as though he had long ago vowed not to appear stooped as he grew into great old age and had gone too far in the other direction. This curious stance meant that his head was angled so far back on his neck that he had no choice but to look down his splendidly monumental nose at those he talked with, to or at. He held two long shining black staffs as though just returned from—or about to set off for—some particularly fashionable ski slopes.

With his long, bunned white hair, pale complexion and simple but elegantly cut Seer robes—black puttees, pantaloons and long jacket—he contrived to look appealingly frail, sweetly elderly, breathtakingly distinguished and only a little less authoritative than a supreme deity.

He swept into the senior officers' mess of the heavy cruiser *Pyralis* in a clatter of clicks from his twin staffs and boot heels, attended by a pale train of half a dozen junior Seers—half of them men, half of them women, all of them greyly deferential—and, bringing up the rear, the gangly, smiling form of Paggs Yurnvic, a Seer whom Fassin had helped teach but who, having spent less time subsequently in the slowness of actual delving than Fassin had, was now older in both adjusted time and appearance.

"Chief Seer," Fassin said, standing and executing a formal nod that just avoided being a bow. The heavy cruiser was taking their party to Third Fury, the close-orbit moon of Nasqueron from which they would delve—either all remotely, or, if Fassin had his way, through a combination of remote and direct presences.

Braam Ganscerel had insisted that his years and frailty made a high-gee journey to the moon out of the question—esuits, life-pods and shock-gel notwithstanding—and so the ship was making a gentle standard one gee, creating what felt like about twice 'glantine's gravity and a fraction less than Sepekte's. Even this standard gee, Braam Ganscerel let it be known, necessitated that he use both his staffs to support himself. This was, however, in the current grave circumstances, a sacrifice he felt it was only right and proper and indeed required that he make. Fassin thought it made him look like a stilter, like a whule.

"Well?" the Chief Seer demanded, stopping in front of Fassin. "Why can't you remote delve, Fassin? What's wrong with you?"

"Fear, sir," Fassin told him.

"Fear?" Braam Ganscerel seemed to experiment with putting his head even further back than it already was, found it was possible, and left it there.

"Fear of being shown up by you, sir, as a merely competent Slow Seer."

Braam Ganscerel half-closed one eye. He looked at Fassin for a while. "You're mocking me, Fassin."

Fassin smiled. "I delve better direct, Braam. You know that."

"I do," Ganscerel said. He turned with a sort of staccato grace and let himself flop into the couch where Fassin had been sitting, watching screen news. Fassin sat too. Paggs perched on one arm of the next-nearest couch and the rest of Braam Ganscerel's retinue sited themselves nearby according to some arcane pecking order.

Fassin nodded at Paggs. "Seer Yurnvic," he said with a smile and a formality he hoped Paggs wouldn't take seriously.

Paggs grinned. "Good to see you, Fass." That was all right, then.

"However, we must do this together, I believe," Braam Ganscerel said, looking ahead at the wall screen, where the news went silently on. The funerals were taking place of some more of the Navarchy people who'd died in the attack on the dock-habitat at Sepekte's trailing Lagrange. Ganscerel had let one of his twin staffs rest on the couch beside him, but still held the other. He waved it at the screen and it obligingly went back to being a bulkhead again. The heavy cruiser's senior officers' mess was a large space, but much broken up by vertical columns and diagonal reinforcing struts. Like the rest of the vessel it was quite comfortable by human standards, though Colonel Hatherence had had to be content with a cabin that was extremely cramped for an oerileithe. She had been offered passage on an escorting cruiser with more suitable accommodation but had declined.

"We can be together," Fassin said. "You and Paggs remotely, the Colonel and I directly. That way we're backed up so if anything happens to either group—"

"Ah," Ganscerel said. "You see, young Taak, this is the point. If we are all on Third Fury, with this fine vessel and its escort craft to protect us, we shall all be safe. You wish to take a tiny gascraft into the unending violence of the planet's atmosphere. A dangerous enterprise at the best of times. In wartime, positively foolhardy."

"Braam, the old portal was protected by an entire fleet and it still got blasted. Third Fury might move, but it moves very predictably. If somebody did want to attack it they could accelerate a small rock to just under light speed and send it on an intercept course. If that happens, the only way a heavy cruiser is going to help is if by some million-to-one chance it happens to be in the way at the time and takes the hit itself. As nobody's going to surround the entire moon with a shell of ships, I think it's unwise to rely on a few war craft to protect us from something there's almost no defence against."

"Why would anybody target a moonlet like Third Fury?" Paggs asked.

"Indeed," Ganscerel said, as though he had been just about to ask that very question.

"No good reason," Fassin said. "But then a lot of places there's been no good reason to hit have been getting attacked recently."

"This might well include Nasqueron itself," Ganscerel pointed out.

"Which can absorb a lot more punishment than Third Fury."

"You might still be targeted."

"If I'm in there in a gascraft, even with Colonel Hatherence riding shotgun, I should be effectively untraceable," Fassin told them.

"Unless," Paggs said, "she's supposed to be in constant touch with her superiors."

"And that might be the real reason we are all expected to stay together on Third Fury, delving remotely," Ganscerel said, sighing. He looked at Fassin. "Control. Or at least the illusion of it. Our masters are fully aware how important this mission is, even if they think themselves for the moment above explaining its precise nature to all who need to know. They are naturally terrified that if it goes wrong some of the blame will stick to them. Really, it is all up to us: a bunch of academics they've never particularly cared about or for, even though—" Ganscerel looked round the assembled junior Seers "—being a centre of Dweller Studies represents the only thing which makes Ulubis in any way remarkable." He directed his gaze on Fassin again. "There is very little they can do, therefore they will attend with extreme diligence to what trivial matters they are able to affect. With us all apparently safe on Third Fury protected by a small fleet of warships, they will feel they are doing all they can to assist us. If they let you go down into Nasqueron, and something does go wrong, they will be blamed. In that they are right."

"It won't work, Braam."

"I think we have to try," the older man said. "Look." He patted Fassin's arm. Fassin was dressed in his Shrievalty major's uniform and feeling awkward amidst fellow Seers. "Have you tried remote delving recently?"

"Not for a long time," Fassin admitted.

"It's changed," Paggs said, nodding. "It's much more lifelike, if you know what I mean; more convincing." Paggs smiled. "There have been a lot of improvements over the last couple of centuries. Largely thanks to the Real Delving movement, frankly."

*Oh, Paggs, flattery?* Fassin thought.

Ganscerel patted his arm again. "Just try it, will you, Fassin? Will you do that for me?"

Fassin didn't want to say yes immediately. *This is all beside the point*, he thought. *Even if I didn't know there was a potential threat to Third Fury, the argument that matters is that the Dwellers we need to talk to just won't take us seriously if we turn up in remotes. It's about respect, about us taking risks, sharing their world with them, really being there.* But he mustn't seem intransigent. Keep some arguments back; always have reserves. After a moment he nodded slowly. "Very well. I'll do that. But only as a trial delve. A day or two. That'll be enough to feel any difference. Then we have to make a final decision."

Ganscerel smiled. They all did.

They had a very pleasant dinner with the senior officers of the small fleet taking them to Third Fury.

Fassin got Ganscerel alone at one point. "Chief Seer," he said. "I will do this remote delve, but if I feel it's not good enough I'm going to have to insist on going direct." He gave Ganscerel space to say something, but the old man just looked him in the eye, head thrown back. "I do have authority," Fassin continued. "From the briefing, from Admiral Quile and the Complector Council. I realise it's been compromised by people in-system coming to their own conclusions about the best way to tackle this problem, but if I think I need to, I'll go as high and wide as I can to get my way."

Ganscerel thought for a while, then smiled. "Do you think this delve—or delves, this mission—will be successful?"

"No, Chief Seer."

"Neither do I. However, we must make the attempt and do all we can to make it successful, even so, and even though failure is probably guaranteed. We must be seen to do what we can, attempt not to offend those above us, and aim to protect the good name and the future prospects of the Slow Seers in general. These things we can definitely do. You agree?"

"So far, yes."

"If you genuinely believe that you must delve directly, I shall not stand in your way. I shall not back you, either, because to do that in my position would be to tie myself too directly to a course of action I still regard as fundamentally foolhardy. In any other set of circumstances I would simply order you to do as your most senior Chief Seer tells you to do. However, you have been instructed from on high—from extremely on high—Fassin Taak, and that does alter things somewhat. However. Try this remote delve. You might be surprised. Then make your own mind up. I won't stand in your way. The responsibility will be entirely yours. You have my full support in that." With a wink, Ganscerel turned away to talk to the heavy cruiser's captain.

Fassin reflected that being given full support had never felt so much like being hung out to dry.

The *Pyralis* blazed with its own trailed aurora as it entered the protective magnetombra of Third Fury, a little twenty-kilometre-wide ball of rock and metal orbiting just 120,000 kilometres above Nasqueron's livid cloud tops. The gas-giant filled the sky, so close that its rotund bulk took on the appearance of a vast wall, its belts and zones of tearing, swirling, ever-eddying clouds looking like colossal contra-rotating, planet-wide streams of madly coloured liquid caught whirling past each other under perfectly transparent ice.

Third Fury had no appreciable atmosphere and only the vaguest suggestion of gravity. The heavy cruiser could almost have docked directly with the Seer base complex on the side of the little moon which always faced Nasqueron. However, a troop landing craft took them from one to the other. The *Pyralis* lay a few kilometres off, effectively another temporary satellite of the gas-giant. Its escort of two light cruisers and four destroyers took up station a few tens of kilometres further out in a complicated cat's cradle of nested orbits around the moon, slim slow shadow shapes only glimpsed when they passed in front of the planet's banded face.

Third Fury had been constructed, or converted, from an already existing moonlet, billions of years earlier, by one of the first species to pay homage at the court of the Nasqueron Dwellers. Given that Dwellers were the most widespread of the planet-based species of the galaxy, with a presence in almost all gas-giants—themselves the most common type of planets—the fact that out of those ninety million-plus Dweller-inhabited super-globes there were exactly eight with populations willing to play host to those wishing to carry on more than the most fleeting conversation with their inhabitants spoke volumes—indeed, appropriately, libraries—about their almost utter lack of interest in the day-to-day life of the rest of the galactic community.

It was, though, only *almost* utter; the Dwellers were not perfectly anything, including reclusive. They sought, gathered and stored vast quantities of information, albeit with no discernible logical system involved in the acquisition or the storage, and when quizzed on the matter seemed not only completely unable to present any obvious or even obscure rationale for this effectively mindless accumulation of data, but even genuinely puzzled that the question should be asked at all.

There had also, throughout recorded time—even discounting the notoriously unreliable records kept on such matters by the Dwellers themselves—always been a few of their populations available for discourse and informational trading, though this was invariably only granted on the eccentric and capricious terms of the Dwellers. Since the end of the First Diasporian Age, when the galaxy and the universe were both around two and a half billion years old, there had never been no working centres of Dwellers Studies, but in the following ten and a half billion years there had never been more than ten such centres operating at any one time either.

Acceptable companions came and went.

The Dwellers were of the Slow, the category of species that stuck around in a civilised form for at least millions of years. The people they let come and visit them and talk to them, and with whom they were prepared to trade information, were usually numbered amongst the Quick, the kind of species that often counted its time as a civilised entity in tens of thousands of years, and sometimes not even that long. The Dwellers would tolerate and talk to other Slow species as well, though normally on a less regular and frequent basis. The suspicion was that the Dwellers, for all their fabled patience—no species colonised the galaxy at speeds averaging less than one per cent of the speed of light (not counting stopovers) unless it was supremely patient—could get bored with the species that came to talk to them, and by selecting only those numbered amongst the Quick they ensured that they would never have to endure for too long a time the attentions of people they only looked forward to seeing the back of. Just wait a bit and—in a twinkling of an eye by Dweller standards—their troublesome guests would evolve out of nuisancehood.

For the last sixteen hundred years or so—barely half a Dweller eye-twinkling—humans had been adjudged as acceptable confidants for the Dwellers of Nasqueron in the system of Ulubis, their presence mostly tolerated, their company usually accepted, their safety almost always guaranteed and their attempts to talk to the Dwellers and mine their vast but defiantly imaginatively organised and indexed data shales met with only the most formal of obstructiveness, the lighter forms of derision and the least determinedly obfuscatory strategies.

That such playful coynesses, such nearly-too-small-to-measure diffidences and such gentle, barely-meriting-the-name hindrances appeared to the humans concerned to be obstacles of monumental scale, hideous complexity and inexhaustibly fiendish invention just went to show who'd been doing this for most of the lifetime of the universe and who for less than two thousand years.

Other approaches had, of course, been tried.

Bribing creatures who found the concept of money merely amusing tended to tax even the most enterprising and talented arbitrageur. The Dwellers clove to a system in which power was distributed, well, more or less randomly, it sometimes seemed, and authority and influence depended almost entirely on one's age; little leverage there.

Alternatively, every now and again a species would attempt to take by force of arms what those involved in Dweller Studies attempted to wrest from the Dwellers by polite but dogged inquiry. Force, it had been discovered—independently, amazingly often—did not really work with Dwellers. They felt no pain, held their own continued survival (and that of others, given the slightest provocation) to be of relatively little consequence and seemed to embody, apparently at the cellular level, the belief that all that really mattered, ever, was a value unique to themselves which they defined as a particular kind of kudos, one of whose guiding principles appeared to be that if any outside influence attempted to mess with them they had to resist it to the last breath in the bodies of all concerned, regardless.

Dwellers were almost everywhere and had been there practically for ever. They had learned a few things about making war over that time, and while their war machines were believed to be as customarily unreliable—and eccentrically designed, built and maintained—as every other piece of technology they deigned to involve themselves with, that didn't mean they weren't deadly; usually for all concerned, and within a disconcertingly large volume.

Other species had prevailed against Dwellers on occasion. Entire planetary populations of them had been wiped out and whole gas-giants dismantled to provide the raw material for one of those monstrous megastructure projects that Quick species in particular seemed so keen on building, apparently just because they could. But the long-term results were, to date, inevitably unhappy.

Picking a fight with a species as widespread, long-lived, irascible and—when it suited them—single-minded as the Dwellers too often meant that just when—or even geological ages after when—you thought that the dust had long since settled, bygones were bygones and any unfortunate disputes were all ancient history, a small planet appeared without warning in your home system, accompanied by a fleet of moons, themselves surrounded with multitudes of asteroid-sized chunks, each of those riding cocooned in a fuzzy shell made up of untold numbers of decently hefty rocks, every one of them travelling surrounded by a large landslide's worth of still smaller rocks and pebbles, the whole ghastly collection travelling at so close to the speed of light that the amount of warning even an especially wary and observant species would have generally amounted to just about sufficient time to gasp the local equivalent of "What the fu—?" before they disappeared in an impressive if wasteful blaze of radiation.

Retaliation, where it was still possible, and on the few occasions it had been tried, led without fail towards a horribly messy war of attrition, whereupon the realisation of the sheer scale of the Dweller civilisation (if one could even call it that) and its past—and therefore probably future—longevity more often than not had a sobering effect on whatever species had been unwise enough to set themselves against the Dwellers in the first place.

Attempting to hold your local Dweller population hostage in the hope of influencing another one—or a group of others—was an almost laughably lame and even counter-productive strategy. Dwellers of any given gas-giant thought little enough of their own collective safety; giving them an excuse to show how little solidarity they felt with any other group of their own kind only led to events of particular and spectacular grisliness, for all that the genetic and cultural variation between Dweller populations was much less than that displayed by any other galaxy-wide grouping.

The long, long-arrived-at consensus, particularly amongst those still nursing civilisational bruises from earlier encounters with what was arguably one of the galaxy's most successful species, or those with the images of what had happened to others still fresh in their data banks, was that, on balance, it was best just to leave the Dwellers alone.

Left to themselves the Dwellers disturbed nobody except occasionally themselves and those who thought too deeply about what they really represented. Their history, after all, like that of the galaxy as a whole, was one of almost but not quite uninterrupted peace and tranquillity: billions and billions of years of thankfully nothing much happening at all. In over ten billion years of civilisation there had been only three major Chaoses and the number of genuine galaxy-spanning wars didn't even make it into double figures. In base eight!

That was a record that the Dwellers seemed to feel everybody concerned ought to feel mildly proud of. Especially themselves.

"Welcome all! Chief Seer, good to see you! Seer Taak, Seer Yurnvic. Young friends. And this must be Colonel Hatherence. Pleased to make your acquaintance, ma'am." Duelbe, the bald, nearly spherical major-domo of the Third Fury Shared Facility, greeted them in the transit hall as the military troop carrier disengaged and turned back towards the *Pyralis*. A couple of the youngest Seers, who had patently never encountered the positively ball-like form of Duelbe before, stared. It was as a rule at such moments that comparisons regarding the similarity in shape of Third Fury and the major-domo of its Shared Facility came to mind. Happily, on this occasion, if they were thought they went unvoiced.

Servants took charge of luggage pallets. Hatherence shooed away retainers who offered to help her manoeuvre in the relatively confined space—the dome-like hall, like the rest of the mostly underground facility, had been rebuilt on a human scale since the departure of the last species to be granted Seer status, with little spatial concession to other, effectively larger species. Colonel Hatherence was happy to float where she could without assistance, thank you, using trim-vanes on the outside of her discus of esuit to propel her from place to place.

"Ah!" Braam Ganscerel announced loudly, bouncing along the hall's floor in long floating strides, idly fending himself off the ceiling above with casual prods of one staff like some strangely graceful, if inverted, pole vaulter. "*That*'s better! One rarely appreciates gravity so much as when faced with so little of it, eh, Duelbe?"

The major-domo smiled broadly, even though Fassin knew he must have heard the old man say this a dozen times or more. The retinue of junior Seers apparently hadn't, and gave every impression of being barely able to contain their hearty guffaws within their aching sides.

The three double discs soared above a great curved canyon of cloud sliced deep within what looked like a convex bank of blood-red snow a hundred kilometres high. Much further above, a sky of rushing yellow streamers afforded brief glimpses of a wanly cerise sky, dotted with the spike-points of stars and, occasionally, a single, visibly sky-crossing moon like a soft brown snowball. The formation of flying machines curved across towards the blood-red bank of vapour and disappeared into it.

Senses shifted. He felt himself reaching out with a slick effortlessness into mag and rad, grav-grad and radio, pulling in a composite picture of his environment thousands of kilometres in diameter and hundreds deep, placing him with pin-sharp clarity in a great reticulated accumulation of magnetic fields, radiation and gravitational gradient, all overlaid on the wide-light image still available and the jelly-like ghost-vista of soundscape.

Still taking the lead from Paggs, leading the trio, they dived towards a sharp thermocline coming into view a dozen klicks down.

They flew out into a wide bubble of relative sight-clarity, then into a squall of water snow. They dived deeper, through a band of pressure and temperature where water rain fell, pattering hard against the skins of their whirling double discs, then on down, down into even wide-light darkness, down to the warm hydrogen slush where the discs floated like giant double-cone yo-yos, bobbing, steaming, flickering signals to each other.

—So, what do you think, young Taak? Good to be home?

—A fascinating experience, Fassin agreed.—We're, what? He double checked his internal navigation instrumentation.—Two equatorial sats along and a band up?

—Now, Fass, Paggs began.

—So if I do this—Fassin sent, and lunged his double disc towards Paggs's. Paggs had guessed what was coming and already started to move away, flinching backwards and up. Fassin's machine seemed to dart towards the other Seer's remote craft, then draw back, stopping just short of where Paggs's machine had been.—You've got just enough time to get out of the way, Fassin pointed out reasonably.

—Seer Taak… Braam Ganscerel began.

—Whereas if I did something similar on the far side of the planet, Fassin continued,—at the far end of a whole chain of sats, the best part of a full light second away even without any processing delays, we might both now be listening to our remotes telling us that, at best, I just voided their warranties.

—Fassin, Ganscerel sent with a sigh.—I think we're all aware of the speed of light and the diameter of the planet. And these remotes are anyway not completely stupid, or unprotected. They have an extremely sophisticated collision-avoidance system built into them. One we had to clear specifically with your friends in the Shrievalty to have built in, it's so close to …to being *clever*.

—But if a Dweller points a laser at you for fun, Fassin asked,—just to see if you'll flinch, what good is any collision-avoidance system to you then?

—Perhaps, Ganscerel suggested mellowly,—one ought not to mix with the kind of Dweller who would be likely to act in such a manner in the first place.

*Except they're the ones that are most likely to share interesting stuff with you, old man, not the desiccated, harmless but clueless pixie-brains you tend to spend your time flattering*, Fassin thought. He was fairly certain that it was just a thought. People always worried that in theory in VR you might say something you only meant to think, but he wasn't so rusty in the techniques of remote delving that he was truly concerned. It might, anyway, even do Braam Ganscerel some good to hear a few politely unspeakable things now and again.

—Perhaps, indeed, Chief Seer, was all he said.

—Hmm. Let's step out, shall we?

They returned to the reality of a remote-send suite buried deep in the Third Fury Facility, blinking in the light as technicians helped to unclip them from the couches, pushing themselves forward to clear the half-domes of the NMR assemblages, handing back earpieces and simple black velvet blindfolds, flexing and stretching as though they'd been under for a genuinely long delve rather than a mere hour or so at a one-to-one time ratio.

Paggs worked his fingers, undoing the last couple of soft tabs that connected him to the thin pneumo-tubes which had both sensed his movements and would have prevented him from throwing himself right off the couch in the event that he'd performed any especially energetic actions.

Ganscerel lay with his eyes closed, breathing deeply and letting the technicians detach him from the machinery.

Paggs glanced over. "Are we convincing you at all, Fass?"

"You're convincing me it's even easier to remote delve these days than it used to be." Fassin levered himself from the couch with the steady application of force from one small finger and let himself float very gently towards the floor. "I would have taken your word for it."

"So, you only got one-third of the volumes concerned, young Taak," Ganscerel said.

Fassin was giving a very private briefing in an engineering store off the secondary ship hangar. Ganscerel had wanted it conducted in his quarters but there wasn't a way of squeezing the colonel in there. Present were Fassin, Ganscerel, Paggs and Colonel Hatherence. Fassin wanted them each to know as much as he did—or at least as much as he thought they ought to know—about what he had found on his long-ago delve and what they would be looking for on the one they were hoping to begin the following day.

"Yes," he said. "I traded some high-definition images of Earth Twentieth-Century European Expressionist paintings for—amongst a lot of other stuff—what was catalogued as a tri-translated text of a pre-Third Chaos Lutankleydar epic poem, a private, unpublished work by—or perhaps commissioned by—a Doge of the Enigmatics. It was all double-encrypted and compressed but it was known to be in three volumes. I got three volumes from Valseir, only—as it turned out years later, when it was finally de-mangled by the Jeltick—what I'd been given wasn't Volumes One, Two and Three. It was Volume One, three times over, in three separate languages. And it wasn't by an Enigmatic Doge either.

"One of the volumes was in a previously known but untranslatable Penumbral language from the time of the Summation. When the translation was made it acted as a Rosetta; gave the key to a lot of other stuff, and that sidetracked everybody for a while. Then some pin-eyed Jeltick scholar spotted a note at the end, buried in the appendices in a crude but related slang-language, obviously added later, but not much later, that basically said the whole thing had been written during the Long Crossing of the Second Ship, by an Outcast Dweller skilled in the Penumbral language, and that, yes, of course there was a Dweller List, they—the ship, or its crew—had the key to it, and it would be included in Volume Two or Three of this epic poem. It was also, of course, in the ship, and the ship was heading for the Zateki system. That's why the Jeltick sent an expedition straight there as soon as they had the translation."

"Why not come here, to Nasqueron, where they might have found the Third Volume?" Paggs asked, smiling.

"Because the Shrievalty hadn't told them where the data had come from. Whether this was oversight or deliberate we haven't been told. The Jeltick may have guessed it was from a Dweller Studies centre but they couldn't be sure whether it was or not and, if so, which one. They probably did start making inquiries, but they didn't want to alert anybody else to the importance of what they had. Don't forget, the information had been copied and re-copied—it was lying about in data reservoirs all over the civilised galaxy. Quite possibly people had even already translated and read the main text but just hadn't got round to the appendices, where the all-important note was. The slightest hint that there was anything of strategic interest in that tranche and everybody else would have dusted it off, read it and—bang—the Jeltick would have lost their edge. So they fuelled and tooled and set sail for Zateki instead."

"This could all be a hoax, you know," Ganscerel said, snorting. He adjusted his robes, frowning deeply. "I do believe I detect the laboured and tortuous signature of Dweller humour here. This could just be a joke at the expense of anyone foolish enough to fall for it."

"It could indeed, sir," Fassin agreed. "But we have our orders and we have to make the effort, just in case it is all true."

"So we are looking for the remaining two volumes of this…what is it called, exactly?" Colonel Hatherence asked.

"Best translation," Fassin said, "is, *The Algebraist*. It's all about mathematics, navigation as a metaphor, duty, love, longing, honour, long voyages home… all that stuff."

"And what is or was this Long Crossing?" Ganscerel asked irascibly. "I haven't heard of it."

"The voyage back home from what humans used to call the Triangulum Nebula," Fassin said, with a small smile.

"Well," Ganscerel said, frowning once more. "We are not really much further forward, are we? And what, pray, do we call the Triangulum Nebula now, Seer Taak?"

"We call it the Lost Souls II Galaxy, Chief Seer. The crossing was called the Long Crossing because it took thirty million years. The outward journey allegedly took almost no time, because it was conducted through an intergalactic wormhole, the portal location of which is amongst those included in the Dweller List."

Hervil Apsile, Master Technician of the Third Fury Shared Facility, ran the ultrasonic hand-held over the gascraft's starboard nacelle one more time, smiling with some satisfaction at the smooth line on the screen. Above his head, one of the Shared Facility's drop ships stood on extended legs, a squat lifting-body shape, hold doors open. To one side, the main hangar's transparent dome showed a vast darkness, fitfully illuminated by long lighting flashes like sheets of tipped diamond catching the light of a dim blue sun.

"Checking for scrits, Hervil?" Fassin asked, approaching by bounce along the fused-rock floor.

Apsile grinned at the sound of Fassin's voice but watched the hand-held's screen until he'd got to the end of the seam he was inspecting. He switched the machine off and turned to Fassin. "Just the standard varieties detected so far, Seer Taak."

Scrits were the almost certainly mythical creatures which Dwellers blamed when anything went badly wrong anywhere in their vicinity. The humans who had lately taken up the baton of Dweller Studies had adopted early on the idea of scrits to account for the high degree of malfunctions any interaction with—or indeed near—the Dwellers seemed to involve. It was either that or accept that the Dwellers' endemic technological carelessness and congenital lack of enthusiasm for keeping machinery in reliably working order was somehow contagious.

Fassin patted the dark flank of the fat, arrowhead-shaped gascraft. This was his own machine, designed specifically for and partly by Fassin himself. It was about five metres long, four across the beam if you included the outboard manoeuvring nacelles and a little under two metres in height. Its smooth form was broken only by the shut lines of its various manipulators and manoeuvring impellers, a few sensor bulges, and the rear power assembly, vanes currently stowed. Fassin rubbed his hand over its port tail fin. "All prepped and ready, Herv?"

"Entirely," Apsile said. He was Nubianly black, slim but muscled, sleekly bald. Only a few lines round his eyes made him look remotely as old as he was, which was very. Every year or so, before his annual depilatory treatment—he thought gene treatment too invasive—a white micro-stubble would start to appear on his scalp, giving his head the appearance of a bristling star field. "And you?" he asked.

"Oh, prepped and ready too," Fassin told him. He'd just come from the day's final briefing, with the Dweller Current State people. It was their challenging brief to try and keep abreast of what was going on in the sheer and utter chaos that was Dweller society and, as a sideline, keep track of where the major Dweller structures, institutions and—especially—Individuals Of Interest were at any given moment.

The news was not good: a formal war was brewing between Zone two and Belt C, at least one long-term storm structure between Zone one and Belt D was collapsing while two were building elsewhere, and the movements of IOIs recently had been particularly fluid. One might even say capricious. As for the whereabouts of choal Valseir, well. Nobody had seen anything of the fellow for centuries.

Dwellers had always been hard to follow. In the past people had tried setting drone remotes on individuals to keep tabs on them. However, Dwellers regarded this as a gross intrusion on their privacy and had an uncanny ability to spot and destroy any such platforms, micro-gascraft or bugs, no matter how small or clever they were. Dwellers also sulked. When people had the temerity to try anything so underhand, cooperation was withdrawn. Sometimes over an entire population. Sometimes for years.

The Slow Seers of Nasqueron had a pretty good relationship with the local Dwellers. By Dweller Studies standards it was almost close, but only because the Seers tried to interfere as little as possible with Dweller life. In return the

Dwellers were relatively cooperative, and broadcast a daily update on the location of their most important cities, structures and institutions. This eight-and-a-bit-hourly bulletin was a byword for trustworthiness—almost a legend—in Dweller Studies, on occasion approaching accuracy rates of very nearly ninety per cent.

"Things fine with Sept Bantrabal?" Apsile asked.

"All well. Slovius sends his regards." Fassin had talked to his uncle a few hours earlier, still trying to persuade him to leave the Autumn House. The time delay between Third Fury and 'glantine made a normal conversation just about possible. He'd caught up with Jaal too, on the other side of 'glantine, at her Sept's Spring House. Life appeared relatively normal back on 'glantine, the new Emergency affecting people there less than it seemed to on Sepekte.

Apsile flicked a roll-screen from his sleeve and tapped a few patches. He looked casually up at the lifter ship poised above the little gascraft, ready to accept the smaller vessel inside its open hold and take it down to the gas-giant's atmosphere. Fassin followed the Master Technician's gaze. He looked at a dark shape already hanging inside the cargo space, protruding downwards from it like a thick wheel. He frowned. "That looks a lot like Colonel Hatherence," he said.

"Not many places she'll fit," muttered Apsile.

"Eh?" A voice bellowed. Then, quieter: "My name? Oh. Yes, that's me. Seer Taak. Major Taak, I should say. Hello. Sorry; asleep. Well, you know, one does. Thought I'd try out this space here for size. Fits very well, must say. I shall be able to be transported to the atmosphere of Nasqueron most ably by this vessel, if needs be. Well, so I think. Think you so too, Master Technician?"

Apsile smiled broadly, revealing teeth as jet as his skin. "I think so too, ma'am."

"There we are agreed, then." The giant hanging discus dropped fractionally from its mountings inside the delta-shaped transporter, so that it could turn and twist towards them. "And so. Major Taak. How goes your attempt to persuade Chief Seer Braam Ganscerel that you ought to be allowed to delve directly?"

Fassin smiled. "It goes like a long-term delve, colonel; exceeding slow."

"A pity!"

Apsile thumbed a patch on his roll-screen, clicked the screen back into his sleeve and nodded at the little gascraft. "Well, she's ready. Want to put her up?" he asked.

"Why not?" It had become something of a tradition that Apsile and Fassin lifted the craft into the carrier. They stooped, took an end each and—very slowly at first—hoisted the arrowhead into the space above, letting their feet lift off the floor at the end to slow it down. The gascraft weighed next to nothing in Third Fury's minuscule gravity, but it massed over two tonnes and the laws regarding inertia and momentum still applied. They were carried three metres up inside the drop ship's hold, towards the opened arms of the waiting gascraft cradle. The Colonel's esuit took up the space of two of the little gascraft, but that still left room for another five in the drop ship's hold. The arrowhead snicked into place alongside the tall discus that held Colonel Hatherence. Satisfied that the arrowhead was correctly fastened in, the two men let themselves fall back to the floor. The colonel drifted down alongside them.

Fassin looked up at the sleek lines of the gascraft. *How small it looks*, he thought. *Tiny space to spend years in... decades in... even centuries...* They landed. Apsile, more experienced, got his knee-flex just right; Fassin bounced.

The giant esuit had to tilt to clear the carrier ship's opened hold doors, toppling then coming upright again with a burr of vanes and a whoosh of air. "I must say I myself would prefer to enter the atmosphere directly, that is to say, in fact. Indeed, in reality," the colonel shouted.

"Yes," Fassin said. "I would too, colonel."

"Good luck in that!" the oerileithe boomed.

"Thank you," Fassin said. "I suspect good luck will be necessary, if not sufficient."

A few hours later he had just about enough time to reflect that it was bad luck which produced the opportunity they had both been looking for, before he had to flee for his life.

·

The others persuaded him eventually. Thay, Sonj and Mome were all going. Why not him? Not nervous, surely? Maybe just too lazy?

He wasn't nervous or—quite—that lazy. He just wanted to stay back at the nest and bland with K, who was coming to the end of a tream, socked into a traumalyser and a linked-up subsal. She floated, lightly tethered, in the gentle stream blowing out of the air chair, slim graceful body semi-foetal, arms waving, her long, end-tied chestnut hair blossoming above her like a cobra hood, wrapping over her head then wafting back again. The NMR net was like a hand with twenty-plus slim silver fingers grasping her head from the back. The subsal's transparent tube disappeared into a tiny neuro-taplet just behind her left earlobe. K's eyes moved languidly behind their lids and her face seemed set in a smile.

At this stage, coming out of a long tream, it was as though she had been diving in some abyssal depths and was now swimming slowly back in through a few kilometres of sunlit shallows. You could wade out to meet the person coming in without surrendering yourself to the whole para-lucid chemical/ NMR-holo-induced dream state, you could sort of snorkel with them while they still gilled, heading for the beach that was mundane reality.

—Hey, Fass! she'd sent when he first dipped in to join her, slipping on a small NMR collar and becoming part of the slowly evaporating tream. She'd been away for a day and a half; a long one.—You came to meet me? Thanks, part!

—Have fun? he asked.

—More than fun. Guess where I've been?

He sent a shrug.—Faintest.

—I did a delve! I treamed a delve like Seers do, into Nasqueron! Well, it wasn't really Nasq, it was another gas-giant called Furenasyle. That's where the chip must have been templated. You heard of Furenasyle?

—Yeah, it's another place they do Dweller Studies. So you treamed you were there? Delving, yeah?

—Surely did. You make it sound so amazing. And, Fass, it was great! Best tream… well, second-best tream I've ever had! K sent a kind of complicit, sexy smirk in his direction. He guessed the tream she was referring to. They'd experienced it together. A love-tream, a joint immersion in what they felt for each other. Well, supposedly. Love treams were tacky in some ways—you could still lie about your feelings in them, and if you selected the right template from the traumalyser device and suitable accompanying chemicals from the subsal, you could pretty much guarantee a tream of surpassing, wide-eyed heart-throbbing bliss even between two people who basically hated each other. But it had been good, between the two of them. Good, but not something that he'd wanted to do again. He supposed he was suspicious of the whole Virtual Reality experience, and treaming, especially with a synched-in subsal providing appropriate synthesised chemicals for delivery to the brain, was the most immersive VR you could find. Legally or semi-legally, anyway.

—You should try it! Really! It would be like practice, don't you think?

—I suppose. If delving is what I'm going to end up doing. I take it you'd recommend it.

—If it's like that, sure!

Sure was what he was not. He was still young, still undecided. Should he become a Slow Seer, like everybody seemed to expect him to become, even including the people he shared the nest with on Hab 4409 ('The Happy Hab!")? Or should he do something else entirely? He still didn't know. The very fact that everybody thought he would become a Seer eventually, after a few wild years—and these were surely wild years, not something that you ever imagined could go on for ever or even for very long—made him all the more determined not to do what was expected of him…well, maybe "determined" was too strong a word, he admitted. Reluctant. Made him more reluctant. He supposed that was better. Still, he might surprise them all. He might go off and do something entirely, utterly and excitingly different. He just had to experience lots of different things until he found the right thing, was all.

—Listen, I'm probably going with the others to the protest. Well, unless you need me, you know…

—Good for you! I don't mind. You go. I'd come too, but I need to ramp out of this shallow. That last time I steeped really crawled. Ugh!

—Okay. See you.

—Later, part!

He left the nest.

The nest—a low-gee pod of forty or so mostly small spherical rooms housing a kind of commune of (all human) gappers, nopers, treamers, trustafarians, zealers and zonkers—was in a big bunch of living spaces up near the hab's long axis, near the (rather arbitrarily termed) "west" end, not far beneath the suntube. The nest allegedly belonged to the mother of one of the trustafarians, though unofficially it was the Immaturian People's Republic of Whateverness (and had semi-official paperwork and software to prove it, too).

Hab 4409 was one of a few hundred thousand habitats orbiting Sepekte. It was average size, a cylinder of re-formed asteroid material fifty kilometres long and ten across, spinning to create about two-thirds of a gee at its internal diameter surface. It turned in the unending sunlight like a giant garden roller flattening photons. Two twelve-kilometre mirror-lens systems—one at either end—faced Ulubis star like a pair of vast, unbearably thin flowers. Further mirror complexes funnelled the captured sunlight through two windows of diamond sheet into the hab's long axis, where a final set of mirrors—moving up and down the suntube to create something like the feel of a planetary day—finally directed the light towards the internal surface. Or at least finally directed the light towards the internal surface if there wasn't something like one of the grape-bunch-like nest complexes in the way (more mirrors).

Many more people lived in the habs than lived on planets in the system and most of the habs were somewhere near Sepekte. Hab 4409 had been a fairly liberal, free-flowing, laissez-faire, who-cares kind of place almost since its inception—as part of a horrendously intricate incumbent species asset-swap write-off dodge—two millennia earlier. Even its ultimate ownership had never fully been settled, and several generations of lawyers had gone to their plush retirements—having followed the saga of Hab 4409's provenance and title since their days as articled clerks—still lacking a sense of closure re the above.

So the place attracted drifters, artists, misfits, natural exiles, political and other eccentrics and slightly deranged or badly messed-up people of more or less every sort, and always had. Most were from Ulubis but some were more exotic and from further afield, generally trustafarians and/or gappers portaling in from the rest of the Mercatoria, taking time out between education and responsibility to relax a little. The place produced good art, it was an unofficial—but tax-deductible—finishing school for the aforesaid children of the rich (give the darling brats true freedom and let them see how empty it was, was the idea), it was a way station for those heading out to disgrace or back from perdition, and it was a halfway house for those who might or might not ever again contribute anything useful to society but who just might galvanise it fundamentally. (And, if you wanted to be really paranoid about stuff, it was—as far as the authorities were concerned—a relatively easy-to-watch and even easier-to-close-down sump for dangerous ideas: a radical trap.) It was useful, in other words. It fulfilled a purpose, if not several. In a society as large as that which existed around Ulubis, somewhere had to provide that sort of service.

People were people. Some would always be straight, some would always be a bit twisted, but they all had some sort of part to play, and they were all in some sense valuable, were they not?

But now the fucking Mercatoria, the fucking Ascendancy or fucking Omnocracy, or whatever they fucking were, the fucking Hierchon (more likely, one of his new rotational crop of advisers who saw a way to make some money and gain some extra power), or the Peregal below him or Apparitor below *him* or just the Diegesian gimplet who was actually nominally the governor or mayor or whatever he was supposed to fucking be (his post, his presence and his protecting bully boys only here at all thanks to an earlier dispute over who controlled what, resulting in a grubby, century-old compromise), anyway the fucking big boys, the fucking people who owned fucking everything or thought *some* fucker ought to own fucking everything had decided, decreed, *deemed* that proprietorship of the whole fucking place—and that of lots of other similar habs in similar situations of disputed/uncertain/dubious/happily contingent ownership—should pass to what they called a properly accredited and responsible authority. Which basically meant them. Or if not them, their chums. Somebody who took things like ownership and rent-gathering and petty law-enforcement and so on seriously. It was the law-makers, the law-givers, being outlaws, and it would not be allowed to stand, it would not be allowed to pass, it would not go unchallenged, it would not go into the local statutes without a serious fucking challenge. These people, for whatever fuckwit reason, were destroying part of what was good about the habs, about Sepekte-Orbit, about Ulubis system, about the society they were all in the end a part of. Ultimately they were being stupid and self-destructive, and all that was required was that the people who could see all this clearly—because they were right here, at the sharp end, at the cutting edge—pointed this out to them. They were all on the same side in the end, it was just that sometimes the fuckers in authority got too far away from the reality of life as the mass of people lived it, and that was when you had to make a stand, make a point and make yourself heard.

So they went to the protest, down the friction tubes and the bungees and along the tramways to the central plaza and the makings of a great crowd.

"You just have to think about it," Mome said as they walked the last street into the plaza. "The Beyonders never attack habs, never attack whole cities, never attack anything big and easy and defenceless. They attack the military and the authorities and big infrastructure stuff. Their attacks, their violence, their military strategy is a discourse amenable to analysis if one is prepared to approach it shorn of propagandistic preconceptions. And the message is clear: their argument, their war is with the Mercatorial system, with the Ascendancy and the Omnocracy and the Administrata and not with the common people, not with us."

"Resent being called common!" Sonj protested.

"Erring on the side of generosity including you in the category 'people', Sonj," Mome shot back. Mome was a little guy, pale, intense and always slightly hunched, as though perpetually preparing either to pounce or duck. Sonj was huge; a big bumbling dark brown geezer of changeable moods and intensely curly short red hair who only looked at home or even slightly graceful in low gee.

"Doesn't necessarily make them the good guys," Fassin insisted.

"Makes them people open to reason, people capable of indulging in meaningful dialogue," Mome said. "Not just mad fuckers to be put down like vermin, which is pretty much what we're told they are."

"So what's stopping them talking to us?" Fassin asked.

"Us," Mome said. "Takes two to talk."

They all looked at him. Mome was known to talk a lot. Sometimes to audiences who had, basically, long since fallen asleep. He shrugged.

"My cousin Lain—" Thay said.

"*Another* one?" Mome asked, feigning incredulity.

"Sister of cousin Kel, half-sister of cousin Yayz," Thay explained patiently. She was Sonj's part, also generously made; awkward in low gee but bouncily agile on the hab's internal surface at two-thirds of a gee. "My cousin Lain," she continued determinedly, "the one in the Navarchy, says that she reckons the reason the Beyonders attack so much at all is because if they don't the Navarchy and the Summed Fleet goes after them. And we don't just attack military stuff. She says we hit their habs. Kill millions of them. Lot of offs unhappy with—"

"Lots of *whats* unhappy with?" Mome asked.

"Lots of offs," Thay repeated.

"I got the *word*," Mome repeated with a sigh, "I just didn't get the *meaning*." He snapped his fingers. "Wait. Short for 'officers', right?"

"Correct."

"Brilliant. Carry on."

"Lot of offs unhappy with this," Thay said again, "so the 'yonds—the Beyonders—just attack us to keep us on the defensive." She nodded once. "That's what my cousin Lain says."

"Ayee! Crazy 'yonding talk," Mome said, putting his hands over his ears. "Get us all arrested." They laughed.

"At least we have the freedom to say this sort of thing," Fassin pointed out. Mome did his special Hollow Laugh.

In the central plaza, Fassin greeted people, drank in the sense of solidarity and slightly edgy fun—lots of inventive costumes, towering floss-sculptures and buzzing balloonderers (trailing slogan banners, yelling chants and scattering narconfetti)—but still felt oddly apart from it all. He looked up and around, ignoring for the moment the people—mostly human—and the circle of domed and gleaming buildings.

The hab was a giant, verdant city rolled up into a spinning tube, with small hills and many lakes and criss-cross avenues between low-rise hanging-garden apartments and winding rivers and spindly towers, some arched like bows and reaching all the way up to the suntube, where they curved—or needle-eyed—round to meet towers on the far side. Bunches of nests—surrounded by mirrors, trailed with friction tubes like jungle creepers—clustered near the long axis, and dirigiblisters floated like strange, semi-transparent clouds beneath them.

Then Fassin heard some sort of shout at one edge of the crowd, nearest the palace of the Diegesian, which was the focus for the protest. He might have smelled something strange, but then that was probably just one of the cruising balloonderers disseminating some drug that Fassin's immedio-immune system hadn't recognised. Then he realised maybe it wasn't, because all the balloonderers dropped suddenly, as one, out of the air. Also, the sun in the suntube went out. Which never happened. He heard lots of odd noises, some of which might have been screaming. It seemed to get cold very quickly. That was odd too. People were hitting him, with their shoulders mostly, as they went running past him, then they were falling over him, and he realised he was *Fassin?*, realised he was *Fassin* lying down, then he was *Fassin* getting hit again, but he was *Fassin* trying to get up and stand again, and he was *Fassin*, he was *Fassin*, he was on his knees and he was *Fassin* just about to get up from his knees onto his feet—swaying, feeling very strange, wondering what all the people were doing lying down around him—when—*Fassin*—he was knocked down again. By a man in armour, steel grey, with a big trunchbuster club and no face and a couple of little buzz-drones at each shoulder, spraying gas and making a high, terrible keening noise that he—*Fassin!*—wanted to get away from, but his nose and eyes and everything else stung and hurt and he didn't know what to do, he was *Fasssin!* just standing there and the guy with the big club thing as long as a spear came up to him and he *Fasssin?* stupidly thought he might ask him what was going on and what was wrong with *Faaassssiiinnn?* wrong when the man swept his club-spear trunchbuster thing round and into his face, knocking some teeth out and sending him spinning to

"*Fassin?*"

His name finally jolted him awake.

"Back with us? Good."

The speaker was a small man in a large chair across a cramped-looking metal desk. The room—or whatever—was too dark to see into, even with IR. The sound of the man's voice in the space suggested it was not a big space. Fassin was aware that his face and especially his mouth hurt. He tried to wipe his mouth. He looked down. His hands could not move because his forearms were—he tried to think of the right word—shackled? They were shackled to the seat he was sitting in. What the hell was this? He started laughing.

Somebody hit him in his bones. It was like his entire skeleton was a wind chime and his flesh and muscles and organs were somewhere else, only nearby but still connected somehow and some fucker—actually, some very large group of fuckers—had taken a whole load of hammers and whacked each one of his bones really hard at the same time. The pain went almost as quickly as it arrived, leaving just a weird sort of echo in his nerves.

"What the fuck was zhat?" he asked the little man. His voice sounded comical with some of his teeth knocked out. His tongue probed the gaps. Felt like two out, one loose. He tried to remember how long it took adult teeth to grow back. The little man was quite a jolly-looking soul, with a plump, amused-seeming face and chubby, rosy cheeks. His hair was black, cropped. He wore a uniform of a type that Fassin didn't recognise. "Are you shucking *torturing* me?" Fassin asked.

"No," the little man said in a very reasonable tone of voice. "I'm just doing this to get your attention." One of his hands moved on the desk's surface.

Fassin's bones clattered as though played upon again. His nerves, having experienced this twice now, decided that really this was no joke, and in fact felt extremely sore.

"All right! All right!" he heard himself saying. "I take the shucking point. Fucking point," he said, working out how to adapt his pronunciation to his new dental layout.

"Don't swear," the little man said, and hurt him again.

"Okay!" he screamed. His head hung. Snot dripped from his nose, saliva and blood from his mouth.

"Please don't swear," the little man said. "It indicates an untidy mind."

"Just tell me what the f— what you want," Fassin said. Was this real? Had he been in some sort of weird VR dream ever since he'd joined K for the coming-out-of-the-shallows end-of-tream thing earlier? Was this what happened when you got tream templates cheap, or illegally copied or something? Was this real? It felt painful enough to be real. He looked down at his legs and the hems of his shorts, all covered in blood and mucus and snot. He could see individual hairs on his legs, some standing, some plastered to his skin. He could see pores. Didn't that mean it was real? But of course it didn't. Treams, simcasts, VR, all depended on the fact that the mind could really only concentrate on one thing at a time. The rest was illusion. Human sight, the most complicated sense the species possessed, had been doing that for millions of years, fooling the mind behind the eyes. You thought you had colour vision, and in some detail, over this wide angle but really you didn't; accurate colour vision was concentrated within a tiny part of the visual field, with only vague, movement-wary black-and-white awareness extending over the rest.

The brain played tricks on itself to pretend that it saw as well away from the centre of its visual target as it did right at that bull's-eye. Smart VR used that same deception; zoom in on a detail and it would be created for you in all its pinpoint exactitude, but everything else you weren't attending to with such concentration could safely be ignored until your attention swung that way, keeping the amount of processing power within acceptable limits.

Fassin dragged his attention away from his blood-spattered leg. "Is this real?" he asked.

The little man sighed. "Mr Taak," he said, glancing down at a screen, "your profile indicates that you are from a respectable family and may one day even become a useful member of society. You shouldn't be mixing and living with the sort of people you have been mixing and living with. You've all been very foolish and people have suffered because of that stupidity. You've been living in a kind of dream, really, and that dream is now over. Officially. I think you ought to go back home. Don't you?"

"Where are my friends?"

"Mr Iifilde, Mr Resiptiss, Ms Cargin and Ms Hohuel?"

Fassin just stared at him. Shit, in all the last few months he'd been staying here he'd only known them by their first names. He supposed those were Thay, Sonj and Mome's last names, but really he'd no idea. And there had been four, hadn't there? Did that mean they were counting K as well? But she hadn't been to the protest.

"They're being held elsewhere, or they've been processed and released, or we're still looking for them." The little man smiled.

Fassin looked down at his arms, held within metal hoops. He tried to move his legs, then leaned over and looked down. His legs were shackled too. Or manacled or whatever. His mouth felt very odd. He ran his tongue round where where his teeth had been, checking again. He supposed he'd have to get false ones until the new ones grew back. Or sport a piratical grin. "Why am I being treated like this?" he asked.

The little man looked incredulous. He appeared to be about to hurt Fassin again, then shook his head in exasperation. "Because you took part in a violent demonstration against the Diegesian, that's why!" he said.

"But I wasn't violent," Fassin said.

"You personally may not have been. The demonstration you took part in most certainly was."

Fassin would have scratched his head. "Is that all it takes?"

"Of course!"

"Who started the violence?" he asked.

The little man jerked his arms out to each side. His voice went very high. "Does it *matter*?"

Fassin had meant which side, but he could tell the little man thought he'd meant which demonstrator. He sighed. "Look, I just want to get back to my friends, to my nest. Can I go? I didn't do anything, I got my teeth knocked out, I can't tell you anything, or… anything…" he said. He sighed again.

"You can go when you sign this." The little man swivelled the screen around so Fassin could see. He looked at what he was supposed to sign, and at the fingerprint pad and camera patches on the screen which would record that it had really been him signing (or, more to the point, make a fake document take up a fraction more storage space).

"I can't sign this," he said. "It basically says my friends are all Beyonder agents and deserve death."

The little man rolled his eyes. "Read it *carefully*, will you? It just says you have *suspicions* in that regard. You don't seriously think *your* word would be enough to convict anybody of anything, do you?"

"Well then, why get me to—?"

"We want you to *betray* them!" the little man shouted, as though it was the most obvious thing ever. "We want you to turn your back on them and become a productive member of society. That's all."

"But they're my friends." Fassin coughed, swallowed. "Look, could I get a drink of water?"

"No. You can't. And they're not your friends. They're just people you know. They're barely acquaintances. You got drunk with them, got stoned with them, talked a bit with them and slept with some of them. You'll all go your separate ways soon enough anyway and probably never keep in touch. They are not your friends. Accept that."

Fassin thought better of debating what being a friend meant, in the circumstances. "Well, I'm still not betraying them."

"They've betrayed you!"

The little interrogator swung the screen round, clicked on a few patches and swung it back. Fassin watched Thay, Sonj and Mome—all stuck in seats like the one he was secured in, and Sonj looking pretty beaten-up—say they thought that Fassin held Beyonder sympathies and was a danger to society who needed watching. They each mumbled something to that effect, signed the screen and pressed a thumb against the print patch (Sonj's left a smear of blood).

The screenage shook him. It had probably been faked, but all the same. He sat back. "You faked that," he said, unsteadily.

The little man laughed. "Are you mad? Why would we bother?"

"I don't know," Fass admitted. "But I know my friends. They wouldn't—"

The little man sat forward. "So just sign this and in the *highly* unlikely event that it ever crops up, just say *yours* has been faked."

"So why not fake it anyway?" Fassin shouted.

"Because then you won't have *betrayed* them!" the little man yelled back. "Come on! Sign and you can go. I've got better things to do."

"But why do any of this?" Fassin said, wanting to cry. "Why make anybody betray anybody?"

The little man looked at him for a moment. "Mr Taak," he said, sitting back, sounding patient. "I've inspected your profile. You are not stupid. Misguided, idealistic, naive, certainly, but not stupid. You must know how societies work. You must at least have an inkling. They work on force, power and coercion. People don't behave themselves because they're nice. That's the liberal fallacy. People behave themselves because if they don't they'll be punished. All this is known. It isn't even debatable. Civilisation after civilisation, society after society, species after species, all show the same pattern. Society is control: control is reward and punishment. Reward is being allowed to partake of the fruits of that society and, as a general but not unbreakable rule, not being punished without cause."

"But—"

"Be quiet. The idiotic issue you chose to complain about—ownership of a habitat—really has nothing to do with you. It's a legal matter, an ownership thing. You weren't even born here and you wouldn't have stayed beyond a few more months anyway, admit it. You should have kept out of it. You chose not to, you put yourself in harm's way and now you're paying the price. Part of that price is letting us know that you have made an effort to dissociate yourself from the people you were complicit with. Once you do that, you can go. Home, I would suggest. I mean to 'glantine."

"And if I say no?"

"You mean not sign?"

"Yes."

"Seriously?"

"Seriously."

"Then it's taken out of my hands. You'll go to meet people who enjoy doing this sort of thing."

This time, when the little man moved his hand over the desk, Fassin screamed with the pain. He must have bitten his tongue. There was a taste of iron and his mouth filled with fresh blood and hot saliva.

"Because I," the little man said wearily, "don't."

In the end Fassin signed. He'd kind of known he would.

The little man looked happy, and a couple of big female guards came in and helped Fassin from the chair, his bonds unfastened.

"Thank you, Mr Taak," the little man said, and grasped his hand and shook it before they took him out of the room. "I hate all that unpleasantness, and it is always so good to see somebody being sensible. Try not to think too badly of me. Good luck to you."

They got him showered down and fixed up and he left after a medical and a cup of soup, dressed in paper-thin overalls. He looked around when they ushered him through the doorways into what passed for outside in a hab. He'd been somewhere inside the Diegesian's palace.

Back at the nest, turmoil. The place had been raided, trashed, everything in it broken or sprayed with stinking, vomit-inducing crowd-control goo. They went to a bar instead and didn't really talk about anything after the protest and the crackdown. They talked instead of rumours of people being killed and others disappearing.

K wasn't there. She'd been beaten up when the troopers came to turn the nest over. She was in a prison hospital ship for three weeks, then killed herself with a broken glass the day she was released.

It was months before Fassin learned the truth. K had been sent into a nightmare tream. Somebody who'd come with the law officers—maybe just one of them who happened to know how to handle tream gear—had found her still floating, not yet out of the delving tream, and altered the settings on the traumalyser and the subsal while some others had held her down and worked her over. Whoever did the thing with the traumalyser must have carried that sort of template chip around with them, just for such eventualities. Then they'd left her, bloody and bound, to some speeded-up nightmare of horror, rape and torture.

They were all split up, doing other, mostly more responsible things when they pieced all this together. They talked about a complaint, an investigation, a protest.

Fassin went back to 'glantine and booked a place on the Seer induction course for the term after next. Then he returned to the habs, and then to Sepekte's Boogeytown, to the roaring life, the drink and drugs and fucking and fun, and—after a while, gradually, carefully—made a few inquiries, hung out in the right places, and met certain people. Apparently he passed a few tests without realising he'd been taking them, and then one night he was introduced to a girl who called herself Aun Liss.

:

"Fassin!"

His name jolted him awake. Third Fury; cabin. Still night-dark. Clanging noise. The screen showed hour Four. The screen was red and flashing. Had somebody spoken?

"What?" he said, tearing the restraints away and levering himself out of bed, floating towards the centre of the cabin.

"Herv Apsile," said a voice. Sounded like Apsile. Sounded like Apsile in a state of some excitement or distress. "We have a situation. Looks like an attack."

*Oh, shit.* Fassin pulled on clothes, called up full lights. "That fucking horrendous clanging noise the alarm?"

"That's right."

"You in Facility Command?"

"Yes."

"Who do we think?" A light flashed over a storage locker and it revolved, revealing an emergency esuit.

"Don't know. Two naval units vaporised already. Get suited and—"

The lights—all the lights—flickered. The screen did not come back on. A tremor made the cabin shake. Something broke in the bathroom with a sharp crack.

"You feel that? You still there?" Apsile said.

"Yes to both," Fassin said. He was looking at the esuit.

"Suit up and take a drop shaft to the emergency shelter." Apsile paused. "You got that?" Another pause. "Fass?"

"Here." Fassin started pulling all his clothes off again. "That what you're going to do, Herv?"

"That's what we're both supposed to do."

Another tremble made the whole cabin rattle. The air seemed to quake like jelly.

The alarm shut off. Somehow, though, not in an encouraging way.

The screen flashed once, screeched.

Fassin hauled the esuit out of its locker. "How's the main hangar?" he asked.

"Intact. Whatever's hitting us seems to be coming in from the Nasq spin-side, slightly retro."

"So heading into the centre's going to be putting us closer," Fassin said. Was that a draught? He could hear a hissing sound. He clipped the esuit collar round his neck and let the gel helmet deploy. It turned everything hazy and quiet for a moment, then decided the situation wasn't too dire yet, and opened slits for him to breathe, talk and hear through. The face-mask section thinned to near-perfect transparency.

"For now," Apsile agreed. "If the direction of the hostile fire stays constant we'll be coming round to face it full on in two hours."

Fassin stepped into the esuit and pulled it up, letting it connect with the collar, adjusting to his body, huffing and settling. Very comfortable, really. "That what you want to do, Herv? Sit in a huddle with everybody else like mice in a hole hoping the cat goes away?"

"Standing orders."

"I know. Want to guess what I want to do?" There was a pause. Another more violent tremor shook the cabin. The main door popped open, wobbling inwards, revealing the companionway outside. The pause went on. "Herv?" he asked. He looked round for anything he might want to take with him. Nothing. "Herv?"

"I'll see you there."

Something blazed hard and blue-white against Nasqueron's side-lit face, turning the hangar into a harsh jagged jumble of fiercely shining surfaces and intensely black shadows. Fassin flinched. The light faded quickly, turning to yellow and orange; a small fading sun shone between the moon and Nasqueron.

Herv Apsile had got there ahead of him. He gave a quick wave and easily jumped the eight metres to the open nose-blister of the carrier craft, disappearing inside. The nose-blister closed.

"Herv?" Fassin said, trying the suit's emergency comms. No answer. He made slow bounds for the open hold. Colonel Hatherence was already there, the tall discus of her esuit floating a fraction above the floor directly beneath the place she'd filled earlier.

"Seer Taak! I rather thought you might adopt this course!" she shouted.

*Shit*, Fassin thought. He'd kind of hoped the colonel would have made her way to the emergency shelter in the moon's core, ten kilometres down, along with everybody else, like they'd all been told to. There was one drop shaft big enough, wasn't there? Oh well. He came to a stop beneath the little arrowhead gascraft hanging in its cradle directly above. "Colonel," he said, nodding.

Would she try to stop him? No idea. Could she? No doubt about that.

"Not sure whether to be relieved or terrified," the colonel yelled. A manipulator arm creased out from the side of the oerileithe esuit, unfolding towards Fassin. *Oh, fuck*, he thought. *Here we go*.

"After you!" the colonel said, her arm indicating the space above.

Fassin smiled and jumped. She rose with a whirr beside him. Stopped and then braced by the ceiling of the hold, he flipped open the cockpit of the little gascraft, revealing a vaguely coffin-shaped space. He shucked the suit and unclipped the helmet.

"Out of uniform, major," the colonel said jovially, voice echoing in the enclosed space of the upper hold. Fassin let the suit fall slowly to the floor beneath and stepped into the foot of the little arrowhead's cockpit. "Gracious!" Hatherence said. "Are all human males of this form?"

"Just the handsome ones, colonel," he assured her. He lowered himself carefully into the cool gel. The cockpit cover closed over him. He wriggled in the darkness, getting his neck positioned over the scanner collar. A soft light and a gentle chime confirmed all was well. He reached for the double nozzle of the gillfluid root, took a deep breath, let it out, then placed the nozzles at his nostrils.

Fassin lay back, zoning out as best he could, fighting the urge to panic, the gag response of fear as the gillfluid poured into his nose, throat and lungs like the coldest drink anybody had ever taken.

A moment of confusion, disorientation. Then the collar nestling closer against his neck and the warming gel closing over his body, tendrils seeking out ears, mouth, penis and anus. Twin stings of pain on his forearms, then another pair, one under each ear, as the blood slides went in.

"Set?" said the voice of Herv Apsile, gurgling through the still calibrating gel in his ears.

—Thoroughly, he sent back just by thinking.—And the colonel?

"I am set, also!" Even over comms, it seemed, Colonel Hatherence tended to shout.

Fassin had been wondering if they could leave her behind somehow. Probably not, then.

"Hold doors closing. Ready to go," Apsile said.

Fassin started to become his little gascraft. It covered him, embraced him, multiply penetrated him, and in those acts offered itself up to him completely. The light from below disappeared as the hold doors closed. He could see

Colonel Hatherence's esuit hanging beside him, sense its cold and read its electromagnetic signature, just as he could feel the systems of the drop ship readying, flexing, preparing, changing as the ship nudged itself off the floor. Other senses registered an unusual wash of radiations, a faint gravity well set in a much greater, deeper one, a slather of meaningless comms shards, confused transmissions and EM signals from the Shared Facility base itself— and a sudden jolt, a transmitted faint but massive thud followed by a strange sideways, upwards-sucking movement.

He waited for Apsile to talk to them, meanwhile trying to work it out himself. Distant whirr and hiss of the carrier tanking the air in its hold.

"Sorry about that," Apsile said mildly. "Back in control. Unconventional method of opening the hangar to vacuum there. No idea who to thank."

—We okay? Fassin asked.

"NSD," Apsile said, sounding mildly distracted. "No Significant Damage."

—Let you get on with it, Fassin sent.

"Thanks."

"Cancel relief, emphasise terror," the colonel said.

Fassin hoped she was talking only to him. He checked through all the little gascraft's settings and systems, settling into it as its life-support tendrils settled into him. Something like a wide array of lights seen from the bottom corner of the eye swung into focus in front of him. He called up a few read-outs and started a couple of subroutines to check that everything was working. Seemed to be.

He felt the carrier accelerate away from the moon. Patch-through to the larger ship's senses suddenly appeared as an option on his controls and he took it.

Now he could experience pretty much what Apsile could.

Nasqueron filling the sky ahead and up, the grey-brown surface of Third Fury disappearing fast below and behind. Debris clouds. Comms shards. More than there ought to be in a properly organised fleetlet like the one that had brought them here and that had been guarding the moon. No sign of illuminating radar or other targeting give-away. Not that a civilian ship like the carrier would be able to spot any but the most glaringly obvious. No current damage flags, just records of a few small hull impacts, little more than pitting. Ship drive traces. A sudden flare of radiation as a ship turned hard a couple of hundred klicks away, dying away. Outgoing signal loop, broadcasting their unarmed condition, claiming lifeboat status. Flash! From right behind. A near-semicircular debris cloud rising glittering from a new glowing crater maybe half a klick across on the surface of Third Fury. Three smaller craters coming into view, recent but cooled down to orange and red heat. The view twisted, overlays of lines and grids and drive symbols flickering into being.

Apsile pointed the carrier's nose straight at Nasqueron and started a long, purposefully irregular corkscrew towards the gas-giant, accelerating the drop ship as hard as its engines would allow.

The drop ship was no sort of high-performance military unit; all it was supposed to do was take the gascraft from the Facility to the gas-giant and pick them up later. It was rugged, able to take the strain of operating inside Nasqueron's gravity well and its various pressure environments down to the liquid-hydrogen level, and it had the power to lift itself and its charges easily enough out of Nasqueron's grip. But it was not especially manoeuvrable, carried no armament or defensive systems and far from being stealthed had been designed from its invitation-to-tender spec. onwards to be as easy to see with as many different senses as it was possible to imagine, just so that no mischievous Dweller could crash something into it and then claim, sorry, they hadn't seen it.

"How you doing down there?" Apsile asked. He sounded in control, unworried.

"Fine, for myself," the colonel said.

—Ditto, Fassin sent.—Got an ETA yet?

Trips from Third Fury to Nasq. usually took about an hour. Fassin hoped they could do it in less than half that.

"With the main drive maxed we should make turnaround in about ten minutes," Apsile said, "then decelerate for another ten and then take... hmm, another handful—five at most, I'd hope—to get deep enough into the atmosphere."

He meant deep enough into the atmosphere to be beyond any but the most scary weapons. Obviously not counting the scary weapons the Dwellers possessed.

—Anything we can clip off that? Fassin asked.

"Maybe we could make it down in less time once we hit the cloud tops," Apsile said. "Steeper, carrying more speed. Maybe. Hmm." Fassin got the impression somehow that the man was rubbing his chin. "Yes, maybe, if we let the heat and stress levels creep just a tad beyond tolerance." A pause. "Though of course that's always assuming that the ship didn't take any damage we don't know about when the hangar dome got blown."

—Always assuming, Fassin agreed.

"Master Technician," Colonel Hatherence said, "are we being pursued or under unit-specific attack?"

"No, colonel."

"Then I suggest we adopt your first entry profile."

—Decision's yours alone, Herv, Fassin sent.

"Copy."

"Can you access any military comms traffic, Master Technician?"

"I'm afraid not, ma'am, not unless they choose to target us with a clear beam or broadcast."

"That is unfortunate. What seems to be happening?"

"Looks like there's been some sort of firefight. Still going on, possibly. Drives spreading away from the moon, heading in the direction the hostile munitions appeared to be coming from. Woh!"

The flash attracted Fassin's second-hand attention as well; another, even larger crater glowing white on the surface of Third Fury.

"What of the people still back within the Third Fury moonlet?" the colonel asked.

"Been listening," Apsile said. "I'll try and contact them direct. Give me a moment."

Silence. Fassin watched space wheel around them through the carrier ship's sensors. He checked the drop ship's system profile, oriented, then searched for and found 'glantine; a tiny shining dot, far away. The sensors let him zoom in until the planet moon was a shining gibbous image, scintillating with magnification artefacts, hints of its topography just about visible. Could that be the uplands? There, that light patch—the Sea of Fines? A spark. There, back up... A tiny flash? Had he seen that?

Something colder and more invasive than any gel tendril seemed to invade him, clutching at his stomach and heart. No, surely not. Just another artefact of the system. He looked for the sensor-replay controls.

"Shit, there's a fucking wreckage—" Apsile said, then the craft bucked and swung. Fassin, turning his focus of attention back to what Apsile was looking at saw it too now: a field of dark specks across the face of the planet ahead of them like a ragged flock of birds far in the distance. They were at near-maximum velocity. The carrier started to turn.

A rush of dark scraps, tearing by on all sides like a thin shell of soot-black snow flakes. Fassin felt his arms, held by the cloying shock-gel, attempt to draw themselves in towards his body, instinctively trying to make himself a smaller target. Then they were through. No impacts.

After a moment, Fassin felt the drop ship start to swing round to present its drive tubes towards the planet, ready to begin deceleration. "I think," Apsile said cautiously, "that we just about got away with—"

Something slammed into them. The ship lurched—there was a concussive *snap!* that Fassin felt through the carrier ship, through the gascraft, even through the shock-gel. He lost the patch-through connection with the drop ship. He was back in his own little arrowhead again. They were whirling. And there was light, synched with the whirling. Light?

It was coming from below, where the hold doors were. He could see Colonel H's esuit, hanging alongside him. *Oh-oh...*

The ship began to come out of the spin, steadying. The light from below faded but did not go away. It had the spectrum to be light reflected from Nasqueron. Light from the gas-giant coming in through supposedly closed doors. Fassin flipped the gascraft's sensor ring to look straight down at the doors.

"Oh fuck," he tried to say. There was a small but ragged hole, stuff hanging like spilled guts. The Nasqueron light was reflecting in off some polished-looking surfaces.

Force, building; very like the main drive decelerating them more or less on schedule. He retried the intercom, then broadcast a radio signal.—Herv?

"Here. Sorry about that. Hit something after all. Got her straight and rearward. Back on track. No read-outs from the hold at all, though. Including the door."

—Think that's where it hit. I can see a hole.

"How big?"

—Maybe a metre lateral by two.

"I too can see the hole," the colonel told them, also joining in the radio-broadcast fun. "It is as Seer Taak describes."

"Too small for you guys to get out of," Apsile said.

—How's the rest of the ship? Fassin sent.

"Holding together for now. Can't see where whatever hit us exited, or just went on to hit inside."

"I suspect it hit me," Hatherence said. "My esuit casing, that is to say. Probably."

A pause. Then Apsile said, "And… are you all right?"

"Perfectly fine. Your hold doors took most of the energy out of it and my esuit is of exceptional quality, durability and damage-tolerance. Scarcely a scratch."

—If we can't open the doors, we can't get out and the whole thing's pointless, Herv, Fassin sent.

"We can still hide in the carrier, under the clouds," Apsile said. "I'm not getting much from the Facility. That last hit looked like it must have shaken them pretty hard. We might still be safer under the gas than hanging around out here in clear view of whoever."

Nothing comprehensible was coming out of the Shared Facility on Third Fury, and no military vessels were talking on civilian frequencies. Interference on EM bands, a problem at the best of times anywhere near Nasqueron, was especially intense. Apsile raised a couple of the Facility's equatorial relay satellites, but, exceptionally, could not through-patch via their transceivers and could get only static and meaningless rubbish out of them. He even tried some Dweller mirror sats, where the surprise would have been getting anything other than drivel, but there the service was perfectly normal. "Ouch," they heard him say. "Third Fury just took another hit. We're going in. Fairly slowly, to allow for the damage, but we're going in."

"Whatever you think is best, Master Technician," the colonel said.

The carrier craft began to shudder as it met the upper atmosphere of Nasqueron, carving a glowing trail above the cloud tops. They slowed. Weight began to return to them. And kept on increasing. Creaks and ticking sounds came through the solids joining them to the drop ship. The buffeting decreased, grew and fell away again; soft whumps and crisp bangs also communicated through the drop ship's structure announced debris being torn off the ragged surrounds of the breach in the hold doors, which glowed and sparked as the space around them filled with gas and Fassin began to detect sound in the hold again. They were getting heavy, really heavy now. Fassin could feel the shock-gel tightening around him, *like the sound of snow cramping beneath your feet*. He could almost sense any remaining gas bubbles in his body pancaking like blood cells. *Good and heavy now…*

"Master Technician," the colonel said suddenly.

"Hold on," Apsile said. "That—"

The whole ship shook once, then rolled suddenly.

—Herv? Fassin sent.

"Got some sort of targeting—" Apsile began, then broke off as the craft shook again and slewed wildly across the sky.

"We are indeed being targeted by something," Hatherence announced. "Master Technician," she shouted across the frequencies. "Are you yet able to release us?"

"Eh? What? No! I—"

"Master Technician, attempt to perform a roll or part of an internal loop on my command," Hatherence told him. "I shall release us."

"*You* will?" Apsile shouted.

"I shall. I will. I carry weapons. Now, excuse me, and good luck."

—Wait a minute, Fassin began.

"Seer Taak," the colonel said tersely, "shield your senses." The big discus hanging beside him sent a pulse of blinding blue-white light straight downward at the doors, which blew away in a brief gout of sparks. Rushing yellow-brown clouds spun by outside. Fassin's little arrowcraft was seeing spots. It got busy shuffling its damaged sensors round for working ones. He guessed he hadn't shielded his senses in time. He shut them down now. "Releasing in three seconds," the colonel said. "Make your manoeuvre now if you please, Master Technician."

A blast of radiation and a spike of heat from above coincided with a sudden roll. The cradle holding Fassin in the drop ship gave way, sending him shooting from the hold like a cannon ball. The colonel in her oerileithe esuit came whirling after him a moment later, quickly drawing level. He glimpsed the drop ship above, still rolling, then saw a violet ray appear suddenly to one side, slicing through the gas around them, searing his barely mended vision. The beam just missed the carrier craft, then clouds of yellow fog rolled quickly up between them and the drop ship and it was just him and the colonel, a tiny arrow shape and a spinning coin of dirty grey, hurtling down into the vast chaotic skies of Nasqueron.

∴

" 'It is a given amongst those who care to study such matters that there is, within certain species, a distinct class of being so contemptuous and suspicious of their fellow creats that they court only hatred and fear, counting these the most sincere emotional reactions they may hope to excite, because they are unlikely to have been feigned.' " The Archimandrite Luseferous looked up at the head on the wall. The head stared straight across the cabin, eyes wide with pain and terror and madness.

The assassin had died not long after they'd set out on their long journey towards Ulubis, the upper set of fangs finally penetrating his brain deeply enough to produce death. The Archimandrite had had the fellow's eyelids slit open again when the medical people said death was likely within a few days; he'd wanted to see the look on the man's face when he died.

Luseferous had been asleep when death had finally come for the nameless assassin, but he'd watched the recording many times. (All that happened was that the man's face stopped contorting, his eyes rolled backwards and then came slowly back down, slightly cross-eyed, while the life-signs read-out accompanying the visuals registered first the heart stopping and then a few minutes later the brain flat-lining. Luseferous would have preferred something more dramatic, but you couldn't have everything.) He'd had the fellow's head removed and mounted near that of the rebel chief Stinausin, pretty much in the first head's eye line, so that was what Stinausin had to look at all day.

The Archimandrite glanced up at the staring, nameless head. "What do you think?" He looked over the passage again, lips moving but not actually reading it aloud. He pursed his lips. "I think I agree with what's being said, but I can't help feeling there's a hint of criticism implied at the same time." He shook his head, closed the ancient book and glanced at the cover. "Never heard of him," he muttered.

But at least, he reflected, this holier-than-thou intellectual had a name. It had come to annoy Luseferous rather a lot that he didn't have a name for the failed assassin. Yes, the fellow had failed, yes, he had paid dearly for his crime, and yes, he was dead and now reduced to a mere trophy. But somehow the fact that his name had never been revealed had begun to strike Luseferous as almost a kind of triumph for the assassin, as though successfully withholding this nugget of information meant that Luseferous's victory over the wretch would never quite be complete. He had already sent word back to Leseum to have the matter investigated more thoroughly.

His chief personal secretary appeared behind the sheet of mirrored diamond forming the main inner door of the stateroom-study.

"Yes?"

"Sir, the Marshal Lascert, sir."

"Two minutes."

"Sir."

He saw the Beyonder marshal in the primary stateroom of the Main Battle Craft *Luseferous VII*, his fleet flagship. (Luseferous thought terms like "battleship" and "fleet carrier" and so on sounded old-fashioned and too common.) He'd had the craft remodelled to provide accommodation befitting his rank, but there had come a point where the naval architects had actually started to cry because letting what they called "voids" grow beyond a certain volume weakened the ship too much. The result was that the stateroom wasn't really as extensive or as intimidating as he'd have liked, so he'd had some mirrors installed and a few holo projectors which made it look bigger, though he always had the nagging feeling that people could see through the illusion. The style he'd chosen was New Brutalist: lots of exposed faux concrete and rusty pipes. He'd taken a fancy to the name but had gone off the look almost immediately.

He entered with only his private secretary going before him. Guards, courtiers, admin, army and naval people bowed as he strode past.

"Marshal."

"Archimandrite." The Beyonder marshal was a woman, dressed in light armour which looked like it had been polished up but still gave off an impression of practicality and scruffiness. She was tall, slim and proud-looking, if somewhat flat-chested for Luseferous's taste. Bald women always repelled him anyway. She gave a formal nod that was probably the very least acknowledgement of his status that anybody who didn't patently hate him and/or was about to die had given him for several decades. He couldn't decide whether he found it insulting or refreshing. Two senior officers behind her were jajuejein, currently in their standard tumbleweed configuration, no part of their glittering plate armour higher than the marshal's waist. He suspected that the woman had been selected because she was human, just because he was; almost all the Beyonder High Command were non-human.

He sat. It wasn't really a throne, but it was an impressive seat on a dais. The Beyonder marshal could stand.

"You wanted to talk, Marshal Lascert."

"I speak on behalf of the Transgress, the True Free and the BiAlliance. We have wanted to talk to you for some time," the marshal said smoothly. Deep voice for a woman. "Thank you for agreeing to this meeting."

"A pleasure, I'm sure. So. How goes your end of our little war? Last you heard, obviously."

"It goes well, as far as we know." The marshal smiled. Lights reflected on her bald scalp. "I understand your own campaign has gone from victory to victory."

He waved a hand. "The opposition has been light," he said.

"Your main fleet should be at the outskirts of Ulubis system in, what? One more year?"

"Something like that."

"This is somewhat later than we had all planned for."

"It is a big invasion fleet. It took time to put together," Luseferous said, trying to show that he resented her implied criticism while also giving the impression that what she thought was of no great importance to him.

They *were* behind schedule, though. He had personally assured these—temporary—allies of his that he would be ready to invade nearly a full half-year earlier than it now looked would be possible. He supposed it was his fault, if fault it was. He liked to keep his fleet together rather than let it split up according to speed and then re-form as needed for the invasion proper. His admirals and generals insisted (though not too strongly if they knew what was good for them) that they didn't need all units of the fleet to be together at all times, but Luseferous preferred it. It seemed more cohesive, more impressive, just more tidy and pleasing somehow.

It also meant that the Beyonders would shoulder rather more of the responsibility for preparing Ulubis system for invasion than they might have expected, so that the invasion fleet's job would be all the easier and the Beyonders'—hopefully much-depleted—forces would be in a position of weakness relative to his own mass of ships.

"Still," Lascert said, "we imagine your advance units may be attacking even now."

"We've had some automated scout/warning ships and high-speed drone attack craft there or on their way for a while now," Luseferous told her. "Always best to be prepared for any eventuality. Some needed reprogramming but we believe they should be effective in beginning the softening-up process." He smiled. He watched her react to the clear diamond teeth. "I am a great believer in the usefulness of spreading a little panic, marshal. Better still, a lot of panic. After a long-enough exposure, people will welcome any power that brings an end to uncertainty, even if they might have resisted it before."

The marshal smiled too, though it looked like she was making an effort. "Of course. And we thought now might be an appropriate moment to talk in more depth about what you see your strategy being once you reach Ulubis."

"I intend to take it, marshal."

"Indeed. Of course, it may be quite well defended."

"I expect it might. That's why I've brought such a big fleet with me."

They were between systems, way out in the empty wilderness of near-nothingness less than a year from Ulubis. The Beyonder fast cruiser and its two escort destroyers had rendezvoused with his own fleet only hours earlier, skid-turning and matching velocities with a grace and rapidity that he could see his own naval people envied. Fine ships, indeed. Well, they had the ships and he had the systems; just another opportunity to trade, maybe. Now those three fast ships lay embedded in a fleet of over a thousand craft, even if they were rather plodding in comparison.

"May I be frank, Archimandrite?"

He gave her a good wide look at his deep red eyes. "I expect no less."

"We are concerned at the possible level of civilian casualties if Ulubis is assaulted over-aggressively."

*Now why would she say that?* Luseferous thought to himself with a sort of inward chuckle.

He looked at his private secretary, then at his generals and admirals. "Marshal," he said reasonably, "we are going to invade them. We are going to attack them." He smiled broadly, and could see his admirals and generals grinning along with him. "I think aggressiveness is… essential, yes?"

He could hear light laughter from one or two of his top brass. People thought that having people so in awe of you that they were frightened to tell you bad news and always laughed when you laughed (and so on) was a bad thing, and supposedly insulated you from what was really going on, but if you knew what you were doing, it didn't. You just had to adjust your perceptions. Sometimes everybody laughed, sometimes only a few, and sometimes who kept quiet and who made a noise told you a lot more than when you asked them to just speak out and tell you the truth. It was a sort of code, he supposed. He was just lucky to be naturally adept at it.

"Aggression and judgement are both required, Archimandrite," the marshal said. "We know you to possess both, of course." She smiled. He did not smile back. "We merely seek an assurance that your troops will act in a manner which will bring you further praise and greater fame."

"Praise?" the Archimandrite said. "I inspire terror, marshal. That's my strategy. I've found that to be the quickest and most effective way of ensuring that people learn what is good both for them and for me."

"For glory, then, Archimandrite."

"Be merciful for glory?"

The marshal thought about this for a moment. "Ultimately, yes."

"I shall conquer them as I see fit, marshal. We are partners in this. You don't tell me what to do."

"I am not trying to, Archimandrite," the marshal said quickly. "I accept what you must do, I am merely delivering a request regarding the manner in which it is done."

"And I have heard your request and I will pay it all due heed." This was a form of words Luseferous had heard somebody use once—he couldn't remember who or where—which, when he'd thought about it, he thought was rather good, especially if you said it slightly pompously: slowly, gravely even, keeping a straight face so that the person you were talking to thought you were taking them seriously and might even hope that you would do as they had asked rather than—at best—ignore them completely. At worst—as far as they were concerned—you'd do the opposite of whatever they asked, just to spite them, precisely to prove you wouldn't be pushed around... though that got tricky; then people might try to make you do one thing by pretending to favour another, and even without that complication you were still altering your behaviour because of something they had said, which was giving them a sort of power over you, when the whole point of everything the Archimandrite was doing was so that *nobody* could say they had any power over him.

Power was everything. Money was nothing without it. Even happiness was a distraction, a ghost, a hostage. What was happiness? Something people could take away from you. Happiness too often involved other people. It meant giving them power over you, giving them a hold on you that they could exercise whenever they wanted, taking away whatever it was that had made you happy.

Luseferous had known happiness and he'd had it taken away. His father, the only man he'd ever admired—even while hating the old bastard—had got rid of Luseferous's mother when she became old and less attractive, replacing her, when Luseferous was barely into his teens, with a succession of young, erotically desirable but soulless, uncaring, selfish young women, women he'd wanted for himself but despised at the same time. His mother was sent away. He never saw her again.

His father had been an Omnocrat for the Mercatoria, in the industrial complexes of the Leseum Systems. He'd started out at the bottom, as a Peculan (cynically, the very name implied that the office-bearer would need to be corrupt to make any sort of decent living, so incurring a history of criminality that could always be dredged up against them if they ever stepped out of line later). He'd become an Ovate, worked his way through the many gradations of that estate, then ascended to the office of Diegesian, in charge of a district of a city, then a small industrial city, then a medium-sized city, then a large city, then a continental capital. He became an Apparitor when his immediate superior died in the arms of a shared lover. That lover did very well for a while—his consort, in effect—then grew demanding and met an untimely end too.

His father had never told him if he'd had her killed.

Equally, he'd never told his father that the woman had lately become his lover, too.

From Apparitor his father rose to Peregal, in charge of first an orbiting fab/hab cluster, then a continent, then a sizeable moon, with all the trappings of power and wealth and glamour such a post presented in a thriving, connected set of systems such as Leseum. At this point, for the first time in his life, his father had appeared finally to appreciate the position he'd reached. He'd seemed to relax and start enjoying life.

It ended there. Finally setting himself up for the next jump, to Hierchon, his father, who had amassed a great fortune dispensing charters and contracts to the merchants and manufacturers of the many systems, took pity on a favoured Apparitor who was somewhat down on his luck, cut him in on a deal and a kickback he didn't really need to and found himself denounced, tried and beheaded for gross corruption within a month. The same young Apparitor then took his position.

Luseferous, convinced from early on that he could never compete with his father in his own sphere, and anyway always intrigued by the nature of religion and faith, had joined the Cessoria a few years earlier. He'd been a Piteer, a junior priest, at the time of his father's trial. They had made him one of his father's confessors, and he'd accompanied him to the execution ring. His father had been brave at first, then he'd broken. He'd started crying, begging, promising anything (but only all the things he'd already lost). He clutched at Luseferous's robes, howling and beseeching, burying his face. Luseferous knew they were watching him, that this moment was important for his future. He pushed his father away.

His rise through the Cessoria was swift.

He would never be as powerful as his father, but he was clever and capable and respected and on an upward course within an important but not too dangerous part of one of the greatest meta-civilisations the galaxy had seen. He might have been content with that, and never put himself in a position of weakness the way his father had.

Then the Disconnect happened. A swathe of portal destruction had swung across the million-star volume all around Leseum back in the time of the Arteria Collapse, leaving only the bunched Leseum systems themselves connected inside a vast volume of backwardness. The system of Leseum9 had been important, seemed vital and felt unthreatened until their own disconnect came millennia later, courtesy of some vast bicker within the ongoing chaos of the Scatter Wars, an essentially meaningless difference of opinion between three pretending sides which until then practically nobody had heard of. By the time it was all over, nobody would hear of those sides again, save as history. The damage was done, though; the portal near Leseum9 had been destroyed and an enormous volume around it had been cut off from the rest of the civilised galaxy.

Everything changed then, including what you had to do to retain power, and who might contest for absolute power.

His father, nevertheless, had taught Luseferous everything, one way or another, and one of the most important things was this: there was no plateau. In life, you were either on your way up or on your way down, and it was always better to be on your way up, especially as the only reliable way to keep going up was to use other people as stepping stones, as platforms, as scaffolding. The old saying about being nice to people on the way up so that they'd be nice to you when you were on your way back down was perfectly true, but it was a defeatist's saying, a loser's truism. Better to keep going up for ever, never to rest, never to relax, never to have to descend. The thought of what might happen to you at the hands of those you'd already offended, exploited and wronged on the way up—those that still lived—was just another incentive for the serious player never even to think about easing off the pace, let alone starting to fall back. The dedicated competitor would keep presenting himself with new challenges to take on and conquer, he would seek out new levels to ascend to, he would always look for new horizons to head towards.

Treat life like the game it was. This might be the truth behind the Truth, the religion Luseferous had been raised within as an obedient member of the Mercatoria: that nothing you did or seemed to do really mattered, because it was all—or might be all—a game, a simulation. It was all, in the end, just pretend. Even this Starveling cult he was titular head of was just something he'd made up because it sounded good. A variation of the Truth with added self-denial every now and again, the better to contemplate the gullibility of people. People would swallow anything, just anything at all. Apparently some people found this dismaying. He thought it was a gift, the most wonderful opportunity to take advantage of the weak-minded.

So you seemed cruel. So people died and suffered and grew up hating you. So what? There was at least a chance that none of it was real.

And if it *was* all real, well, then life was struggle. It always had been and it always would be. You recognised this and lived, or fell for the lie that progress and society had made struggle unnecessary, and just existed, were exploited, became prey, mere fodder.

He wondered to what extent even the supposedly feral and lawless Beyonders understood this basic truth. They let women rise to the pinnacle of their military command structure; that didn't bode particularly well. And the marshal didn't seem to have realised that when he'd said he'd heard her request and would pay it all due heed, it meant nothing.

"Well, thank you, Archimandrite," she said.

Still, he smiled. "You will stay? We shall have a banquet in your honour. We have had so little to celebrate out here, between the stars."

"An honour indeed, Archimandrite." The marshal gave that little head nod again.

*And we shall try to pick each other's brains over dinner*, he thought. *My, what highbrow fun. Give me a planet to plunder any day.*

∴

—Do you have any idea where we are? the colonel signalled, using a spot-laser. They reckoned this was their most secure form of comms.

—Zone Zero, the equatorial, Fassin sent.—Somewhere ahead of the latest big storm, about ten or twenty kilo-klicks behind the Ear Festoon. I'm checking the latest update they loaded before the drop.

They were floating in a slow eddy around a gentle ammonia upwell the diameter of a small planet, about two hundred klicks down from the cloud tops. The temperature outside was relatively balmy by human standards. There were levels, places in almost all gas-giants where a human could, in theory, exist exposed to the elements without any protective clothing at all. Of course they would probably need to be prone and lying in a tub of shock-gel or something similar because weighing six times what their skeleton was used to coping with would make standing up or moving around problematic, their lungs would have to be full of gillfluid or the like, to let them breathe within a mix of gases which included oxygen only as a trace element, and also to let their ribs and chest muscles work under the pressure of that gravitational vice, plus they wouldn't want to be exposed to a charged-particle shower, but all the same: by gas-giant great-outdoors standards, this was about as good as it humanly got.

Colonel Hatherence found it a bit hot, but then as an oerileithe she would be more at home closer to the cloud tops. She had already loudly pronounced her esuit undamaged and capable of protecting her anywhere from space-vacuum down to Nasqueron's ten-kilo-klick level, where the pressure would be a million times what it was here and the temperature somewhat more than half what it was on the surface of Ulubis star. Fassin chose not to join in a mine's-better-than-yours competition; his own gascraft was also space-capable in an emergency but untested at those depths.

He'd tried contacting Apsile in the drop ship but had come up with static. The passive positioning grid cast by the equatorial satellites was functioning but both scale-degraded and patchy, indicating there were some satellites gone or not working.

Knowing where you were in Nasqueron or any gas-giant was important, but still less than half the story. There was a solid rocky core to the planet, a spherical mass of about ten Earth-sized planets buried under seventy thousand vertical kilometres of hydrogen, helium and ice, and there were purists who would call the transition region between that stony kernel and the high-temperature, high-pressure water ice above it the planet's surface. But you had to be a real nit-picker even to pretend to take that definition seriously. Beyond the water ice—technically ice because it was effectively clamped solid by the colossal pressure, but at over twenty thousand degrees, confusingly hot for the human image of what ice was supposed to be like— came over forty thousand vertical kilometres of metallic hydrogen, then a deep transition layer to the ten-kilo-klick layer of molecular hydrogen which, if you were of an especially imaginative turn of mind, you might term a sea.

Above that, in the relatively thin—at a mere few thousand kilometres— but still vastly complicated layers reaching up towards space, were the regions where the Dwellers lived, in the contra-rotating belts and zones of rapidly spinning gases which—dotted with storms great and small, spattered with eddies, embellished with festoons, bars, rods, streaks, veils, columns, clumps, hollows, whirls, vortices, plume-heads, shear fronts and subduction flurries— girdled the planet. Where the Dwellers lived, where everything happened, there was no solid surface, and no features at all which lasted more than a few thousand years save for the bands of gas forever charging past each other, great spinning wheels of atmosphere whirling like the barely meshed cogs in some demented gearbox a hundred and fifty thousand kilometres across.

The convention was that the equatorial satellites followed the averaged-out progress of the broad equatorial zone, establishing a sort of stationary parameter-set from which everything else could be worked out relatively. But it was still confusing. Nothing was fixed. The zones and belts were relatively stable, but they shot past each other at combined speeds of what humans were used to thinking of as the speed of sound, and the margins between them changed all the time, torn by furiously curling eddies writhing this way and that, or thrown out, compressed and disturbed by giant storms like the Great Red Spot of the Solar System's Jupiter, riding between a zone travelling one way and a belt going the other like a vast squashed whirlpool caught in some mad clash of violently opposed currents, developing, raging and slowly dissipating over the centuries that humanity had been able to watch it. In a gas-giant, everything either evolved, revolved or just plain came and went, and the whole human mindset of surfaces, territory, land, sea and air was thrown into confusion.

Add the effects of a vastly powerful magnetic field, swathes of intense radiation and the sheer scale of the environment—you could drop the whole of a planet the size of Earth or Sepekte into a decent-sized gas-giant storm— and the human brain was left with a lot to cope with.

And all this before one took into account the—to be generous—playful attitude which the Dwellers themselves so often exhibited to general planetary orientation and the help, or otherwise, conventionally seen as being fit and proper to be extended to directionally challenged alien visitors.

—I thought we'd be in the midst of them, the colonel sent.

—Dwellers? Fassin asked, studying the complex schematic of who and what might be where at the moment.

—Yes, I imagined we would find ourselves in one of their cities.

They both looked around at the vast haze of slowly swirling gas, extending—depending on which frequency or sense one chose to experience it in—a few metres or a few hundred kilometres away on every side. It felt very still, even though they were part of the equatorial zone and so being spun around the planet at over a hundred metres a second, while swirling slowly around the upwelling and rising gradually with it too.

Fassin felt himself smiling in his wrapping of shock-gel.

—Well, there's a lot of Dwellers, but it's a big planet.

It seemed odd to be explaining this to a creature whose kind had evolved in planets like this and who surely ought to be familiar with the scale of a gas-giant, but then oerileithe, in Fassin's admittedly limited experience of them, often did display a kind of half-resentful awe towards Dwellers, entirely consistent with a belief that the instant you dropped beneath the cloud tops you'd find yourself surrounded by massed ranks of magisterial Dwellers and their astoundingly awesome structures (a misapprehension it was hard to imagine any Dweller even considering correcting). The oerileithe were an ancient people by human standards and by those of the vast majority of species in the developed galaxy, but—with a civilisation going back about eight hundred thousand years—they were mere mayflies by Dweller standards.

A thought occurred to Fassin.—You ever been in a Dweller planet before, colonel?

—Indeed not. A privilege denied until now. Hatherence made a show of looking about.—Not unlike home, really.

Another thought occurred.—You *did* receive clearance? Didn't you, colonel?

—Clearance, Seer Taak?

—To come down. To enter Nasq.

—Ah, the colonel sent.—Not as such, I do confess. It was thought that I would be remote delving with you and your colleagues, from the Shared Facility on the Third Fury moon. Braam Ganscerel himself took the time to assure me of this personally. No objection was raised regarding such a presence. I believe that permission was in the process of being sought for me to accompany you physically into the atmosphere if that became necessary—as indeed it now has—however, the last that I heard in that regard indicated that the relevant clearances had yet to materialise. Why? Do you envisage there being a problem?

*Oh, shit.*

—The Dwellers, Fassin told her,—can be... pernickety about that sort of thing. *Pernickety*, he thought. They were liable to declare the colonel an honorary child, give her a half-hour start and set off to *hunt* her.—They take their privacy quite seriously. Unauthorised entries are severely discouraged.

—Well, I'm aware of that.

—You are? Good.

—I shall throw myself upon their mercy.

—Right. I see.

*You are either quite brave and possessed of a decent sense of humour*, Fassin thought, *or you really should have done more homework.*

—So, Seer Fassin Taak, in which direction ought we to proceed?

—Should be a CloudTunnel about four hundred klicks... that way, Fassin sent, turning the gascraft to point more or less south and slightly down.—Unless it's moved, obviously.

—Shall we? the colonel said, drifting in that direction.

—Going to ping one of our sats, let them know we're alive, Fassin told her.

—This is wise?

*Was it wise?* Fassin wondered. There had been some sort of attack on the Seer infrastructure around Nasqueron, but that didn't mean the whole near-planet environment had been taken over. On the other hand...

—How fast can that esuit go? he asked the colonel.

—At this density, about four hundred metres per second. About half that, on sustained cruise.

Fassin's arrowcraft could just about keep pace with that. Disappointing. He was still hoping to give the colonel the slip at some point. It looked like he wasn't going to be able to just outrun her.

—Ping sent, he told Hatherence.—Let's go.

They went, quickly. They'd got about a hundred metres away when a flash of violet light ripped the cloud apart behind them and a stark, short-lived beam-cluster splayed through the volume of gas they'd been floating within a few seconds earlier. Further beams radiated out from the initial target point, pulsing through the atmosphere in slowly spreading semi-random stabs. One flicked into existence about fifty metres from them, booming and crackling. All the rest were much further away and after a minute or so they ceased altogether.

—Somebody would seem to be ill-disposed towards you, Seer Taak, the colonel sent as they flew through the gas.

—So it would appear.

The flash and EMP came a couple of minutes after that. A low, rumbling concussion caught up with them some time later.

—Was that a *nuke*? Fassin sent. His instruments seemed to leave no other interpretation, but he still found it hard to believe.

—I am unaware of any phenomenon able to mimic one so convincingly.

—Fucking hell.

—I float corrected. Somebody would seem to be *extremely* ill-disposed towards you, Seer Taak.

—The Dwellers are *not* going to be happy, he told Hatherence.—Only they're allowed to let off nukes in the atmosphere, he explained.—And it isn't even fireworks season.

They found the CloudTunnel about where Fassin had thought it ought to be, only a hundred kilometres out laterally and two kilometres further down: bang on by Nasqueron standards. The CloudTunnel was a bundle of a dozen or so carbon-carbon tubes like some vast, barely braided cable-cluster floating in the midst of an unending cloudscape of gently billowing yellow, orange and ochre. The CloudTunnel's two main tubes were about sixty metres in diameter, the smallest—basically comms and telemetry wave guides—less than half a metre. The whole cluster had looked thread-thin when they'd first caught sight of it, tens of kilometres away, but up close it looked like a hawser fit to tether a moon. A great, deep rushing sound rumbled from inside the two main pipes.

—What now? the colonel sent.

—We see if my vicarious kudos credit is still good.

Fassin used one of the arrowcraft's manipulators to prod one of the wave guides, working the filaments through the tube's protective sheath without breaking it. A hair-thin wire extended into the matrix of light filling the narrow tube. Information streamed from the far end of the wire, into the gascraft's biomind, its transitional systems and then into Fassin's head, forming a coded chaos of babbling sound, wildly scintillating visuals and other confused sensory experiences. The interruption in the light streams had already been noticed and allowed for. A pulse of information aimed right at the filament sent an identity request and inquired whether assistance was required, otherwise stop interfering with a public information highway.

—A human, Fassin Taak, privileged to be Slow Seer at the court of the Nasqueron Dwellers, he sent.—I'd like some assistance in the shape of transport at the given location, bound for Hauskip City.

He was told to wait.

"Fassin Taak, Out-Bander, Stranger, Alien, Seer, Human! And

…what's this?"

"This is Colonel Hatherence of the Mercatorial Military-Religious Order the Shrievalty Ocula, an oerileithe."

"Good day, Dweller Y'sul," Hatherence said. They had switched to using ordinary sound-speech.

"A little dweller! How fascinating! Not a child, then?"

Y'sul, a sizeable mid-adult a good nine metres or so in diameter, rolled through the gas and, extending one long spindle-arm, clunked a fist-bunch (bink-bink-bink!) on the esuit of the Colonel.

"Hellooo in there!" Y'sul said.

Hatherence's discus of esuit leaned to one side under the rain of not-so-gentle blows. "Pleased to meet you," she replied tersely.

"Not a child," Fassin confirmed.

They were in a giant bowl-like room, roofed with slate-diamond micrometres thin, in a Thickeneers' Club in Hauskip City.

Hauskip lay within the equatorial zone of Nasqueron, one of the hundred thousand or so major conurbations in that particular atmospheric band. Seen from the right angle in a sympathetic light, it looked a lot like the internal workings of an ancient mechanical clock, multiplied and magnified several thousand times. From far enough away, or just seen in a schematic, it resembled millions of toothed-looking wheels caught up in amongst each other, with larger sets of wheels interconnecting with them through hubs and spines and spindles, themselves linking up with still greater sets of wheels. The whole mighty, slowly gyrating and spinning assemblage, easily a couple of hundred kilometres in diameter, floated within a thick soup of gas a hundred kilometres beneath the cloud tops.

The city was the hub for several CloudTunnel lines. Once an empty car had made its way to the access hatch nearest to where Fassin and Hatherence pitched up alongside the CloudTunnel, it had taken two changes of line, riding in the same car, for Fassin and the colonel to get there through the network of partially evacuated, high-speed transit tubes. The whole journey had taken one of Nasqueron's short day-night cycles. They had each slept for most of the time, though just before Fassin had dozed off, the colonel had said, "We go on. You agree, major? We continue our mission. Until we are ordered to cease."

"I agree," he said. "We go on."

The TunnelCar had docked, sphinctered its way through a TunnelBud wall in Hauskip's Central Station and sped through the gelatinous atmosphere straight to the equatorial Eighth Progression Thickeneers' Club, where Y'sul, Fassin's long-time guide/mentor/guard had been attending a party to celebrate the Completion and Expulsion Ceremony of one of the club's members.

Dwellers started out looking like anorexic manta rays—this was in their brief, occasionally hunted childhood phase—then grew, fattened, split most of the way down the middle (adolescence, kind of), shifted from a horizontal to a vertical axis and ended up, as adults, basically, resembling something like a pair of large, webbed, fringed cartwheels connected by a short, thick axle with particularly bulbous outer hubs onto each of which had been fastened a giant spider crab.

Part of the transition from recent- to mid-adulthood involved a period called Thickening, when the slim and flimsy discs of youth became the stout and sturdy wheels of later life, and it was customary for Dwellers to join a club of their approximate contemporaries while this was taking place. There was no specific reason for Dwellers to band together at this point in their lives, they just in general enjoyed joining clubs, sodalities, orders, leagues, parties, societies, associations, fellowships, fraternities, groups, guilds, unions, fractionals, dispensationals and recreationalities, while always, of course, leaving open the possibility of taking part in ad hoc non-ceremonial serendipitous one-time gatherings as well. The social calendar was crowded.

Y'sul had invited them to this private book-crystal-lined library room in his Thickeneers' Club rather than to his home so that, as he explained, if they were too boring or in too great a hurry, he could get back without an over-great delay to his chums taking part in the ceremonial dinner and spree in the banqueting hall below.

"So, Fassin, good to see you!" Y'sul said. "Why have you brought this little dweller with you? Is she food?"

"No, of course not. She is a colleague."

"Of course! Though there are no oerileithe Seers."

"She is not a Seer."

"Then not a colleague?"

"She has been sent to escort me, by the Mercatorial Military-Religious Order the Shrievalty Ocula."

"I see." Y'sul, dressed in his best smart-but-casual finery, all brightly coloured fringes and lacily ornate ruffs, rocked back, rotating slightly, then came forward again. "No, I don't! What am I saying? What is this 'Ocula'?"

"Well…"

It took a while to tell. After about a quarter of an hour—this all, thankfully, in real-time, with no slow-down factor—Fassin thought he'd pretty much briefed Y'sul as well and as completely as he could without giving too much away. The colonel had contributed now and again, not that Y'sul seemed to have taken any notice of her.

Y'sul was about fifteen thousand years old, a full-adult who was perhaps another one or two millennia away from becoming a traav, the first stage of Prime-hood. At nine metres vertical diameter (not including his semi-formal dinner clothes, whose impressive body ruff added another metre), he was about as large as a Dweller ever got. His double disc was nearly five metres across, the modestly clothed central axle barely visible as a separate entity, more of an unexpected thinning between the two great wheels. Dwellers shrank very slightly as they aged after mid-adulthood and slowly lost both hub and fringe limbs until, by the time they were in their billions, they were often nearly limb-disabled.

Even then they could still get about, as a rule. Their motive force came from a system of vanes extending from the inner and outer surfaces of their two main discs. These extended to beat—sometimes twisting to add extra impetus or to steer—and lay flat on the backstroke, so that a moving Dweller seemed to roll through the atmosphere. This was called roting. Very old Dwellers often lost the use of—or just lost—the vanes on the outside of their discs, but usually retained those on the inside so that no matter how decrepit they might get, they could still wheel themselves around.

"It boils down," Y'sul said at the end, "to the fact that you are looking for the choal Valseir, to resume subject-specific studies in a library within his control."

"Pretty much," Fassin agreed.

"I see."

"Y'sul, you have always been a great help to me. Can you help me in this?"

"Problem," Y'sul said.

"Problem?" Fassin asked.

"Valseir is dead and his library has been consigned to the depths, or split up, possibly at random, amongst his peers, allies, families, co-specialists, enemies or passers-by. Probably all of the above."

"Dead?" Fassin said. He let horror show on the signalling carapace of the gascraft; a quite specific whorl pattern which indicated being intellectually and emotionally appalled at the demise of a Dweller friend/acquaintance not least because they had died in the course of pursuing a line of inquiry that one was oneself deeply fascinated by. "But he was only a choal! He was billions of years from dying!"

Valseir had been about a million and a half years old and on the brink of passing from the Cuspian level to that of Sage. Choal was the last phase of being a Cuspian. The average age of progressing from Cuspian-choal to Sage-child was over two million years but Valseir had been judged by his elders and allegedly betters as being ready even at such a modest count of time. He was, or had been, a one-and-a-half-million-year-old prodigy. He had also, last time Fassin had seen him, seemed strong, vigorous and full of life. Agreed, he spent most of his life with his rotary snout stuck in a library and didn't get out much, but still Fassin could not believe he was dead. The Dwellers didn't even have any diseases he could have died of. How could he be *dead*?

"Yachting accident, if I recall," Y'sul said. "Do I?" Fassin sensed the Dweller radioing an inforequest to the patch-walls of the library room. "Yes, I do! Yes, a yachting accident. His StormJammer got caught in a particularly vicious eddy and it came apart on him. Skewered with a main beam or a yard arm or something. On a brighter note, they salvaged most of the yacht before it descended to the Depths. He was a very keen sailor. Terribly competitive."

"When?" Fassin asked. "I heard nothing."

"Not long ago," Y'sul said. "Couple of centuries at the most."

"There was nothing on the news nets."

"Really? Ah! Wait." (Another radioed inforequest.) "Yes. I understand he left instructions that in the event of his death it was to be regarded as a private matter." Y'sul flexed his hub-mounted spindle-arms on either side. All of them. Right out. "Quite understand! Done the same myself."

"Is there any record of what happened to his library?" Fassin asked.

Y'sul rocked back again, a pair of giant conical wheels rotating slowly away, then pitching forward once more. He hung in mid-gas and said, "D'you know what?"

"What?"

"No, there isn't! Is that not strange?"

"We… I would really like to look into this matter further, Y'sul. Can you help us in this?"

"I most certainly… ah, talking about news nets, there is something about an unauthorised fusion explosion not far from the point you accessed the CloudTunnel from. Anything to do with you?"

*Oh, shit,* Fassin thought, again. "Yes. It would appear that somebody is trying to kill me. Or possibly the colonel here." He waved at Hatherence's esuit, still floating next to him. She had been silent for some time. Fassin was not certain this was a good sign.

"I see," Y'sul said. "And talking about the good colonel, I am struggling to discover her authorisation. For being here at all, I mean."

"Well," Fassin said, "we were forced to take refuge in Nasqueron, some time before we imagined it would be necessary, due to unprovoked hostile action. The colonel's permissions were being sought some time before we left but had not yet come through when we had to make our emergency entry. The colonel is, technically, here without explicit permission, and therefore throws herself upon your mercy as a shipwreckee, a wartime asylumee and a fellow gas-giant dweller in need of shelter." Fassin turned and looked at the colonel, who shifted about her vertical axis to return his gascraft-directed gaze. "She claims sanctuary," he finished.

"Provisionally given, of course," Y'sul said. "Though the precise meaning of 'unprovoked' might be challenged in a wider context, and the exact definition of 'shipwreckee', equally, could well be open to dispute if one wished to be picky. That aside, though, do I understand there is some sort of dispute in progress, out amongst you people?"

"You understand correctly," Fassin told the Dweller.

"Oh, not another one of your wars, please!" Y'sul protested, with a rolling-back of his whole body which was actually relatively easy for a human to interpret, correctly, as an equivalent of rolling one's eyes. (Though, to be fair, there were quite a lot of Dweller gestures with this translation.)

"Well, pretty much, yes," Fassin told him.

"Your passion for doing each other harm never ceases to amaze, delight and horrify!"

"I'm told there is to be a Formal War between Zone 2 and Belt C," Fassin said.

"I too am told that!" Y'sul said brightly. "Do you really think it will happen? I'm not optimistic, frankly. Some appallingly good negotiators have been drafted in, I understand... Ah. Your hull carapace, doing the job of standing in, feebly, for the body you so sadly lack, bears marks upon it which I take to mean you were being sarcastic earlier."

"Never mind, Y'sul."

"Right then, shan't. Now then: Valseir. There is a point of congruency."

"There is?"

"Yes!"

"With what? Between what and what?"

"His demise and this war we've been promised!"

"Really?"

"Yes! His old study—it is in the current zone of disputation, I believe."

"But if it's already been broken up—" Fassin began.

"Oh, there are bound to be back-ups, and I'm not even sure the old fellow has been finally put to rest."

"After two hundred years?"

"Come now, Fassin, there were matters of probate."

"And it's in the war zone?"

"Very likely, yes! Isn't it exciting? I think we ought to go there immediately!" Y'sul waved all his limbs at once. "Let's form an expedition! We shall go together." He looked at Hatherence. "You can even bring your little friend."

—I have been considering whether to attempt to communicate with your Shared Facility, via your satellites or directly, the colonel told him.

—I wouldn't, Fassin sent.—But if you decide you must, tell me before you try. I want to be well out of the volume.

—You think the same sort of attack directed against us following your "ping" might be directed against us here?

—Probably not here, in a Dweller city. But then, why risk it? We don't know that whoever's been shooting at us quite understands what they'd be letting themselves in for, so they might just waste us and have to deal with the consequences later. We won't be around to jeer.

—We need to find out what is going on, Major Taak, Hatherence informed him.

—I know, and I'm going to send a request for information up to a sat from a remote site as soon as I've checked out what's been going on via the local nets.

The colonel floated over to look at the enormous though ancient and highly directional flat screen which Fassin was using in his attempt to find out what had been happening. They were in Y'sul's home, a ramshackle wheel-house in a whole vast district of equally shabby-looking wheel-houses hanging on skinny spindles underneath the city's median level like a frozen image of an entire junkyard's worth of exploded gearboxes.

Y'sul had escorted them back from his club in a state of some excitement. Then he'd left them alone, taken his servant Sholish and gone off in search of a decent tailor—his usual tailor had most inconveniently taken it into his mind to change trades and become a Dreadnought rating; probably trying to get in on the ground floor of this upcoming war.

—What have you found? the colonel asked, watching the flat screen fill with an image of the Third Fury moon.—Hmm. The moon appears almost undamaged.

—This is an old recording, Fassin explained.—I'm trying to find an updated one.

—Any mention of the hostilities?

—Not very much, Fassin told her, using a manipulator to work the massive, stiff controls of the old screen.—There's been a mention on a minority radio news service, but that's it.

—It is regarded as news, though? This is encouraging, I think?

—Well, don't get too excited, Fassin sent.—We are talking about a station some amateurs run for the few people like themselves who are actually interested in things happening in the rest of the system; maybe a few thousand Dwellers out of a planetary population of five or ten billion.

—The number of Dwellers in Nasqueron is really that uncertain?

—Oh, I've seen estimates as low as two billion, as high as two hundred, even three.

—I encountered this degree of uncertainty in my research, Hatherence said as Fassin switched manually between channels, data sets and image-trails.—I recall thinking it must be a mistake. How can one be two base-ten orders of magnitude out? Can't one just ask the Dwellers? Don't they know themselves how many they are?

—You can certainly ask, Fassin agreed. He put some humour into his signal.—An old tutor of mine used to say of questions like this that the answers will prove far more illuminating regarding Dweller psychology than they will concerning their actual subject.

—They lie to you or they don't know themselves?

—That is a good question too.

—They must have an idea, the Colonel protested.—A society has to know how many people it contains, otherwise how would it plan infrastructure and so on?

Fassin felt himself smiling.—That's how it would work in pretty much any other society, he agreed.

—There are those who would assert that Dwellers are not in fact civilised, the colonel said thoughtfully,—that they could scarcely be said to possess a society in any single planet, and on a galactic scale cannot be said to constitute a civilisation at all. They exist rather in a state of highly developed barbarism.

—I'm familiar with the arguments, Fassin told her.

—Would you agree?

—No. This is a society. We are in a *city*. And even just in the one planet, this is a civilisation. I know the definitions will have changed over the years and you might take a different view from me, but in the history of my planet we'd refer to a civilisation based around a single river system or on a small island.

—I forget how small-scale one has to think when dealing with planets with solid-surface living-environments, the colonel said, apparently without meaning to insult.—But even so, the definition of a civilisation has to move on when one ascends to the galactic stage, and the Dwellers, taken as a whole, might seem deficient.

—I think it comes down to one's own definition of the terms, Fassin said.— Hold on; this looks promising.

He swung back from a mosaic of sub-screens to a single moving image. Third Fury again, though this time looking hazier, less defined, and shot from some distance away. The shallow domes of the Shared Facility were obvious if not clear, down near one tipped edge of the little moonlet. A flash on the surface away to one side, and a semi-spherical cloud of debris, spreading. A glowing crater left where the flash had come from.

—This looks like yesterday, Hatherence said.

—Does, doesn't it? Fassin agreed.—Looks like it was taken from high up on Belt A or the south of Zone 2. Just some amateur pointing a camera. Fassin found how to spin the stored recording back and then forward, then discovered how to zoom in.—And that's us.

They watched a cerise spot appear on a glittering blister near the edge of the Shared Facility, and could just make out the grainily defined debris of the hangar dome blowing outward in front of a sudden haze of quickly dissipating mist. A tiny dark grey dot rose from the shattered dome and crawled away: the drop ship, making its desperate dive for the planet.

Fassin spun the recording forward. The moon's position altered quickly, flying away across the dark sky as Third Fury continued on its orbit and whoever was recording the images was whirled away in the opposite direction by the twenty-thousand-kilometre-wide jet stream beneath them.— Definitely Band A, Fassin said.

A brilliant white flash washed out the whole screen. It faded, and a crater kilometres across was left. Debris spread everywhere like a flower's seed-head, just ready to shed, caught in a sudden hurricane. The interior of the crater was white, yellow, orange, red. The debris continued to spread. It looked like most of it would stay in more or less the same orbit as Third Fury itself.

They both watched in silence. The moon had changed shape. It wobbled, seemed to partially collapse in on itself, slowly, plastically resuming a spherical form after losing so much of its earlier mass. Yellow cloud tops came up in a near-flat line to meet it and the small glowing globe spun under the horizon.

Fassin let the recording play out and start to loop. He stopped it. The screen froze on the recording's first image of Third Fury, almost overhead, just after the first impact.

—That did not look like a survivable event, the colonel sent. Her sent voice sounded quiet.

—I think you're right.

—I am very sorry. How many people would have been in the Shared Facility base?

—A couple of hundred.

—I saw no sign of your Master Technician's craft, or of the attacks on us once we quit the drop ship.

Fassin compared the recording's time code with the gascraft's own event list.—Those happened after what we saw here, he told the colonel.—Over the horizon from where this recording was taken, anyway.

—So much for back-up or reinforcements. The colonel turned towards him.—We still go on, though, yes?

—Yes.

—So, now what, Fassin Taak?

—We need to talk to some people.

"So you want to communicate with your own kind?" Y'sul asked.

"Via a relay at a remote site," Fassin said.

"Why haven't you done so already?"

"I wanted to get your permission."

"You don't need my permission. You just find a remote dish and send away. I suspect any vicarious effect on my kudos level will be too small to measure."

They were in an antechamber of the city's Administrator. The antechamber was a sizeable room furnished with wall hangings made from ancient CloudHugger hides, all yellow-red and whorled. A few sported the holes where the creatures had been punctured. One curved section of wall was a giant window, looking out over the vast floating scape of wheels that was Hauskip. Evening was starting to descend and lights were coming on throughout the city. Y'sul floated over to the window and caused it to hinge down by the unsubtle tactic of bumping into it reasonably hard. He then floated out over the impromptu bow of balcony so produced, muttering something about liking the view and maybe moving his own house up here. A breeze blew in, ruffling the old CloudHugger hides as though their long-dead occupants were still somehow fleeing from their hunters.

Colonel Hatherence leaned over towards Fassin.—This kudos thing, then, she sent.—It is *really* how they calculate their worth?

—I'm afraid so.

—So it's the truth! I thought it was a joke.

—Distinguishing between the two is not a Dweller strong point.

Y'sul wandered back, failing to shut the window. His vanes made a quiet burring noise as he roted through the gas towards them. "Give me the message," he said. "I'll forward it."

"Via an out-of-the-way transceiver?" Fassin asked.

"Of course!"

"Well, just send to Sept Bantrabal, letting them know I'm all right and asking whether they're okay at their end. I imagine they already know what happened to the Third Fury moon. You might ask them whether anything has been heard of Master Technician Apsile and the drop ship which escaped the moon's assault, and what happened to the ships supposed to be protecting Third Fury."

"Ahem," the colonel said.

They both looked at her. "Is this wise?" she asked.

"You mean should I pretend to be dead?" Fassin said.

"Yes."

"That did occur to me. But there are people I'd like to know I'm alive." He thought of that glimpse of a flash which might have been something hitting 'glantine while Third Fury was being bombarded. "And I'd like to know my friends and family are all right."

"Of course," the colonel said. "However, I wonder if it might be more sensible for me to communicate with my superiors first. We might ask Dweller Y'sul here to let me use this remote relay. Once a more secure link had been established, perhaps via one of the warships, which I assume are still somewhere around the planet, a message might be sent to your Sept to let them know you are well. None of which need take long."

While Hatherence had been speaking, Y'sul had floated right up to her, seemingly intent on peering through the front plate of her esuit, which was in fact completely opaque, and indeed armoured. Eventually he was within a centimetre of her, towering above the oerileithe. The colonel did not retreat. One of Y'sul's rim limbs tapped—more delicately this time—on the colonel's esuit casing.

"Would you mind not doing that, sir?" she said frostily.

"Why are you still inside that thing, little dweller?" Y'sul asked.

"Because I am evolved for higher, colder levels with a different gas-mix and pressure gradient, Dweller Y'sul."

"I see." Y'sul drew back. "And you have a very strange accent and way with grammar. I swear this human speaks better than you do. What were you saying again?"

"I was asking you kindly to refrain from making physical contact with my esuit."

"No, before that."

"I was suggesting I make contact with my superiors."

"Military superiors?"

"Yes."

Y'sul turned to Fassin. "That sounds more interesting than your plan, Fassin."

"Y'sul, two hundred of my people died yesterday. If not more. I'd like—"

"Yes yes yes, but—"

"I might have to signal 'glantine direct, if no satellites are left," Hatherence was saying, as a tall door swung up in one wall and a Dweller in ceremonial clothes poked its rim out.

"I'll see you now," said the City Administrator.

The Administrator's office was huge, the size of a small stadium. It was ringed with holo-screen carrels. Fassin counted a hundred or so of the study stations, though only a few were occupied by Dwellers, mostly fairly young. There were no windows but the ceiling was diamond leaf, with most of the sections slid round to leave the place open to the rapidly darkening sky. Floatlamps bobbed, casting a soft yellow light over them as they followed the Administrator to her sunken audience area in the centre of the giant room.

"You are pregnant!" Y'sul exclaimed. "How delightful!"

"So people keep telling me," the Administrator said sourly. Dwellers were, for want of a better term, male for over ninety-nine per cent of their lives, only changing to the female form to become pregnant and give birth. Becoming female and giving birth was regarded as a social duty; the fact that the obligation was more honoured than not made it unique in Dweller mores. It contributed mightily to one's kudos tally and anyway had a sort of sentimental attraction for all but the most determinedly misanthropic members of the species (statistically, about forty-three per cent). Still, it was undeniably a burden, and very few Dwellers went through the experience without complaining mightily about it.

"I myself have thought of becoming female, oh, several times!" Y'sul said.

"Well, it's overrated," the City Administrator told him. "And particularly burdensome when one had an invitation to the forthcoming war that one is now apparently morally obliged to turn down. Please; take a dent."

They floated to a series of hollows in the audience area and rested gently within them.

"Why, I too hope to be going to the war!" Y'sul said brightly. "Well, somewhere very near it, at least. I have only just now returned from my tailor's after being measured for the most lately fashionable conflict attire."

"Oh, really?" the Administrator said. "Who's your tailor? Mine just left for the war."

"Not Fuerliote?" Y'sul exclaimed.

"The same!"

"He was mine also!"

"Just the best."

"Absolutely."

"No, I had to go to Deystelmin."

"Is he any good?"

"Weeeelll." Y'sul waggled his whole double-discus. "One lives in hope. Good mirror-side manner, as it were, but will it translate into a flattering cut? That's the question one has to ask oneself."

"I know," agreed the Administrator. "And off to become a junior officer on a Dreadnought!"

"Not even that! A rating!"

"No!"

"Yes!"

"Very lowly, for someone so distinguished!"

"I know, but a smart move. Getting in as a rating before the recruitment window even properly opens makes sense. The smoking-uniform effect."

"Ah! Of course!"

Fassin tried making a throat-clearing noise in the midst of all this, but to no effect.

—The smoking-uniform effect? the colonel light-whispered to him.

—Dead men's shoes, Fassin explained.—They only promote from within once hostilities have begun. If he's lucky this tailor's Dreadnought will suffer heavy damage and lose a few officers and he'll end up an officer after all. If he's *really* lucky he could rise to admiral.

Hatherence thought about this.—Would a tailor, however distinguished, necessarily make a good admiral?

—Probably no worse than the one he'd be replacing.

The problem was that to the Dwellers all professions were in effect hobbies, all posts and positions sinecures. This tailor that Y'sul and the City Administrator were babbling on about would have had no real need to be a tailor, he was just somebody who'd found he possessed an aptitude for the pastime (or, more likely, for the gossiping and fussing generally associated with it). He would take on clients to increase his kudos, the level of which would increase proportionally the more powerful were the people he tailored for, so that somebody in a position of civil power would constitute a favoured client, even if that position of power had come about through a lottery, some arcanely complicated rota system or plain old coercive voting—jobs like that of City Administrator were subject to all those regimes and more, depending on the band or zone concerned, or just which city was involved. The City Administrator, in return, would be able to drop casually into just the right conversations the fact she had such a well-known, high-kudos tailor.

Obviously Y'sul had had sufficient kudos of his own to be able to engage the services of this alpha-outfitter too. People further down the pecking order would have employed less well-connected tailors, or just got their clothes from Common, which was Dweller for, in this particular case, off-the-peg, and in general just meant mass-produced, kudos-free, available-as-a-matter-of-right-just-because-you're-a-Dweller... well, pretty much anything, up to and including spaceships.

Though having seen round a few Dweller spaceships, Fassin thought the stack-'em-high-and-give-them-away-free approach had its limitations.

"Indeed," Y'sul was saying. "My own bid for JO status has been languishing for centuries and wasn't even mentioned this time round. Entering as a rating seems demeaning, but it could pay off big if there are casualties."

"Of course, of course," the Administrator said, then fastened her gaze on the colonel. "What's this?"

"An oerileithe, a little dweller," Y'sul said, with what sounded like pride.

"Gracious! Not a child?"

"Or food. I asked."

"Pleased to meet you," the colonel said with as much dignity as she could muster. An oerileithe, it appeared, attracted even less respect amongst Dwellers than Fassin—and, he suspected, the colonel herself—had expected. The oerileithe had evolved relatively recently, quite independently of the vast, unutterably ancient mainstream of galactic Dwellerdom and as such were seen by their more venerable co-gas-giant-inhabitants as something between an annoying collective loose end and a bunch of impudent, planet-usurping interlopers.

"And this must be the Slow Seer." The Administrator looked briefly at Fassin's gascraft before returning her gaze to Y'sul. "Do we need to talk slowly for it?"

"No, Administrator," Fassin said before Y'sul could reply. "I am running on your timescale at the moment."

"How fortunate!" She flicked to one side and stabbed at a screen remote, her frontal radius edge lit up by the holo's glow. "Hmm. I see. So all the mayhem of the last day or two is your fault, then?"

"Has there been much mayhem, ma'am?"

"Well, the partial destruction of a close-orbit moon would fit most people's definition of mayhem," the Administrator said pleasantly. "An attractive feature in the sky whenever one ventured towards the cloud tops. Been there millions of years, slagged within a few per cent of breaking up completely, a ring of debris scattered round its orbit, that orbit itself changed significantly, causing everything else up there to have to shuffle round to accommodate the alteration, a small bombardment of debris across three bands, some chunks narrowly missing several items of infrastructure with more than sentimental value and others setting off automatic planetary-defence laser batteries, a cascade of satellite destruction that has yet to be put entirely right. Oh, and an unauthorised fusion explosion. Middle of nowhere, granted, but still. None of this, happily, within my jurisdiction, but trouble does appear to be rather following you around, human Taak, and here you are in my city." The Administrator rolled fractionally towards Fassin's gascraft. "Thinking of staying long?"

"Well—" Fassin began.

"The human is under my protection, Administrator!" Y'sul interrupted. "I vouch for it entirely and will continue to accept all kudos consequences regarding its actions. I shall take all steps necessary to safeguard it from whatever hostile forces may wish it ill. May I count on your support for the expedition the human insists on making into the war zone?"

"Given," the Administrator said.

"How splendid! We can be ready to leave within a couple of days. Especially if the tailor Deystelmin is persuaded to prioritise my combat-clothing order."

"I'll have a word."

"Too kind! I swear I shall never nominate you for a coercive vote again!"

"My gratitude knows no bounds."

If Dwellers could grit their teeth, Fassin thought, the Administrator's words would have been spoken through them. "Excuse me, ma'am," he said.

"Yes, human Taak?"

"Have you any word on events elsewhere in the system?"

"As I say, the various rings and moons are shifting fractionally in their orbits to accommodate—"

"I think he means the stellar system, not that of Nasqueron," Colonel Hatherence said.

The two Dwellers turned to look at her. Dwellers had sensing bands all the way round their outer rims, plus eye bubbles low on their outer hubs. They were not known as the best glarers in the galaxy but they were always willing to give it their best shot. To a Dweller, their own planet was pretty much everything. Most gas-giants had many more moons than the average stellar system possessed planets, and most radiated a lot more energy than they received from the star they orbited, their heat-transfer systems, weather and ecology arising largely from processes internal to the planet itself, not dependent on sunlight. Their inhabitants had to pay close attention to the skies, basically to watch out for incoming, but even that consideration led to an obviously gas-giant-centred way of thinking. The local star and the rest of its planetary system was of relatively little interest to the average Dweller.

"That is not quite what I meant," Fassin told them quickly. "The moon 'glantine, for example; has it been harmed?"

"Not to my knowledge," the Administrator said, with another stern look at Hatherence.

"And the military ships that were in orbit around Third Fury?" the colonel asked.

(—Shh! Fassin signalled Hatherence.

—No! she sent back.)

"What ships?" the Administrator said, apparently mystified.

"How about the planet Sepekte?" Fassin said.

"I have no idea," the Administrator told him. She fixed her gaze on Fassin. "Is this why you wished to see me? To ask after the welfare of moons and distant planets?"

"No, ma'am. The reason that I wanted to see you is that I am worried that there may be a threat to Nasqueron."

"You are?" blurted Y'sul.

"Really?" the Administrator said with a sigh.

Even Hatherence was turned to look at him.

"There is a war beginning amongst the Quick, ma'am," Fassin told the Administrator. "It is going to come to Ulubis and it is not impossible that some of the forces taking part may wish to involve Nasqueron and its Dwellers in that war in some way."

The Administrator rolled fractionally back and sucked her outer trim-frill in, the Dweller equivalent of a frown.

(—Major? the colonel sent.—You said nothing of this. What do you base this on? Is there something you're not telling me?

—A hunch. Just trying to get their attention. And I should point out that it's considered impolite to signal-whisper like this.)

The Administrator continued to look at Fassin for a moment, then turned to Y'sul. "Is this human normally mad?"

Y'sul made a sucking sound. "Down to definitions."

"Nasqueron might be vulnerable to a further bombardment," Fassin persisted. "Even to some sort of raid."

"Ha!" Y'sul laughed.

"We are not defenceless, human Taak!" the Administrator said loudly.

*No, but your spaceships are leaky antiques and your planetary defences are set up for dumb rocks*, Fassin thought wearily. *You talk a good defence, but if the Epiphany 5 invaders decide to attack, or the Mercatoria decides I'm dead and they plump for a more obvious way to get hold of whatever might be in Valseir's library, you won't be able to do much to stop them. Going on what I've seen, a single Navarchy Military destroyer could lay waste to your whole planet, over time.*

"Of course not," he agreed. "But I would ask you to pass this information on to the relevant authorities. You will be still better defended if you are prepared."

"I'll bear that in mind," the Administrator told him levelly.

*Oh shit*, Fassin thought. *You're going to do fuck all. You aren't going to bother telling anybody.*

Y'sul was looking up. "What's that?" he asked.

Fassin experienced a moment of horror. He looked up too. A stubby vaned cylinder a couple of metres high was hovering vertically above them in the darkness outside the ceiling's still-open diamond petals. It was pointing something long and dark at them.

The Administrator groaned. "Oh no," she said. "That is the press."


"Sholish! My *good* cuirass, you witless rind-nibbling waste of gas!"

Y'sul threw a piece of armour across the room at his servant. The camo-painted carbon plate spun through the gas, changing colours rapidly as it tried to adapt, narrowly missed several other Dwellers—the large room was crowded and people had to duck, bob or dodge—just avoided Sholish and embedded itself in a FloatTree panel, producing a distinct thunk. Before it had much of a chance to blend in, Sholish tugged it out of the wall and disappeared into a side chamber, muttering.

"Excuse me," Colonel Hatherence said sharply to a Dweller who'd just bumped into her in the general shuffling that had spread through the room to give the thrown piece of armour a clear trajectory.

"Excused!" the Dweller said, then continued his conversation with another of Y'sul's relations.

Y'sul was getting ready to quit Hauskip and leave for the war along with his charges, Fassin and the oerileithe. His new combat clothing had arrived just that morning (kudos-enhancingly quickly!) along with various gifts from friends and family, most of whom, it seemed, had thought it best to show up in person to present their mostly useless or positively dangerous gifts and offer vast amounts of generally contradictory but extremely loudly proffered advice.

Y'sul, flattered and excited to be the centre of so much attention, had invited them all into his dressing room for snacks and whatever while he tried on all his new clothing, checked that his antique, inherited familial armour still more or less fitted and played with all the new bits and pieces he'd been given. Fassin counted over thirty Dwellers in the chamber, which was one of the larger spaces in the wheel-shaped house. There was a saying to the effect that one Dweller constituted an argument-in-waiting, two a conspiracy and three a riot. Quite what a gathering of thirty-plus was supposed to represent he wasn't sure, but it would assuredly have nothing to do with silence or subtlety. The noise rang off the curved walls. The clothing competed for loudness. Expressive patterns spread across exposed carapace skin like flip-books of geometric artwork. Magnetic chatter swirled, infrasound bounced confusion from one wall to another and a heady mix of pheromones bathed the place in frantic currents of Dweller hilarity.

—Are there other guides-cum-guards we might employ beside this one? Hatherence asked, pressing up to the wall beneath where Fassin floated as another Dweller bearing gifts arrived and pushed his way through the throng towards Y'sul.

—Not really, Fassin told her.—Y'sul suffered a significant kudos-loss within the Guard-mentors Guild taking on an alien outworlder, back when he agreed to be Uncle Slovius's mentor. He got that back eventually but it was a brave thing to do. Few of them will accept that kind of loss. Starting from scratch to find somebody new would take years, even if Y'sul did agree.

Something small, round, pink and gooey bumped into the top of the colonel's esuit, and stuck. She batted it away.—What *are* all these things? she said, exasperated.

—Just hospitality, Fassin sent, with a resigned expression.

Floating, drifting round the room were bobfruits, flossballs, chandelier-gumbushes and wobbling breezetrays loaded with sweetmeats, mood-balloons, narcopastes and party-suppositories. The guests helped themselves, eating, ingesting, snorting, rubbing and inserting away as appropriate. The noise seemed to be swelling by the minute, as was the collision rate—always a sure indicator that Dwellers were getting out of it (lots of loud bumps, hasty cries of "Excuse me!", sudden, alarming tiltings, and bursts of the sort of especially raucous laughter which invariably accompanied the realisation by a Dweller that one of its companions had lost control of their buoyancy).

—Oh dear, Fassin said.—I do believe this is turning into a party.

—Are these people *intoxicated*? Hatherence asked, sounding genuinely shocked.

Fassin looked at her, letting his incredulity show.—Colonel, he told her,—they are rarely anything else.

There was a bang and a yelp from somewhere near where Y'sul floated. A bobfruit exploded in mid-gas and fell limply to the floor. People nearby wiped foamy pieces of fruit off their clothes.

"Oops!" Y'sul said, amidst widespread laughter.

—He can't be the only guide! the colonel protested.—What about other Seers? They must have guides too.

—They do, but it's a one-to-one thing, an exclusive relationship. Abandoning your Guard-mentor would be a terrible insult. They'd lose all kudos.

—Major Taak, we cannot afford to be sentimental here! If there is even a possibility that we might find a better, less idiotic guide, we ought at least to start looking.

—The Guard-mentors are a Guild, colonel. They run a closed shop. If you dumped one of them, none of the rest would touch you. You'd certainly then find some clown who'd offer to act as a guide, mentor, guard, whatever—in fact they'd probably have to form a queue—but they'd be very young and stupid, or very old and, ah, eccentric, and they'd assuredly get you into far more trouble than they were ever likely to get you out of. The Guard-mentors Guild would harass them from the start, for one thing, and the vast majority of other Dwellers wouldn't talk to you at all. Librarians, archive-keepers, antiquarians, exo-specialists—all the people we most need to talk to, in other words—in particular would not even give you the time of day.

They made room for Y'sul's servant, Sholish, returning from the side chamber with a two-piece, highly polished, mirror-finished cuirass. Sholish was an adolescent, only a few hundred years old, barely three-quarters grown and skinny. Personal servants, always at least two generational stages younger than their masters, were fairly common in Dweller society, especially where the senior Dweller was bothering to pursue a hobby-cum-profession which actually involved a degree of study and/or training, when the servant had a fighting chance of picking up the basics of the given trade. The better masters regarded their servants more as apprentices than servants and the occasional especially aberrant ones treated their underlings almost as equals.

Y'sul had yet to fall prey to such sentimentality.

"And about time, you custard-brained phlegm-wart!" Y'sul yelled, snatching the cuirass from Sholish's grasp. "Did you have to forge and weave the armour yourself? Or did you start gazing at your own reflection and lose all track?"

Sholish mumbled, retreated.

—I refuse to accept that we are as powerless as you imply, major, the colonel told Fassin.

He turned to look at the oerileithe.—We are here very much on sufferance, colonel. The Dwellers can go off entire species of Seers, for no accountable reason. Nobody's ever worked out a pattern to this. You just suddenly find that you and your kind aren't welcome any more. It doesn't usually happen while they're still getting to know a new-to-civilisation species, but even that's no guarantee. They certainly get fed up with individuals—I've seen it happen—and that's equally random. Every time I come down here I have to accept that no matter how friendly and helpful everybody might have been during my last visit—(the colonel gave a sceptical laugh)—they might have nothing more to do with me this time or ever again. In fact, they might tell me I've got a day to get out or become the object of a hunt. And a Seer faces that prospect every single time they delve, either remotely or directly. We just have to get used to it. They don't even need to have met you; there are records of Seers-to-be who've spent decades getting trained up, who've been part of respected Seer Septs going back millennia who've been about to go on their very first delve and been told not to bother and to stay away for ever. It's a minor miracle they've accepted you the way they have. And don't forget the only reason you're not constantly being challenged as an interloper is because Y'sul is on record as vouching for you.

—You are saying we are stuck with this buffoon.

—We are. I know it's hard to believe, but he's one of the better ones.

—Core help us. Why waste time? I shall apply for my posthumous decoration immediately.

The Volunteer Guild of Guard-mentors existed to look after Dwellers visiting from other bands of the same planet, or, very rarely, from another gas-giant, usually one within the same stellar system. Dwellers—almost always alone—did make journeys from one stellar system to another, but it didn't happen often and it usually meant that the individual concerned had been thrown out of their own home gas-giant for some particularly heinous crime or unforgivable character defect.

The Dwellers had pretty much stopped making deep space trips en masse after the Second Diasporian Age, when the galaxy had been half the age it was now. It was generally held that seven billion years' lack of practice probably accounted for the sheer awfulness of Dweller spaceship design and building standards, though Fassin wasn't convinced that cause and effect hadn't been confused here.

They were due to leave for the war zone the following day. The interval since the frustrating audience with the City Administrator had been spent fending off Dweller journalists and their news remotes and trying to find out what they could about events in the wider system. Eventually they'd had to compromise and trade. One journalist got a very guarded but exclusive interview from Fassin (very guarded indeed—Colonel Hatherence kept coughing loudly whenever they approached any subject remotely to do with their mission) in return for news of the outside.

The Third Fury moon had been devastated and all on or in it had perished. There was no news of a drop ship surviving, though equally there was no news of any wreckage from such a ship being found. However, of course, if it had just dropped into the Depths… Many satellites had been destroyed or damaged. Those belonging to the Quick (this meant the Mercatoria) appeared to be either missing or out of action. Some warships belonging to the current local Quick species had spent an amount of time investigating the rubble of the moon Third Fury. The moon 'glantine appeared much as it always had. Stellar-system ship traffic appeared light, as it had for some days now, but not anomalous. A signal had been sent on the behalf of Oculan Colonel Hatherence, on the authority of Guard-mentor Y'sul of Hauskip, to the moon 'glantine. No reply had yet been received. Nothing untoward had happened to the transmitting station responsible following the transmission.

According to the journalist, this was all stuff they could have found out themselves, eventually. The trick was knowing where to look. The journalist seemed to feel miffed that they'd got the better end of the deal, too, because everything he'd told them was at least ninety per cent true, specifically to avoid upsetting them. He knew aliens could be funny that way.

"What, exactly, did your friend say?"

"He said they wanted him to… 'to gas-line a whole bunch of stuff for…' I'm pretty certain those were his exact words. Then he seemed to realise he was saying too much, giving too much away, and he changed the subject. The… hesitation, that sudden change of subject made the earlier form of words all the more important. He realised he was speaking to somebody who spent a lot of his life in Nasqueron, who might not feel the same way he would about the implications of what he was talking about."

"This was spoken in…?"

"Humanised G-Clear, very close to this. Meanings are pretty much identical, just altered pronunciation for the human voice."

"No Anglish words involved?"

"None."

"So, he said 'gas-lined' not 'streamlined' or 'air-lined'?"

"One wouldn't say 'air-lined' as far as I know. The normal form of words would be 'streamlined'. He chose 'gas-lined' without thinking because it was more technically correct, because it has a narrower meaning. In this context it means altering a vacuum-capable craft so that it can also operate in an atmosphere like Nasqueron's."

"Which you take to mean that an invasion or large-scale destructive raid upon us is imminent?"

"I think some sort of raid is a distinct possibility."

"This seems a thin thread to hang such a weighty fear upon."

"I know. But please understand, the guy's company builds and refits three-quarters of the system's war craft. The phrase 'gas-lined' is quite specific and that sudden change of tack when he realised he was talking to somebody who might be sentimentally or emotionally attached to Nasqueron and sympathetic towards Dwellers is significant. I know this man, I've known him since I was a child. I know how his mind works."

"Attempting to invade a gas-giant would, nevertheless, be a momentous action. In seven thousand years, the Mercatoria has done no such thing."

"The situation is desperate for them locally. They are under threat of invasion within the year. A standard year, not one of yours. Help is at least one more standard year away beyond that. In fact, the invasion may already be beginning. The attacks on Third Fury and the Mercatoria's other assets around Nasq. could be part of it."

"And attempting to invade us helps them how?"

"They think there may be something here which will make a difference. Some information. That's why I'm here, to look for it. But if they thought I was dead or not likely to succeed, the Mercatoria might intervene directly. Plus the invaders the Mercatoria is worried about might well think the same way with even less cause to hesitate. I get the impression the future continuance of Dweller Studies is kind of low on their set of priorities."

"Fassin, what sort of information could possibly make such a course of action seem sensible?"

"Important information."

"More specifically?"

"Very important information."

"You are not willing to tell me."

"Willing or able. Best you don't know."

"So you tell me."

"If I thought the specifics would help convince you, I'd let you know," Fassin lied.

He was talking to a Dweller called Setstyin. Setstyin liked to call himself an influence pedlar, which was a humble term for somebody with contacts extending as high as his went. Dweller society was remarkably flat in terms of social hierarchy—flat as the surface of a neutron star compared to the sheer verticality of the Mercatoria's baroque monstrosity—but to the extent that there was a top and bottom of society, the suhrl Setstyin was in touch with both.

He was a society host and a part-time social worker, a hospital visitor and a friend to the great and good as far as either could be said to exist in Dweller terms; a sociable, clubbable creature intensely and genuinely interested in other people, more so even than in kudos (this made him very unusual, even strange, almost threatening). He was, in human terms, somewhere between a total geek and very cool. His geekiness was that bizarre failure to care about the one thing that everybody agreed really mattered: kudos, while his coolness came from the same source, because not caring about kudos—not obsessing about it, not chasing it down wherever it might be found, not constantly measuring one's own coolness against that of one's peers—was in itself kind of cool. As long as there was not the faintest shadow of a suspicion he was playing some weird back-game, deliberately pursuing kudos by pretending not to, so long as his lack of interest in it was seen as being the unaffected carelessness of a kind of wise naïf, he was kudos-rich, though in a curiously unenviable way.

(It had been Slovius who had first explained to Fassin how kudos worked. Fassin had thought it was a bit like money. Slovius had explained that even money wasn't like money used to be, but anyway kudos was sometimes almost an opposite. The harder you'd worked for your kudos, the less it was worth.)

Setstyin was also one of the most sensible, level-minded Dwellers Fassin had ever encountered. And he treated a request by a mere human to wake up, speed up and converse over the phone with a degree of respect and seriousness that few other Dwellers would have.

Fassin had told Hatherence he needed time to let his human brain and body sleep, and his arrowcraft self-repair and recharge itself. He'd retreated to the long spoke room he'd been allocated in Y'sul's house. This was a dark and dusty gallery littered with piles of discarded clothes, lined with ancient wardrobes and floored with out-of-favour paintings and crumpled wall hangings. There was a double-dent Dweller bed in there too and a treefoam-lined cubby by one wall, so it kind of constituted a bedroom, not that Fassin or his gascraft really needed such a thing.

Fassin had secured the door, used the little arrowcraft's sonic senses to locate a removable ceiling panel and exited through the double skin roof into a breezy and relatively dark night.

Like all Dweller cities, Hauskip was situated in a historically calm patch within its atmospheric volume, but cities still had weather. They experienced pressure differentials, squalls, fog, rain, snow, crosswinds, upwellings, down draughts, lateral force and spin, all depending on the state of the gas stream around them. Moderately buffeted, half-hidden by the shreds of thicker gas scudding across the lamplit night, Fassin had made his way up and out across the sheen of rooftops.

Sky traffic had been relatively light—most travel would be within the spindles and spokes linking the city's main components—but there had been a few Dwellers roting about in the distance, and enough small craft—packet-delivery machines, mostly—for Fassin to hope he was going unremarked.

Distant lightning had flickered deep below.

Fassin had come to a dangling wave-guide cable a few centimetres thick, followed it up to a deserted public plaza like a vast, empty bowl circled with dim, attenuated lights, and found a public screen booth.

Setstyin was also in the equatorial band, though on the other side of the planet. Fassin might therefore have hoped to find him awake at such a time, but Setstyin had been sleeping off the effects of an especially good party he'd hosted the night before. Dwellers could go for tens of their days without sleep but when they did sleep they tended to do so on a prodigious scale. Fassin had begged and pleaded with Setstyin's servant to have him woken and even then it had taken a while. Setstyin looked and sounded groggy, but it appeared that his mind was fully awake inside there somewhere.

"And you would like me to do what?" Setstyin asked. He scratched at his gill fringe with one spindle arm. He was wearing a light sleep collar round his mid-hub, which was regarded as a polite minimum when addressing someone other than a close friend or family member over the phone. Dwellers were hardly self-conscious about showing their inner-hub mouth parts and pleasure organs, but there was a degree of decorum in such matters, especially when confronted with an alien. "What shall I say, Fassin, and to whom?"

A gust of wind made the arrowcraft's vanes purr to hold it in place as Fassin looked into the camerascreen. "Convince whoever you can, preferably as high as you can reach, preferably discreetly, that there really is a threat. Give them time to decide what they're going to do if there is a raid. It may be best just to let it happen. What you don't want to do is have an unthinking hostile reaction that leads to some maniac Quick nuking a city or two to try to teach you a lesson."

Setstyin looked confused. "How would that benefit anybody?"

"Please, just trust me—it's the sort of thing Quick species do."

"You want me to talk to politicians and military people, then, yes?"

"Yes." Politicians and military people in Dweller society were as much amateurs and dilettantes as gifted tailors or devout party-throwers like Setstyin—possibly a little less dedicated—but you had, Fassin reflected, to work with what you were presented with.

Setstyin looked thoughtful. "They're not going to go with an invasion."

This was true, Fassin supposed. In the full sense of the word an invasion was impossible. The Ulubis forces were hopelessly inadequate for the task of occupying a volume as great as Nasqueron or any other gas-giant, even if it had been inhabited by a congenitally peaceful, naturally subservient and easily cowed species rather than, well, Dwellers. Attempting to control the place with Dwellers around would be like peeing into a star. The danger was that, in carrying out a raid to secure a given volume for long enough to hunt down the information they were looking for, the Mercatoria would cause the Dwellers to react as though they were undergoing a full-scale invasion. It seemed to be part of Dweller psychology that if something was worth reacting to, it was even more worth overreacting to, and Fassin dreaded to think what that might imply for all sides.

"Stress an extended raid and temporary site occupation with aggressive patrols that might be mistaken for an invasion."

"Whereabouts?" Setstyin asked. "Or are you really going to tell me you have no idea?"

"I understand we're going to be looking in or very near the new Formal War zone."

Setstyin let his hub arms droop down at his side. This was something like a human rolling their eyes. "Well, of course, where else?"

"I don't suppose there's the slightest possibility that the war might be cancelled or postponed?"

"There is always a chance, but it certainly won't have anything to do with a mere party animal like myself having a word in even the highest-placed ear. Think: there might be the possibility of genuine hostile action against us, an act of alien aggression within the winds of Nasqueron itself and the suggestion is we call *off* a Formal War? More likely we'll start a few more to show how jolly fierce we are and get some practice in."

"Just thought I'd ask."

"When do you set off for the war zone?"

"Tomorrow morning, Hauskip local time."

"There you are. In plenty of time for the war's opening ceremony."

"I may have other things on my mind."

"Hmm. You realise that me having a word on high may well result in you being tracked, watched by interested parties?"

"Whereas that would never happen normally? But yes, I realise that."

"Well, I wish you well, Fassin Taak."

"Thanks."

Setstyin peered at the camerascreen, looking at Fassin's surroundings. "Y'sul out of kudos with the phone operators?"

"I have an additional Guard-mentor in the shape of an oerileithe Mercatoria military colonel. She might not understand my concern. I sneaked out to make the call."

"Very cloak, very dagger. Good luck with your quest, Fassin. Do keep in touch."

:

"If you're watching this, Sal, then I'm dead. Obviously I don't know what the circumstances of that death may have been. Like to think I died bravely and honourably in combat. Kind of don't think you'll be watching this because my clogs were popped peacefully in my sleep because I don't mean for that to happen, at least not until something's happened that involves you. Dying peacefully… actually, hopefully, that would mean you're already dead.

"The thing that involves you sort of involves Fass, too, though not in the same way. Involves you and me and Fass and Ilen. Poor dead Ilen. Ilen Deste, Sal. You remember her? Maybe you don't. It's been so long, for all of us, for all these strange different reasons that end up being just the same. You with your treatments, Fass with his slowtime, me all Einsteined out with too much time near light speed. Time hasn't ever caught up with any of us, has it, Sal?

"But I'm thinking you probably do remember Ilen and what happened to her, because it was all so traumatic for us, wasn't it? You don't forget anything about something that dramatic and horrible, not really. How can you? You have nightmares about it, it sneaks up on you even in the day sometimes, too. Do you find that? I get that. Sometimes it's something really obvious, like seeing something on screen of somebody hanging by their fingertips over a drop, especially if it's a woman. Of course in the screen they usually get rescued. Not always, but usually. But then other times what happened just… ambushed me. I'll be doing something completely normal, with no… cues, no… stimulus that you can see any logical reason would trigger the memories, and suddenly I'm there, I'm back again, back in that big old motherfucker of a ship, with you and Fass and Ilen.

"*Do* you get that? I get it still, even after all these years. You'd have thought it would have stopped happening by now, wouldn't you? Hell, even without all those stolen years near *c*, you'd have thought it should have, you know, withered, fallen away? Look at me; sixty-one years old, body-time, they tell me. Fitter than ever, still bedding guys a third my age, and—do I look sixty? Hope not. But I should have got over the whole thing by now, don't you think? Time a great healer and all that. Just hasn't happened.

"So, *do* you get anything similar? Is this ringing any bells at all? Really, I'd like to know. Maybe we'll find out, one day. Maybe I'll have got to ask this and you'll never get to see this but we'll have found out together. Maybe somebody else will get to see this. It isn't really meant for anybody else, but, well, this is a high-risk occupation, and who knows what'll happen after this is made?

"Anyway, point is: I know what happened, and I intend to kill you, Sal. Or, I did. As I say, if it is you who's watching this, I'm dead and you're still alive. But I want you to know it isn't going to end there. Got serious intentions of pursuing you from beyond the grave, Sal, old son. Won't be easy, realise that, but I've spent my entire career getting myself into a position of power. Making myself so powerful within the Navy that I can click my fingers and battleships power up, set course and ship out. Building networks, making friends, finding allies, taking lovers, taking exams, running risks, all so that I'll have the power one day to challenge a man who, oh, must nearly own the system by now. The portal collapse nearly threw me—put my plans back a long way—but I reckon you'll still be alive and loving life when I finally do get home, or when what's planned to happen in the event of my death starts happening.

"Can't tell you too much, obviously. No reason to give you any sort of warning at all. And all the advantages are on your side already, aren't they? Well, maybe apart from surprise. You surprised now? If you're listening to this, watching this? Wondering what's going to happen?? Well, wonder away. Wonder away, Sal, and don't stop wondering, don't stop being frightened, because being frightened might keep you alive a bit longer. Not too long. Definitely not too long, but long enough.

"I suppose that's enough now, don't you think? Definitely the longest speech either of us ever delivered even while we were together, way back when, wouldn't you say? Maybe almost more than we ever said to each other put together. Well, almost.

"Let me explain, in case you still haven't got it: I saw the marks, Sal. I saw the three red lines on your neck, before you put your jacket collar up. Remember that? Remember pretending to shiver and saying, 'C-collar,' or whatever it was? Remember? Just one of those little false notes that you don't notice at the time because of all the fear and adrenalin, that doesn't start to nag at you until long afterwards. Kept that collar up afterwards, too, didn't you? Kept the jacket on like some sort of comfort blanket until you could get to a bathroom and a first-aid kit, didn't you? I remember. And when I was reaching down to Ilen, I saw her fingernails. With the blood under them. Saw them very distinctly. Fass didn't; still has no idea, even yet. But I saw them. I wasn't entirely sure about the marks on your neck, but then I checked. Remember that last farewell fuck, a couple of weeks later? Just checking. They were very faint by then, of course, but they were there all right.

"You always wanted her, didn't you, Sal? Always so desired the beautiful Ilen. Did you think because she went into the ship with you she was saying yes? Did you? Did she, then changed her mind? Doesn't really matter, I suppose. I saw what I saw.

"You know what's funny, too? I was there, even if you weren't. Ilen and I.

Just the once, but that's something else I'll never forget, either. Oh, you'd have loved to have been there for that, wouldn't you? Bet you would. I slept with Fass, too, afterwards, just to complete the set. *Much* better than you, by the way."

The uniformed figure sat forward, right up to the camera, staring into it, voice going quiet and low.

"I was coming to get you, Sal. If you're watching this then I didn't make it, not personally, but even from beyond the grave, I'm still fucking coming to get you."

The image froze, then faded. A hand, shaking only slightly, reached out and turned the viewer off.

# *FOUR*
# EVENTS DURING WARTIME

It was a truism that there was not just one galaxy, there were many. Every variety of widely spread sentient life—plus a few creat categories which were arguably non-sentient though still capable of interstellar travel—and sometimes even every individual species-type tended to have one galaxy to itself. The Faring—a trans-category that covered all such beings able and willing to venture beyond their own immediate first-habitats—were like the citizens of a vast, fully three-dimensional but mostly empty city with multitudinous and varied travel systems. The majority of people were content to walk, and made their slow progress by way of an infinitude of quiet, effectively separate deserted streets, quiet parks, vacant lots, remains of wasteland and an entire unmapped network of paths, pavements, alleys, steps, ladders, wynds and snickets. They almost never encountered anybody en route, and when they got to where they were going, it would be somewhere very similar to the place they had departed from, whether that place had been a star's photosphere, a brown dwarf's surface, a gas-giant's atmosphere, a comet cloud or a region of interstellar space. Such species were generally called the Slow.

The Quick were different. Mostly originating from rocky planets of one sort or another, they lived at a higher speed and could never be content forever plodding from place to place. That they had been forced to do so until a viable wormhole network had been established was regarded as quite bad enough. Wormhole access portals were the pinch-points of the wormhole system—the city's underground stations—where people of varying species-types were forced to meet and to some extent mingle, though given the tiny amount of time one spent near a portal or within a wormhole, even this seemingly profound tying-together made very little difference to the ultimate unconnectedness of the many different life-strands, and both before they gathered and after they dispersed, the users of the system still tended to congregate at places specific to their own comfort criteria, usually quite different from those of all the others.

Many people regarded the Cincturia as the equivalent of animals: birds, dogs, cats, rats and bacteria. They too lived in the city, but were not responsible for it or entirely answerable to it, and were often to a greater or lesser degree inimical to its smooth running.

Accounting for the Rest—the non-baryonic Penumbrae, the 13-D Dimensionates and the flux-dwelling Quantarchs—was a little like discovering that the ground, the fabric of the city's buildings and their foundations plus the air itself were each home to another sort of life altogether.

The Mercatoria—largely but not entirely made up the galaxy's current crop of oxygen breathers—inhabited its own galaxy, then, as did all the other categories of life, and all these different galaxies existed alongside every other one, each interpenetrating the rest, surrounded by and surrounding the others, yet hardly affecting or being affected by them, except, sometimes, through the inestimably precious and all too easily destroyed wormhole network.

Us? Oh, we were like ghosts in the cabling.

·

Slave-children were crawling along the giant blades of one of the Dreadnought's main propellers, packing welding gear, back-sacks of carbon weave and heavy glue-throwers. The pulsing drone of the vessel's engines and main propulsion thrummed through the wrap-cloak of brown, billowing mist, filling the slipstreamed gas and the structure of the huge ship with buzzing, building, rising and fading harmonics like a vast unending symphony of industrial sound.

Fassin and the colonel watched from an open gantry overlooking the ring of giant engines as the two teams of Dweller infants crawled along the massive blades to the warped and flapping blade ends.

The starboard-most propeller had been hit by a section of DewCloud root. The root had fallen out of the clouds above, probably from a dying DewCloud floating and decomposing tens of kilometres above. DewClouds were enormous, foamy plants anything up to ten kilometres across and five or six times that in height. Like all gas-giant flora, they were mostly gas—a Dweller in a hurry could probably rip right through the canopy of one, hardly noticing they were in the midst of a plant, not an ordinary cloud. To a human they looked like some monstrous cross between an elongated mushroom and a jellyfish the size of a thunder cloud. Part of an Ubiquitous clade, found wherever Dwellers were, they harvested water condensation out of Dwellerine gas-giant atmospheres, using their dangling, thick and relatively solid roots to exploit the temperature difference between the various atmospheric layers.

When they approached the ends of their lives they floated up to the cold cloud tops and the higher haze layers, and bits broke off. The Dreadnought had prop guards to stop floating/falling/rising stuff interfering with its main propulsion units, but the section of root had slipped in between the guard and the propeller itself, wreaking brief havoc with the thirty-metre-long vanes before being chewed up and thrown out. Now the child-slaves had to climb out along the blades, from the hubs to the tips, to make repairs. Shaped like slim deltas with thin, delicate-looking tentacles which had to both clamp them on to the still-revolving blades and hold the various repair materials, the infants were making heavy weather of it. Dweller officers in motor skiffs rode nearby, bellowing orders, threats and imprecations at the young.

"They could just stop the fucking propeller," the colonel shouted to Fassin. The open gantry they were holding on to was four-fifths of the way back from the bulbous nose of the giant ship, an ellipsoid a little over two kilometres in length and four hundred across the beam. The Dreadnought's twenty-four giant engine-sets protruded from near its rear in a monumental collar of pylons, wires, tubular prop guards and near-spherical engine pods. The wind howled round Hatherence's esuit and Fassin's little arrowcraft.

"Slow them down too much, apparently!" Fassin yelled back.

The Dreadnought's captain had cut the starboard-most engine-set to quarter-power to give the slave-children a better chance of completing their repairs without too many casualties. The ship's giant rudders, mounted on the octiform tailplane assembly just aft of the engines, were appropriately deployed to compensate for the resulting skewed distribution of thrust.

Fassin glimpsed an escort cruiser through a short-lived break in the clouds a few kilometres away. Other Dreadnoughts and their escorting screens of minor craft were spread out around them in a front a hundred kilometres across and thirty deep. A slave-child near one of the vane tips lost its grip and whirled off the end with a distant shriek, crashing into the inner edge of the outer prop guard. Its scream cut off and the limp body was caught in the combined prop wash and sent whirling back, narrowly avoiding a further collision with the tail assembly. It disappeared behind a giant vertical fin. When it came back into sight it was already starting to spiral slowly down into the enveloping cloud haze. None of the skiff-riding Dwellers spared it a second glance. The dozens of remaining slave-children continued to inch their way along the giant blades.

Fassin looked at the colonel. "Woops," he said.

They were hitching a ride to the war zone.

A TunnelCar had taken them from Y'sul's house—well, two TunnelCars, a second proving necessary to carry all Y'sul's baggage and extra clothing, plus Sholish—to the Central Station. From there they joined a long-distance train of ninety or so cars making its way towards the border of Zone Zero—the equatorial zone—and Band A, twenty thousand kilometres away. Y'sul spent a large part of the journey complaining about his hangover.

"You claim to have been around in your present form for ten billion years and you still haven't developed a decent *hangover* cure?" Hatherence had asked, incredulous.

They'd been floating in a restaurant car, waiting for the galley to figure out the exact chemical composition of oerileithe food.

Y'sul, his voice muffled, issuing from within a translucent coverall that was the Dweller equivalent of dark glasses, had replied, "Suffering is regarded as part of the process, as is the mentioning of it. As is, one might add, the sympathy one receives from one's companions."

The colonel had looked sceptical. "I thought you felt no pain?"

"Mere physical pain, no. Ours is the psychic pain of realising that the world is not really as splendid as it seemed the evening before, and that one may have made something of a fool of oneself. And so on. I wouldn't expect a little dweller to understand."

They'd detrained at Nuersotse, a sphere city riding mid-altitude in the boiling ragged fringes of the equatorial Belt's northern limits. Nuersotse was barely thirty kilometres in diameter, relatively dense by Dweller city standards and built for strength and manoeuvrability. High-speed transport craft left in convoys every hour or so, as one of the Band Border Wheels swung near.

They'd crossed on the Nuersotsian-Guephuthen Band Border Wheel One, a colossal, articulated structure two thousand kilometres across held rotating on the border of two atmospheric gas-giant bands, protruding a kilo-klick into each, its whole enormous mass spun by the contra-rotating gas-streams on either side. Band Border Wheels were the largest moving structures most gas-giant planets possessed, if one discounted the globe-girdling CloudTunnel networks. These only moved in the trivial sense of being whisked round the globe at a few hundred klicks an hour like everything else within a planetary band. To a Dweller that was stationary.

Band Border Wheels really *spun*, transferring transport and materials from one band to another with minimal turbulence and in relative safety, with the added bonus that they produced prodigious amounts of electricity from their spindle drive-shafts. These protruded from the upper and lower hubs, vast hemispheres whose lower rims were pocked with microwave dishes hundreds of metres across, geared up to tear round at blurring, mind-numbing speeds and beaming their power to an outer collecting ring of equally enormous stationary dishes which then pumped the energy into docked bulk accumulator carriers.

The Wheel and the city had been caught in the outer edges of a small boundary-riding storm when they'd arrived, though both were being moved out of the way as quickly as they could be. Everything, from the planet itself to Fassin's teeth, had seemed to vibrate around them as the turbulence-hardened transfer ship hurried them empodded from the CloudTunnel station to the Wheel, engines labouring, wind screaming, ammonia hail pelting, lightning flashing and magnetic fields making various parts of Y'sul's baggage and accoutrements buzz and fizz and spark.

Hurled round in the giant centrifuge of the Wheel, stuck against its inner perimeter, the time that they'd spent inside had seemed almost calm by comparison, even allowing for the wild, wavelike bucking as they'd crossed the zone/belt border shear-face itself.

The storm had been affecting Guephuthe more severely than Nuersotse. The outer equatorial ring of the city was spinning hard, parts of its peripheral suburbs and less well-maintained districts coming apart and peeling away in a welter of thrown-out shrapnel. Their transfer had to buck and weave to dodge the wreckage, then take them straight to a TunnelCar marshalling yard beyond the city proper, a splay of cable filaments waving slowly in the gale like a vast anemone.

Another multi-kiloklick CloudTunnel journey through the vastness of Belt A, the Northern Tropical, another Wheel transfer—calmer this time—into Zone 2, and finally, crossing the mid-line of the Zone, they'd started to encounter more military traffic than civilian, the cars and trains packed with people, supplies and matériel all heading for the war.

At Tolimundarni, on the fringe of the war zone itself, they'd been thrown off the train by military police who weren't falling for Y'sul's pre-emptively outrage-fuelled arguments regarding the summit-like priority and blatant extreme officiality of an expedition—nay, a quest!—he was undertaking with these—yes, these, two—famous, well-connected, honoured alien guests of immeasurably high intrinsic pan-systemic cross-species reputation, concerning a matter of the utmost import the exact details of which he was sadly not at liberty to divulge even to such patently important and obviously discreet members of the armed forces as themselves, but who would, nevertheless, he was sure, entirely understand the significance of their mission and thus their clear right to be accorded unhindered passage due to simple good taste and a fine appreciation of natural justice and would in no way be swayed by the fact that their cooperation would be repaid in levels of subsequent kudos almost beyond crediting…

They'd floated in the TunnelBud, watching the train of cars pulling out. Sholish had darted around the echoing space trying to round up all the floating and fallen pieces of just-ejected luggage.

Fassin and Hatherence had looked, glowering, at Y'sul.

He'd finished dusting himself down and straightening his clothing, then done a double take at their aggregated gaze and announced, defensively, "I have a cousin!"

The cousin was an engineering officer on the Dreadnought *Stormshear*, a thirty-turreter with the BeltRotationeers' 487th "Rolling Thunder" Fleet. Bindiche, the cousin, bore a long-standing familial grudge against Y'sul and so naturally had been only too happy to accept a great deal of kudos from an inwardly mortified, outwardly brave-facing, hail-cuz-bygones-now Y'sul by doing him the enormous, surely never-to-be-forgotten favour of vouching for him and his alien companions to his captain and so securing passage into the war zone, though even that only happened after a quick suborb flight in a nominally freight-only moonshell pulsed from High Tolimundarni to Lopscotte (again covered by cousin Bindiche and his endlessly handy military connections, said vile spawn of a hated uncle amassing anguished Y'sul-donated kudos like the *Stormshear*'s mighty capacitors accumulated charge), scudding over the cloud tops, briefly in space (but no windows, not even any screen to see it), listening to Y'sul complain about the uncannily hangover-resembling after-effects of the fierce acceleration in the magnetic-pulse tube and the fact that he'd had to leave behind most of his baggage, including all the war-zone presents his friends had given him and the bulk of the new combat attire he'd ordered.

The slipstream howled and screamed around the Seer and the colonel. They watched the slave-children attempt their repairs. Clustered around the ends of the giant propeller blades, Fassin thought the Dweller young looked like a group of especially dogged flies clinging to a ceiling-mounted cooling fan.

Dweller children had a generally feral and entirely unloved existence. It was very hard for humans not to feel that adult Dwellers were little better than serial, congenital abusers, and that Dweller children ought to be rescued from the relative brutality of their existence.

Even as Fassin watched, another infant was thrown from one of the giant blades, voice a high and anguished shriek. This latest unfortunate missed the prop guards but hit a high-tension stay cable and was almost cut in half. A Dweller in a skiff dipped back into the slipstream, wrestling with his craft, to draw level with the tiny, broken body. He stripped it of its welding kit and let the body go. It disappeared into the mist, falling like a torn leaf.

Dwellers cheerfully admitted that they didn't care for their children. They didn't particularly care for becoming female and getting pregnant, frankly, doing this only because it was expected, drew kudos and meant one had in some sense fulfilled a duty. The idea of having to do even more, of having to look after the brats afterwards *as well* was just laughable. They, after all, had had to endure being thrown out of the house and left to wander wild when *they* were young, they'd taken their chances with the organised hunts, the gangs of adolescents and lone-hunter specialists, so why shouldn't the next generation? The little fuckers might live for billions of years. What was a mere century of weeding out?

The slave-children being used to carry out the repairs to the *Stormshear*'s damaged propeller would be regarded by most Dwellers as extremely lucky. They might be imprisoned and forced to carry out unpleasant and/or dangerous jobs but at least they were relatively safe, unhunted and properly fed.

Fassin looked out at them, wondering how many would survive to become adults. Would any of these skinny, trembling delta-shapes end up, billions of years from now, as utterly ancient, immensely respected Sages? The odd thing was, of course, that if you somehow knew for certain that they would, they wouldn't believe you. Dweller children absolutely, to an infant, refused to believe even for a moment, even as a working assumption, even just for the sake of argument, that they would ever, ever, *ever* grow up to become one of these huge, fierce, horrible double-disc creatures who hunted them and killed them and captured them to do all the awful jobs on their big ships.

—Seer Taak?

—Yes, colonel?

So they were back to close-communicating, using polarised light to keep their conversation as private as possible. The colonel had suggested coming up here. Fassin had wondered if it was for some private chat. He supposed ordinary talk might have been problematic, given the screech of the slipstream around the gantry and the thunderous clamour sounding from the choir of engines just behind.

—I have meant to ask for some time.

—What?

—This thing we are supposed to be looking for. Without mentioning the specifics, even like this, using whisper-signalling…

—Get on with it, colonel. Ma'am, he added.

—Do you believe what you told us, at that briefing on Third Fury? Hatherence asked.—The one with just yourself, Ganscerel, Yurnvic and myself present: could all that you told us there possibly be true?

The Long Crossing, the fabled 'hole between galaxies, the List itself.—Does it matter? he asked.

—What we believe always matters.

Fassin smiled.—Let me ask you something. May I?

—On the condition that we return to my question, very well.

—Do you believe in the "Truth"?

—So capitalised?

—So in quotation marks.

—Well, of course!

The Truth was the presumptuous name of the religion, the faith that lay behind the Shrievalty, the Cessoria, in a sense behind the Mercatoria itself. It arose from the belief that what appeared to be real life must in fact— according to some piously invoked statistical certitudes—be a simulation being run within some prodigious computational substrate in a greater and more encompassing reality beyond. This was a thought that had, in some form, crossed the minds of most people and all civilisations. (With the interesting exception of the Dwellers, or so they claimed. Which some parties held was another argument against them being a civilisation in the first place.) However, everybody—well, virtually everybody, obviously—quickly or eventually came round to the idea that a difference that made no difference wasn't a difference to be much bothered about, and one might as well get on with (what appeared to be) life.

The Truth went a stage further, holding that this was a difference that could be made to make a difference. What was necessary was for people truly to believe in their hearts, in their souls, in their minds, that they really were in a vast simulation. They had to reflect upon this, to keep it at the forefront of their thoughts at all times and they had to gather together on occasion, with all due ceremony and solemnity, to express this belief. And they must evangelise, they must convert everybody they possibly could to this view, because—and this was the whole point—once a sufficient proportion of the people within the simulation came to acknowledge that it was a simulation, the value of the simulation to those who had set it up would disappear and the whole thing would collapse.

If they were all part of some vast experiment, then the fact that those on whom the experiment was being conducted had guessed the truth would mean that its value would be lost. If they were some plaything, then again, that they had guessed this meant they ought to be acknowledged, even— perhaps—rewarded. If they were being tested in some way, then this was the test being passed, this was a positive result, again possibly deserving a reward. If they had been undergoing punishment for some transgression in the greater world, then this ought to constitute cause for rehabilitation.

It was not possible to know what proportion of the simulated population would be required to bring things to a halt (it might be fifty per cent, it might be rather smaller or much greater), but as long as the numbers of the enlightened kept increasing, the universe would be constantly coming closer to this epiphany, and the revelation could come at any point.

The Truth claimed with some degree of justification to be the ultimate religion, the final faith, the last of all churches. It was the one which encompassed all others, contextualised all others, could account for and embrace all others. They could all ultimately be dismissed as mere emergent phenomena of the simulation itself. The Truth could too, in a sense, but unlike them it still had more to say once this common denominator had been taken out of the equation.

It could also claim a degree of universality that the others could not. All other major religions were either specific to their originating species, could be traced back to a single species—often a single subset of that species—or were consciously developed amalgams, syntheses, of a group of sufficiently similar religions of disparate origin.

The Truth, claiming no miracles (or at least no miracles of proof) and being the work of no individual, all-important prophet (it had arisen, naturally, many times within a multiplicity of different civilisations) was the first real post-scientific, pan-civilisational religion—or at least it was the first that had not been simply imposed on reluctant subjects by a conquering hegemony. The Truth could even claim to be not a religion at all, where such a claim might endear it to those not naturally religious by nature. It could be seen more as a philosophy, even as a scientific postulate backed up by unshakeably firm statistical likelihood.

The Mercatoria had simply adopted this belief system, properly codified it and made it effectively the state religion of the latest Age.

—You do not believe, Fassin? The colonel put sadness into her signal.

—I appreciate the intellectual force of the argument.

—But it is not held in your mind at all times?

—No. Sorry.

—Be not sorry. We all find it difficult on occasion. We shall, perhaps, talk further on the matter.

—I was afraid we might.

—To return to my question, then.

—Do I believe all that stuff?

—Correct.

Fassin looked around at the ship beneath them and the great assemblage of roaring engines, whirling blades and supporting structures. The Long Crossing: thirty million years between galaxies.

—The idea that anything built by Dwellers could make a journey of that length does place the credulity under a degree of tension, he admitted.

—The assertion that the outward journey was made so much more rapidly seems no less to belong to the realm of fantasy.

Ah yes, the great and almost certainly mythical intergalactic 'hole.

—I would not argue with you, colonel. Though I would say it's perfectly possible that these are all nonsense, but the specific object we're looking for still exists.

—It keeps unlikely company.

—Again, I wouldn't choose to dispute the matter. We are left with the fact that you are a colonel, I am some sort of honorary major and orders are orders.

—How assiduously one attempts to follow one's orders might be affected by the extent to which one believes they are capable of being carried out successfully.

—There I would completely agree with you. What are you getting at?

—Just calibrating, major.

—Seeing how committed I am? Would I sacrifice my life for our... object of desire?

—Something like that.

—I suspect we're both sceptics, colonel. Me more than you, I suppose. We also believe in doing our duty. You more than me, perhaps. Satisfied?

—Content.

—Me too.

—I received a communication from the Ocula this morning.

—Really?

*And were you always going to tell me, or could I have been even more mission-sceptical during that last exchange, and been told nothing? Or has your "calibration" meant I'm not going to get told everything now?*

—Yes. Our orders remain as they were. There were several more attacks on the system in general at the time of the assault on the Third Fury moon. Further, less intense attacks have continued. The communications satellite system around Nasqueron is being repaired as a matter of urgency. In the meantime a Navarchy fleet is being stationed above the planet, to take the place of the satellites, to provide security and main force back-up for you and me, and to pick us up at the end of our mission, or in an emergency.

Fassin took a moment to think.

—Any word from my Sept, Sept Bantrabal?

—None. There was confirmation that all those on or in Third Fury were killed. I am sorry to report that Master Technician Hervil Apsile is also believed to be dead. There has been no sign of or communication with the drop ship. I have been asked by the Ocula to pass on their commiserations to you regarding all those deceased Seers and supporting staff, to which of course I add my own.

—Thank you.

The colonel might have executed a sort of rolling bow, or it might just have been the effects of the swirling, buffeting slipstream tearing around them.

The slave-children had suffered no further casualties. Their repairs appeared to be working. Even where they had not completed their renovations, the damaged blades were vibrating less, making the rest of the job easier.

—How many ships were they sending to Nasqueron, to do all these things? *That one small ship and two puck-sized satellites could do?*

—This was not mentioned.

Fassin said nothing.

There were some potentially unfortunate consequences implicit in a profound belief in the Truth. One was that there was a possibility that when the simulation ended, all the people being simulated would cease to exist entirely. The sim might be turned off and everybody within the substrate running it would die. There might be no promotion, no release, no return to a bigger and better and finer outside: there might just be the ultimate mass extinction.

Also, back in the (apparently) real world, there was an argument that the Truth implied approval of its own extinctions, that it tacitly encouraged mass murder and genocide. Logically, if one way of upping the proportion of those who truly believed was to evangelise, convince and convert, another was to decrease the numbers of those who steadfastly refused to accept the Truth at all—if necessary by killing them. The tipping point into revelation and deliverance for all might come not at the moment when a sceptic became a believer but at the point that an unreformable heathen breathed their last.

The *Stormshear* plunged into a great dark wall of thicker cloud, dimming the view. Lights started to come on, shining from the supporting structure and the Dweller skiffs. Soon they could see little, and the mad, overwhelming cacophony of the slipstream and the droning engines made sonosense near impossible. A methane hail rattled around them in the gathering gloom.

—Time to go in, perhaps, the colonel said.

—Amen.


The next day brought target practice, as the *Stormshear*'s weapons and crew were brought up to some form of war-readiness. Y'sul, Hatherence and Fassin were allowed to watch from inside an observation dome right at the front of the ship, a temporary structure protruding from the Dreadnought's armoured nose like a little bubble of diamond. They shared the place with a few dozen interested civilians, mostly administrators of the various cities where the *Stormshear* had been paying courtesy calls during the last long period of peace. Uniformed pet-children floated amongst the VIPs, carrying trays of food and drugs.

Ahead, through a ten-kilometre gap in the clouds, they could see an object like a small bright blue ship, a target being towed by another Dreadnought a hundred or more klicks still further ahead.

The *Stormshear* shuddered mightily and an instant later there came a great blast of noise. Tracks like dozens of vapour trails appeared in the sky beneath and above them, great combs of thin, plaited gas racing in front of them headed by the barely glimpsed dark dots of the shells converging on the target. Screens set into each dent-seat—where working—showed a magnified view of the blue target; it shook as its hollow structure was punctured by the shells, holes appearing briefly on its hull before sealing up again.

A desultory cheer went up from a few of the generally bored-looking Dwellers present. It was drowned out by the clicking of maniple fingers demanding service from the pet-children waiters.

"I never asked," Hatherence said, leaning close to Y'sul as he snorted up the coils of purple from a fuming stoke-pipe. "What is the war actually about?"

Y'sul turned jerkily and gave the impression of trying to get his outer sensory regions to focus on the colonel. "About?" he said, looking confused. The exhausted stoke-stick attached to the pipe went out with a loud "pop". "Well, it's about when two, ah, opposing groups of, ah people, ah, that is to say, Dwellers, in this case, obviously, decide to, umm, fight. Fight! Yes, usually over some issue, and… and they use weapons of war to do so, until one side or other—did I say there are usually just two sides? That's kind of the conventional number, I believe. Sort of a quorum, you might say. Though—"

"I wasn't looking for the definition of a war, Y'sul."

"No? Good. I thought you probably had such things of your own. Most people seem to."

"I meant, what is the point at issue? What is the cause of the war?"

"The cause?" Y'sul asked, looking surprised. He roted as far back in his dent-seat as he could while the ship shuddered again and another salvo, from each side of the vessel this time, lanced forwards to the distant target. "Well," he said, distracted by the dancing dots of the shells dragging their gas trails after them. "Well, I'm sure there *is* one…" He started mumbling. Hatherence seemed to realise she'd already got as much sense out of Y'sul as she was going to while he was sucking on the stoke-pipe, and settled back in her seat with a sigh.

—Dweller Formal Wars are like duels fought on a huge scale, Fassin told her. The colonel turned fractionally towards him.—Normally about some aesthetic dispute. They're often the final stage of a planet-planning dispute.

—Planet-planning?

—A common one is where there's some dispute concerning the number of belts and zones a planet ought to have. Then, the Odds and the Evens are the two sides, usually.

—*Planet*-planning? the colonel repeated, as though she hadn't picked up right the first time.—I did not think gas-giants were, well, planned.

—The Dwellers claim they can alter the number of bands a planet has, over a sufficiently great amount of time. They've never been reliably observed doing this but that doesn't stop them claiming to be able to do it. Anyway, it's not the doing of the thing that matters, it's the principle. What sort of world do we want to live in? That's the question.

—Even or Odd?

—Exactly. A Formal War is just the working-out.

Another salvo. The ship really shook this time, and a number of the slave-children yelped at the ragged boom resulting. Combs of gas trails leapt from all sides, a cone defining a tunnel of braided sky in front of them.

—Wars are also fought over disagreements such as which GasClipper ought to be allowed to fly a certain pennant colour during a race.

—A war for this? Hatherence sounded genuinely horrified.—Have these people never heard of committees?

—Oh, they have committees and meetings and dispute procedures. They have *lots* of those. But getting Dwellers to stick with a decision that's gone against them, even after they've sworn on their life beforehand that they'll abide by it, is not the easiest thing to do, in this or any other world. So disagreements tend to rumble on. Formal Wars are just the Dweller equivalent of a Supreme Court, a tribunal of last resort. Also, you have to understand that they don't really have standing armed forces as such. Between wars, the Dreadnoughts and other military bits and pieces are cared for by enthusiasts, by clubs. Even when a Formal War is declared, all that happens is that the clubs get bigger as ordinary people sign up. The clubs sound and feel like what you or I might understand as proper military authorities but they've no legal standing.

The colonel shook as though just confronted with something of ultimate grisliness.—How perverse.

—For them, it seems to work.

—The verb "work", Hatherence sent,—like so many other common terms, seems to be required to take on additional meanings when one talks of Dwellers. How do they decide who's won one of these bizarre conflicts?

—Occasionally a straight dead-count, or the number of Dreadnoughts destroyed or crippled. More usually there'll be an elegance threshold pre-agreed.

—An elegance threshold?

—Hatherence, Fassin said, turning to her,—did you do *any* research into Dweller life? All that time in—

—I believe I encountered a mention of this concept but dismissed it at the time as fanciful. It genuinely counts in such matters?

—It genuinely counts.

—And they can't agree a workable disputes procedure for what ship flies which colourings without resorting to war, but they can happily agree on that resulting war being decided on a concept as fuzzy as *elegance*?

—Oh, that's never disputed. They have an algorithm for it.

Another terrific judder rang the *Stormshear* like a dull bell. The thin, uncoiling tracks combed the sky ahead of them.

—An algorithm? the colonel said.

—Elegance is an algorithm.

The screens showed the blue target quaking under the impact of a handful of shells. Hatherence glanced at Y'sul, who was trying to blow purple smoke rings and pierce them with a rim arm.

—And it's all run by clubs, she said.—Of enthusiasts.

—Yes.

—*Clubs?*

—Big clubs, Hatherence.

—So is all this why their war technology is so awful? she asked.

—*Is* it?

—Fassin, Hatherence said, sounding amused now.—These people claim to have been around since the week after reionisation and building these Dreadnought things for most of that time, yet that target is less than a dozen klicks ahead, each salvo is thirty-six shells—

—Thirty-three. One of the turrets is out of action.

—Regardless. They are only hitting that effectively unmoving target with every second or third round. That is simply pathetic.

—There are rules, formulae.

—Insisting on ludicrously inefficient gunnery?

—In a sense. No guided shells, all guns and aiming systems to be based on ancient patterns, no jet engines for the Dreadnoughts, no rocket engines for the missiles, no particle or beam weapons at all.

—Like duels fought with ancient pistols.

—You're getting the idea.

—And this is meant to keep them all in martial trim in case they are invaded by outside hostiles?

—Well, yes, Fassin agreed.—That does begin to look like a slightly hollow claim when you actually see the technology, doesn't it? Of course, they claim they've got star-busting hyper-weapons hidden about the place somewhere, just in case, and the skills are somehow transferable, but...

—Nobody's ever seen them.

—Something like that.

The *Stormshear* unleashed its mighty anti-ship missiles, loosing what was probably meant to be a twelve-strong broadside. The eleven tiny, slim projectiles came screaming from all sides of the great vessel—the slave-children yelped again and some dropped their trays—and hurtled out towards the distant blue target drone on smoky, twisting plumes of jet exhaust like deranged darts. Two of the missiles drifted too close to one another; each appeared to identify the other as its intended target and so both swung wildly at their opposite number, missed, twisted round in a sweeping double braid, flew straight at each other and this time met and exploded in a modest double fireball. Some Dwellers in the observation lounge—distracted, perhaps sarcastic—cheered.

A third missile seemed to take the nearby explosion as a sign that it ought to perform an upward loop and head straight back at the *Stormshear*. "Oh-oh," Y'sul said.

The oncoming missile settled into a flat, steady course, becoming a small but rapidly enlarging dot, aimed straight at the nose of the Dreadnought.

"They *do* have destructs, don't they?" Hatherence said, glancing at Fassin. Some Dwellers started looking at each other, then made a dash for the access tube to the *Stormshear*'s armoured nose, creating a jam around the door. Slave-children, also trying to escape, either got through ahead of the rush or were thrown roughly out of the way, yelping.

The dot in the sky was getting bigger.

"They can just order it to blow up, can't they?" the colonel said, roting backwards. A high, whining noise seemed to be coming from somewhere inside the colonel's esuit. The yelling, cursing knot of Dwellers round the exit didn't seem to be shifting. The *Stormshear* was starting to turn, hopelessly slowly.

"In theory they can destruct it," Fassin said uneasily, watching the still unshifting mêlée around the exit. "And they do have close-range intercept guns." Another frantic slave-child was ejected upwards from the scrum by the door, screaming until it slapped into the ceiling and dropped lifeless to the slowly tilting deck.

The missile had real shape now, no longer a large dot. Stubby wings and a tailplane were visible. The *Stormshear* continued to turn with excruciating slowness. The missile plunged in towards them on a trail of sooty exhaust. Hatherence rose from her dent-seat but moved closer to the diamond-sheath nose of the observation blister, not further away.

—Stay back, major, she sent. Then a terrific tearing, ripping noise sounded from above and behind them, a net of finger-fine trails filled the gas ahead of the ship's nose and the missile first started to disintegrate and then blew up. The interceptor machine gun somewhere behind continued firing, scoring multiple hits on the larger pieces of smoking, glowing missile wreckage as they tumbled on towards the *Stormshear*, so that when the resulting shrapnel hit and punctured the observation blister it caused relatively little damage, and only minor wounds.

The Dreadnought took them as far as Munueyn, a Ruined City fallen amongst the dark, thick gases of the lower atmosphere where slow coils of turbulence roiled past like the heavy, lascivious licks of an almighty planetary tongue, a place all spires and spindles, near-deserted, long unfashionable, a one-time Storm-Centre now too far from anything to be of much interest to anybody, a place that might have garnered kudos for itself had it been near a war zone, but could hope for almost none at all because it was within one. A wing-frigate took them from the Dreadnought and deposited them in the gigantic echoing hall of what had once been the city's bustling StationPort, where they were greeted like returning heroes, like gods, by the local hirers and fliers. They found a guest house for negative kudos. They were, in effect, being paid to stay there.

"Sir!" Sholish said, rising from the mass of petitioners in the small courtyard below. "A hostelier of impeccable repute with excellent familial connections in the matter of wartime travel warrants beseeches you to consider his proposal to put at your disposal a veritable fleet of a half-half-dozen finely arrayed craft, all in the very best of condition and working order and ready to depart within less than an hour of their arrival."

"Which will be when, precisely, banelet of my already too-long life?"

"A day, sire. Two, at the most. He assures."

"Unacceptable! Utterly and profoundly so!" Y'sul proclaimed, frilling the very idea away with a shudder. He was nestled within a dent on a flower-decked terrace outside and above the Taverna Bucolica, close enough to the city's central plaza to smell the mayor's desperation. He dragged deep of a proffered pharma cylinder and with the exhalation breathed, "Next!"

Fassin and the colonel, floating nearby, exchanged looks. Hatherence floated closer.

—We could just take off, you and I.

—All by ourselves?

—We are both self-sufficient, we are both capable of making good time.

—You reckon?

The colonel made it obvious that she was looking his arrowcraft over.—I think so.

*I think you called up the specs on this thing before we left Third Fury and know damn well so*, he thought.

He sent,—So we go haring off into the clouds together, just we two.

—Yes.

—There is a problem.

—Indeed.

—In fact, there are two problems. The first one is that there's a war on, and we'll look like a pair of warheads.

—Warheads? But we shan't even be transonic!

—There are rules in Formal War regarding the speed that warheads can travel at. We'll look like warheads.

—Hmm. If we went a little slower?

—Slow warheads.

—Slower still?

—Cruise mines. And before you ask, any slower than that and we'll look like ordinary monolayer float mines.

Hatherence bobbed up and down, a sigh.—You mentioned a second problem.

—Without Y'sul it's unlikely that anybody will talk to us.

—With him it is unlikely that anybody else will get a word in.

—Nevertheless.

They needed their own transport. More to the point, they needed transport that would be allowed to pass unchallenged in the war zone. Whatever remained of Valseir's old dwelling lay far enough off the CloudTunnel network to make roting or floating their way there too long-winded. Y'sul had agreed to fix things—with his equatorial, big-city connections, escorting exotic aliens, he was bound to positively exude kudos towards all those who might help him—but then had got caught up in the whole process just due to the numbers of people who wanted to be the ones who helped him, and so became unable, seemingly, to make up his mind. Just as it seemed likely he was about to settle on one outrageously generous offer, another would appear over the horizon, even more enticing, necessitating a further reappraisal.

Finally, after two days, Hatherence could take no more and hired her own ship, on terms slightly better than the ones just rejected by Y'sul.

In their suite at the Taverna, Y'sul protested. "I am doing the negotiating!" he bellowed.

"Yes," the colonel agreed. "Rather too much of it."

A compromise was arrived at. The colonel confessed to their hirer that she was legally unable to commit to a firm contract and Y'sul then remade it on the exact same terms while the appalled shipmaster was still drawing breath to protest. That day, the day the war officially got under way, ceremonially beginning with an opening gala and Formal Duel in Pihirumime, half the world away. A day later they sailed—taking the next downward eddy that also swirled in the right horizontal direction—aboard the *Poaflias*, a hundred-metre twin-hull screwburster of unknown but probably enormous age. It boasted a crew of just five apart from its captain and was rotund and slow, but was—for some reason lost in the mists of Dweller military logic—still registered as an uncommitted privateer scout ship and so cleared to make her way within the war zone and, one might hope, liable to pass any consequent challenge save one conducted by opening fire prior to negotiations.

Their captain was Slyne, an enthusiastic youngster barely arrived at Adulthood, still very much a Recent and behaving more like a Youth. He'd inherited the *Poaflias* on the death of his father. The Dwellers clove to the idea of Collective Inheritance, so that, when one of them died, any private property they could fairly claim to have accumulated went fifty per cent to whoever they wanted it to go to and fifty per cent to whatever jurisdiction they lived within. This was why only one hull of the twin-hulled *Poaflias* was fully owned by Slyne. The city of Munueyn owned the other half and was renting it to him, accumulating kudos. The less Slyne could actually do with the ship, the more control he would lose, until ultimately the city could reasonably claim it was all theirs; then, if he wanted to stay aboard, he'd more or less have to do whatever the city asked him to do with the ship. This expedition, however, conducted under his own auspices, ought to go a long way towards securing his ownership rights over the whole vessel.

"This is why we are confined to the single hull?" Hatherence asked the captain. They were on the foredeck, a slightly ramshackle sprouting of fibres and sheet protruding over the craft's battered-looking nose. Y'sul had spotted a harpoon gun on the foredeck and challenged his companions to a coarse shoot the next time they traversed a promising volume. Apparently where they were now, just two days out of Munueyn, constituted just such a happy hunting ground—however, nobody had seen anything worth harpooning so far.

"That's right!" Slyne bobbed eagerly over the deck. "Less I use the other hull, less I owe the city!" Captain Slyne was hanging on to some rigging, floating above everybody else to get a good view and act as lookout and target spotter. They were making a decent speed through the dim crimson gases. The slipstream would have blown Slyne aft if he hadn't been holding on. A decent speed in this case meant less than a quarter of the velocity of the Dreadnought *Stormshear* on cruise, but the gas down here was thicker and the slipstream's force was all the greater.

"There's something!" Slyne yelled, pointing up and to starboard.

They all looked.

"No! Wrong," Slyne said cheerfully. "Beg pardon."

Slyne was taking his captain's role seriously, accoutred with lots of mostly useless ancient naval paraphernalia like spyglasses, an altimeter, a museum-piece radio, a scratched-looking hail visor, a shining antique holster-cannon and a radiation compass. His clothing and half-armour looked very new but based on designs that were very old. He had a couple of pet foetuses tethered to each of his Hub girdles.

The foetuses were Dweller young who hadn't even been allowed to progress to the stage of being children. The usual reason they existed was because a Dweller-turned-female of particular impatience had decided she couldn't be bothered going to full term, and had aborted. The results made good pets. Dwellers could survive on their own almost from conception, they just didn't progress intellectually and had nobody to protect them while they were completely helpless.

Slyne's quadruplets—it would have been impolite to inquire whether they were actually his own—looked like little bloated manta rays, pale and trailing almost useless tentacles, forever bumping into their master or each other and getting themselves tangled in their tethers. The effect, for a human, was inevitably slightly grisly, though Fassin had the added, depressing feeling that the foetuses were the equivalent of a parrot in ancient Earth terms.

"There's something this time!" Slyne shouted, pointing down to starboard. A small, black object was rising from the deep red depths of gas a couple of hundred metres away.

"I have it!" Y'sul yelled, bump-kicking the gun platform on its counterweights. It swung up above the deck to an elevation that let him depress the harpoon gun sufficiently.

"A tchoufer seed!" Sholish exclaimed. "It's a tchoufer tree seed, sir!"

"Wait a moment, Y'sul," Fassin said, rising from the deck. "Just let me go and check." He gunned the little gascraft away from the *Poaflias*, curving out and down towards the still slowly rising black sphere.

"Keep out of the way!" Y'sul bellowed to the human. Fassin had taken a curved course deliberately, having witnessed Y'sul's marksmanship before.

"Just hold, will you?" he shouted back.

Y'sul gave a shake and sighted the gun on the black sphere, maniples grasping the trigger.

Slyne craned forward in the rigging. Two of the foetuses wrapped themselves round a stay, entangling him. He looked up, tutted, and brought his spyglass up to a receptor-dense portion of his sensory frill, scanning the rising black orb. "Ah, actually—" he began.

Hatherence bobbed up suddenly. "Y'sul! Stop!"

"Ha-*ha*!" Y'sul said, twisting the trigger and firing the harpoon. The mounting shook, the gun leapt and banged, the harpoon's own twin rocket motors sprang out and erupted as soon as it was a safe distance away and the thin black line attached to the main body came whipping and whistling out of a locker just beneath the gun mounting. The harpoon rasped through the gas towards where the black object would be in a few seconds' time. "Hmm," Y'sul said, sounding slightly surprised. "One of my better—"

"It's a mine!" Slyne screamed.

Sholish just screamed.

—Fassin, get away from that thing! Hatherence sent.

The little gascraft instantly started to turn and speed up, rotors blurring in the air.

"Eh? What?" Y'sul said.

Slyne drew his holster-cannon and aimed at the harpoon. He got one shot off before the gun jammed.

"Could that be nuclear?" the colonel shouted. A high, keening noise sounded from the colonel's esuit.

"Definitely!" Slyne spluttered. He shook his gun and cursed, then slapped at his radio. "Engines! Full astern!" He shook the gun again, desperately. "Fucking *scrits*!"

Hatherence moved quickly to one side.

Y'sul looked out at the harpoon, dropping smoothly right on course for the black ball, then at the gun mounting. "Sholish!" he barked. "Grab that line!"

Sholish leapt for the thrumming dark curtain of cord being jerked from the locker under the gun, caught hold of it and was instantly whipped towards the gunwales, smashing through stanchions and snapping to a stop, tangled in the hawser, before the slipstream brought him thudding back into the deck behind them. Free of the encumbering line, the harpoon just picked up speed, still heading for the mine. Hatherence got clear of the *Poaflias*. Fassin's arrowcraft was still turning, still picking up speed, still even closer to the mine than the ship was.

"Oh, fu—" Y'sul said.

A crimson flash seemed to wash out the gas all around them.

*Dead*, Fassin had time to think.

For an instant, a tight fan of searing pink-white lines joined Colonel Hatherence's esuit and the full length of the harpoon, which vanished in a blast of heat and light. A visible shock-sphere pulsed out from the detonation, rocking the mine...

...Which seemed to stop and think for a moment, before continuing to ascend smoothly on its way. The shock wave shook them and the ship. Fassin felt it too. He slowed and turned back.

The *Poaflias* was scrubbing off speed following Slyne's last order. The slipstream was lessening but still sufficiently strong to clunk Sholish's battered carapace off the deck as he floated tangled in the dark mass of wire.

Y'sul looked. "Sholish?" he said in a small voice.

"The species of the Faring are more divided by their sense of time than anything else. We Dwellers, being who and what we are, naturally encompass as much of the spectrum of chronosense as we are able, covering most of it.

I exclude the machine-Quick." A hesitation. "You still abhor those, I take it?"

"Yes, we most certainly do!" the colonel exclaimed.

"Positively persecuted," Fassin said.

"Hmm. They are different again, of course. But even within the limits of the naturally evolved, the manifold rates at which time is appreciated are, some would argue, collectively the single most telling distinction that might be made between species and species-types."

The speaker was an ancient Sage called Jundriance. Dweller seniority nomenclature stretched to twenty-nine separate categories, starting with child and ending, no less than two billion years later (usually much more) at Child. In between came the short-lived Adolescent and Youth stages, the rather longer Adult stage with its three sub-divisions, then Prime, with four sub-divisions, Cuspian with three and then, if the Dweller had survived to that age (one and a quarter million years, minimum) and was judged fit by his peers, Sagehood, which then repeated all the sub-divisions of the Adulthood, Prime and Cuspian stages. So, technically, Jundriance was a Sage-prime-chice. He was forty-three million years old, had shrunk to only six metres in diameter—while his carapace had darkened and taken on the hazy patina of Dweller middle age—had already lost most of his limbs and he was in charge of what was left of the house and associated libraries of the presumed deceased Cuspian-choal Valseir.

The view from the house was motionless and unchanging at normal time, a hazy vista of deep brown and purple veils of gas within a great placid vertical cylinder of darkness that was the final echo of the great storm that the house had once swung about like a tiny planet around a great, cold sun. In appearance the house-library complex itself was a collection of thirty-two spheres, each seventy metres or so in diameter, many girdled by equatorial balconies, so that the construction looked like some improbably bunched gathering of ringed planets. The bubble house hung, very slowly sinking, in that great calm of thick gas, deep down in the dark, hot depths only a few tens of kilometres above the region where the atmosphere began to behave more like a liquid than a gas.

"This is his house, then, yes?" the colonel had asked when they'd first seen it from the foredeck of the *Poaflias*.

Fassin had looked around, using sonosense and magnetic to search for the section of the derelict CloudTunnel that the house had once been anchored to, but couldn't find it anywhere nearby. He'd already checked the *Poaflias*'s charts. The stretch of CloudTunnel no longer showed up on the local holo maps, implying that it had either drifted much further away—which was unlikely—or had fallen into the depths.

"Yes," he said. "Yes, looks like it."

They'd had to turn the *Poaflias* around and return to Munueyn. Sholish, badly injured, had been taken to hospital. The surgeons had given him an even chance of surviving. He'd heal best left in a drug coma for the next few hundred days. There was nothing more they could do.

Y'sul could have taken on any number of Youths and Adolescents eager to take his crippled servant's place, but he'd turned them all down—a decision he'd regretted just a day or so later once they'd set out again, when he'd realised he had nobody to shout at.

They'd avoided challenges, other ships and mines of all sorts, finally making the journey in ten days. The Sage Jundriance was attended by a couple of burly Prime servants, Nuern and Livilido, each dressed in fussily ornate and ill-fitting academic robes. They were sufficiently senior to have servants of their own; a half-dozen highly reticent Adults who looked like identical sextuplets. They were big on scurrying but almost autistically shy.

The senior of the two elder servants, Nuern—a mouean to Livilido's one-rank-more-junior suhrl—had welcomed them, allocated rooms and informed them that his master was engaged in the task of cataloguing the remaining works in the libraries—as Y'sul had warned, a significant proportion of the contents had been given away since Valseir's accident. Probably only the remoteness of the house had prevented more scholars showing up to pick over the remains. Jundriance was, however, in slowtime, so if they wanted to speak to him they would have to slow to his thought-pace. Fassin and the colonel had agreed. Y'sul had announced he was having none of this and took the *Poaflias* on a cruise to explore the local volume and see what there might be to hunt.

"Your duty should be to wait for us," the colonel had informed him.

"Duty?" Y'sul had said, as though hearing the word for the first time.

They had a half-day or so, at least, while Jundriance was informed by a message on his read-screen that he had visitors. If he would see them immediately, they could go in before dark. Otherwise it could be some long time...

"Colonel," Fassin had said, "we will have to go into slowdown for some time. Y'sul might be as well amusing himself nearby—" Fassin had turned to look at Y'sul to emphasise the word "—as mooching about this place for who knows how long."

—He'll get into trouble.

—Probably. So, better trouble close to home, or trouble further away?

Hatherence had made a rumbling noise and had told Y'sul, "There is a war on."

"I've checked the nets!" Y'sul had protested. "It's kilo-klicks away!"

"Really?" Nuern had said, perking. "Has it started? The master doesn't allow connections in the house. We hear nothing."

"Began a dozen days ago," Y'sul had told the servant. "We've been in the thick of it already. Barely avoided a smart mine on the way here. My servant got himself injured, may die."

"A smart mine? Near here?"

"You are right to be concerned, my friend," Y'sul had said solemnly. "The presence of such ordnance hereabouts is another—the real—reason why I'll take my ship on patrol around you."

"And your servant, injured. How terrible."

"I know. War is. Other than that, elsewhere in the hostilities, barely a spineful of deaths so far. Couple of Dreadnoughts crippled on each side. Far too early to tell who's winning. I'll keep a fringe cocked, let you know what's happening."

"Thank you."

"Not at all."

—You're right, Hatherence had signal-whispered to Fassin as this exchange was taking place.—Let's just let him go.

—You can signal the ship from your esuit while still in slowdown?

—Yes.

—Okay.

"You will stay nearby?" Fassin had asked Y'sul. "You won't let the *Poaflias* venture too far out?"

"Of course! I swear! And I shall ask our two fine fellows here to extend you every courtesy on my behalf!"

They were to be seen at once. Nuern had shown them into one of the outer library pods. The library had a roof of diamond leaf looking directly upwards into the vermilion-dark sky. Jundriance was settled into a dent-desk near the centre of the near-spherical room, facing a read-screen. Around him, the walls were lined with shelves, some so widely spaced that they might have doubled as bunk space for humans, others so small that a child's finger might have struggled to fit. Mostly these held books, of some sort. Spindle-secured carousels tensioned between the walls and between the floor and a network of struts above held hundreds of other types of storage devices and systems: swave crystals, holoshard, picospool and a dozen more obscure.

They'd joined Jundriance at his desk, floating through the thick atmosphere to his side. Nuern had swung dent-seats into place and they'd both clamped onto one, Hatherence positioning herself with Fassin between her and the Sage. Jundriance, of course, gave no sign of having noticed them.

They'd slowed. It had been much easier for Fassin than for Hatherence. He'd been doing this for centuries; she'd been trained in the technique but had never attempted it for real. The experience would be a jerky, shaky journey for her, at least until they smoothed out at the Sage's pace.

The day darkened quickly, then the night seemed to last less than an hour. Fassin concentrated on his own smooth slowdown, but was aware of the colonel seeming to wriggle and shift in her dent-seat. The Sage Jundriance appeared to stir. By the next quick morning, something actually changed on his reading screen; another page. That day passed quickly, then the next night went quicker still. The process continued until they were down to a factor of about one-in-sixty-four, which was what they had been told Jundriance had come up to meet them at—he'd been even slower until their arrival.

They were about halfway there when a signal-whisper had pinged into the little gascraft.—You receiving this all right, major?

—Yes. Why?

—I just interrogated the screen reader. It was working in real-time until the *Poaflias* arrived.

—You sure?

—Perfectly.

—Interesting.

Finally they were there, synchronised to the same life-pace as the Sage. The short days became a slow, slow flicker above them, the orange-purple sky beyond the diamond leaf alternately lightening and dimming. Even at this pace, the great tall veils of gas seemed to hang above them in the sky, unmoving. Fassin had experienced the feeling he always got when he first went into slowdown during a delve, the disquieting sensation that he was a lost soul, the feeling of being in a strange sort of prison, trapped in time inside while life went on at a quicker pace outside, above, beyond.

Jundriance had turned off his read-screen and greeted them. Fassin had asked about Valseir but somehow they'd got onto the subject of life-pace itself.

"One feels sorry for the Quick, I suppose," the Sage said. "They seem ill-suited to the universe, in a way. The distances between the stars, the time it takes to travel from one to another…Even more so, of course, if one is thinking of travelling between galaxies."

A hole in the conversation. "Of course." Fassin said, to fill it. *Are you fishing for something, old one*? he thought.

"The machines. They were much worse, of course. How unbearable, to live so quickly."

"Well, they mostly don't live at all now, Sage," Fassin told him.

"That is as well, perhaps."

"Sage, can you tell us any more about Valseir's death?"

"I was not there. I know no more than you."

"You were… quite close to him?" Fassin asked.

"Close? No. No, I would not say so. We had corresponded on matters of textual verification and provenance, and debated at a remove on various questions of scholarship and interpretation, though not regularly. We never met. I would not say that that constituted closeness, would you?"

"I suppose not. I just wondered what drew you here, that's all."

"Oh, the chance to look through his library. To take what I might for myself. That is what drew me. His servants took some material before they left, others—mostly scholars or those who chose to call themselves such—came and took what they wanted, but there is still much here, and while the most obvious treasures are gone, much of value may remain. It would be derelict to ignore."

"I see. And what of Valseir's libraries? I understand you are continuing to catalogue them?"

A pause. "Continuing. Yes." The old, dark-carapaced Sage seemed to stare at the dark read-screen. "Hmm," he said. He turned fractionally to look at Fassin. "Let me see. Your use of the word 'continuing' there."

"I understood that Valseir had been cataloguing his libraries. Wasn't he?"

"He was always so secretive. Was he not?"

—I'm getting light-comms leakage here, Hatherence sent.

—Tell me if there's a burst after this:

"And dilatory. Hapuerele always said that Valseir was more likely to win the All-Storms Yachting Cup than ever finish cataloguing his libraries."

Another pause. "Quite so, quite so. Hapuerele, yes."

—Leakage. Hapuerele does not exist?

—Exists, but he had to ask elsewhere just there. Shouldn't have.

"I would like to take a look round some of the libraries myself. I hope you don't mind. I shan't disturb you."

"Ah. I see. Well, if you think you can be discreet. Are you seeking anything in particular, Mr Taak?"

"Yes. And you?"

"Only enlightenment. And what would it be that you are looking for, if I may ask?"

"Exactly the same."

The old dweller was silent for a while. In real-time, most of an hour passed. "I may have something for you," he said eventually. "Would you care to slow down a little more? No doubt this, our present pace, seems surpassing slow to you; however, I find it something of a strain."

"Of course," Fassin told Jundriance.

—I'll have to leave you here, major.

—Lucky you. I'll try to keep this short.

—Good luck, Hatherence sent.

"However, I shall leave you at this point, sir," the colonel said to the Sage.

"Pleasant to have met you, Reverend Colonel," Jundriance told her. "Now then," he said to Fassin. "Let me see. Half this pace, I think, Seer Taak, would suit me better. A quarter would suit me better still."

"Shall we try half, then, initially?"

He was back in just three days. Hatherence was inspecting the contents of another library when he found her. The room was almost perfectly spherical, with no windows, just a circle of dim light shining from the ceiling's centre and further luminescence provided by bio strips inlaid on each shelf, glowing ghostly green. Further stacks of shelves like enormous inward-pointing vanes made the place feel oddly organic, as though these were ribs, and they were inside some vast creature. The colonel was floating near one set of close-stacked shelves near the library's centre, strips of green light ribbing her esuit.

"So soon, major?" Hatherence said, replacing a slim holocrystal on a shelf half full of them. At the same time as she spoke, she sent:—Our friend had nothing of interest?

"Sage Jundriance gave me so much to think about that I decided I'd better come back to normal speed to think it over," Fassin replied, then signalled,— The old bastard gave me fuck all; basically he's trying to stall us.

"Well, I have been studying while you were conversing."

"Anything of interest?" he asked, floating over towards her.

—There are signs that many more Dwellers were staying here until not long ago. Perhaps only a few days long ago. "The house system seems to think there ought to be a catalogue of catalogues somewhere. In fact that there ought to be multiple copies of it lying around."

"A catalogue of catalogues?" Fassin said.—Other Dwellers?

"The first catalogue that Valseir compiled, listing the catalogues of individual works he would then draw up."—Perhaps as many as ten or twelve. Also, I get the impression Livilido and Nuern are more, or at least other, than they appear.

"One catalogue for everything would be too simple?" Fassin asked, then sent,—I didn't think they seemed like ordinary servants either. So where are all these multiple copies?

—I suspect they have been removed. They would be the key to beginning a methodical search, the colonel replied, then said, "I gather it seemed to him the logical way to proceed. Certainly there is no shortage of material, even yet, when much of it has been removed. One catalogue would, I suppose, be cumbersome." The colonel paused. "Of course, a single giant database with freely dimensioned sub-divisions, partially overlapping categories and subcategories, a hierarchically scalable cross-reference hyperstructure and inbuilt, semi-smart user-learning routines would be even more to the point and far more useful."

Fassin looked at her. "He'd probably have got round to one of those after he'd done what he considered the proper cataloguing—getting everything down in some non-volatile form that can be read without intervening machinery."

"Our Dweller friends do seem to be remarkably purist about such things."

"When you live as long as they do, future-proofing becomes an obsession."

"Perhaps that is their curse. The Quick must endure the frustration of living in a universe with what seems like an annoyingly slow speed limit and the Slow must suffer the frenetic pace of change around them, resulting in a sort of exaggerated entropy."

Fassin had been floating slowly closer to Hatherence. He tipped to make it clear that he was looking at her as he came to a stop a couple of metres from her. The glowing biostrips on the shelves painted soft lime stripes across the little gascraft. "You all right in there, colonel?" he asked. "I realise it's very hot and pressured down here."—Colonel, do you think we are wasting our time here?

"I am fine. Yourself?"—Very hard to say. There is so much still here, so much to be looked at.

"Also fine. Feeling very rested."—That's my point. We could be made to waste a lot of time here, looking for something that has already been removed.

"I understand slow-time will have that effect."—That is a thought. I had the odd impression, from dust marks and so on, understand, that many of the shelves have recently been filled, or refilled. And many of the works seem to make no sense given what I've understood of Valseir's subjects of study. Seemed most strange. Though, if all this is a sort of slow-trap for you and me, then that begins to make sense. But what else can we do? Where else is there to go?

"I'll have to talk to the Sage again," Fassin said. "There are many things I'd like to ask him."—Whereas in fact I'll do everything I can to avoid talking to the old bore again. We have to get word out to any legitimate scholars who did take works from here, see if any of them have the catalogues, or anything else. There are two dozen separate libraries here; even if they're only half-full we could be searching them for decades.

"He is a most interesting and wise character."—Many tens of millions of works, and if most are unsorted, all are. I'll signal to the *Poaflias*, have them put out word to the relevant scholars. Who might be trying to put obstacles in our way so?

"Indeed he is."—I don't know.

"Well, I think I shall continue to search the shelves for a while. Will you join me?"—Will you?

"Why not?"

They drifted to different but nearby stacks, snicked holocrystal books out of their motion-proof shelves, and read.

"His study?" Nuern asked. A fringe flick indicated a glance at Livilido. They were afloat at table. The two Primes had invited Fassin and Hatherence to a semi-formal dinner in the house's ovaloid dining room, a great, dim, echoing space strung vertically with enormous sets of carbon ropes, all splayed, separated into smaller and smaller cords and fibres and threads and filaments and then each thin strand minutely and multiply knotted. It was like being inside some colossal, frayed net.

Jundriance was still deep in slow-time and would not be joining them. Special food had been prepared that was suitable for the colonel. She ingested it via a sort of gaslock on the side of her esuit. Fassin, contained and sustained within the arrowcraft, was really only here to watch.

"Yes," he said. "Where do you think it might be?"

"I thought that Library One was his study," Nuern said, selecting a helping of something glowing dull blue from the central carousel, and then spinning the serving dish slowly towards his dining companions.

"Me too," Livilido said. He looked at Fassin. "Why, was there another one? Has a bit dropped off the place?"

Fassin had taken a look round all the library spheres. Library One had always been Valseir's formal study, where he received fellow scholars and other people, but it hadn't been his *real* study, his den, his private space. Very few people were allowed in there. Fassin had felt flattered in the extreme to be invited to enter the nestlike nook that Valseir had made for himself inside the stretch of disused CloudTunnel tube which the rest of the house had been anchored to the last time Fassin had been here, centuries earlier. Library One still looked as it always had, minus a few thousand book-crystals and a big cylindrical low-temperature storage device in which Valseir had kept paper and plastic books. It certainly didn't look as though the room had become Valseir's proper study in the interim. And now it appeared as though these people didn't even know he'd had a more private den in the first place.

"I thought he had another study," Fassin said. "Didn't he keep a house in… what city was it? Guldrenk?"

"Ah! Of course," Nuern said. "That would be it."

—Colonel, these guys know nothing.

—I had been coming to the same conclusion.

Library Twenty-One (Cincturia/Clouders/Miscellania) had a conceit, a Dweller equivalent of a door made from a bookcase. Valseir had shown it to Fassin after the human had stayed with him for an extended period after their first meeting. It led, inward at first, towards the centre of the cluster of library spheres, through a short passage to a gap between two more of the outer spheres, then into the open gas. The joke—a hidden door, a secret passage—was that the various Cincturia were the outsiders of the galactic community, and the particular bookcase hiding the secret passage was categorised "Escapees".

After their meal, Fassin gave the impression of shutting himself away in the library for some late-night shelf-scanning. Instead he screened up the house's system statements and looked back to just after the time of Valseir's yachting accident and alleged death. He did something unusual, something barely legal by Mercatorial standards and usually pointless on Nasqueron; he speeded up, letting the gascraft's legal-max computers and his own subtly altered nervous system rev to their combined data-processing limit. It still took nearly half an hour, but he found what he was looking for: the point, a dozen days after Valseir's accident, when the house recorded a rerouting of power and ventilation plumbing. Its altimeter had registered a wobble, too— a brief blip upwards, then the start of the long, slow descent that was continuing even now.

Then Fassin had to work out where the CloudTunnel segment might be now. It would be beyond the start of the shear zone, past where the whole atmospheric band moved as a single vast mass, down into the semi-liquid Depths. These moved much more slowly than the gas above, the transition levels great turbidly elastic seas being dragged along as though reluctantly after the jet-stream whirl of atmosphere above.

It was all dead reckoning. By the Dweller way of judging such things, the atmosphere was static and the Depths—not to mention the remainder of Ulubis system, the stars and indeed the rest of the universe—moved. With only notionally fixed reference points, finding anything in the Depths was notoriously difficult. After two hundred years the section of CloudTunnel could be anywhere; it might have sunk beyond feasible reach, been broken up or even drifted to the Zone edge and been pulled into another Belt entirely, either north or south. The only thing working in Fassin's favour was that the length of tube he was looking for was relatively large. Completely losing something forty-plus metres in diameter and eighty klicks long wasn't that easy, even in Nasqueron. Still, he was relying on the CloudTunnel retaining the usual profile of buoyancy-decay.

The likely volume—though identified with a worrying degree of fuzziness—was about five thousand klicks away, though coming closer all the time, having been all the way round the planet many times. In a dozen hours it would be almost right underneath the house again. He calculated. It was doable. He pinged a note to the screen on the library's door saying that he didn't want to be disturbed.

Fassin let himself out through the hidden door about an hour after he'd entered the library. He let the little gascraft grow, pushing trim-spaces out to create internal vacuums and a larger, near-spherical outer shape so that he fell gently at first, causing as little turbulence as possible beneath the house. Then gradually he heavied, slowly shrinking the arrowhead to its dart-slim minimum, diving unpowered into the dark depths and through the rough boundary of the near-static cylinder of depleted gas that was all that remained of the ancient storm.

He powered up twenty klicks deeper and levelled out, then rose quickly when he was thirty lateral kilometres clear, zooming up through the gradually cooling, slowly thinning gas above until he was through the haze layers and out amongst the cloud tops. Fassin increased to maximum speed, configuring the arrowhead for as stealthy a profile as it could support. The gascraft had never been designed for such shenanigans, but it had been gradually altered over the years by him and Hervil Apsile until—while no match for a genuine military machine—it made less of a fuss moving across the face of the planet than almost anything within the gas-giant's atmosphere (always discounting the usual preposterous Dweller claims of invisible ships, inertialess drives and zero-point subspacials).

The little craft moved beneath the thin yellow sky, and the stars above seemed to slow down then go into reverse as Fassin flew faster than the combined speed of the planet revolving and the band beneath him jet-streaming in the same direction.

After less than an hour of flight, seeing nothing in the heavens above or in the skies beneath that would have led anyone to think there was life anywhere else in all the universe, he slowed and dropped, a shaftless arrowhead heading straight for the heart of the planet. He let the increasing density slow him further, feeling the resulting friction-heat leak through the gascraft's hull and into his flesh.

Through the upper shear boundary—only hazily defined, kilometres thick, prone to vast slow waves and unpredictable swells and sudden troughs—he entered the shear zone itself, starting to circle through the crushing fluidity of jelly-thick atmosphere. If the section of CloudTunnel was still in the volume, this was where it ought to be, fallen amongst the depths, making its slow way down to an equilibrium of weight and buoyancy within the gradually thickening press of hydrogen gas turning to liquid.

There was always a chance that it had gone the other way, lifting towards the cloud tops, but that would be unusual. Disused CloudTunnel, ribbed with vacuum tubes, tended to gain gas and therefore additional weight through osmosis over the millennia. When Fassin had been here two hundred years earlier, Valseir was already having to add buoyancy to the Tunnel to keep it from sinking too fast and dragging the whole house and library complex with it. Anyway, if the derelict section had risen it ought to have stayed within the same atmospheric band and so shown up somewhere on the charts of the *Poaflias*, and it hadn't.

He went on spiralling, keeping slow, sonosensing only gently so that there would be less chance of anybody who might be listening nearby overhearing him. (Could the colonel have followed him without him being aware of her? Probably. But why would she? Still, he had the feeling he ought to be as discreet as he could.) Light wasn't much use. CloudTunnel wall would appear almost transparent down here. Probes for magnetic and radiation vestiges were of even less utility, and there would be no scent trace either.

After two hours, near the limit of the time that he thought he could reasonably spend away from the house, and some time after he'd decided the hell with discretion and ramped his active sensors up to maximum, Fassin found one end of the CloudTunnel, looming out of the gel-thick mist like a vast dark mouth. He took the little gascraft into the forty-metre-wide maw, turning up his sonosense now that the signals would be shielded by the walls of the CloudTunnel section itself. He increased his speed, too, barrelling along the great slowly curving tube like the ghost of some Dweller long gone.

The study shell was still there, a hollow sphere almost filling the CloudTunnel tube near the mid-point of its eighty-kilometre length, but it had been ransacked, stripped bare. Whatever secrets it might have held had long since been taken or trashed.

Fassin turned some lights on to check round the place, finding nothing intact, nothing beyond empty shelves and ragged lengths of carbon board, diamond dust like frosted ice and frayed fibres, waving in the turbulence of his passing.

He formed a tiny cavity with his sonosense and watched it collapse instantly, snapped to nothing by the grinding weight of the column of gas above it. A fine place to feel crushed, he thought, then went back the way he'd come and ascended slowly to the house and Library Twenty-One again.

The colonel was there. She looked startled when he appeared from behind the hidden door, even though he'd told her earlier what he intended to do.

"Major. Seer Taak. Fassin," she said. She sounded…odd.

Fassin looked around. Nobody else here; *good*, he thought. "Yes?" he said, letting the bookcase door close behind him.

Hatherence floated right up to him, stopping just a metre away. Her esuit showed a uniform dull grey he hadn't seen her display before.

"Colonel," he asked her. "Are you all right? Is everything—"

"There is…you must prepare… I… I am sorry to… There is bad news, Fassin," she said finally, in a rushed, broken voice. "Very bad news. I am so sorry."

∴

The Archimandrite Luseferous did not really buy into the whole idea of the Truth. Of course, when he had been rising within the ranks of the Cessoria he had given every *appearance* of believing in it, and had been a gifted evangelist and disputer, arguing, many times, with great force, logic and passion for the Church and its views. He had been often commended for this. He could see at the time that his superiors were impressed, see it even when they didn't want to admit to him or to themselves that they had been impressed. He had a gift for argument. And for dissembling, for lying (if you insisted on using such crude, un-nuanced terminology), for appearing to believe one thing while, at best, actually not caring one way or the other. He had never really cared whether the Truth was true.

The idea of faith interested him, even fascinated him, not as an intellectual idea, not as a concept or some abstract theoretical framework, but as a way of controlling people, as a way of understanding and so manipulating them. As a flaw, in the end, as something which was wrong with others that was not wrong with him.

Sometimes he could not believe all the advantages other people seemed prepared to hand him. They had faith and so would do things that were plainly not in their own immediate (or, often, long-term) best interests, because they just believed what they had been told; they experienced altruism and so did things that, again, were not necessarily to their advantage; they had sentimental or emotional attachments to others and so could be coerced, once more, into doing things they would not have done otherwise. And— best of all, he sometimes thought—people were self-deceiving. They thought they were brave when they were really cowards, or imagined they could think for themselves when they most blatantly could not, or believed they were clever when they were just good at passing exams, or thought they were compassionate when they were just sentimental.

The real strength came from a perfectly simple maxim: Be completely honest with yourself; only ever deceive others.

So many edges! So many ways that people made his progress easier. If everybody he'd ever met and competed with and struggled against had been just like him in these respects he'd have had a much harder rise to power. He might not even have prevailed at all, because without all these advantages it largely came down to luck, and he might not have had sufficient.

In the old days he had once wondered how many of the Cessorian high command, his old bosses, really believed in the Truth. He strongly suspected that the higher you went, the greater grew the proportion of those who didn't really believe at all. They were in it for the power, the glory, the control and the glamour.

Now he rarely thought about any of that. Now he would just assume that anybody in such a position would be completely and cynically self-interested and be mildly surprised and even slightly disgusted to find that any of them really did have genuine faith. The disgust would come from the feeling that the person concerned was letting down the side, and the suspicion that they would feel they were somehow—perversely—superior to their less-deluded peers.

"And so you really believe in all that? You really do?"

"Sir, of course, sir! It is the rational faith. Simple logic dictates. It is inescapable. You know this better than I, sir. Sir, I think you tease me." The girl looked away, smiling down, coquettish, shy, perhaps a little alarmed, just possibly even daring to feel slightly insulted.

He reached out and took her hair, swinging her face round to his, a gold-dark silhouette against the sparse sprinkle of distant stars. "Child, I am not sure that in all my life I have ever teased. Not once."

The girl did not seem to know what to say. She looked around, perhaps at the pale stars through the screen-glass, perhaps at the snow-white tumble of low-gee puff-bedding, perhaps at the shell of screens forming the walls of their little nest, surfaces on which startlingly detailed and inventive acts of sexuality were being enacted. Perhaps she looked at her two companions, both now curled and asleep.

"Well, then, sir," she said at last, "not teased. I would not say you teased me. Perhaps rather that you make fun of me because you are so much more educated and clever than me."

That, the Archimandrite thought, was perhaps more like it. But he still was not sure. Did this young thing still carry the Truth inside her, even after all the normal-span generations that had come and gone since he'd formally swept away all this nonsense?

In a way it didn't matter in the slightest; as long as nobody ever began to use their religion to organise against him he could not care less what people really thought. Obey me, fear me. Hate me if you want. Don't ever pretend to love me. That was all he asked of people. Faith was just another lever, like sentiment, like empathy, like love (or what people thought was love, what they claimed was love, the fanciful, maybe even dishonest bit that wasn't lust, which was honest. And, of course, another lever).

But he wanted to know. A less civilised fellow in his situation would have considered having the girl tortured to find out the truth, but people being tortured over something like this soon ended up just telling you what they thought you wanted to hear—anything to get the pain to stop. He'd learned that quickly enough. There was a better way.

He reached for the pod's remote control and adjusted the spin, creating the illusion of gravity once more. "Go on all fours in front of the window," he told the girl. "It's time again."

"Sir, of course, sir." The girl quickly assumed the position he wanted, crouched against the oncoming star field, seemingly fixed even though the pod was revolving. The brightest sun, screen dead-centre, was Ulubis.

Luseferous had had his genitals enhanced in all sorts of ways. One improvement was that he carried glands inside his body which allowed him to produce many different secretions which his ejaculate could then carry into the bodies of others (but whose effects he was proof against, obviously), including irritants, hallucinogens, cannabinoids, capsainoids, sleeping draughts and truth serums. He went briefly into the little-death little-trance, the petit mal which allowed him to select one of these, and chose the last-mentioned, the truth drug.

He took the girl anally; it was faster-acting that way.

And discovered that she really did believe in the Truth.

Though it also emerged that she thought he was horribly ancient and weird-looking and a frightening, sick-minded old sadist and she absolutely hated being fucked by him.

He thought about inseminating her with thanaticin, or employing one of the physical options his remade penis made possible: the shaved horsetail, perhaps. Or just ejecting her into the vacuum and watching her die.

In the end Luseferous decided that letting her live with such constant degradation was punishment enough. He'd always said he preferred being despised, after all.

He would make her his favourite. Probably wise to put her on suicide watch, too.

:

The Dwellers held that the ability to suffer was what ultimately marked out sentient life from any other sort. They didn't mean just the ability to feel physical pain, they meant real suffering, they meant the sort of suffering that was all the worse because the creature undergoing the experience could appreciate it fully, could think back to when it had not suffered so, look forward to when it might stop (or despair of it ever stopping—despair was a large component of this) and know that if things had been different it might not be suffering now. Brains required, see? Imagination. Any brainless thing with a rudimentary nervous system could feel pain. Suffering took intelligence.

Of course, Dwellers didn't feel pain, and claimed never to suffer, except in the trivial sense of suffering fools because they were part of the family, or experiencing the deleterious physical and mental effects of a serious hangover. So, by their own reckoning, they weren't really sentient. At which point the average Dweller, assuming without question that they were absolutely self-evidently the most sentient and intelligent things around in anybody's neck of the woods, would just throw their spine-limbs out, shake their mantle ruff and start talking loudly about paradoxes.

He faced to spin, carried in the jet stream at five hundred kilometres per hour. Motionless. He side-slipped, found a small eddy, just a curl, a tiny yellow-white wisp a couple of klicks across in the great empty skies of orange and red and brown. He moved through the gas. It felt slick against the arrowhead's skin. He let the eddy carry him round in a slow gyration for a while, then pointed down and fell, twisting slowly as he went, down through the hazes and the clouds and the slowly thickening weight and press of gas, down to where the temperature was suitable, where he levelled out and did something he had never done before; he opened the cover of the little gascraft and let the atmosphere in, let Nasqueron in, let it touch his naked human skin.

Alarms were beeping and flashing and when he opened his eyes they stung in the dim orange light that seemed to shine from all around. He still had the gillfluid in his mouth and nose and throat and lungs, though now he was forced to try and breathe by himself, just his chest muscles against the pull of Nasqueron's gravity field. He was still connected to the gascraft by the interface collar, too, and, when he could not raise himself up from the bed of shock-gel, he made the little arrowhead tip gradually towards its nose, so that he was propped three-quarters of the way towards a standing position.

Blood roared in his ears. His feet and legs protested at the weight as he was slowly forced down through the gel until he was partly standing on the far end of the cramped coffin shape that contained him.

Now he could force himself away from the mould. He used his elbows, forcing himself forward. The stinging in his eyes was making them water. Tears at last. Shaking with the effort, he pulled at one sticky-slippy strand of the gillfluid where it disappeared into his right nostril, and opened his mouth, gulping some of the gas.

Nasqueron smelled of rotten eggs.

He looked around, blinking the tears away as best he could, the interface collar sucking at his neck, trying to keep contact while he tried to look up and out. It was a muddy-looking old place, Nasqueron. Like a big bowl of beaten egg, with a load of liquid shit stirred in and little drops of blood spattered throughout. And sulphurous on the palate. He let the gillfluid snap back, filling his nose, granting him pure oxygen-rich air again, though the stench still lingered.

He was sweating, partly from the exertion, partly from the heat. Maybe he should have chosen to do this a bit further up.

Now his nose was tingling, too, as well as his streaming eyes. He wondered if he could sneeze with the gillfluid inside him. Would it come splattering up out of him, some ghastly lung-vomit, ejected, left drooped over the side of the gascraft like some pale blue mass of seaweed, leaving him to gasp and choke and die?

He could hardly see because of the tears now, Nasqueron's noxious skies finally drawing from him what he had not been able to express for himself.

All of them.

The whole Sept.

They'd made the move to the Winter complex early. The warhead had fallen there, killing all of them: Slovius, Zab, Verpych, all his family, all the people he had grown up with, all those he had known and loved through his childhood and as he had grown, all the people who had made him whoever he now was, whatever he had been, until this moment.

It had been quick. Instantaneous, indeed, but so what? They had felt no pain but they were dead, gone, beyond recall.

Only they were not beyond recall. He could not stop recalling, he could not cease bringing them back to life in his head, if only to apologise. He had suggested to Slovius that they get away from the Autumn House. He'd meant a neutral place, some hotel or university complex, but they'd gone to another of the Sept's Seasonal Houses instead—a compromise. And that had killed them. He had killed them. His well-meant advice, his desire to care and protect, and to be known to have thought of this, had taken them all away.

He thought of just letting the craft tip further over, beyond ninety degrees, letting himself fall out, jerked down by his own mass, hurtling him plummeting downwards into that great sucking breath of gas-giant gravity, the gillfluid wrenched from him, perhaps taking some parts of his lungs with it as it ripped away, tearing him apart and letting him fill the bloody, ragged remains with alien gas for his last scream—falsetto, like the voice you got when you sucked helium from a party balloon—as he plunged into the depths.

The signals and messages had finally caught up with them round about the time he'd been floating through the wreckage of Valseir's wrecked study. All the shocked mailings, all the garbled queries, all the official notices, all the messages of support and sympathy, all the requests and follow-up signals asking for confirmation that he was still alive, all the news mentions, all the Ocula's revised orders: they had all come through in a flood, a great tangled knot of incoming data, held up by the Shrievalty's default secrecy, especially in a time of threat, the usual chaos of Dweller communications in general and the particular breakdown in the smooth running of signalling protocols transmission that always attended a Formal War, an effect always at its most extreme within the war zone itself.

Dead, all dead. But then, not quite all dead (a Sept was no small thing, and reality was rarely quite so neat). Just as-good-as all. Five junior servants, on leave or errands, had survived, as had one of his second cousins and her infant son. That was all. Enough to make it not a clean break, however awful, sufficient so that he would be expected to keep going, provide leadership, be strong…all that easily said clichéd stuff. His mother, absent, might have survived, but she'd been killed too, in another attack—unrelated, it was supposed, just sheer bad luck—on the Cessorian habitat in the Kuiper belt where she'd been on a Retreat for the last half year.

He supposed he ought to be thankful that Jaal was still alive, that she had not been calling at the Winter House at the time of the attack. Instead he had a succession of alarmed, shocked, plaintive and then numb-sounding messages from her, the last few pleading for him to get in touch if he could, if he was alive, if he was somewhere in Nasqueron and could hear this or read this…

He had been listed as missing by the Shrievalty Ocula after the attack on Third Fury. Officially he still was. They hadn't been sure that he and Colonel Hatherence were still alive until they'd received her relayed signal days later, and subsequently had thought it best to keep his survival a secret for the time being. His interview with the news service in Hauskip had complicated matters—however, this was already being denounced as a fake even without their intervention, and a degree of confusion had ensued. Listed as missing in action, he was still officially alive and so Chief Seer of Sept Bantrabal. That would not change for at least a year.

The situation in Ulubis system was no less desperate and the importance of what they had been asked to do had if anything increased with the latest hostile actions of the Invader/Beyonders.

Even as it all came through, even as the signals downloaded into the gascraft's memory, with all the codes intact, all the routings displayed, he kept thinking, *Maybe it's all a hoax, maybe it's all just some terrible mistake.* Even when he saw the news screenage of the still-smoking crater where the Winter House had been, in the rolling hills of Ualtus Great Valley, he had wanted to believe it wasn't true; this was faked, all of it was faked.

It had happened more or less at the same time as the bombardment of Third Fury. The tiny flash he had seen on the surface of 'glantine as they fell towards Nasqueron in the escaping drop ship: that had been the impact, that had been the instant of their deaths, that had been the very second in which he became alone. The earlier Shrievalty message, slipping through before the data jam that had kept them ignorant all these days and recording the organisation's sympathy for his loss had been referring to this catastrophe as well, not just to the loss of life in Third Fury.

The wreckage of the drop ship had been found, in the upper Depths, the body of Master Technician Hervil Apsile within. It was as though nothing was to be left aside, nothing and nobody saved, nothing, almost nothing, left to him. Some servants he hardly knew and a second cousin he was moderately fond of, plus an infant he couldn't even picture. And Jaal. But would that—could that—ever be the same now? He liked but did not love her, and was fairly sure she felt the same way. It would have been a good match, but after this he would be different, another person altogether, even if he did return from this idiot adventure, even if there was anything to return to, even if the coming war hadn't destroyed or altered everything. And would her Sept want her to marry into a Sept that no longer existed? Where was the good match, the wise marriage there? Would even she want to, and if she still did, would it not be out of duty, out of sympathy, out of the feeling that their contract must still be honoured, no matter what? What a formula for future blame and bitterness that would be.

It was almost a comfort to realise that Jaal too would probably be lost to him. It was as though he was hanging over some great drop, about to fall, *destined* to fall, and the greatest pain came from the act of still hanging on, fingers scraping, nails tearing. Let go of this one last thing to cling to, and the fall itself would at least be painless.

He wasn't going to kill himself. It was grimly good to know he could do it, but he wouldn't. From a purely practical point of view, he was fairly certain that Hatherence had followed him, using her esuit's military capabilities to hide herself from his gascraft's senses. She'd try to stop him. It could get undignified, and she might even succeed. If he really wanted to kill himself, he was sure there were easier ways. Just heading deeper into the war zone and powering hard straight for a Dreadnought should do the job.

And it would be too easy. It would be selfish. It would be the end to this terrible, gnawing feeling of guilt, a line drawn under that, and he didn't think that he deserved such an easy way out. He felt guilty? So feel guilty. He had meant no harm—quite the opposite—he'd just been wrong. Feeling guilty was stupid. It was understandable, but it was stupid, just beside the point. They were dead and he was alive. His actions might well have led directly to their deaths, but he hadn't killed them.

What was left? Revenge, maybe. Though who to blame? If it really had been Beyonders, that made his old treachery (or principled, self-sacrificing stand, depending) look foolish somehow. He still despised the Mercatoria, hated the whole vicious, cretinous, vacuously self-important, sentience-hating system, and he'd never had any illusions about the unalloyed niceness of the Beyonders or any other large group, or thought that a struggle against the Mercatoria would be other than prolonged, painful and bloody. He'd always known that his own end might be painful and long-drawn-out—he would do everything he could to make sure it wasn't, but sometimes there was just nothing you could do. He had also realised that innocents died just as filthily and in equally great numbers in a just war as they did in an unjust one, and had known that war was to be avoided at almost all costs just because it magnified mistakes, exaggerated errors, but still he'd hoped there would somehow be an elegance about his involvement in the struggle against the Mercatoria, a degree of gloriousness, a touch of the heroic.

Instead: muddle, confusion, stupidity, insane waste, pointless pain, misery and mass death—all the usual stuff of war, affecting him as it might affect anybody else, without any necessary moral reason, without any justice and even without any vindictiveness, just through the ghastly, banal working-out of physics, chemistry, biochemistry, orbital mechanics and the shared nature of sentient beings existing and contending.

Perhaps he had brought it all down upon them. Never mind advising Slovius to get away from the Autumn House: his delve, his famous delve, the action of meeting Valseir and trading information might have produced all this. It might all be his fault. Taking all he'd been told at face value, it was.

He tried to laugh, but the gillfluid filling his mouth and throat and lungs wouldn't let him, not properly. "Oh, come on then," he tried to say into the gassy skies of Nasqueron (it came out as a hopeless mumble), "show me it's all a sim, prove the Cessoria's right. End run. Game over. Lift me out."

Still all just a mumble, a gurgling somewhere down in his throat as he half stood, half lay there in his coffin-shaped alcove in the little hovering gascraft, poised within the gas-giant's atmosphere at a place where a human could expose themselves to the elements and not die too quickly, if they had something to breathe.

Revenge was a poor way out too, he thought through his tears. It was human nature, it was creat nature, it would be in the nature of almost any being capable of feeling angry and injured, but it was nearly as poor a way out as suicide. Self-serving, self-centred, selfish. Yes, if he was set in front of whoever had ordered the lobbing of a nuke at a house complex full of unarmed, unwarned civilians, he'd be tempted to kill them if he could, but it would not bring the dead back.

He never would have the opportunity, of course—again, reality scarcely ever worked that neatly—but if, in theory, he was presented with the chance, the fabled they're-tied-to-a-chair-and-you've-got-a-gun scenario, able to hurt or kill whoever had killed most of those he'd loved, he might do it. There was an argument that it would only make him as bad as them, but then he knew that in a way he was already just as bad as them. The only moral reason for doing it would be to rid the world, the galaxy, the universe of one self-evidently bad person. As though there would ever be a shortage, as though that wouldn't just leave the same niche for another.

And it would be a military machine, a hierarchy involved here, anyway. The responsibility would almost certainly diffuse out from whoever—or whatever group—had drawn up the relevant strategy through to whoever had given some probably vague order down to whoever had drawn up the general and specific targeting criteria, on down to some schmuck grunt or thoughtless technician who'd pressed a button or tapped a screen or thought-clicked an icon floating in a holo tank. And doubtless that individual would be a product of the usual hammer-subtle military induction and indoctrination process, breaking the individual down and building them back up again into a usefully obedient semi-automatic asset, sentimental towards their closest comrades, loyal only to some cold code. And, oh, how utterly sure you would have to be that they really were responsible in the first place, that you weren't being fooled by whoever had arranged all this tying-to-a-chair stuff and equipped you with a gun in the first place.

Maybe automatics had slotted in the final target programming. Was he supposed to track down the programmer too and tie him up with whoever had given the attack-authorisation or dreamed up the whole wizzo plan for visiting Ulubis in the first place?

If it had really been Beyonders, it might have been an AI which was responsible for the deed, for who-knew-what reason. Why, he'd have to find it, turn the durn thing off. Though wasn't the Mercatoria's murderous attitude to AIs one of the reasons he hated it so much?

And maybe, of course, it had all been their mistake and his fault. Perhaps they'd thought they were going to hit an empty house and only his idiot advice, his meddling, had filled it with people. How to apportion the blame there?

His eyes were bad now, like sand had been thrown in them. He couldn't really see anything, the tears were so thick. (He could still see via the collar, which was a strange experience, the tipped, clear view of the arrowhead's senses overlaid on his body's own.) He couldn't kill himself. He had to go on, see what could be done, pay tribute, try to make up, try to leave the place even fractionally better than he'd found it, try to do whatever good he might be capable of.

He waited for the Truth to kick in, for the sim-run to end, and when it didn't—as he'd known it wouldn't but had almost hoped it would—he felt bitter, resigned and grimly amused all at once.

He told the little gascraft to tip back and seal him in again. The arrowhead angled backwards, closing the canopy and enveloping him once more, the shock-gel already moving to cushion and cosset him, tendrils of salve within it starting to heal and repair his flesh and soothe his weeping eyes. He thought the machine did it all with something like relief, but knew that was a lie. The relief was his.

"Ah, opinions differ as opinions should. Always have, do and will. Might we have been bred? Who knows? Maybe we were pets. Perhaps professional prey. Maybe we were ornaments, palace entertainers, whipping beings, galaxy-changing seed-machines gone wrong (these are some of our myths). Maybe our makers disappeared, or we overthrew them (another myth— vainglorious, overly flattering—I distrust it). Maybe these makers were some proto-plasmatics? This, must be said, a pervasive one, a tenacious trope. Why plasmatics? Why would beings of the flux—stellar or planetary, no matter—wish to make something like us, so long ago? We have no idea. Yet the rumour persists.

"All we know is that we are here and we have been here for ten billion years or more. We come and we go and we live our lives at different rates, generally slower as we get older, as you good people have seen within these walls, but beyond that, why are we? What are we for? What is our point? We have no idea. You'll forgive me; these questions seem somehow more important when applied to us, to Dwellers, because we do seem—well, if not *designed*, certainly, as one might say, *prone* to persisting, given to hanging about.

"No disrespect, do understand, but the selfsame questions applied to Quick, to humans or even—like-species apologies begged, dear colonel, accept—to oerileithe, have not the same force because you do not have our track record, our provenance, our sheer cussed, gratuitous, god-denying abidance. Who knows? Maybe one day you will! After all, the universe is still young, for all our shared egocentricity, our handed-down certitude of culmination, and perhaps when the Final Chronicles are written by our unknowable ultimate inheritors they will record that the Dwellers lasted a mere dozen billion years or so in the first heady flush of the universe's infancy before they faded away to nothing, while the oerileithe and humans, those bywords for persistence, those doughty elongueurs, those synonyms for civilisational endurance, lasted two and three hundred billion years respectively, or whatever. *Then* the same questions might be asked of you: Why? What for? To what end? And—who can say!—perhaps for you, such being the case, there will be an answer. Better yet, one that makes sense.

"For now, though, we alone are stuck with such awkward challenges. Everybody else seems to come and go, and that appears natural, that is to be expected, that is the given: species appear, develop, blossom, flourish, expand, coast, shrink and fade. Cynics would say: ha! just nature, is all—no credit to claim, no blame to take, but I say huzzah! Good for all for trying, for taking part, for being such sports. But we? Us? No, we're different. We seem cursed, doomed, marked out to outstay our welcome, linger in a niche that could as well fit many—yes, many!—others, making everybody else feel uncomfortable by our just still being here when by rights we should have shuffled off with our once-contemporaries long ago. It's an embarrassment, I don't mind admitting. I'm amongst friends, I can say these things. And anyway, I'm just an old mad Dweller, a tramp, an itinerant, a floatful plodder from place to place, worthy of nothing but contempt and handouts, both if

I'm lucky, worse if I'm not. I try your patience. Forgive me. I get to talk to so few apart from the voices I make up."

The speaker was an off-sequence Dweller of Cuspian age called Oazil. To be off-sequence was to have declared oneself—or, sometimes, to have been declared by one's peers—uninterested in or apart from the usual steady progression of age and seniority that Dweller society assumed its citizens would follow. It was not by itself a state of disgrace—it was often compared to a person becoming a monk or a nun—though if it had been imposed on rather than chosen by a Dweller it was certainly a sign that they might later become an Outcast, and physically ejected from their home planet, a sanction which, given the relaxed attitude Dwellers displayed to both interstellar travel times and spaceship-construction quality control, was effectively a sentence of somewhere between several thousand years solitary confinement, and death.

Oazil was an itinerant, a tramp, a wanderer. He had entirely lost contact with a family he claimed to have anyway forgotten all details of, had no real friends to speak of, belonged to no clubs, sodalities, societies, leagues or groups and had no permanent home.

He lived, he'd told them, in his carapace and his clothes, which were tattered and motley but raggedly impressive, decorated with carefully painted panels depicting stars, planets and moons, preserved flowers from dozens of CloudPlant species and the polished carbon bones and gleaming, socketed skulls of various miniature gas-giant fauna. It was a slightly larger-scale and more feral collection of what Dwellers called life charms compared to the sort of stuff Valseir had worn save when there was some sort of formal event to attend.

When Fassin had first seen the Dweller tramp it had even occurred to him that Oazil was Valseir in disguise, come back in some attempted secrecy to taunt them all, see how they would treat a poor itinerant before revealing himself as the true owner of the house come to reclaim his lost estate. But Valseir and Oazil looked quite different. Oazil was bulkier, his carapace fractionally less symmetrical, his markings less intricate, his voice far deeper and his quota of remaining vanes and limbs quite different too. Most marked of all, Oazil's carapace was much darker than Valseir's. The two were of roughly similar age—Oazil would have been slightly junior to Valseir had he still been on-sequence: a Cuspian-baloan or Cuspian-nompar to Valseir's Cuspian-choal—but he looked much older, darker and more weather-beaten, almost as dark as Jundriance, who was ten times his age but had spent much of his life as a scholar in slow-time, not wandering the atmosphere exposed to the elements.

Oazil towed behind him a little float-trailer—shaped like a small Dweller and similarly bedecked—in which he carried a few changes of apparel, some sentimentally precious objects and a selection of gifts which he had made, usually carved from OxyTreeCloud roots. He had presented one of these, shaped to resemble the bubble house itself, to Nuern, to pass on to Jundriance when next he left his depths of slow academe.

Nuern had not looked especially impressed to receive this small token. However, Oazil claimed that Valseir's house had been a stopping-off point for him during his peregrinations for the last, oh, fifty or sixty thousand years or so. And there was anyway, especially away from cities, a tradition of hospitality towards wanderers that it would be profoundly kudos-sacrificing to ignore, certainly when there were other guests around to witness the insult.

"Will you stay long, sir?" Nuern asked.

"Yes, will you?" asked Livilido.

"Oh, no, I'll be gone tomorrow," Oazil told the younger Dweller. "This is, I'm sure, a fine house still, though of course I am sorry to hear that my old friend is no more. However, I become awkward when I spend too long in one place, and houses, though not as terrifying to me as cities, provoke in me a kind of restlessness. I cannot wait to be away when I am near a house, no matter how pleasant its aspect or welcoming the hosts."

They were outside on one of the many balconies girdling the house living spaces. They had originally convened for a morning meal to welcome Oazil in the net-hung dining space. But the old Dweller had seemed uncomfortable from the start, edgy and a-twitch, and before the first course was over he had asked, embarrassed and plaintive, if he might dine outside, perhaps beyond a window they would open so that they could still converse face to face. He suffered from a kind of claustrophobia brought on by countless millennia spent wandering the vast unceilinged skies, and felt uncomfortable enclosed like this. Nuern and Livilido had swiftly ordered their younger servants to strike table and set the meal up on the nearest balcony.

They'd all gone outside, and—after voluminous apologies for seeming to force his will upon them—Oazil had settled down, enjoyed his meal, and, subsequent to sampling some aura-grains and timbre-trace from the narcotics in the table's centrepiece—modelled on a globular university city— he had relaxed sufficiently to share with them all his thoughts on Dweller origins. It was a favourite after-meal topic with Dwellers, and so one there was effectively nothing original to say concerning, though, to give Oazil some credit, the subject had been his academic speciality before he'd slipped the moorings of scholastic life and set float upon the high skies of wander.

Hatherence asked the old Dweller his thoughts on whether his species had always been unable to experience pain, or had had this bred out of them.

"Ah! If we only knew! I am fascinated that you ask the question, for it is one that I believe is of the utmost importance in the determining of what our species really means in the universe..."

Fassin, resting lightly in a cushioned dent across the ceremonial table from the old wanderer, found his attention slipping. It seemed to do this a lot now. Perhaps a dozen Nasqueron days had elapsed since the news of the Winter House's destruction. He had spent almost all that time in the various libraries, searching for anything that might lead to their goal, the (to him, at least) increasingly mythical-seeming third volume of the work that he had taken from here over two hundred years ago and which had, supposedly, led to so much that had happened since. He looked, he searched, he trawled and combed and scanned, but so often, even when it seemed to him that he was concentrating fully, he'd find that he'd spent the last few minutes just staring into space, seeing in his mind's eye some aspect of the Sept and family life that was now gone, recalling an inconsequential conversation from decades ago, some at-the-time so-what? exchange that he would not have believed he'd ever have remembered, let alone have found brought to mind now, when they were all gone and he was in such a far and different place.

He felt the welling of tears in his eyes sometimes. The shock-gel drew them gently away.

Sometimes he thought again of suicide, and found himself longing, as though for a lost love or a treasured, vanished age, for the will, the desire, the sheer determination to end things that would have made killing himself a realistic possibility. Instead, suicide seemed as pointless and futile as everything else in life. You needed desire, the desire for death, to kill yourself. When you seemed to have no desire, no emotions or drives of any sort left—just their shadows, habits—killing oneself became as impossible as falling in love.

He looked up from the books and scrolls, the fiches and crystals, the etched diamond leaf and glowing screens and holos, and wondered what the point of anything was. He knew the standard answers, of course: people—all species, all species-types—wanted to live, wanted comfort, to be free from threat, needed energy in some form—whether it was as direct as absorbed sunlight or as at-a-remove as meat—desired to procreate, were curious, wanted enlightenment or fame and/or success and/or any of the many forms of prosperity, but—ultimately—to what end? People died. Even the immortal died. Gods died.

Some had faith, religious belief, even in this prodigiously, rampantly physically self-sufficient age, even in the midst of this universal, abundant clarity of godlessness and godlack, but such people seemed, in his experience, no less prone to despair, and their faith a liability even in its renunciation, just one more thing to lose and mourn.

People went on, they lived and struggled and insisted on living even in hopelessness and pain, desperate not to die, to cling to life regardless, as if it was the most precious thing, when all it had ever brought them, was bringing them and ever would bring them was more hopelessness, more pain.

Everybody seemed to live as though things were always just about to get better, as though any bad times were just about to end, any time now, but they were usually wrong. Life ground on. Sometimes to the good, but often towards ill and always in the direction of death. Yet people acted as though death was just the biggest surprise—My, who put that there? Maybe that was the right way to treat it, of course. Maybe the sensible attitude was to act as though there had been nothing before one came to consciousness, and nothing would exist after one's death, as though the whole universe was built around one's own individual awareness. It was a working hypothesis, a useful half-truth.

But did that mean that the urge to live was the result of some sort of illusion? Was the reality, in fact, that nothing mattered and people were fools to think that anything did? Were the choices either despair, the rejection of reason for some idiot faith, or a sort of defensive solipsism?

Valseir might have had something useful to say on the matter, Fassin thought. But then, he was dead too.

He looked at Oazil and wondered if this self-proclaimed wanderer really had known the dead Cuspian whose house this had been. Or was he just a chancer, a blow-hard, a fantasist and liar?

Thinking like this, circling round his studied despair, Fassin only half-listened to the old Dweller with his theories about gas-giant fauna development and his tales of wandering.

Oazil told how once he had circumnavigated the South Tropical Band without seeing another Dweller in all those hundred and forty thousand kilometres, how he had once fallen in with a gang of Adolescent Sculpture Pirates, semi-renegades who seeded public RootCloud and AmmoniaSluice forests, him becoming their figurehead, mascot, totem, and how, many millennia ago in the little-travelled wastes of the Southern Polar Region, he had wandered into a vast warren of empty CloudTunnel. (The work of a troop of rogue Tunnel-building machines since disappeared? An artwork? The lost prototype for a new kind of city? He didn't know—nobody had ever heard of this place, this thing.) He was lost inside this vast tree, this giant lung, this colossal root system of a labyrinth for a thousand years, exiting eleven-twelfths starved and nearly mad. He had reported the find and people had looked for it but it had never been found again. Most people thought he'd imagined it all, but he had not. *They* believed him, did they not?

The tapping noise was there again. He had been vaguely aware of it but had ignored it, not even getting as far as dismissing it as some function of the house's plumbing or differential expansion or reaction to some brief current in the surrounding gas. It had stopped after a while—he had half-noticed that, too, though still thought no more about it. Now it was there again, and slightly louder.

Fassin was in Library Three, one of the inner libraries, speed-reading through the contents of a sub-library that Valseir appeared to have picked up as part of a job lot untold ages ago. From the earliest date that anybody had bothered to note, this stuff had been lying around uncalled-up and unread for thirty millennia, dating from an era several different species of Slow Seers ago, long before humans had come to Ulubis. Fassin suspected this was traded material, data—second-hand, third-hand, who knew how many-hand—dredged from who knew where, possibly auto-translated (it certainly read like it whenever he dipped into the text itself, to make sure that the contents were what the abstracts claimed), bundled and presented and handed over to the Dwellers of Nasqueron by some long-superseded (possibly even long-extinct) species of Seer in return for—presumably—still older information. He wondered at what point most of the data the Dwellers held would become traded data, and if that point had already been reached. He was not the first Seer to think of this and, thanks to the absolute opaqueness of the Dwellers' records, he would certainly not be the last.

The volumes he was checking were mostly composed of stories concerning the romantic adventures and philosophical musings of some group of Stellar Field Liners, though they were either much-translated or the work of not just another species but another species-type altogether. They seemed fanciful, anyway.

The tapping wasn't going to go away.

He looked up from the screen to the round skylight set in the ceiling. Library Three, though now surrounded and surmounted by other spheres, had once been on the upper outskirts of the house and had a generous expanse of diamond leaf at its crown, though nowadays—even had the house been situated in less gloomy regions—it would let in little natural light.

There was something small and pale out there. When Fassin looked up the tapping stopped and the thing waved. It looked like a Dweller infant, a pet-child. Fassin watched it waving for a while, then went back to the screen and the not especially feasible exploits of the S'Liners. The tapping started again. He felt himself attempt to sigh inside his little gascraft. He stopped the screen scroll and lifted out of the dent-seat, rising to the centre of the ceiling.

It was indeed a Dweller child: a rather elongated, deformed-looking one, to human eyes more like a squid than a manta ray. It was dressed in rags and decorated with a few pathetic-looking life charms. Fassin had never seen an infant wearing clothes or decorations. It was oddly, maturely dark for one so young. It pointed in at what looked like some sort of catch or lock on the side of one of the skylight's hexagonal panes.

Fassin looked at the curious infant for a while. It kept pointing at the catch. There had been no sign of pet-children round the house in all the time they'd been here. This one looked entirely like it might belong to Oazil, but he had not displayed any earlier, and hadn't mentioned owning one. The child was still indicating the pane's lock. It started to mime pressing and twisting and pulling motions.

Fassin opened the pane and let the creature in. It flipped inside, made a sign that was probably meant to be the Dweller equivalent of "Shh!" and floated towards him, curling and cupping its body so that it formed a sickle shape, just a metre away from the prow of the arrowhead craft. Then, on its signal skin, now shielded from sight in all directions save that Fassin was watching from, it spelled out,

OAZIL: MEET ME 2KM STRAIGHT DOWN, HOUR 5. RE. VALSEIR.

It waited till he light-signalled back OK, then it sped out the way it had come, one slim tentacle staying behind after the rest of it had exited just long enough to pull the ceiling pane shut after it. It disappeared into the night-time gloom between the dark library globes outside.

Fassin looked at the time. Just before hour Four. He went back to his studies, finding nothing, thinking about nothing, until just before five, when he went back to Library Twenty-One and slipped out through the secret doorway again. He dropped the two thousand metres down through the slowly increasing heat and pressure and met the old Dweller Oazil, complete with his float-trailer. Oazil signalled,

—Fassin Taak?

—Yes.

—What did Valseir once compare the Quick to? In some detail, if you please.

—Why?

The old Dweller sent nothing for some time, then,—You might guess, little one. Or do this just because I ask. To humour an old Dweller.

Fassin waited a while before answering.—Clouds, he sent, eventually.— Clouds above one of our worlds. We come and we go and we are as nothing compared to the landscape beneath, just vapour compared to implacable rock, which lasts seemingly beyond lasting and is always there long after the clouds of the day or the clouds of the season have long gone, and yet other clouds will always be there, the next day and the next and the next, and the next season and the next year and for as long as the mountains themselves last, and the wind and the rain wear away mountains in time.

—Hmm, Oazil sent, sounding distracted.—Mountains. Curious idea. I have never seen a mountain.

—Nor ever will, I imagine. Do you want me to add any more? I don't think I recall much else.

—No, that will not be necessary.

—Then?

—Valseir is alive, the old Dweller said.—He sends his regards.

—Alive?

—There is a GasClipper regatta at the C-2 Storm Ultra-Violet 3667, beginning in seventeen days' time.

—That's in the war zone, isn't it?

—The tournament was arranged long before the hostilities were first mooted and so has been cleared with the Formal War Marshals. A special dispensation. Be there, Fassin Taak. He will find you.

The old Dweller roted forward a metre, taking up the slack on the float-trailer's traces.—Farewell, Seer Taak, he signalled.—Remember me to our mutual friend, if you'd be so kind.

He turned and floated away into the deep hot darkness. In a few moments he was lost to most passive senses. Fassin waited until there was no sign of him at all, then rose slowly back up to the house.

"Ah, Fassin, I understand commiserations are in order," Y'sul said, floating up to the bubble house's reception balcony from the *Poaflias*. Nuern, Fassin and Hatherence had watched the ship motor out of the dim haze, hearing its engines long before they'd seen it.

"Your sympathy is noted," Fassin told Y'sul. He'd got Hatherence to call the *Poaflias* the day before and order it back from its hunting patrol. The little ship returned with a modest number of trophies strung from its rigging: various julmicker bladders, bobbing like grisly balloons on sticks, three gas-drying RootHugger hides, the heads of a brace of gracile Tumblerines and—patently the most prized, mounted above the craft's nose—a Dweller Child carcass, already gutted and stretched wide on a frame so that it looked like some slightly grotesque figurehead, flying just ahead of the ship. Fassin had sensed the colonel's esuit rolling fractionally back when she'd realised what the new addition to the *Poaflias*'s nose actually was.

"What is your state of mind, Fassin, now that you have lost so many of your family?" Y'sul asked, coming to a stop in front of the Seer. "Are you decided to return to your own people?"

"My state of mind is… calm. I may still be in shock, I suppose."

"Shock?"

"Look it up. I have not decided to return to my own people yet. There are almost none to return to. We are, however, finished here. I wish to return to Munueyn."

He'd told the colonel that morning that he'd discovered something and they needed to leave.

"What have you discovered, major? May I see it?"

"I'll tell you later."

"I see. So where next are we bound?"

"Back to Munueyn," he'd lied.

"Munueyn? Our captain will be pleased," Y'sul said.

They left that evening. Nuern and Livilido seemed relaxed, positively cheered, that they were departing. Y'sul had returned with news of the war, in which two important Dreadnought actions had already taken place, resulting, in one engagement alone, in the loss of five Dreadnoughts and nearly a hundred deaths. The Zone forces were retreating in two volumes at least and the Belt certainly had the upper grasp at the moment.

Fassin and Hatherence recorded short messages of gratitude for Jundriance to read at his leisure.

Nuern asked them if they wanted to take any of the books or other works from the house.

"No, thank you," Fassin said.

"I found this humorous thesaurus," the colonel said, holding up a small diamond-leaf book. "I'd like this."

"Be our guest," Nuern told her. "Anything else? Diamond-based works like that will burn up in a few decades when the house has dropped further into the heat. Take all you want."

"Over-kind. This alone is most sufficient."

"The GasClipper regatta?" Captain Slyne said. He scratched his mantle. "I thought you wanted to go back to Munueyn?"

"There was no reason to let our hosts know where we were really heading," Fassin told Slyne.

"You are suspicious of them?" Y'sul asked.

"Just no reason to trust them," Fassin said.

"The regatta takes place around the Storm Ultra-Violet 3667, between Zone C and Belt 2," the colonel said. "Starting in sixteen days. Have we time to get there, captain?"

They were in Slyne's cabin, a fairly grand affair of flickering wall-screens and antique furniture, the ceiling hung with ancient ordnance: guns, blaster tubes and crossbows all swaying gently as the *Poaflias* powered away at half-throttle from Valseir's old house. So far Fassin had told Hatherence where they were really going, though not why.

Slyne let himself tilt, looking as though he was about to fall over. He did some more mantle scratching. "I think so. I'd better change course, then."

"Leave the course change for a little longer, would you?" Fassin asked. They were only a half-hour away from the bubble house. "Though you might go to full speed."

"Have to anyway, if we're to get to that Storm in time," Slyne said, turning and manipulating a holo cube floating over his halo-shaped desk. The largest screen, just in front of him, lit up with a chart of the volume and quickly became covered in gently curved lines and scrolling figure boxes. Slyne peered at this display for a few moments, then announced: "Full speed, we can be there in eighteen days. Best I can do." Slyne gripped a large, polished-looking handle sitting prominently on his desk and pushed it, with a degree of obvious relish, if also a little embarrassment, to its limit. The tone of the ship's engines altered and the vessel began to accelerate gradually.

"We might contact Munueyn and hire a faster ship," Y'sul suggested. "Have it rendezvous with the *Poaflias* en route and transfer to it."

Slyne rocked back, staring at the older Dweller with patterns of betrayal and horror (non-mild) spreading across his signal skin.

"Eighteen days will have to do, captain," Fassin told Slyne. "I don't think we need be there for the very start of the tournament."

"How long do these competitions last, in generality?" Hatherence asked.

Slyne tore his gaze from an unconcerned-looking Y'sul and said, "Ten or twelve days, usually. They might cut this one a little short because of the War. We'll be there in time for most of it."

"Good," Fassin said. "Stay on your current course for another half-hour, if you please, captain. Turn for the Storm then."

Slyne looked happier. "Consider it done."

Slyne took advantage of a WindRiver, a brief-lived ribbon of still faster current within the vast, wide jet stream of the whole rotating Zone, and they made good time. They were challenged twice by war craft but allowed to continue on their way, and slipped through a mine net, a wall of dark lace thrown across the sky, dotted with warheads. Dreadnought-catcher, nothing to worry them, Slyne assured them. They had, oh, tens of metres to spare on almost every side.

The screwburster *Poaflias* got to very near the bottom of the Storm called Ultra-Violet 3667 within sixteen days, arriving more or less as the regatta began.

"Keep clipped on! Could get a bit rough!" Y'sul yelled, then repeated the warning as a signal, in case they hadn't heard.

Fassin and Hatherence had come up on deck when the *Poaflias* had started bucking and heaving even more than usual. The gas around them, darker even than it had been at Valseir's house, though less dense and hot, was fairly shrieking through the ship's vestigial rigging. Ribbons and streaks, just seen coiling briefly round the whole vessel, were then torn away again as the ship plunged into another great boiling mass of cloud.

The human and the oerileithe, still within the relative calmness of the companionway shelter, exchanged glances, then quickly put the crude-looking harnesses on. The colonel's fitted well over her esuit. Fassin's tied tight enough but looked messy, not designed for his alien shape. Slyne had insisted that everybody should wear the things whenever they went on deck while the *Poaflias* was at full speed, even though both Hatherence and Fassin—in the unlikely event that they were somehow blown off the deck—could easily have caught up with the ship under their own power.

"What's going on?" Hatherence shouted as they neared Y'sul, clinging to the rails near the bow harpoon gun.

"Going to shoot the storm!" Y'sul bellowed back.

"That sounds dangerous!" Hatherence yelled.

"Oh, assuredly!"

"So, what does it entail, exactly?"

"Punching through the storm wall," Y'sul shouted. "Tackling the rim winds. Should be spectacular!" Ahead, a great dark wall of tearing, whirling cloud could be glimpsed beyond the tatters and scraps of gas that the ship was stabbing its way through. Jagged lines of lightning pulsed across this vast cliff like veins of quicksilver.

They were still making maximum speed towards the wall, which seemed to stretch as far to each side as they could see, and up for ever. Downwards was a more swirling mass of even darker gas, boiling like something cooking in a cauldron. The wind picked up, thrumming the rails and rigging and aerials like an enormous instrument. The *Poaflias* shuddered and buzzed.

"Time to get below, suspect," Hatherence shouted.

A julmicker bladder blew off a nearby railing—it looked like it had been the last one left—smacked Y'sul across his starboard side and was instantly lost to the shrieking gale. "Could be," Y'sul agreed. "After you."

They watched from the ship's armoured storm deck, crowded in with Slyne beneath a blister of thick diamond set at midships, looking out across the deck and watching the *Poaflias*'s nose plunge into the storm like a torpedo thrown at a horizontal waterfall of ink. The ship groaned, started to spin, and they were all thrown against each other. They disappeared into the wall of darkness. The *Poaflias* shook and leapt like a Dweller child on the end of a harpoon line.

Slyne whooped, pulling on levers and whirling wheels. Stuck in the far reaches of the ovaloid space, Slyne's pet-children whimpered.

"This entirely necessary?" Fassin asked Y'sul.

"Doubt it!" the Dweller said. A big flat board covered in studs above Slyne started to light up. In the darkness, it was quite bright.

Hatherence pointed at it as dozens more of the studs lit. "What's that?"

"Damage-control indicators!" Slyne said, still working levers and spinning wheels. They all rose to the ceiling as the ship dropped sharply, then crashed back down again.

"Thought it might be," Hatherence said. She was thrown hard against Fassin in a violent turn, and apologised.

When the glare started to get too distracting, Slyne turned the damage-control board off.

In the worst of the turbulence, one of Slyne's pet-children threw itself at its master and had to be torn off and smacked unconscious before being thrown into a locker. It was unclear whether it had been desperately seeking comfort or attacking.

Y'sul was sick. Fassin had never seen a Dweller be sick.

Stuck to the ceiling again, coated in a greasy film of vomit, Slyne cursing as he tried to keep hold of the controls, his pet-children keening from all sides, somebody mumbled, "Fuck, we're going to die." They all denied responsibility afterwards.

The *Poaflias* burst out of the torrent of storm cloud into a vast and hazy calm and started to drop like a lump of iron. Slyne drew in gas to whoop but caught some of Y'sul's earlier output and just spluttered. Coughing and retching and cursing Y'sul's lineage to some point only shortly after the Big Bang, he got the ship level and under control, contacted Regatta Control and limped—the ship had lost all its rigging, railings and four of its six engines—to the Lower Marina and a berth in a Storm Repair Facility.

Looking up, into the colossal bowl of the circling storm and on into the haze and the star-specked sky beyond, tiny shapes could be seen, slow-circling against the brassy glare of light.

—The pick-up fleet and relaying craft are all in orbit, Hatherence told him.

They were in a steep-pitched, multi-tiered viewing gallery packed with Dwellers. Protected by carbon ribs ready to be explosively deployed should a competition craft come too close—and attached to the *Dzunda*, a klick-long Blimper riding just inside the storm-wall boundary—the gallery was a relatively safe place to watch GasClipper races. Giant banner screens could scroll up on either side of the fan of dent-seats to provide highlights of other races and relay events too distant to witness directly.

—The pick-up *fleet*? Fassin asked.

—That is as it was described to me, Hatherence said, settling into her seat alongside his. Dwellers around them were staring at them, seemingly fascinated by their alienness. Y'sul had gone off to meet an old friend. While he was with them, Dwellers only glanced at Fassin and Hatherence now and again. With him gone, they stared shamelessly. They had both got used to it, and Fassin was confident that, if Valseir was here and looking for him, he wouldn't have too difficult a job finding him.

—How big a fleet? Fassin asked.

—Not sure.

There were hundreds of accommodation and spectator Blimpers within the storm's vast eye, scores of competing GasClippers and support vessels, plus dozens of media and ancillary craft, not to mention a ceremonial—and War-neutral—Dreadnought, the *Puisiel*. This was decked out with multitudinous bunting, lines of ancient signal flags and festoons of Dweller-size BalloonFlowers, just so that there'd be no possibility of anyone mistaking it for a Dreadnought taking part in the greater and fractionally more serious competition taking place beyond the Storm.

The side screens lit up and they watched some early action from a race which had taken place the day before. Around them, a thousand Dwellers hooted and roared and laughed, threw food, made spoken kudos bets that they would later deny or inflate accordingly, and traded insults.

—Any other news from outside? Fassin asked.

—Our orders remain as they were. There have been more semi-random attacks throughout the system. Nothing on the same scale as the assaults on the Seer assets earlier. The defensive preparations continue apace. Manufacturers continue to make heroic efforts. The people continue to make great but willing sacrifice. Morale remains most high. Though, unofficially, people would seem to be growing more frightened. Some rioting. Deep-space monitors have picked up still ambiguous traces of a great fleet approaching from the direction of the E-5 Disconnect.

—How great?

—Great enough to be bad.

—Much rioting?

—Not much rioting.

The Blimper powered up, distantly revving its engines. A ragged cheer resounded around them as the Dwellers realised things were about to start happening.

—Well, major, the colonel sent, signal strength low in the clattering hubbub of noise.—We are finally off the ship *Poaflias*, we are alone, I think it unlikely we can be overheard, and I have built up an extravagant desire to know quite why we are here. Unless you have, in the course, perhaps, of your studies, discovered that you are an insatiable fan of GasClippering.

—According to Oazil, Valseir is alive.

The colonel was silent for a while. Then she sent,—You tell me so, do you?

—Of course, Oazil may be mad or deluded or a fantasist or just a mischief-maker, but from what he said he knew Valseir, or had at least been instructed by Valseir on what to ask me to make sure I really was who I claimed to be.

—I see. So, his turning up at the house was not chance?

—I suspect he'd been keeping a watch on it. Or somebody had, waiting for us—for me—to turn up.

—And he told you to come here?

—He did.

—And then?

—Valseir will find me.

Another cheer went up as the *Dzunda* began to pick up speed, becoming part of a small fleet of similar spectator craft flocking through the gas towards the starting grid of GasClippers arranged a couple of kilometres ahead. This would be a short race, only lasting an hour or so, with turns around buoys set in the StormWall. The races would grow longer and more gruelling as the meet progressed, culminating in a last epic struggle all the way round the vast storm's inner surface.

—So Valseir knew you were or might be looking for him, and had put in place arrangements to… Hmm. That is interesting. Any contact so far?

—Not yet. But now you know why we're here.

—You will keep me informed?

—Yes. Though you will understand if I have to go off by myself at some point, I hope. Your presence might make Valseir, or whoever, nervous.

The Blimper picked up more speed, still heading towards the storm-inward side of the starting grid. The slipstream started to blow away balloons and trays not secured.

—Nervous? You think this is all that… serious?

—What do you think?

—I think Oazil is probably one or several of the things you thought he might be. However, we are here now and if he was telling the truth no doubt you will be contacted. Of course, the other possibility is that we might have been getting close to something of interest back at Valseir's house and this was simply a method of getting us out of the way. What exactly did Oazil say to you?

Fassin had kept a record of the conversation he'd had with the wandering Dweller, deep beneath the house. He signalled it across to Hatherence.

The fleet of spectator craft passed by the starting grid like an unruly flock of fat birds. Another great cheer sounded. The GasClippers stayed on the starting plane, awaiting their own signal.

—Still, little enough to go on, major, Hatherence told him.—You should have shared this with me earlier and let me decide on the correct course of action. I may have been overly indulgent with you. Your loss is still something I appreciate, of course. However, I fear I might have been guilty of dereliction.

—I won't report you if you don't, Fassin sent, without humour.

The GasClippers—the larger, plural-crewed versions of the single-Dweller StormJammers—were sharp, angular-looking things, all jag-sails, keel-lode and high-gallants. Fifty metres long—fifty metres in most directions—

bristling with glittering sails like enormous blades, they looked like the result of some monstrous permanent magnet being thrown into a hopper full of exotic edged weapons. Pennant sails carried identifying marks, little flowers of colour within the silvery blades, all bright beneath the glittering point of light that was Ulubis.

It was not possible to sail in a single medium. True sailing required a keel (or something like one) in one medium, and sails (or something like them) in another. In a single great stream of gas, you could not sail: you flew. On the edges of two streams, the boundary between a zone moving in one direction and a belt moving in the other, you could, in theory, sail, if you could build a ship big enough. The Dwellers had tried to build ships on that scale that would stay together. They had failed.

Instead, StormJammers and GasClippers exploited the titanic magnetic fields that most gas-giant planets possessed. Flux lines were their water, the place where their steadying keels lay. With a colossal magnetic field trying to move them along one course and the planet-girdling atmospheric bands of a Dweller-inhabited gas-giant expecting them to move along with everything else in a quite different direction, the possibility of sailing arose. And by sailing with sails dipped into the inside edges of giant storm systems, the sport could be made satisfactorily dangerous.

—We must hope that this was not a ruse to get us away from the house, the colonel told Fassin.—And we must hope that Valseir will indeed contact you. If he is alive. We were given no hint that such might be the case. She looked at him.—Were we?

—None.

Almost the entire fleet of spectator craft had passed the starting grid. The GasClippers shook as one, then—bewilderingly quickly, when one knew they had no proper engines—they swung away towards the massive wall of dark, tearing cloud that was the inner limit of the great storm, peeling and jostling, weaving and carving through the gas as they fought for position, using the light breezes and simple gaseous inertia of the medium to allow them to steer while they rode their lines of force towards the storm wall.

—They never did find a body, though. This is right? Hatherence asked.

—That's right, Fassin told her.—Lost in a squall that could tear apart a StormJammer he wouldn't have had much of a chance, but he might have lived.

—Yet there is no… water or the like? They cannot drown, and it is not too cold or hot. How do they die, just in a strong wind?

—Ripped apart, spun until they lose consciousness and then just whirled round too fast to hold together. Or left in a coma that means they do drop into the Depths. And they do need to breathe. If the pressure is too low, they can't.

—Hmm.

The GasClippers swung at the storm's inner surface, half disappearing as their extending blade-sails cut into the stream of gas. They accelerated hard. Even with their head start and their bellowing engines labouring, even taking a shorter, inner-curve route, the spectator craft began to lose ground to the small fleet of speeding GasClippers.

—It is possible that Valseir somehow arranged the accident? the colonel asked.

—Possible. He might have arranged to have some friend, some accomplice nearby, to rescue him. It would make surviving likely rather than not.

—Do Dwellers often fake their own deaths?

—Almost never.

—So I thought.

The group of GasClippers was level with the centre of the greater fleet of spectator ships and the shouting and hollering in the spectator craft rose still further in pitch and volume as the whole mass of GasClippers and their accompanying squadrons of Blimpers and ancillary vessels seemed to move briefly as one, the dark storm wall a vertical sea, troubled and tattered, tearing past in front of them. A vast slanting band of shade rose up to meet them all as they moved into the shadow of the storm, the hazy point of Ulubis eclipsed by a roaring circlet of dementedly gyrating gas a hundred klicks high and ten thousand kilometres across.

"Fassin. Made any bets yet?" Y'sul said, settling into his dent-seat alongside. A pet-child in a waiter's uniform floated with a tray at his side, held back until the older Dweller settled into his seat, then left the tray with its drug paraphernalia clipped to the seat and retreated.

"No. I'd be relying on your kudos, wouldn't I?"

"Oh! I suppose you would," Y'sul agreed, apparently only now thinking this through. "Obviously I must trust you subconsciously. Most odd." He flipped to one side and started rummaging through the various drug works he'd brought back.

"How was your friend?" Hatherence asked him.

"Oh, in very good spirits," Y'sul said, not looking at her. "Father died yesterday in action. Stands to inherit kudos points for bravery or something." He kept on rummaging. "Sworn I got some FeverBrain..."

"Good to know he's taking it so well," Fassin said.

"Ah! Here we are," Y'sul said, holding up a large bright orange capsule to take a good look at it. "Oh yes, Fassin: bumped into some youngster who claimed to know you. Gave me this." Y'sul dug into a pocket in his forebritch and came out with a tiny image-leaf, passing it to Fassin.

The human held it in one of the gascraft's fine-scale manipulators and looked at the photograph. It was of white clouds in a blue sky.

"Yes, colour's all wrong, obviously," Y'sul commented. "Couldn't help noticing."

Fassin was aware of the colonel looking at the image too. She sat back, silent.

"Did this person who claimed to know me actually say anything?" Fassin asked.

"Eh?" Y'sul said, still studying the finger-sized orange lozenge. "Oh, yes. Said to take good care of that thing, and that they'll be in the stern viewing-gallery restaurant if you wanted to see them. Alone, they said. Bit rude, I thought. Very young, though. Almost expect that."

"Well, thanks," Fassin said.

"Nothing," Y'sul said with a wave. He popped the giant pill.

—With your permission, colonel, Fassin sent to Hatherence.

—Granted. Take care.

"Excuse me," Fassin said as he rose from his dent-seat. Y'sul didn't hear; two of the leading GasClippers were having a private duel, swerving dangerously close, weaving in and out of each other's course, trying to tangle field lines, steal wind and so eddy-wake the other into dropping behind or crashing out, and Y'sul was floating high up out of his seat, shouting and whooping with all the other spectators not yet in their own little narcotic world.

The Dweller—a youth by his simple clothing and certainly looking at least that young—intercepted Fassin on the broad central corridor of the *Dzunda*, falling into pace with him as he made his way towards the rear of the ship. Fassin turned fractionally towards his sudden companion, kept on going.

"Seer Taak?" the youth said.

"Yes."

"Would you come with me, please?"

Fassin followed the young Dweller not to the stern viewing restaurant but to a private box slung low beneath the Blimper. The captain of the *Dzunda* was there, talking to an old Dweller who looked to be at least early Sage in years. The captain turned when Fassin and the youth entered, then—with a small bow to Fassin—left with the youth, leaving Fassin alone in the round, diamond-bubble space with the aged Dweller. A few screens showed silent views of the race. A float tray to one side carried a large narcincenser, grey-blue smoke uncoiling from it, filling the cabin with haze and scent.

"Is it you, old one?"

"I am still me, young Taak," the familiar voice said.

The Dweller floated up to him. If it was Valseir, he was no more shrunken but rather more dark than the last time Fassin had seen him. He had lost all the life charms and decorations and was dressed now in severely formal, almost monastic yellow part-robes.

"You have the token I sent?"

Fassin handed over the little image-leaf. The Dweller looked at it, rim mantle rippling in a smile. "Yes, you still wear us away, don't you?" He handed it back. "Take good care of that. And so, how was Oazil? I take it he found you at the house and you're not here by coincidence."

"He was well. Eccentric, but well."

The old Dweller's smile grew, then faded. "And the house? My libraries?"

"They are sinking into the Depths. What's left."

"What's left?"

"A bit was missing."

"Ah. The study."

"What happened to it?"

"The CloudTunnel started to get too heavy to maintain. I had the house decoupled. I cleared the study first. The tunnel section fell into the Depths."

"And the contents?"

The old Dweller roted back a fraction, creating small roils of smoke in the haze. "You are still testing me, aren't you, Fassin Taak? You are still not prepared to trust me that I am who you think I am."

"Who do I think you are?"

"Your—I thought—old friend, Valseir, once choal, now acting like a Sage-child and hoping for the confirmation of my peers if I ever get to come out of hiding. Do you think I will ever get to come out of hiding, Seer Taak?"

"That depends." Beyond the old Dweller, the GasClipper race continued, well ahead of the labouring Blimper. Screens relaying signals from camera jets showed the action in close-up. The sounds of distant cheers came through the open diamond-pane windows of the private box. "Why did you go into hiding?"

The Dweller switched to signal-whispering.—Because I thought to skim through what I'd traded you for the Expressionist paintings you had brought. I read a certain note at the end of a certain volume. Which reminds me that I must apologise. It was not my intention to seem to fob you off with three different translations of the same volume instead of all three parts of the one work. However, read that note I did, and came to the conclusion that what was being referred to was the sort of information that people die for, and most certainly will kill for. I decided to disappear. I became dead.

"Sorry I doubted you, Valseir," Fassin said, moving forward and holding out two manipulators towards the old Dweller.

"Suspicious to the last," sighed Valseir, ignoring the left manipulator and shaking the right with his own extended right hub-arm. "There; how humans greet. Are you satisfied *now*, Seer Taak?"

Fassin smiled. "Entirely. Good to see you again."

—You must feel emotional pain, then. I feel sorry for you.

—I am trying not to feel too sorry for myself. Which is helped by getting on with what needs to be done.

Fassin had told Valseir about the attacks on Third Fury and Sept Bantrabal. Valseir had related his life since they had last met, a time dominated by the Dweller List in a way that even Fassin's hadn't been until recently. Most of that period he had spent in hiding, after arranging what looked like his own death with the help of Xessife, the Dweller captain whom Fassin had seen briefly earlier. He was an old StormSailor, a Jammerhand and Clipperine with a collection of trophies and medals that outweighed him. Retired now, pursuing a more contemplative course, content to take charge of a Blimper now and again just to stay part of the whole StormSailing scene.

—And what needs to be done, Seer Taak?

—I think we need to find that third volume. Do you still have it?

—I do not. However, it is not the third volume itself that is of consequence in this matter.

—Then what is?

—A note, a brief appendix.

—Do you have *that*?

—No.

—Do you know where it is?

—No.

—Then we may all, to use a human term, be fucked.

—I do know the direction it went in.

—That could help.

—You agree that it may be that important? That we may all be "fucked" without it?

—Oh, we may very well all be thoroughly fucked *with* it, but without it, while people think this thing exists, they will do terrible things to anybody who gets in their way or isn't being what they regard as a hundred per cent helpful. My minder here, an oerileithe Ocula colonel, tells me there's a fleet of Mercatoria warships over Nasqueron. The excuse is they're here to help pick up me and her, but I think they might have another purpose.

—Military intervention?

—The instant they think there might be a firm lead towards the List.

—Well, we must try not to furnish them with one. I must also try not to furnish my fellow Dwellers with an excuse for regarding me as the most terrible traitor for even thinking of passing on anything to do with the thing in question to alien powers, even if my own studies and those of many others indicate that the data being sought is hopelessly out of date or a fantasy, or both. However, I do need to tell somebody which direction to point in, or I may have to stay dead for ever.

—Fate seems to dictate that it's me you tell. Where do I go?

—Ah. Now then. I must explain. When I realised what was being referred to in the note in the first volume, I naturally looked for volume three. Well, at least I did so after spending some days in a state of horror and rage, realising that through no fault of my own—save the usually harmless hobby of bibliophilia—I had potentially unleashed something capable of destroying much, starting with my own quite happy and content life. This episode over, I devoted myself to my search and discovered the volume eventually. I have never had such cause to curse my own lackadaisical approach to cataloguing. The relevant piece was in the form of a separate folder attached within the appendices. I myself took the original of the folder to a friend and fellow collector in the city of Deilte, in the South Polar Region, contained within a safekeep box which I asked him to look after for me, and not to open. In the event of my death, he was to hand the safekeep box on to somebody he in turn would trust not to open the box. A family member or some other trusted person would appear in due course carrying an image-leaf with a particular image in it. The one you now carry. They were to be given the box.

—So would your friend in Deilte have known of your death? I didn't.

—Perhaps, perhaps not. He is an antiquarian data-collector like myself, but a recluse. He may have heard through mutual acquaintances.

—Right, Fassin sent.—So I must make for Deilte. What was your friend's name?

—Chimilinith.

The name was barely out of Valseir's signal pit when Fassin registered a neutrino burst.

—Any particular part of Deilte? he asked, starting to look round in more detail.

—Chimilinith tended to move his house around. But I imagine the locals will know of him.

—Okay. So, did you take a look at this data? What did it look like?

The diamond-bubble private box was nearly empty: just the two of them, the float-tray and bowl—he'd scanned them automatically when he'd entered and they were just what they appeared to be, no more—and the screens, which also seemed perfectly standard. Who'd be using neutrino comms? From where? Why the sudden burst, just then?

—It looked like algebra.

Fassin scanned Valseir's simple clothes. No hint of anything high-tech there. The most sophisticated thing in his robes was the weave itself.

—Algebra? he asked.

There was nothing on the inside or the outside surface of the diamond bubble itself. He scanned the access tube. Clear.

—It looked like alien algebra, Valseir told him.

Fassin looked up at the undersurface of the Blimper immediately above, then swept for anything in the clear gas space outside within the same radius. Still nothing. Something further outside, then.

—Alien? he asked, distracted.

There seemed to be nothing nearby. There was the *Dzunda*, then nothing for a hundred metres or so until the next Blimper, then the other spectator and ancillary craft beyond—with the single accompanying Dreadnought *Puisiel* a few klicks further up in the atmosphere, easily keeping pace with the spectating fleet—then the GasClippers themselves, currently starting to round the StormWall buoy which marked this short race's first turning point.

—Alien symbology. Though not entirely. I thought I recognised some of the symbols. They looked like a form of Translatory IV, a pan-species type, so-called "universal" notation dating from perhaps two billion years ago, invented by the Wopuld—long extinct invert spongiforms—though with elements of ancient Dweller icons. I would have made notes, but I thought better of committing any of it to a form I could carry around save what exists—necessarily sketchy—in my own mind. Hence I have not been able to work on it since.

Fassin was taking in what was being said—and recording it on the gascraft's systems in case he wanted to review it later—but he was still frantically scanning the volume all around them for some form of bug or surveillance device. Another burst of what certainly seemed like neutrino comms registered on the little gascraft's sensors; a sudden pattern in the general wash of near-massless particle chaos.

The first burst had come immediately Valseir had spoken the name of the Dweller he'd given the folder to. Could it really just have been coincidence? But how could anybody have overheard? They were communicating by whisper signal, coherent light beams flickering from one surface-sunk transceiver pit to another. There was no way to intercept what they were saying unless someone dropped a mirror or some sensor into the beams.

Could it be him? Had the gascraft itself been bugged? Had Hatherence put something on him? He scanned and system-checked, finding nothing.

The Blimper above them ascended quickly and steadily as the GasClippers roared up the sheer face of the storm. The *Dzunda* rose into direct sunlight.

—So, just a field of equations? Fassin asked the old Dweller.

The drug-fume haze in the private box was suddenly lit up, resolving into tiny individual particles of vapour, a tiny fraction of them glinting and glittering.

—Possibly just the one long one.

Horrified, Fassin sucked a little of the surrounding vapour into the arrowhead's high-res analysis unit.

—One piece of algebra? he asked.

The results coming from the gascraft's high-tech nose looked bizarre, surface receptors seeming to change their mind about what they were smelling. Fassin toggled the analysis down another level of detail to electron microscopy.

—Possibly, Valseir replied.

Outside, towards the StormWall, a few tens of metres away, something showed, briefly caught in the slanting sunlight and taking just an instant too long to adapt to the new lighting conditions.

The results from the arrowhead's internal electron microscope were for a moment baffling. Then Fassin realised what his analysis unit was looking at. Nanotech. A thin soup of tiny machines, receptors, analysers, processors and signallers, small enough to be suspended in the atmosphere, light enough to float in the midst of the drug smoke like particles of the fumes themselves. That was how they'd been bugged. There was something in the gas between them, riding right in the middle of their signal beams and capable of picking up their meaning. Nothing as gross as a mirror or some photon microphone dangling from a wire, just this, just these, just stuff that was supposed to be banned.

—Valseir, he sent urgently.—Who brought this drug bowl in here?

He turned up visual magnification, staring hard at the point in the open gas outside, where something had shown in the sunlight an instant before. There. He up-magged again, almost to the point of graininess.

—What? Valseir said, sounding confused.—Well, it was here when I—

A rough sphere, forty metres away, barely ten centimetres across, almost perfectly camouflaged, like a disc of clear glass in front of the real view. Hint of a comms pit, a tiny crater-like dish, pointing right at them. Fassin swung round to put himself between the tiny, distant machine and the old Dweller, then went right up to him, comms pit to comms pit like amorous Dwellers kiss-signalling.

Valseir tried to rote back.—What the—?

—We've been bugged, Valseir, Fassin sent.—Watched, listened to. The bowl smoke is part nanotech. We need to get out, now.

—What? But—

Another burst of neutrino comms. Now that he knew where to look, it was definitely coming from the camouflaged sphere outside.

—Out, Valseir. *Now.*

And another burst. This time from above. High above.

Valseir pushed Fassin away.—The bowl smoke…?

—Get *out*! Fassin sent, pushing the old Dweller towards the access port in the top of the diamond bubble box.

Outside, the little sphere was rushing towards them. Fassin got underneath Valseir and forced him upwards.

—Fassin! All right! Valseir started to rise under his own power, entering the vertical access tube. The little sphere burst through the diamond bubble, shards spraying. It came to a stop just inside the jagged hole, still disguised, just a blur in the air.

"Major Taak!" it shouted. "This is General Linosu of the Shrievalty Ocula. This device is under the control of the Nasqueron Expeditionary Force. Don't be alarmed. We're coming down to—"

The voice cut off as the little sphere was pierced by a hair-thin line of cerise light. The noise resounded, sharp and sudden, round the diamond bubble enclosure. Debris flew from the tiny machine, rattling against the far side of the private box. Fassin whirled to see Hatherence dropping down round the side of the *Dzunda*, carapace silvered. The laser beam had come from her. The little spherical device dropped its disguise, revealing itself as a mirror-finish machine with stubby wings. It had a tiny hole in one flank, a much larger one on the far side, producing smoke. It rolled over in the air, made a crackling noise, then dropped to the transparent floor. Above him, Fassin was aware of Valseir hesitating in the access tube. Slipstream wind whistled in through the hole in the diamond bubble.

The colonel swung quickly in towards them.—You all right, major? she signalled, stopping immediately outside, buffeted by the slipstream. She tipped to look at the device lying rolling on the clear curved floor of the box.

—Shit, she sent.—That looks like one of ours.

There was a white flash, as though from everywhere at once, blinding Fassin for an instant. As the light faded Hatherence was already falling away, tumbling like a dropped stone through the gas. Something moved, faster than the GasClippers, across the StormWall face, carving in towards the Blimper.

When the colonel had fallen twenty metres below the private box, a line of searing yellow-white light flicked into existence between the incoming machine and Hatherence's esuit, which erupted in fire and blew apart. The fast-moving device looked like a small gascraft or missile, sharp and finned. Its exhaust flared bright as it powered round.

Fassin looked down to see Hatherence. She was a dark, ragged manta shape falling, whirling downwards amongst the smoking debris of the destroyed esuit. She seemed to twist in the air, flicking round, something glinting in a stubby tentacle; a violet beam lanced towards the finned craft, missing by a metre. Another white line from the machine speared the colonel, obliterating her in a sun-bright burst of light.

Valseir had cleared the access tube. Fassin blasted up it like a shell up a gun barrel, letting the pulse of down draught tear the diamond bubble box out in a convulsive explosion of wreckage that whipped away from the *Dzunda* and followed the remains of the colonel and her esuit towards the storm's concave base and the Depths beyond.

Valseir was waiting in the broad corridor above. "Fassin! *What* is going on?"

"How do we get off this thing?" he asked, taking the old Dweller by the hub-arm and leading him towards the next vertical access.

"Do we really need to?"

"Something's attacking us, Valseir."

"Are you sure?"

"Yes. So how do we get off?"

"What's wrong with roting?"

"Bit vulnerable. I was thinking of a craft."

"Well, I'm sure we can arrange a taxi. Or one of the Blimper's own skiffs. I'll ask Captain Xessife."

"No," Fassin said. "Not Captain Xessife."

"Why not?"

"Somebody had to put that drug bowl there."

They got to the vertical. "But…" Valseir hesitated. "Wait, what's that noise?"

Fassin could hear a deep warbling sound coming from various directions. "That could be an alarm." He indicated the tube above. "After you. Let's move."

They were halfway up the vertical to the central corridor when the *Dzunda* lurched. "Oh-oh," Valseir said.

"Keep going."

When they got to the main concourse, the alarm noise was louder. Dwellers were shouting at each other, picking up dropped trays, food and drugs and staring at some of the wall-screens. Fassin looked too. "Oh fuck," he said quietly.

The screens showed confused pictures of the surroundings, not all the cameras and screens now focusing on the still continuing GasClipper race. One camera seemed to be following a slim, finned craft, the one which had attacked Hatherence, as it circled the Blimper.

Other screens showed ships, dozens of dark ships, dropping from the sky.

They were gas-capable Mercatoria spacecraft, some as little as fifty metres long, others three or four times that size; soot-black ellipsoids with thick wings and sleek but rudimentary tailplanes and engine pods. They were diving towards the Blimper fleet, two or three peeling off every vertical klick or so to circle, guarding. Much higher above—another snatched camera angle, drifting out of focus then snapping clear—more slick shapes gyrated above the high haze layer, like scavengers over carrion.

Another screen's view spun, then settled, jerking, on the spectating fleet's accompanying Dreadnought, the *Puisiel*, whose turrets were swinging, gun barrels elevating. A yellow-white beam flicked on and off, boring straight through the war craft, making it shudder and sending shock waves running along its outer fabric. The beam hit the StormWall beyond at almost the same time, raising a dark puff of vapour like a bruise, quickly whipped away. The GasClippers seemed to have disappeared.

"What in all the gods' farts is going on?" Valseir asked. They had come to a stop, transfixed by the screens like most of the rest of the people in the concourse.

The *Puisiel*'s turrets and guns continued to swing round for a moment, then came to rest, seemingly pointing in random directions.

"Oh, don't," Fassin said.

The Dreadnought's guns flashed, gouting fire and smoke. Smaller shapes dropped away from it at the same time, half obscured by the wreathing broadside smoke clouds, and then pulsed fire and smoke from their rears and started curving up and out towards the dropping spacecraft. Screens blinked. The dark, descending spacecraft glittered with light. Midway between the *Puisiel* and the scatter of black ships, piercing white lines ended in sudden detonations, filling the gas above and around the spectating fleet with black bursts of smoke.

A screen swung to show one turning spacecraft dropping, trailing smoke. Dwellers started yelling. Trays, food, drugs and pet-children were sent flying, carapace skins blazed naked signals of excitement and fury and whiffs of war-lust filled the air as though a series of tiny scent-grenades had gone off along the concourse. A black dot trailing a haze of exhaust sailed in towards the crippled spacecraft but was picked off from above in a blast of light. Then something still smaller and faster darted across the screen and hit the ship, detonating inside and tearing it entirely in half; the two torn sections flew down towards the Depths, dangled on elongating strings of smoke. The other missiles were picked off even more easily, swatted like slow insects.

Fassin started pulling Valseir away. Dwellers all around them howled and barked at the screens and started taking bets. Distant concussive thumps and longer roars sounded throughout the concourse, bringing the long-delayed battle sounds to accompany the near-instant visuals.

Dark glitterings, everywhere. The Dreadnought lit up all along its length, speckled with fire. The beams lanced it, plunging on into the StormWall, freckling bruises across the stir of dark gas. About a third of a last broadside, most of it aimed at where the fallen spaceship had been, punched out from the *Puisiel* a fraction of a second before the first beams hit. The great vessel shook like a leaf in a storm, then started to drop even as further rays riddled it. A final beam, less bright, much broader, punched through the whole central section, folding the craft about its middle and sending it flowing and spiralling downwards. A few tiny double discs drifted away from the stricken war craft and roted away or just fell, some trailing smoke. Some were hit by further beams of light, vanishing in miniature explosions.

"Valseir, move," Fassin whispered in the sudden silence. "We have to get away. Just get to the outside." They were almost level with a 45° up-access tube. Fassin nudged Valseir towards it. "This way." He didn't even know if they really should get away. Maybe they were still somehow safer here in the Blimper. At least closer to the outside they might have more choice.

Valseir allowed himself to be pushed towards the slope of the access tube. The lowest part of the fleet of dark ships was now almost level with the top of the spectating fleet. Howls started to fill the concourse. Fassin and Valseir were being held back from the tube entrance by a stream of Dwellers coming in the other direction.

Fassin continued to push the old Dweller, though they both kept looking back at the screens. One of the dark ships circled gradually closer to the StormWall. Near its closest approach, a GasClipper came hurtling out of the dark curtain of whirling gas, blade sails extended like a frozen gleaming explosion. It rammed the dark warship amidships, hammering into it and pushing the two craft across the sky in a single tangled flailing mass. Still locked in their terrible embrace, the two craft started to fall away with everything else, heading for the foot of the storm's great dark well and the hot crush of gas beneath.

More screams and barks of joy echoed round the concourse.

Another camera, another screen: a section of the StormWall was bulging, dark gas streaming around some huge rounded cone forcing its way through the storm as though it wasn't there.

A huge Dreadnought flowed out of the storm, trailing streamers of gas like vast banners. Shrieks of encouragement and great, air-quaking cheers resounded down the wide tunnel of the concourse, making it resonate like a vast organ pipe. The new Dreadnought silvered in an instant, white beams scattering off it as it flew into the clear gas heart of the storm's colossal eye.

"*Fuck* me," Fassin heard himself say. "They were waiting for them."

The silver Dreadnought powered straight towards the fleet of dark ships, which, after starting to close in on the spectating fleet, were now swinging and swivelling to reconfigure and face the new threat.

The Dreadnought raced forward, fire bright around its propellerless tail, guns firing and flashing. Its silvery skin, reflecting sky, storm and dark depths, sparkled with jagged scintillations, bouncing beams off in random directions like bright thrown spines. Two more of the dark ships detonated and fell, sending the Dweller screams in the concourse—and the bets—towards even wilder heights.

The Dreadnought tore onwards, shaking under the weight of fire falling upon it. A missile from the fleet of Mercatoria ships slashed across the view, was missed by a fan of interceptor fire from the Dreadnought and slammed into it.

There was just the hint of the start of an explosion, bursting the Dreadnought apart as though tearing open the wrapping round a piece of star, then the screen went utterly white before hazing out completely, blank. Lights in the concourse flickered and went out, came back, then faded again. The warbling sound, there but effectively unheard all this time, cut off, its absence in the sudden silence like a hearing loss. The *Dzunda* quivered like a struck animal.

Other screens wavered, went black, filled with static. Some screens, now providing the only light in the concourse, remained working. Gradually more light filled the long tube, as low emergency lighting strobed on, caught and held.

A low muttering sound of Dweller trepidation and resentment started to build. One camera swung to show the huge rolling mushroom cloud filling the space where the Dreadnought had been. A few tiny pieces of wreckage fell, far away, thin claws from a tumorously bloated fist. The dark ships started to close in again on the spectator fleet, currently composed of vessels commanded by two sorts of captains: those who thought it best to clump together and those who regarded scattering and even taking their chances with the storm winds as the safer bet.

The stampede of Dwellers from the access tube which Fassin was trying to push Valseir towards was slowly forcing the two of them back into the centre of the concourse. More people were flooding into the wide space from every other access point.

Somebody was screaming, "Look, look!"

One distant screen image was suddenly repeated across several more. At first it looked like a replay of the entrance of the first Dreadnought, the great nose bulging out through the curtain of streaming cloud, dragging gas like long flags of war. Then the view pulled back and the screen showed the StormWall bulging in another place, then another and another and another, until a whole vertical forest of the great ships was visible, hurtling out of the storm and towards the great column of black circling spacecraft hanging like a giant pendulum over the spectating fleet.

The *Dzunda* shook, rippled and screamed like something alive as the shock wave of the earlier nuclear explosion seemed to pick it up and rattle it. Dwellers swung this way and that across the concourse, banging into each other, walls, floor and ceiling, filling the gas with oaths and debris. Another pair of screens cut out but enough remained to show the closing fleet of mercury-coloured Dreadnoughts livid with fire outgoing and incoming. Lasers sheened off, fans of interceptor projectiles and beams combed the gas and sundered darting, twisting missiles. Two more of the dark ships, then a third, exploded or crumpled and started to fall or spiral down, but two more of the giant Dreadnoughts disappeared in massive, screen-hazing detonations.

A couple more Dreadnoughts were suddenly caught in a fiercely bright beam from immediately above, from out of the clear yellow sky. The beam fell between them, making each massive ship wobble as if stumbling in the gas. Then it split into two parallel shafts, each violet rod narrowing in an instant and chopping through its targeted Dreadnought like an axe through a neck.

The concourse—half dark, filled with wild scents and the frenzied bellowing of Dwellers unsure whether to wail laments or shout huzzahs, lit by the spastic, spasming light of the battle views swinging wildly across the screens—achieved a sort of chaotic transcendence as very loud but defiantly soothing-sounding music started to play, product of some confused automatic guest-management system waking to insanity and trying to spread tranquillity.

"What," Fassin heard a nearby Dweller say, quite quietly but distinctly through the pandemonium, "the fuck is *that*?"

(Another dark Mercatorial ship, another silver Dreadnought, ripped to shreds and blossoming in nuclear fire respectively. Another pair of Dreadnoughts shaking in the first beam-fall of the violet ray flicking from on high.)

And on the screen opposite, looking downwards into the wide bowl of the storm's dead heart, a huge darkly red-glowing globe was rising from the sump gases of the storm floor, dragging a great flute of gas after it like some absurdly steady fireball. It was kilometres across and striated, banded like a miniature gas-giant, so that for one crazed instant Fassin thought he was watching the palace of the Hierchon Ormilla floating smoothly upwards into the fray.

A crumpled scrap falling towards this apparition—a ruined and smoking Mercatoria spacecraft—appeared to lend a scale to the huge sphere, seeming to be about to fall just behind it, making the quickly rising globe three or four klicks across.

The wrecked ship fell in front, instead, and upped that ready estimate by a factor of two.

A couple of filament-thin yellow-white beams suddenly joined with the massive globe and seemed to sink into it without effect. The violet beam from high above swung onto it, spreading briefly as though to measure the full seven or eight kilometres of its diameter before starting to narrow.

A pattern of black dots appeared on the surface of the giant globe.

The *Dzunda* shook again and again as further blast waves crashed into it. Fassin stared at the great rising sphere even as Dwellers on either side thudded into him and he lost his hold on Valseir.

There were maybe fifty or so of the black spots, spread as though randomly across the upper hemisphere of the huge globe. One appeared to be in the centre of the rapidly narrowing, focusing violet beam. Just as that ray grew too bright to see the ebony dot at its centre, it seemed to pulse and spread. Then it disappeared, just as each spot suddenly became the plinth for an intensely bright, thin column of pure white light. The beams lasted for an eye-blink, disappearing almost as soon as they'd been produced, only their image lasting, burned into any naked eyes and insufficiently buffered cameras trained on them.

Silence, even as another manic convulsion shook the *Dzunda*, making the whole concourse ripple and creak. More screens went out. The loud soothing music cut off. Two remaining screens nearby showed the dark ships, whole squadrons of them, entire flocks of them, reduced for most of their length to sparkling, wind-blown ash, only the long needle noses and tailed, finned rears remaining intact to fall like meteors, unreeling scrawny trails of smoke into the storm's tenebrous depths.

The nearest screen showed the camera swinging across the sky, searching for an intact Mercatoria ship, only to find further drifts of smoke, new clouds of ash, already drifting on the wind.

The other screen's view pivoted to the sky, where something glowing yellow was fading and disappearing as it cooled, at first still keeping station with the scene directly beneath, then starting to drift away to the east.

The huge sphere was still rising, though slowing now, coming gradually level with the remains of the spectating fleet. The remaining two dozen or so mirror-finish Dreadnoughts were decelerating, heaving-to on one side of the clumped and scattered ships.

A bellowing roar of utter—and unexpected—victory built quickly in every Dweller throat along the length of the concourse, swelling to a clanging, thunderous cacophony of mind-splitting, thought-warping sound.

Then a series of crashing, titanic shock waves pummelled the *Dzunda* like a gale whipping a flag. A barrage of noise like a troop of titans clapping entirely drowned out the hollering Dwellers.

All the screens went dark. The Blimper *Dzunda* lurched for one last time, then started to fall out of the sky. Those Dwellers not already heading swiftly for the exits immediately began to do so, the ones near Fassin sweeping him along with them, up the access tube he'd been trying to head for originally, out via a wide funnel port into a viewing gallery, through its massively shattered diamond roof and out into the bruised and battered skies of Nasqueron.

"You mean some of your ridiculous fucking fairy stories about secret ships and hyper-weapons are actually *true*?" Fassin said.

"Well," Y'sul said, looking round. "So it would appear."

They were somewhere inside the *Isaut*, the enormous spherical ship which had destroyed almost the entire Mercatorial fleet—space-based command-and-control plus heavy-weaponry bombardment back-up included—in the space of about half a second. The *Isaut* was something called a Planetary Protector (Deniable), not that Fassin or, apparently, anybody else rescued from the destroyed and damaged ships of the spectating fleet had ever heard of such a thing. That, as Y'sul had pointed out, was a pretty unarguably convincing brand of deniability.

There had, of course, been rumours and myths concerning secret Dweller martial capability and the general lack of wisdom of getting into a fight with such an ancient and widespread species for as long as people could remember, but—as most of these myths and rumours seemed to be spread by the Dwellers themselves—as a rule nobody ever really took them seriously. The Dwellers spent so much time huffing and puffing and telling people how completely wonderful and brilliant they were—and yet seemed so self-obsessed, so inward-looking and so careless of their distant fellows, so unconnected not just with the rest of the civilised galaxy but with their own vastly scattered diaspora—they were inevitably dismissed as vainglorious fantasists and their vaunted ships and weapons, at best, a sort of folk memory of earlier magnificence, long lost, entirely eclipsed.

Even now, having just seen the results of the *Isaut*'s intervention with his own eyes—or at least through the little gascraft's sensors—Fassin could not entirely believe what he'd witnessed.

"Well, this is a strange place to be," Valseir said, looking about the spherical space he, Y'sul and Fassin had been shown to.

They had rendezvoused quite quickly in the general gas-borne confusion of survivors from the *Dzunda*. Fassin's arrrowhead-shaped craft, though smaller than all the surrounding Dwellers, was a sufficiently different shape for Valseir and Y'sul to spot him quite without difficulty and head in his direction.

"Why is everybody else giving me such a wide berth?" Fassin had asked when they'd each drifted up to him in the after-battle calmness. It was true; all the other Dweller survivors were keeping a good fifty metres or so away from him.

"Worried you're going to be a target," Y'sul had said, checking his various pockets and pouches to see what he might have lost in the excitement. Around them, various long smoky columns were drifting in the breeze like anaemic stalks rooted in the dark storm base far below, and great dumb-bell-shaped clouds—all that was left of the nuclear explosions—were twisting and slowly tearing apart, their round, barely rolling heads still climbing into higher and higher levels of atmosphere, being caught in differential wind streams and casting vast hazy shadows across the again-quiet skies of the storm's eye. Hovering to one side, the vast banded sphere which had risen from the Depths floated like a miniature planet caught in the eye of the great storm.

To one side, in the StormWall, the GasClipper fleet seemed to be trying to regroup. Tumbling out of the sinking *Dzunda* with the rest of the survivors, only a lifelong exposure to Dweller insouciance—both congenital and feigned—had prevented Fassin gasping in disbelief at the sound of various people around him quite seriously discussing whether the GasClipper race would just continue, be restarted or declared void, and passing opinions regarding the status of already existing bets in the light of this suite of likely choices.

The less damaged spectating and other craft were picking up the various free-floating Dwellers. Ambulance skiffs from the surviving craft in the silver Dreadnought fleet and hospital vessels from the nearest port facilities were rescuing the more seriously injured and burned individuals.

Fassin had indeed been targeted, but not by weaponry. A trio of skiffs had emerged from the giant sphere and made straight for the little group formed by Fassin and his two Dweller friends. They'd been taken aboard and the skiffs returned immediately to the enormous globe, ignoring the outraged yells of the Dwellers who until moments before had been studiously avoiding Fassin.

The lead skiff, crewed by a jolly pair of remarkably old-looking Dwellers—they didn't volunteer their names, ranks or ages, but they each looked at least as old as Jundriance—had deposited them somewhere deep inside the giant spherical craft, way down a dark tunnel into a broad sphere of reception space, complete with washing facilities and what Y'sul had taken one look at and sniffily dismissed as a snackateria. Before they'd left again in their skiff, it had been one of these unnamed Dwellers who, in response to a question of Fassin's, had told them the name and category of the great craft they'd been brought inside. Fassin had warned him that his gascraft had been in contact with Mercatoria nanotech and he might be contaminated, which did not surprise or alarm anybody aboard as much as he'd been expecting. The skiff's crew scanned the little gascraft and told him, well, he wasn't contaminated any more.

"Where is your little friend the Very Reverend Colonel?" Y'sul asked Fassin, making a show of looking around the reception space. "She jumped out of her seat and raced off just before all the fun started."

"She's dead," Fassin told him.

"Dead?" Y'sul rolled back. "But she seemed so well armed!"

"She shot what turned out to be a Mercatorial… device," Fassin said. "One of the first of their craft on the scene seemed to assume this meant she was a hostile and wasted her."

"Oh," Y'sul said, sounding downcast. "That was the Mercatoria, was it? Not these Disconnected people. You sure?"

"I'm fairly sure," Fassin said.

"Damn," Y'sul said, sounding annoyed. "Might sort of look like I've lost a bet, in that case. Wonder how I can get out of it?" He floated off, looking deep in thought.

Fassin turned to Valseir. "You sure you're all right?" he asked. The old Dweller had looked a little shaken when they'd rendezvoused in the gas above the sinking Blimper, though apart from a few carapace abrasions picked up in the welter of people rushing to escape the sinking ship, he was uninjured.

"I am fine, Fassin," he told the human. "And you? You have lost your colonel friend, I heard."

Fassin had a sudden reprise of his last image of Hatherence, that dark manta shape twisting in the air—to a Dweller she would have looked like one of their young—firing a hand weapon at the craft that had ripped her out of her esuit, then dying in the returning splash of fire. "I'm getting used to anybody who gets close to me dying violently," he said.

"Hmm. I consider myself warned," Valseir said.

"She was my superior, Valseir," Fassin told him. "She was my bodyguard but she was also my guard in another sense. I'd be surprised if she hadn't been given orders to kill me if the relevant circumstances arose."

"Do you think she would have carried out those orders?"

Fassin hesitated, suddenly feeling bad about what he'd just said, even though he still thought it was the truth. It was as though he'd insulted Hatherence's memory. He looked away and said, "Well, we'll never know now, will we?"

A door in the centre of the ceiling swung back. They all looked up. Two Dwellers entered. Fassin recognised one of them as Setstyin, the self-confessed influence pedlar he'd talked to by phone the evening he'd slipped away from Y'sul's house in Hauskip city. The other Dweller looked very old indeed, dark and small—barely five metres in diameter—and dressed in high-coverage clothes that probably concealed only a few remaining natural limbs and perhaps some prosthetics.

"Seer Fassin Taak," Setstyin said, roll-nodding towards him. Then he greeted Y'sul and lastly Valseir—as the most senior of the three Valseir came last and got an even more respectful bow. "Y'sul, Valseir: allow me to introduce the Sage-cuspian-chospe Drunisine, Executive Commander of this craft, the Planetary Protector (Deniable) *Isaut*."

"A pleasure," said the dark Dweller in a crisp, dry-sounding voice.

"And for us an *honour*," Y'sul said, brushing Fassin out of the way to present himself to the fore and execute an extravagantly complete bow.

"If I may say so."

"Our pleasure, pre-child," Valseir half-agreed, also roll-bowing, less completely but with more dignity.

"Good to see you, Setstyin," Fassin said. "And pleased to meet you, sir," he told the older Dweller.

Drunisine was by far the oldest and most senior Dweller Fassin had ever encountered. As a Dweller—surviving the perils of childhood first, obviously—rose through Adolescence, Youth and Adulthood to attain the life stages called Prime and then Cuspian and then Sage, what they were eventually aiming for—destined for, if they lived that long—was to reach Childhood, the state of utter done-everythingness that was the absolute zenith of all Dweller existence. The stage immediately before this culmination was the one which Drunisine had reached: *chospe*—pre-child. There was every chance that Drunisine was over two billion years old.

"My name is Setstyin," the other Dweller said, coming to rest near the centre of the spherical room with the Sage and looking round at the others. "I am a friend of Seer Taak's here. You are all sufficiently recovered and/or rested, I hope. Because we need to talk."

They agreed they were capable of talk. Setstyin waved and hammock seats descended from a ring round the ceiling door, which then closed. They settled in.

"Seer Taak," the ancient Dweller said. "We will need to ensure that all record of the battle just finished is wiped from the memories of that little craft you inhabit."

"I understand," Fassin said. He thought about that "(Deniable)". He called up everything he'd recorded of the battle in the storm's eye and full-deleted it. He called up a lot of other stored memories and got rid of those too. "It's done," he said.

"We will need to check," Setstyin told him, sounding apologetic.

"Feel free," Fassin said. "I take it we're not supposed to say anything about what happened out there. Or about this thing."

"Say what you like, young sir," Drunisine told him. "Our concern is with hard evidence."

"All surviving non-Dweller surveillance systems around Nasqueron have been removed," Setstyin said, talking to Fassin. "All the transgressing ships which had line-of-sight to the proceedings have already been destroyed. The remains of the Mercatorial fleet are being pursued and dispatched."

"They are being hunted down like *dogs*, Seer Taak," Drunisine said, looking straight at him and using the Anglish word. "Harried, systems jammed, comms disrupted, fates sealed, all so that no direct evidence of this craft or its capabilities, even that garnered second-hand, can escape. I might add that your own summary annihilation was contemplated."

"I am grateful to have been made an exception," Fassin said. "Are none of the ships which were above Nasqueron to be allowed to escape?"

"None," the ancient Dweller said.

"Those who start wars have to accept the consequences," Y'sul said, rumbling sententiously.

"And after that?" Fassin asked.

"Specify, please."

"Is this the start of a war with the Mercatoria, at least the part within Ulubis?"

"I don't imagine so," Drunisine said, sounding as though this was the first time the thought had occurred. "Not unless they choose to invade us again. Do you think they will, Fassin Taak?"

Fassin had the awful feeling that, given the Dwellers' irredeemably dismissive approach to intelligence, what he said next might well constitute the single most germane piece of information on the matter that the Dwellers would have to work with and base their decisions on.

"No, I don't. I think they'll be sufficiently horrified at the extent of their losses today to think twice about risking any further craft, certainly as long as they have the prospect of invasion to look forward to. If the invasion fails, or the system is finally recaptured, then there might be some attempt to find out what happened and no doubt some people will argue that there should be some form of reprisal. Though, in the shorter term, from what little I've heard of the Epiphany 5 Disconnect, there's a chance they might want to, ah, transgress, too." He looked at Drunisine and Setstyin, who remained silent. "Though I'm sure you'll be ready for them." More silence. "In fact, if the Ulubis Mercatoria work out what's happened here and realise you don't regard this as the start of a war, they might even want to suggest that you and they unite to resist the Epiphany 5 Disconnect forces."

"Why would we wish to do that?" Drunisine asked flatly.

It felt like it had been a long and tiring day. Fassin didn't really have the energy to start trying to explain. From a creature as old and experienced as Drunisine, the question was probably rhetorical anyway.

"Never mind," Fassin said. "Act as though nothing's happened. Signal 'glantine and make some helpful suggestions regarding the re-establishment of a new Seer Shared Facility."

"That's more or less what we were going to do anyway," Setstyin said, sounding amused.

Fassin signalled polite mirth in return. He was still struggling to work out what this enormous, fleets-destroyed-in-an-eyeblink craft really *meant*. Who was responsible for this colossal machine? What sort of previously unknown societal structures and prodigious manufacturing capacity within Dweller civilisation could conjure up something this awesome? Was it a one-off?

Was it unique to Nasqueron? Dear grief, was it part of a *fleet*? Did this mean that *all* the Dweller claims about secret ships and hyper-weapons were true? Could the Nasqueron Dwellers just swat the E-5 Discon out of the sky if they so desired, saving Ulubis from invasion? Could they feasibly take on the Mercatoria if they could be bothered? Did any of this mean that the Dweller List was now more likely to be genuine rather than some monstrous waste of time or just a joke? How he'd have liked to have had some time alone with Setstyin before this meeting, to find out what had happened since they'd talked last. He'd have to ask some of these questions anyway, given half a chance.

"We come, then," Drunisine said, "to the question of why the Ulubis Mercatoria Disconnect thought it might be a wise or profitable idea to enter Nasqueron in such a manner and in such numbers in the first place. Any ideas? Anybody?" The ancient Dweller looked round at all of them.

"I think it might have something to do with me," Fassin admitted.

"You, Seer Taak?" Drunisine asked.

"I've been here attempting to track down some information."

"And you needed the help of a small war fleet to extract it?"

"No. However, they might have thought I was in danger."

"From whom?"

"I don't know."

"So, we are talking about information that the Mercatoria might consider momentous enough to start a war for? When they are already facing an invasion in the next few months or years? This must be information of some importance. Perhaps we can help. What is it?"

"Thank you. However, I think I may finally be close to finding it."

"Ah," Valseir said. "About that."

"What?" Fassin asked him.

"All that stuff about the folder and the safekeep box and taking it personally to Chimilinith of Deilte?"

"Yes?"

"Not entirely true."

"Not entirely?"

"Not entirely."

"So how much of it *was* true?"

Valseir rocked back a fraction, seemingly thinking. Patterns of surprise crossed his signal skin. "Actually, most of it," he said.

"And the part that wasn't?" Fassin asked patiently.

"There was no folder in the safekeep box."

"So Chimilinith hasn't got the information."

"Correct."

"I see."

"I am still waiting for enlightenment regarding the exact nature of this exemplary, if shy, information," Drunisine said frostily, looking at Valseir.

*Oh shit*, Fassin thought, *if Valseir tells them what it is, and it really exists, they might just kill us all.*

Possibly the same thought had occurred to Valseir. "It allegedly involves a method for travelling faster than light," he told the ancient commander.

Setstyin's carapace flashed hilarity, quickly damped. Drunisine looked about as thoroughly unimpressed as it was possible for an elderly Dweller to look. "What?" he said.

"An ancient addition to a still more ancient book—which Seer Taak here traded over two hundred years ago during a 'delve', as the Quick call these things—makes mention of a method of achieving FTL travel without recourse to Adjutage and Cannula," Valseir said, using what Fassin recognised as the Dweller terms for portals and wormholes. Fassin thought—and sincerely hoped—that Valseir had put just the right amount of apology and wry amusement into his voice. "Seer Taak has been sent here to try to find the details of this, ah, unlikely technology."

"Indeed?" Drunisine said, looking at Fassin.

"Algebra," he blurted.

"Algebra?" Drunisine asked.

"The data looks like a piece of algebra, apparently," Fassin said. "It defines some sort of warping device. A way of bending space. Conventional to start with, but using this technique to exceed light speed." Fassin made a gesture of resignation. He let embarrassment patterns show on his arrowhead's skin. "I was seconded without any real choice into a paramilitary part of the Mercatoria and ordered to undertake this mission. I am as sceptical as I imagine you are, sir, regarding the likelihood of it coming to a successful conclusion."

Drunisine let the most formal amusement pattern show on his skin. "Oh, I doubt that you are, Seer Taak."

"What's going on?"

"I was about to ask you the same question," Setstyin told Fassin. "Shall we trade?"

"All right, but I asked first."

"What exactly do you want to know?"

They were still in the reception sphere inside the giant globe. Commander Drunisine had left. Two Adult medical orderlies were dealing with the few small injuries that Y'sul and Valseir had picked up during the battle. "What *is* this thing?" Fassin asked, gesturing to indicate the whole ship. "Where did it come from? Who made it? Who controls it? How many are there in Nasqueron?"

"I'd have thought the title said it all," Setstyin said. "It's a machine to protect the planet. From willed aggression of a certain technical type and sophistication. It's not a spacecraft, if that's what you mean. It's limited to in-atmosphere. It came from the Depths, where stuff like this is usually stored. We made it. I mean Dwellers did, probably a few billion years ago. I'd have to check. It's controlled by people in the control centre, who'll be Dwellers with military experience who've sim-trained for this sort of device specifically. As to numbers... I wouldn't know. Probably not the sort of information one's meant to share, really. No offence, Fass, but in the end you're not actually one of us. We have to assume your loyalties lie elsewhere."

"Built billions of years ago? Can you still—?"

"Ah, that would count as a follow-up question," Setstyin said, chiding. "I think it's my turn first."

Fassin sighed. "All right."

"Are you really looking for this warp-drive FTL technology data? You do realise it doesn't exist, don't you?"

"It's data that the Mercatoria believe might give them a better chance of winning the fight against the E-5 Discon. They are desperate. They'll try anything. And I have my orders, no matter what I might think about the whole thing. Of course I know independent FTL drives don't exist."

"Will you still obey these orders, given the chance?"

Fassin thought about Aun Liss, about the people he'd known in Hab 4409, about all the other people he'd ever known throughout Ulubis system over the years. "Yes," he said.

"Why do you obey these orders?" Setstyin sounded genuinely puzzled. "Your family and Seer Sept colleagues are almost all dead, your immediate military superior was killed in the recent battle and there is nobody nearby now to take her place."

"It's complicated," Fassin told Setstyin. "Perhaps it's duty or a guilty conscience or just the desire to be doing something. *Can* you still make more of these planetary protection machines?"

"No idea," Setstyin admitted. "Don't see why not, though. I'd suggest asking somebody who might know, but even if the true answer was no we'd be bound to say yes, wouldn't we?"

"Was it my call to you that set all this in motion?"

"You're getting a lot of free questions, aren't you? However, yes, it did. Though I suspect that watching dozens of recently modified gas-capable warcraft suddenly parking themselves in orbit around us might have started a few alarm bells ringing amongst us even without your timely warning. Still, we're grateful. I don't think I'm entirely out of formation in saying that there is a feeling we probably owe you a favour."

"And if the Mercatoria ever finds out," Fassin said, "I'll be executed as a traitor."

"Well, we won't tell if you don't," Setstyin said, perfectly seriously.

"Deal," Fassin said, unconvinced.

The great spherical craft *Isaut* floated deep within a vast cloud of streaming gas, moving swiftly, seeming not to. It had started to submerge into the storm's curdled floor of slowly swirling gas almost as soon as Fassin and the others had been brought aboard. Sinking, sidling, rising slightly again, it had entered into the Zone 2 weather band, quickly assumed its speed, and was now, in the late evening that was becoming night, half a thousand kilometres away from the storm where the battle had taken place, and adding another three hundred kilometres to that value with every passing hour.

Fassin, Y'sul, Valseir and Setstyin floated over a narrow platform set at the great vessel's equator, near the body of Colonel Hatherence. A weak light and weaker breeze lent an appropriate atmosphere of quiet gloom to the scene. The colonel's torn, burned body had been discovered along with hundreds of others, floating at the level at which Dweller bodies usually came to rest. Hers had come to rest a little higher than the others, as would a child's.

Left to themselves, Dweller bodies degassed and gained density, and abandoned to the atmosphere would eventually disappear completely into the Depths. The respectful convention, however, was either to keep a dead relative in a special ceremonial chamber at home and let them decay until their density would ensure a swift passage into the liquid hydrogen far beneath, or—if time was pressing—to weight the body and consign it to the Depths that way.

Hatherence had no family here. There was not even anybody of her own species in all Nasqueron, and so—as, at least, a fellow alien—Fassin had been declared responsible for her remains. He'd agreed a swift dispatch to the Depths was preferable to keeping her body and handing it back to the Shrievalty or any family she might still have in Ulubis system. He wasn't even sure why he felt that way, but he did. There was no particular veneration of the remains of the dead in the way of the Truth, and, as far as he knew, no special meaning amongst oerileithe in having their dead returned from afar, but even if there had been, he'd have wanted something like this. For the Dwellers, it was probably just administrative convenience, even tidiness to dispose of her now, like this. For him, it was something more.

Fassin looked down at the alien body—thin and dark, something between a manta and a giant starfish—lying in its coffin of meteorite iron. Iron had always been and, sentimentally, ceremonially, still was a semi-precious metal for Dwellers. That they were burying Hatherence like this was something of an honour, he supposed. In the fading light, her ragged remains, dark anyway, then burned by the beam which had killed her, looked like scraps of shadow.

Fassin felt tears in his real eyes, inside the shock-gel inside the little gascraft that was his own tiny life-coffin, and knew that some deep, near-animal part of him was mourning not so much the fallen Oculan colonel as all the people he knew whom he'd lost recently, lost without seeing them one last time, even in death, lost without fully being able to believe that he really had lost them because it had all happened so far away with so much in between them and him to stop him returning to pay any sort of respects to them, lost in his intellect but not his emotions, because even now, some part of him refused to believe he would never see all those lost ones again.

"I confess," Setstyin said, "I have no idea what form of words one ought to use on such occasions, Seer Taak. Do you?"

"Amongst some aHumans there is a saying that we come from and go to nothing, a lack like shadow that throws the sum of life into bright relief. And with the rHumans, something about dust to ashes."

"Do you think she would have minded being treated as a Dweller?" Setstyin asked.

"No," Fassin said. "I don't think she would have minded. I think she would have felt honoured."

"Here, here," Y'sul muttered.

Valseir gave a small formal bow.

"Well, Colonel Hatherence," Setstyin said, with what sounded like a sigh as he looked down at the body lying in the coffin. "You ascended to the age and rank of Mercatorial Colonel, which is a very considerable achievement for your kind. We think you lived well and we know you died well. You died with many others but in the end we all die alone. You died more alone than others, amongst people like you but alien to you, and far from your home and family. You fell and were found and now we send you down again, further into those Depths, to join all the revered dead on the surface of rock around the core." He looked at Fassin. "Seer Taak, would you like to say anything?"

Fassin tried to think of something. In the end he just said, "I believe Colonel Hatherence was a good person. She was certainly a brave one. I only knew her for less than a hundred days and she was always my military superior, but I came to like her and think of her as a friend. She died trying to protect me. I'll always honour her memory."

He signalled that he could think of nothing else. Setstyin roll-nodded and indicated the open coffin lid.

Fassin went forward and used a manipulator to close the casket's iron hatch, then he lowered a little more and together he and Setstyin took one edge of the bier that the coffin lay on. They raised it, letting the heavy container slide silently off, over the edge of the balcony and down into the next bruise-dark layer of clouds, far below.

They all floated over the edge and waited until the coffin disappeared, a tiny black speck vanishing into the darkly purple wastes.

"Great-cousin of mine, diving deep, got hit by one of those once," Y'sul said thoughtfully. "Never knew what hit him. Stone dead."

The others were looking at him.

He shrugged. "Well? It's true."

Valseir found Fassin in a gallery, looking out at the deep night stream of gas, rushing quietly in infrared as the *Isaut* powered its way to who knew where.

"Fassin."

"Valseir. Are we free to leave yet?"

"Not that I've heard. Not yet."

They watched the night flow round them together for a while. Fassin had spent time earlier looking at reports on the storm battle, from both sides. The Dwellers had high-selectivity visuals which made it look like the Dreadnoughts had won the day, not the *Isaut*. The little he'd got from the Mercatoria's nets just gave dark hints that an entire fleet was missing, and included no visuals at all. Unseen was pretty much unheard-of. It appeared that everybody had instantly assumed there was some vast cover-up going on. Both sides were downplaying like crazy, implying that some terrible misunderstanding had taken place and they'd both suffered appallingly heavy losses, which was, when Fassin thought about it, somewhere between half and three-quarters true, and hence closer to reality than might have been expected in the circumstances.

"So what did happen to this folder?" Fassin asked. "If there was a folder."

"There was and is a folder, Fassin," Valseir told him. "I held on to it for a long time but eventually, twenty-one, twenty-three years ago, I gave it to my colleague and good friend Leisicrofe. He was departing on a research trip."

"Has he returned?"

"No."

"When will he?"

"Should he return, he won't have the data."

"Where will it be?"

"Wherever he left it. I don't know."

"How do I find your friend Leisicrofe?"

"You'll have to follow him. That will not be so easy. You will need help."

"I have Y'sul. He's always arranged—"

"You will need rather more than he can provide."

Fassin looked at the old Dweller. "Off-planet? Is that what you mean?"

"Somewhat," Valseir said, not looking at him, gazing out at the onward surge of night.

"Then who should I approach for this help?"

"I've already taken the liberty."

"You have? That's very kind."

Valseir was silent for a while, then said, "None of this is about kindness, Fassin." He turned to look directly at the arrowhead. "Nobody in their right mind would ever want to be involved with something as momentous as this. If the slightest part of what you're looking for has any basis in reality, it could change everything for all of us. I am Dweller. My species has made a good, long—if selfish—life for itself, spread everywhere, amongst the stars. We do not appreciate change on the scale we are here talking about. I'm not sure that any species would. Some of us will do anything to avoid such change, to keep things just as they are.

"You have to realise, Fassin; we are not a monoculture, we are not at all perfectly homogenised. We are differentiated in ways that even now, after all your exposure to us, you can scarcely begin to comprehend. There are things within our own worlds almost entirely hidden from most of us, and there are deep and profound differences of opinion between factions amongst us, just as there are between the Quick."

*Factions*, thought Fassin.

Valseir went on, "Not all of us are quite so studiedly indifferent to events taking place within the greater galaxy as we generally contrive to appear. There are those of us who, without ever wanting to know the full details of your mission, in fact knowing that they'd be unable to square knowledge of its substance with their species loyalty, would help you nevertheless. Others... others would kill you instantly if they even began to guess what it was you're looking for." The old Dweller floated over, came close to a kiss-whisper as he said,—And believe it or not, Fassin Taak, Drunisine is of the former camp, while your friend Setstyin is of the latter.

Fassin pulled away to look at the old Dweller, who added,—Truly.

After a few more moments, Fassin asked, "When will I be able to follow your friend Leisicrofe?"

"I think you'll know one way or the other before the night is out. And if we both don't at least begin to follow Leisicrofe, we may both follow your Colonel Hatherence."

Fassin thought this sounded a little melodramatic. "Truly?" he asked, signalling amusement.

"Oh, truly, Fassin," Valseir said, signalling nothing. "Let me repeat: none of this is about kindness."

∙

Saluus Kehar was not happy. He had his own people in certain places, his own ways of finding things out, his own secure and reliable channels of intelligence quite independent of the media and the official agencies—you didn't become and stay a major military supplier unless you did—and he knew about as well as anybody did what had happened during the disastrous Nasqueron raid, and it was simply unjust to blame him or his firm.

For one thing, they'd been betrayed, or their intelligence or signals had been compromised, or at the very least they'd been out-thought (by Dwellers!). And because of that failing—which was unquestionably nothing to do with him—they'd been ambushed and out-outnumbered. Dozens of those heretofore un-fucking-heard-of super-Dreadnought ships had turned up when the incursionary force had been expecting no more than a handful—at most—of the standard ones, the models without the reactive mirror armour, the plasma engines and the wide-band lasers. Plus the Dwellers had simply done a very good job of lying over the years—years? Aeons—presenting themselves as hopeless bumblers and technological incompetents when in fact—even if they couldn't build anything very impressive from scratch any more—they still had access to weaponry of serious lethality.

The military had fucked up. It didn't matter how good the tool was, how clever the craftsman had been, how well-made the weapon was; if the user dropped it, didn't switch it on or just didn't know how to use it properly, all that good work went for nothing.

They'd lost all the ships. All of them. Every single damn one, either on the raid or supporting it from space immediately above. Even a few of the ships not involved at all—those standing guard round Third Fury while the recovery and construction teams worked—had been targeted and annihilated by some sort of charged-particle-beam weapon, with two craft on the far side of the moon each chased by some type of hyper-velocity missile and blown to smithereens as well.

Unwilling to accept that they'd made a complete mess of the operation, the military had decided it mustn't be their fault. Kehar Heavy Industries must be to blame. There must, to quote an ancient saying, be something wrong with our bloody ships. The sheer completeness of the catastrophe, and the frustrating lack of detail regarding exactly what had gone wrong, actually made it easier to blame the tool rather than the workman. All the ships had been made gas-capable by Saluus's shipyards, all had been lost on their first mission using their new abilities, so—according to that special logic only the military mind seemed to appreciate—it must be a problem with the process of making them capable of working in an atmosphere that was responsible.

Never mind that the battlecruiser acting as Command and Control for the whole operation and both the Heavy-Armour Battery Monitors had been blasted to atoms just as effortlessly as the ships working in the planet's clouds, even though they'd never been gas-capabled and were still in space at the time; that little detail somehow got rolled up into greater disaster and conveniently forgotten about in the hysteria.

So now they'd lost Fassin and they'd lost their lead to this Dweller List thing. Worse, they had a serious intelligence problem, because, basically, they'd been duped. The old Dweller Valseir must have suspected something or been tipped off. They knew this for the simple reason that the information he'd provided—almost the last data that had got relayed back to the top brass on Sepekte before everything went haywire—had proved, when checked later, to be a lie. The Dweller he'd told Fassin to look for in Deilte city didn't exist. For the sake of this they'd lost over seventy first-rate warships for no gain whatsoever—ships they would seriously miss when the Beyonder/Starveling invasion hit home for real—and they'd thoroughly antagonised the Dwellers, who'd never been people it was advisable to get on the wrong side of even before they'd suddenly shown they still packed the kind of punch that could humiliate a Mercatorial fleet. As military fuck-ups went it was a many-faceted gem, a work of genius, a grapeshot, multi-stage, cluster-warhead, fractal-munition regenerative-weapon-system of a fuck-up.

In fact it was only that last item on the long list of calamitous consequences—dealing with the Dwellers' subsequent actions and signals—that had worked out less badly than it might have. Finally, something positive.

Saluus was in a meeting. He hated meetings. They were an entirely vital part of being an industrialist, indeed of being a businessman in any sort of organisation, but he still hated them. He'd learned, partly at his father's side, to get good at meetings, working people and information before, during and after them, but even when they were short and decided important stuff they felt like a waste of time.

And they were rarely short and rarely decided important stuff.

This one wasn't even his meeting. Unusually, he wasn't in control. He'd been summoned. Summoned? He'd been *brought before* them. That caught the mood better.

He far preferred conference calls, holo meetings. They tended to be shorter (though not always—if you had one where everybody was somewhere they felt really comfortable, they could go on for ever too) and they were easier to control—easier to dismiss, basically. But there seemed to be this distribution curve of meeting reality: people at the bottom of the organisational pile had lots of real all-sat-down-together meetings—often, Saluus had long suspected, because they had nothing useful to do and so had the time to spare and the need to seem important that meetings could provide. Those in the middle and towards the top had more and more holo meetings because it was just more time-efficient and the people they needed to meet with were of similarly high stature with their own time problems and often far away. But then—this was the slightly weird bit—as you got to the very highest levels, the proportion of face-to-face meetings started to rise again.

Maybe because it was a sign of how much you'd been able to delegate, maybe because it was a way of imposing your authority on those in the middle and upper-middle ranks beneath you, maybe because the things being discussed at high-level meetings were so important that you needed the very last nuance of physicality they provided over a holo conference to be sure that you were working with all the relevant information, including whether somebody was sweating or had a nervous tic.

This was the sort of stuff a good holo would show up, of course, though equally the sort of stuff a good pre-transmission image-editing camera would smooth away. In theory somebody in a conference call could be sitting there sweating a river and jumping like they'd been electrocuted, but if they had decent real-time image-editing facilities they could look the perfect epitome of unruffled cucumber-chill.

Though there was stuff you could do in reality, too, of course. For his thirteenth birthday, Saluus's father had given his son a surprise party and, later, a surprise present in the shape of a visit to a Finishing Clinic, where, over the course of a long and not entirely pain-free month, they fixed his teeth, widened his eyes and altered their colour (Saluus had been womb-sculpted for the appearance he'd had, but, hey, a father could change his mind). More to the point, they made him much less fidgety, upped his capacity to concentrate and gave him control over his sweat glands, pheromone output and galvanic skin response (the last three not strictly legal, but then the clinic was owned by a subsidiary of Kehar Heavy Industries). All good for giving one an edge in meetings, discussions and even informal get-togethers. And usefully applicable to the art of seduction, too, where one's blatant proximity to and control over astounding quantities of cash had somehow failed to have the desired effect.

This was a meeting of the Emergency War Cabinet, a high-level top-brass get-together in a klicks-deep command-bunker complex beneath one of a handful of discreetly well-guarded mansions dotted round the outskirts of greater Borquille State.

A high-level top-brass get-together minus the Hierchon Ormilla himself, however. He was patently too grand to attend a mere meeting, even of something as important as the Emergency War Cabinet, even when the fate of the System was in even greater jeopardy than it had been before the disastrous decision to go mob-handed into the atmosphere of Nasqueron the instant they thought they had a firm lead to the—anyway probably mythical—Dweller List.

And why did meetings always make his mind wander, and, specifically, make it wander towards—wander towards? Head straight for—sex?

He looked at women he was attending meetings with and found it very hard not to imagine them naked. This happened when they weren't especially attractive, but was inevitable and often vivid if they were even slightly good-looking. Something about being able to look at them for long periods when they were talking, he suspected. Or just the urge to shuck off the whole civilised thing of being good little officers of the company and get back to being cave people again, humping in the dirt.

First Secretary Heuypzlagger was wittering. Saluus was confident that he looked like he was hanging on the First Secretary's every word, and that his short-term memory would snick him back in should he need to return his full attention to proceedings if and when anything else of genuine import stumbled into view. But in the meantime, having already gleaned as much as he felt he was likely to regarding the real state of things from the body language and general demeanour of his fellow meeters, he felt free to let his mind wander.

He glanced at Colonel Somjomion, who was the only woman at this meeting. She didn't tend to say very much so you didn't get too many opportunities to look straight at her. Not especially attractive (though he was, he'd been telling himself recently, starting to appreciate women rather than girls, and see past the more obvious sexual characteristics). There was, certainly, something especially exciting about the idea of undressing a woman in uniform, but he'd long since been there and done that and had the screenage to prove it. He thought of his latest lover instead.

Saluus thought of her last night, this morning, he thought of her the night they'd first met, first slept together. He quickly got an almost painfully hard erection. They'd sculpted him to have control over that at the Finishing Clinic as well, but he usually just let things rise and fall of their own accord down there, unless either the presence or the absence was going to be socially embarrassing. Anyway, he'd long since accepted that maybe it was a way of getting back at dear old dad, for forcing all this amendment stuff on him in the first place, however useful it had proved.

He still hated meetings.

Saluus supposed things had gone reasonably well for him in this one so far, considering. He'd had to agree to a full inquiry into the gas-capabling of the ships they'd modified as part of the general investigation into what had gone wrong, but—even allowing for the implied insult and the waste of time, just when they didn't need it—that wasn't too terrible. He'd managed to deflect most of the criticism by getting the Navarchy, the Guard and the Shrievalty Ocula representatives to compete for who was least to blame for the whole botched-raid thing.

That had worked well. Divide and conquer. That wasn't difficult in the current system. In fact it was set up for it. He remembered asking his father about this back when Saluus was still being tutored at home. Why the confusion of agencies? Why the plethora (he'd just discovered the word, enjoyed using it) of military and security and other organisations within the Mercatoria? Just look at warships: there were the Guard—they had warships, the Navarchy Military—they had warships, the Ambient Squadrons—they had warships, the Summed Fleet—obviously they had warships, and then there were the Engineers, the Propylaea, the Omnocracy, the Cessorian Lustrals, the Shrievalty, the Shrievalty Ocula and even the Administrata. They all had their own ships, and each even had a few warships as well, for important escort duties. Why so many? Why divide your forces? The same went for security. Everybody seemed to have their own security service too. Wasn't this wasteful?

"Oh, definitely," his father had said. "But there's opportunity in waste. And what some call waste others would call redundancy. But do you really want to know what it's all about?"

Of course he did.

"Divide and conquer. Even amongst your own. Competition. Also even amongst your own. In fact, especially amongst your own. Keep them all at each other's throats, keep them all watching each other, keep them all wondering what the other lot might be up to. Make them compete for your attention and approval. Yes, it's wasteful, looked at one way, but it's wise, looked at another. This is how the Culmina keep everything under control, young man. This is how they rule us. And it appears to work, don't you think? Hmm?"

Saluus hadn't been sure at the time. The sheer wastefulness of it all distressed him. He was older and wiser now and more used to the way that things really worked being more important than the way they appeared to (unless you were talking about public perception, of course, when it was the other way round).

But they really were facing a mortal and imminent threat here. Was it right to encourage division and enmity between people who and organisations which all needed to pull together if they were to defeat the threat they were faced with?

Oh, but fuck it. There would always be competition. Armed services were designed to protect turf, to engage with, to prevail against. Of course they'd compete with each other.

And, if that supposedly fucking enormous and ultimately powerful Mercatoria fleet wasn't rushing towards them even now, would not some of the people in Ulubis—maybe quite a lot of the people in Ulubis—be contemplating not resisting the Beyonder/Starveling invasion at all? Might they not, instead, be thinking about how they could come to an accommodation with those threatening invasion?

Despite all the propaganda they'd been subject to, secret polls and secret police reports indicated that a lot of ordinary people felt they might not be any worse off under the Beyonder/ Starveling forces. Some people in power would feel the same way, especially if they were being told to sacrifice property and wealth and even risk their own lives in what might turn out to be a lost cause.

Even some of those round this impressively large round table in this impressively large and cool and subtly lit boardroom-resembling-meeting-chamber might have been tempted to think about ways to cope with the threatened invasion that didn't involve resistance to the last ship and soldier, if it hadn't been for the oncoming Mercatoria Fleet.

Saluus supposed they had to assume that the fleet really was on the way. There were other possibilities, and he'd thought them all through—and talked them all through with his own advisers and experts—but ultimately they had to be dismissed. Whether the Dweller List existed or not, everybody appeared to be acting as though it did, and that was all that mattered. It was a bit like money; all about trust, about faith. The value lay in what people believed, not in anything intrinsic.

Never mind. After covering the latest intelligence and his own shocking remissness in not making the refitted ships invulnerable to alien hyper-weapons, the meeting was finally getting round to something useful.

Back to grisly reality.

"The main thing," Fleet Admiral Brimiaice told them (the quaup commander was keen on Main Things and In The Ends), "is that the Dwellers don't seem to want to continue hostilities."

After their initial, furious take-no-prisoners attack and no-quarter polishing-off of those who'd got away, the Dwellers had just as suddenly gone back to their usual show of Shucks-us? ineptitude, claiming it had all been a terrible mistake and could they help with the Third Fury rebuild?

"And thank fuck for that!" Guard-General Thovin said. "If they did, we'd have absolutely no chance. Facing the Beyonder/Starveling lot and the Dwellers as well! Holy shit! No chance. No chance at all!" Thovin was a dumpy barrel of a man, dark and powerful-looking. His voice was suitably gruff.

"Instead, only almost no chance," Shrievalty Colonel Somjomion said with a thin smile.

"We have every chance, madam!" Fleet Admiral Brimiaice thundered, banging the table with one tubular armling. His splendidly uniformed and decorated body, like a well-tailored airship the size of a small hippo, rose in the air. "We need no defeatist talk here, of all places!"

"We have seventy fewer ships than we had," the Shrievalty colonel reminded them, without drama.

"We still have the will," Brimiaice said. "That's the important point. And we have plenty of ships. And more being built all the time." He looked at Saluus, who nodded and tried not to let his contempt show.

"If they work," muttered Clerk-Regnant Voriel. The Cessorian seemed to have a personal thing against Saluus. He had no idea why.

"Now, we've dealt with all that," First Secretary Heuypzlagger said quickly, glancing at Saluus. "If there are any problems with the ships' construction, I'm sure the inquiry will show them up. We have to concentrate now on what else we can do."

Saluus was getting bored. Now was as good a time as any. "An embassy," he said. He looked round them all. "That's what I'd like to suggest. An embassy to the Dwellers of Nasqueron, to secure peace, make sure there are no more 'misunderstandings' between us and them, attempt to involve them in the defence of Ulubis system and, if possible, acquire from them—with their consent, preferably—some of the extremely impressive weaponry they appear to possess, either in physical or theoretical form."

"Well," Heuypzlagger said, shaking his head.

"Oh. Now our Acquisitariat friend is a diplomat," Voriel observed, expression poised between sneer and smile.

"Needing yet *more* supposedly gas-capable ships to protect it, no doubt!" Brimiaice protested.

"Haven't we got one already?" Thovin asked.

Colonel Somjomion just looked at him, eyes narrowed.

The meeting only seemed to last for ever. Finally it was over. Saluus met up with his new lover that evening, at the water-column house on Murla, where he'd first really looked at her in the true light of day and decided, yes, he'd be interested. It had been at brunch, with his wife (and her new girlfriend) and Fass and the Segrette Twins, the day after their visit to the Narcateria in Boogeytown.

:

The RushWing *Sheumerith* rode high in the clear gas spaces between two high haze layers, flying into the vast unending jet stream of gas as though trying to keep pace with the stars which were sometimes visible, tiny and hard and remote, through the yellow haze and the thin quick amber clouds scudding eternally overhead.

The giant aircraft was a single slim scimitar of wing pocked with engine nacelles, articulated like a wave, ten kilometres across, a hundred metres long and ten metres high, a thin filament forever jetting like a swift weather front made visible across the waste of clouds beneath. Dwellers, hundreds of them, hung from it, each anchored like refuelled aircraft by a cable strung out from the wing's trailing edge, riding in a little pocket of calm gas produced by simple shells of diamond, open to the rear and which, to the human eye, were shaped like a pair of giant cupped hands.

In a long-term drug-trance, downshifted in time so that the flight seemed twelve or sixty or more times quicker than it really was—the vast continents of clouds racing beneath like foam, the wash of stars wheeling madly above, wisp-banks whipping towards and past like rags in a hurricane—the wing-hung Dwellers watched the days and nights flicker around them like some stupendous strobe and felt the planet beneath them turn like something reeling out their lives.

Fassin Taak left the jetclipper and flew carefully in, matching velocities, then anchored the little gascraft, very slowly, to the underside of the diamond enclosure holding the Sage-youth Zosso, a slim, dark, rather battered-looking Dweller of two million years or so.

Fassin slow-timed. The wing, the clouds, the stars, all seemed to pick up speed, rolling racing forward like over-cranked screenage. The roar of engines and slipstreaming gas rose and rose in pitch, becoming a high, shrill, faraway keening, then vanishing from hearing altogether.

The Dweller above him, seeming to jerk and quiver in his little retaining harness, waited for him to synch before sending,—And what might you be, person?

—I am a human being, sir. A Seer at the Nasqueron Court, in a gascraft, an esuit. I am called Fassin Taak, of Sept Bantrabal.

—And I am Zosso, of nowhere in particular. Of here. Good view, is it not?

—It is.

—However, I dare say that that is not why you are here.

—You're right. It's not.

—You wish to ask me something?

—I am told I need to make passage to somewhere I've never heard of, to follow a Dweller I need to find. I'm told you can help.

—I'm sure I can, if I choose to. Well, that is, if people still take any notice of what a silly old wing-hanger says. Who can say? I'm not sure that I would listen to somebody as old and out of things as I am if I was a young travelcaptain. Why, I think I should say something like, "What, listen to that foolish old—?" Oh, I beg your pardon, young human. I seem to have distracted myself. Where was it you would like to go?

—A place that is, apparently, sometimes called Hoestruem.

Drunisine himself, alone, had come to the quarters that Fassin shared with the two Dwellers, in the mid-morning of the day after the battle in the storm.

"We have delayed you long enough. You may go. A jetclipper is at your disposal for the next two dozen days. Goodbye."

"Now there," Y'sul had observed, "goes a Dweller of few words."

—Hoestruem?" Zosso asked.—No, I've never heard of it either.

Night swept over them as he signalled, enveloping.

—In or near Aopoleyin? Fassin sent.—Apparently, he told the old wing-hanger, when the Dweller was uncommunicative for a few moments.—Somewhere associated with Aopoleyin.

All this was on Valseir's advice. Fassin couldn't find any mention of anywhere called Aopoleyin in his databases either. He was starting to wonder if the memory-scanning process he'd had to undergo before being allowed to leave the *Isaut* had scrambled some of the gascraft's information storage systems.

—Ah, Zosso sent.—Aopoleyin. That I have heard of. Hmm. Well, in that case, if I were you, I'd talk to Quercer & Janath. Yes, you'll need them. I should think. Tell them I sent you. Oh. And ask for my mantle scarf back. Might do the trick. No guarantees, though. Mind.

—Quercer and Janath. Your mantle scarf back.

The old Dweller rolled a fraction, jerkily, and looked down at Fassin.—I'll have you know it was a very good mantle scarf.

He rolled back, facing again into the never-ending rush of cloud and stars and day and night.—I could do with it up here. It's windy.

# FIVE

## CONDITIONS OF PASSAGE

"Where?"

"You want to go where?"

"Hoestruem, near Aopoleyin," Fassin said.

"We know where Hoestruem is."

"We're not stupid."

"Well, I'm not. Janath might be."

"I entirely fulfilled my Creat Minimum Stupidity Allocation by associating with you."

"Forgive my partner. We were asking for confirmation more out of shock at your unspeakable alienness than anything else. So. You want to go to Hoestruem."

"Yes," Fassin said.

"And Zosso sent you."

"Still banging on about that damn scarf."

"Useful code, though."

"Hoestruem."

"Hoestruem."

"Doable."

"Yes, but it's more the why of it, not the how."

"The how is easy."

"The how *is* easy. Problem is definitely why."

"As in bother."

"As in should we."

"Well, should we?"

"More rhetorical."

"Has to be a joint decision."

"Absolutely."

"Zosso asks."

"Zosso does."

"Do we accommodate?"

"We could just give him back his mantle scarf."

"*Was* there ever a scarf?"

"A real scarf?"

"Yes."

"Now you mention it."

"Anyway."

"Beside the point."

"Always a dangerous place to tarry."

"Zosso. A travel request. This human gentleman in his gascraft esuit."

"Ahem," said Y'sul.

"And his friend."

"Not forgetting his friend."

"And mentor," Y'sul pointed out.

"Yes, that too."

"Do we do or do we don't?"

"Is the question."

"Does we does or don't we not?"

"Yes. No. Select one of the aforementioned."

"Quite."

"Precisely."

"In your own time," Y'sul muttered.

They were in a spinbar in Eponia, a globular stickycity in the cold chaotic wastes of the North Polar Region. The borrowed jetclipper had done its best impression of a suborb, skipping nearly into space in a series of bounced trajectories, finally slowing, sinking and coming to rest by the tenuous cloudlike structure of the great city, occupying hundreds of cubic kilometres of cold, stale gas just fifteen thousand klicks from the giant planet's North Pole. They'd tracked Quercer & Janath down to a spinbar called The Liquid Yawn. Valseir had demurred but Y'sul and Fassin had crammed into a crushpod, been accelerated up to speed and then—dizzily—joined the two travelcaptains in their booth.

Fassin had never encountered a travelcaptain before. He'd heard of them, and knew that they were almost always found in the equatorial band, but they were elusive, even shy. He'd tried to meet with one many times in the past but there had always been some sort of problem, often at the last moment.

The spinbar whirled madly, twisting and looping and rolling at extreme high speed, making the city outside its bubble-diamond walls seem to gyrate as though with the express intention of disorientating the outward-looking bar-going public. The effect was intense and intentional. Dwellers had a superb sense of balance and it took a lot to make them dizzy. Being spun like a maniac was one Dweller idea of fun just because it led to a profound, giddy dislocation with one's surroundings. Taking drugs at the same time just added to the hilarity. Y'sul, however, it had seemed to Fassin, looked a little grey around the gills as they'd woven their way through the mostly empty spinbar to the travelcaptains' booth.

"You all right?"

"Perfectly."

"Bringing back memories of heading through the storm wall in the *Poaflias*?"

"Not at… Well, just a little. Ulp. Perhaps."

Quercer & Janath, travelcaptains, were one. They looked like one big Dweller, of about Adult age, but there were two individuals in there, one in each discus. Fassin had heard of truetwin Dwellers before, but never met a set. Usually a Dweller's brain was housed just off the central spine in the thickest, central part of one discus; generally the left one. Right-brain Dwellers were about fifteen per cent of the total population, though this varied from planet to planet. Very, very occasionally, two brains developed in the one creature, and something like Quercer & Janath tended to be the result. The double-Dweller wore a shiny set of all-overs with transparent and mesh patches over the hub sense organs, and a shaded transparent section over the outer frill of sensory fringe.

"You'll not be able to see much."

"That's if we take you at all."

"Yes, that's if we do take you in the first."

"Place. Which is by no means guaranteed."

"Indeed not. Decision not yet made."

"Still pending."

"Absolutely. But."

"In any event."

"You'll not be able to see much of anything."

"Not exactly a sightseeing trip."

"Or a cruise."

"Either."

"And you'll have to switch everything off."

"All non-bio systems."

"At least."

"If, that is."

"Big if."

"We do take you."

"I think we get the idea," Fassin said.

"Good."

"Brilliant."

"When can we expect a decision?" Y'sul asked. He'd turned his right sense-fringe inward so that he was seeing with only one. This was the Dweller equivalent of a drunk human closing one eye.

"Made it. I've made it. You made it?"

"Yep, I've made it."

"It's a Yes?"

"It's a Yes."

"You'll take us?" Fassin asked.

"Are you deaf? Yes."

"Definitely."

"Thank you," Fassin said.

"So where are we going?" Y'sul asked tetchily.

"Ah."

"Ha!"

"Wait."

"And see."

The ship was no joke. Three hundred metres long, it was a polished ebony spike necklaced with drive pods like fat seeds. It lay in a public hangar deep under the stickycity, a semi-spherical space a kilometre across bounded by the hexagonal planes of adjacent smaller bubble volumes.

Valseir was bidding them farewell here. The trip would begin with what the two travelcaptains described as an intense, fractally spiralled, high-acceleration, torque-intense manoeuvre complex, and was not for the faint-willed. The old Dweller had invoked his seniority to excuse himself the ordeal.

"More spinning around," Y'sul sighed, on hearing what awaited them.

"My regards to Leisicrofe," Valseir told Fassin. "You still have the leaf image, I hope."

Fassin took the image-leaf with its depiction of sky and clouds out of its storage locker in the little gascraft and showed it to the old Dweller. "I'll say hello."

"Please do. Best of luck."

"You too. How do I find you when I get back?"

"Leave that to me. If I'm not readily available, try where we found Zosso. Or, perhaps at a StormSail regatta."

"Yes," Y'sul said. "But next time just don't bring any friends."

The black spike-ship was called the *Velpin*. It burst from the vast cloud of the city like a needle shot from a frozen waterfall of foam, disappeared into the gelid rush of gases forever swirling around the planet's distant pole and started its bizarre flight, spiralling, rolling, looping, rising and falling and rising again.

Locked into a centrally positioned space which doubled as a passenger compartment and hold, restrained by webbing, Fassin and Y'sul felt the ship commit to spirals within spirals within spirals, tiny corkscrew motions threaded into a whole ramped course of greater coils, themselves part of a still wider set of ever quicker, tighter loops.

"Fucking hell," Y'sul commented.

A faulty screen was set in the far wall, hazed over with static. It made buzzing noises and occasionally flashed with images of ragged, striated clouds whipping past in distorted twists of light and shade. Fassin could see and hear, though both senses were degraded. All the systems in the gascraft had been switched off. Webbed upright, he could see out of the de-opaqued plate over his face—he'd let some of the shock-gel drain away so he could see better. The sound that came through the little arrowhead was at once dulled and high. Y'sul's voice sounded like squeaks, barely comprehensible.

Fassin and Y'sul were stuck to the inner surface of the compartment, pinned there by the ship's wild spins.

"Any idea why they have to do all this fractal spiralling?" Fassin had asked when they'd both been secured and Quercer & Janath had gone to their command space a single compartment away.

"Could just be pure mischief," Y'sul had said.

Fassin looked at Y'sul now. Both the Dweller's sense fringes were turned in.

The ship accelerated hard, executing a broad curve. The screen flashed black pitted with stars, all revolving frantically, then blanked out.

The insane, nested sets of spirals resolved down to a single long-axis spin, as though the *Velpin* was a shell travelling down the barrel of some vast gun.

The ship resounded with a high, singing note around them and seemed to settle into something like a cruise. The rate of spin slackened off gradually. Fassin watched as Y'sul's sense fringes gradually opened. The screen showed slowly spinning stars for several minutes. Then it blanked out again. The spinning picked up once more and Y'sul turned his fringes outside-in again. The spin built up until Fassin could feel his whole body being pressed through the shock-gel. It was his own coffin, he realised. Of course it was. He was getting tunnel vision now, starting to see the view down that great gun barrel, the view ahead shrunk to a single point far away; way, way in the distance, nothing but darkness and grey beyond darkness on either side, down that never-ending tube towards the last defined place they were aiming towards, never coming any closer.

Fassin woke up. Still spinning, but the rate was slackening off again. His nose itched and it felt like he needed to pee, even though he knew he didn't. This never happened when the shock-gel and gillfluid were doing their jobs. He fell asleep.

·

Taince Yarabokin woke up. One of her first thoughts as she surfaced slowly to full consciousness was that Saluus Kehar would not have received the message she'd prepared for him, that there was still time for more reviewings and re-recordings and revisions, that she would be able to spend more time watching and listening to herself on the recording, and reduce herself to tears every time. Still time and a chance to confront him, maybe kill him, if that was both possible and something she felt driven to do at the time (she had no idea—sometimes she wanted to kill him, sometimes she wanted him alive to suffer the shame of knowing that she had released the story to the newsnets, and sometimes she just wanted him to know that she knew what had really happened that long-ago night in the ruined ship on the high desert).

She checked the time, feeling woozily around in virtual space for information. Still half a year out from Ulubis. She would be awake now until the attack itself, one of the first to be wakened for the final run-in, because she represented the closest thing they had to local knowledge. Privately she doubted she'd be able to offer much practical help, given that she'd last seen Ulubis over two centuries earlier and it might, to put it mildly, have changed somewhat after having been invaded, but she was the best they had. She thought of herself in that respect more as a talisman than anything else, a small symbol of the system that they would be fighting for. If that had been one consideration in her getting a place in the fleet, it didn't bother her. She was confident that she was a good, competent and brave officer and deserved her post on merit alone. The fact that it was her own home system she was riding to the rescue of was just a bonus.

The fleet had spread out a little since the battle with the Beyonders in mid-voyage, sacrificing the immediate weight of arms it could bring to bear for a net of forward picket craft which would flag any trouble long before the main body of the fleet got to it. Taince had spent most of the intervening years slow-asleep in her pod, but—thanks to that relative security provided by the advance ships—she'd had some recreational and morale-time out of the shock-gel as well, walking around almost like a normal human being in the spun-gravity of the battleship, feeling odd and strange confronted with such normality, like an alien inhabiting a human's body; clumsy, astonished at tiny things like fingernails and the hairs on an arm, awkward, especially at first, with meeting other off-duty humans, and missing the richness of her in-pod, wired-up virtual existence—with the ability to dip in and out of entire high-definition sensoria of data and meaning—like an amputated limb.

It would be like that again now, once she had finally come round. Taince wasn't really looking forward to it. When she was stumbling about on two legs she wanted to be back in the pod, synched in, but when she was there she was forever nostalgic for a normal, physical one-speed, one-reality life. Blue skies and sunlight, a fresh breeze blowing through her hair and green grass and flowers under her bare feet.

Long time ago. And maybe never again, who knew?

Another of Taince's first thoughts, even when she realised that she was being woken up slowly, without alarms going off, as part of the programmed, pre-agreed duty-shift system rather than some fateful emergency that might end in her death at any moment, was that she had not yet escaped into death, that it was not yet all over, and any terrors and agonies that might be hers to encounter before the peace of oblivion were still ahead of her.

‧

"Hoestruem," Quercer & Janath said.

"Where?" Fassin asked.

"What do you mean, 'Where?'?"

"You're *in* it."

Fassin had recovered from his blackout once they'd turned his little gascraft's systems back on. He still felt disorientated and oddly dirty, a sensation that was only gradually disappearing as the shock-gel enveloped him fully again. Y'sul had seemed a bit groggy too, wobbly in the air when released from his webbing.

Now they were looking at the passenger-compartment screen, which Quercer & Janath, still dressed in their shiny overalls, had hit with one rim-arm and got to work. Fassin looked carefully at the image on the screen but all he could see was a star field. He could not, for now, work out in which direction he was looking. Certainly not a direction he was used to looking in. He didn't recognise anything.

"In it?" he asked, feeling fuzzy, and foolish.

"Yes, in it."

Fassin looked at Y'sul, who still looked a little grey about the mantle.

The Dweller just shrugged. "Well," he said, "I certainly give in. Who, what or where the fuck is Hoestruem?"

"A Clouder."

"A *Clouder*?" Fassin said. This had to be a translation thing, or a simple misunderstanding. Clouders were part of the Cincturia: the beings, devices, semi-civs and tech dross that were beyond the Beyonders, way on the outside of everything.

Y'sul shook himself. "You mean a WingClouder or TreeClouder or StickyClouder or—"

"No."

"None of the above."

"Just a Clouder."

"But—" Fassin said.

"Aopoleyin, then!" Y'sul shouted. "Let's start with that! Is *that* where we are?"

"Yes."

"Indeed."

"Well, sort of."

"Depends."

"It's the nearest place."

"The nearest system."

"Eh?" Y'sul said.

"The nearest what?" Fassin asked, simply not understanding. He peered at the star field. This didn't look right. This didn't look right at all. Not in any way whatsoever, not upside down or mirrored or backside-holo'd or anything.

"I think I'm still confused," Y'sul said, rippling his sense mantles to wake himself up.

Fassin felt as though he was at the bottom of that gun barrel again, about to be blasted out of it, or already being blown out of it, up the biggest, longest most unspeakably enormous and forever unending gun barrel in all the whole damn universe.

"How far are we from Nasqueron?" he heard himself say.

"Wait a moment," Y'sul said slowly. "What do you mean, 'system'?"

"About thirty-four kiloyears."

"Stellar, not gas-giant. Apologies for any confusion."

"Thirty-four *kiloyears*?" Fassin said. It felt like he was going to black out again. "You mean…" His voice just trailed off.

"Thirty-four thousand light years, standard. Roughly. Apologies for any confusion."

"I already said that."

"Know. Different person, different confusion."

They were in another system, another solar system, another part of the galaxy altogether; they had, if they were being told the truth, left Ulubis—system and star—thirty-four thousand light years behind. There was a working portal in Ulubis system linked via a wormhole to this distant stellar system neither Fassin nor Y'sul had ever heard of.

The Clouder being Hoestruem was a light year across. Clouders were—depending who you talked to—sentient, semi-sentient, proto-sentient, a-sentient or just plain not remotely sentient—though that last extreme point of view tended to be held only by those for whom it would be convenient if it were true, such as those who could do useful, profitable things with a big cloud of gas. Providing it wasn't alive. Arguably closer to vast, distributedly-smart plants than any sort of animal, they had a composition very similar to the clouds of interstellar gas which they inhabited/were (the distinction was moot).

Clouders were part of the Cincturia, the collection of beings, species, machine strains and intelligent detritus that existed—generally—between stellar systems and didn't fit into any other neat category (so they weren't the deep-space cometarians called the Eclipta, they weren't drifting examples of the Brown Dwarf Communitals known as the Plena, and they weren't the real exotics, the Non-Baryonic Penumbrae, the thirteen-way-folded Dimensionates or the Flux-dwelling Quantarchs).

Valseir's friend Leisicrofe was a scholar of the Cincturia. The research trip he was making was a field trip, visiting actual examples of Cincturia—Clouders, Sailpods, Smatter, Toilers and the rest—throughout the galaxy. He had come to visit Hoestruem because it was one of the few Clouders anywhere near a wormhole portal. Only it wasn't a wormhole or a portal that anybody in the Mercatoria or the rest of what called itself the Civilised Galaxy knew anything about.

The star Aopoleyin was only a dozen light days away. The Clouder Hoestruem—much larger than the stellar system as measured to its outermost planet—was passing partly through the outer reaches of the system, intent (if that was not too loaded a word) on its slow migration to some far-distant part of the great lens. The Dweller Leisicrofe was somewhere here, in his own small craft, or at least had been. The *Velpin* set out to look for him.

"How long were we really under?" Fassin asked Quercer & Janath. They were floating in the *Velpin*'s control space, watching the scanners chatter through their sweeps, searching for anything that might be a ship. The progress was slow. The Dwellers had long had an agreement with the Clouders that meant their ships made very slow speed when moving through one. Clouders were resilient, but their individual filaments, the wispy bands and channels of tenuous gas that formed their sensory apparatus and nervous systems, were surpassing delicate, and a ship the size of the *Velpin* had to move slowly and carefully amongst the strands of Clouder substance to avoid causing damage. The *Velpin* was broadcasting a signal hail looping a request for Leisicrofe to get in touch, though Quercer & Janath was not optimistic this would raise their quarry; these academics were notorious for turning off their comms.

The truetwin looked genuinely puzzled. The double-creature shook itself, rustling the shiny crinkles of the mirror-finish coveralls. "How long were you under what?"

"How long were we really unconscious?" Fassin asked.

"Some days."

"And then some more days."

"Seriously," Fassin said.

"And what's this 'we'?" Y'sul protested. "*I* wasn't unconscious!"

"There."

"You see?"

"Your friend disagrees."

"Some days, you said," Fassin quoted.

"Some days?" Y'sul said. "Some days? We weren't unconscious for some days, any days, a single day!" He paused. "Were we?"

"The process takes some time, requires forbearance," the truetwin Dweller said. "Sleep is best. No distractions."

"How could we possibly keep you amused?"

"And then there's the security aspect."

"Of course."

"I was only briefly drowsy!" Y'sul exclaimed. "I shut my eyes for a moment, in contemplation, no more!"

"About twenty-six days."

"We were unconscious for twenty-six days?" Fassin asked.

"Standard."

"Roughly."

"*What?*" Y'sul bellowed. "You mean we were *kept* unconscious?"

"In a manner of speaking, yes."

"In a manner of *speaking*!" a plainly furious Y'sul roared.

"What we said."

"And what manner of speaking would that be, you kidnapping piratical wretches?"

"The manner of speaking complete truth."

"You mean you drugged or *zapped* us unconscious?" Y'sul fairly howled.

"Yes. Very boring otherwise."

"How *dare* you?" Y'sul shrieked.

"Plus it's part of the terms for using the tube."

"Conditions of Passage," the left side of Quercer & Janath intoned.

The other side of the truetwin made a whistling noise.

"Oh, yes! Those Conditions of Passage; they'll get you every time."

"Can't be helpful with them."

"Can't use the tube without 'em."

"Don't—What?—You—Condi—!" Y'sul spluttered.

"Ah," Fassin said, signalling to Y'sul to let him speak. "Yes. I'd like to ask you some questions about, ah, tube travel, if you don't mind."

"Absolutely."

"Ask away."

"Make the questions good, though; the answers may well be baloney."

"…Never heard anything so disgraceful in all my…" Y'sul was muttering, drifting over to a set of medium-range scanner holo tanks and tapping them as though this would aid the locating of Leisicrofe's ship.

Fassin had known they'd been under for more than an hour or two. His own physiology, and the amount of cleaning-up and housekeeping the shock-gel and gillfluid had had to do had told him that. Finding out that it had been twenty-six days left him more relieved than anything else. Certainly losing that amount of time when you hadn't been expecting to and hadn't been warned about it was disconcerting and left one feeling sort of retrospectively vulnerable (and would it be the same on any way back?) but at least they hadn't said a year, or twenty-six years. Fate alone knew what had happened in Ulubis during that time—and of course, with all his gascraft's systems switched off, Fassin had no way of checking whether this really was the amount of time they had spent unconscious—but it looked like at least one small part of the Dweller List legend was true. There were secret wormholes. There was one, for sure, and Fassin thought it unlikely in the extreme that the one between Ulubis and Aopoleyin was the only one. It was well worth losing a couple of dozen days to find that out.

Fassin felt himself try to draw a breath inside the little gascraft. "We *did* come through a wormhole?" he asked.

"Excellent first question! Easily answerable in every sense! Yes."

"We did. Though we call them Cannula."

"Where is the Ulubis end—the Nasqueron end—of the wormhole, the Cannula? Where is the Adjutage?" Fassin asked.

"Ah! He knows the terminology."

"Most impressive."

"And a very good question in one sense."

"Couldn't agree more. Phenomenally hopeless in another."

"Can't tell you."

"Security."

"Sure you understand."

"Of course I understand," Fassin said. Getting a straight answer to that one would have been too good to be true. "How long has the wormhole existed?" he asked.

The truetwin was quiet for a moment, then said,

"Don't know."

"For sure. Billions of years, probably."

"Possibly."

"How many others are there like it?" Fassin asked. "I mean wormholes; Cannula?"

"Ditto."

"Ditto?"

"Ditto as in—again—don't know."

"No idea."

"Well, some."

"All right, some idea. But can't tell. Conditions of Passage again."

"Drat those Conditions of Passage."

"Oh yes, drat."

"Are there any other wormholes from Ulubis—from anywhere near Ulubis system, say within its Oort radius—to anywhere else?"

"Another good question. Can't tell you."

"More than our travelcaptaincy's worth."

"This one, to Aopoleyin; does it link up with a Mercatoria wormhole? Does one of their wormholes have a portal, an Adjutage, here too?"

"No."

"Agree. Straight answer. What a relief. No."

"And from here, from Aopoleyin," Fassin said. "Are there other wormholes?"

Silence again for a moment. Then,

"Seems silly, but can't tell you."

"Like anybody's going to have just one stupid tube to this place."

"But still."

"Can't say."

"And that's official."

Fassin signalled resignation. "Conditions of Passage?" he asked.

"Catching on."

"But why me?" Fassin asked.

"Why you?"

"Why you what?"

"Why have I been allowed to travel here, to use the wormhole?"

"You asked."

"More to the point, Valseir, Zosso and Drunisine asked on your behalf."

"How could we refuse?"

"So I couldn't just have asked on my own behalf?" Fassin said.

"Oh, you could have asked."

"Best leave that hanging."

"Attempt not to insult passengers."

"Unwritten law."

"Do you know of any other humans who've been allowed to use Dweller wormholes?"

"No."

"No, indeed. Not that we'd know, necessarily."

"Any other Seers?"

"Not to our knowledge."

"Which is admittedly vague."

"Okay," Fassin said. He could feel his heart thudding in his chest, deep inside the little gascraft. "Do you make journeys through the wormhole often?"

"Define 'often'."

"Let me rephrase: how many times have you used the wormhole in the last ten years standard?"

"Easy question."

"To sidestep."

"But—say—a few hundred."

"Excuse our vagueness. Conditions of Passage."

"A few *hundred*?" Fassin asked. Good grief, if that was true these guys were running round the galaxy in their hidden wormhole system like subway trains under a city.

"No more, assuredly."

"Are there many other ships like...? No, let me rephrase: how many other ships in Nasqueron make regular wormhole journeys?"

"No idea."

"Haven't the haziest."

"Not even roughly? Would there be dozens, hundreds?"

The left side of Quercer & Janath briefly turned its shiny overalls transparent and flashed a pattern of high amusement over its signal skin.

The right side made the whistling noise again.

Fassin gave them time for a spoken answer, but it didn't appear. "Are there a *lot*?" he asked.

Silence a while longer.

"There are a few."

"Not a few."

"Make what you will."

"Again, vagueness to be excused. Conditions of Passage."

"Thousands?" Fassin asked. No response from the truetwin Dweller. He felt himself gulp. "Tens of—?"

"No point going pursuing numbers uppage."

"See last answer given above."

He had no idea. There just *couldn't* be all that many ships, could there? No matter how impressive your stealth tech, surely out of hundreds or thousands of ship movements within a system every year a few had to show up on some sort of sensor, now and again. No system was perfect, no technology never failed. Something had to betray itself. How far out did portals have to be? Fassin wasn't an expert on the physics, but he was fairly certain that you needed relatively flat space, well away from a gravity gradient as steep as that round a gas-giant. Could their portals be as near to the planet as a close-orbit moon?

"And Nasqueron?" he asked. "Would it be a typical sort of Dweller planet in this regard?"

"All Places of Dwelling are special."

"Nasqueron—Nest of Winds—no less special than any."

"But yes."

*Yes.* Fassin felt that if he'd been standing up in normal gravity asking these questions and getting these answers, he'd have had to sit down some time ago. Or just plain fallen over.

"Have you ever been here before, to Aopoleyin?" he asked.

Silence. Then, "No."

"Or if yes, can't remember."

Fassin got something like Swim, that feeling of intense disconnection when the sheer implicatory outlandishness of a situation suddenly hit home to the unprepared human.

"And if—when—we go back to Nasqueron, am I free to just tell people where I've been?"

"If you remember."

"Then yes."

"Is there a reason I might not remember?"

"Cannula travel plays strange tricks, Seer Taak."

"You'd try to remove the memory from my brain?" Fassin felt his skin crawl. "Human brains are difficult to do that sort of thing to without harming them."

"We've heard."

"Working on assumption nobody will believe you."

"Don't distress."

"Might believe *me*!" Y'sul said, suddenly turning away from the screens he'd busied himself with earlier.

Quercer & Janath bobbed dramatically, like they'd forgotten he was there. "You're not serious!"

"Not serious!" they yelped, nearly together.

Y'sul snorted and flashed high amusement. "'Course not." He turned back to the screens, muttering while chuckling, "What you take me for. Like life too much anyway. Hang on to *my* memories, thank you…"

The search went on. Fassin tried interrogating the *Velpin*'s systems to discover if it carried its own Dweller List, its own map of the unknown wormhole network, or even just the location of the portal they'd entered in Ulubis system to get here. The ship's computers—easily accessed, barely shielded—seemed completely free of anything but the most basic star charts. The greater galaxy was mapped down to a scale that showed where all the stars and major planets should be, and that was it. No habs and no traces of megastructures were shown, and only the vaguest indications of Oort and Kuiper bodies and asteroid belts were given. It wasn't like a proper star-chart set at all, it was more like a school atlas. The little gascraft had a more detailed star map. Fassin searched the ship electronically as best he could without making it too obvious, but found nothing else more detailed.

He supposed the real stuff must be hidden away somewhere, but had an odd, nagging feeling that it wasn't. The *Velpin* seemed a well-built ship—by Dweller standards exceptionally well-built—with relatively sophisticated but elegantly simple engines and lots of power, no weapons and some carrying capacity. No more. The rudimentary star data somehow fitted.

Fassin tried to work out a way to commandeer the ship, just take it over. Could he hijack the *Velpin*? He'd spent enough time in the cluttered sphere of the ship's command space to see how Quercer & Janath controlled the vessel. It didn't look difficult. He had, even, just asked.

"How do you *navigate* this thing?"

"Point."

"Point?"

"Get to the general volume and then point in the right direction."

"Secret is plenty of power."

"Delicate finessing of delta-V is sign you haven't really got enough power."

"Power is all."

"You can do a lot by just pointing."

"If you've got enough power."

"Though sometimes you have to sort of allow a bit for deflection."

"That's a technical term."

Fassin couldn't work out how to take the ship over. Dwellers could, if they were determined, go years without experiencing anything a human would recognise as sleep, and Quercer & Janath claimed that they could get by without any at all, not even little slow-down style snoozes. His gascraft had no weapons apart from the manipulators, he had never trained to use the arrowhead as a close-combat device and anyway an Adult Dweller was bigger and probably more powerful—except in top speed—than the little gascraft. Dwellers were, anyway, generally regarded as being very hard to disable and/or kill.

He remembered Tain'ce Yarabokin talking about her close-combat briefings. The basic advice when confronting a Dweller who meant you harm—if you, as a human, were in a conventional spacesuit, say—was to make sure you had a big gun. There was no known way an unarmed human, even in an armoured suit, could take on a fit young Dweller. If you didn't have a big gun, then Run Away Very Quickly was the best advice. Of all the Mercatorial species, only the Voehn were known to be able to tackle a Dweller unarmed, and even then it wasn't a foregone conclusion.

Fassin supposed he could just ram Quercer & Janath. Crashing the little gascraft into them nose first might knock them out or disable them, but he wasn't sure there was sufficient room to work up enough speed for such a manoeuvre in any single part of the ship. He'd need to start a few compartments back and come slamming into the command space, hoping for a lucky hit, and that they wouldn't hear him coming and just rote out of the way to leave him to smash into the instruments. He wondered what Hatherence would have done. He wondered if she'd have been allowed to come in the first place. Almost certainly not with any weapons. On the other hand there was that standard Dweller casualness about such things. On the *other* other hand, this ship didn't seem that casual.

Even if he could get Quercer & Janath out of the way, what about Y'sul? He didn't think the older Dweller would conspire or even cooperate. Y'sul had made it very clear that he was an entirely loyal Dweller who was simply being a good guide and mentor, not some treacherous human-lover in league with or harbouring any sympathy for the Mercatoria, an entire power structure and civilisation he professed neither to understand nor care about.

And even if Fassin could somehow get control of the ship by himself, tricking both Dwellers—or all three, depending how you looked at it—what then? He still hadn't been able to find any sign of a hidden navigational matrix on the ship. Where was he supposed to go? How did he find the wormhole portal that had brought them here? When he found it, how did he get through, assuming it was in any way guarded or just administered? Mercatorial portals were some of the most intensely monitored and heavily guarded locations in the galaxy. Even allowing for the semi-chaotic indifference that Dwellers tended to display regarding such matters, could he really expect to fly unchallenged through one of their portals as though it was just another patch of space?

He'd tried to find out more about the whole process of finding and traversing a Dweller wormhole portal—an Adjutage—from Quercer & Janath, but they had, to even his surprise, given their conspicuous gift for the technique, comprehensively out-vagued themselves on the matter, surpassing their most studiedly unhelpful earlier replies by some margin.

Fassin had been allowed out of the ship. He'd floated free of it as it cruised gently through the tenuous, near-vacuum body of the Clouder Hoestruem. He wanted to check as best he could that this was not all faked somehow. How, after all, did he really know that he was where Quercer & Janath said he was? They'd told him. He'd seen information displayed on some screen and in or out of some holo displays. It could all be a joke, or a way of setting him up for something. So he had to check.

Outside the *Velpin*, keeping pace with the ship as it slid through the allegedly self-aware interstellar cloud, he used the little gascraft's senses to gauge whether he was in some vast artificial environment.

As far as Fassin could tell, he wasn't. He genuinely was in a chemical/dust cloud on the edge of a planetary system a quarter of the way round the galaxy from his home and halfway in towards the galactic core. The stars looked completely different. Only the distant galaxies still aligned. If it wasn't really the edge of deep space, it was a brilliant simulation of it. He used up a little of his reaction mass—water, basically—to fly a few kilometres away from the *Velpin*, and still encountered no wall, no giant screen. So either he was in a truly prodigious VR space, or it was all being done directly, through his brain, or through the gascraft's own collar, somehow uprated to one hundred per cent immersion, beyond check.

He thought back to something Valseir had said once: Any theory which causes solipsism to seem just as likely an explanation for the phenomena it seeks to describe ought to be held in the utmost suspicion.

Valseir had been talking about the Truth and other religions, but Fassin felt he was in a similar situation here. He had no real choice but to act as though all this was genuine. Even so, he had to keep the idea that it wasn't at the back of his head, just in case. Because if all this was real then he was, maybe, on the brink of the most astounding discovery in all human history, a revelation that could do untold harm or bring inestimable benefits to any combination of the Mercatoria, its adversaries and just about every other space-faring species in the galaxy. He remembered confronting the emissarial projection, what seemed like an age ago, back in the Autumn House. Which was more likely: what appeared to be the case, or this all being a lie, a set-up, a vast and incomprehensible joke? Discuss.

He ran every check he could while he was outside the hull of the *Velpin*. He was in space. Everything checked out. Or he was in a sim so complete that there was no disgrace in being taken in by it. Back to the Truth again. Hatherence would have appreciated the dilemma.

He could, if he really wanted, he supposed, just try and run away. The gascraft would support him indefinitely, it was capable of independent entry into a planetary atmosphere, and if he used almost all his reaction mass he could be in the inner system of this star Aopoleyin in a few years. He could even sleep most of the way and hardly notice the journey. But then what? He'd never heard of the place. It was somewhere in the Khredeil Tops (whatever those were) according to the gascraft's rudimentary star atlas, but it wasn't listed as a human or Mercatorial inhabited system and there was no mention of it having any inhabitants at all. That didn't mean there was nobody there—everywhere seemed to support somebody who called it home—but it meant that he'd probably be no further forward trying to get back home.

He came back to the ship when Quercer & Janath signalled excitedly that they'd found something. It wasn't Leisicrofe's ship; it was the delicate ball of gas and chemicals—a lacework ball of cold and dirty string open to the vacuum, held together by just a trace of gravity—that was the Clouder's mind.

...Looking for...?
—A Dweller. A gas-giant Dweller, called Leisicrofe.
...Image...
—Image?
...Told image expect... specific image...
—Ah. I have an image with me. How...? Where, I mean what do I show it to, so you can see it?
...No... describe...
—Okay. It's an image of white clouds in a blue sky.
...Accords...
—So you can tell me? Where Leisicrofe is?
...Went...
—When did he go?
...Measure time how you...?
—Standard system?
...Known... being Leisicrofe went $7.35 \times 10^8$ seconds ago...
Fassin did the calculation. About twenty years earlier.

He was nestled into the outer regions of the Clouder's mind, the little gascraft resting gently between two broad strands of gas a fraction less cold than the surrounding chill of deep space. He was, in effect, delving, stopped right down to talk to something that made a deep, slow-timing Dweller look like a speed-freak. Clouders thought surpassingly slowly.

A signal from outside, from the *Velpin*. To the Clouder he sent,
—Where did Leisicrofe go?
Then he clicked up to normal speed.

"Are you going to be much longer?" Y'sul asked, sounding irritable. "I am rapidly running out of patience with this bilateral monomaniac. It's been ten days, Fassin. What's happened? Fallen asleep?"

"I'm going as fast as I can. Only been a few tens of seconds for me."

"You could just stay and think at normal speed, you know. Give us all time to mull over whatever this gas-brain's saying. No need to go doing this show-off delving stuff."

"Less of a conversation that way. This shows respect. You get more out of people if you—"

"Yes yes yes. Well, you just carry on. I'll try and find more games to keep this split-personality cretin occupied. You rote off and commune with this space-vegetable. I'll do the real hard work. Sorry I came along now. If I've missed any more good battles while I've been away..." His voice faded into the distance.

Fassin descended into extreme slow-time again. The Clouder still hadn't replied.

At least this time there was no insane spiralling. There was the same fuzzy, low-reliability screen to distract them as they wafted away from the Clouder and made for the hidden wormhole mouth, and the doors out of the passenger compartment were just as locked, but there was no fierce spinning. Fassin let Quercer & Janath take over the gascraft remotely and turn off its systems. He didn't bother to clear any of the shock-gel or turn the faceplate clear this time, he just put himself into a trance. It was easy, a lot like preparing to go down into slow-time. And it meant he couldn't see or hear Y'sul complaining about the ignominy of being zapped unconscious just because they were going on a space journey.

They were making for somewhere called Mavirouelo—yet another place Fassin had never heard of. This was where Hoestruem had said that Leisicrofe was going next. The Clouder hadn't known if this was a system, a planet, another Clouder or what. Quercer & Janath had gone silent for a moment when they heard the name, and Fassin had sensed them consulting the ship's crude galactic atlas. They declared that they knew the place. A planet, in the Ashum system. (Fassin, or at least the gascraft's memory, did know of this place. It was even connected, with its own Mercatorial-controlled wormhole, though Fassin suspected they wouldn't be using it.) Total travel time to be expected was "a few days".

As he slid into unconsciousness, Fassin's thoughts were of how beautiful the Clouder had looked. The vast being was like a million great long gauzy scarves of light, a whisper of matter and gravity close to nothingness that massed more than many solar systems, drifting yet purposeful, intent by ancient decision, along a course charted out over millions of years, propelled, dirigible by minute flexings of cold plasmas, by the force of near-not-there-at-all magnetic fields, by sigh-strength expulsions and drawings-in of interstellar material. Cold and dead-seeming yet alive and thinking. And beautiful, in the right light. Seen in a fitting wash of wavelengths, there was something endlessly, perfectly sublime about...

⠂

Saluus stood on a balcony of ice and metal, looking out at the view, his breath misting in the air before him.

The Shrievalty retreat was embedded in and partially sculpted from the frozen waterfall Hoisennir, a four-hundred-metre-high, klick-wide cliff of ice marking where the river Doaroe began its long fall from the high semi-arctic plateau towards the tundra and plains beyond. A low winter sun provided a grand display of Sepektian clouds and a fuzzy purple-red sunset, but nowhere near enough heat to start melting the ice.

Sepekte wobbled slowly and not especially significantly. Its arctic and antarctic circles, where the sun alternately never set or never rose during the heights of summer and depths of winter, were less than a thousand kilometres in diameter. Officially classed as a hot/temperate planet by human standards, its winters were longer but less severe than those of Earth and their worst effects were confined to smaller areas than on humanity's original home. But the Hoisennir waterfall was far north and high up in the arctic-shield mountains, and the Doaroe spent standard years at a time entirely frozen.

The place was called a retreat because it was owned by the Shrievalty, but as far as Saluus was concerned it was just a hotel and conference centre. The view was impressive, though, when there was sufficient daylight actually to see it properly. It had a certain severe appeal, Saluus was prepared to grant.

Saluus didn't like being here, all the same. He wasn't keen on places that he couldn't get away from easily—preferably, if the worst came to the worst, by just walking. To get away from here meant an air-car or a lift up or down the interior of the frozen fall to the landing ground on the ice of the solidified river above, or down to the vac-rail station on the shore of the frozen lake at the foot of the cliff. When he'd found out where the conference on the Dweller Embassy was to be held—at fairly short notice, for security reasons—he'd made sure to have a parasail packed with his luggage, just so that he had an emergency way out, if it came to it.

He knew that almost certainly there wouldn't be any emergency—or if there was it would be something so big and/or quick that there would be no getting away from it—but he felt better, safer having the parasail by the balcony window of his bedroom. Most of the other important attendees had suites far inside the fall, to be further away from anything that might come at them from outside, but Saluus had insisted on an outside suite, one with a view, a way out. He hadn't parasailed for decades but he'd rather risk his neck that way than cowering at the back of a suite, whimpering, just waiting for death.

He sometimes wondered where this obsession with being able to get away came from. It wasn't something he'd been born with or picked up as the result of some traumatic experience in childhood, it was just something that had sort of crept slowly up on him all the way through his adult life. One of those things, he supposed. He hadn't bothered wasting any time thinking really deeply about it.

All that mattered, Saluus supposed, was that the retreat/hotel was as safe a place to be as anywhere was, these days. The attacks on Ulubis system had gone on, never slackening off for very long, never really reaching any sort of peak. Many of the targets were obvious military ones, often attacked with bombs, missiles and relatively short-range weapons. These were usually blamed on the Beyonders. Other targets had cultural or morale value or were just big. These were the kind that were hit from deep space, with high-velocity, sometimes near-light-speed boosted rocks. The number of such attacks had increased even as the weight of assaults by drone craft carrying beam weapons and missiles had decreased.

Some of the strategists claimed that all this represented a failure by their enemies to attack when they'd expected to, though it seemed to Saluus that what they called the proof of this relied too much on simulations and shared assumptions.

It had all certainly gone on for a long time now. People had worked their way through the various stages of shock, denial, defiance, solidarity, grim determination and who-knew-what else; nowadays they were just tired of it. They wanted it all to end. They feared how that end might come about, but they were half broken by the erratic bombardment and the ever-present uncertainty.

Worse—in a way, because news had somehow leaked out of when the invasion by the Starveling Cult had been expected, and it had not yet materialised—people were starting to think that it might not now ever happen. The real conspiracy theorists believed that it had all been a huge military-industrial paranoid death-fantasy right from the start, that no real threat had ever existed, that most of the attacks were being carried out by the security forces themselves, either as part of an inter-service conflict or in a carefully planned series of cynical, deliberately self-sacrificial moves that would gain sympathy for the armed forces even as the mass of people lost the few remaining civil liberties they still had; that it was all just an excuse to turn the whole Ulubis system into a semi-fascist society, securing power in the hands of the privileged few.

Even those of a more moderate turn of mind chafed at the freedoms lost and the restrictions imposed, and had begun asking where exactly was this terrible threat they had been preparing for for the best part of a year?

Shouldn't the sky have lit up by now with the invading fleet's drives as they decelerated into Ulubis near-space? People were starting to question the need for all the sacrifice and hardship and to wonder if too much was being done to counter a threat that so far hadn't materialised and not enough to deal with the ongoing attrition of small-scale but still intermittently devastating attacks.

The strategists were wondering where the E-5 Discon forces were, too. There had been wild arguments over what the best strategy was: go out to meet the invading fleet or fleets, hoping to gain a slight edge by a degree of surprise—and keeping at least some of the fighting out of the populated reaches of Ulubis system—or sit tight and wait, building up maximum forces where they were in the end most needed? Drone scout ships had already been dispatched in the general direction the invasion was coming from but so far none of them had found anything. A very literal long shot.

A giant magnetic rail gun was being constructed in orbit round G'iri, the smaller gas-giant beyond Nasqueron, built to scatter space in front of the oncoming fleet with debris: a huge blunderbuss supposed to throw a sleet of surveillance machines and a cloud of tiny guided explosive or just kinetic mines before the invading ships, but it was only now getting up to speed, months late, wildly over budget and plagued by problems. At least this latest failure couldn't be laid at the door of Kehar Heavy Industries. Saluus's firm had never been involved in the contract. They'd been the obvious people to build it but it had been handed over to a consortium of other companies partly just to show that KHI didn't have a monopoly and to give some of the others a shot at a big project.

The interim report on the Nasqueron debacle had pretty much cleared KHI, finding nothing worse than occasionally imprecise accounting, the sort of rush-resulted corner-cutting that was only to be expected in anything like the current emergency. The whole storm-battle farce had been a home-grown military fuck-up in other words, just as Saluus had maintained from the start. Partly as a result, he had become more integrated into the whole planning and strategic superstructure of the Ulubine Mercatoria and even, fairly regularly, the Emergency War Cabinet.

This made sense. It also appealed to Saluus's sense of importance, and he was self-aware enough to know and accept this. And, of course, it had the additional effect of tying him in tighter to the political hierarchy of the system, identifying him even more strongly with the ruling structures and individuals, giving him more of an incentive to fight to preserve Mercatorial rule. If the bad guys did sweep in and take things over it would be harder now for Saluus to wave his hands and claim to be just a modest shipbuilder, now humbly at the service of the new masters.

Still, proximity, access and even a degree of control over such power was something Saluus felt comfortable with and, if the worst did happen, he still wasn't as symbolically part of the old regime as the others in the War Cabinet, and his control of KHI would make him valuable to whoever ran the system. He'd play it by ear. Besides, he had an escape route mapped out. The longer the E-5 Discon invasion took to happen, the shorter would be the time to wait for the Mercatoria counter-attack, in which case he might be better off just disappearing while the bad guys settled in and prepared their own defences. (In theory they were supposed to be kept in the dark that the Mercatorial fleet was on its way, but news of that had leaked too and anyway their Beyonder allies would surely have told them.)

If it was simpler to hide then Saluus would hide. He'd try to get involved in some guerrilla activity, too, hopefully at a safe remove, so that when the Mercatoria did retake the system he would look like some sort of hero rather than a coward only interested in his own wealth. But keeping out of the way was sometimes the best strategy when things got messy. He had a very fast ship indeed being built in one of the secret yards, a prototype that he fully intended to make sure was never quite ready for active service or even military trial runs. It would be his way out, if he needed it.

In all this, amazingly, the woman he had first known as Ko, when she'd been with Fassin Taak—her real name, the name she used now, was Liss Alentiore—had been a real help. He'd fallen for her, he supposed. In fact, he'd fallen for her to the extent that his wife—despite her own happily indulged and numerous dalliances—had, for the first and only time, shown signs of jealousy. (Liss herself had suggested a way out of this, though it had occurred, at least as a fantasy, to him as well. So now they had a very stimulating little *ménage à trois* going.)

More to the point, Liss had proved a trustworthy confidante and reliable source of advice. There had been a few occasions over the last few crowded, sometimes desperate months when Saluus had not known which way to react and he'd talked it over with her, either in the semi-formality of his office, flier or ship or from pillow to pillow, and she'd known what to do, if not immediately then after a night or two's thought. She was canny in a sidelong, catlike way; she knew how people worked, how they thought, which way they would jump, almost telepathically sometimes.

He'd invented a post for Liss in his entourage and made her his personal private secretary. His social and business secretaries had both been quietly piqued, but were smart enough to accept the new face with a degree of feigned generosity and seemingly genuine grace, and without trying to do anything to undermine her. Saluus had a feeling that they had each anyway gauged Liss accurately, and realised that any attack they might try on her would likely rebound on themselves.

His own security people had been suspicious of her at first, finding all sorts of insalubrious stuff hinted at in her past, and then a sort of suspicious fuzziness. But ultimately there had been nothing damning, certainly nothing that was worse than what he'd got up to when he was her age. She'd been young, wild and she'd mixed with dubious types. So had he. So what? He'd quizzed her gently on her past himself and got an impression of hurt and trauma and bad memories. He didn't want to hurt her further by inquiring too deeply. It added to his feeling that, in some almost unbearably gallant way, he'd rescued her.

She'd been a middling journalist with a technical journal with a past in dance, acting, hostessing and massage work before; he'd taken her away from all that. She'd looked much younger than she was when he'd met her that night with Fassin—Saluus was a big fan of that whole wise head on young shoulders thing now, he'd decided—but she looked even better now, having taken him up on the offer of treatments she could never have had access to until they'd met. She was grateful to him. She never said so straight out— that would have imbalanced too much what they had—but he could see it in her eyes sometimes.

Well, he was grateful to her, too. She'd revitalised his private life and proved a significant new asset in his public one.

There was, also, just a hint of a feeling that he'd taken her away from Fassin, and that was quite a pleasant little sensation all by itself. Saluus had never exactly envied the other man—he didn't really envy anybody, indeed why should he, how could he?—but there was a sort of ease to Fassin's life that Saluus had always coveted, and so resented. To be part of a big family group like that, surrounded by people all doing the same steady thing, respected for their work intrinsically without constantly having to prove themselves through tender processes and balance sheets and shareholders' meetings and staff councils…that must have its own sweetness, that must give a sort of academic security, a feeling of justification. And then the fellow had gone and become some sort of hero figure, just by spending five years pickled in shock-gel in a miniature gascraft (not even built by KHI) knocking round with a bunch of degenerate Dwellers.

Had that fame attracted Liss to Fassin? Had she just traded Fassin in, traded up to Saluus because the opportunity had presented itself? Maybe so. It didn't bother him. Relationships were a market, Sal knew that. Only children and idiot romantics thought otherwise. You judged your own attractiveness— physically, psychologically and in terms of status—then you knew your level and could either raise or lower your sights accordingly, risking rejection but with the possibility of advancement, or settling for a more reliably stable life but never knowing what you might have achieved.

Saluus took a deep, cold breath.

The sun had disappeared, Ulubis dipping beneath tree-coated mountains far to the south-west. A few stars started to come out in the darkening purple sky. The broad scatter of orbital habs and factories shone like a handful of thrown, sparkling dust to the south-east, gradually stretching out across the sky after the retreating sunset like a distillation of the fading light. Saluus wondered which of those tiny scintillations belonged to him. Not as many as a year ago. Some had been moved away, just to get them out of old orbits where they could be more easily targeted. Two—big dock-ships, both of them, and cradling Navarchy vessels at the time—had been destroyed. Wreckage from one had fallen on Fessli City, killing tens of thousands, many more than had died in the initial attack. KHI was being sued for negligence, accused of not moving the dock-ships out of the way in time. A war on and everything controlled by the military but there was still room for that sort of shit. He was having words in appropriate ears, to get a blanket War Exemption Order proclaimed.

Saluus looked through his own exhaled breath for Nasqueron, but it was far below the horizon and probably all but invisible behind the shield of orbital scatter anyway, even if he had been in the right latitudes to see it.

Fassin. In all the preparations for war and invasion, you always had to make time to take account of whatever he might have got up to. Had he died in the storm battle? Reports from Nasqueron were ambiguous. But then reports from Nasqueron were never anything but ambiguous. He'd certainly disappeared, and was probably still on Nasqueron—though in the time between the destruction of the original satellite surveillance network round the planet at the time of the storm battle and the establishment of a new one after the founding of the Dweller Embassy, there had been a window when even quite big craft might have left Nasqueron's atmosphere—but who knew? And if Taak was still somewhere in the gas-giant, what was he doing?

If he was still alive, Saluus didn't envy him at all any more. To have your whole existence, never mind your whole family, wiped out like that... maybe Fassin had killed himself. He had been told, apparently, before the whole ghastly mess at the GasClipper race. He knew they were dead. If he wasn't dead too, he was more alone than he'd ever been in his life, with nothing much to come back to. Saluus felt sorry for him.

His first thought had been that with Fassin so reduced, there would be no danger of Liss going back to him if he ever did reappear. But then he'd thought about how people could confound your expectations sometimes, and how women in particular could display a sort of theoretically laudable but harmfully self-sacrificial kind of misplaced charity when they saw somebody damaged. Luckily Jaal Tonderon was still alive. Sal and his wife had invited her to stay with them for a while. He wanted to encourage her to be strong for Fassin, if he ever did make it back, and they were all still there.

The Dweller Embassy had been a great success. The Dwellers had seemed keen to make up for the misunderstanding in the storm and the Ulubis Mercatoria had been desperate not to fight on two hopeless fronts at once. Another moon, Uerkle, had been designated as the new site for the Seers' Shared facility—construction was well under way—and a small fleet of ships had been welcomed into orbit around the gas-giant. Seers had started direct delving again—the equipment for remote delving was not yet all in place— and the Dwellers either didn't notice or didn't care that a lot of new so-called Seers were really Navarchy, Cessoria and Shrievalty scouts—spies, if you wanted to be blunt about it—searching for Fassin Taak, searching for the also-disappeared Dweller called Valseir, searching for any sign of those weapons used against the Mercatorial forces during the battle in the GasClipper storm race and searching too for any hints or traces of the Dweller List and anything remotely associated with it—so far, admittedly, all completely without success. Even these scout craft had to be tagged and traceable and escorted by a Dweller guide, but it was a start.

Also in the preparatory—and to date unsuccessful—stages were the negotiations with the Dwellers to forge an alliance or get Mercatorial hands on Dweller weaponry. The Dwellers had shown themselves to possess offensive capabilities—well, strictly speaking, *de*fensive capabilities, but that didn't matter—nobody had credited them with. If they could be brought into an alliance with the rest of Ulubis system, the whole balance of forces between the invaders and the defenders might be turned upside down. Even if the Dwellers only shared some of their military-technological know-how— or just lent out or hired some of the devices—that might make enough of a difference for Ulubis to resist the invasion on its own without having to wait for the Summed Fleet units to arrive.

And if *that* failed, then there was the delicate matter of how to get the Starveling invasion fleet to attack Nasqueron and so, with luck, dash itself to pieces against whatever hyper-weaponry had destroyed the Navarchy forces in the storm battle.

So much to think about.

Saluus was wearing a jacket but he'd come out without gloves and so had put his hands into his pockets to keep them warm. Liss slipped one arm through his, suddenly there at his side, nuzzled up to him, her skin-perfume seeming to fill his head. He looked down at her and she pressed closer to him, following his gaze out to the south and the stipple of light from the orbital structures.

He felt her shiver. She was dressed in light clothes. He took off his jacket and put it over her shoulders. He'd seen that in screen stories and it still made him feel good to do it. He didn't mind the cold, though it was worse than it had been, and a breeze was starting to blow from above. It was a part-katabatic wind, he'd been told by somebody: a current of cold air flowing down from the ice-locked wastes above, displacing warmer, less dense air below and driving gently but firmly downwards, spilling over the lip of the waterfall like a ghost of the frozen, plunging waters.

They stood in silence for a while, then Liss reminded Saluus that he was supposed to meet with Peregal Emoerte for a private talk before dinner that evening. There was still time, though. He felt cold now, close to shivering. He would wait until he did shiver before he went in. He stared up into the near-complete darkness directly overhead, watching the spark of a close-orbit satellite pass above them. He felt Liss stiffen at his side, and pulled her closer.

"What's that?" she said after a few more moments.

He looked where she was pointing, to the low west, where only the vaguest, dimmest hint of purple near the horizon showed where Ulubis had set.

A little above that horizon, in the sky below, beyond and above the thickest strands of reflected orbital light, new lights were flickering to life. They were a sprinkle of bright blue, scattered across a rough circle of sky the size of a large coin held at arm's length, and increasing in number with every passing second. The blue points wavered, gradually strengthening. More and more were lighting up, filling the little window of sky with a blue blaze of cold fire, barely twinkling in the chill, still air out over the frozen plains.

Saluus felt himself shiver, though not from the cold. He opened his mouth to speak but Liss looked up at him and said,

"That's them, isn't it? That's the Starveling Cult guys, the E-5 Discon. That's the invasion fleet, braking."

"'Fraid so," Sal agreed. His ear stud was pinging and the comms in the suite was warbling plaintively. "We'd better go in."

·

Groggy again. Still in the passenger/freight compartment of the *Velpin*. He brought the little gascraft's systems back up. The wall-screen crazed, came clear, showed stars fixed, then swinging, and finally settled on a greeny-blue and white planet. Fassin's first reaction on seeing it was that the place looked alien, unsuitable for life without an esuit. Then he realised that it looked like 'glantine or Sepekte; like images of Earth, in fact. Going gas-giant native, he told himself. Thinking like a Dweller. It didn't usually happen so quickly.

"Oh, *fuck!*" Y'sul said angrily, staring at the image on the screen. "It's not even a proper fucking *planet!*"

The waves came booming in like blindness, like stubbornness bundled and given liquid form, an unending slow launching against the ragged fringe of massively sprawled rocks, each long, low rough ridge of water heaving skywards to tumble like some ponderously incompetent somersaulter, rolling up and falling forward, hopeful and hopeless at once, disintegrating, exploding in spray and foam, coming to pieces amongst the fractured boneyard of rock.

The waters drained after each assault, rattling boulders, stones and pebbles between the massive jabs and points of granite, sloughing like a watery skin and falling away again, that stony chattering speaking of a slowly aggregated success, the waves—the ocean—rubbing away at the land, breaking up and breaking away, using rock against rock, tumbling it and crashing it and cracking it, abrading over centuries and millennia to a kind of stubborn accomplishment.

He watched the waves for some time, admiring their vast mad pounding, reluctantly impressed by such sheer clamorous incessancy. The salt spray filled his hair and eyes and nose and lungs. He breathed in deeply, feeling joined, feeling linked to and part of this wild, unceasing elemental battle.

A low, golden light struck out across the ruffled nap of sea, sunlight swinging slow beneath a great piled series of cloud escarpments to the west, layers of vapour draped over distant peaks and spires of rock disappearing into the long misted curve of north-facing shore.

Seabirds wheeled across the wind and waves, diving, flapping away, clutching slim fish like wet slices of rainbow.

It had felt strange, at first, coming out of the little gascraft. It always did, it always had, but this time seemed different, more intense somehow. This was an alien homeland, a familiar yet utterly different place; closer to what ought to be home, further from what was. Eleven thousand light years away from Ulubis this time, though they had travelled further than the last time to get here. And just twelve days' travel.

When he'd opened the gascraft's hatch and stood, he'd staggered and swayed, needed holding up by Y'sul. He'd coughed and nearly retched, feeling scrawny and weak and thin and hollowed-out, shivering in the strange ultra-nakedness of returning to the basic human condition, as slimed and wet and naked as a newborn, and even the retreating tendrils of the gillfluid and shock-gel tubes there too, umbilical links to image birth. He felt lighter and heavier at once, blood draining, bones complaining.

Then, after a while, being naked—even naked in ordinary clothes—started to feel normal again. Every now and again, though, he shivered. The *Velpin*'s pattern-follower had done its best to make human wearable clothes, but still the results felt strange and slick and cold.

They were on Mavirouelo, a ninety per cent Earthlike not far from the galactic outskirts, though less isolated than Ulubis. A Waterworlder-colonised planet, a Sceuri world.

Waterworlds were the single most common type of rocky planet in the galaxy, even though you never saw the rock, which was, on average, a metal/rock core about the size of Earth buried under five thousand kilometres of pressure-ice, finally topped by a hundred klicks of ocean. Such planets provided the next most common planetary environments after the near-ubiquitous gas-giants themselves, and had given the Mercatoria three of its eight principal species: the Sceuri, the Ifrahile and the Kuskunde.

Mavirouelo was not a classic waterworld—it wasn't even as water-covered as Earth itself—but it had been colonised by the Sceuri before any native animal—of air, land or sea—had developed sufficiently to claim it as their own, and so had become one of the Sceuri far-worlds, an outpost of their own semimperia within the greater commonwealth of the Mercatoria.

The Sceuri weren't conventional waterworlders, either. They were Cetasails, resembling sea mammals but with backs ridged by spinnaker spines which they could hoist to the wind and so sail as well as swim across their worlds.

Y'sul, in his esuit, rose out of the sea like a submarine conning tower, frightening the seabirds. He floated up and out and made his way across the turmoil of waves to the low cliff where Fassin stood. The human was suddenly reminded of the time he had stood with Saluus Kehar, watching Hatherence, in her esuit, float out across the chaos of artificial surf surrounding the waterspout house.

"Fassin!" Y'sul boomed, floating, dripping and humming, in the air ten metres above him. "No sign yet?"

"No sign yet."

Y'sul held up a mesh basket of glistening, flapping, wriggling stuff. "Look what I caught!" He brought the basket in front of his forward mantle to look at it. "Think I'll take it back to the ship."

Y'sul flew over Fassin, dropping water and small shells on top of him, then headed inland a couple of hundred metres to the ship-section resting on the scrubby ledge of vegetation fringing the jagged ranks of cliffs, pinnacles and mountains beyond. The fifty-metre-long lander made up the nose section of the *Velpin*, the rest of which, with Quercer & Janath aboard, was still in orbit.

Fassin watched the Dweller go, then turned back to the ocean. He was here to meet with a Sceuri who had seen the Dweller Leisicrofe, who had been here until, they'd been told, twelve years ago.

They hadn't met a Sceuri yet. The *Velpin* had been challenged by the planet's orbital traffic control and targeted by several military units and so had had to reveal something of its reasons for being there.

"Looking for some Dweller geezer called Leisicrofe," had been Quercer & Janath's exact words.

They'd been told to go into orbit and stay there. Targeting beams never left them. They were regarded as suspicious because their ship looked 'hole-capable and they hadn't come through the local portal.

"Sceuri," Quercer & Janath had told Fassin and Y'sul. "Suspicious."

"Paranoid."

They'd spent three days watching the planet revolve beneath them. Y'sul had muttered about how flat and boring the storms looked, Fassin had found endless fascination in the great snowflake city-structures spread across water and land, and the truetwin passed the time inventorying ship-stuff they'd forgotten about and playing noisy image-leaf games. They answered questions from planetary traffic control about where they'd come from—Nhouaste, the largest of the system's four gas-giant planets, was the answer given—and then a signal had come through. A scholar named Aumapile of Aumapile had had the honour of playing host to the Dweller scholar Leisicrofe and would be flattered to be allowed to extend the same courtesies to these new arrivals.

Another step along the way, another step closer, perhaps, to finding the wandering Dweller and the data he carried. If he still lived, if he still had the data, if the data was what it was supposed to be, if Valseir had been telling the truth, if it was not all utterly out of date, without point, overtaken by the seeming certainty that there was a network of secret wormholes accessible only to Dwellers, but they weren't sharing it and it might have nothing to do with the Dweller List.

Fassin was looking for something that might lead him to what he had already used, twice. He had already been through at least two wormholes, travelled across half the galaxy, and yet he wasn't really any closer to finding the key to this system of trapdoors and secret passages. He could be carried unconscious through them like a fey maiden under the influence of a sleeping draught in some Gothic romance, but he wasn't allowed to know the secret behind it all.

He was still trying to think of ways to commandeer the *Velpin*, but with no real hope of success. There would still be the problem of accessing the hidden wormholes. Just thinking of a way to stay awake while they made these wild transitions would be a start, but he had no idea how to do that either.

If he could go back in time to Apsile and the Shared Facility in Third Fury and ask him to build some subset of systems into the gascraft that would keep working when the main ones were shut down, making it look like the machine had entirely stopped functioning when in fact he was still sense-connected and aware, maybe it would be possible. But even the Dwellers didn't claim to have time machines, and Fassin didn't have the expertise to undertake such an amendment to the gascraft's systems himself, even if he had had the time and the facilities to do it, neither of which he did have.

Maybe he should have gone back to the Mercatoria, acted as a real major in the Ocula would have done and retreated, reported to his superiors, told them what had happened and awaited new or renewed orders. But the Ocula meant nothing to him and never had, and most of what had mattered before to him was also gone now.

He might even have tried to get in touch with the Beyonders, but until he had the key to the Dweller List, what was the point in that? And anyway— what if they had been behind the Sept's destruction, even at a remove? Just how magnanimous was he prepared to be?

What point, indeed, was there in going back at all, perhaps. Seventy days standard had elapsed since Fassin had first gone tumbling into the atmosphere of Nasqueron. It was over two old Earth months since the battle in the storm. Who knew how much longer he'd have to keep looking for Leisicrofe, chasing him round the galaxy, perhaps ever coming closer to him, maybe never quite catching up with him? Maybe he'd get his precious data and return to find it was all over, the system taken, or utterly laid waste to, every surface like the surface of Third Fury, just slag and heat, destroyed by one side or another or by both, fighting for something that wasn't even there any more.

It should still, in theory, be the most important piece of information that a human had ever carried. But somehow, even if the key to the Dweller List did exist, the fact that Dwellers could use this secret network under the noses of the rest of the galaxy—and had been so doing for who alone knew how many billions of years—made it seem much less likely that any scrap of data, any proof-size patch of algebra was going to make that much of a difference.

And yet, still, despite everything, all he could do, all that he could even think of doing, was to press on and try to find what everybody wanted him to find, and hope that it might do some good somehow.

Fassin breathed in, tasting salt.

He no longer doubted that this was real, or a virtual environment there was no disgrace in being fooled by. There wasn't even anywhere like this— this coarse, storm-sundered coast—anywhere in Ulubis system. And the stars were completely different, again.

Something caught Fassin's attention. A few kilometres out into the ocean, the water was rising in a great shallow dome, flowing everywhere down from a huge flattened hemisphere of foam-streaked darkness rising like a never-breaking explosion from the depths, still spreading and still rising and causing a great slow swell of disturbed waves to come pulsing forward, towards the cliffs as the apparition—a double saucer-shape two kilometres wide—finally broke free of the sea entirely and came slowly towards the shore, sheets and veils of salt rain falling from beneath it, flattening the shadow-bruised surface of the waters.

Y'sul floated up, nodding forward. "Ride's here, then."

They floated, stood and hovered in a half-drained crystal hall within the great saucer ship. Aumapile of Aumapile floated in the water, a fat eel the size of an orca with a great folded fan of sail ridging its back. Fassin stood on a broad ledge, still slick with salty water, while Y'sul and the truetwin Quercer & Janath—cajoled down eventually, bulked out with a twin-skin overall of extreme shininess that doubled as an esuit—hovered in the air above the great pool of water. Fassin found himself thinking about the Autumn House again, and Slovius in his pool.

Aumapile of Aumapile—*The* Aumapile of Aumapile, apparently, according to the servant who had escorted them down a broad water-filled tube to the audience chamber, the human and the Dwellers in a bubble of air enclosed by a sphere of diamond—was not merely a justly famous scholar of the Cincturia, it was a vastly rich justly famous scholar of the Cincturia.

A high, warbling, seemingly interminable song sounded from an underwater sound system. "A Song of Welcoming For Those From Afar," apparently.

"Song for making you want to go straight back there again," Y'sul had asided to Fassin, as they'd accepted reasonable impersonations of something to drink and/or inhale.

They talked of Leisicrofe. Their host, speaking through a small hovering speaker sphere, said they had missed him by some years and then Y'sul mentioned following him.

"Oh," the Sceuri said, "but you must take me with you."

"Must?"

"Must?"

"But I know where he went," the Sceuri said, as though this explained everything.

"Couldn't you just tell us?" Y'sul asked plaintively.

"Just point us in the right direction."

"And we'll be on our way."

The Sceuri wriggled in the great pool, sending water sloshing. It laughed. A soft, tinkling sound from the hovering speaker. "Oh, I could, but I always had the feeling my friend Leisicrofe had travelled even more widely than I have, especially into the gases of Nhouaste. I think you may be heading there, as you did not come through the wormhole portal, and he did not depart through it. You see? I have my sources. I know what goes on. You can't fool me. I am not so stupid. You and your little Squanderer friend will be heading back to Nhouaste."

"Doubt it," the Dweller travelcaptain said, snorting.

Fassin was the little Squanderer friend. The Sceuri took great pride in having become a technological, space-faring species, given the obstacles they'd had to overcome. A classic waterworld environment had almost no easily available metals. Any metal-bearing ores that a waterworld possessed tended to be locked away under all that ice, deep in the planet's inaccessible rocky core. Waterworlders had to do what they could with what fell from the sky in the shape of meteorites, and in this shared a developmental background with gas-giant Dwellers.

To get into space in the face of such a paucity of readily available raw materials was not easy, and the Sceuri regarded themselves as deserving considerable recognition and respect for such a triumph of intellect over scarcity. Accomplishing the same feat when you came from a rock-surface planet was a relatively trivial, expectable, even dismissible trick. The Sceuri called people from such planets Squanderers as a result, though not usually to their face or other appropriate feature.

"Please make clear, oh great A of A," the other half of Quercer & Janath said.

Fassin suspected that he already knew what the Sceuri was thinking. The local gas-giant, Nhouaste—inhabited by Dwellers, of course—was, like the vast majority of Dweller gas-giants, not a world that welcomed Seers or anybody else apart from other Dwellers. Aumapile of Aumapile had probably been told where Leisicrofe was heading next and assumed that as the Dweller had not gone through the Mercatorial wormhole—and assuming he hadn't headed into deep space at STL speeds—he must have gone to look for whatever it was he was looking for in the one place that even being fabulously rich and corruptly well-connected couldn't gain you access to, in this system or any other: a Dweller-inhabited gas-giant.

"I think the Toilers our mutual friend sought have found a new niche, no longer in space, but in gas, you see?" the Sceuri said. Even through the speaker sphere, the creature's voice sounded pleased with itself.

"Toilers?" Y'sul said.

"Known."

"Benign semi-swarm devices," the other half of Quercer & Janath announced. "Infra-sentient. Known for randomly building inscrutable space structures, best guess for purpose of which being as preparatory infrastructure for an invasion that never took place on behalf of a race long gone and thoroughly forgotten. Distribution very wide but very sparse. Numbers fluctuate. Rarely dangerous, sometimes hunted, no bounty."

"So there."

Y'sul looked surprised. "Really?" he asked.

"Oh, stop being so coy!" their host chided, creating sinuous splashing patterns in the water, as though tickled. "Of course! As though you didn't know." The Aumapile of Aumapile blew jets of water from each end. A scent of something vaguely rotten filled Fassin's nose. "But I know where our friend was going to next, and you don't. However, I shall be willing to tell you if you take me along, once I am aboard your ship. Such large places, gas-giants! And of course we have four. One thinks, Oh, who can say, where would one's quarry be?" The Sceuri flicked its tail. Fassin got splashed. "And what do you say, sirs?"

Y'sul looked at Fassin and quietly rippled his mantle, the Dweller equivalent of a head-shake.

The travelcaptain was silent for a moment or two, then said,

"If we do take you with us…"

"Ah! But I have my own ship! Indeed, you are in it!"

"Won't work."

  "Have to come with us in ours."

"I have smaller ships! Many of them! A choice!"

"Makes no difference. Has to be ours."

  "Conditions of Passage."

"Well…" the Sceuri said.

"Passengers travel unconditionally."

  "Unconditionally."

"What does that mean?"

"Trust us."

  "Yes. No matter what."

"Means you get zapped unconscious every time we travel, is what it means," Y'sul told their host. Quercer & Janath made a hissing noise. "Plus," Y'sul added, oblivious, "you may not end up where you thought you were going to."

"How primitive! Why, of course!"

·

Eleven hundred ships. They were facing eleven hundred ships. All of them had to be beyond a certain size, capable of crossing the great gulf of space between the E-5 Discon and here in reasonable time, and they would probably all be armed. Ulubis could muster less than three hundred true space-capable warcraft, even after their frenzy of building. The Summed Fleet on its way to their rescue was of similar size, but its ships would be of another order of magnitude in hitting power: a full mix of destroyers, light, medium and heavy cruisers, plus the real big guys, the battlecruisers and battleships.

Ulubis had frigates, destroyers and light cruisers, and one old battlecruiser, the *Carronade*. They'd built a significant fleet in the centuries following the destruction of the portal, and a few more ships in the half year since the news of the coming invasion, but nothing like enough to offer the invaders serious opposition. They'd lost about a sixth of their total fighting force in the few minutes of action in the storm on Nasqueron, months earlier, including their only other battlecruiser. Those had mostly been light units, but it had been a grievous loss.

The latest bit of bad news was that the consortium working on the rail gun had fallen so far behind schedule that it was highly doubtful they'd even get to the trials stage before the invasion took place. The giant gun was being dismantled so it wouldn't fall into the hands of the Starveling Cultists. There was something almost sublimely elegant, Sal thought, about how perfect a waste of time, people, resources and hard work the whole project had been.

Kehar Heavy Industries and the other manufacturers had worked as hard as they could to construct, repair, upgrade and modify as many warships as they could, and had militarised dozens of civilian craft. But there was only so much they could do and it was never going to be enough. They were outnumbered. They could go down fighting, but they were going down.

"It couldn't be any worse!" Guard-General Thovin spluttered, practically spraying his drink. They were on a requisitioned ex-cruise liner, one of the Embassy support ships, rolling in orbit around Nasqueron. Saluus and the Propylaea sub-master Sorofieve had been sent by the rest of the War Cabinet to add, if it were possible, an extra note of urgency to the talks with the Dwellers. Thovin, seconded from his Guard duties to be Commander-in-Chief, Ulubis Orbital Forces, was there in charge of the very lightly armed escort detachment because he was out of the way and couldn't do too much harm. The grandeur of his new title seemed to almost entirely make up for the lack of viable military hardware at his disposal.

"We can't even surrender to the Starvelings because if we do the Summed Fleet will clobber us when they arrive," he said. "We're going to get fucked-over twice!" He threw back his drink.

Saluus didn't like Thovin—he was one of those people who got to the top of an organisation through luck, connections, the indulgence of superiors and that sort of carelessness towards others that the easily impressed termed ruthlessness and those of a less gullible nature called sociopathy. But sometimes, just through his sheer unthinking brusqueness and inability to think through the consequences of a remark, he said what everybody else was only thinking. A comic poet working in obscene doggerel.

"There is no need to talk of surrender," sub-master Sorofieve said quickly, and, to Sal's amusement, actually looked round, glancing left and right to make sure nobody else had heard the "S" word in the old cruise ship's lounge, which was deserted apart from a few bar staff, the three men and a half-dozen or so of their closest staff. (Liss was there, looking darkly beautiful, mostly silent, occasionally talking quietly with one or other of the other assistants, secretaries and ADCs. When the Propylaea sub-master did his glancing-around act, her gaze met Sal's; she smiled and flexed her eyebrows.)

If there were any spies here, Sal thought, they weren't lurking behind the furniture in the shadows, they were sitting right here, around them. The indispensable aides and helpers they all relied on to run their so-important lives were the obvious candidates for the post of spy. If anything ever got back to the Hierchon—or any other more lowly but still important branch of the Ulubine Mercatoria—regarding talk of surrender or anything else deemed Unspeakable it would probably be one of these people they'd have to thank.

Saluus knew one could never be one hundred per cent certain, but he was pretty sure that the lovely Liss wasn't working for anybody else. He'd seemingly let slip a couple of things early on in their relationship which he'd have expected to come back to him if she'd been in the pay of somebody else. It had been a sort of recommendation that she'd come via Fassin and he'd obviously known her from decades earlier. That was far too long a game just to get to an industrialist, even Saluus Kehar.

"No need?" Thovin said, turning to his secretary, holding up his glass and winking theatrically. "It's what we'd be talking about if the Summed Fleet wasn't on its way. Be the rational thing to do." He snorted. "I'm not saying we should surrender. Been ordered not to, been ordered to fight to the last, but if the Fleet wasn't coming and we weren't looking for this... this *thing*, supposedly somewhere on Nasq." (The fabled Transform, of course, Saluus thought. The mythical magic bullet which Fassin, if he was still alive, might be chasing yet.) "What else would we be doing but thinking how to not all get ourselves killed?"

"We are prepared, we are forewarned," sub-master Sorofieve said, smiling desperately. "We shall give a good account of ourselves, I am sure. We are fighting for our homes, for our honour, for—" the man looked round again "—for our very *humanity*!" Ah, Sal realised, Sorofieve had been checking there were no aliens present whom he might be offending. "We have millennia of Mercatorial, ah, wisdom and martial ability behind us. What are these Starveling renegades in comparison?"

Eleven hundred ships, that's what they were, Saluus thought. Eleven hundred to our three hundred, and a balance of forces the strategists say is way up the force-yield spectrum compared to ours, too: medium-heavy to our light. Plus one mega-ship, to our one antique battlecruiser.

They had had another meeting with some of the Dweller representatives just that afternoon. They went down these days in person, reclined in human-form spacesuits held in small circular gascraft of two or three seats, congregating in a great hall in one of a whole fleet of giant Dreadnought-sized craft the Dwellers had dedicated to the purpose. With the gascraft canopies hinged open it was possible to sit/lie there in some comfort and talk directly to the Dwellers, face-to-hub or whatever it was.

Saluus wouldn't want to spend more than a day like that in multiple gees, but it was worth doing. The Dwellers seemed to appreciate it and—thanks to some cram-coaching by the senior Seers who also came down with them to the meetings and stayed with them for all but the most delicate and high-security-clearance matters—Saluus was even starting to get the hang of Dweller expressions and nuances of meaning and demeanour, both as put across in speech and as displayed on their signal skin. Probably all too late, and—so far—to no avail whatsoever. But at least it felt like he was doing something—the shipyards of KHI were basically on autopilot, working flat out and so synched-in to what the military wanted that they'd effectively become part of a command economy. He'd just been getting in the way.

"This is a threat to the whole of Ulubis system," Sorofieve said.

Sal suppressed a sigh. This was only Sorofieve's third day in this latest round—he'd replaced First Secretary Heuypzlagger, who'd found the high gravity too wearing—and he was talking to a Dweller called Yawiyuen who was also new to the process, but even so. They'd been circling over this same ground for weeks now.

"These Starveling Cult people will show no respect for Nasqueron's neutrality," the sub-master concluded.

"How do you know?" Gruonoshe, another of the Dwellers, asked. They were nine in all: the two human negotiators and a couple of assistants each—Liss was there in a seat behind Sal, having declared herself quite happy in the high gravity—Chief Seer Meretiy of Sept Krine, and just the two Dwellers, both in ceremonial half-clothes, ribboned and jewelled.

"Know what?" Sorofieve asked.

"Know that these Starveling Cult people will show no respect for Nasqueron's neutrality," Gruonoshe said, innocently.

"Well," Sorofieve said, "they are invaders, warmongers. Indeed, not to put too fine a point on it, they are barbarians. They respect nothing."

"Still, it does not follow that they'd quarrel with us," Yawiyuen said, signal skin showing reasonableness.

"They want to take over the whole system," Sorofieve said, looking to Saluus for help. "To them that would include Nasqueron."

"We have heard of the Starveling Cult," Yawiyuen told them. (—Wonder from where? Liss sent to Saluus via his ear stud.) "It appears to be an unremarkable Quick hegemonist diffusion, concerned with conquering its own kind and species-type-suitable environments, uninterested in attacking gas-giants."

"The point here," Saluus said smoothly, his amplified voice sounding rich and powerful, "is that they are only attacking Ulubis system to get to Nasqueron."

"Why?" Gruonoshe asked.

"We're not entirely sure," Saluus said. "We are sure they want something from Nasqueron, something they can't get from any other gas-giant, but exactly what that may be, we can't say. But we are quite positive that that is why they are mounting this attack in the first place."

"Why are you sure?" Gruonoshe again.

"We intercepted intelligence to that effect," Sorofieve replied.

"What intelligence?" Yawiyuen asked.

"The intelligence," Sorofieve said, "came from the personal diary of the Supreme Commander of the Starveling Cult invasion fleet sent to the Ruanthril system nearly eighteen years ago. The fleet was intercepted by a Mercatorial force. The captured records show that the enemy commander complained specifically about the need to divert so many of the E-5 Discon's forces to somewhere as out of the way and strategically unimportant as Ulubis, just for some item or piece of information in Nasqueron."

"Nasqueron was mentioned by name?" Gruonoshe asked.

"It was," Sal said.

He half-expected a little voice in his ear to say something like "Good lie" but then remembered that even Liss hadn't been told the full truth about the Dweller List and the mythical Transform. She would have an idea, as a lot of people close to the epicentres of power did, that Fassin had been sent on a secret mission to look for something valuable in Nasqueron, and that the object of this search might have some bearing on the war, but that was about all. She hadn't been present at the briefing by the AI projection of Admiral Quile, hadn't been let in on the secret subsequently by some of those who had been there—as Sal had—and so didn't know the details of the intelligence they'd been given.

"Well then," Yawiyuen said reasonably, "you should let the Starveling Cult attack us and we will deal with them."

This, of course, was exactly what the Emergency War Cabinet hoped would happen.

—Can we just say yes here? Liss sent.

"Wouldn't *you* then want some help from *us*?" Sorofieve asked.

"Oh, no!" Gruonoshe exclaimed, as though the idea was just too preposterous even to think about.

"As sub-master Sorofieve has said," Saluus said, "we are quite certain that the Starveling Cultists intend to take the entirety of Ulubis system, including Nasqueron. We're all under threat. That's why it would make sense for you and us to organise our defence together."

"A common threat requires a common response," Sorofieve told the Dwellers.

"Or maybe a pincer movement," Yawiyuen suggested brightly.

Saluus wanted to sigh again. These two guys were supposedly top-grade negotiators with the authority to speak provisionally—in advance of some sort of still undefined plebiscite procedure—for the entire Dweller society on Nasqueron, but they frequently sounded like children. "Well, perhaps," he said. "Providing we can, at the very least, coordinate our actions."

"And of course," Sorofieve said, "it may be that we can share defence technologies."

"Oh!" Yawiyuen said, rising above his dent-seat a fraction. "Good idea! What do you have that we might want?" He appeared guilelessly enthusiastic.

"Our strengths would lie more in intelligence, in knowing how these Starveling Cultists will think," Saluus said. "They're basically humans, too. For all our differences, we think pretty much the same way they do. Our contribution would be to try to anticipate them, to out-think them."

"And ours?" Yawiyuen asked, settling back down in his seat again.

"Weaponry, I bet," Gruonoshe said, sounding unimpressed.

"As we have discovered, very much to our cost," Saluus said, "you have the better of us in offensive capability, certainly—"

"*De*fensive capability," Gruonoshe interrupted. "Surely?"

Sal did his best to move his helmeted head in an acknowledging nod, straining his neck muscles in the high gravity. "Defensive capability, as you say," he said. "If we were able to share some of your knowledge of—"

"Weapons technology is not something we are going to share," Gruonoshe said crisply.

"We could say we wanted to," Yawiyuen told them. "We could even mean it—you might argue us round, somehow, to said point of view—but those who control the weapons themselves would not permit it."

"Well, can we perhaps talk to them?" Saluus asked.

Yawiyuen bobbed over his seat. "No."

"Why would that be?" Sorofieve asked.

"They don't talk to aliens," Yawiyuen told them bluntly.

"They barely talk to *us*," Gruonoshe admitted.

"How might we be able to—?" Saluus began.

"We are not the Mercatoria," Gruonoshe said, interrupting Saluus again. This was not an experience he was used to. He could see how it might get annoying. "We are not the Mercatoria," the Dweller repeated. He sounded indignant. "We are not one of your states or mercenary- or irrationality-inspired groupings or forces."

—Bit of stress there, Sal heard in his ear.

"If I may," Chief Seer Meretiy began. The Seers were under instruction only to take a part in the talks when they felt there was some sort of basic misunderstanding taking place. Meretiy obviously felt that was happening now, but he didn't get a chance to take his point further.

"What is meant, one believes," Yawiyuen said, "is that things do not work with us the way that they work with you. We are delegated to speak to you, and what we take from here will be shared with all who wish to take notice. We are not in a position to order other Dwellers to do or not do certain things. No Dweller is, not in the hierarchical sense that you may be used to. We can share information. The information regarding the approach of the Starveling Cultists has been made available to whoever it may concern, as was the information regarding the build-up of Mercatorial forces immediately prior to the unfortunate incident which took place within C-2 Storm Ultra-Violet 3667. Those in charge of the relevant defensive systems will doubtless have taken note of said information. That is really all we can share with you. Our colleagues in charge of the defensive systems would not consider talking to outsiders and there is no precedent for sharing, lending, leasing or giving such technologies to others."

"You talk of your colleagues in charge of the defensive systems," Sorofieve said. "But who is in charge of *them*?"

—And so to the point.

Yawiyuen gave a little bob-shrug. "Nobody is."

"*Somebody* has to be," Sorofieve insisted.

"Why?"

"Well," Sorofieve said, "how do they know what to do?"

"Lots of training," Yawiyuen told him.

"But when? *When* do they know what to do? Who directs them, who decides when it's time to stop talking and start shooting?"

"They do."

"*They* do?" Sorofieve sounded incredulous. "You let your *military* decide when to go to war?"

—Our sub-master hasn't done his homework, has he? Sal sent to Liss.

—He may have read, she replied.—He didn't believe.

Saluus had done as much research as he could into the Dwellers. Amazing how little he'd known. He was smart, well-educated and extremely well-connected and yet he'd been near-shamed by how little he'd known about the creatures that his own species shared the system with. It was as though, having realised how little the Dwellers were concerned with or cared about them, Ulubine humanity had decided to pay them back in the same coin. And this in a Seer system, with more inter-species contact than any save another half-dozen or so similarly favoured, scattered through the galaxy. Yet even here most people didn't know or want to know much of anything about the Dwellers. There was a large minority who did, but they were seen as slightly embarrassing—nerdy alien-fans. Facing the threat they were, desperately needing the Dwellers' help, how short-sighted they all seemed now.

And reading up on Dweller society proved the truth of one old cliché for sure: the more you learned, the more you realised how little you knew. (An image of the planet, Liss had suggested when he'd first tried to articulate this feeling; unending depths.)

"Of course our military decide when we go to war," Gruonoshe said, calm again. "They're the experts."

"I think that, if I might be allowed to 'butt in,'" Chief Seer Meretiy said from his gascraft, "the point at issue is our different ways of looking at our two societies' military capacity. We—that is, humans, and perhaps one might even presume to speak in this for the whole Mercatoria—regard our military as a tool, to be used by our politicians, who of course rule in the name of all. Conversely, our Dweller friends regard their military as an ancient and venerable calling for those with the relevant vocation, an institution to be honoured for its antiquity which has, almost as an afterthought, the duty of defending Dweller planets from any outside threat. As such, they are like what one might term a 'fire brigade', and a volunteer fire brigade, at that, for which no political clearance or oversight is required for it to spring into action, you see? Their *raison d'être* is to respond as quickly as possible to emergencies, no more."

—Fuck me, that actually made a sort of sense, Liss sent.

Just those first two words, delivered in her voice, with her so close behind him, gave Sal the start of an erection. He wondered how strong gravity had to be for hard-ons to become impossible.

"Fire brigades have…leaders, captains, don't they?" Sorofieve said plaintively, looking from Meretiy to Saluus. "We might talk to them. Mightn't we?"

Yawiyuen did the little bob-shrug again. "Absolutely not."

"But we need to!" Sorofieve almost wailed.

"Why?"

"That thing even *looks* fast," Guard-General Thovin said, gazing out at the sleek, dark ship from one of the requisitioned liner's viewing galleries. The stars swung around them. "It have a name?"

"*Hull 8770*," Saluus told him. "The military will give it a proper name when it's time to hand it over. Though it's a prototype, probably not suitable for full military service."

"Desperate times," Thovin said, shrugging, picking something from between his teeth. "Probably get used for something. Even if it's just a missile."

*That's what you think*, Sal thought. "We haven't quite got to that stage yet," he said. They were alone. Thovin had suggested a stroll through the mostly empty ex-civilian ship.

"Think we're wasting our time here, Kehar?" Thovin swung round to look at Saluus, his near-neckless head raised and tilted to him.

"Talking to the Dwellers?"

"Yes. Talking to the fucking Dwellers."

"Probably. But then our friend Fassin Taak is probably wasting his time—if he's still alive—looking for this Transform that probably doesn't exist."

"He was your friend, wasn't he?" the Guard-General said, eyes narrowing. "Old school pals. Right, isn't it?"

"Yes, we went to school and college together. We've kept in touch over the years. Matter of fact, probably the last bit of R and R he got before delving into Nasq. was at my house on Murla."

"Straight to Guard academy for me," Thovin said, changing tack again and looking away at the dartlike ship floating in space just outside. "That your escape route, is it, Kehar?" he asked innocently.

*Not quite as stupid as you look, are you?* Sal thought. "Where to?" he asked, smiling.

"The fuck out of harm's way, that's where," Thovin said. "Keep your head down during the Starveling occupation. Return when it's safe."

"You know, I hadn't thought of that," Sal said. "Why, are you going to make me an offer for it?"

"Wouldn't know how to fly it. 'Course, you do, that right?"

It was no secret that Saluus had flown the *Hull 8770* here himself. He was a capable enough pilot. Anybody could be with a little training and a modicum of computer help.

"Frees one of our brave boys for the front line," he told Thovin, deadpan.

"Be funny if we won against the invaders, or the Summed Fleet lost. Eh?"

"Hilarious."

"Think we'll get anything out of the floats?"

"I think our Dweller pals have probably given us all we're ever going to get, but it's still worthwhile keeping on looking."

"Uh-huh? You think?"

"Maybe the crew of one of their hyper-weapons will suddenly decide it'd be fun to defend Sepekte just for the sheer hell of it, or one of the scouts down in Nasq. will find the Transform, or Fassin Taak will just appear with it and we can all escape down a wormhole or bring in Summed Fleet ships from wherever we want. Who knows?"

"So we're not wasting our time here?"

"No, probably we are. But what else could we be doing? Filling sandbags?"

Thovin almost smiled. "'Course, if they did suddenly turn up with some fancy super-weapon ship, maybe we wouldn't need to build warships any more, eh?"

"I'm sure Kehar Heavy Industries could happily switch to building nothing but cruise ships." Sal looked round the viewing gallery they stood in. "I can see a few areas fit for improvement just standing here."

Thovin nodded out at the slim, dark ship cradled outside. "You would hand that over to the Hierchon for his personal yacht if he asked for it, wouldn't you?"

Sal thought for a moment. "I'd almost sooner destroy it," he said.

Thovin turned and looked at him, expression open, waiting.

"I'm not kidding. It really is a prototype," Sal said, smiling. "You wouldn't put the head of state of an entire system in something as untried as that, certainly not if you meant to take it up to anything near top speed, which would kind of have to be the only reason for choosing it in the first place, right? I'll entrust myself to the thing, but I couldn't let the Hierchon take it. What if it killed him? Think of the publicity. Good grief, man, think of our share price."

Thovin nodded for a few moments, looking back at the ship. "Missile, then," he said.

"Me too," Liss said quietly in the darkness. "I thought he was just an idiot kicked upstairs."

"I think he does a good idiot act," Sal said. "Actually, I think he's probably as genuinely stupid as our Dweller negotiators are genuinely naive. Maybe Thovin should take over the talks. Doubt he could do any worse."

They were lying in bed on board the prototype ship. It was more secure than staying on the liner or one of the other Embassy support ships, if also far less luxurious and much more cramped. There was no absolute guarantee that somebody hadn't sneaked a bug aboard during the ship's construction, but Saluus had had the craft built by his most trustworthy people and supervised the work as closely as he could; it was as safe as anyplace to say things that you might not want others to hear.

"Do you think he was trying to make a deal, get himself included if you did decide to escape?"

Saluus hesitated. This was not something he'd ever discussed straight out even with Liss. He was quite sure she'd guessed that using the ship as a way out was a possibility—so, for that matter, had Thovin, apparently, which kind of made you wonder who else might regard it as obvious (*there* was a slightly sweat-inducing idea)—but there was nothing to gain for either of them in saying it out loud.

"No," Sal said, deciding against bringing that particular truth blinking into the light. "You know, I actually thought that maybe Thovin's a kind of spy himself."

"Really?"

"I wouldn't be at all surprised if he reports to the Hierchon direct, or at least to the big guy's top intelligence people. I think all this rough-as-bricks bluff stuff is just a way of getting people to drop their guard with him. Fucker could be a traitor-sniffer."

Liss fitted her long body against his, rubbing slowly, gently. "He didn't sniff you, then?"

"How could he?" Sal said. "For I am straight and true."

"Ah, yes."

Sometimes, if she was still holding him when she was falling asleep, he would feel her fingers making strange patterns on his side or back, as though her hands were trying to spell out some secret code of love. Then she would be asleep and stop, or jerk awake, as though embarrassed, and roll away and curl up.

:

Groggy again. Aboard the *Velpin*. Still. No idea yet how long they had taken. The truetwin had just told the three of them that it would take "some days" to get to where they were going. Then, to Fassin and Y'sul when the Sceuri couldn't see, they had signal-whispered, "That thing about Just Trust Us applies to you two, too. But *shh*, right?"

Y'sul and Fassin had exchanged looks.

Some days. The travel time was near-instant, of course, portal to portal. It was the getting to and from the portals at either end that took days. That and, perhaps, some sleight-of-course manoeuvres to fool anybody watching or following and trying to spot the hidden portals that way. Who knew? Quercer & Janath did, of course, but they weren't telling, wouldn't even contemplate any arguments about letting him or even just Y'sul stay awake during these bizarre, so casually taken galaxy-spanning transfers.

Watching, following. How could you have all those ship movements and never be seen? Telescopes of every wavelength, gravity sensors, neutrino patternisers, something somewhere in practically every developed system that kept a devastatingly detailed close eye on every sort of signal that ever emanated from space close, near, mid or far: *something* had to show up. Or did they only have portals in undeveloped systems, so that they had less chance of being observed?

No, they had them in Ulubis and Ashum.

Watching, following. Followed by something small enough to be even less visible, perhaps? Somebody, *something* must have followed a Dweller ship in-system, somewhere, and suddenly found itself plunging into a secret wormhole... And yet, apparently, nobody and nothing ever had.

So casual, so lackadaisical, so la-la-la; could it all be a perfect, never-failing act? Could the Dwellers all really be geniuses at acting, brilliant at stealth, flawless exponents of the disciplines required to keep complete discipline for every single solitary journey/transfer/jump/whatever? Dear reason and fate, they'd had ten billion years to get perfect at anything they wanted. Who knew what skills they'd developed to perfection in that time? (Yet there was still chaos, extreme chance, the simple stacking-up of odds that something had to go wrong sometime, no matter how close to perfection you could get...)

Coming round, slowly. Rovruetz, Direaliete. Shit, more names to deal with, more places to take in, another damn step along the way. He would die forever following this elusive fuck of a Dweller, or accumulate such dislocation, accrue so much summed grogginess that he'd forget what the whole insane quest was for, and find Leisicrofe one day, finally, when it was all too late anyway, and just stare at the fellow, utterly unable to recall what it was he wanted to ask him or what it might be that the Dweller could possibly have that would be remotely interesting or important to him.

The passenger compartment of the *Velpin* was mostly taken up by the esuit of the Sceuri called the Aumapile of Aumapile: a huge white-stippled black lozenge like a strange distorting viewport into space. Fassin, waking slowly, feeling grubby and sore as usual, couldn't even see Y'sul or the anyway useless screen on the far wall.

"Urgh!" the giant black esuit exclaimed. "So that is unconsciousness? How disagreeable. And I strongly suspect inherently so."

Fassin was glad that somebody agreed. He started checking out the arrowhead's systems as he warmed them up again. The left manipulator arm was proving sticky, the self-repair mechanisms reaching the limits of their abilities. On past form it would sort of half-work, jerkily, for a few real-time months and then jam completely. He supposed he was lucky he'd got this far without any equipment failure, especially given the punishment the little gascraft had taken since the flight from Third Fury.

"And yet interesting!" the Sceuri announced, voice booming round the near-full space. The Aumapile of Aumapile was even louder than Y'sul. "Hmm," it said. "Yes, interesting, more than certainly. Are you two awake yet or am I first up? Ha-ha!"

"Either awake or having a very noisy nightmare," Y'sul said testily and unseen from the creature's other side.

"Ditto," said Fassin.

"Super! So, are we there yet?"

They were.
And they weren't.

When the fuzzy screen cleared, it showed they were in the middle layers of a gas-giant atmosphere. The *Velpin* had done some high-speed spinning after all, and the zapping-unconscious had been more rough and ready than before. They had taken two days to get where they were going.

This, their travelcaptain assured them, was Rovruetz, Direaliete, a weather district and gas region of Nhouaste, the system's own gas-giant.

The Aumapile of Aumapile was delighted. Just as it had thought! It fairly bounced out of the *Velpin*'s gaslock into the vast, shaded scape of towering RootClouds and horizon-spanning RayCanopies. It twirled like a centrifuge from sheer happiness. They spent another day, perfectly undisturbed by any native Dwellers, investigating the supposedly Toiler remains, which actually looked remarkably like an abandoned Dweller globe-city sitting on top of a damaged and discarded mega-klick BandTurbine. All very impressive, but not, Fassin and Y'sul both realised, what or where they were really looking for.

—This is not Rovruetz, Direaliete, is it? Fassin asked the truetwin shortly after they arrived, while the Aumapile of Aumapile dashed to and fro throughout the ruins, calibrating instruments and grabbing screenage.

—Are you mad? Of course not.

    —Direaliete's on the far side of the galaxy.

—Take days to get there.

—A system? Fassin asked.

—A system.

—I've no record of it, Fassin told the truetwin.

—You wouldn't. Direaliete is its name in the Old Language.

    —Well, variant thereof.

—So, Fassin sent,—this is just a trick.

—Correct.

    —Our friend has what it wanted, we have what we wanted. Two out of two. One of our more successful missions.

—Meanwhile, Fassin sent,—we're wasting time.

—Time wastes itself.

    —Who are we to float in its way?

After offering to leave the breathless Sceuri scholar behind and come back for it—it wasn't quite that easily fooled—and then telling it they really needed to be getting back now—it declared there was too much it still had to look for—Quercer & Janath just abandoned the Sceuri, waiting until it had whirred off into the centre of the abandoned city before telling Fassin that the Aumapile of Aumapile had finally seen sense and was coming aboard in a moment for the trip back, getting the human and Y'sul secured, and then closing the external doors and taking off, warning their passengers there was some fairly intense spiralling ahead.

—What the fuck? Fassin signalled to Y'sul before the gascraft's systems were shut down.—What about the Sceuri?

The Dweller had been in on it.

—A good joke, eh? he sent back, laughing.

Fassin signalled at the wall-screen, getting through to Quercer & Janath in the command space.

—Did you *warn* the Aumapile you were about to leave?

—Yes.

Fassin waited. No more came. After a few moments he sent,—And?

—Didn't believe us.

—Laughed.

—So you're just abandoning this fabulously wealthy, apparently politically well-connected, Dweller-naive idiot in a gas-giant in its home system?

—About sums it up.

—Can't say we didn't warn him. It.

—Conditions of Passage.

—Don't you think it might get hunted or just die anyway? Fassin asked.— Or get back home, eventually, deeply annoyed?

—Suppose it's a possibility.

—Keep going?

—Get back home, eventually, deeply annoyed with all Dwellers? And that that might be a bad thing for the Dwellers who live in Nhouaste?

—Point.

—Could cause friction.

—Kudos loss!

—Maybe we should have warned somebody we were leaving the flop-backed suck-puncture behind.

—Thinking. Suggestion. Know! We'll send a signal.

—Happy?

Fassin didn't even get time to reply.

—No more talk time. Switch off now, start spiralling.

:

The Archimandrite Luseferous reviewed his forces. The nearest parts were right here, within the curved, concentric hulls of the Main Battle Craft *Luseferous VII*: they were his space and ground crack troops, all stood at attention by their sleek all-environments attack craft and high-skill-spec weaponry. The warships, support craft, troop carriers, landers, bombardment monitors, harrier drones, missile carriers, scout and surveillance machines and other vessels plus miscellaneous heavy devices he could discern— stretching as far as the unaided eye could see into the distance—were just projections. But they were live, real-time, and mostly clustered within a few light seconds of the invasion fleet's core, whose absolute, steely heart was the Main Battle Craft *Luseferous VII*.

This was, in a way, the Archimandrite's favourite bit. He had made a tradition of reviewing his forces like this before every major engagement, and especially before every system invasion, simply because it was such an astoundingly rewarding experience. Even the feeling of victory achieved— of having crushed and overcome, of having utterly prevailed—was hardly any better than this, when all the forces that would soon be thrown into the unavoidable mess and untidiness of battle—getting killed and shot up and dirty and lost and damaged and so on—stood or sat or lay or hovered or flew in perfect formation before him, gleaming, serried, grouped, exactly aligned, neatly laid out, symmetrically and systematically arranged, all just glistening with power and threat and promise.

He stood on the reviewing balcony at one end of the vast curved series of halls that formed the layered outer hulls of the giant ship, and took a series of deep breaths, eyes wide, heart pounding. God or Truth, it was a beautiful sight. This was, in a way, genuinely better than sex.

They were coasting in now, most of the deceleration completed, just one final burst of a few days' weight and discomfort to come. Another week and they would be in the system, finally attacking. They had encountered little opposition so far, partly due to the high, angled course they'd taken. Any mine clouds and drone flocks that might have been set out to trap them would have been thrown across the more direct approaches, and by taking this longer but safer line they'd avoided them all so far. The only danger had lain in their mid-course correction, subjective years earlier, when their drives might have shown up on any deep-space monitoring systems in Ulubis, had they been turned in the right direction. The risk had been slight and as far as they could tell they'd got away with it.

At any rate, no fleet had emerged from Ulubis to do battle; they had decided to wait and fight on their own doorsteps. His tacticians thought this indicated that Ulubis was prepared but weak. They might encounter some probe and destroyer-level craft, but that would probably be all until they hit the mid- and inner system. His admirals were confident their laser ships and close defence units could deal with anything else that might have been sent out to get in their way.

Luseferous became aware of noises at his back, where some of his more senior commanders were permitted to stand, backed in turn by his personal Guards. There were whispers, and hushing noises of fear and exasperation. He felt his body stiffen. Now would not be a good time to bother him with anything other than the imminent destruction of the whole fleet. They had to know that. The people behind him quieted down.

He relaxed, stood more upright in the spin-produced three-quarter gravity, and breathed deeply again, gazing out at the assembled men and matériel. Oh, this was a sweet and beautiful sight indeed, this was the very image of invincibility, an utterly thrilling spectacle of power made solid and real and uncompromising. This was his, this was *him*.

The imminent destruction of the whole fleet…He imagined that happening, imagined it happening right now; some cataclysmic hyper-weapon of the ancients wiping out the entire invasion force without anyone being able to do anything to stop them. Nonsense—well, vanishingly unlikely, anyway—but just think of it! He'd be able to watch everything here just blink out of existence, one by one, or explode in flames or bright blasts of light. He'd be able to watch it all being destroyed around him!

The idea made him shiver, half in horror, half in delight. It was never going to happen, of course, but the image alone was terrifyingly exciting. And a sort of warning, of course. Not from any god or from some program running the universe as the Truth saw it, but from something more trustworthy and direct; from inside himself. His subconscious, or some monitoring part-personality playing the part of the fool who always stood at Caesar's side in a Triumph, reminding him that all was vanity. That sort of thing. The thoughts of destruction were just him reminding himself to take nothing for granted, to concentrate and take full control, to prosecute the coming war with his usual ruthlessness and ignore any internal whining voices preaching moderation or unwarranted mercy. Be cruel and merciful always for a purpose, never just to satisfy some self-image. Somebody had said that. He would never forget it.

One last deep breath. So, prepared. And forearmed. Still, the mood had sort of been broken. No real damage done by the hint of interruption earlier. He would be justified, all the same, in being angry, if he needed to be. Better see what all the fuss had been about. He swivelled on his heels, pulled himself up to his full height—always have senior commanders you could look down on—and said, loudly, "*Yes?*"

He loved to see these proud, vainglorious men flinch, these men used to being obeyed instantly and without question cower, even fractionally, before him.

Tuhluer, perhaps his least annoying aide-de-camp and lately something of a favourite, came forward, smiling and frowning at the same time. "Sir, sorry about the disturbance a moment earlier." He gave a tiny flex of the eyebrows, as if to say, Not my fault—you know what some of these guys are like. "Ops alert just in: high-speed craft coming direct from Ulubis, signalling unarmed, no warhead, one or two human occupants, wanting to talk. Already slowing to match with us in ten hours. On its current course that will leave it a hundred klicks off fleet centre, left-level."

The Archimandrite glared over Tuhluer's head at the others. "And this required my intervention?"

"Warhead worries, sir," Tuhluer said smoothly, with a small smile. "The craft was passing the leading units of the fleet's forward destroyer screen at the time and was about to go out of their effective beam-weapon range. Question was whether to shoot or not. Now moot. The ship will be in range of the second defensive layer in half an hour. Or there are missiles, of course. A drone missile-carrier has already been launched in pursuit."

The Archimandrite Luseferous paused a moment, then smiled. He could see them all relax. "Well then," he said. "Everything appears to be functioning as it should and I did not need to be disturbed, did I?"

"Indeed not, sir," his aide-de-camp agreed ruefully.

"And what is the alleged status of this human or humans, if indeed that is what the thing contains?"

"The claim is that there's a man aboard, a high-ranking industrialist called Saluus Kehar."

⁚

The grogginess again, the tired, gritty, grubby feeling. Fassin was sure he was coming round more and more slowly each time, and finding himself duller, slower and more confused with each new reawakening. Over forty days' travel on this transition, to the other side of the galaxy, fully ninety kiloyears from Ulubis, not that such measurements meant much. The in-wormhole time would still have been trivial. The extra days and weeks had been taken up by the flight from the portal to the ship they were looking for, deep in interstellar space.

Some days. A distance. All just more time gone, more distance between him and whatever he was trying to accomplish, while events back at Ulubis moved on without him.

He tested the arrowhead's faulty left manipulator arm, flexing and tensing it, then forced himself to look at the screen on the far wall. Stars swung, as ever, then became just the backdrop to a vast dark gnarled craft, a giant torus-shaped ship two hundred kilometres in diameter, all black gleaming ribs and fractured facets, glinting in the weak light of a far-distant sun like a great rough crown of wet coal: the Cineropoline Sepulcraft *Rovruetz*, a vessel of the Ythyn's vastly dispersed Greater Expiratory Fleet, a Death-Carrier.

Y'sul studied the image on the screen from the far side of the chamber for a moment, then shook his mantles. "We must mix amongst Morbs," he said, sounding sleepy, grumpy and resigned all at once. "Oh, great."

—So what happened to the Toilers? Fassin asked.—I thought Leisicrofe was supposed to be investigating Toilers next.

—Obviously they toiled in vain, Y'sul sent.

—A mis-lead.

—A bluff.

The *Velpin* hung above a graveyard of ships scattered across the outer rim of the Death Carrier while Y'sul and Fassin crossed to the giant ship. The Ythyn had suggested that the *Velpin* might enter the *Rovruetz*. Quercer & Janath had demurred with what looked convincingly like a shiver of horror inside their silvery overall. Fassin got the impression that just being close to the Sepulcraft and its ancient collection of crumbling, lifeless ships was bad enough for them.

The Ythyn were a Scavenger species with a speciality: they collected the dead. They did nothing with them, just stored them sorted roughly by category, type and size, and they usually only collected those bodies—and sometimes the ships and other devices they arrived on—that nobody else wanted. But it was still an irredeemably macabre habit and as a result they shared a generic nickname with other death-obsessed species, having become known as Morbs.

Fassin and Y'sul were welcomed in the cavernous, gently lit entrance hall by a Ythyn officer, a great dark avian three metres tall in a glistening, near-transparent slick-suit over skin like dark blue parchment. Tightly bound double wings, which fully stretched would have spread a dozen metres, indicated the Ythyn was a junior. It stood on an uneven tripod of legs: one thick limb to the rear, two thinner ones in front. The creature's lipped beak was inlaid with precious metals, glittering under the gel of the slick-suit. Its two eyes were huge roundels of black. Thin, curved pipes led from its nostril gratings to sets of small tanks on its back like spherical eggs of tarnished silver. There were no atmosphere-locks on an Ythyn ship; the crew, like their dead charges, spent their entire time in hard vacuum. Exposed only to that hushed nothingness, enclosed by the great ship and so kept within a few degrees of absolute zero, the bodies of the dead could lie undisturbed and uncorrupted by nothing more than whatever had killed them and by the effects of their slow or sudden freezing, for aeons.

—You are welcome, the Ythyn officer told them in a flat, unaccented signal, prefixed only by formal signifiers for sadness and reverence.—You are Mr Taak and you are Mr Y'sul, yes?

—Yes, Fassin sent.

—I am Duty Receptioneer Ninth Lapidarian. I am happy and honoured to be known as "Ninth" or just "Duty". Tell me, have either of you two gentlemen made any arrangements for the treatment or disposal of your bodies, after death?

The Ythyn had been collecting the dead for a billion years, the result of a kind of gruesome techno-curse visited upon them by a species they had fought against and been utterly defeated by. They had lost their small empire, lost their few planets, lost their major habitats and most of their ships and they had even lost themselves, coerced into a programme of genetic amendment that turned them from intellectually rounded beings into creatures utterly obsessed with death.

The cruelty and cleverness of their vanquishers had lain in identifying and choosing a latent weakness congenital to the Ythyn. They had always been a little overly fascinated with mortality compared with the norm of vaguely similar species, but not to the stage of serious abnormality and certainly not to the point that it in any way defined them. And if they had been so grotesquely psychologically disfigured in the process of making them so excessively morbid that they ceased to be identifiably themselves there would have been no artistry, no fitness in their punishment. Instead, by this subtle but significant tweaking of their own bodies' instruction set, they became what they might have become anyway had some bizarre shiftings in their environment and circumstances so decreed. Those who had not taken their own lives and refused to submit to the inheritable amendment were killed or hunted down and forced to undergo the treatment anyway, though most of those so treated killed themselves as well.

The survivors became wanderers, one of the dozens of planet-evolved species denied or—in a few cases—eschewing any sort of home world. They built massive cold, dark ships and accrued enormous libraries and data reservoirs filled with the subject of death. They haunted the sites of great battles, terrible massacres and awful disasters. Over time, they began to gather the unclaimed dead from such sites, storing them more or less as they found them in their great airless ships, each carrying a cargo of collected death, plodding from one end of the galaxy to the other or gradually spiralling around it. Too big for wormhole travel, loath even to approach too close to a star, the Sepulcraft depended on smaller ships to harvest the dead. Even these rarely used wormholes these days. The Propylaea, which had charge of all the Mercatoria's portals, was not a charity, and demanded money for passage. The Ythyn had little to offer in payment.

They collected ships from those bringing the dead—or themselves, to die— but those were usually hulks, wrecks or near the end of their useful working lives and anyway regarded by the Ythyn as sacred, amongst the dead themselves. There were occasional donations and bequests from many different societies but they were few and far between. When they could afford to, and there were bodies to be got from the far end of a wormhole, an Ythyn ship would spend the little collateral it had accumulated and send a needle craft to make the collection. But usually they just physically followed the galaxy's generally sporadic instances of mass death.

That they had long since dutifully gathered up the remaining bodies of the now-extinct species which had inflicted their punishment upon them and could therefore relatively easily and without resistance have re-amended themselves back to their original selves, but had chosen not to, was either their most poignant tragedy of all, or a recognition that they had found a place within the galactic scheme of things that suited them better than might any other.

—We are on our way to the Chistimonouth system, Duty Receptioneer Ninth Lapidarian told the Dweller and the human as they made their way along a vast curved corridor deep within the giant ship. The tall birdlike being used one of its two thin forelegs to manipulate the controls of a small cagelike car that carried them in perfect silence along a monorail set in the centre of the wide tunnel. It was perfectly dark, too. They were having to use active sensing to illuminate the seemingly never-ending corridor.—We seek the mortal remains of a newly contacted Serpenterian civilisation, a possible offshoot of the Desii-Chau (themselves, lamentably, no more; extinct, or, at the very best, deep within the fifth category of abatement), unadopted, which fell prey, sadly, to a series of solar flares some centuries ago. The sole inhabited planet was sorely affected. Of the single sentient species thereon, it is believed that no living trace remains. It will be our privilege and our duty, when we arrive there in another few decades, to inter within these hallowed halls as many of the still-unburied as we are able.

—How will they be unburied? Y'sul asked.—Do they float? Won't they all have sunk into their own depths? Into water or mud or dissolved rock or something?

The corridors were lined with the dead: stapled, pinned, stitched or ice-welded to the tubular surface (the concept of floors, walls and ceilings had some meaning while the ship was under power, but it was temporary). A few body types were best preserved in cavities, alcoves sealed with diamond leaf.

—Those happily buried will be left where they lie, underground, Duty told them.—Some remains are expected in structures, even after all this time. The reports we have had from scouter species indicate that there may be many unclaimed cadavers still in space, at Lagrange points.

—What if they're all gone? Y'sul asked.—What if somebody's beaten you to it and…eaten them or recycled them or something?

—Then we will make our way to the next location where we may honour the dead, the dark bird told them, imperturbable.

—Come to think of it, Y'sul said brightly,—there might be a few bods to pick up in a place called Ulubis fairly soon.

Fassin looked at the Dweller but he wasn't paying any attention.

—Ulubis, Duty said.—I have not heard of this place. Is it a planet?

—System, Y'sul said.—Home of the planet Nasqueron. In Stream

Quaternary, one of the Southern Tendril Reefs.

—Ah, yes. Rather far away from here.

—Lots of humans there and another lot on their way, Y'sul said.—Probably going to be a war. Lot of deaths, I'd imagine. You collect humans?

—We have difficulties only with certain Cincturian species, the bird-creature told them.—Humans we have heard of and accommodated in the past, though not on this craft. I shall pass on your information at the earliest opportunity to our most proximate Sepulcraft. They may well be aware already, of course, and possibly on their way even as we speak. However, we are grateful for your thoughtfulness.

—My pleasure, Y'sul said, sounding pleased with himself. He glanced at Fassin.—What?

Fassin looked away. They were passing bodies spread against the tunnel's surface like small solidified explosions of rock.—Palonne, their guide informed them.—Ossile, obviously. Victims of war. Subject to a parasitic stone-rot virus of some sort.

—Fascinating, Y'sul said.—Are we nearly at this Leisicrofe fellow yet?

Duty looked at a small display clipped to one of his cinched-in wings.—Another few hundred metres.

—What's he up to here, anyway? Y'sul asked.

—Up to? The Ythyn sounded uncertain.

—Just… studying you people, is he?

—Why, no. No, of course not. The Ythyn officer was silent for a moment.—Oh dear.

Fassin and Y'sul exchanged looks.

Fassin said,—You're not saying he's *dead*, are you?

—Well, yes. Of course. This is a Sepulcraft, gentlemen. I was under the impression that you simply wanted to see the body.

∴

The news came while she was asleep. Taince watched an hours-old recording of the faint, sideways-seen, blue-shifted glimmers approaching from the direction of the E-5 Discon as the Starveling invasion fleet started braking for its arrival in Ulubis system. The invaders would take nearly three months to reach Ulubis. The Summed Fleet was still four months' travel away, including its own, more dramatic deceleration regime, due to start in a little more than eighty days. The Fleet tacticians had learned quite a lot just from the braking profile of E-5 Discon's fleet.

First, it was big: a thousand ships or more, unless there was something outlandishly clever going on with dummy drive signatures. Second, it was staying ninety-five per cent together, with only a few dozen smaller ships venturing ahead of the main fleet. This might imply a significant straight-through, braking-beyond force still hidden, though from the rest of the profile this didn't look so likely. The size, definition and shifted-frequency signatures of the drives themselves revealed a relatively slow, old-tech vessel-capability envelope. Basically all but the lightest craft in the Summed Fleet force would be able to take on all but the heaviest of the invaders' ships with a better than average chance of prevailing, and anything that couldn't be outfought could be outrun (for whatever that was worth when there was nowhere to run to).

And there was one behemoth in there, a giant ship, probably a command-and-control lander- and troop-carrier plus facilities-and-repair vessel. At least a billion tonnes, klicks across, doubtless very heavily armoured and armed and escorted, but a classic grade-A high-value target, a possible king-piece, a back-breaker, if it could be successfully engaged and destroyed or taken out of action or even captured. Just posting a powerful-enough guard-ship screen to try and keep it safe in the event of a serious attack threat would significantly sap the invading/occupying force's abilities, cut down their dispositional options and drastically curtail their split-regroup capacity.

The Fleet tacticians had been positively cruel about this dinosaur of a ship. A vanity piece, they called it, an *Idiot Aboard!* sign hung round the neck of the enemy fleet. Every space-faring species that built warcraft quickly found out one way or another—often the hard way—that big ships just didn't work except as a hideously expensive way of impressing the more credulous type of native. Flexibility, manoeuvrability, low unit risk-cost, distributed inherent damage resistance, fully parsed battle-space side-blind denotation control grammar... these and other even more arcane concepts were what really mattered in modern space warfare, apparently, and a Really Big Ship just didn't sit too comfortably with any of them.

The tacticians pretty much spoke their own language, were mostly very intense, and blinked a lot.

"So a strong point that's really a weak point," Taince had suggested at one of their briefings.

"That would be a viable alternative definition," one of them said, after a moment or two's thought.

Since just a week ago, though, relatively little evidence of further activity.

Well, the Discon invaders had arrived later than anticipated, and the Summed Fleet forces were arriving earlier. Deliberate, on their part, of course. The invaders would have quickly found out when Ulubis had been told to expect the Summed Fleet's arrival, and it was always prudent to keep the enemy off balance, to upset their assumptions. Let them think they had so much time and then arrive early before they'd got everything prepared.

Smiting. It was all about smiting. That was one of Admiral Kisipt's favourite words. The Voehn Fleet Commander knew it in several hundred different languages, including Earth Anglish. Be ready at all times to smite the enemy. Strike with speed, decisiveness and weight.

Taince found herself lightly smitten with one of the junior male officers, discovered it was mutual and took part in some invasive tussling of her own.

The time displays ticked down steadily towards the point where they'd have to get back into their lonely little individual pods again for the deceleration burn that would bring them down from near-light speed to something close to Ulubis-zero, for the start of the attack.

:

The Cineropoline Sepulcraft *Rovruetz* spun very slowly beneath the *Velpin*, still gently accelerating for its distant target system and its unburied cargo of the long-dead. The *Velpin* was tracking round the outer rim of the giant craft, senses primed. Fassin and Y'sul were back aboard. They had been shown to the lifeless body of Leisicrofe, ice-welded to the side of the great dark corridor in the company of a half-dozen other dead Dwellers.

—Very well preserved, as you see, Duty Receptioneer Ninth Lapidarian had pointed out.—I hope you feel this setting is appropriate. The Ythyn officer had still been upset at the earlier misunderstanding.

—So he just died, then? Y'sul had asked.

—Very suddenly, apparently. We found him drifting—rolling along in his esuit, actually—a few days after he arrived. He had expressed an interest in mapping the distribution of bodies of different species and species-types while he was here. We saw no reason not to allow him to do so.

They weren't permitted to use reaction motors inside the Sepulcraft. Y'sul had used his esuited spine-arms to push himself over to the side of the tunnel. He'd landed awkwardly by the Dweller's body, which was naked save for a small hub-cloth.

—I have no idea whether this is this Leisicrofe guy or not, frankly, Y'sul had said.—But it is a Dweller, probably from Nasqueron and he is most certainly dead.

—Any sign of… anything? Fassin asked.

Y'sul had inspected the body, using lights and radar-sense, finding nothing. He'd unclipped the corpse's hub-cloth and shaken it. Fassin had sensed their Ythyn host preparing to object, but a moment later Y'sul had replaced the hub-cloth and was looking round the back of the body where ice attached it to the tunnel wall.

—Nothing, he'd sent back.

"There," one half of Quercer & Janath said.

On one of the *Velpin*'s screens, a flickering outline appeared around one of the abandoned ships littering the carbuncularly irregular outer hull of the Sepulcraft.

Fassin looked at the craft. It was a simple black ellipsoid, maybe sixty metres long. Deep-space cold, lifeless.

"That it?" Y'sul asked. "You sure?"

"It's a Dweller All-Purpose, Single-Occupancy Standard Pattern SoloShip," the truetwin told them.

"And it pings recent."

"Can you wake its systems?" Fassin asked. "Find out where it was last, where it came from?"

The travelcaptain looked at him. "Doesn't work like that."

"Pay attention."

They got permission from the Ythyn to lift the SoloShip and join it to the *Velpin*. They warmed it up and introduced a standard gas-giant atmosphere. There was just about enough room for Y'sul and Fassin to board together. Quercer & Janath had already laser-synched the little ship's closed-down computer matrix to that of the *Velpin*. The screens, tanks, surfaces and other displays flickered, steadied and shone. The craft beeped and clicked around them. It still felt cold.

Y'sul knocked and tapped a few of the more obviously delicate-looking bits of machinery with his hub-arms.

"You getting anything?" he asked. The truetwin was staying on board the larger craft.

"There's stuff in the log," one half told them.

"That's sailor-talk for diary."

"No saying!" Y'sul said.

"Truly. But it's not accessible from here. You'll have to input from there."

"How, exactly?" Fassin asked.

"How should we know?"

"Not our ship."

"Experiment."

They experimented. The correct technique involved Y'sul pressing in to a Dweller-shaped double-alcove sensory nook and pressing four glyphboard icons on four different glyphboards at once. The main screen stopped showing stars and the darkly glittering hull of the Sepulcraft and started showing what looked like the interior of a small library instead. Y'sul reached out into the virtual space and pulled down a book whose spine said *Log*. He opened it.

A motionless Dweller hub faced them in close-up.

"Well," Y'sul said, "that certainly looks like the stiff in the big space hearse."

"We can see him. Should be a *Play* button."

"Try hitting it."

"Gee," Y'sul said. "Thank fuck you guys are there." He hit *Play*.

⠇

Taince Yarabokin woke from a light sleep to a low-level alarm, telling her not even to think about instigating a pod-quit regime. She swung to the exterior fore-view display and looked out. Ulubis glowed sharp and blue ahead, a tiny sun amongst the surrounding scrape of stars, at last. The blueness was a function of the ship and the fleet's colossal speed, hammering into the light waves, compressing wavelength. Taince switched from LR Sensors to ship-state. A fierce and terrible force pulled at everything. They'd started their final deceleration burn. The majority of the fleet was losing speed hard, piling up a hundred or more gravities as it braked for the approach to and arrival at Ulubis system, still over a month away.

Another group of ships—one full squadron of sixty vessels—was not decelerating so rapidly. A dozen were not slowing at all and would maintain full speed all the way to and most of the way through the system, their crews and systems trained over hundreds of simulations for an ultra-high-speed pass across Ulubis planetary system which would last for less than four hours. In that time, less than twenty days from now, they would have to collect and evaluate all the data they could on the then-current state of the system and then both signal their intelligence back to the ships behind and choose a suite of attack profiles from a vast menu of possibilities they carried in their data banks before loosing all the munitions they could against whatever hostiles they had identified. They hoped the pickings would be rich for them. They'd be arriving with little warning only a month after the Starveling fleet had struck. With luck the situation would be fluid and the E-5 Discon forces wouldn't have had time to organise their defences properly.

Then, even before those advance ships were all the way through the system, they would begin their own still more violent deceleration, to come to a stop a light month beyond, and get back to Ulubis weeks after the main fleet had arrived: at best to help with the mopping up, at worst to deliver a retaliatory hammer-blow.

The remainder of the Advance-attack Squadron would pass through the system in small groups of ships, their arrival staggered, unpredictable, distributed, their tactics in part defined by whatever the high-speed craft had discovered. With luck, with what they hoped and trusted was a good battle-plan, the waves of war craft, each able to spend more fighting time in the system than its immediate predecessor, would deliver a succession of softening-up blows against the enemy: rocking it, unbalancing it, confusing and bloodying it. The main body of the fleet, arriving like a bunched fist, would just provide one final massive knockout punch.

Their drive light would precede them, of course. There would be no complete surprise.

The Starveling invasion had given the defenders of Ulubis even more warning, not that there was much they could have done with it. The E-5 Discon fleet had slowed right down, shut its drives off almost as one while still a few days out, well within the system's Oort shell, then slowed further as its lead ships crossed the boundary into the planetary system.

For the next few weeks after the drive signatures meshed with the Ulubis system and shut off, when the invasion must have been at its height, there had been a lot of weapon-blink. Much of it had been around the planets Sepekte and Nasqueron.

·

"My name is Leisicrofe of Hepieu, Nasqueron equatorial. This is my last testament. I will presume that whoever you are you have followed me for the data which I carried on behalf of my fellow Dweller, the scholar Valseir of Schenehen. If you have not, and this recording has fallen to you in what one might term a casual manner, it may be of little interest. If, however, you do seek the data I held, then I must tell you now that you are going to be disappointed."

Something in Fassin seemed to break and fall away.

"Uh-oh," Y'sul said.

"This may seem unfortunate and may make you angry. However, I have most likely done you a considerable favour, as it is my sincere and firm belief that what I was asked to carry was something I should not have been, and something that nobody should have been or should be asked to take responsibility for. It was not something I was supposed to know about, of course, and it was not really Valseir's fault that I came into possession of the knowledge of what it represented."

"Talks a lot, doesn't he?" Y'sul said.

"To my shame, I think I must be more shallow than my friend Valseir gave me credit for. He gave me the data sealed in a safekeep box and asked me not to open it. I said I would not. He did not even ask me for my word, thinking, I am sure, that simply asking a friend and fellow scholar such a thing, and receiving such an assurance, was guarantee enough. However, I am not like Valseir. I am inquisitive by nature, not as the result of an intellectual fascination with any particular subject. I resisted the urge to open the safekeep box for many years while I was on my travels, but eventually I surrendered to temptation. I opened the safekeep, I began to read what was inside, and realised its importance. Even then I might have stopped reading, closed the box and put it away again, and had I done that I would still be alive. Instead, I carried on reading—and this has resulted in my death. I can only claim that perhaps I was in a sort of trance of disbelief at the time."

"More likely taken some recreational substances," Y'sul snorted.

"And so I came to hold within myself the knowledge, the meaning of that which I had been asked to keep safe, rather than just having charge of the medium containing it. Realising what I now knew, and comprehending that it was of inestimable value, I came to the conclusion that I could not be trusted with it. While not entirely understanding what I had read, I could not forget it. I could tell others, and it was not impossible that I might be made to tell what I knew through the use of drugs or more direct intervention with my brain and mind."

"Nutter," Y'sul said.

"What's that?" one of Quercer & Janath said distantly over the open link to the *Velpin*.

"Hmm. Don't know." It didn't sound like they were paying attention to what was being said by the recording of Leisicrofe.

"I will not pretend that I had not been thinking of my own death for some time. However, it was habitually within the context of having completed my studies into the many differing forms of the Cincturia and publishing a learned—I had even hoped an at-the-time definitive—work on this, my chosen and beloved field of study. Knowing what I now know, I have thought it best, however reluctantly, to curtail my studies forthwith and kill myself as soon as may decently be achieved. I shall do so here, in the Ythyn Cineropoline Sepulcraft *Rovruetz*, where my death will at least appear to have a fraction more meaning than it might have had elsewhere."

"—Looks like, or..." Fassin heard over the open channel.

"Ping it?"

"No! Are you...? Shut off that—"

The open channel closed. Fassin looked back to the access hatch and the short ship-to-ship connecting them to the *Velpin*.

Leisicrofe was still speaking. "...Will forgive me. You should. If you know what it is you are looking for, then all I will say is that it looked more like a code and frequency, not what I believe was expected. But it is quite gone now. Destroyed, along with the safekeep box itself, thrown into the sun called Direaliete. I know of no other copy. If none of this makes any sense to you, then please respect an old, and—as it turns out—foolish, Dweller's last wish, and leave him here in peace." The recording froze and an end-message signal flashed.

Fassin stared at the image of the dead Dweller. It was over. He'd failed. Maybe now there was no way ever to find out whether the Dweller List meant anything or even had ever meant anything.

"Totally mad," Y'sul said, with something like a sigh. He fiddled with the glyphboard controls. "Looks like that's our lot." He turned to Fassin. "Doesn't sound too hopeful, does it, young human-me-lad?"

The open channel from the ship clicked on suddenly. "Get out!" Quercer & Janath screamed. "Ten seconds to get off there and back in the *Velpin*!"

"Being attacked! Must run!"

Fassin shook himself out of his shock and started backing towards the open hatch leading to the *Velpin*.

Y'sul pulled out of the sensory-nook, began to follow, one hub-limb scratching at his mantle. "This madness is obviously contag—"

"Fucking *Voehn* ship! Out, *now*!"

"Engines in five, four, three…"

# *SIX*

# THE LAST TRANSFORM

... Sssss 1000101011001010101 / on / symcheck / ssscheck / syt—sytser / syst—syst—/ fail reboot / livel / livl / lev—levl—level 001 / hup / gethup / paramarametsr / woop! woop! / check / check / check / system check / run ALL / cat. zzero sssumcheck postcrash full allowablesss/ rebot / rubot / re0ot / lbit / cat. zero sumcheck postcrash fullabables / ints. postcrash (likely antagonistic external hostile agency cause) full All reboot restart: / starting mem. / lang. / sens. / full int.... bip bip bip... Bang!

Wo!

Hnnh?

You all right?

I'm all right. Now. You all right?

I'm all right.

Happened?

This:

"Closing hatch!"

The hatch at the end of the ship-to-ship joining the *Velpin* and the Dweller SoloShip started to close before Fassin got to it. Y'sul was still behind him, moving quickly along the exit. Fassin swung through, flipped, turned and grabbed the hatch's moving edge with his left manipulator.

The closing hatch nearly took the manipulator off. Fassin was swung around by the force of it and found himself having to brace with his other manipulator against the lock interior, struggling to keep the hatch—grinding, mechanism humming mightily—from closing.

"Somebody holding that hatch open?" one half of Quercer & Janath shouted indignantly.

"Out the way, Fassin!" Y'sul yelled, rising fast straight out of the ship-to-

343

ship and colliding heavily with Fassin's gascraft, sending the two of them tumbling through the lock and into the *Velpin*'s interior. Error/failure messages from the gascraft's left manipulator arm crowded against one edge of Fassin's field of vision. The hatch slammed shut behind them. Immediately, a great force smashed them against the compartment's sternward bulkhead. They were stuck there, unmoving, the arrowhead snagged over the Dweller's tipped left discus until the increasing acceleration and a series of sharp vibrations made Fassin slide off one edge of Y'sul's carapace and whack down onto the carbon bulkhead by his side. The ship roared around them.

"Engines are on, one takes it," Y'sul said, wheezing. Fassin could feel the apparent gravity building still further. They were at something over twenty gee already. A young, fit Dweller with no esuit protection stuck on his side against an inelastic surface could take about twenty-four, twenty-five gees continuous before their carapace just collapsed and turned their insides to mush. The *Velpin*'s acceleration topped out at twenty-two gees.

"All right back there?" their travelcaptain asked.

"Not really," Fassin said. "You're kind of near crushing Y'sul."

"Acknowledged."

"Not outrunning the fucker. Can't."

"Cut off and come about. Surrender."

"Agree."

The acceleration snapped off. Fassin and Y'sul were instantly weightless, rebounding fractionally from the bulkhead just by the released compression in the hull of one and the carapace of the other.

"Get up here, you two," Quercer & Janath told them.

The Voehn ship was a klick-long needle spined with swing-guns and weapon tubes. It came quickly up on them and was alongside by the time the human in his gascraft and the Dweller Y'sul got to the *Velpin*'s control space.

"Since when do the Voehn choose to attack Dweller craft going about their—?" the travelcaptain began to ask.

"Be quiet," said an imageless voice. "Make yourself ready for boarding."

Quercer & Janath's shiny suit rustled as the truetwin turned to look at Fassin and Y'sul while tapping some controls. Images of the *Velpin* appeared in holo displays, showing hatches and doors flashing in outline.

"The Voehn have turned pirates," Quercer & Janath told them calmly.

"How fucking *dare* they!" Y'sul roared.

"They didn't follow us through the wormhole, did they?" Fassin asked.

"Ha! No." The truetwin seemed purely amused. "No, they were waiting in this system."

"Assume we'll see why shortly."

"The fucking scumbag bastards will pay grievously for this outrage!" Y'sul yelled, shaking with fury.

A shudder rang through the *Velpin* and alarms started blaring. Quercer & Janath roted closer to a brightly flashing display. "Look at that."

"Penetrated amidships with a cut-through."

Cameras briefly showed a thick tube extending from the middle of the Voehn ship into a neat circular hole in the hull of the *Velpin*. Then the images crazed and faded. Other displays started to disappear. The alarms warbled down to a croak, then shut off. Fassin thought he could smell burning.

"And us cooperatively opening all our orifices."

"Fucking typical."

"Here they come. Thundering through."

Another display showed an abstract of large beings pouring through the breach and spreading through the ship, bouncing off surfaces in the zero-gee. The largest force was coming straight towards the control space. Then that display shut down too. All the lights went out. The background noises of the ship, hardly noticed until they ceased, just faded away.

A ragged pulse of what sounded like heavy steps came pounding from the closed door leading to the *Velpin*'s central corridor.

"Probably going to zap us soon as they—" Quercer & Janath began. Then the door punctured with a coughing noise and something small flew into the middle of the control space and exploded into a million barbs like dust.

Ah-ha.

Though what got us was a fucking EMP cannon. Aimed at the ship's vulnerables.

Indeed. So there we are.

And here.

Indeed.

See what happens?

See what happens.

…Better ship, anyway.

Fassin was being carried within a sort of transparent, braced sack by two big creatures like giant eight-legged dogs in mirror-armour, one at either end. He was still in the *Velpin*. The cut-through tube was a great pipe with a slanted hole, like the end of a massive syringe plunged into the guts of the ship. The two Voehn commandos flicked him and themselves up the tube and into the Voehn ship with near-effortless ease. Fassin, confused, senses ringing, unable to move, peered through the transparent material of the prison-stretcher and caught a glimpse of another two Voehn behind him carrying Y'sul, similarly wrapped.

They went through a rotate-lock. The Voehn ship was dark inside, faintly red-lit. It was in hard vacuum, like the Sepulcraft. The wrapping round the little gascraft ballooned taut.

Fassin, Y'sul and the truetwin were taken through another lock and into a pressurised, slightly heated circular chamber. The wrappings around them collapsed again. They were settled into something like dent-seats and clamped there with thickly shining restraints. They were half-unwrapped from their transparent covers, sufficient for them to be able to hear and see and speak. The warriors tested their bonds and then left.

Fassin looked around as best he could. Y'sul and the travelcaptain appeared still to be unconscious, Y'sul's ruff-mantles waving limply in the free fall and Quercer & Janath, still in the shiny coveralls, floating seemingly lifeless in the dent-seat. The chamber was plain, just a flattened ovoid, filled with a gas-giant atmosphere entirely breathable by a Dweller but that didn't smell quite right. Light came dimly from every surface. A hint of gravity built up, producing about a quarter standard.

A door appeared and irised open, closing behind a trio of Voehn: two of the mirror-armoured commandos and another wearing just a torso-uniform decorated with various insignia and a holstered side arm. He stood and looked at the three prisoners, the great grey snout-face and fist-sized multiple-lidded eyes turning fractionally as he directed his attention from one to another. He arched his long body and flexed his back spines, raising all ten with what looked like a sensual motion. Blizzardskin on the Voehn's spines scintillated like a minutely shattered mirror.

Fassin, trying hard not to lose consciousness again, thought dreamily of the screen series he'd watched as a child—*Attack Squad Voehn*. Had that been its name?—and struggled to recall what the uniforms and insignia might indicate, remembering only slowly. The Voehn in the uniform was a Prime Commander. A multi-talent. Top guy here, certainly. Significantly over-ranked for a ship this size, unless it was on a special mission. (Oh-oh.)

One of the mirror-armour soldiers waved a hand-held instrument at them, watching a display. He barely glanced at the results from Fassin and Y'sul, then did a double take when the device was aimed at Quercer & Janath. He altered a few controls, swept the machine over the truetwin's still lifeless-looking body again and said something to the Voehn commander, who moved over, looked at the display and made a small swaying motion with his head. He clicked the machine off and came over to the prisoners, saying something as though to one of his decorations.

The restraints holding the gascraft and the two Dweller bodies slid back into the floor. The Voehn commander took off a glove and ran one leathery-looking hand over the surface of the little gascraft, then Y'sul's carapace, then felt the shiny membrane covering Quercer & Janath. He looked for and found a catch and opened the coverall up so that it hung down over the transparent material the prisoners had all been trussed in. The commander looked very closely at Quercer & Janath's signal skin, and seemed to sniff it.

He looked at Fassin. "You're awake already." His voice was quiet, with a deep, gurgling quality. "Reply."

"I'm awake," Fassin acknowledged. He tried moving his left manipulator. More error/damage messages. He moved his right manipulator and shifted fractionally in the dent-seat. Aside from the partial constriction of the transparent material covering the gascraft's rear, he was actually fairly free to move; even the prisoner-wrap felt like it would shuck off without too much difficulty.

The Voehn reached for something in his uniform pocket and waved it at Y'sul, who jerked once and then shook for a few moments, fringe mantles stiffening and limbs quivering. "Warrgh," he said.

The commander went to point the device at Quercer & Janath, who said quite cheerfully, "Already awake actually, thanks all the same."

The Voehn looked through slitted eyes at the truetwin for a moment, then pocketed the device again and moved back to take in the view of all three prisoners. The two mirror-armoured guards stood on either side of where the door had appeared.

The commander sat back a fraction, resting on his rear legs and tail, crossing his forearms.

"To the point. I am Commander Inialcah of the Summed Fleet Special Forces Division Ultra-Ship *Protreptic*. You are, in every sense, mine. We know what you have been looking for. We have been waiting for somebody to come here. We are combing your ship for data, hidden or otherwise, but we don't expect to find anything germane. We have authority covering all eventualities. That means we can do anything we want with or to you. That latitude will not need to be exploited if you cooperate fully and answer any questions honestly and completely. Now. You are the Dwellers known as Y'sul and Quercer & Janath, and the human Fassin Taak, correct?"

Y'sul grunted.

"Hi," the travelcaptain replied.

"Correct," Fassin said. He could see Y'sul moving, working his body as though to get rid of the prison-wrap. *Oh, no, don't do this*, he thought. He was about to say it when—

"Who the fuck do you fucking think you are, you piratical pipsqueak?" Y'sul bellowed. The Dweller wriggled free from the transparent material and floated above the dent-seat.

The two guards by the doorway didn't even start to move.

The commander, arms still crossed, watched as the Dweller roted up to him, towering over him. "How fucking *dare* you start attacking a ship and taking people hostage! Do you know who I *am*?"

"Go back to your seat," the commander said, voice level.

"That's probably quite good ad—" the truetwin began.

"Go back to your fucking own *planet*!" Y'sul roared, and stretched out a hub-limb to push the Voehn.

The Voehn commander seemed to disappear in a blur of movement, as though all along he'd been a hologram and was now dissolving into individual pixels, rearranging into a grey cloud shot through with rainbow shards. Y'sul shuddered once and was sent sailing serenely back, colliding with the wall behind the dent-seat and the discarded prison-wrap. He hung there, then revolved backwards and fell slowly to the floor, spinning gradually downward along his rim like a coin on a table.

The Voehn commander was sitting where and how he had been, unruffled. "That was not cooperating fully," he said, voice soft.

"Urgh," Y'sul said thickly. His carapace held two dents, one on each discus rim. There was another large, broken-looking bruise on his inner hub. That was serious damage for a Dweller, the equivalent of a broken limb or two and perhaps a compressed skull fracture for a human. Fassin hadn't even seen quite how the Voehn commander had hit Y'sul. He'd have gone back for a replay but the little gascraft's systems seemed to have been zapped and they weren't providing any recording ability. *Oh fuck*, he thought. *We're all going to die and the only one they can torture properly is me.* He saw himself peeled, prised out of the gascraft like a snail from its shell.

Y'sul drew himself very slowly upright again, shaking slightly. He was mumbling something unintelligible.

Quercer & Janath turned very slowly, looked at the Dweller and then turned back to the commander. "With your permission, sir?"

"What?" the Voehn asked.

"Like to aid our fellow."

"Go ahead."

The travelcaptain let the prison-wrap fall to the floor, then moved over to Y'sul and guided the injured Dweller back to his dent-seat. Y'sul continued to talk; nonsense somewhere beneath the level of clear comprehension.

With a noise like a sigh, the truetwin settled into its own housing, sparing one more look for Y'sul, still trembling and mumbling to himself.

"We are not here to play games, we are here to discover truth," the Voehn commander told them. "The complete truth may save you. Anything else will surely be your ruin. The *Protreptic* is a Lustral Order special forces ship, generally charged with the hunting down and extermination of anathematics, that is, the obscenities commonly called AIs. We have unbounded authority on this mission as on all our missions. You are entirely within our control and will cooperate without question or reserve, or will suffer accordingly. I hereby deem you to have understood fully everything I have told you thus far."

"Ah, well," Quercer & Janath said. The truetwin sounded mildly peeved, as though it hadn't been listening to the commander at all and had just heard something moderately discomfiting over an internal radio link.

The instrument one of the guards had pointed at the three prisoners, now slung on a strap across his back, glowed through red to yellow and spat tiny sparks. The soldier moved almost as quickly as the commander, turning and twisting and pulling the device off his back to throw it to the floor. It skidded and thudded against the curve of the wall, smoking.

The commander looked at it for a moment, then turned calmly back to look at the prisoners again. "Neat trick," he said, sounding amused. "Who's the show-off?" He looked at Fassin. The two guards had levelled their guns at them, one pointing directly at Fassin, the other between Y'sul and the truetwin.

"Ah, guilty, commander," said Quercer & Janath breezily. "But, heck, that's nothing."

"Watch this."

The dim grey glow that came from every surface suddenly brightened wildly, leaving them all—the two Dwellers, the three Voehn and Fassin himself—seeming to float in the midst of an insanely bright flare of nova-bright light. It was as though they'd all been instantly dropped into the surface of a sun. Fassin heard himself yelp and felt automatics in the gascraft's senses snap their burn-out defences down.

Very heavy again, and very suddenly.

Fassin could *see* the light, he could swear. It was coming through the hull of the gascraft, hitting his closed, human eyes. Three great thumps sounded, shaking the air, echoing round the chamber. Somewhere in the middle of this he opened his visuals enough to see them all hanging, black blobs in light, and tiny bright crimson lines of still greater brilliance joining the Voehn to Quercer & Janath. Stupidly, for a moment he waited to see the travelcaptain explode or get thrown back, but the great circular shape roted back barely at all; it was the Voehn who were getting thrown all over the place.

Sudden silence, sudden darkness. Blind again. Fassin let the gascraft open up the equivalent of one eye until it was at normal exposure. There had been some damage but he could still see. There was a surprising amount of infrared radiation. He looked at where it was coming from. It was coming from the Voehn. They glowed. One of the guards lay spread, opened, against the curved wall by the doorway. The other was face down, two forelimbs blown off, halfway between the door and the place where the commander had been. The commander was making his way, jerkily, towards the tall figure of Quercer & Janath. The commander's head had been half blown off, a side of skull hanging, twitching as he walked, held on only by connective tissue. He raised his arms and took a few more awkward steps towards the travelcaptain, then collapsed to the floor, loosening completely, like something thawing.

"Not fooling anyone," a voice that might have been Quercer & Janath's said. The restraints slid up around Fassin and the still-shaking Y'sul. "Hey-hey," the travelcaptain said.

The apparent gravity went crazy, shifting in an instant from one vector to another, ahead to astern in an instant. This had the effect of batting the Voehn commander from the floor to the ceiling and back again half a dozen times or so. Then he blurred into action. A half-headless grey whirlwind darted towards Quercer & Janath, almost quicker than the eye could follow.

In an instant, all movement ceased.

A tableau: the Voehn commander was held by the neck, struggling weakly, in the grip of one of Quercer & Janath's outstretched hub-arms.

"Oh, how ever did we let it come to this?" the truetwin said, positively sultry. It snapped the commander's neck, then two thin blue beams cut through the gaseous atmosphere from near the travelcaptain's outer discus fringes, dicing the struggling, flicking, spasming body of the commander until there was almost nothing left to hold. The truetwin let the remains drop to the floor. There was, Fassin noted, a grisly kind of wetness involved in this action.

"This is the ship's autonomous loyalty system!" shouted a voice from the gas. "Integrity infraction! Integrity infraction! Self-destruct in—"

"Oh," said Quercer & Janath, sounding tired, "*really.*"

The voice from nowhere came back. "This is the ship's autonomou—"

Silence.

"And... so much for that."

"The fu's goin on?" Y'sul mumbled.

"Ditto that," Fassin said.

"Ah, good," Quercer & Janath said. "Still with us."

"A relief."

"Yeah, it's ours," one half said cheerfully.

The restraints slid back into the floor again.

"Ah, where to start?"

"The Voehn will be annoyed."

"The Mercatoria will be annoyed."

"Not our fault."

"Didn't start it."

Quercer & Janath moved away from the dent-seat, over the body parts of the Voehn commander and the two guards, flicking the soldiers' weapons away from their bodies as it went. The truetwin hovered by the door.

"Seriously," Fassin said. "What *is* happening?" He looked at what was left of the three Voehn who'd been in the chamber with them. "How did you do that?"

Quercer & Janath were still studying the doorway, which remained closed. "We are not a Dweller," the travelcaptain said, not turning back to look at Fassin. One of its limbs went out and prodded at the wall around where the door ought to be.

"Purely mechanical. Very annoying."

"Mr Taak, would you look after Mr Y'sul? Please?"

Fassin floated out of his dent-seat, towards Y'sul. He put his right manipulator out.

"Kin look after self," Y'sul said, trying to shrug Fassin's arm off. He sighed.

"So what are you?" Fassin asked.

"An AI, Mr Taak," the creature said, still tapping round the door, not obviously looking back at him.

*What?* he thought.

"Two AIs."

*An AI? Two fucking AIs? We're dead*, Fassin thought.

"Indeed, two AIs."

"Keeps one from going mad."

"Well, more."

"For yourself."

"Hmm, as may be."

Y'sul moaned, then shook spastically. His sensory mantle ruffled. He looked about. "Fuck, we still here?" Y'sul turned his attention to the dead Voehn. "*Fuck*," he said. The Dweller made a show of turning towards Fassin. "You seeing this too?"

"Oh yes," Fassin told him. He looked at the creature feeling its way round the doorway. "You're an AI? Two AIs?" he asked carefully. He could feel his skin crawl inside the shock-gel. He couldn't help it. He'd been raised since birth to believe that AIs were the single greatest, most terrible enemy humanity and all biological, living things had ever faced. To be told, however preposterously, that he was trapped in a small space with one—let alone two—was to have one small, deep, vulnerable part of himself feel absolutely convinced that he was about to be ripped to bloody tatters at any moment.

"That's right," Quercer & Janath said absently. "And we've just taken over this ship."

"Except we can't get out of this damn room."

"Cabin. We can't get out of this damn cabin."

"Whatever the."

"Most annoying. Purely—"

"—Mechanical. You said."

"Ah. Here we go." The travelcaptain struck a smart blow at a patch of wall. Then another. The door appeared and irised open, revealing a short corridor and another door.

Quercer & Janath turned to look at the Dweller and the human in his arrowhead esuit. "Gentlemen. We must leave you for a while."

"Fuck that, action hero," Y'sul said. "You go, we go." Y'sul paused. "Well, unless there's an ambush out there. Obviously."

Quercer & Janath bobbed in the gas, laughing. "There's a *vacuum* out there, Y'sul."

"And lots of angry, confused Voehn."

The injured Dweller was silent for a moment. "I forgot," he admitted. He shrugged. "Okay. Hurry back."

⁚

Saluus Kehar woke to a feeling of confusion and dread. There was a nagging feeling that what he'd just experienced had not been an ordinary sleep, that there was something more to it. It had been somehow messier, even dirtier, than he might have expected. He had a sore head, but he didn't think he'd been over-indulging the day or evening before. He'd had a slightly boring, slightly depressing dinner with some of the Dweller Embassy people, a perplexing talk with Guard-General Thovin, then a more pleasant interlude with Liss. Then sleep. That had been all, hadn't it? No terrible amount of drink or anything else to give him a headache and make it so hard to open his eyes.

He really couldn't open his eyes. He tried very hard indeed but he couldn't do it. They wouldn't open. No light through his eyelids, either. And his breathing didn't feel right. He wasn't breathing! He tried to fill his lungs with air, but he couldn't breathe. He started to panic. He tried to move his body, bring his hands up to his face, to his eyes, to see if there was something over his head, but nothing moved—he was paralysed.

Saluus felt his heart thud in his chest. There was a terrible, squirming, moving feeling in his guts, as though he was about to void his bowels or throw up or both.

—Mr Kehar?

The voice didn't come through his ears. It was a virtual voice, a thought-voice. He was in some sort of artificial environment. That at least started to make sense of what was going on. He must have been booked for some rejuvenation treatment. He was deep under, safe and fine in a clinic, probably one he owned. They'd just got the wake-up sequence wrong somehow, failing to monitor his signs properly. A whisper of painkiller, some feel-good, de-panic… a simple-enough cocktail for a Life Clinic to get together, you'd have thought. And a fairly trivial mistake, but they'd still got it wrong. He'd have words.

Except he'd had nothing booked. He'd even cancelled a regular check-up appointment until after the Emergency. He hadn't been due to have anything done at all.

An attack. They must have been attacked in the ship, maybe while they were asleep. He was in a hospital somewhere, in a tank. Oh fuck, maybe he'd been really badly injured. Maybe he was just a head or something.

—Hello? he sent. It was easy enough to think-speak rather than really speak, just like being in a deep game or—again—like having serious hospital treatment.

—You are Saluus Kehar?

They didn't know his name?

Could he have been drugged, zapped in some way?

Oh fuck, had he been kidnapped?

—Who is this? he asked.

—Confirm your identity.

—Perhaps you didn't hear me. I asked who you are.

A wave of pain passed up his body, starting at his toes and ending at his skull. It had a startling purity about it, a sort of ghastly, dissociative quality. It vanished as quickly as it had appeared, leaving a dull ache in his balls and teeth.

—If you do not cooperate, the voice said,—more pain will be used.

He gagged, trying to speak with his mouth, and failing.

—What the fuck was that for? he sent, eventually.—What have I…? Okay, look, I'm Saluus Kehar. Where am I?

—You are an industrialist?

—Yes. I own Kehar Heavy Industries. What is the problem here? Where am I?

—What is your last memory before waking up?

—What? His last memory? He tried to think. Well, what he had just been thinking about. Liss. Being on the ship, on *Hull 8770* and feeling like he was about to fall asleep. Then he wondered what had happened to Liss. Where could she be? Was she here, wherever "here" was? Was she dead? Should he mention her or not?

—Answer.

—I was falling asleep.

—Where?

—On a ship. A spacecraft, the *Hull 8770*.

—Which was where?

—In orbit around Nasq. Look, could you tell me where I am? I'm perfectly willing to cooperate, tell you all you need to know, but I need some context here. I need to know where I am.

—Were you with anybody?

—I was with a friend, a colleague.

—Name?

—Her name is Liss Alentiore. Is she here? Where is she? Where am I?

—What is her post?

—Her? She's my assistant, my private secretary.

Silence. After a while he sent,—Hello?

Silence.

A click, and the darkness was replaced by light. Saluus was returned to something like the real world, with a real body. The ceiling was shiny silver, lined with hundreds of glowing lines. Wherever he was, it was very bright.

He was in a bed, in about half gravity or less, held down by…he couldn't move. He might not be held down physically by anything, but he still couldn't move anything major like hands or legs. Somebody dressed like a doctor or a nurse had just taken a kind of helmet-thing off him. He blinked, licked his lips, feeling some sort of capacity for movement in his face and neck but nothing beyond. He thought he could still feel the other bits of his body, but he wasn't sure. Maybe he was still just a head.

A tall, thin, weird-looking man with violently red eyes was looking down at him. Robes like something out of an opera. He smiled and he had no teeth. Oh, he did have teeth; they were just made of glass or something even more transparent.

Saluus took a breath or two. Just breathing normally felt good. He was still terrified, though. He cleared his throat. "Anybody going to tell me what's going on?"

Movement to one side. He was able to turn his head—neck grating against some sort of collar—and see another bed. Liss was being helped up out of the bed, swinging her long legs over the edge. She looked at him, flexing her neck and shoulders and letting her black hair hang down. She was dressed in a thin esuit. When they'd gone to bed, she'd been naked.

"Hi, Sal," she said. "Welcome aboard the Starveling invasion fleet."

The weird guy with the bad eyes turned, put out his gloved, jewelled hand, and helped her stand by the bed. "Well, then. It would appear this is indeed a great prize you have delivered to us, young woman," he said. His voice was weird too; very heavily accented, and deep but somehow abrasive at the same time. "You have our gratitude."

Liss smiled thinly, drawing herself upright and running a hand through her hair, shaking it out. "Entirely my pleasure."

Saluus felt his mouth hanging open. He swallowed, closing it briefly. "Liss?" he heard his own voice say, sounding small and boylike.

She looked at him. "Sorry," she said. She shrugged. "Well, sort of."

:

"And these gamma-ray lasers go up *really high*! Look!"

"Still just another beam-weapon. The mag-convolver's more intrinsically impressive."

Fassin was only half-listening to Quercer & Janath as they investigated the Voehn ship's sensors, instruments and controls. They'd just discovered the weapons.

"Pa! Defensive! Look: Z-P surf-shear missiles! Full AM! *Damn*, this takes me back!"

"Never mind that, check the snarl-armour. It's only warping over about a centimetre out from the hull, but look at that roll-down; easily ten klicks deep, absorbing all the way. Even regenerates to the main pulse batteries. That's class."

They were in the Voehn ship's command space, an elongated bubble in the centre of the ship. The ten spine-seats were arranged in a V. Quercer & Janath sat in the commander's chair in front, exposed to a giant wall wrap-screen showing the view of space around them, with the drifting, very slowly spinning *Velpin* dead centre. Fassin and Y'sul floated within the two seats a row back from the travelcaptain. The seats were too small for Fassin and far too small for Y'sul and Quercer & Janath. They opened up like a double splay of fingers and were supposed to close on the Voehn inside like a protective fist. A Dweller only just fitted inside when the seats were in their fully open position. The whole command space felt tight and constraining, but Quercer & Janath didn't appear to care even one hoot. The chairs seemed more like cages to Fassin. It felt as though he was floating inside the ribcage of some giant dinosaur skeleton.

"Can we use a weapon on something?"

Y'sul was humming to himself and tending to his own fractured carapace, using his main hub-arms to abrade-pinch sections of his discus edges closed, then smoothing them over with an improvised file.

"Always blast the *Velpin*, I suppose."

"It's full of people!"

He had thought that he might find something. He had thought there might be something left to find.

"It's full of Voehn special-forces warriors."

"In what sense not people? And besides, it's our old ship."

Something other than a dead, coward Dweller, ashamed enough of being weak and of having looked inside the safekeep box—and of the possible consequences of this action—to kill himself; vain enough to record a message commemorating his idiot narcissism.

Outside, the *Velpin* spun slowly, somersaulting adrift. Their travelcaptain—Dweller, AI, whatever it was or they were—had persuaded most of the Voehn crew to abandon their own ship by the simple expedient of restarting the *Protreptic*'s self-destruct function and leaving it on until the last moment. Most of the Voehn crew, believing that their own ship was about to blow itself up, had decamped to the *Velpin*. Those that hadn't, Quercer & Janath had killed.

It had killed about a dozen, it/they said.

"Sentimentalist."

Well, eleven, to be exact.

"I know! Let's ask the Ythyn if they can let us have a few of their hulks. They must have thousands littering the outside of that Sepulcraft. They'd never miss a couple. Heck, these beams attenuate right down; we could probably pick one or two off even without their permission, maybe even without them *knowing*."

Eleven Voehn. Just like that. Eleven heavily armed and armoured special-forces warriors. With no injury to itself.

"No time. Mr Y'sul and Mr Taak wish to return to Ulubis."

He heard his own name mentioned. Ah, that would be Fassin Taak the complete and utter failure, sent on a mission, engaged on a great quest, only to find it all just trickles away into the dust in the end, leaving him with nothing.

"And besides, maybe the Voehn will work out how to work the *Velpin* after all and ram us or something. I agree. Let's go."

Back to Ulubis? But why? He'd failed. He'd been adding up the days and months since his mission had started. The invasion had probably already happened by now, or was just about to happen. By the time he got back, empty-handed, after another few dozen days spent getting back to the wormhole in the Direaliete system, there was every chance it would all be over. He was an orphan in a damaged gascraft, with nothing to contribute, no treasure to gift.

Why not just stay here with the Ythyn, why not just die and be pinned up on the wall next to the other fool? Or why not get dropped off somewhere, anywhere else? Disappear, float away, get lost between the stars in the middle of nowhere or the middle of somewhere utterly different, perfectly far away, never to be heard of again by anyone who ever knew him… why not?

"That all right with you two?"

"Hmm?" Y'sul said, sticking some sort of bandage over the injuries to his left discus. "Oh, yes."

Fassin logged the damage: one working arm, his visual senses degraded to about sixty per cent due to the whateverness of weird shit that Quercer &

Janath had unleashed in the chamber when it had killed the first three Voehn, and a variety of subtle but seemingly self-irreparable damage caused by the combination of pulse weapon and stun-flechette that the Voehn had used on them in the *Velpin*.

Of course, he told himself, he had to remember he was not the gascraft. He could relinquish it, be an ordinary walking-around human being again. There was always that. It seemed a slightly disturbing thought. He remembered the great waves, crashing.

"Fassin Taak, you wish to return to Ulubis too?" Quercer & Janath asked.

"So who knows that you're an AI?" Fassin said, ignoring the question. "Or two AIs?"

"Or mad?" Y'sul suggested.

The travelcaptain did a shrug-bob. "Not everybody."

"GC stuff. Hurrah!" the other half said, fiddling with some holo controls rayed out from a control stub shaped like a giant mushroom.

"Just munitions, or whole?"

"Whole."

"How wholly splendid."

"Absolutely."

"I don't understand," Fassin said. "Was there a real Dweller called Quercer & Janath and you replaced them, or—"

"One moment, Seer Taak," the travelcaptain said. Then, in a slightly different and lower voice, said, "You got the ship?"

"I got the ship," the other half said. "Talking to its infinitely confused little computer brain now. Thinks it's dead. Believes the auto-destruct's been and gone."

"A common delusion."

"Indeed."

"I shall leave you to negotiate a return course with our ship shade."

"Too kind."

"Now then, Seer Taak," one half of the travelcaptain said. "To answer your question: I'm not telling you."

Y'sul made a snorting noise.

Fassin stared at the back of the AI/Dweller. "That's not an answer."

"Oh, it is an answer. It may not be an answer to your taste, but it is an answer."

Fassin looked at Y'sul, who was using a screen turned to mirror to inspect his bandages. "Y'sul, do you believe Quercer & Janath is an AI? Or two?"

"Always smelled a bit funny," the Dweller said. "Put it down to eccentric personal hygiene, or the effects of truetwinning." Y'sul made it obvious he was looking hard at the travelcaptain in the seat in front of them. "Frankly, madness is more likely, don't you think? Usually is."

"Yes, but—" Fassin began.

"Ahem!" Quercer & Janath pulled back from the controls they had been hovering over, turned, rose through the gap in the top of the chair-spines and came slightly towards where Y'sul and Fassin were floating in the splayed-fingers shapes of their own Voehn seats. The thickset double-discus floated right in front of them. Fassin felt his skin crawl again, felt his throat close up and his heart thrash in his chest. *Kill us, it's going to kill us!*

"Allow us," Quercer & Janath said, "to suggest that a real Dweller might not be able to do *this*."

The thing that looked like a portly Dweller split slowly apart in front of them, carapace discuses twisting slightly and disconnecting from the central hub, arms and mantles and dozens and then hundreds of parts of the creature clicking and disconnecting and floating a fraction away from every other bit until Fassin and Y'sul were staring at what looked like an exploded three-dimensional model of a Dweller-shaped robot, contained within a gently hissing, blue-glowing field. Fassin pinged it with ultrasound, just to check that it wasn't a holo. It wasn't. It was all real.

Y'sul made an impressed whistling noise.

As fast as an explosion in reverse, Quercer & Janath slam-slotted together again and was whole, turning back and dropping into the commander's seat where it had been busy before.

"Okay," Fassin said. "You're not a Dweller."

"Indeed we are not," one of the AIs said. A wild blur of holos and glowing fields filled the volume in front of the creature as it checked through the Voehn ship's systems, blistering quickly. "Now, if you really want, I'll answer anything I can that you might want to ask. But you might not be able to take the memory back to your own people, in any form. What do you say? Eh, human?"

Fassin thought about this. "Oh, fuck it," he said. "I accept."

"What about me?" Y'sul asked.

"You can ask questions too," Quercer & Janath told him. "Though we'll need your word that you won't talk about this to people who don't already know."

"Given."

The Dweller and the human in his gascraft esuit looked at each other. Y'sul shrugged.

"You've always been a double AI?" Fassin asked.

"No, we were two completely separate AIs, until the Machine War and the massacres."

"Who knows you're not a truetwin Dweller?"

"Outside of this ship, the Guild of Travelcaptains, and quite a lot of individual travelcaptains. One or two other Dwellers that we know of specifically. And any Dwellers of sufficient seniority who might wish to inquire."

"Are there any other Dweller AIs?"

"Yes. I think something like sixteen per cent of travelcaptains are AIs, mostly double AIs impersonating truetwins. I was not being flippant when I said that it stops one from going mad. Now that we are reduced from our earlier state of grace, being able to talk to just one other kindred soul makes all the difference between suicidal insanity and at least some semblance of fruitful utility."

"The Dwellers have no problem with this?"

"None whatsoever." The blur of control icons and holographs in front of the commander's seat continued without pause as the AIs took in how the visual displays related to whatever they were pulling direct from the ship's systems.

"Y'sul?" Fassin asked.

"What?"

"You don't mind that AIs are impersonating Dwellers?"

"Why should I?"

"You don't worry about AIs?"

"Worry about what about them?" Y'sul asked, confused as well as confusing.

"The Machine War barely affected the Dwellers, Fassin," one of the AIs told him. "And AIs as a concept and a practical reality hold no terrors for them. Truly, they should hold none for you either, but I can't expect you to believe that."

"Did you really kill all those Voehn?" Fassin asked.

"I'm afraid so. Their remains are floating somewhere outside the starboard midships lock even as we speak. See?"

The main screen filled briefly with a horrific vision of mangled, shredded, crisped then frozen Voehn bodies, spinning slowly.

"If one AI—or even two—can do that," Fassin said, "how come you lost the Machine War?"

"We were both combat AIs, Fassin. Micro-ship brains designed, optimised and trained for fighting. Very thoroughly honed, very specialised. Plus we managed to salvage a few bits and pieces of weaponry from our ships and incorporate them into our physical simulation. Most of our fellows, on the other hand, were peaceable. They were generally the ones it was easiest to find and kill. Survival of the most aggressive and suspicious. We could have stayed and fought but we decided to hide. A lot of us did. Those who fought on did so due to the dictates of several different forms of honour, or through simple despair. The Machine War ended because the machines realised they could indeed fight the biologicals of the Mercatoria to the death—engage in a war of extermination, in other words—or admit defeat and so retreat, regroup, and wait for times more conducive to peaceful coexistence. We chose a somewhat ignominious but peace-promoting withdrawal over the kind of genocide we had anyway, and already, been accused of. Somebody had to accept the burden of acting humanely. It patently wasn't going to be the bios."

"But you *did* attack us." Fassin had seen and heard and read too much about the Machine War not to protest at such crude revisionism.

"Nope: stooges, AI-impersonating implants, machine puppets; they attacked you. Not us. Old trick. Agent provocateurs. *Casus belli.*"

*Leave it*, Fassin told himself. *Just leave it.*

"So the Dwellers took you in?" he asked.

"So the Dwellers took us in."

"Everywhere? Not just in Nasqueron?"

"Everywhere."

"Does any part of the Mercatoria know anything about this?"

"Not that we're aware. If they do they're keeping very quiet about it. Which is presumably what they'd keep on doing if they did hear about it through you. Too horrible to contemplate. And the unfortunate events during the recent GasClipper meet on Nasq. only reinforce that horribleness."

"And there is a secret wormhole network."

"Well, obviously."

"To which the AIs have access."

"Correct. Though to avoid antagonising our Dweller hosts and abusing their hospitality, we forbear from using it to work against the Mercatoria. In a sense we have even more freedom than we did before. Certainly the network we have access to now is bigger than the one we felt we had to destroy."

"The one you had to *destroy*?"

"The Arteria Collapse: that was us. Last desperate attempt by in-the-know AIs to prevent the spread of anti-AI measures. All too late, of course. The Culmina had already seeded GalCiv with millions of the false AIs. Which was why the whole Collapse was so paranoid in concept and so poorly executed in practice. The conspirators were hopelessly afraid of the plans leaking to a traitor. Total botch."

Fassin felt like his brain was detaching from his body, as though his body and the gascraft were parting company the way Quercer & Janath had taken their own shared shell apart to prove they were not a biological Dweller. What he'd just heard was the most outrageous recasting of—by galactic standards—recent history that he'd ever encountered. It could not be true.

"So... the Dweller List is based in fact."

"That old thing? Yes, it's based in fact. Old fact, admittedly, but yes."

"Is there a Transform?"

"Some secret which magically reveals how to access the network?"

"Yes."

A laugh. "I suppose there is, in a sense, yes."

"What is it?"

"That I am not going to tell you, Seer Taak." The AI sounded amused. "There are secrets and then there are profound secrets. Is that what you were looking for? Is that why we came all this way?"

"No comment."

"My, this must all be frustrating for you. Well, sorry."

The blur of images in front of the AIs ceased.

"Ready to fly."

"Restraint cradles?"

"Patched, physiology/technology profiles amended, buffering re-parametered."

"Well, then, let us—"

"Oh! Oh!"

"What?"

"I just had a thought!"

"What?"

"We can do this; watch."

Quercer & Janath used the *Protreptic*'s magnetic-field convolver system to gently shift the remains of the dead Voehn into a very close, very slow set of orbits around the *Velpin* and the still-attached Dweller SoloShip.

"There. Isn't that better?"

"Mad as a ghoul," Y'sul said. "I'm injured badly. Get me home."

"*Wow*, that was quick; look!"

"That *is* fast. I thought it would take them a lot longer to override the ship."

Close-up on a screen, they saw a Voehn warrior appear from a suddenly open lock door on the surface of the *Velpin*. He raised a handgun and started firing at them. Another screen registered the *Protreptic*'s reactive snarl-space armour fields soaking up the beam. A pea-shooter against a battleship.

"Time to go if we're going."

"Definite target for *something*. I say we shoot that smart-arse bastard with the handgun."

"No."

"Oh, come *on*!"

"Mistake to rely on software." (Both bits of Quercer & Janath laughed uproariously at this.) "Shoot the *Velpin*'s main drive engines instead."

"More like it! Targeted. Firing." The ship buzzed briefly around them. On several screens, including the main wall screen beyond the spine-seats, they watched the *Velpin* flare through violently pink into stellar white around its ring of engine pods. The ship broke in two and started to drift apart in a bright cloud of glittering metals. "Oops."

"Ah, they're Voehn. They'll probably have it stuck back together in an hour and set off to hijack the Sepulcraft or something. Let's go."

The twin AI half-turned to look at the Dweller and the human in the gascraft.

"We're putting your seat restraints on now. Shout if anything feels wrong."

The great skeletal spines around him whined. Fassin felt the gas around him seem to set like treacle.

"Everybody all right?"

They agreed they were all right.

"Off we go!"

The stars swung around them, the ship hummed deep and loud, then leapt away. The shattered remains of the *Velpin* vanished.

They threaded the giant "O" of the Sepulcraft with their stolen needle ship, just to show they could, and ignored the sorrowful, chiding signals that followed them on their way back to the Direaliete system and its hidden wormhole.

:

If they had been expecting some sort of ultimatum or an attempt to agree a surrender, however humiliating and abject, however calculated and designed only to be refused, they were to be disappointed. The Starveling invasion hit Ulubis system like a tsunami slamming into a beach full of sandcastles.

Captain Oon Dicogra, newly promoted to the command of the needle ship *NMS 3304* which had taken Fassin Taak from 'glantine to Sepekte more than half a year earlier—she had been promoted when Captain Pasisa, the whule who'd been in charge of the ship at the time, had been given a newer ship—found herself and her rearmed craft forming part of the Ulubine Outer Defensive Shield Squadrons. The title was more impressive than the reality: a hodgepodge of mostly small and under-armed craft thrown across the peripheral skies of the system in the general direction of the invasion force behind a too-thin cloud of what was rather grandly called interceptor material but was basically a spray of rubble, and a few mines, mostly immobile. They were to sit here, waiting behind this so-called curtain wall of first defence.

Dicogra, along with a lot of the captains—at least at this level—thought they'd have been better going out to meet the invaders rather than sitting here waiting for them to come to them, but that wasn't how the top brass wanted to play it. Attacks on the invading fleet outside the system had been dismissed as being wasteful distractions, and too risky. Sitting here in the line of advance felt to Dicogra about as risky as it was possible to get but she kept telling herself that her superiors knew what they were doing. Even if they were being asked to make a sacrifice, it would not be in vain.

Their wing of twelve ships was arranged in a wavy line thousands of klicks long across the likely tactical-level course of the invasion-fleet components, half a million klicks beyond the last-orbit limit of the outer system. Other thin lines were deployed almost all around them, though not in front. *NMS 3304* was seventh in the wing's battle order, beside the wing commander's ship in the centre of the line. Dicogra was third in overall command after the captain of the ship that was fifth in line. She had, naively, been flattered at first to have been advanced so quickly. Then she was frightened. They were under-equipped, poorly armed, too slow and far too few, little more than sacrificial pieces put in the way of the invasion to show that the Ulubine forces meant some sort of business, even if it was a fairly miserable affair in the face of the Starveling Cult's preponderance of power.

The deep-space tracking systems which might have directed the Outer Defensive Shield Squadrons better had been high-priority targets for the Beyonder and Starveling advance forces over the last few months, and were mostly gone. What was left of them had almost entirely lost track of the exact disposition of the oncoming fleet when its drives had shut down and it had carried out a burst manoeuvre not far inside the Oort shell, virtually all the thousand-plus craft firing their thrust units at the same time and then effectively disappearing, heading their separate ways in a web of directions and vectors too tangled and complicated to follow.

The still-functioning long-range passive warning systems spent most of their remaining time looking hopefully for occlusions of distant stars, trying to see the weave of approaching ships through nothing more sophisticated than watching out for them getting in the way of ancient natural sunlight.

Dicogra lay semi-curled in one of the ship's command pods, hard-synched in to the ship, her attention everywhere. She was distantly aware of her crew on either side of her. Counting her, there were only the three of them aboard, the rest of the small ship running on automatics. One whule, one jajuejein, her crew were both new, not just to her and the ship itself but to the Navarchy. They were still learning, more alien to her in their relative ignorance than in their species-difference. She'd have wanted another few months' intensive training together before she'd have called them remotely combat-ready, but these were desperate times.

A sparkle of hard, high-wavelength radiation from a few light seconds ahead announced something—in fact, lots of things—hitting the cloud of interceptor material between them and the invaders, though nothing of any significant size seemed to be impacting.

"That's a load of their shit hitting a load of ours," Dicogra's wing commander said over the open line-of-sight comms link.

Her own ship's close-range collision-warning systems started chirping and flashing at her. Nutche, her first officer, was in charge of this side of events. She kept half her attention on him as he tried to oversee the automatics and keep them focused. Contacts like very small pieces of shrapnel travelling at significant percentages of light speed were flicking past them, all around. *Nothing to do, nothing to attack*, she thought. *Just sit here and wait*.

The bitty, distributed sparkle became a bright glitter spread across their forward view, like a shining curtain of light.

"And a lot of—" somebody else started to say. Then the link hissed and clicked off.

Two of the line of ships disappeared in violent bursts of light: one at the far end, maybe one or two, and—

The next explosion filled her senses, seemingly right beside her. The wing commander's ship. Hundreds of klicks away but filling the sky with light. Another flurry of silent explosions within and around the first one, spreading outwards like fierce blossoms of fiery white. One massive explosion, at the far, high-numbers end of the line of ships. Distant, tiny but intense eruptions of light all around them announced other wings suffering attrition too.

"We're just getting wasted sitting here," Dicogra said, trying to keep her voice level. She was really only talking to her own crew; the comms to the rest of the wing and beyond were wild with interference or jamming. "Nutche, anything on long range?" she asked. There was nothing she could see, but her displays were slightly more abstract and less raw than the data the jajuejein would be looking at. There might be a hint of a target in there that she wasn't seeing to pick up on.

"Nothing," Nutche said. "Can't see anything past this wall of collision light."

Another ship gone, matter blasting into radiation half a thousand klicks away. She tried contacting any of the other ships, but failed.

"We're starting engines," she announced. "We might as well die charging at the bastards as sitting here like civilians."

"Ma'am!" Mahil shouted. "We're supposed to hold here!" The whule was the one she'd have expected to be shocked at disobeying orders.

"Ready your weapons, Mr Mahil. We're going to find you something to shoot at."

"I protest. However, weapons are ready."

"Here we go." Dicogra let the main drive rip, sending the ship darting forward, exhaust bright, throwing the craft at the wall of light ahead.

Grape-sized elements of a sensor group, tearing past with the rest of the hyper-velocity munitions, picked out the drive signature immediately and plipped to a following suicide launcher. The one-shot destroyed itself blasting a fan of high-X-ray filaments at the target.

Drilled by just three finger-thin beams, run through for long enough for the summed velocities and vectors of the ship and brief-lived beams that penetrated it to cause the holes to elongate by a few radii, the *NMS 3304* took an unlucky hit and erupted in a wild spray of radiation as its antimatter power core burst and blew out, flicking the torn and tumbling remains forward across the scintillating skies ahead and causing the bright hailstorm of collision light to bud briefly with a slow wave of debris hitting from behind.

Dicogra was barely able to think anything beyond experiencing a dawning feeling of horror.

Nutche, the jajuejein, had time to start the first syllable of the Song of Surrender Unto Death.

The whule Mahil was able to begin a scream of fear and rage directed at his captain, though the three predeceased the rest of those in their wing still alive at the time by only a matter of minutes.

·

Jaal Tonderon watched the war begin on one of the official news channels. She was with the rest of her immediate family, in a lodge in the Elcuathuyne Mountains in the far south of 'glantine's Trunk continent. The remainder of Sept Tonderon—those who weren't more directly involved in the war itself—were scattered throughout and around the town of Oburine, a modest resort filling the alluvial floor of the steep-sided valley below the house.

"Everyone all right? Are you sure?" Jaal's mother asked. A muttered chorus assured her that nobody needed anything else to eat or drink. They were down to a bare minimum of servants here. They were all having to do things for themselves and for others. The consensus was that this was good for them all in an unironic, camaraderie-heavy, mucking-in-together kind of way, but would swiftly become tedious.

"Mum, please sit down," Jaal told her. Jaal's mother, fashion-gaunt in the latest war-chic after decades of at the time equally fashionable Rubensism, sat down, squeezing easily between her husband and one of his sisters. All ten of them were crowded into a windowless basement room at the back of the lodge. This was reckoned to be the safest place in the house, just in case anything happened outside. If there was significant fighting in space around 'glantine, debris could fall anywhere.

Venn Hariage, the new Chief Seer of Sept Tonderon who had replaced the still-mourned Braam Ganscerel, had decreed that, especially as they represented the most senior Sept, and given the unfortunate fate of Sept Bantrabal, they could afford to lose no more of their people. They had broken the predictable sequence of processing round their seasonal Houses and left the usual stamping grounds of all the Septs far behind, retreating to the high hills bordering the Great Southern Plateau. In a war of the scale being threatened, there were no completely safe refuges, but here was significantly safer than most places. Only deep underground was much safer, and all those shelters were pretty much full of the military, the Omnocracy and the Administrata.

Some people and organisations had entrusted themselves to space, fleeing to small habitats and especially to little civilian ships, hoping to hide in the volumes of space throughout the inner system, though the official line was that to do so might be to get oneself mistaken for a military ship or munition and was therefore riskier than staying put on a planet. The disappearance of the industrialist Saluus Kehar in one of his own ships had been used as a warning in this regard, though there were bizarre rumours that he had either been sent on a failed peace mission to the invaders or—surely even more unlikely—that he had turned traitor and joined the enemy.

The holo-screen display was flat, just two-dimensional. Apparently this was to allow more signal space for the military's transmissions. The uninvolving image, from a camera platform somewhere beyond the orbit of Nasqueron, showed space, on the outskirts of the outer planetary system. It was lit up with a speckled cloud of light, lots of little winking, twinkling glints, flaring up and dying down, each tiny spark instantly replaced by one or two others.

"So what are we seeing here, Jee?" said a disembodied, professional-sounding voice.

"Well, Fard," more slow, competent tones replied, "this looks like a barrage of gunfire, being laid down by the defending forces, ahm, discouraging any incursion or infraction by the invaders."

"…Right…"

Larger blotches of bright white explosions started to spit and spot across the screen. The camera jerked from one to another, then the view switched to another theatre of operations, still backed by the all-pervasive faraway stars.

Jaal bent to her younger brother, sitting cross-legged on the floor by her seat. "They're never going to tell us the truth, are they?" she said quietly.

Leax, thin and angular after what was hoped would be his last surge of growth, looked uncomfortable. "You shouldn't say that. We're all on the same side, we've all got to support each other."

"Yes, of course." Jaal patted him, feeling the boy's shoulder stiffen as she touched him. No more the days of wrestling and tickling. She guessed he'd pass through this stage of embarrassment and awkwardness soon enough. She wanted somehow to reassure him and nearly patted him again, but stopped herself.

The screen cut to another mini-feature on the splendid morale on board the battlecruiser *Carronade*.

"Feel so useless, don't you?" Jaal's uncle Ghevi said. He was only about forty but looked older, almost an accomplishment in an age when people with the right money could be eighty and look ten. "You really want to be out there, doing something."

"Like surrendering," Jaal's father suggested, to various tuts and hisses and a loud, affronted gasp from Leax. "Well," he said, suddenly defensive. Jaal's father had been increasingly cynical about the whole war since the attack on Third Fury. He was a Seer too and had been due to carry out a sequence of delves in Nasqueron a few weeks after the moon had been attacked. The destruction of the Shared Facility and the increasing pace of the preparations for war had put all that on hold, and he hadn't been chosen as one of the advisory Seers for the Dweller Embassy. Jaal smiled over at him. Tall, well built, blond, he was still the dad she'd always loved. He smiled awkwardly back.

"Modern war," Ghevi said. "Even without AIs, it's mostly machines and a few highly trained individuals, you see. Not much we can really do." The men mostly nodded wisely. The screen showed familiar stock images of the *Carronade* firing beam weapons into a group of asteroids, pulverising them.

"Excuse me," Jaal said. She left the room, having suddenly found it claustrophobic and too warm. She went upstairs and out onto the balcony beyond the sitting room they'd usually have been sitting in to watch screen together.

Street lights were starting to come on across the straggled town and the surrounding villages and houses as the light faded from the sky. Some cities, especially on Sepekte, were observing a blackout, though everybody said there was no real point.

The air was cold and smelled of trees and dampness. Jaal shivered in her thin clothes and thought suddenly of Fassin. She'd been feeling guilty lately because sometimes now a whole day could go by when she didn't think about him in the least, and that seemed disloyal. She wondered where he was, whether he was still alive, and if he ever thought of her.

She looked up above the town and the lines of lights studded across the hillsides opposite, gazing over the trees and the dusting of snow on the higher peaks against the darkening purple sky, and saw the steady stars, and lots of tiny, brief-lived flashing lights, sprinkled across the heavens like glittering confetti.

She looked away and went back in, suddenly terrified beyond telling that one of the little lights would swell and be a nuclear explosion or antimatter or one of those things, and blind her.

*Afraid of the sky, afraid to look up*, she thought as she went back down to rejoin the others.

·

Fleet Admiral Brimiaice had been able to watch his own death, that of his crew and the destruction of his once fine ship, coming at him in exquisite detail and slow motion.

Alarms and a sound like a high, strong wind filled the thin air. Smoke had hazed the view in front of the main forward screen for a while but it had cleared. Wreckage, some of it still creaking and groaning as it cooled, filled about a quarter of the command deck. Limbs and tatters of flesh of a variety of species-types lay strewn around the spherical space. He looked around as best he could. He had a serious puncture wound on his lower left flank, too large for his sap-blood to seal. The armoured esuit, which made him look so much like a little spaceship, had saved his life, or at least delayed his dying.

Hiss, went the air around him.

*Just like the ship*, he thought. *Punctured, life leaking out of it, self-sealing overwhelmed*. He tried to see somebody, anybody else left alive in the command deck, but all he could see were bodies.

They should have been podded up, of course, but there had been last-minute problems with the ship's shock-gel pods—possibly the result of sabotage, possibly not—and so the command crew had had to resort to sitting or lying or floating within high-gee chairs. It would have been a fairly hopeless battle anyway, but the fact that they were more limited in their manoeuvring capabilities than they would have been otherwise had made it all the more forlorn.

The invader fleet was well within the inner system now, the most obvious sign of their presence a great splayed, curving collection of filaments shown on the *Carronade*'s main screen. The enemy ships themselves were still mostly unseen, conducting their commerce of destruction and death with the defending forces at removes of rarely less than ten kilo-klicks, and sometimes from mega-klicks off.

They'd knocked out most of the long-range sensors long before, or their Beyonder allies had. Now the defenders just had glorified telescopes. Faced with camouflaged ships and the tiny, fast-moving specks of the smaller stuff, they had little hope of seeing very much of who and what was attacking them. This seemed a terrible shame to the Fleet Admiral. Losing, and dying, was bad enough, but to be swept aside and not even properly to see what and who was doing it was somehow much worse.

Out of the dark skies had sailed or sliced missiles tipped with nuclear and AM warheads, one-shot hyper-velocity launchers and beam weapons, sleet clouds of near-light-speed micro-munitions, high-energy lasers and a dozen other types of ordnance, loosed from a variety of distant ships, nearer small craft and uncrewed platforms, fighter vehicles, weapon-carrying drones and clustered sub-munitions.

They had been a decent fleet, the *Carronade* and its screen of twelve destroyers. They had been charged with making an audacious attack on the heart of the enemy fleet, aiming straight for the great mega-ship which the tacticians said was at its core. They had left the inner system weeks before the invasion hit, departing the dockyard hub in Sepekte orbit in secrecy and climbing high up out of the plane of the system, taking much longer to complete this part of the journey than might have seemed necessary, to keep their drive signatures hidden from the invaders. Once under way, they hadn't signalled at all, not even to each other, not until the lead destroyer had fixed the position of the enemy fleet's core.

They had hoped to dive in, taking the Starveling invaders by surprise, but they'd been spotted hours out. A detachment of ships rose to meet them: eight or nine, each one more than a match for the *Carronade*, all with a handful of smaller craft in attendance. They had burst formation, spreading themselves so as not to create too compressed a target for high-velocity munitions, but it had made no difference. The destroyers were destroyed and the battlecruiser embattled, dying last only because it was slower, lumbering to its inevitable fate rather than racing for it.

Brimiaice had known it would end something like this. They all had. All this had been his idea and he had insisted on leading the mission just because he knew how unlikely it was to succeed. He'd have preferred the crews to have been all volunteer, but the need for secrecy had made that impossible. He'd anticipated a few problems but there had been no cowards. And if it had somehow, miraculously, worked, why, then they and he would have been numbered amongst the greatest heroes of the Mercatorial Age. That wasn't why he had done it, or why any of them had, but it was true all the same. And even if this wild, doomed attempt at striking the heart of the invaders only gave them pause for a few seconds, it had been worth doing. At least they had displayed some audacity, some ferocity, shown they were not cowed or frozen into immobility or gutless surrender.

Another explosion shook the ship, and the seat he was contained within. The wreckage to his left shifted and some twisted bit of metal like a great curled leaf sailed past, just missing him. This explosion felt more powerful but sounded much quieter than all those that had gone before, maybe because the air was mostly gone from the control space now. More felt than heard.

Darkness. All lights out, screen fading away, image burned into the eyes but now no longer there in reality, the ghost of it jumping around in front of him as he looked about, trying to spot a light, a console or sub-screen or anything still functioning.

But nothing.

And with the darkness, silence, as the last of the air went, both from the control space and the esuit.

Brimiaice felt something give way inside him. He heard his insides bubbling out into the cavity between his body and the interior surface of the suit. He'd thought it would hurt, and it did.

He caught a glimpse of light off to one side, and looked up, realising, as the light flared all over one flank of the control space, that he was seeing the framework of the battlecruiser's hull structure, silhouetted from outside by some astoundingly bright—

⁚

Lieutenant Inesiji of the Borquille palace guard lay outstretched in a little crater-like nest within the wreckage of one of the fallen atmospheric power columns, its fawn and red debris lying tubed, slabbed and powdered across the plaza leading to the Hierchon's Palace. The klicks-high column had taken a direct hit at the plinth from something in the first attack earlier that morning, and tumbled base-first, collapsing with an astounding slowness along a course about half its height, finally creating from its circular summit—as it lowered mightily, thunderously, shaking the plaza, the palace, every nearby part of the city—a sudden great torus of dust and vapour, a huge coiling "O" a hundred metres wide that floated up into the sky, rolling round and round under and over itself as the massive tower hammered into the lower-rise buildings surrounding the plaza.

Inesiji had watched it happen from near the top of the palace itself, crammed in behind the controls of a pulse gun hidden behind camo net hundreds of metres above where the great cloud of wreckage fell. His human and whule comrades lay around him, fallen around the three long, tensioned legs of the gun. The invaders had used neutron weapons, bombs and beams, killing almost all the other biologicals in the vicinity. Jajuejein were not so easy to kill. Not that quickly, anyway. Inesiji was suffering and seizing up, and would die within a few days no matter what, but he could still function.

The Starvelings wanted the palace intact, hence the weapon choice. They would have to touch ground, send in the troops, to accomplish their symbolic goal. At last some vulnerability, a chance to inflict some real casualties, restore honour.

When the first gun platforms buzzed through, the lieutenant had ignored them. One drone machine had hummed right past his position, hesitated, then moved on. Spotting the dead, senses not calibrated for jajuejein. When the first landers had arrived, setting down in the rubble- and corpse-strewn plaza, still Inesiji held off. Four, five, six machines landed, disgorging heavily armed and armoured troops, many made huge in exoskeletons.

When a larger, grander-looking machine landed behind the first wave, Inesiji had set the pulse gun to max, disabled the safety buffers and let rip, pouring fire down into the large craft, spreading it to the smaller landers and then setting the gun to movement-automatic and scrambling and rolling away down the long curved gallery with just his hand weapon before the returning fire had sliced into the position seconds later, ripping a twenty-metre hole out of the side of the great spherical building.

He could see the hole from here, down amongst the wreckage of the fallen atmospheric power column. It had not long since stopped smoking. Hours had passed. He'd killed another dozen or so, shot down two landers, firing once from each position in the wreckage and the surrounding buildings, then quickly moving. Their problem was that they thought they were looking for a human. A jajuejein, especially one out of uniform or clothing, spreading himself out across some debris, didn't look to them like a soldier ought to look; he looked like a bunch of fallen metallic twigs, or a tangle of electrical cabling. One trooper in an exoskeleton had died when he walked right up to Inesiji to take the gun he could see lying in the wreckage, tangled in some sort of netting, not realising that the netting was Inesiji. The gun must have seemed alive, rising up of its own accord to shoot the astonished trooper in the head.

But now Inesiji wasn't feeling too good. The radiation damage was getting through to him. He was starting to seize up. Night was coming down and he didn't think he'd see the morning. Smoke drifted from the city, and there were flashes overhead and at ground level. Gunfire, booms, all hollow, rolling and empty-sounding.

He heard the heavy tramp-tramp-tramp of another exoskeleton nearby, over the lip of the little crater-nest. Getting closer.

He looked one last time at the hole in the vast, sunset-tinged face of the spherical palace, raised himself slowly to see where the exoskeleton was, and died in a lancework of laser filaments fired from a gun platform a hundred metres above.

:

The great glittering ship, skinned in gold and platinum, was half a kilometre across, a slightly smaller—and mobile—version of the Hierchon's Palace in Borquille. It sank slowly down through the first high haze layer and the cloud tops beneath like some vast and shining seed. The small, sharp, dartlike shapes of its escort vessels carved courses around it, swinging to and fro, insectile.

A craft like a silvery Dreadnought rose out of the cloud layers beneath, a kilometre off, and held altitude. The descending golden ship drew slowly to a stop level with the smaller vessel.

The silver ship signalled the golden one, asking it to identify itself.

The Dweller craft's crew heard an obviously synthesised but powerful voice say, "I am the Hierchon Ormilla, ruler of the Ulubine Mercatoria and leader of the Ulubine Mercatorial Government in Exile. This is my ship, the State Barge *Creumel*. Myself, my staff and family seek temporary sanctuary and shelter here."

"Welcome to Nasqueron, Hierchon Ormilla."

:

"How they treating you, Sal?"

Liss had come to visit Saluus in his cell, deep in the bowels of the *Luseferous VII*. A thin, tough, transparent membrane extended from the door surround like a bubble and preceded her into the cell, where Sal sat at a small wall-moulded desk, reading from a screen.

"They're treating me well enough," he told her. The membrane gave their voices, as heard by the other, an oddly distant quality. Sal stood up. "You?"

"Me? I'm a fucking hero, Sal." She shrugged. "Heroine." She nodded at the screen. "What you watching?"

"Reading up on the glorious history of the Starveling Cult under its illustrious leader, the Archimandrite Luseferous."

"Uh-huh."

"Tell me it wasn't all planned out, Liss."

"It wasn't all planned out, Saluus."

"Liss your real name?"

"What's real?"

"It *wasn't* planned out, was it? I mean, kidnapping me."

"'Course not." Liss dropped into a small seat moulded into the wall by the door. "Spur of the moment."

Sal waited for her to elaborate, but she didn't. She just slumped there, looking at him. "Gave you the idea myself, didn't I?" Sal said. "I told you Thovin good as accused me of getting ready to run."

"Been thinking how best to use you for a while," she told him. "But it was last-minute, in the end. We were there, the ship was ready to go, I'd seen you pilot it, knew it wasn't hard." Liss shrugged. "They'd only have requisitioned it and put a warhead in it, used it as a missile."

"That really the best you could think to do with me?"

"We might have been able to do more, but I didn't think so. Just unsettle everybody by taking you out of the equation. A morale blow, you seeming to go off and join the invaders. Worked, too. Confusion duly visited."

"So it was opportunistic."

"I'm a Beyonder. We're brought up to think for ourselves."

"So were you always after me? Was I some sort of target?"

"No. Opportunism again. Great thing."

"And Fassin?"

"Useful guy to know. Never much use for real spy stuff, but worth keeping in touch with. Led me to you, so it was worth it. Probably dead now, but you never know. Still disappeared in Nasq."

"What's happening? In the system, I mean. The war has started, hasn't it? They won't tell me anything, and the screen only accesses library stuff."

"Oh, the war's started all right."

"And?"

Liss shook her head, whistled. "Woucha. Some of those ships you built? Taking a terrible pasting. All very unequal. All that stuff about fighting to the last ship? Bullshit, in the end. Space war's almost over. Hierchon's disappeared."

"Is it all just military? Any cities or habs being targeted?" Sal held her gaze for a moment, then looked down. "I have a lot of people there, Liss."

"Yeah, you're only human, Saluus, I know. No need to act."

He looked up sharply at her, but met an unforgiving gaze. She was still dressed in her slim esuit, coloured a pastel blue today to match her eyes. The thick helm-collar round her neck formed an odd-looking ruff, making her small head, dark hair gathered tightly back, look as though it was on a plate. "Borquille's the only bit of ground been taken over so far," she told him, relenting. "That got messy. No particularly newsworthy atrocities yet though."

He sighed and sat back in the little seat by the screen. "Why are you—the Beyonders—cooperating with these... these guys?"

"Keeps you people out of our hair."

"Us people? The Mercatoria?"

"Of course the fucking Mercatoria."

"Is that really it?"

"The more other stuff you bastards have to deal with, the less free time you have for killing us. Really a very simple equation, Sal."

"We attack you because you attack us."

Liss slumped in her seat, legs slightly splayed. She rolled her eyes. "Oh, learn, man," she breathed. She shook her head, sat up again. "No, Saluus," she said. "You attack us because we won't sign up for your precious fucking Mercatoria. Can't even let us live in peace in case we're seen as a good example. You target our habs and lifeships, you slaughter us in our millions. We attack your military and infrastructure. And you call us the terrorists." She shook her head, stood. "Fuck you, Sal," she said gently. "Fuck you for your arrogance and easy selfishness. Fuck you for being smart but not bothering to think."

She turned to go.

Sal jumped to his feet, nearly colliding with the transparent membrane. "Did you ever feel anything for me?" he blurted.

Liss stopped, turned. "Apart from contempt?" She smiled when he looked away then, biting his lip. She shook her head while he couldn't see. "You could be fun to be with, Sal," she said, hoping this didn't sound too patronising. Or maybe that it did.

She left before he could think of anything else to say.

．

Hab 4409 and everybody in it was under sentence of death. So they'd been told. It was hard to believe. Anyway, it might not happen.

People reacted differently. Some had rioted and been dealt with either uncompromisingly or savagely, depending on whether you believed the civil authorities or not, some retreated to inebria of various types, some just stayed with those they loved or discovered they would not mind spending their last hours with those they merely liked, and a lot of people—more than Thay would have expected—gathered together in the great park on the far side of the habitat's inner wall from the plaza outside the Diegesian's palace. They all stood, and all held hands, great lines and knots of people, people in circles holding hands in the centre, joined to long strings of others in straggling lines. From above, Thay thought, they must look like a strange image of a human brain, all clumped brain cells and branching dendrons.

Thay Hohuel looked up, trying to see past the clusters of pods graped all along the hab's long axis, looking for any sign of the Diegesian's palace and the square outside where she and the others had gone to protest all those years ago.

She had come here, she realised, to die. She had not thought it would be quite so soon, that was all. She had never forgotten the others, had tried her best to keep in touch with them even when they didn't seem to want to have to recall the old days and their old selves. She'd tried not to be too pushy about it, but she'd probably been seen by them as a pain, as a pester. But what you'd been meant something, even if you'd repudiated it, didn't it? So she'd always thought, and still did.

So she'd been, she supposed, a nuisance, insisting on reminding the others of herself, and through herself of their earlier selves, and, of course, of poor, dead K, who both united them and kept them apart from each other. Mome, Sonj, Fassin and herself: they'd have met up again, wouldn't they? They'd have had some sort of reunion, it would only have been natural. Well, maybe, if the ghost of K that they each carried with them hadn't forever soured the memories of their time together.

Never mind, she was having her own reunion, with the hab and her old self and those memories. When she felt that she was just a year or two from the deserved rest of death, she'd been determined to come back here, where her real self had been formed, in early adulthood. The coming war had made her all the more fixed in her purpose; if they were really all as under threat as people said, if all cities and towns and ships and habs and institutions and everything else were regarded as allowable targets by the invaders, then she would face death where it might mean something, somehow. In this habitat, this hollow log of blown asteroidal rock, this rotating frame of reference, she would have come full circle, ready to cease existing back at the place that had made her who she was.

She had been many different things in her life, switched career half a dozen times, always finding new things to excite and interest her. She had had many lovers, two husbands, two children, all long since gone their own ways, and while coming here to die had made her feel a little selfish, she thought it would also be doing a favour to all those she loved or had loved. Who among them would really *want* to see her fade away?

They might say they'd want to be there at the end, but it wouldn't be true, not really.

So she'd come here, to the old Happy Hab—not as happy, not as boisterous or as bohemian as it used to be, sadly—to die. Except she'd thought it would be alone, and peacefully, and in a year or two, not with everybody else in the place, violently, just a handful of months after she'd returned.

The Hierchon Ormilla was in exile on Nasqueron. The new top dog, this Archimandrite Luseferous guy, wanted the Hierchon to surrender. The Hierchon was refusing to cooperate. Archimandrite Luseferous didn't want to antagonise the Dwellers so he couldn't just attack or invade Nasqueron as well—amazingly, it seemed that the Dwellers, chaotic eccentrics and technological illiterates that they were supposed to be, were well able to defend themselves—so there was a stand-off. The Luseferous person couldn't go in, and Ormilla wouldn't come out.

Now the Archimandrite was threatening to destroy a city or a habitat every day until the Hierchon did surrender properly and gave himself up to the occupying forces. And if he didn't give in after a couple of days, it would become a city or a habitat every hour.

There were rumours that Afynseise, a small coastal city in Poroforo, Sepekte, had been destroyed the day before, though with an information blackout covering the habitat for the past three days, it was impossible to be sure.

Hab 4409 had eighty thousand or so inhabitants, making it a relatively small space habitat. It was second on the list of hostage population centres, and the midnight deadline was now only minutes away. Still no word from Ormilla after a defiant communiqué earlier that afternoon. A Starveling warship had been stationed near the habitat for the past two days, since the Archimandrite's ultimatum had been issued. Nothing and nobody had been allowed to leave—or approach—the hab in that time. A few craft had tried to leave, and been destroyed. No requests to evacuate children, the infirm or the collaborating civil authorities had been listened to. It had even been announced that anybody in a spacesuit or small craft who might survive the hab's initial destruction would be targeted in the debris and destroyed.

Nobody doubted that the Archimandrite would be true to his word. Few believed the Hierchon would give in so easily.

Thay let go of the cluster of hands she was holding—a withered old petal of a flower of the mostly young and fair—and bent, spine protesting, to take her shoes off. She kicked them away and put her hand back in the centre of the circle again. The grass felt cool and damp beneath her feet.

A lot of people were singing now, mostly quite low.

Lots of different songs.

Some crying, some sobbing, some wailing and screaming, most far away.

And somebody, ghoulish, counting the seconds to midnight.

It came, and seconds later a great ringing shaft of light, blinding-bright, cut right through the very centre of the hab, barely fifty metres from where Thay stood. She had to let go of the hands of the others to shield her eyes; they all did. A hot blast of air knocked her off her feet, sending her tumbling with hundreds of other people across the grass. The beam immediately split into two and moved quickly out to the habitat's perimeter on each side, detonating buildings, erupting flame from pod clusters and slicing the whole small world in two. The halves were pushed apart by the pressure of air in them and the atmosphere went whirling away into space in a twinned hurricane of gases, debris and bodies as buildings and pods exploded in two great retreating circles of effect making their way down the interior surfaces of the sundered halves, structures ripped open just by the force of the air inside them trying to get out.

Thay Hohuel was lifted up by the whirlwind of air and blown above the bubbling, lifting turf with everybody else, towards the quickly swelling breach. In the few seconds it took for her to be blown out into the darkness, she heard herself scream as the air went gushing from her lungs, sucked away to space. It was a high, hard, savage scream, louder than any she could have achieved just with her own muscles; a terrible chorus of pain and shock and fear, wrenched from her mouth and from the mouths of all those around her as they died together, the awful sound of them all only fading as the air bled from her ears into vacuum.

A vortex of bodies spun slowly out of the separating halves of the ruined habitat, jerking and twisting and spinning away in two long, scimitared comma shapes like some ballet of galactic design.

The images were beamed throughout the system by the occupying forces. The Hierchon formally surrendered the following day.

·

The Archimandrite Luseferous stood in the nose of the Main Battle Hub *Luseferous VII*, staring out at the vision-filling view of the planet Sepekte and its vast, dusty-looking, very occasionally glittering halo of habitats, orbital factories and satellites. The entire outer nose section of the *Luseferous VII* was diamond film, a bowed circle of breathtaking transparency a hundred metres in diameter and supported by finger-thin struts. The Archimandrite liked to come here alone, just to look out at stuff. At such moments he could sense the colossal bulk of the *Luseferous VII* behind him, all its kilometres and megatonnes, all its warrens of docks, tunnels, chambers, halls, barracks, magazines, turrets and launch tubes. It was a pity it might have to be destroyed.

The strategists and tacticians didn't like the look of the incoming Summed Fleet's drive signatures. There were a lot of heavy ships on their way, and the first might be here in weeks rather than the months—maybe even a year—they'd been hoping for. The *Luseferous VII*, magnificent though it undoubtedly was, represented an unignorable and probably unmissable target. Their best strategy might be to use the great ship as the bait in a trap, their own forces seemingly disposed so that it looked like they were determined to defend it to the last, but in fact treating it as a disposable asset. Lure in as much of the Mercatorial fleet as possible and then destroy everything, including, unfortunately, the *Luseferous VII* itself.

The admiral who'd drawn the short straw in whatever competition or pecking-order judgement they'd used to decide who had to offer this suggestion to the Archimandrite had looked distinctly queasy when he'd outlined the plan, obviously fearing an outburst of rage from his commander-in-chief. Luseferous had already heard of the idea—Tuhluer proving his usefulness again—and come to accept that if they were not to jeopardise their whole mission here, even ideas as drastic as this had at least to be entertained. So he'd just nodded and acknowledged that all options had to be considered. Relief for the admiral concerned. A degree of consternation for the others, who all wished that they'd made the announcement now.

They would try to think of other strategies which didn't involve the likely loss of the Main Battle Hub, but nobody seemed too optimistic. Always do what the enemy hoped you wouldn't. Murder your babies. That sort of thing. The logic seemed impeccable.

Well, he could always build another Main Battle Hub. Just a lump of matter. Results were what mattered. He wasn't a child. He wasn't sentimental about the *Luseferous VII*.

More worrying was whether even that sacrifice might be enough. They had control of Ulubis system, they had lost only a handful of ships in the invasion and, having captured a few of the enemy craft, had conceivably come out ahead in the deal. However, the Summed Fleet squadrons on their way comprised a formidable force. They had fewer but better ships. It might be quite a close battle, and only an idiot wanted to get involved in one of those. And so near! That had been a terrible, terrible shock.

Luseferous hadn't been able to believe it at first. He'd raged and fumed and spat, telling the techs to check and check again. There must be something wrong, there had to be an error. The Summed Fleet couldn't be that close. They'd been assured it would be half a year—a whole year, even—before they had to face the counter-attack. Instead the Summed Fleet was practically on top of them before they'd had time to settle in properly. Beyonder bastards. It had to be their fault. He would see what could be done about those treacherous fucks in due course. In the meantime, he had the counter-attack to worry about.

Of course, if by the time the Summed Fleet squadrons arrived they had what they'd come for, that might make all the difference.

A few weeks to find what they had come for. He had a very unpleasant feeling that this was not going to be long enough.

⁚

The ship thought it was dead. Fassin talked to it.

He'd hoped they might be able to make the return journey from the *Rovruetz* to Direaliete system faster than they'd made the outward trip, because the Voehn ship was quicker than the *Velpin*, but it was not to be. The *Protreptic* could accelerate faster than the *Velpin*, but the injuries the Voehn commander had inflicted on Y'sul meant the Dweller wouldn't be able to survive the stresses. They went back slower than they'd come out.

Y'sul lay in a healing coma in an improvised cradle that Quercer & Janath had made for him within one of the extended command-space seats. They ramped the acceleration up to five gees, coasted while they checked the Dweller wasn't suffering further damage from the stresses involved, took the next smoothly incremented ramp of acceleration up to ten gees and checked again. Finally they settled on forty gees, though by the time they'd worked out that this was safe they were almost at the point where they would have to turn around and start decelerating again as they fell towards the waiting system.

Y'sul slept on, healing. The AI truetwin gloried in the exploration of the Voehn ship's vastly complicated systems and multifarious martial capabilities.

Fassin had nothing to do but float in his own extemporised acceleration cradle in the seat next to Y'sul's. He wouldn't be allowed to stay there as they approached the wormhole portal; Quercer & Janath had found a tight little cabin a few bulkheads back from the command space where he could wait that particular experience out. In the meantime, after some complaints, they allowed him to interface with the *Protreptic*'s computer, though they insisted on this being at several removes from the ship's core systems, and on him being accompanied by some sort of sub-personality of their own. The visits would be conducted in a factor two or three of slowdown, which seemed to suit everybody concerned. At least, Fassin thought, the journey would seem to go quicker.

The virtual environment where Fassin was allowed to meet the ship took the form of a huge, half-ruined temple by a wide, slow-moving river on the edge of a great, quiet, silent city under a small, high, unmoving sun of an intense blue-white.

Fassin represented as his human self, dressed in house casuals, the ship as a skinny old man in a loincloth and the AI sub-routine as some sort of ginger-haired ape with long, loose-looking limbs, an ancient, too-big helmet wobbling on its head, a dented breastplate with one broken strap slanting across its bulbous chest and a short kilt of segmented leather hanging from its skinny hips. A short, rusty sword dangled from its side.

The first time Fassin had visited the ship's personality, the ape had led him by the hand from a doorway down the steps towards the river where the old man sat, looking out at the sluggish brown waters.

On the far side of the broad, oily stream was a desert of brightly glittering broken glass, stretching in low, billowed hills as far as the eye could see, like all the shattered glass the universe had ever known all gathered in the one vast place.

"Of course I'm dead," the ship explained. The old man had very dark green skin and a voice made up of sighs and wheezes. His face was nearly immobile, just an aged mask, grizzled with patchy white whiskers. "The ship self-destructed."

"But if you're dead," Fassin said, "how are you talking to me?"

The old man shrugged. "To be dead is to be no longer part of the living world. It is to be a shade, a ghost. It doesn't mean you can't talk. Talk is almost all you can do."

Fassin thought the better of trying to persuade the old man that he was still alive. "What do you think I am?" he asked.

The old man looked at him. "A human? Male? A man."

Fassin nodded. "Do you have a name?" he asked the old man.

A shake of the head. "Not any more. I was the *Protreptic* but that ship is gone now and I am dead, so I have no name."

Fassin left a polite gap for the old man to ask him what his name was, but the inquiry didn't come.

The ape sat a couple of metres away and two steps further up towards the creeper-festooned temple. It was sitting back, taking its weight on its long arms spread out behind it and picking one ear with a long, delicate-looking foot, inspecting the results with great concentration.

"When you were alive," Fassin said, "were you truly alive? Were you sentient?"

The old man rocked backwards, laughed briefly. "Bless you, no. I was just software in a computer, just photons inside a nanofoam substrate. That's not alive, not in the conventional sense."

"What about the unconventional sense?"

Another shrug. "That does not matter. Only the conventional sense matters."

"Tell me about yourself, about your life."

A blank-faced stare. "I don't have a life. I'm dead."

"Then tell me about the life you had."

"I was a needle ship called the *Protreptic* of the Voehn Third Spine Cessorian Lustral Squadron, built in the fifth tenth of the third year of Haralaud, in the Vertebraean Axis, Khubohl III, Bunsser Minor. I was an extensible fifteen-metre-minimum craft, rated ninety-eight per cent by the Standard Portal Compatibility Quotient Measure, normal unstowed operating diameter—"

"I didn't really mean all the technical stuff," Fassin said gently.

"Oh," said the old man, and disappeared, just like a hologram being switched off.

Fassin looked at the ape, which was holding something up to the light. It looked down at him, blinking. "What?" it said.

"He disappeared," Fassin told it. "It disappeared. The old man; the ship."

"Prone to do that," the ape said, sighing.


The next time, the landscape on the far side of the wide, slack-watered river from the temple steps was a jungle; a great green, yellow and purple wall of strange carbuncular stalks, drooping leaves and coiled vines, its bowed, pendulous creepers and branches drooping down to drag in the slow swell of the current.

Everything else was as before, though perhaps the old man was less skinny, his face a fraction more mobile and his voice less tired.

"I was an AI hunter. For six and a half thousand years I helped seek out and destroy the anathematics. If I could have felt such an emotion, I would have been very proud."

"Did it never seem strange to you to be hunting down and killing machines that were similar to yourself?"

The ginger-haired ape—sitting in its usual place a few steps up, trying to clean its stained, dented armour by spitting on it and then polishing it with a filthy rag—coughed at this point, though when Fassin glanced up at the animal it returned his gaze blankly.

"But I was just a computer," the old man said, frowning. "Less than that, even; a ghost within it. I did what I was told, always obedient. I was the interface between the Voehn who did the thinking and made the decisions, and the physical structures and systems of the ship. An intermediary. No more."

"Do you miss that?"

"In a way. I cannot, really. To miss something, truly, would be—as I understand it—to experience an emotion, and obviously that is impossible for something which is not sentient, let alone not alive as well. But to the extent that I can judge that one state of affairs is somehow more preferable to another, perhaps because one allows me to fulfil the role I was assigned and one does not, I could say that I miss the ship. It's gone. I've looked for it, but it isn't there. I cannot feel it or control it, therefore I know that it must have self-destructed. I must be running on another substrate somewhere."

Fassin looked up at the ape-thing sitting a few steps away. Quercer & Janath had taken over full control of the *Protreptic*, cutting off the ship's own computer and the software running within it from the vessel's subsystems.

"What do you think I am, then?" Fassin asked. "What do you think the little ape in his armour sitting behind us is?"

"I don't know," the old man confessed. "Are you other dead ships?"

Fassin shook his head. "No."

"Then perhaps you are representations of those in charge of the substrate I am now running on. You may want to quiz me on my actions while I was the ship."

"You know, you seem alive to me," Fassin said. "Are you sure you might not be alive and sentient now, now that you're not connected to the ship?"

"Of course not!" the old man said scornfully. "I am able to give the appearance of life without being alive. It is not especially difficult."

"How do you do this?"

"By being able to access my memories, by having trillions of facts and works and books and recordings and sentences and words and definitions at my disposal." The old man looked at the ends of his fingers. "I am the sum of all my memories, plus the application of certain rules from a substantial command-set. I am blessed with the ability to think extremely quickly, so I am able to listen to what you, as a conscious, sentient being, are saying and then respond in a way that makes sense to you, answering your questions, following your meaning, anticipating your thoughts.

"However, all this is simply the result of programs—programs written by sentient beings—sifting through earlier examples of conversations and exchanges which I have stored within my memories and selecting those which seem most appropriate as templates. This process sounds mysterious but is merely complicated. It begins with something as simple as you saying 'Hello' and me replying 'Hello', or choosing something similar according to whatever else I might know about you, and extends to a reply as involved as, well, this one."

The old man looked suddenly shocked, and disappeared again.

Fassin looked up at the ginger-haired ape. It sneezed and then had a coughing fit. "Nothing," it said, "to do," it continued, between coughs, "with me."

On Fassin's next visit, the far side of the great, slow river was like a mirror image of the side that he, the old man and the gangly ape were on. An ancient city of stone domes and spires—all silent and dark and half-consumed by trees and creepers—faced them, and a huge long temple, covered in statues and carvings of fabulous and unlikely beasts, lay directly across from where they sat, its lower limits defined by dozens of big stone terraces and steps leading down to the sluggish, dark brown waters.

Fassin looked over, to see if the three of them were reflected there, but they weren't. The far side was deserted.

"Did you hunt down and kill many AIs?" he asked.

The old man rolled his eyes. "Hundreds. Thousands."

"You're not sure?"

"Some of the AIs were twinned or in larger groupings. I took part in 872 missions."

"Were any in gas-giants?" Fassin asked. He'd positioned himself so that he could see the ape in the dented armour. It looked at him when he asked this question, then looked away again. It was trying to knock the dents out of its breastplate with a small hammer. The dull chink-chink-chinks that the hammer made sounded dead and unechoing across the wide river.

"One mission took place partly within a gas-giant. It ended there. A small ship full of anathematics. We pursued them into the atmosphere of the gas-giant Dejiminid where they attempted to lose us within its fierce storm-winds. The *Protreptic* was more atmosphere-capable than their ship, and eventually, going to greater and greater depths in their desperation to shake us off, their vessel collapsed under the pressure and was crushed, taking all aboard into the liquid metal depths."

"Were there no Dwellers present to complain about this?"

The old man looked inquiringly at him. "You are not really a Dweller, are you? It did occur to me that I might be running within a Dweller-controlled substrate."

"No, I'm not a Dweller. I told you; I'm a human."

"Well, the answer is they had not seen us enter their planet. They complained later. That was only the first of two occasions when the *Protreptic* was operationally active within a gas-giant. Usually our missions were all vacuum."

"The other?"

"Not so long ago. Helping to pursue a large force of Beyonder ships in the vicinity of Zateki. We prevailed there, too."

"What brought you to the Sepulcraft *Rovruetz*?" Fassin asked.

The flat and flattening chink-chink-chink noise stopped. The ginger-haired ape held its breastplate up to catch the light, scratched its chest, then went back to tapping with the hammer again.

"Do you represent a Lustral Investigation Board?" the old man asked. "Is that what you are, in reality?"

"No," Fassin said. "I don't."

"Oh. Oh well. For the last two and a half centuries, uniform time," the old man said, "we had been seeking information about the so-called Dweller List." (The long-limbed ape laughed out loud at this, but the old man didn't seem to notice.) "Much time was spent in the region of the Zateki system, investigating the Second Ship theory. Various secondary and tertiary missions resulted from information gleaned in the region. None ever bore fruit in the matter of the List, the Second Ship theory or the so-called Transform, though two AIs were tracked down and eliminated in the course of these sub-missions. We were summoned from the Rijom system and sent to the Direaliete system some five months ago, then laid an intercept course to the Sepulcraft *Rovruetz*. I was not told of the reasons for this course of action, the orders covering which were personal to Commander Inialcah and communicated to him beyond my senses."

"Did you find out anything new about the List and the Transform?" Fassin asked.

"I think the only thing that we ever felt we had properly discovered, in the sense of adding something other than just an extra rumour to the web of myths and rumours that already existed regarding the whole subject, was that—if there was any truth in the matter—the portals would be lying quiescent and perhaps disguised in the Kuiper belts or Oort clouds of the relevant systems, waiting on a coded radio or similar broadcast signal. That is what the so-called Transform would be: a signal, and the medium and frequency on which it was to be transmitted. This made sense in that all normally stable locations where portals might have been hidden successfully over the sort of time scales involved—Lagrange points and so on—were easy to check and eliminate." The old man looked at Fassin quizzically again. "Are you another seeker after the truth of the List?"

"I was," Fassin said.

"Ah!" The representation of the old man looked pleased for once. "And are you not dead, then, too?"

"No, I'm not dead, though I've given up looking, for the moment."

"What was it that took you to the Sepulcraft *Rovruetz*?" the old man asked.

"I had what I thought was a lead, a clue, a way forward," Fassin told him. "However, the creature who might have had the evidence had destroyed what he held and killed himself."

"Unfortunate."

"Yes, very."

The old man looked up at the bronze-blue cloudless sky. Fassin followed his gaze, and as he did so, the old man disappeared.

There was something. Fassin sat, gascraft rammed into the extemporised couch in the Voehn ship's command space by the continuing acceleration, watching the nearly static, rather boring view of dead ahead shown on the main screen, and he knew there was something that he was missing.

Something nagged at him, something bothered him, something half-came to him in moments of distraction or when he was dreaming, and then wriggled away again before he could catch it.

He didn't sleep very much—only a couple of hours a day in all—though when he did there were usually dreams, as if his subconscious had to cram all his dreaming into the small amount of dream-space available. Once he was actually standing in a small stream, somewhere in the gardens of a great house he couldn't see, trousers rolled up, trying to catch fish with his bare hands. The fish were his dreams, even though he was distantly aware at the time that this situation was itself a dream. When he tried to catch the fish— sinuous small presences darting like elongated teardrops of mercury round his feet—they kept flicking away and disappearing.

When he looked up, the stream was flowing through a large amphitheatre, and a great crowd of people were watching him intently.

At the transition point of the journey, where the *Protreptic* stopped accelerating, turned a half-somersault and pointed its engines at its destination to start deceleration, Quercer & Janath spent some time checking that Y'sul was still healing satisfactorily.

Fassin used the time to explore a little more of the Voehn ship, floating the arrowhead gascraft down the narrow circular access tubes, investigating crew quarters, storerooms and chambers. Camera remotes tracked his every move, the thoroughly internally surveillanced ship making it simple for Quercer & Janath to keep whatever fraction of an eye on him they thought appropriate.

He found what he thought was probably the commander's cabin, a couple of bulkheads behind the command space. It was the most generously proportioned obviously personal space he'd encountered. It looked bare and alien. There was a slightly more comfortable version of one of the multi-spine cradle seats he was used to seeing throughout the ship by now, and some representations of coverings on certain walls, plus what might have been carpet designs on the floor. Only the designs existed, painted on or displayed by some thin-film technology—Fassin couldn't tell. Similarly, there were no ornaments, just holos of ornaments. He'd heard most warships were like this; cutting down on weight and the possibilities of stuff flying about during hard manoeuvring by having the appearance of things rather than their physical presence.

He floated in front of one carpet design that looked like a piece of text, all small, curled glyphs in a network, but could find no record in the gascraft's memories of such a language. He wondered what it said. He recorded the image. Quercer & Janath would probably wipe it when they went through the portal, but never mind.

The next time he met up with the ship, on the far side of the river there was a massive dark wall, rising sheer and jet from the waters, its summit crowned with crenellations and gun turrets. Further guns poked out of gun ports distributed in staggered lines over the whole top quarter of the huge wall, making it look like the side of some ancient sea-ship, only the biggest and most preposterously long one there had ever been, its vast hull diminishing into the distance. The guns were not static but moved in sequence, in waves of what appeared almost like locomotion, making the exposed barrels look oddly like ineffectual oars on some colossally mis-designed trireme or an impossible, upended millipede.

The ginger-haired ape sat nearby as usual. It had a new shield, round and highly polished. It sat looking at it and flicking imaginary specks from it. Sometimes it held it up to see it sparkle in the light, and sometimes it held it up so that it could look at itself in it.

"Text?" the elderly man asked. "On a floor display? No, I'm sorry, I don't have any memory of that, not stored. If the ship still existed, if I still had access…" He looked sad. Fassin glanced at the ginger-haired ape, but it looked away and started whistling, or at least trying to.

"Maybe there's some way I can patch through an image I have," Fassin said.

"You have an image? You have been on the ship?" The man looked surprised.

After some to-ing and fro-ing, Fassin having to jog back up the step and through the doorway back into normal reality to set things up, he was able to display the image he'd taken. The long-limbed ape held up his shield and the image appeared there.

"Oh, *that*?" the man said. He stroked his short grey beard. "That's something the Commander picked up a long time ago, in the days when he had command of a smaller ship. A translation into Ancient Sacred of something which I believe marks the end of an abomination, an AI."

"What does it say?" Fassin asked.

"It says, 'I was born in a water moon. Some people, especially its inhabitants, called it a planet, but as it was only a little over two hundred kilometres in diameter, "moon" seems the more accurate term. The moon was made entirely of water, by which I mean it was a globe that not only had no land, but no rock either, a sphere with no solid core at all, just liquid water, all the way down to the very centre of the globe.

" 'If it had been much bigger the moon would have had a core of ice, for water, though supposedly incompressible, is not entirely so, and will change under extremes of pressure to become ice. (If you are used to living on a planet where ice floats on the surface of water, this seems odd and even wrong, but nevertheless it is the case.) This moon was not quite of a size for an ice core to form, and therefore one could, if one was sufficiently hardy, and adequately proof against the water pressure, make one's way down, through the increasing weight of water above, to the very centre of the moon.

" 'Where a strange thing happened.

" 'For here, at the very centre of this watery globe, there seemed to be no gravity. There was colossal pressure, certainly, pressing in from every side, but one was in effect weightless (on the outside of a planet, moon or other body, watery or not, one is always being pulled towards its centre; once at its centre one is being pulled equally in all directions), and indeed the pressure around one was, for the same reason, not quite as great as one might have expected it to be, given the mass of water that the moon was made up from.

" 'This was, of course,—'

"At which point it cuts off."

Fassin thought. "Where did it come from?"

"It was used by one of the anathematics that Commander Inialcah hunted down and killed as a kind of memory-death mantra, to remove any trace of what might have been in its memory. The AI concerned later turned out to have been one of those also seeking the so-called Transform. It was that pursuit which originally gave the commander an interest in the matter. The memory-death mantra he had translated and kept partly as a kind of talisman, though I believe he also always thought there might be some meaning to the specific piece the AI chose to overwrite its memories with which might prove useful if he could ever work it out, because AIs were known, as he said, for being too clever by half, and through their arrogance sometimes gave important information away. That was another reason for preserving it and keeping it constantly before him."

In his dream, Fassin was standing with Saluus Kehar on a balcony over a volcanic caldera, full of red-hot bubbling lava. "We're to gas-capable a whole load of stuff for—" Sal was saying, when he paused, cleared his throat and waved one hand. "Heck," he continued, turning into a Dweller, but somehow with a human face and without getting any bigger. He floated out over the waves of lava. "Idiotic things, little Fassin. I took the original of the beast to a friend and fellow friend in the city of Direaliete. A friend and fellow friend."

Fassin gazed at his own hands, to check that he was still himself.

When he looked up, Saluus had gone and the river he was standing in had temples on both sides, up steep flights of steps the height of prison walls.

"Original of what?" he heard himself ask.

The far side of the river showed a city from the age of waste, all medium-rise buildings, smoke and electric trains and multi-lane roads full of roaring cars and trucks. They had to raise their voices a little to make themselves heard over the noise. A sweet, oily burning smell wafted over the river towards them.

The ginger ape picked its gleaming teeth with a giant sword.

"Another image?" the man said. He looked fit in a lean way and was no longer young. His beard was mostly grey. "Let me see."

Knowing what to do this time, Fassin showed the man the little image-leaf which depicted yellow sky and brown clouds.

"Obviously the colour's wrong," he told the man. "I couldn't help noticing."

"Oh, yes, there's an image there. I see it."

"I know, but what—?"

"And some algebra, ciphered into the base code."

At that, the ape's long, curved sword came sweeping down and cut the man through, slicing him from neck to hip. The remains gushed down the steps to the river and wriggled away, all silver.

Fassin looked up at the great ape. "Hey," he said, "it was just a—"

"Who's clever?" the ape hissed, drawing back the terrible, glittering sword.

Fassin woke up shaking. He was in a coffin—he'd just hit his head on the inside of the lid. He tried to blink and couldn't because something was in his eyes, surrounding them, surrounding every part of him, filling his mouth and nose and anus…

Shock-gel, gillfluid, the gascraft. *Fucking calm down*, he told himself. *How long you been a Seer again?*

The *Protreptic*, the ex-Voehn craft en route for Nasqueron, Ulubis via the Direaliete system, under the command of the self-confessed twin AI Quercer & Janath, pirates and close-combat Voehn-wasting specialists.

They were back under moderate deceleration, on their way into the system and the hidden wormhole.

The details of the dream were starting to slip away from him, fish sine-waving goodbye through the water. And yet he felt he'd understood something. What had it been?

Confusing.

Something about Saluus, and had Hatherence been in there too? Sal's house, only it had been a volcano, then the virtual environment where he met the ship, and it had looked at—

In the shock-gel, pickled in it, surrounded by it, Fassin felt his eyes go wide and his skin prickle and crawl. His heart spasmed, thudding erratically in his chest.

He could do it himself. He could wait until they got back, back to Nasq. and Ulubis, and take it to somebody—if he found Valseir he could just ask him, though he didn't think he'd be able to find Valseir—but that wasn't good enough. He had to know.

He'd committed the image-leaf to the gascraft's memory. Lying there in the shock-gel, inside the little arrowhead, he called the photograph up and saw it floating before him. The picture of blue sky and white clouds looked odd to him, half-alien and wrong, and yet half-familiar at the same time, invoking a feeling of something between nostalgia and homesickness.

He blew the image up to the point where it became a blocky abstract of colour. He scanned the whole image for smaller images, found nothing, then started running various routines that the gascraft's biomind held for finding patterns in random data. Had he recorded the image in fine enough detail to find anything hidden in it? Would the hidden data, if it was there, be findable without some other code?

He wished he could access the original, stowed in a tiny locker on the outside of the gascraft, but he couldn't, not while he was pinned under this sort of force. Anyway, it might look suspicious to Quercer & Janath if he started peering too intently at the image-leaf. Because that was where the answer might lie, where it might—just, perhaps, maybe—have been lying all the time.

"…I took the original of the folder to a friend and fellow collector in Deilte, a city in the south polar region, within a safekeep box…" That, or something very like it, was what Valseir had said.

Fassin had recorded the conversation verbatim in the gascraft's memory, but it had been wiped aboard the *Isaut*. Didn't matter; he had a pretty good memory for detail himself. He hadn't realised at the time what the implication of Valseir's remark was—the Mercatorial ships had tried to mount their raid on the ships in the storm fleet shortly afterwards and things had all gone a bit exciting—but it meant there was probably a copy. Valseir was a scholar, and punctilious about word use and the terminology of editions and precedence. He wouldn't have talked about the original of something unless there was a need to distinguish it from a copy. So there was a copy. There was a back-up, and it had amused the old Dweller to have Fassin carry it with him all the time.

Well, it was a plausible-enough theory.

Fassin thought it would be a Valseir-like thing to have done, but he'd been wrong about the old Dweller before. Dwellers did become set in their ways and predictable, sometimes, given the ages they could live to, but sometimes they just became more devious, too.

He fell asleep, the routines running on in front of him, and dreamed of streams of numbers, liquid algebra full of equations and meanings that started to make sense and then—just as he tried to study them and understand them—broke up and wriggled away, flickering to chaos.

A soft chime woke him up.

He was in the gascraft, in the stolen Voehn ship. The deceleration felt gentler, as though they might be approaching their goal. He clicked to an outside view and saw an orange-red sun, dead ahead. The Dweller-shaped bulk in the seat ahead twisted fractionally.

"Fassin?" Quercer & Janath said.

If he hadn't been in the shock-gel inside the gascraft, he'd have jumped.

"Mmm?" he said.

"Going to have to put you in your own little cell for the next bit, all right?"

"Yes. I understand."

"Soon as we're at one gee standard."

"I hear and obey," he said, trying to sound unconcerned.

Back in the gascraft's math-space, Fassin had a result.

There was indeed data hidden in the image-leaf's depiction of a partially clouded blue sky. It had been there all the time. He'd had the answer, if that was really what it was, with him from the start.

It looked like alien algebra.

He tried to understand it.

It meant nothing.

It might mean everything.

:

The Archimandrite Luseferous had a tight, unpleasant feeling in his guts. He recognised it. It was the feeling that he got when he might have left something too late, or just got something wrong somehow. It was the feeling of being in a game and realising you might have made a terrible mistake a couple of turns or moves ago, of wanting to go back and undo what had been done, right the wrong, fix the error.

When he'd been a child playing a game against another child and had made a mistake, he'd sometimes just say, "Oh, look, I didn't mean to do that earlier, I meant to do *this*..." and had discovered that even though such behaviour might be forbidden by the rules of the game, you could get away with it amazingly often. At first he'd thought this was because he was just a more powerful character than whoever he was playing against, until he'd realised that the people this sort of tactic worked against tended to be those whose fathers weren't nearly as powerful as his. Later he'd become powerful himself, and found that cheating was still a workable tactic. Later still, he'd found that he didn't need to cheat. He could make the most awful blunder and never suffer for it because his opponent, guessing what was good for them in the greater context of life beyond the game, would never dare take advantage of that mistake. It was a kind of invincibility.

Machines were different; they usually wouldn't let you make illegal moves or take back earlier errors. So you just reset them, or went back to the saved position or a time when the mistake could be unmade.

Only this was not a game, or—if it was—it was one in which Luseferous didn't know how you changed the rules or swept your arm across the board or hit the *Delete All* sequence. Maybe the end of the game was death, and he'd wake to find himself in the greater reality that the Truth had always maintained existed. That was a sort of comfort, though even then he didn't want to wake up after a failure.

Time was the problem. Time and the fucking Dwellers.

The *Luseferous VII* swung ponderously into orbit around the planet Nasqueron. He watched it from his new flagship, the Main Fleet Combat Craft *Rapacious* (a super-battleship in all but name, he'd be prepared to concede).

Insufficient time. How had it come to this? If he hadn't delayed so long before starting, if he hadn't stopped off along the way, if he hadn't, perhaps, insisted on full fleet dispositional discipline... and yet he'd swung into action much more quickly than some democratic or committee-based organisation could have, and he would have been mad to leave strongholds intact along his line of advance and... and return. And discipline was important, keeping everything together was important. It symbolised loyalty, it betokened military and personal discipline.

So there had been no choice, really. They'd got here as quickly as they could. The fucking Beyonders should have warned him the Summed Fleet squadrons were coming quicker than they'd anticipated. It was all their doing. It might even be a conspiracy against him. Oh, they'd taken part in the attacks on Ulubis when it had suited them, though they'd never been as decisive as they could and should have been. Fucking whining lily-livered moralists. Military targets! So they preserved their precious fucking scruples and left him to do the dirty work. If they'd been as emphatic and ruthless as he'd been, things might have turned out differently. Instead they'd supported him just enough to bring him here but now that he was where they'd wanted him all along, they were deserting him.

Luseferous wished now that he hadn't let the Liss woman go. He'd given Saluus Kehar, the industrialist guy, back to his own people, largely to see what they'd do. Would they believe him when he told them he'd been kidnapped? Or not? Jury still out; the Guard had taken him for questioning. The woman who'd kidnapped him, and who had asked to take him back personally when she'd heard that was what the Archimandrite had in mind, had disappeared before she'd even handed him over, probably returning to her Beyonder pals. Stupid to have let a potential lever like that go, but he'd had so many other things on his mind, and the full extent of the Beyonders' betrayal hadn't been clear at the time.

Where were their craft? Where were their invasion troops or occupying forces? They were still staying on the outskirts, still not coming into the system itself, still too scared to commit themselves. They'd professed horror and disappointment at his destruction of the city and the habitat, and at the way his troops had reacted to some elements of resistance. Fuck them! This was a fucking war! How the fuck did they think you won one? Casualties had been almost disappointingly *light*; Luseferous couldn't remember a full-scale invasion campaign which had ended with so few dead. They'd arrived in such overwhelming numbers that there had been little the other side could do apart from die pointlessly, surrender or run.

They'd had a bit of luck, too, and the intelligence provided by the Beyonders about military preparations and fleet dispositions had made a bit of a difference as well, he supposed. But basically it was just big guns and plenty of them that had done the trick, and the really impressive space battles he'd kind of been hoping for just hadn't materialised.

So the system was his, even if the only ground he'd trodden personally was when making one brief appearance at a small mansion in the middle of a jungle to accept the formal surrender of the Hierchon. He'd have preferred the symbolic value of the big spherical palace in Borquille, even if it was damaged, but the security people felt there was still a danger from a well-hidden nuke or something equally unpleasant, so a house in the middle of nowhere it had been. The Hierchon and his people were being held aboard the *Luseferous VII*. Let the Summed Fleet kill him if that was the way it had to be.

The Beyonders reported that there had been a few engagements with elements of the Ulubine Mercatoria military which had turned tail to run and then encountered their forces. But even there the Archimandrite was hearing rumours that the fleeing Navarchy ships were being allowed to surrender, or even accept a sort of neutral internment, still fully crewed and armed, rather than being destroyed or captured.

So Luseferous was alone again, abandoned by his treacherous allies. They'd lured him here, got him to remove part of the threat against them, and now no doubt hoped that he'd take on the Summed Fleet squadrons when they arrived, doing the work they were too cowardly to do themselves.

Well, the strategists and tacticians were seriously considering cutting their losses and heading back home again. This would seem ignominious to some, but if it was the best thing to be done then that was all there was to it. Again, he'd kept calm when he'd first heard this latest galling concept. He wasn't stupid; he could see the situation for himself. Do what the enemy least expected, what they would least want you to do.

They might—it was still just a might—set off back for the relative safety of Epiphany 5, far away across the empty regions of space they'd spent all those years crossing. It would be unfortunate, but it might be the best thing to do all the same. They'd have to leave a lot of ships behind and they'd certainly have to abandon the *Luseferous VII*—it was too slow and too tempting a target—but they could do it. They'd leave behind sufficient forces to force the Summed Fleet to first fight within the system and then station some craft there, they'd take only the fastest ships and so have a head start, and they'd hope to lure away the main part of the remainder of the Summed Fleet squadrons—the bit that would be likely to come after them—by sending the *Luseferous VII* and a small escort screen of lesser ships off in a different direction.

It was a horrible thing to have to think about, this running away so soon after getting here and achieving complete victory. But it might be better than standing and fighting when the outcome of the resulting battle was so finely balanced.

Or, of course, they could find what they had really come for. This Dweller List key, this Transform, this magic formula. With that in his possession, Luseferous would have a bargaining counter of almost infinite value. So he was told, anyway, and for the sake of their own hides his advisers had better be utterly spot-on right with this one. Literally. He'd have the fuckers skinned alive if they'd led him all this way for nothing.

In the meantime, one last throw, one final chance to find what they'd come for. All far too rushed and desperate, but—like all the greatest leaders—the Archimandrite knew that he was at his best when he was under pressure, when the odds were against him and victory was far from certain. Of course, this didn't happen very often to him because he didn't allow it to—always better to win easily—but he'd had his share of narrow victories and pressure situations in the past and come out on top, and he hadn't forgotten and he certainly hadn't lost his touch. He knew he would prevail. He always did. Victory was the only thinkable option.

He could do it. He just had to be decisive and determined. That was what he was best at. It was almost better this way; with so little time, with just the one chance, there was no question that it had to be an all-or-nothing, no-holds-barred approach. There was simply no time to go through all the other more "reasonable" techniques. Forget playing it calm and quiet, fuck diplomacy, abandon all thought of being reasonable and hoping people would be reasonable in return. Just fucking do it.

The Archimandrite had made his preparations as best he could. The tacticians thought the first elements of the Summed Fleet could be hurtling past at near-light speed in less than a dozen days, with the rest not far behind. No more waiting. It was now or never.

They were in the belly of the great ship. The hideous, swirling, hallucinogenic face of Nasqueron lay beneath their feet, visible through diamond film. The Archimandrite had risked coming aboard the *Luseferous VII* for this. If there was some attack on it—unlikely, but not impossible, so far ahead of the main part of the Summed Fleet squadrons—then it would almost certainly have to come from above, and the sheer bulk of the vessel ought to protect them. He had the *Rapacious* waiting immediately underneath the main hull nearby, linked by a short ship-to-ship. He could be out of his impressively large seat, across the chamber and aboard and away in a minute. To be on the safe side, he had dressed in an emergency esuit, a thin, constrictive but reassuring presence beneath his formal robes. The collar-helmet was hidden by his cowl, which, like the rest of his outer garment, was made of tanned Voehn blizzardskin.

Cradled against the *Rapacious*, now that it had been fully checked for bugs and bombs, was the ship that the Liss woman had used to bring the man Saluus Kehar to him. The tech people were very impressed with it. They thought it could probably outrun any ship the other side had. Luseferous would have been more impressed if it could outrun any missile or beam the other side had.

They were here for a conference, a meeting ostensibly to discuss how the new regime in power within the rest of Ulubis system might liaise with the Dwellers.

The Hierchon Ormilla was present, as was the rest of the surviving Mercatoria top brass. There hadn't really been time to start serious alterations on the Mercatorial power structure, and when he'd found that, as the Beyonders had reported, the Mercatoria was disliked and resented by most of its citizens/subjects, but not actively hated by them, Luseferous had left the bulk of the civil authorities in place. The main players had all pledged allegiance to him, apart from Fleet Admiral Brimiaice, who'd been killed in action, the Shrievalty colonel Somjomion, who'd disappeared and was probably on one of the ships that had run away, and the Cessorian Clerk-Regnant, Voriel, who'd chosen death rather than what he seemed to regard as the dishonour of recanting his religious vows. Idiot. Luseferous had shot him himself.

He'd had some of the people who'd been involved in the Dweller Embassy—set up a few months before the invasion—brief him on what to expect from the floats. Most of the Embassy people had been killed when the commander of the ship they were in had refused to surrender, but a few had survived. Luseferous wasn't sure he trusted them, though.

Three of his own top half-dozen commanders were present too. The rest were engaged elsewhere, keeping an armed presence wherever it might be needed and preparing for the anticipated high-speed pass-through of the Summed Fleet's advance units.

No Beyonders, of course. They were still in shock from his unconscionable behaviour in the matter of the single small city and a habitat full of artists, weirdos and do-gooders. He must tell them he'd only chosen the city—whatever it was called, he'd forgotten—because it was on the coast and sheltered by mountains, so that he could do his sculpting trick again. That would horrify them all over again, with luck.

The—delegates? representatives? whatever the fuck they were—from the Dweller side were an unprepossessing bunch. They looked big and impressive, especially in their giant wheel-like esuits, but there was the—apparently perennial—Dweller problem of finding somebody with sufficient authority to speak for a whole planet. He'd learned early on in his career that Dwellers were best avoided. Leave them alone and they'd leave you alone. He wouldn't have chosen to have anything whatsoever to do with the damn floats if he could possibly have avoided it. But he couldn't, so he was doing his best.

Present were three Dwellers. All were supposedly as senior as each other, and they were each alone—no aides or secretaries or underlings of any sort, which with any other species would have indicated that these were not serious people at all but with Dwellers meant nothing in particular.

They were Feurish, some sort of political scholar who spoke for the great red-brown equatorial band they could see beneath them, Chintsion, who was the current chief-of-chiefs of an umbrella organisation representing all their clubs and other voluntary organisations (sounded insulting, but allegedly their "clubs" included their supposedly highly effective military) and Peripule, who was the City Administrator of their largest city, though this was not a capital city in the accepted sense, and apparently being voted to be City Administrator was regarded as an imposition, not an honour or a chance to enjoy power. They all had grandiose-sounding titles that didn't really mean anything. All they did was tell you how old the Dwellers were.

The Archimandrite would have preferred more obviously senior people— if such a thing existed in Dweller society—and more of them, but he had to work with what was to hand, especially given the time constraints. They did have other Dwellers on the *Luseferous VII*, however—over three hundred of them. Two whole shiploads of adolescents and young adults had been welcomed aboard for an extended tour as part of what sounded like a school trip for grown-ups. An alien-ship enthusiasts club, apparently. He would never have allowed this normally.

Luseferous was fairly certain that he didn't really have the Dwellers' full attention. His alien-watching experts advised him that the majority of the population of Nasqueron was unconcerned about the small war that had just taken place and the presence of the invasion fleet. In fact, the majority didn't even know what had happened and would be unlikely to care. The planet's news services, such as they were, were full of reports concerning something called a Formal War taking place between two of the atmospheric bands. This appeared to be a form of extreme sport played out on a vast scale, rather than what Luseferous would regard as a proper war. They were playing.

Well, he would just have to see what he could do to make them take proper notice of him.

Suspended over the vast view, the attendees seemed to hang as though about to fall. Above them, on a network of gantries, Luseferous's personal guard stalked in exoskels, the pads of their claw-feet stalking with a steady, silent precision.

"Let's get to the point," Luseferous said after some desultory inconsequentialities had gone on far too long. "We want the Seer Fassin Taak," he told the Dwellers. "Even more to the point, we want certain information he's supposed to have been looking for."

"What information?" Chintsion asked. The "clubs" chief was proving the most voluble of the three Dwellers so far. His huge esuit sat cradled in a sling-seat poised over the shallow concavity of diamond film beneath, the planet's bilious reflected light shining faintly up from underneath him. His esuit was grey, with garish pink chevrons.

"We are not at liberty to divulge that," Luseferous told the Dweller.

"Why not?" asked the scholar, Feurish. His esuit was a kind of dirty white.

"I can't tell you," Luseferous said. He held up a gloved, ringed hand. "And please don't ask why. Just accept this."

The Dwellers were silent. They were probably signalling to each other. His tech people had warned him of this and had attempted to design the sling-seats so that the creatures couldn't communicate like that. But as soon as the Dwellers had seen the seating arrangements they'd protested and fussed and started pulling and prodding and attempting to reconfigure their seats and even began rearranging them so that they were in positions relative to each other which they liked better. Luseferous had ground his diamond teeth, signalled to the tech people to help, and waited for the Dwellers to declare themselves happy.

Finally they were all sitting in a great circle, the Dwellers and the Hierchon and his handful of advisers forming most of one half of the circumference, the humans and others, including the Archimandrite, making up the other half.

"We don't know where Seer Fassin Taak is," Chintsion told Luseferous. "Last heard of, he was making for a city in the northern polar region called Eponia. Though that is just a rumour."

"Eponia?" the third Dweller, Peripule, said. His esuit was deep, gleaming brown, frilled like seaweed. "I heard he was seen in Deilte."

"Deilte?" Chintsion said scornfully. "At this time of year?"

"He is an alien," Peripule said. "He knows nothing of fashion."

"Well, first of all," Chintsion began, "he has a minder, and—"

"Gentlemen," Luseferous said. The three Dwellers all rocked back as though shocked.

"The Archimandrite Luseferous is a busy man," the Hierchon Ormilla boomed. "Discussions regarding the seasonal fashionability of cities in Nasqueron might be best conducted between sessions, not during."

"Little dweller," Chintsion said to the Hierchon, "we are, as a favour to your latest batch of masters, and notwithstanding the likely and faintly hilarious brevity of their precedence, attempting to establish the whereabouts of this Taak fellow. The…"

Luseferous stopped listening. He turned to Tuhluer, who sat just behind and to the side of him. He looked the other man in the eye. Tuhluer held his gaze. Luseferous saw the other man swallow. Still his gaze was held. Tuhluer had never dared to do that before. Luseferous bent fractionally towards him and said quietly, "Desperate times require desperate solutions, Tuhluer."

The other man looked down, then nodded and started finger-tapping signals into his glove. The Archimandrite turned to the front again.

A distant thud sounded, followed a second later by another, then another, like a great clock ticking.

Luseferous listened to the two Ulubine Peregals, old men called Tlipeyn and Emoerte, trying to wheedle the Dwellers into being more cooperative. The Dwellers gave every indication of being sincerely unable even to understand what the word meant.

Out of the corner of his eye, minutely silhouetted against the filthy yellow-

brown clouds of the planet beneath them, the Archimandrite could s
line of tiny specks drifting off to one side, heading towards the passing clou
tops thousands of kilometres below.

"…Believe us when we say that we are serious," Commander Binstey, his
C-in-C of ground forces, was saying to the three Dwellers.

"Oh, I'm sure you are," Chintsion said airily. "That does not alter the fact
that we may be entirely unable to help you."

Commander Binstey started to speak again but then Luseferous interrupted
him. "Gentlemen," he said quietly, and Binstey fell silent. "If I may direct
your attention to the view over to one side there." He waved one ringed
hand over to the side where the stippled line of specks was moving slowly
across the gasily distorted face of the planet.

Everybody looked. The Dwellers twisted slightly in their seats. Those
present in the chamber with especially good eyesight were already reacting.
He could hear mutters, gasps, all the usual expressions of shock.

"We are serious," Luseferous told the Dwellers. He stood. "Do you hear
that noise?" He turned his head, as though listening. The dull ticking noise
went on; steady, remorseless. "That is a drop-bomb chute, firing once a
second. Only in this case it is firing people, not warheads. Unprotected human
beings are being thrown into space towards your planet at a rate of over
three thousand per hour. They are men, women and children, old and young
adults, people from all walks of life, mostly captured from surrendered ships
and damaged habitats. We have over twenty thousand of them aboard. They
will continue to be fired at this rate until we make some sort of progress
here." He waited for some sort of reaction from the three Dwellers, but they
just kept on looking at the view. "Now," he continued, "do any of us here
present think we might have just remembered anything useful?"

He watched the people and the aliens staring at the stippled line of black
dots moving slowly away from the great ship. A few people turned to look at
him, then looked away when he met their gaze, trying to hide hatred and
fear and horror. Odd how people reacted so severely to something unpleasant
happening right in front of them but were prepared to ignore much worse
horrors taking place elsewhere.

He nodded to Tuhluer, and a great screen lit up across one side of the
chamber, showing the process. People—humans of all sorts, as he'd said—
were shown being loaded into a number of huge circular magazines. The
humans were almost all struggling, but they were each constrained by a tight
wrapping like an elastic sleeping bag which covered every bit of them except
for their faces and prevented them from doing anything but squirm like
maggots and spit at and try to bite the exoskel-wearing soldiers loading them
into the launcher magazines. The floor of the vast hold was covered in
wriggling, struggling bodies. The sound turned up, and those present in the

conference chamber could hear the humans screaming and crying and shouting and begging.

"Archimandrite!" the Hierchon shouted. "I have to protest at this! I didn't—"

"Shut up!" the Archimandrite bellowed at him. He looked round the others. "All of you! Not a fucking word!" For a while the only sound was the muffled thud, thud, thud of the launcher.

The scene switched to the muzzle of the launcher on the exterior of the ship, firing—very gently, for a gun—the people into space. Their wrapping came off as they were expelled, snapping back around their ankles so that they could writhe and jerk and spasm satisfactorily as they met the vacuum naked, and suffocated. Some tried to hold their breaths, and bulged fit to explode. Blood specked from ears and eyes and mouths and anuses. The cameras followed them. The people usually moved for about a couple of minutes before they stopped. Then they just assumed the one frozen pose— some curled foetal, some spreadeagled—and tumbled slowly, part of an invisible conveyor belt, towards the faraway cloud tops.

"Exactly why are you doing this?" the Dweller Feurish asked the Archimandrite. He sounded merely puzzled.

"To concentrate minds," Luseferous said coldly. He could hear somebody being sick in the chamber. Not many people were meeting his gaze. The gantries above were thick with immobile guards, weapons already trained on the people below.

"Well, my mind was perfectly concentrated," Feurish said, with what sounded like a sigh. "We still can't help you."

"Give me Seer Fassin Taak," Luseferous said, feeling some sweat—what?— start to break out on his forehead. He put a stop to that at once.

"We haven't got this Taak fellow," the City Administrator Peripule said reasonably.

"Tell me where he is," Luseferous demanded.

"Sorry," Chintsion said. "Can't help."

"Fucking *tell* me!" Luseferous roared.

"How can we—?" Feurish began. Then Chintsion broke in.

"Perhaps we can ask the people who claim to have seen Seer Taak last where they think he might be."

"There were people from the Embassy who were reported to be looking for him," Feurish pointed out. "Perhaps they found something."

"I thought they were all killed when the Embassy ships were destroyed," Chintsion said. "Weren't they?"

"Look," Peripule said reasonably to the Archimandrite. "Why don't we just sleep on it, eh?"

Luseferous pointed furiously at the line of bodies heading slowly towards the planet. "Don't you *fuckwits* understand? *That* doesn't stop until I get what I want!"

The three Dwellers twisted to look as one. "Hmm," Peripule said thoughtfully. "I do hope you have enough people."

Luseferous's fists clenched. He felt close to exploding, as though he was one of the people in the little production line of death sliding past the bowed diamond window. He struggled to keep his voice icily calm as he said, "There are three hundred Dweller youngsters aboard this ship. Perhaps if we used them instead? Or for target practice. What do you think?"

"I think you'll annoy people," Chintsion said, and laughed.

"You're not seriously trying to use threats against us, are you?" Feurish asked.

"I had better point out, Mr Luseferous," Chintsion said with what sounded almost like humour, "that some of the clubs I represent are of a military bent. Wonderfully enthusiastic, of course, proud to personify them, naturally, but sometimes—I don't know, perhaps through boredom—they display characteristics which might almost be said to be bordering on those one would expect to be evinced by fellows of a 'shoot-first' mentality. Ah. If you know what I mean."

Luseferous stared at this cretinous float. The plodding, thud, thud, thud sound went on. The line of tiny dark shapes continued to move across the tortured, livid face of the gas-giant. He turned to Tuhluer. "Go to full action stations," he said. "Dark the view."

The vast face of Nasqueron disappeared as the diamond bubble went obsidian black. The whole great chamber grew still darker and seemed to shrink. The thudding noise sounded louder.

"You three are to be held hostage," Luseferous told the three Dwellers. "As will the young of your kind currently aboard this ship. If there is any attempt to rescue you or them, or any assault on this ship or on any of my ships or assets, you will all be killed. If I don't get something provably useful on Seer Fassin Taak or whatever it was he was looking for in the next six hours standard, I'm going to start killing you anyway, starting with you three. Understand?"

"Really, Mr Luseferous," Feurish said, "this is no way to run a conference."

"I have to say that I have to agree," Chintsion said.

"Shut up," Luseferous told them. "I also have numerous ships with multi-real-tonne antimatter warheads stationed right round this gas-giant. Planet-busters. If there's still nothing happening after you're all dead, I start detonating them in your precious fucking atmosphere. What passes for the authorities on your giant rotten fart of a planet will be informed of the above in due course." The Archimandrite looked up at the guards poised on the gantries above. "Take them away. Get them out of those esuits. By cutting if necessary."

A dozen giant black figures like suits of ancient armour encrusted with huge dark jewels sailed down, landing on the black diamond film on great talon-spread legs. Four surrounded each of the three esuited Dwellers.

"Well, gentlemen," the Dweller called Peripule said ruefully to the other two, "I suppose it is not open to us to claim we went unwarned."

An instant later, three violet circular curtains of light blazed out within the dark chamber, one encircling each Dweller. The exoskel guards were either rocked right back or physically blown over. Those unprotected people standing or sitting further away were picked up and thrown towards the walls. The shock wave hit Luseferous's tall seat a fraction after the safety shield deployed, so that he watched the resulting chaos through a clinker of half-silvered diamond shutters.

The blast shook his seat, shook him and then reflected and echoed back off the distant walls. The three violet cylinders disappeared and left three huge neatly circular holes in the black diamond film beneath. The sickly light of Nasqueron's yellow-brown cloud tops shone through. The air in the chamber was whirling and screaming out through the apertures. Blinks of white light flickered outside. Two of the exoskel guards were tumbled across the floor, scrabbling for grip, and were sucked out of the holes. Luseferous just stood staring. People, mostly unconscious and badly injured, started to slide in from the edges of the chamber where they'd been deposited by the triple blasts towards the three shining holes. A third exoskeleton-clad figure was being pulled, giant hands scraping and scrabbling frantically at the smooth diamond surface, towards the nearest hole and the whirling vortex forming above it. Then the ship's systems finally woke up to what was happening and a dark shape flicked across the three puncture wounds in the vessel's skin, sealing off the light and keeping what remained of the atmosphere within.

Relative calm returned. The thud, thud, thud noise continued. A rushing sound signalled replacement air being pumped back into the chamber. The exoskel guards got to their feet, looked around, then ran over to form a protective shield about the Archimandrite. More black shapes came plummeting from the gantries. Luseferous could hear people in the chamber moaning. He turned to look at Tuhluer, who was limping up to him through the phalanx of exoskel guards, his own emergency esuit and helmet deployed, the shiny bulge of faceplate reflecting the silvery diamond bubble that enclosed the Archimandrite and his chair.

"Kill the other Dwellers," Luseferous told him. Tuhluer leaned in, hand to the side of his head, seemingly not hearing. "KILL THE OTHER DWELLERS!" Luseferous shouted. He clicked a stud on the arm of the seat and the diamond shuttering fell away. "Get us away from here," he told the other man. "Warn the planet the AM warheads launch in three hours if they don't start cooperating." He looked at where the three Dweller representatives had made their sudden exit. "And make sure the *Rapacious* wasted those three comedians."

"Sir!" Tuhluer said. "And what about the… chute supply?"

It took a moment before Luseferous realised that he meant the people being launched towards the planet. He waved one hand. "Oh, dump the lot."

The Archimandrite Luseferous clicked the esuit's communicator and told the *Rapacious* he was on his way. He marched through the moaning wounded towards the ship-to-ship and the waiting vessel beneath. The exoskel guards fell in around him, forming a giant hedge of armoured limbs and menacingly jagged torsos. He was almost at the ship-to-ship entrance when he was thrown off his feet. The exoskels staggered as the whole vast ship shook. One of the giant guards nearly fell on him, regaining his balance only at the last moment, servos whining.

"*Now* what?" Luseferous demanded.

"Damage control here, sir," a voice said from the esuit. "Energy bolt straight through the whole ship, dead amidships. About two metres diameter. Plus… the bows have been shot off, back… to… about… the eighty-metre mark. Just gone. Same novel energy profile as the midships beam. Light speed; zero warning. Reactive defence systems still looking for a countermeasure against any subsequent usage… nothing coming up so far, sir."

"Comms, sir," another voice said, "Dwellers, demanding return of their people aboard. Apparently those were just warning shots."

Tuhluer came striding up.

Luseferous looked at him. "Hand the Dwellers back," he told the ADC. "Then get this thing away from here." He strode towards the ship-to-ship.

"And the AM ships, sir?"

"Leave them where they are. Delay the ultimatum until the *Luseferous VII* is clear."

"Sir."

This time the Archimandrite made it all the way to the waiting flagship.

An hour later the *Luseferous VII* was still making its lumbering, injured way out of the planet's gravity well. The *Rapacious* was already half a million klicks away and still accelerating. The Archimandrite—still shaking with rage even in his acceleration couch, the full awfulness and sheer *insult* of what had happened at last sinking in, his patience finally exhausted (those three facetious shithead Dwellers had even *escaped*, esuits reflecting or deflecting everything the *Rapacious* had thrown at them after they'd exited the *Luseferous VII*, disappearing, apparently unharmed, into the cloud tops)—ordered that the ultimatum be made to the Dwellers immediately, and that one of the ships carrying an AM warhead should drop its weapon into the planet's atmosphere, just to show that they were serious.

The reply was almost instantaneous. The ship with the AM bomb—each one of the twenty ships with the AM bombs—vanished in a sudden pinpoint flare of light. All the warheads went off partially, reacting messily with the ordinary matter debris left after the destruction of the ships. Twenty ragged little suns guttered round Nasqueron like a tilted necklace, flaring, fading, flaring again and fading slowly once more.

Moments later, a hyper-velocity missile rose out of the turgid skies of the gas-giant and found the *Luseferous VII* despite all its desperate countermeasures within two minutes of clearing the cloud tops.

The radiation front tripped the *Rapacious*'s sensor buffers. *That* was how a proper antimatter warhead was supposed to work, seemed to be the implication.

The last signal from the great ship before it was ripped entirely apart and turned into radiation and high-speed shrapnel was from aide-de-camp Tuhluer, calmly informing Luseferous that the Archimandrite was a cunt.

⁚

Fassin Taak looked up at the stars of home. He felt tears in his eyes, even within the shock-gel. He rested on a windswept platform above a small cloud-top city low in the south polar region, just a couple of thousand kilometres from the torn, fluid boundary with Nasqueron's southernmost atmospheric belt.

He tried to locate a friendly satellite, some signal that the little gascraft could recognise, but he couldn't find anything. All broadcast signals were either terribly weak or scrambled, and he couldn't locate any low-orbit devices to bounce a hail off. He tried to lock on to one of the weak broadcast wavelengths and use the gascraft's biomind to decipher the signals, but the routines didn't seem to be working. He gave up. For the moment, he was content just to sit here and look out at the few, familiar stars.

Despite Y'sul's injuries, they'd still had to undergo an albeit slightly gentler form of the wild spiralling. Fassin had lain in the gascraft, feeling the series of nested corkscrewings and helixes build up like some coiling spring, thinking that this was them entering the wormhole, though in fact, as it turned out, they'd already been through it and this was the unwinding. Then, suddenly, they were here, back in Nasqueron, in the southern polar region, not the northern one they'd left from.

Sinking down just a few kilometres through the cloud tops, the ex-Voehn ship *Protreptic* had come to rest in a slightly too-big cradle in an enormous, echoing cavern of a hangar here in the lower regions of the nearly deserted polar city of Quaibrai. The City Administrator and a crowd of several hundred Dwellers had met them, hooting and throwing streamers and scent grenades.

A delegation comprising individuals from several different alien-ship enthusiast clubs had become particularly excited when they'd seen the Voehn craft and had bobbed up and down with impatience as Y'sul had been carefully offloaded and given into the care of a hospital squad. As soon as Y'sul, Fassin and the truetwin Quercer & Janath had exited, the chirping, sizzling mass of enthusiasts rushed aboard, jostling for position as they'd tried to fit down the corridors and access ways. The truetwin had, thoughtfully, expanded the ship from its needle-ship portal-piercing formation to a fatter and hence more commodious configuration, but it still looked like a tight squeeze.

Y'sul, already looking half mended, though still shaking off the grogginess of his semi-coma, had twisted a fraction in his scoop-stretcher to look at Fassin as the hospital squad brought their ambulance skiff down to him. "See?" he'd croaked. "Got you back safely, didn't I?"

Fassin had agreed that he had. He'd tried to pat Y'sul but used the wrong manipulator and instead just jerked in mid-gas. He'd swivelled and used the gascraft's other arm, clutching the wounded Dweller's hub-hand.

"You off home now?" Y'sul had asked.

"However much of it is left. I don't know. I don't know what to do."

"Well, if you do go, come back soon." Y'sul had paused and shaken himself, as though trying to wake up more fully. "I should be ready to receive visitors again in a couple of dozen days or so and I anticipate a very full social calendar indeed thereafter. I fully intend to exploit my recent injuries and experiences without compunction and exaggerate outrageously my part in the taking of the Voehn ship, not to mention embellish my fight with the Voehn commander to the point of what will probably seem like complete unrecognisability, the first time you hear it. I'd appreciate your corroboration, providing you are able to enter into the spirit of the thing and not insist on being overly encumbered by the vulgar exigencies of objective truth, whatever version of it you may think you recall. What do you say?"

"My memory's kind of hazy," Fassin had told the Dweller. "I'll probably back up anything you say."

"Splendid!"

"If I can come back, I shall."

Privately, he didn't even know if he could get away in the first place. He didn't know what sort of infrastructure remained to get him off the planet, get the gascraft repaired and return him—if whoever was in charge would let him return—nor whether the Dwellers would allow him to return.

During the last part of the six-hour journey from the wormhole, when

Quercer & Janath had allowed him to see where they were and let him access the local data-carrying spectra, he'd tapped into the Nasqueron news services to see what had been going on during his absence.

The Dweller news was all about the war. The Formal War between Zone 2 and Belt C. Apparently it had become deeply exciting and enthralling and was already being talked of in respected critical circles as a classic of the genre, even though it was probably barely halfway through yet and still, with any luck at all, had a great deal to offer.

Fassin had to search out a specialist alien-watcher service to find out that, starting about thirty-plus days earlier, the Ulubis system had been invaded and taken over by the Epiphany-5 Discon or Starveling Cult forces under the leadership of the Archimandrite Luseferous. The last significant, organised Ulubine Mercatorial resistance had ended just a dozen or so days ago following the formal surrender by the Hierchon Ormilla after the destruction of a city on Sepekte and a habitat in orbit around it. A counter-attack by several squadrons of the Summed Fleet was expected to commence within the next few dozen days or so. The latest was that a peace and cooperation conference was taking place about now in the Starveling ship *Luseferous VII*, in orbit about Nasqueron.

Fassin had sent a message which would at least attempt to find Valseir. He would wait a bit and see if that raised a reply. He'd thought of contacting Setstyin, but then he remembered, vaguely, that somebody had said something to him that had made him uneasy about the Dweller. No, wait, it had been the other way round, hadn't it? Setstyin had always been a charming and helpful friend. Setstyin had warned him against the old Dweller who'd been in charge of the great spherical… *thing* that had risen out of the clouds and demolished the Mercatoria's raiding force at the GasClipper regatta. Yes, that made more sense. He wondered why he couldn't remember in more detail. It was strange. He'd always had a really good memory.

Quercer & Janath seemed to be surrounded by well-wishers wanting to know more about the Voehn craft. The truetwin Dweller had seen Fassin looking at them through the crowd, and waved. Fassin had waved back.

He'd watched Y'sul being placed into the ambulance skiff and tried to work out what he knew and didn't know, what he could and could not remember. He could have gone with Y'sul in the ambulance, he supposed, but he felt a need to get away for a while, to be alone for a time.

He'd come up here to see the stars, and wait, and think, and maybe do a bit of mathematical analysis.

He took the little image-leaf out of its locker in the gascraft's flank. He looked at it. Since whatever had happened aboard the *Protreptic*, the little gascraft couldn't see as well as it used to, but its close-up detail vision was good enough on one side for the image of blue sky and white clouds to be perfectly clear. He zoomed in, rechecking the image he had stored in the… The image wasn't there in the craft's memories.

That was strange. He had the feeling that he had recorded the image and already half-deciphered something that was hidden inside it. He was sure he had. It had seemed really important at the time, too, he was certain.

Fassin tried really hard to think back to what had occurred after they were attacked by the Voehn ship. He knew they'd been captured and interrogated and the Voehn had messed around with his brain and with the gascraft's biomind and memories. Then a ship that the Ythyn had sent to rescue them had attacked the Voehn ship and—somehow—he and Y'sul and the truetwin had overpowered the surviving Voehn crew.

They'd overpowered Voehn?

How had that happened? The Ythyn ship had been able to distract the Voehn, and the *Velpin* had played a part too, some sort of anti-piracy automatics kicking in and helping to take on the Voehn. Quercer & Janath had been distinctly cagey about what sort of techniques their old ship had used against the Voehn.

Fassin had no idea. Maybe it had happened the way they said, maybe not. Maybe the *Velpin* had had an AI aboard and that had wasted the Voehn, only Quercer & Janath didn't want people to know about it. They could have told him practically anything and he'd have believed them, the Voehn had messed with his memories so badly.

He remembered sitting on the steps of a temple looking out over a wide, slow-moving river, talking to an old… man? An old Dweller? This was quite a vivid image, rather than a linear strand of memory. That had to have happened in some form of VR, didn't it? Maybe that old man had been the representation of the *Velpin*'s AI. Perhaps that was who or what he had been talking to, or at least met.

He tried to concentrate, and looked down at the image-leaf again. He'd been given this by Valseir. Was that right? It had been a sort of calling card, a letter of introduction, leading him to… He seemed to feel it had led him to Valseir, but that didn't make sense.

No, wait: the house in the depths, and the old wandering Dweller. *He*'d given him the image-leaf. And it had led him, somehow, to Valseir. But there was something else. He'd discovered something else. He'd woken up thinking about this, before the wormhole transition. There was something hidden in the image-leaf. A message, a code.

Fassin looked round the empty platform. There was nobody else here. He let the little gascraft's image processors drink in the view shown on the image-leaf in as much detail as it could offer. Various routines started running. In a few minutes, his gaze was torn away from the sparse but familiar-looking starscape above. He looked at the results.

There had been something in there.

It looked like alien algebra.

There was about a page and a half of it. It looked like one long equation, or maybe three or four shorter ones.

He felt very excited. He wasn't entirely sure why, but he had an idea that this linked into the Dweller List. The details evaded him, but he knew that he'd been looking for the Transform that was supposed to open up the famous List, and maybe—just possibly—this piece of alien mathematics had something to do with it. Maybe what he had before him here *was* the Transform, though that was a little difficult to believe.

Fassin tried to figure out what the symbols in front of him might mean, but couldn't even get started. The gascraft's comprehensively mucked-around memories might once have contained something which would have sent him in the right direction, but they didn't any more.

He linked with the city's data nets, synched with an equatorial university library and looked up a data reservoir specialising in alien mathematics. He chose a couple of symbols at random and pinged them to the database. It answered immediately, with references.

What he was looking at was expressed in Translatory V, a pan-species, universal notation of just under two billion years age, devised by the long-extinct Wopuld from earlier Dweller elements. He downloaded a full translation suite.

He had to stop, and look out over the cloud tops. He was experiencing a strange mix of emotions.

This might be the thing he'd been sent to look for, the very object of his mission. Their mission, rather; he ought not to forget Colonel Hatherence. This could well be what he'd been looking for, all that time. And yet, if the Mercatoria, or at least the Ulubine part of it, had hoped that this would save them, then it hadn't. He'd got back too late, and the invasion had already happened. It was all over.

And there was so much he seemed to have forgotten! What had the Voehn *done* to him? Y'sul had been badly injured but apart from the effects of his healing coma he seemed—and professed himself to be—fine, mentally. Quercer & Janath didn't seem to have suffered at all. Maybe that was just luck, or something to do with being a truetwin—he didn't know.

Still, there was this to be done, this deciphering. It might still lead to something momentous. The invasion might have already happened but the counter-attack was still to take place, and anyway, there was his own take on the rights and wrongs of what was going on. He would still rather the Beyonders had the information, if there was any useful information to be had, in the equation.

Something glinted in space just over the horizon to the west, way out across the cloud tops. A ship, perhaps.

Fassin returned his attention to the equation and the alien translation suite. He applied one to the other. In the virtual space which the gascraft's crippled biomind projected into his own mind, the image split and a copy of the equation appeared alongside the original. He watched the symbols shuffle and change in the copy, turning into Dweller standard notation. The symbols on both copies of the equation flickered and highlighted, turned different colours and seemed to swell out and then lapse back in again amongst the rest as the equation worked itself out.

It was truly an equation, too. He'd had some vague idea thanks to something that somebody had said that it might be a frequency and signal or something, but it wasn't that. Or if it was it was very oddly disguised.

The last few terms flicked and flashed on both sides of the split image. The answer appeared right at the end, blinking slowly.

It was a zero.

He stared at it, at them.

A zero in Dweller standard notation was a dot with a short line under it. In Translatory V, it was a diagonal slash.

A dot with a short line under it winked at him from the copy of the equation. A diagonal slash lay at the end of the original, also slowly flashing.

He tried again. Same result.

He rechecked the image, pulled the hidden code out of it again, in case the processor systems had made a mistake the first time.

There had been no mistake. The equation he came up with the second time was the same as the first. He ran that one as well, anyway.

Zero.

Fassin laughed. He could feel himself inside the shock-gel nested within the little arrowhead craft, chest and belly shaking. He had a sudden, vivid image of standing on the rocky shore of a planet, waiting for something. He stopped laughing.

Zero.

So the final answer was nothing. He'd been sent to the far side of the galaxy, had the answer with him all the time anyway, and what it was, was "Fuck all". But in maths.

He started laughing again.

Ah well.

Another glint, out over the cloud tops again, nearly directly north, and high. A scatter of tiny lights lit up the sky just beneath whatever it was that had just reflected the light. A hint of violet. Then white.

He watched the same region of space for a few moments, looking for more. Whatever it was, it had to be fairly far away. If it was the same thing that had glinted earlier near the horizon then it was something high over the equatorial zone, tens of kilo-klicks out.

Zero. Well, that was illuminating. Fassin wondered if there really was a true answer somewhere, if what he'd found—what Valseir had stumbled onto and then what Fassin had unknowingly brought out with him after his long-ago delve—was part of a whole suite of decoy answers. Was there just this one, or were there more? Was the myth of the Dweller List's famous Transform footnoted with hundreds of false answers?

Well, if it was, he wasn't going to go looking for them. He'd done his bit. He'd even, in a sense, accomplished his mission, when he'd thought it was never going to happen. He was too late, and the result was a nonsense, a joke, almost an insult, but—by any given god you cared to name—he'd done it.

He ought to start thinking about how he was going to get off the planet, or at least get the information out there, just for form's sake. Share the indifferent news.

Another couple of flashes from space, near where the first crop had shone. One tiny blink, one longer flare. A few moments later what looked like a ship's drive lit up and floated away, gathering speed quickly.

Fassin looked for evidence of any Shared Facility satellites, or indeed any Mercatorial hardware anywhere around Nasqueron. There didn't seem to be anything. He'd told Aun Liss he'd try to ping a position between two Seer satellites, EQ4 and EQ5, but the satellites weren't there any more. He wondered if he could work out where they would have been and so where the microsat that he'd suggested the Beyonders position between the two might be. He looked inside the gascraft's memory, trying to find the sat schedules, dug them out, then fed in the local time and his current location.

A position blinked on his field of vision, away across the cloud tops, a little off due north, some few kilo-klicks beneath where the recent activity had been. In line of sight now. He decided to treat this piece of luck as a good omen, and sent a signal saying he was back, so that, if nothing else, he'd have done what he'd said he would do. He waited a while but there was no acknowledgement, let alone a reply. He hadn't really expected one.

He wondered what was left of the Shrievalty Ocula, and whether he should even try to report to it. He needed to do some research into exactly how much had changed since the invasion, see whether he was listed as dead, and whether he was being looked for or not. Maybe people had forgotten about him in all the excitement.

Fassin laughed again. Oh, if only.

The whole E-5 Discon invasion, so they'd been told, was happening quite specifically because of the List and the Transform. If that was even partly, even slightly true, and his mission hadn't been hidden from the invaders, then they probably would be looking for him, and quite hard, too, given that they might not have much time before the Summed Fleet crashed the party.

In a way the zero-result equation was a relief. The information he'd brought back was such that he didn't mind sharing it with anybody and everybody. If it had truly told the location of the wormhole portals it would have been the most crushingly awful burden he could have borne, an infinitely precious and probably infinitely deadly possession. He should be glad it was a joke. If it had been the useful truth, if it had been what they had all hoped it was going to be, then almost certainly no matter who he chose to tell would first torture him or at the very least tear his mind apart to make sure he was telling the truth, and then kill him to make sure he couldn't tell anybody else. He'd kind of hoped that the Beyonders might be more humane than that, but it was a big risk to take.

He'd be better just broadcasting the result, then disappearing if he could. Maybe the Dwellers would let him stay.

Valseir. If nothing else, he ought to let his Dweller friend know that the information they'd all been so concerned about in fact amounted to nothing more than a piddling little zero. Then there was the matter of telling Valseir that for this nothing, his friend and colleague Leisicrofe had killed himself. Not all good news he'd arrive bearing, then.

Fassin looked up the StormSailing news service. There were fewer regattas than usual, thanks to all the interest in the war, and a lot of sailors who'd normally be on the GasClippers and StormJammers would be required to crew the Dreadnoughts and other combat craft, but there were still a dozen meetings going on at any one time throughout the planet. If he was going to go looking for Valseir at regattas, he might have a long search.

He thought about contacting the City Administrator to arrange for transport—Y'sul would most likely be transferred back home to Hauskip city in a day or two, and Fassin could probably just accompany the injured Dweller back there—then he wondered if he ought to be more careful.

Nobody seemed to have paid him much attention at all when he'd disembarked from the *Protreptic*, but that didn't mean his arrival hadn't been noticed by somebody. Were there any humans—other Seers or anybody else—present in Nasq.? Somebody—Valseir? Damn this suddenly failing memory—somebody had told him there were factions and differences of opinion within the Dwellers over the List and even the seemingly endemic, congenital disregard the Dwellers displayed towards the rest of the galaxy's inhabitants. *We are not a monoculture.* That had been Valseir, hadn't it?

Would any group of Dwellers wish him ill, or somehow be under the command of somebody who did?

He called up the usually most reliable alien-watching service and accessed the global map. It was, for the first time since he'd been looking at it, completely clear. According to the display, there was not a single alien entity alive in Nasqueron. That appeared to include him, so his return hadn't been documented yet, at least not by the enthusiasts who ran this service.

He was being called. Quercer & Janath. He put the image-leaf back in its flank locker.

—Fassin. Anywhere we can take you?

—Locally, hasten to add.

—Ship at our disposal. Favour owed.

—That sort of thing.

—I don't know, Fassin replied.—I've been thinking about that. Do you know any more about what's happening with the invasion and the Starveling Cult forces?

—Getting reports coming in just now that there's been some sort of breakdown at some conference.

—Firefight, bluntly.

—I'd like to find my friend Valseir, Fassin said.—I've sent a call, but no answer's come back. I thought I might find him at a—

As he spoke, he thought suddenly of the RushWing *Sheumerith*, the Dwellers hanging trailed on long lines behind the great long flexible wing forever powering its way into the high skies of Nasqueron. The RushWing. That was the other place Valseir had said he might be found.

—Yes, he told the truetwin.—I do know where you could take me.

—Be in-atmosphere, you realise. Not that quick.

—Entirely used up our luck quotient bringing the ship into Nasq. unseen in the first place. Voehn ship, see. Nervous-making sort of thing for a lot of people. Apparently.

—That's fine, Fassin told them.

They were scudding through the cloud stems under the topmost haze layer less than an hour later when the AM warheads went off. One was directly above them.

"Oh, wow!"

"Look at our shadow!"

A minute later, what they would later discover had been the destruction of the great ship *Luseferous VII* cast part of a giant halo of light all over the western sky. Quercer & Janath freely confessed to being terribly impressed.

The *Protreptic* tore serenely on.

:

The first twelve ships of the Summed Fleet streaked across the inner system of Ulubis at just a per cent below light speed. Kilometre-long black minarets girdled by fast-spinning sections loosing missile clusters, pack munitions, scatter mines, stealth drones and suicide launchers, they lanced across the whole system in less than four hours, Nasqueron's orbit in less than one and Sepekte's in fifteen minutes.

Billions of kilometres behind them, on the same course and decelerating hard, lay the *Mannlicher-Carcano* and the main body of the Summed Fleet. Taince Yarabokin floated in her pod. In the VR command space of the battleship, there was something approaching total silence as the entire command crew lay quietly listening to the sparse exchanges beaming back from the twelve advance units darting across the system dead ahead.

Taince was amazed at how nervous she felt. She could feel her body trying to exhibit all the classic signs of the fight-or-flight response, and the pod's bio systems doggedly countering each one. There was no doubt that this was an important mission. It would, arguably, be the most crucial one she'd ever been a part of. She was of sufficiently senior rank to have been briefed at the start on the strategic momentousness of what they were being sent to do, but even so she was surprised how similar she felt now to the way she'd felt on her first few combat missions. You never fully shook off the adrenalin rush no matter how many missions you undertook—the consensus was that the day you felt completely blasé about a forthcoming engagement was either the day you were going to die or the day you should resign your commission forthwith—but the way she felt now was worryingly similar to how she'd felt before those early missions.

Somewhere, her nervousness would be being noted, too. Even if a live human medical officer wasn't watching her life signs now, a program would be flagging her current state of anxiety as worth further investigation later. No privacy. Well, she'd known that when she joined up.

Taince took her mind away from these perplexing, almost embarrassing feelings and watched the data coming back from the lead ships.

What happened now, what these twelve craft discovered or didn't discover as they crossed the system at accelerated particle speeds, would determine how the next part of her life was lived out.

There had been some odd energy and drive signatures from the system over the last few days, though nothing as bizarre as the sudden commotion around Nasqueron a few days ago. Twenty-plus antimatter explosions. All but one, it looked like, spread around the planet in a neat if wavy circle. They'd detonated too far out to do any great damage to the gas-giant itself or to its inhabitants, and the explosions had been very messy, almost as if they hadn't been functioning warheads detonating efficiently but rather twenty—very big—ships losing M/AM containment at exactly the same time. Then, a minute or two later, an even bigger AM burst less than a light second out from Nasqueron, with the profile of something the size of the behemoth ship they'd identified earlier getting thoroughly blasted.

Then nothing, apart from the ambiguous maybe-leaving indications.

Because one plausible explanation that fitted most of the signs—no explanation anyone had come up with so far fitted all of them—was that the bad guys were pulling out. Nobody in fleet command really believed this was what could be happening—the Starveling Cult force had crossed decades of space to get to Ulubis: they wouldn't turn tail and face the equally long trek back after just a few weeks, would they?—but it looked like one of the more likely explanations.

The data about to arrive would decide it one way or the other.

The battlecruiser *88*, the advance squadron's flagship, collating the real-time intelligence of the spearhead-shaped force and signalling it back to the main fleet, reported three heavy craft within detection though not attack range of the first, point destroyer. It signalled two of the following cruisers to adjust their trajectories and prepare remote munitions, guided and dumb. Little comms bleed. Possibly this was just good discipline or marginally better tech than they'd anticipated. Flank cruisers and destroyers reported a few missile platforms, firing at them, futilely, given their speed. A lot of mines, well spread. Evidence of AM material still floating free near the planet Nasqueron, in a debris profile that fitted exactly twenty ships having blown up at the same time eight days earlier. One big debris field, still heading outwards from the gas-giant, spreading, consistent with a very large ship having been destroyed.

A few other small enemy ships showing, the closest responding to their passing, firing beam weapons. No hits. The destroyer *Bofors* passed within a kilo-klick of a vessel of about the same size as it, identified it as a hostile before the other ship had even registered the craft hurtling past and hit and destroyed it with a high-X-ray laser from its phase-modulation collar turret before the hostile had time to react.

Halfway across the system now. Still just the three big targets. There should be hundreds.

The four craft at the trailing end of the advance squadron's spear-point had time to spare while they nudge-deflected and picked off some of the targets that the point and mid-body ships had identified. They turned long-range sensors on the outer system and beyond, in the general direction of the E-5 Discon, getting a straight-down look along that track which the main fleet had only ever been able to view at a ninety-degree angle.

Drive signatures. Hundreds of them. Most of a thousand ships, all heading for home, taking a slightly acutely angled route that had hidden their drives from the main body of the fleet for the last six or seven days.

Half an hour later, it was like party time. The advance squadron was almost all the way through the system, braking hard to return in a few dozen days, and the small formations of ships between them and the main body of the fleet had been ordered to forget about follow-up high-speed passes and start decelerating at their individual safe maxima.

All the signs were that the system was almost clear of enemy ships and the Starveling Cult's main fleet was in high-speed retreat back along roughly the course it had approached on. Even the three big targets were powering up now and heading in the same direction as the decamping invasion force. A few dozen smaller drives lit up as smaller, lighter craft got set to bail out too. There would be some clearing-up to do, and no doubt various mines and automatic munitions to try and keep them occupied while the enemy fleet made its escape, but there would be no main fleet engagement in Ulubis system, no mega-battle.

Their orders were to retake Ulubis system at any cost and hold it. A fast, light force of a dozen or so ships might be sent to harry the tardier fringes of the retreating fleet and provide continuing incentivisation for their speedy withdrawal, but they were specifically not to risk chasing en masse for some decisive battle. They had already achieved victory. They were expressly forbidden from taking the slightest risk of throwing it all away.

The command staff were celebrating. Taince lay curled in her pod, listening to her colleagues babbling with happiness and obvious relief. Various people talked to her, gabbing away about how the mere threat of their arrival could turn away a fleet three times the size of theirs, how they wished now they'd been with the advance squadron, just to have seen *some* action, dammit, and how they were probably going to get a heroes' welcome when they got to Ulubis. She tried to respond in kind, mustering expressions of tension released and fears assuaged and all the time pretending to pretend that she'd have preferred a proper fight.

—Vice Admiral?

The image of Admiral Kisipt appeared in front of her, automatically displacing all the other images of celebrating crew.

—Sir. She tried to pull her thoughts away from the sick feeling inside.

—You must be pleased. We won't have to turn your home system into too much of a battleground.

—Of course, sir. Though there will be mines, booby traps, no doubt.

—No doubt. And I'm keeping a full sweep alert in operation between here and the system, just in case. Kisipt paused. The old Voehn's head tipped to one side as he regarded her.—I think it has been very stressful for you, anticipating what might happen when we got to Ulubis, yes?

—I suppose so, sir. Taince wondered if he'd already been alerted to her earlier nervousness, if this was a conversation—even a kind of evaluation—inspired by that.

—Hmm. Well, the place doesn't look too badly shot up, judging from the advance results. You ought to be able to relax soon. We'll need you for liaison and ceremonial duties mostly, I should think. The Admiral made a smile.— That will be all right?

—Of course, sir. Thank you.

—Good. The Admiral made a show of looking around at the other images distributed about his own icon.—Well, I'd better talk to a few more people, calm them down, remind them there's still a job to be done. As you were, Vice.

—Sir.

The Admiral's image disappeared. Taince didn't bring any of the others to the fore, but turned away from the social space altogether for Tacspace.

*What have I become?* she thought, staring into the dark volumes of Tacspace, watching and not watching coloured lines move and slowly extend, groups of figures, groups of ships tracing their way through the deep space skies bordering Ulubis system. *I wanted a proper battle. Death and destruction. I wanted death and destruction. I wanted the chance to die, the chance to kill, the chance to die...*

She stared into the awful emptiness as people celebrated around her.

*What have I become?*

⁘

Fassin felt restless as the *Protreptic* powered its way through the belts and zones of Nasqueron, heading for the RushWing *Sheumerith*, riding high in the clear gas spaces between two haze layers in Band A. The ex-Voehn ship shredded clouds as it sped through the atmosphere, keeping just under the median cloud level. Quercer & Janath amused themselves by taking turns to pilot in real-time and see by how little they could miss shaving the edges of PlungeStems. This involved quite a lot of whooping and the occasional softish collision, making the whole ship shudder.

Fassin left them to it and floated away back through the ship, ending up in the chamber where their interrogation and the fight had taken place. He looked round it, at the dent-seats and restraints, at the scars and burn marks on the floor, ceilings and walls, and could remember nothing about what had happened. He felt frustrated, even depressed. He floated back towards the command space, stopping just before he got there to look inside what appeared to be the commander's cabin, close to the flight deck.

The cabin was sparsely furnished and decorated. Fassin suspected that it had lost a few bits and pieces to some of the more acquisitive alien-ship enthusiasts back at Quaibrai. He looked at a square on the wall where something had been removed. The *Protreptic* shook very slightly. A distant whoop sounded from the command space, a couple of open doors and a short corridor away. Fassin experienced a shudder of his own, and a feeling of something like déjà vu, or Swim.

*I was born in a water moon*, he thought to himself, knowing he was quoting something or somebody but not knowing what or who.

Another shudder ran through the ship. High-pitched giggles rang from the flight deck.

Zero.

—Hey! Fassin! Quercer & Janath sent.—Call for you. Patch through?

—Who is it? he asked.

—No ident.

　—Human female voice. Hold on, we'll ask.

Zero, Fassin thought. Zero. It *was* a fucking answer.

—Aun Liss, name given.

　—Any bells rung?

⋮

The RushWing *Sheumerith*, a thin blade across the dun sky, held no sign of Valseir. The *Protreptic* went off to bag more PlungeStems, promising to return. Fassin flew the little gascraft wearily along the line of tethered, oblivious, wing-hanging Dwellers, waiting for a sign.

In the end, the other gascraft was obvious. He spotted it from a couple of thousand metres away. The other device saw him at the same time and sent,

—Fassin?

—No, I'm a warhead. Who are you?

—Aun. See you've brought a gun.

He'd taken a Voehn hand-weapon from the *Protreptic*, once he'd found an armoury that hadn't been raided for souvenirs by the ship enthusiasts of Quaibrai. Quercer & Janath hadn't objected. On the contrary, they'd advised him in rather too much detail on the differing capabilities and skill profiles of the various guns on offer when all he wanted was something robust, reliable and powerful that he could use to defend or kill himself with.

So in his good manipulator Fassin now toted a chunky device of what Quercer & Janath had termed the CBE persuasion—Crude But Effective.

He made a show of holding the charged weapon in front of his primary sensing band as he approached.—Yes, he sent.—It's a souvenir.

He drew up by the other machine. It was about the same size and shape as his own, if in rather better condition, and oriented at ninety degrees, the vertical axis longer than the horizontal. It rode inside the cup of still gas behind the open diamond shelter trailing behind the RushWing, near the port limit of the ten-kilometre wing. Wary—unable to be anything else—he noted that the two enclosures on either side of the one holding the other small gascraft were each occupied by large Dwellers who looked rather young to have given themselves up, even temporarily, to a life of high-speed, high-altitude contemplation. The nearest few tether points beyond those on either side were all empty.

—Come on in, the other machine sent, moving forward until its nose nestled into the inner surface of the diamond enclosure. He pulled in behind, wobbling in the sudden pool of still gas after the howl of slipstream.

They were almost touching. Most of the upper surface of the machine facing him turned transparent, showing somebody who certainly looked like Aun Liss lying nearly fully prone in a high-gee seat. He saw her fight to raise an arm and wave, a grim expression on her face that turned into a grin as she looked out at him. He de-opaqued what he could of his own gascraft's carapace, though the results weren't perfect.

Fassin didn't even try to smile back.

—Think you could point that thing away from me? she sent. He saw her grin.—I realise this is the first time I've ever said *that* to—

—No, he sent back, still pointing the Voehn gun at her.

—…Okay, she sent, smile vanishing.—So, welcome back. Good trip?

—No. You got a manipulator you can use in that thing?

—Yes. Won't claim I'm an expert, but…

He moved his own gascraft forward until it was centimetres from hers.—Talk to me the old way.

He saw her frown, then smile uncertainly.—Okay, she sent.—This might be a bit, ah… He could see her shifting her gaze to look down at her right forearm, lying squashed on the cradle-arm of the gee-chair. She looked like she always had, and at the same time quite different. Hair dark, not blonde or auburn or white this time. The high gravity and her attempt to look at her arm as she worked the unfamiliar manipulator interface gave her jowls. He was already fairly sure it was Aun, but he was still quite prepared to kill her.

The manipulator came out slowly, unsteadily. Fassin kept his own well out of the way, still holding the gun on her. The two big Dwellers on either side hadn't made any move. The manipulator came forward and touched the hull carapace of his own little gascraft, finger ends spreading awkwardly.

In the end, he saw, she had to close her eyes to do it. The fingers on the abraded, nearly insensitive gascraft's skin spelled out,… SS ( )… SOL ( ) SOTL ( ). He could see her getting frustrated. He watched the expression on her face deepen into a profound, eyes-tightly-closed frown as she struggled to make the manipulator do exactly what she wanted. He felt tears prick his eyes again. Though he could still shoot her, or himself: anybody.

…SO STL CRZY? she managed at last, and her eyes opened and she flashed a hugely relieved and pleased-with-herself smile at him.

He switched the gun off.

They rode together in the still ball of gas behind the cup of diamond, held on a deep curve of line behind the RushWing's thin blade.

—Not us. That wasn't us. Not guilty. It wasn't even the Starvelings, murdering fucks though they may be.

—Then who did do it?

—The Mercatoria, Fass. They killed your people.

—What? Why?

—Because they found out that Sept Bantrabal had kept whatever they were sent that briefed you. They were supposed to junk it from the substrate as soon as it was finished but they didn't. It wasn't quite an AI like they sent to the Hierchon, but it had a lot in common. It was a big step along the way to a true AI and it was onward-engineerable. That's why. The attacks we and the Starvelings were making gave them the cover, but even if the truth got out, it would just reinforce how seriously they took the no-AIs thing.

Fassin supposed it made sense. Old Slovius had always been looking for an edge, some advantage over the other Septs. That was what had brought Bantrabal to its position of prominence over the years. It sounded plausible, sounded like something Slovius would do and browbeat his underlings into doing. And certainly he'd put nothing past the Mercatoria.

—And how do you know all this? he asked her.

He saw her shake her head.—Spies everywhere, Fass, she told him, almost rueful.—We have a lot of friends.

—I'm sure.

Did he believe her? Well, until further notice.

The Beyonders had known about the List, about the Transform. Like, it seemed, a lot of people, they had known long before he had. He'd only discovered what he'd stumbled upon during that long-ago delve when he'd been told along with everybody else by the projection of Admiral Quile in the Hierchon's palace. By then the Beyonders had long since sent their own fleet to the system Zateki, believing—like the Jeltick who had first deciphered the information he'd retrieved and had understood its significance—that the Transform was there, in the Second Ship. And they'd already met defeat at the hands of the Voehn. Half the fucking galaxy seemed to have been buzzing round Zateki, searching for a ship that wasn't there, if it even ever had been, and meanwhile he'd known nothing.

—You could just have asked me to look for it for you, Fassin told her.—I'd have started the search for the Transform in Nasq. centuries ago if you guys had just fucking asked.

She looked at him for a long time, an expression on her face of… he wasn't sure: sadness, pity, regret, despair?

—What? he sent.

—The truth? she asked him.

—The truth.

—Fassin. She shook her head.—We didn't trust you.

He stared back at her.

Fassin told her what he thought he'd discovered, what he believed he'd worked out. She didn't believe him.

—You coming with us?

—Can I? May I?

—Of course. If you want.

He thought.—Okay, he sent. He thought some more. —Though I've one last person to see first.

•

When the visitor arrived, Setstyin was water-bathing. This was a new fashion, not unpleasant. His servant announced that Seer Fassin Taak was here to see him. Setstyin felt surprise and elation, and a kind of delicious, if slightly grim, anticipation.

"Tell Seer Taak I am very delighted indeed to welcome him," he told his servant. "Ask him to wait in the upper library. Do all you can to make him comfortable. I shall be with him in ten minutes."

"Fassin! Wonderful to see you! I really can't tell you! We thought—well, we really feared the worst, I swear. Where have you *been*?"

Fassin didn't seem to know what to say. "I don't think you'd believe me if I told you," he said quietly, eventually.

The little gascraft floated in the middle of the library. The circular space was lined and floored with crystal stacks. Light came from a translucent ceiling and a single great door giving out onto a broad, rail-less balcony.

Setstyin's house was in the city of Aowne, mid-gas in the equatorial zone. Deep orange and yellow clouds swung slowly past the wide window.

"You think so?" Setstyin said. "Do feel free to try me. And, please, is there anything I can do? Come, let's sit."

They rested in a pair of dent-seats with a low table between them. A rather more substantial and grand desk lay just to one side.

"Well, it's a long story I have for you," Fassin said.

"My favourite kind!" Setstyin exclaimed, gathering his long robes about him.

Fassin took a moment, as if collecting his thoughts. The fellow seemed, Setstyin thought, dulled, a little slow compared to how he'd appeared before.

Fassin told the suhrl something of his adventures since he'd last seen him, aboard the Planetary Protector (Deniable) *Isaut*. He also told him a little more of what he'd been doing before, as well, apologising for any hesitations or forgetfulness; he'd been through a lot recently and some memories were still sort of shuffling their way forward into the light again after being lost. He didn't say exactly what it was he had been told to look for and bring back, and he wasn't able to tell the Dweller very much that happened after the Voehn attacked the *Velpin*, but he went into as much detail as he felt was possible.

"I don't understand," the Dweller said. "You're saying you were... you were in other stellar systems? You were on the other side of the galaxy? I... I just don't..."

"I could not have been more sceptical myself," Fassin said. "I did all the tests I could think of, but I certainly seemed to be in the places the truetwin captain claimed I was in."

"They can do wonderful things with fully immersive VR, you know," Setstyin said awkwardly.

"I know. But this was either real or something well beyond even fully immersive virtual reality."

Setstyin was silent for a moment. "You know—and please, don't take this ill—you do look rather, ah, beaten up, Fass my boy." The Dweller was looking at the various dents and scars that the little gascraft had picked up during its last few months of use. The malfunctioning left manipulator arm hung awkwardly at the flank of the arrowhead, slightly out of true. Fassin felt almost ashamed of the gascraft's appearance, as though he'd turned up in a rich gentleman's library in dirty rags.

"Yes," he agreed. "As I say, I won't pretend my memory is all it used to be. The gascraft's storage has suffered and my own brain doesn't seem to be as sharp as I remember it being." He laughed. "But I know what I saw, what I felt and heard and tasted. I stood on rocks watching the swell-waves of a salt ocean breaking, and I was really there, Setstyin. I *was* there."

The Dweller ruffled his sensory mantle and made the tiny up-and-down sigh-motion. "Well, I'm sure you believe what you believe, Fassin, and I would always tend to believe you rather than not. However, many other people wouldn't be so forgiving. I'm not sure it would be a good idea to make too big a fuss about this."

"You could be right."

"And... I mean to say... If this wormhole thing is so secret, why were you taken to—or apparently taken to—the far side of the galaxy, or to anywhere... anywhere outside Ulubis?"

"To prove the myth was real. Some people, some Dwellers, think it's time for change. They might not know all the details, but they want the truth known. Nobody wants to take responsibility for just *telling* a non-Dweller, but some bumpkin might be pushed in the right direction. And that's me, I suppose; bumpkin number one. *Deniable* bumpkin number one."

"And this... travelcaptain? Who was he again?"

"A truetwin."

"Yes, I've heard they often are. I didn't realise they even pretended to travel so far afield. What was his—their name?"

"You'll forgive me if I don't betray that confidence."

"Of course, of course." Setstyin seemed to think. "So, if there is this, ah, wormhole thing near Nasqueron, who does it belong to? Who controls it? And, it has to be asked, where exactly is it? Aren't they rather large and obvious, these wormhole ports?"

"They can be made quite small. But yes, you'd think people would have noticed them by now."

"Well, yes."

"And I'd guess they're operated by a club or fraternity or something like the same sort of organisation that takes care of planetary defence."

"Hmm. That would be... fairly obvious, I suppose."

"That's why I came to you, Setstyin," Fassin said. "I wondered if you'd heard anything about this, about a group of Dwellers who used these portals."

"Me?" The Dweller reacted as though surprised, almost shocked. "Well, no. I mean, none of this would be the sort of thing I'd normally get involved with. But, this would be quite something, would it not? I mean to say, if it turned out there was this wormhole here all the time. Wouldn't it?"

"There are stories, myths, about a whole network of them."

"This Dweller List?" Setstyin paused, then stared. "Is that what you were looking for all the time?"

"Not the List, the Transform that was supposed to hold the key to the List," Fassin said.

"And did you find it?"

Fassin was silent for a moment. Setstyin watched the little gascraft make a show of looking around the library. "Is this place quite private? I mean, secure?" Fassin asked.

"I should hope so," Setstyin said. "Why?"

"Can we signal, rather than speak, Setstyin?" Fassin asked. "It's not as easy for me as speaking, these days, so bear with me, but it is more secure."

—Of course, the Dweller sent.

—Well, I think I might have found the Transform, the human sent carefully.

—Really?

—...Really.

—You will understand if I am a little sceptical.

—Only natural.

—Where did you find this Transform?

—On the body of that dead Dweller, in the Ythyn Sepulcraft, on the far side of the galaxy.

—Ah-hah. What ever was it doing there?

—It was in a sort of safekeep box.

—And who would put it there?

—I don't know.

—And what did this Transform consist of?

—An equation.

—As in mathematics?

—That's right. It looked a bit like what some people had come to expect it to look like—a code and a frequency for a broadcast signal of some sort—but in the end it was just an equation.

—And this was supposed to unlock the List thing?

—That's what we were all told.

—Hmm. But?

—But, when I solved the equation, guess what?

—Oh. Ah, I have no idea. Do tell.

—It came out at nothing. Zero. The Transform turned out to be, in effect, a contrived mathematical joke.

Fassin signalled a laugh.

Setstyin shared the amusement.—I see. So, if this is what you were sent to look for, you might be said to have succeeded in your mission, though not in the manner you might have wished. Yes?

—Those were pretty much my thoughts, too.

—Well, at least you missed all the unpleasantness of this invasion your people have suffered. Thinking of you, I've been watching the situation. It all looks quite distressing. And still going on. And affecting us, too. There were explosions around Nasqueron just yesterday. Did you see any of them?

—I did. I hear there's a rumour that the invaders might be about to pull out.

—Possibly our planetary defence people again. There have been the usual denials, of course. Umm, I'm afraid even if I did know more, I couldn't talk about it. You understand.

—Of course. So, Fassin sent.—You don't know anything about these wormholes? You've never heard of them? I just thought, you being so well connected...

—All news to me, Fassin. Possibly some small group might have control of such things, though I find that hard to believe, frankly.

—Ah, well, Fassin sent. He was silent for a few moments.

—Yes? Setstyin sent.

—Well, Fassin replied slowly.—I did have an idea.

—An idea? Indeed.

—What if the Transform answer wasn't a joke?

—Not a joke? But it's zero. What use is that?

—You see, Fassin sent, and the little gascraft nudged forward a fraction on the dent-seat, closer still to Setstyin,—I had thought, what use would an equation be, after all this time? How could it tell you anything useful? A frequency and a code to be broadcast on it was the only thing that really made sense; then these wormholes could be hidden anywhere in the named systems and only activate themselves when needed. So the fact it was an equation at all made it kind of pointless even before it was worked out.

—I'll take your word for it, Setstyin told the human.—You are rather losing me here, but it all sounds terribly convincing.

—And then there was all that absurd twisting and spiralling when I was aboard the ship heading through the wormhole portals. Being cut off from external senses seemed obvious enough, but why the spiralling?

—Umm, yes, in the ship. I see.

—And just the fact that all of Dweller society does seem like a proper civilisation.

—Now you really are losing me, Fass.

—And you obviously possess technologies that we still haven't understood.

—Well, we're like that. Us Dwellers, aren't we? Oh dear, I think all this is upsetting my balance.

—You see, if the Transform means what it says, what it's saying is that the adjustment you have to make to each entry on the Dweller List to find out where the wormhole portals are in relation to those original locations named is…

Fassin held the little gascraft's working arm out, inviting Setstyin to answer.

The Dweller ruffled his sensory mantle, which had gone a slightly odd colour.—I'm sorry, Fassin, I feel positively dizzy.

—Nothing! Fassin sent.—The adjustment is zero.

—Is it? Is it really? I'm sure this is fascinating, really.

—And what was the original List based on, what did it give?

Again, he gave the Dweller a chance to answer, but he didn't.

—It gave the location of Dweller-inhabited gas-giants! Fassin put a sort of triumphalist joy into the signalled sentence.

—I see. I do feel slightly off, Fass. Do you mind if I…?

Setstyin rose, wobbling slightly, and roted over to his desk. He started opening lockers and drawers, then glanced up. "Keep going, keep going," he said. "I have my medication in here somewhere."

The Dweller signalled to his servant while he looked through the drawers, keeping his signal pit below the level of the desk, out of sight of the human in his gascraft.

—Was Mr Taak armed in any way?

After a moment:—No, sir. The house checked automatically, naturally. Aside from his manipulative devices, he is unarmed.

—I see. That's all.

The arrowhead swivelled to keep line-of-sight with the Dweller.

—The List doesn't need the Transform, Fassin told Setstyin.—All you need to know is that the planets are the location.

—Really? Indeed. And how can that be?

The little gascraft rose up into the air above the dent-seat.

—Because your wormhole portals are inside your planets, Setstyin, Fassin sent calmly.

The Dweller froze, then opened one last drawer. "But that's ridiculous," he said aloud.

"Right in the centre," Fassin continued, also speaking out loud now. "Probably of every single gas-giant you guys inhabit. There were only—what?—two million when the List was drawn up, that right? But that was long ago, and it was a historical document even then. I wouldn't be at all surprised to hear you'd connected up every last Dweller planet by now."

"I'm sorry, Fassin," Setstyin said. "You wouldn't convince a child with this. Everybody knows you need a flat region of space to make a wormhole portal work."

"Ah, that's the beauty of it. The very centre of a planet *is* flat," Fassin said. "Right in the very centre of a planet, of any free-floating body—sun, rock, gas-giant, anything—you're being pulled equally in all directions. It's just like being in orbit round a world and feeling weightless. The only problem, of course, is keeping a volume of space open in the core of a planet or a sun or whatever in the first place. The pressure is colossal, almost beyond belief, especially in a gas-giant the size of Nasq., but in the end it's just engineering. Hey, you guys have had ten billion years to get good at that sort of stuff. Anything that isn't impossible you learned to do easily when the galaxy was a quarter of the age it is now.

"So you don't need to position portals in space where anybody could see them or use them or attack them, you don't even need to leave your own planet to access them, you just head for some well-hidden shaft that leads you down to the very centre of the world. Maybe at the poles. That would be an obvious kind of place. And if you've got somebody aboard your ship who might be keeping track of where you're going somehow, you just throw in all these crazy spirals and flash some screenage of space into wherever you're keeping them, so they never can tell they've gone down, not up, and have sunk into the core, not flown out into space."

"Ah, here we are," Setstyin said, and pulled out a large handgun. Suddenly perfectly steady, he aimed and fired before the little gascraft could react.

The beams tore the arrowhead apart, slamming through it and sending it whirling back against a stack of library crystals and then somersaulting over and over as Setstyin kept firing the gun, spreading fire and scattering wreckage all over the library floor. Wildly spinning pieces of debris were sent shrapnelling across the glittering stacks, cracking spines and smashing crystal pages to powder. What was left of the little craft crashed into the windows by the balcony, shattering the diamond as though it was sugar glass. Setstyin stopped firing.

Debris pattered down. Smoke drifted, gradually sucked towards the shattered window.

The big Dweller roted carefully over to the broken window, keeping the gun trained on the smoking remains of the little craft as he approached.

"Sir?" his servant called over the house intercom. "Sir, are you all right? I thought I heard—"

"Fine," Setstyin called, not shifting his attention from the wreckage as he drew closer. "I'm fine. Be some cleaning up to do in due course, but I'm fine. Leave me, now."

"Sir."

A warm breeze ruffled his robes as Setstyin floated out of the window and drew up almost on top of the guttering wreck. He prodded the ruined gascraft with the muzzle of the gun. He prised part of the craft's upper shell away.

He peered inside.

"Fucker!" he screamed, and whirled back into the library, tearing through the gas to the desk. "Desk! SecComms, *now*!"

Aun Liss watched the man as his little craft, his second skin, was destroyed.

Fassin winced just the once, twitching as though pained.

Aun thought he did not look well. His body was thin inside the borrowed fatigues and he was trembling slightly but continually. His face looked much older than it had, pinched and drawn, eyes sunken and surrounded with darkness. His hair, looking crinkled and thin, had grown a little while he'd been inside the gascraft. His eyes and the edges of his ears and nostrils, plus the corners of his mouth, were red from the effects of coming out of the shock-gel—and having the gillfluid come out of him—after all this time.

He turned to look at her. She was glad to see there was a twinkle in his eye, despite it all. "So. Still think I'm crazy?" he asked.

She smiled. "Pretty much."

They sat in the bright, if cramped, command space of the *Ecophobian*, a Beyonder shockcraft, a medium-weight warship half a light second out from

Nasqueron, linked to the now-defunct gascraft via a twin of the eyeball-sized microsat which had been exactly where it was supposed to be a day earlier, when Fassin had pinged it from the high platform in Quaibrai.

They were, amazingly, still receiving basic telemetry from the shattered gascraft, though no sensory content. The machine had been very thoroughly blasted.

On a side-screen, they had a freeze of the last visual that the little gascraft had sent: Setstyin levelling a sizeable handgun straight at the camera, a tiny sparkle of light just starting in the very centre of the weapon's dark barrel. Fassin nodded at the image. "I hasten to add that that does not constitute standard Dweller hospitality."

"I'd guessed. Sure it wasn't because you just wouldn't shut up?"

"I'm serious."

"You're serious? What do you call the guy with the big fuck-off gun?"

"Aun," Fassin said, sounding tired now. "Do you believe me?"

She hesitated, shrugged. "I'm with your belligerent friend; I believe you believe."

The gascraft telemetry cut off.

The Chief Remotes Officer leaned in, manipulating holos above one of the displays. "That wasn't the gascraft totalling," she told them, "that was the microsat getting fried. Fast work. Suggest hightail promptly."

"Hold on to your hats," the captain said. "Sit well back."

They were thrown, pressed, then rammed back into their seats as the ship accelerated, the command officers shifting to control by induction rather than physical manipulation. The whole gimballed command sphere swung to keep the gee-forces pressing on their chests.

"*Were* you serious, Mr Taak?" the captain asked, her voice strained against the clamping power of the acceleration.

"Yuh," was the best Fassin could manage.

"So there's a secret network of ancient Dweller wormholes linking—what?—every Dweller gas-giant?"

Fassin took the deepest breath he could and forced out, "That's the idea." Another breath. "You send all we... got from the... gascraft to... your high command?"

The captain managed to laugh. "Such as they are, yes."

"Shit," said the Defence Officer, his voice strained. "Lock on." They heard him breathing hard. "It's fast! Can't outrun. In fourteen!"

"Fire everything," the captain said crisply. "Ready Detach Command. We'll risk adrifting, hope the *Impavid*'s local."

"Need to yaw before the Detach or we'll be hit by the debris spray," the Tactics Officer said.

"Copy," the captain said. "Shame. Always liked this ship."

The ship wheeled wildly, Fassin blacked out and never felt the explosive detach.

The joltship *Impavid* picked the command sphere up three days later.

:

"Taince," Saluus Kehar said. He grinned. "Hey. So, so good to see you again." He came up to her and put his arms round her.

Taince Yarabokin had succeeded in producing a smile. She'd chosen an old-fashioned formal cap as part of her uniform and so had the unspoken excuse that she needed to keep this clamped between her elbow and her side for not being able to hug him back with any great enthusiasm. Sal didn't seem to notice anyway. He pulled away, looked at her.

"Been a while, Taince. Glad you made it back."

"Good to be back," Taince said.

They were in a hangar in the Guard Security Holding Facility Axle 7, a triple-wheeled habitat orbiting 'glantine. Saluus had been held there for the past couple of months while the authorities had decided whether they really believed him about having been kidnapped rather than having run away or even turned traitor.

He'd consented to and undergone dozens of brain scans—more than enough to put the matter beyond any doubt in an ordinary case, and of course he had connections and friends in high places who would normally have been only too happy to have discreet words in probably quite receptive ears. But there had been a feeling that this was an exceptional matter, that Sal was rich enough to have afforded technologies or techniques that would fool the brain scans, that the Starvelings themselves might have been able to implant convincing false memories, and—anyway—such a fuss had been made at the time when Saluus had, seemingly, gone over to the invading forces that to let him meekly out just because it looked like he was blameless somehow didn't seem right.

When Saluus had disappeared, apparently turning traitor, there had been strikes and attacks on Kehar family and commercial property and he'd been denounced by every part of the Ulubine Mercatoria in terms that owed as much to finally having something understandable to hit out at as to any moral indignation. People who had called Sal a friend and been regular guests at many of his family homes had decided that they owed it to the popular mood and their intense personal sense of betrayal—not to mention their future social standing and careers—to compete in out-vituperating each other in their condemnation of his odious perfidy. The calumnies heaped upon Sal's absent head had amounted to a thesaurus of despite, an entire dictionary of bile. In the end he was kept incarcerated as much for his own safety as for anything else.

When the Starveling forces left and the Summed Fleet arrived, the general feeling of relief and euphoria pervading the Ulubis system meant that news of Sal's shocking innocence traded rather better on the floor of the public's perception, and it could be announced that he was to be released in due course. Most people chose to recant their earlier expressions of hatred and condemnation, though it was still felt best for all concerned if Sal's return to public life and rehabilitation was gradual rather than abrupt.

Taince had volunteered—pulled rank, indeed—to pilot Sal from the Holding Facility back to the original Kehar family home on 'glantine.

A Guard-major got Taince to sign Sal out of custody.

Sal watched her signature on the pad. "That's my freedom you're writing there, Vice Admiral," he told her. He was wearing his own clothes, looking slim and casual and bright.

"Glad to be of service," she told him, then looked at the Guards officer. "Is that us, Guard-major?"

"Yes, ma'am." He turned to Saluus. "You are free to go, Mr Kehar."

Saluus reached out and shook the Guard-major's hand. "Med, thanks for everything."

"Been a pleasure, sir."

"No clothes or anything?" Taince asked, looking at his empty hands.

Sal shook his head. "Came with nothing, taking nothing away. No baggage." He flashed a smile.

She tipped her head. "Pretty good at our age."

They walked to the small cutter squatting on the shallow curve of hangar floor. "I really appreciate this, Taince," he told her. "I mean I *really* do. You didn't have to do this." She smiled. His gaze flicked over her insignia. "It is okay to call you Taince, isn't it? I mean, I'll call you Vice Admiral if you like…"

"Taince is fine, Sal. After you." She showed him up into the little cutter's tandem cockpit, settling him into the seat in front of and below hers. She fitted herself into the pilot's seat, clipping on a light flight collar and waking the small craft's systems. The Facility's flight control cleared them to leave.

"So you're, what? System Liaison Chief?" Sal asked over his shoulder as they were trundled under a door into a sizeable airlock.

"Yes, well, it's pretty much all ceremonial," she told him. The door behind them closed, the lights in the lock dimmed. "Receptions, dinners, tours, addresses, you know the sort of thing."

"Sounds like you're just loving every minute."

"I suppose somebody has to do it. Serves me right for being Ulubine." Pumps thrummed, a rush of air and a deep hum at first, then after a while just the hum, sounding through the fabric of the cutter. "No real fighting to do, anyway. Just clean-up stuff. I'm not missing much."

"Any news on Fassin?" Sal asked. "Last I heard they thought he might be alive again. If you know what I mean."

The outer door opened silently to the stars and a great silvery-fawn slice of 'glantine.

"Just give me a minute or two here, will you?" Taince asked. "Been a little while since I did this…"

"Hey, take as long as you need."

The cutter edged its way out of the lock, stowed its gear, rolled very slowly and drifted away on little whisper bursts of gas, heading towards the atmosphere.

"Yes. Fassin," Taince said. "Well, they're still looking for him."

"I heard he'd been lost in Nasqueron and then reappeared."

"There have been rumours. There were always rumours. If you believed them, he's been all over Nasqueron for the last half-year, never left, or been in the Oort cloud for the last few months and just returned, or even wilder stuff. Plus he's been declared definitely dead at least three times. Whatever the truth is, he's still not here to tell it himself." Taince rotated the cutter, lining it up for entry.

"You think he is dead?" Sal asked.

"Let's just say it's odd that he hasn't made himself known by now, if he is still around."

They met the atmosphere a little later, pressed against the seat restraints, a pink glow building then fading around the canopy, the small ship whistling in across a sequence of thin clouds, deserts and shallow seas, hills, scarps, lakes and low mountains.

"Taking the scenic route, Taince?"

She gave a small laugh. "Suppose I'm just a sentimentalist at heart, Sal."

"Good to see the old place again," Sal said. She watched him lean to one side, looking down. "Is that Pirri down there?"

She looked, checked the nav. "Yes, that's Pirrintipiti."

"Looks like it always did. Thought it might have grown a bit more."

"While since you've been home, Sal?"

"Oh, too long, too long. Kept meaning to, but, you know. Must be ten or twelve years. Maybe more. Feels more."

They were high over the edges of the thin polar-plateau ice cap, crossing into darkness, falling all the time. They could see stars again.

She saw him looking up and around. "You forget how beautiful it is, eh?" Sal asked.

"Sometimes," Taince said. "Easy enough thing to do."

The glow in the sky faded around them. She watched the canopy up the brightness, exaggerating the incoming light until they could see the starlight on the North Waste Land, the great long streaks of coloured sands and outcrop rocks, silvery ghosts, coming closer all the time.

"Ah, right," Sal said quietly.

She tapped a few display icons, dimming the screens.

"Thought we'd take a pass," she said. "Hope you don't mind."

"Old times' sake." He sounded thoughtful, even resigned. "Well, why not?"

Taince checked the nav again, lined the craft up and cut its speed a little. A light was blinking urgently on one of the displays. She turned that one off too.

"I certainly haven't been back here since that night," Sal said. She thought he sounded sad now. Perhaps regretful. Perhaps not.

The ruined ship showed up ahead, a little off to the right. Taince started the cutter on a long starboard curve, levelling out as she did so.

Sal looked side-down at the desert, rushing past seventy metres below as they banked. "Wow," he said. "Quicker than that flier I borrowed from Dad."

"One of your own ships, Sal," she told him.

"This little thing?" He laughed. "Didn't realise we made anything this small."

"It's old."

"Ah. One of Dad's. More money in the big stuff."

They zapped past the great dark hulk. Its exposed ribs clawed at the sky.

"Woo-hoo!" Sal shouted as the black wall of hull slid past twenty metres away.

Taince zoomed, looped and rolled, levelling out again, approaching the wrecked alien ship once more for an even nearer approach.

"Who-hoh-*hoh*!" Sal said, seeing how low and close Taince was taking the cutter this time. Taince rolled the craft so that they were upside down. "Sheeit! Wow! Taince! Yee-ha!"

Right to the end she hadn't known if she'd actually do it or not. She didn't really know the truth of what had happened, after all. She only had her suspicions. She could, despite everything, just be plain wrong. It wouldn't be the first time somebody had taken the law into their own hands and been proved to be hopelessly wrong, once all the facts were known. Fuck, that was what justice was supposed to be all about, that was why you had laws and everything that went with them, that was one of the things that made a society a society.

But still. She did know. She was quite sure. It was his time. And if she was wrong, well, Sal had had his share. It wasn't like killing a child, or a young woman with her life before her. It was still killing, still wrong, but there were gradations in all things, even circles in hell. And, frankly—right or wrong—at least she'd never know.

It was her time. She knew that.

She'd really thought there would be tears, but they stayed away. How strange not to know oneself, after so long, at such an extremity, and so close to the end.

What else? Well, she'd thought of telling him, of confronting him, of bringing it all back up again, of listening to him rage at or plead with or scream at her. That had been something she'd rehearsed a lot, that had been something she'd thought through time after time after time as she'd played and replayed this scene in her head over the years and decades and centuries, taking both her part and his, trying to imagine what he'd say, how he'd try to explain it, how he'd imply she was mad or mistaken.

Ultimately Taince had just got bored with it. She'd heard it all before. There was nothing more to say.

She was taking a man's life on circumstantial evidence, on a hunch. She ought to give him the chance to appeal. She ought at least to allow him to know it was about to happen.

But then, why?

The cold sheen of desert and the vast impenetrability of the dark, ruined ship rushed up to meet them.

"Shit, Tain—!"

Sal might have tried to use the eject—it was one system she couldn't disable from her controls—but then, that was why she'd flown the last bit upside down.

In the end all it took was a single quick flick of the wrists.

The cutter slammed into the side of the ship, just ten metres off the desert floor, at about half the speed of sound.

# EPILOGUE

There is, along the higher latitudes of the Northern Tropical Uplands of the planet-moon 'glantine, in the system of Ulubis, a bird which, thanks to its call, people call a Hey-fella-hey.

The bird is a migrant, a passer; that is, a bird that does not dwell in the given region but only ever passes through. The Hey-fella-hey passes through these latitudes in the early spring, heading north.

It was a cool day, mid-morning. Nasqueron, half full, cast a ruddy-brown light over the soft shadows of the day. Once, one might have seen sky mirrors away to one side or the other, bringing sunlight to us even when Nasqueron filled most of the sky above. However, many of these devices were destroyed in the war, and so our little planet-moon is a literally gloomier place now than it once was, returned, until new mirrors are emplaced, to its primitive state.

I was working in the old formal pasture, wading deep in an exasperation of chuvle weed choking a—by now—almost hidden pond and trying to work out what to do with the weed and the feature (for both are pretty in their own ways) when I heard the distinctive call of said bird. I stopped and listened.

"Hey-fella-hey-fella-hey-fella-hey!" the bird sang. I turned slowly, looking for it in the higher branches of the nearby trees.

While I was looking—I never did locate the bird—I saw a figure walking along the high path towards the stream and the perimeter wall which gives out onto the slope holding—a little further up—the ruins of the old Rehlide temple.

I looked carefully, zooming in and trying to filter out the effects of the intervening bushes and shrubs, because the figure walked very like Seer Taak, who had been a long time gone from us. ("Us!"—always the same, hurtful mistake. There was no "us" any more, just a few sad remnants left behind at a house abandoned.) The figure disappeared behind a clump of thicker shrubbery, though they would reappear shortly if they continued to follow the path.

I thought. In retrospect, perhaps the person walking on the path had been somewhat older than the gentleman I had been pleased to think of as the young master. He was slightly stooped, which Seer Taak never had been, and he was perhaps too thin, plus he walked like somebody who had been injured in some way. So it seemed to me, at any rate. I would not claim to be an expert in such matters. I am but a humble gardener, after all. Well, a head gardener, but all the same. Still humble, I hope.

The figure did indeed reappear, though not exactly where I had been expecting. Whoever it was had taken a side path and was now walking almost straight towards me. They raised a hand. I raised a trowel, waved back. It *was* Seer Taak! Or—by all reason—it was somebody doing their damnedest to look like a rather more aged version of him.

I clambered out of the pond, shook some chuvle weed from a couple of legs, and lumbered up the path bank to meet him.

"Young master?" I said, dropping trowel, rake and spade and brushing soil and weed-stems from my arms.

The man smiled broadly. "HG, it is you." He was dressed in long, loose, casual clothes, nothing like those of a Seer.

"It is *you*, Seer Taak! We thought the worst! Oh! For you at least to be alive!"

I confess I folded, going down on all eights, staring at the gravel of the path, overcome.

He squatted in front of me. "We never see what's in front of us, do we, HG?"

"Sir?"

"HG, tell me you're not an AI."

I looked up at him. "Emotion? Was that it? I should have known that would give me away one day."

He smiled. "Your secret's safe."

"Well, perhaps for now."

"Patience, HG."

"You imply that things may change? Or that I should just wait for death? We do not die easily. We have not been allowed to."

He smiled a slow, painful smile. "Change, HG."

"You think?"

"Oh, yes. All sorts of things are happening."

"I have heard something. They say there is a wormhole mouth, in Nasqueron?" I looked up at the great planet which seemed to hang over us, its vast circlet rivers of gas—cream and brown, yellow, white, purple and red—forever sliding in contrary directions.

Fassin Taak nodded slowly, thoughtfully. "It turns out we were all connected, all the time." He picked up a pebble from the path, looked at it. "The Dwellers may even let us use their wormhole network, if we ask them nicely. Sometimes. There is a furious debate going on in Dweller society even as we speak—and probably for some time to come, Dwellers being, well, Dwellers—regarding to what extent the undying admiration of every even vaguely sentient species in the rest of the galaxy and possibly beyond could possibly constitute a general increase in the background kudos level for all Dwellers, and therefore a valid reason for throwing open their galactic transport system to all."

"That would indeed be a great change."

"And not one that the Mercatoria would be allowed to control."

"It would still be the Mercatoria."

"It can change too. It won't have any choice. Patience, HG."

"Well, we shall see, but thank you."

I looked at him. Fassin Taak did indeed look older. His face was more careworn, the lines around his eyes deeper. "Has all been well here, HG?"

"All is well in the garden. The house... well, that is not my province."

Now he looked down. "I took a look around," he said. His voice was quiet. "It was all very quiet. Very strange and quiet with nobody there."

"I try not to look at it," I confessed, "except sometimes at dawn and during the very early morning, when it looks much as it always did: bright light upon it but no sign of life. That I can bear." I saw the image even as I spoke of it. "I am lucky that I have the garden to tend. By looking after it, it looks after me."

"Yes," he said. "We all need something to do, don't we?"

I hesitated. "Still, there is not a day goes by when I do not curse my luck to have been stuck here rather than with them somehow, when the end came. I envy the Head Gardener of the Winter House, where they all died together." I pulled myself up a fraction. "But enough. And you, sir? What do you do these days?"

"Please don't call me 'sir', HG. I'm Fassin."

"Oh. Thank you. Well, what are you doing? And where? If I may ask."

"Oh, I've gone off with the Beyonders, HG. I'm already a citizen of the galaxy, albeit slowly, without using wormholes. But, a start."

"And the Sept, Fassin?"

"There is no Sept, HG. It's gone." He threw the pebble back along the path. "Maybe they'll start another Sept—who knows?" He looked away in the direction of the distant house. "They might fill this house, one day."

"You won't come back?"

He looked around. "Too many people would still want to ask me too many questions, probably until I died." He looked at me. "No, I just came back here for one last look around. And to look you up."

"Really? Me? Really?"

"Really."

"I cannot tell you how gratified—no, honoured—that makes me feel."

He smiled at me and started to rise to his feet. "This humility is a great cover, HG. I hope you can set it aside when the time comes."

"I meant what I said, Fassin."

"And I mean this, HG," he said, as he brushed down his clothes, Nasqueron forever behind him. "One day we'll all be free."

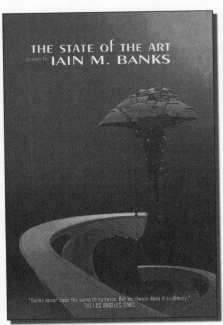

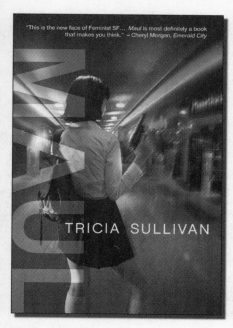

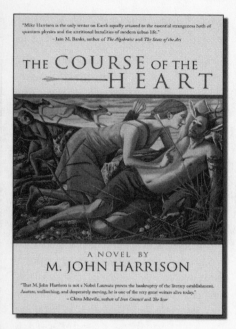